"A real love, a real marriage, is struggling to make life better for the person you love."

"That's just how women do it." He ground out the words, crumbling. Hell, he was like a granite rock disintegrating. "They say all the right words. Do all the things meant to fool a man into thinking..."

He choked back the rest of the memories too bleak to examine. Images that whirled like black wraiths before his eyes. "Women know just what to do to make you think how wonderful they are. So sweet and dainty and feminine and loving until your heart is caught like a fish on a line and you don't even know enough to escape until you're out of the water. Struggling to breathe. Seeing the glint of the knife before it slices you wide open. So when I say get away from me, I mean *get away from me!*"

* * *

Rocky Mountain Man
Harlequin Historical #752—May 2005

Praise for Jillian Hart's recent books

High Plains Wife

"Finely drawn characters and sweet tenderness tinged
with poignancy draw readers into a familiar story that
beautifully captures the feel of an Americana romance."
—*Romantic Times*

Bluebonnet Bride

"Ms. Hart expertly weaves a fine tale of the heart's
ability to find love after tragedy. Pure reading pleasure!"
—*Romantic Times*

Cooper's Wife

"A wonderfully written romance full
of love and laughter."
—*Rendezvous*

DON'T MISS THESE OTHER
TITLES AVAILABLE NOW:

#751 THE DUCHESS'S NEXT HUSBAND
Terri Brisbin

#753 THE MISSING HEIR
Gail Ranstrom

#754 HER DEAREST ENEMY
Elizabeth Lane

JILLIAN HART

ROCKY MOUNTAIN MAN

HARLEQUIN®

TORONTO • NEW YORK • LONDON
AMSTERDAM • PARIS • SYDNEY • HAMBURG
STOCKHOLM • ATHENS • TOKYO • MILAN • MADRID
PRAGUE • WARSAW • BUDAPEST • AUCKLAND

ISBN 0-373-29352-6

ROCKY MOUNTAIN MAN

Copyright © 2005 by Jill Strickler

www.eHarlequin.com

Printed in U.S.A.

Please address questions and book requests to:
Harlequin Reader Service
U.S.: 3010 Walden Ave., P.O. Box 1325, Buffalo, NY 14269
Canadian: P.O. Box 609, Fort Erie, Ont. L2A 5X3

Prologue

Montana Territorial Prison, 1879

Sweat crept like a spider down the middle of his back and stung in the open gashes made fresh with the edge of a bullwhip. Duncan Hennessey didn't mind the harsh midday sun fixing to blister his skin. No, he'd grown used to the burning heat so that he hardly noticed it. Nor was he bothered by the thirst so strong his mouth had turned to sandpaper and his tongue felt thick and dry.

He did not feel hunger chewing through his stomach. Or the cuts on his calloused hands or the rough stones scraping away the calluses on the insides of his fingers. He'd grown accustomed to it because there was no other choice. For ten cruel winters and as many brutal summers, he'd bent and lifted, bled and labored behind the tall stone walls that caged him.

Today, at sundown, it would all come to an end. For at the end of the day, he would be set free. It was unbelievable, but it was true. His name was on the short list—he'd glanced at it over the shoulder of one of the prison guards. It was really going to happen. He simply had to make it through the rest of this day. That was all. When the sun inched behind the Bitterroot Mountains, his punishment would be over.

He'd been afraid to think of this day. Hopelessness was the killer here, more than the cold or heat or beatings. More rampant than sickness and the endless violence. His soul had hardened into impenetrable iron. He no longer felt. Not hope. Not fear. Not sorrow.

Not even today, as the sun crept along its course through the sky, did he feel a single hope. He knew better. He might be a free man come dusk, but he had to be alive to enjoy it.

"You!" A voice as hard as Montana granite seemed to come out of nowhere. As did the whip snap—the only warning of what was to come. "You're not sweatin' hard enough, you worthless rat. Don't think you get outta puttin' in your fair share a work. You ain't free yet."

It was a game to the guards. To brutalize especially those who were leaving. They thought it funny that while the Territory of Montana might grant a man his freedom at the end of his time served, they held the greater power, to keep him from it. Many had failed to live through the beatings that marked their last day. So he was not surprised by the hiss as the whip sailed through the air.

He knew better than to stop working. As he bent to lift a heavy rock torn apart by the pickax crew, he saw the whisper-thin shadow undulate across the yellow-hued earth. Like a snake rising back to strike and then attacking.

Duncan relaxed his back muscles, surrendering to the pain instead of bracing against it. Pain wasn't as bad when you gave in to it. The lash sliced through his skin. He bit the inside of his mouth to keep from groaning, for the keen bite of the whip pierced bone-deep.

He breathed in, let the pain course through him until it seemed to flow outward and away from the wound. He heaved the chunk of granite into the wagon, a second slash gnawed into his shoulder blade. He hardly felt it. He was made of steel and no whip made could defeat him.

He chucked another rock into the wagon. More sweat trickled into the newer open gashes and stung like hell. This punishment was meant to reduce him, to defeat him, but he was stronger. Warrior's blood of the proud Nez Perce tribe flowed through his veins. The Territory of Montana had done its best to strip him of all he held valuable, but it had failed.

He was Duncan Hennessey, grandson of the respected Gray Wolf, and no territorial law and no prison guard could take that from him or beat it from him.

He winced as his torn back muscles spasmed, but he refused to slow the pace of his work. He pushed harder and labored faster. Much awaited him outside the walls. He would not give the guards any further reasons to use their whips. Even as the sun began to slide down from its zenith, marking the day as half over, he controlled his thoughts.

He would not look ahead to seeing the outside world. It would make him yearn, and yearning came hand in hand with need. And need was like a sharp knife—one edge but two sides. It was both strength and weakness that cuts, either way. A man who showed any weakness did not survive.

He intended to survive. He made himself of stone, like the arrowheads of his mother's people. Like the mountains that ringed the great prairie and rose proudly above the jagged foothills around him. His grandfather had named him "Standing Tall" for the mountains and their jagged profiles that seemed to watch over him as he struggled to lift what had to be a hundred-pound boulder and dispose of it with the other waste rocks.

His wounds could bleed. The guards could strike again. But those great mountains reminded him of who he was. He was strong. He was a warrior.

He would survive this day and then— He banished the image of lush green forests and the sweet tang of pine that rolled into his mind. Not yet. He would not dare to think of the day's end, for he had the rest of the day to live through.

Only then would he dare to dream of home.

Light from the setting sun flared brightly, spearing over the faces of the mountains and painting the land and sky with bold pink and purple strokes. It was pleasant on Duncan's face as he walked through the steel gate in the twelve-foot-high stone walls and listened to it clatter closed behind him.

Locking him out. Not in.

I'm free. Duncan found that he could not take a step. The sky stretched out in a brilliant celebration of the coming twilight before him. Such beauty, his eyes had not seen, for the prisoners were marched east at the workday's end, to the food hall and cells beyond.

Whispers of his identity began to stir within him. Places he'd kept hidden and protected behind walls of steel. He took pleasure in watching an eager owl, spotted white on soft down of brown, glide through the shadows to roost on the top branches of a lodgepole pine. No wind stirred the drying grasses that fringed wagon ruts in the road.

The land seemed to be waiting, holding itself still, and like the owl, he waited. For what, he did not know. An eternity had passed since he'd been able to do as he pleased and go where he chose. For the first time in a decade he did not have to move, not until he wanted to. He could follow the road through the upslope of the rolling hill or take off through the fields or climb into the tree. Whatever he wanted, if he had a mind to.

He was free. Truly free. Gratitude stung his eyes. His throat thickened so he could not swallow. He looked behind him to make sure it was still real. Sure enough, the locked gate reflected the bold fire left from the setting sun. A guard in the tower overhead was watching with a rifle leaning against his shoulder. There was no mistaking the message in the man's gaze—move along.

Duncan did. He followed the road, for it would lead through mountains and valleys and towns. It would lead him home.

As the last light bled from the sky and stained the faces of the great mountains so it looked as if they were crying tears, Duncan ambled past the owl in the tree. He lifted his tired feet and walked until the prison was nothing more than a small glint of light in the distance. He did not stop until there was no sign of it at all. Until that hellish place was good and truly behind him.

Only then did he kneel and untie the cheap shoes the prison had presented him with. The stiff new clothes rustled and tugged uncomfortably at his skin, the garments courtesy of the Montana territory. How generous. Bitterness welled up, draining his spirit and darkening the twilight. Stars winked to life as he cupped his hands as he knelt beside a small creek and let the coolness trickle over his skin.

The gurgling sound of the rushing water made his vision blur and the thickness in his throat grow worse. He'd never noticed before, but the music from a creek was a beautiful sound. He filled his palm with the fresh goodness and sipped.

He swore he'd never tasted anything more delicious. The clear, clean water wet his tongue, trickled down his throat and refreshed him. It had been too long since he'd tasted such water. While he drank his fill, he considered the grove surrounding him. Pines stretched upward, their sparse limbs and long, fine needles casting just enough cover from view of the road, although he'd encountered no other late-night traveler.

By the looks of things, he was not the only creature to visit the creek. In the damp yellow-brown clay, he recognized the small clefted tracks of deer and antelope and the larger elk, and the wide pads with claw marks of the great black bear. That told him fishing was good here. Yes, it would be a fine place to spend the night.

As he had not done since he was twenty-one, he chose a slim pine branch and broke it to use as a spear. He sharpened it well against the useful edge of a granite rock and chose a quiet place to wait, in an eddy where the creek widened before it whispered down an incline.

His eyes grew accustomed to the night as the last twilight shadows vanished. The pale, luminous darkness was like an old friend. He stirred the quiet water slowly, startling the resting fish. He speared a ten-inch summer trout on the first try.

Gratitude. It filled him like the slow, sweet scents of the night. It brought him hope as he watched the stars flicker to life between the coming clouds and the reach of the silent pines. Rain scented the night breeze, while Duncan cleaned the fish, built a fire and gathered wild onions and lemon grass greens for seasoning, as his grandfather had taught him.

While the fish roasted above an open flame, he made a shelter for the night. By the time raindrops stirred the pine needles overhead, Duncan turned the trout on the spit until it was done. Rain sang with the wind's moaning accompaniment to tap a rhythm against the earth, while, beneath the thickest of the spreading pine boughs, he remained dry as he ate. The moist, tender meat tasted so good, his mouth ached with the flavors of the seasoned trout. Nothing beat wild lemon grass, his ma used to say.

Ma. I get to see you again. His chest filled with the old grief he'd locked away, for he hadn't seen her since his sentencing. He allowed himself to remember, to pull out the image of that sad time and look at it. It had been a dark day, for he'd been awaiting transport from Dewey to the territorial prison, and his mother had come to see him.

A regal, proud woman, she'd worn a calico dress, her long dark braids coiled and hidden beneath the matching sunbonnet. No one could ever mistake her for being just a farmer's wife. She was a warrior's daughter. Her dark almond eyes, her delicate bronze face, her voice low and sonorous, spoke of strength.

She'd come to comfort him. She'd come to vow she would prove his innocence at any cost.

Through the bars of steel caging him in, he'd seen at once the future. His mother risking all the good that had finally come into her life on the impossible. No jury was going to believe him, for he was a half-breed, and the woman accusing him was the prettiest daughter of the finest family in the county.

The young lady was lying—he'd never touched her—but the chances of proving that…well, there was no way to prove it absolutely. Folks believed what they wanted to, and it was easier to see him as a rapist and a violent felon than to find a seemingly perfect lady guilty of perjury. A daughter of a judge didn't lie.

He'd wanted to save his mother endless heartache. She'd had a happy life and she should not risk it. He'd done the right thing in telling her to leave and to never look back. To return to her house and her husband and tend her garden and raise her horses and live her days in happiness. To forget she had a son. For he'd been all but as good as dead.

After the first day laboring in the brutal winter cold, he'd realized that he'd told his mother the truth. The young man he'd been, the boy she'd raised, was dead. Only a man as hard and fierce as a Montana blizzard could survive. Only a man without heart or soul would last long in endless labor and brutal conditions. He was no longer Duncan Hennessey, Standing Tall, son of Summer Rose, grandson of Gray Wolf.

He stepped out from under the shelter. But as he lifted his face to the rain and let the soothing coolness wash the day's grime from his skin, Duncan felt alive. He shucked off the government-issue trousers and button-up shirt, scratchy and rough with cheap starch, and the creek water rushed over his toes. The rain washed over him. And he dared to hope that maybe a part of that young man he used to be had survived.

Lightning burned through the angry clouds. He let thunder crash through him. The years of despair and defeat sluiced away and he lifted his arms to the sky, welcoming the deluge as it pounded over him. Hope winged up within him.

He was Duncan Hennessey, a free man, and he was going home. After what was behind him, what lay ahead could only be better. He had family waiting for him. A life to return to. A future to build. Joy lifted him up like the steam from the warm and wet earth.

Joy, he marveled at the emotion. From this moment on, what despair could there be for a man who had his life, his family and his hope returned to him?

He could not know that what lay ahead would be worse than the cruel years in prison.

Far worse.

Chapter One

Bluebonnet County, 1884

The ancient evergreens grew tall and thick, their wide limbs stretching overhead to block out the deep beautiful blue of the Montana sky.

Betsy Hunter, huddled on her buggy's comfortable springed seat, pulled the Winchester rifle closer, so it was snug against her thigh. As many times as she'd traveled across the high prairie from her hometown of Bluebonnet to the rugged edges of the great Rocky Mountains, not one frightening thing had happened.

Still, she was jumpy. The wind moaned through the trees and those thick, dark branches swung like monstrous arms and thumped and scraped the buggy top as if those trees had come alive and were trying to get at her. Of course, it was only her fanciful thoughts getting away with her. They were trees rooted into the ground and not menacing predators with sharp claws and big teeth and an appetite for town ladies.

She was perfectly safe from the army of innocent pines and cedars and firs. Not that it made driving along this forgotten road any easier. There was always something about this part of the mountain that felt menacing.

Perhaps, it was because she knew *he* was close—Mr. Hennessey. A loner, a mountain man and the most rude human being she'd ever met, and since she was an optimist who believed there was something good to like in everyone, that was saying a lot.

Mr. Duncan Hennessey was the most cynical, caustic and bitter human being in existence, if he was human at all. He avoided her as if she brought an epidemic of small pox and the plague, so she didn't see him often on her weekly trips to deliver and fetch his washing. Her first impression of the man was that he seemed more like a great black bear, although shaven and wearing a man's clothes, snarling and growling at her from his front step.

"This is the way I want it." He'd commanded as he'd handed her payment up front, plus additional delivery charges for driving out so far from town. "I'll leave the bag of clothes here on the step. You come, get it, put the clean bag in its place and leave. Don't knock on the door. Don't try to talk to me. Just get in that frilly buggy of yours and go back where you came from."

"But what if you need special services, like a repaired button?"

He'd seemed to rear up even taller at her perfectly necessary question, although he hadn't actually moved a muscle. His face, his eyes and his entire mood had turned as dark as a moonless night when a storm was building.

"Just repair the damn thing and leave a note in the bag when you return the clean clothes. I'll pay you next time around. Never—" he'd lifted his upper lip like a bear ready to attack "—never get anywhere near me, you hear?"

What a perfectly disagreeable man—no, beast. That's what he was. Really. As if she would want to get anywhere near him! "There's no need to shout. There is nothing wrong with my hearing," she'd told him as sweetly as she could manage. "I'll do as you ask, of course."

She needed his business.

"See that you do!" His dark eyes had narrowed with a fierce threat before he'd turned and slammed the door to his log cabin shut with the force of thunder.

It was his mood that was tainting the forest, she was sure of it. Every time she drove the rutted and barely visible road, for it was always in danger of growing over, she was probably the only vehicle that used it, she could feel the hate like a dark cloud that emanated from him. It was a far-reaching cloud.

It was not only her imagination, for Morris, her faithful chestnut gelding was uneasy in his traces. He swiveled his ears and lifted his nose, scenting the wind. Alert for danger—alert for any sign of *him*. Morris didn't like Mr. Hennessey, either. It was hard to imagine that anyone—or anything—could.

Oh, Lord, she'd reached the end of the road. The trees broke apart to make a sudden clearing. There was the small yard, the stable and paddock, and beyond that the little log cabin on a rise. Halfway between the stable and the house there was a bright honey pile of logs. And a man with an ax.

It was him. He had his back to her as he worked. Sunlight streamed from a hazy sky to shine on the finest pair of men's shoulders she'd ever seen. Muscles bunched and played in smooth motion beneath skin as stunning as polished bronze. Mr. Curmudgeon himself, shirtless, his dark hair tamed at his nape with a leather thong, was splitting wood like an ordinary man, but there was nothing ordinary about her least favorite customer.

As sunlight worshiped his magnificent shape, he drew back the ax and sent it hurling toward the split log. A great rending sound echoed through the clearing as the blade of steel cracked the wood and two pieces tumbled apart.

The hairs stood up on Betsy's nape as he set down his ax. He hadn't looked around, but he'd sensed her presence, for he became larger and taller, if that were possible, so that he looked more than his impressive six-plus feet. His shoulders braced, his arms bowed, his big hands curled into fists. Even from her buggy seat, she saw his jaw clamp tightly and the tendons in his neck bunch.

She was early, she knew it. Judging from the grimace on Mr. Curmudgeon's face, he was not only surprised, but also angry to see her. Well, that was too bad. He didn't have to talk to her. She didn't plan on saying a single word. She had his bag of clean and ironed laundry to deliver, neatly folded as always. He could be as unpleasant as he wished, it was his right and this was his property, after all.

But she didn't have to let it bother her.

It was difficult, but she managed to nod politely as

she drove past where he stood, unabashedly scowling at her unexpected arrival. She'd prepared for him not to be happy, but honestly, she'd never seen such an offensive sneer. His powerful dislike rolled over her like wind off a glacier and it seemed to dim the brightness and warmth of the sun.

Okay, he wasn't just unhappy. He was furious. She shivered in the suddenly cool air. Where was she going to go? She was already here. Her dear horse had tensed and his soft brown coat flickered nervously as he broke his trot to speed away from the disgruntled beast starting to huff and puff, as if working himself up into a temper.

"I don't blame you a bit," she whispered to Morris as she pulled him to a stop in the shade of the cabin's front door. She climbed out to calm him, the poor thing, and rubbed his forehead the way he liked.

Between the gelding's erect and swiveling ears, she spotted *him* stalking toward her like an angry bear, head up, hair whipping in the wind—somehow it had come out of its thong—and his gaze was one black blaze of mad.

"Don't you worry, Morris, I know just how to handle him." Betsy lifted the large rucksack from the back of her buggy, careful not to disturb the others. She could feel his approach like a flame growing closer, but she wasn't afraid. There wasn't a creature on earth that she couldn't tame—eventually.

"Mr. Hennessey, good day to you." She tossed him her most winning smile.

He seemed immune to it. "You're early."

"No, this is my new delivery time. It's changed. If you would have read last week's note—"

"I have no time for reading idle chatter. Do I owe you more money or not?"

"Goodness, no, it's just that I gained another client out this way, if you can believe that—"

"I can't." Duncan remembered to count to ten, but all he could see was red. Anger built in his head like steam. The top of his head felt ready to blow right off. "Then this will be your new regular time?"

"Exactly!" The woman beamed at him from beneath her yellow sunbonnet's wide brim. She was everything he'd come to hate—it wasn't her fault. She didn't seem to understand how her friendliness provoked him.

He took one wary step back and kept going. Distance. It's all he wanted. Distance from her. From town, where she came from. In fact, he'd rather be completely alone forever, until the day he died. He hated doing laundry almost as much, and in fact, he rather preferred the somber laundress who used to come. She was sharp, bitter and never had a kind word. He understood that.

But this new woman—he couldn't get used to her. He didn't understand her at all. She was naive. Sheltered. She probably came from one of those happy-looking families on one of those pleasant, tree-lined streets—nothing bad ever happened to those people. They didn't end up doing hard time in prison for another's crime. They didn't fail their families. Those people had never lost everything.

The image of his mother's grave, marked by only a small stone that did not even bear her name, flashed into his vision. Bitterness filled his mouth and choked him. His heart had stopped existing years ago. The fact that it was beating in his chest made no difference. Like a dead man, he had no future, no hopes, nothing at all.

Nothing but resentment for the slender female and those like her. She wore that frilly yellow calico dress— the one that irritated him the most—for it swirled around the toes of her polished black shoes. She left the rucksack of clean clothes neatly on the front step, as she always did, walking with light, bouncing steps as if her feet didn't quite reach the ground.

Something so delicate and sunny did not belong anywhere near him.

He turned his back, hefted up the ax again and sank it into the pine log with all his strength. The wood rent, two halves flew into the air and tumbled to the ground. He took his time positioning the wedge before he struck again.

He could feel her watching him. Her wide, curious gaze was like an unwanted touch on his bare back. It was indecent, he knew, to work in the presence of a lady without wearing his shirt, but this was his land. He lived far away from civilization for a reason, so he could do what he wanted. There was nothing this woman, or any woman like her, had that he needed.

He didn't care if he offended her, and if he did, then all the better. Maybe she'd leave faster.

But no, she was taking her time. Carefully positioning the laundry in the back of the buggy—apparently there was a complicated system. She seemed intent, half bent over the small boot of the vehicle, and he could only see the bottom half of her skirt. Good. That was an improvement. Maybe all of her would be gone and he would be alone and safe.

He learned long ago what a woman could do to a man. They were the fairer sex, or so he'd been told, but he knew better. A pretty face could hide a deceitful and ruthless heart more easily than an ugly one. He had to admit that Betsy Hunter was one of the prettiest women he'd ever seen.

Not beautiful, she wasn't exactly that. He'd seen enough women in his time to know that beauty had its own aloofness. Betsy Hunter was not a cool vision. No, she was something far more appealing. She was like the sun. She shone from the inside out. Her lovely brown hair always seemed to be tumbling down from its pins to blow in the wind and tangle around her face. She was as slender as a young willow and she moved like a wild mustang, all power and grace and fire.

She straightened from her task and he could see more than just the swirling hem of her skirt. That was not an improvement. He was a man, and a man with needs long unfulfilled, and his eyes were hungry, he could not deny that. He watched her soft round bosom shiver as she hurried to her horse's side. Her lush bow-shaped mouth had to taste like sugar, he decided, when she leaned close to speak to her gelding.

No wonder the animal preened and leaned into her touch. Duncan envied the gelding for the way it enjoyed the light strokes of her gentle fingers.

Desire pulsed in his blood, growing stronger with each beat. He watched her spin on her dainty black shoes. Her ruffled hem swirled, offering a brief look at her slim, leather-encased ankles. Which made him think of her legs. Walking as she was, with the wind against her, her petticoats were no protection. The cotton fabric molded to her form and his gaze traced the curve of her hips and the length of her fine thighs—

"I'll see you next week, Mr. Hennessey!" she called cheerfully, waggling her fingertips to wave goodbye.

It was such an endearing movement, and it shocked him that he noticed. That longing roared up within him for what he could never have, for what he could never let himself want. What was wrong with him? He forced the heat from his veins. He turned into cold steel.

One pretty woman had cost him everything. He would never be fooled again, not by Miss Hunter or by anyone like her. It was fitting that she climbed into her fancy little buggy and hurried her horse down the road. Good riddance. He didn't like how her gentle smile twinkled in her sky-blue eyes. He really disliked the lark-song music of her voice.

In fact, he hoped to never see her again. Next Friday at one in the afternoon he would make sure he was long gone. Out hunting or just out for a twenty-mile walk. Gunmen could attack, a wolf could stalk her, or she could break an axle on that expensive buggy of hers, and he wouldn't care. He'd keep away from her.

No woman was his lookout. No, not ever again.

He gave thanks when the fir and pines guarding his land closed her from his sight. All he heard was the faint *squeak-squee-eak* of a buggy wheel and then nothing but silence.

Just the way he liked it.

Well, that hadn't gone too badly, considering. Betsy waited until she was certain Mr. Hennessey was well out of sight before she retrieved her lunch pail from beneath the seat.

As she unwrapped her tomato, lettuce and salt pork sandwich, she felt sorry for her least-favorite customer—although, on objective terms, he was her best client. He paid extra delivery fees, for he was far out of her usual delivery area. It was nearly an entire afternoon's round trip. Twenty miles one way. Mr. Curmudgeon—oops! Mr. Hennessey—paid more to have his laundry brought to him than for the actual washing and ironing itself. With the county having come upon hard times from storms and drought, she couldn't afford to alienate a single customer.

Which is what troubled her as she bit into her sandwich. The crisp salty pork and sweet fresh tomato and her ma's rye bread made her stomach growl all the harder, it was so good. She chewed, planting the water jug between her thighs to hold it steady while she worked the stopper with her free hand. It gave with a pop and she took a long cool swing.

Much better. Dealing with Mr. Difficult was always a trial, but she'd managed to do fairly well this time. He'd been surprised to see her—she'd known he would be. He'd growled and given a very intimidating scowl, but he hadn't fired her. He wasn't going to. He couldn't fool her. She had taken his measure long ago. Her Mr. Curmudgeon was a wounded beast whose snarl was much worse than his bite.

He was simply an unhappy and distrustful loner. She wondered what had made him like that. Had he always been so bitter? What heartbreak could have possibly made him that way? What would compel a man to retreat from civilization and live alone in the wilderness, over twenty miles from the nearest town?

Whatever happened to him, it had to have been terribly tragic. Betsy tried to imagine the possibilities as she transferred the half-eaten sandwich into her driving hand and dug in her little lunch pail with the other. The image of Duncan Hennessey, shirtless, his glorious male form kissed by the brazen sun, troubled her. He was one fine-looking man. Too fine for the life of a recluse. It was a woman that had broken his spirit. Maybe she'd jilted him. Or maybe she'd died.

Yes, she knew that pain. Although she'd been a widow for over five years now, the sadness of losing Charlie remained. If she hadn't had a loving family and wonderful friends to keep her firmly in this world, she could see how that painful grief could drive a person to a solitary life.

Losing a loved one hurt more than anything. It was one reason she'd never been able to remarry. The thought of being so vulnerable again frightened her. Her life, her heart, her very soul had been devastated. Maybe that was why Mr. Hennessey was so unpleasant. He never wanted to let anyone into his heart again.

Her heart twisted in sympathy. As beastly as he was on the outside only pointed to a deep, private pain. The poor man. That's why she never allowed his surly behavior to trouble her. As she unwrapped her slice of strawberry pie, she vowed to be even friendlier the next time she crossed his path.

With her mouth watering, she took a rich, creamy bite. Sweet berries burst on her tongue and she moaned in delight. She savored the lovely flavors, for she believed that the enjoyment of a good dessert should never be rushed.

For no reason, Morris froze in the middle of the path and the buggy jerked at the sudden stop. She looked up in surprise as the fork tumbled out of her fingers, taking her next bite of pie with it. She watched the steel utensil and ruby-red strawberries tumble between the dash and the whiffletree. Before dismay could settle in, she realized her horse was twitching, as if a thousand flies were crawling over his warm coat, but there wasn't a single fly anywhere.

What was wrong with Morris? There was no danger in sight, although it was very shadowy. The ancient trees blocked most of the light from the sky and they seemed to moan, but that was just the rising wind rubbing limbs together.

"It's all right, sweet boy." She reached to set the brake so she could hop out and retrieve her fork.

Morris's ears swiveled, as if he heard some danger approaching, and he gave a frightened whinny. That simply couldn't be a good sign. Betsy pushed her meal aside, her dessert forgotten and reached for the Winchester.

It wasn't on the seat where it was supposed to be. Her tin lunch pail sat there instead, emitting the scent of wonderful strawberries. Where did the gun go? The tiny hairs along Betsy's nape stood straight on end and tingled. She wanted her rifle.

As Morris whinnied again, she dropped to her knees on the floorboards. There it was. She grasped the sun-warmed barrel in time to see a shadow move between the trees—a tall figure with wide shoulders and brawny arms. She caught a glimpse of dark hair above harsh black eyes. That wasn't Mr. Hennessey, was it?

The branches parted and it wasn't Mr. Hennessey breaking through the thick undergrowth. It was a bear.

The blood rushed from her head as the great black bear reared up on his hind legs, using his powerful limbs and claws to break away the impeding evergreens. Thick boughs snapped like gunfire, but it was a small sound compared to the bear's furious roar. His enormous jaws twisted open, exposing huge rows of teeth. Sharp, jagged teeth made for tearing his prey into small, manageable bites.

Time seemed to slow. She couldn't lift the gun fast enough. The bear was reaching out with his enormous humanlike hands, except for the lethal claws at the tips. As he roared again, saliva dripped from his mouth. The beast was looking for lunch, and she doubted he wanted her sandwich or her pie, although they were both very good. He was eyeing her horse!

In a strangely eerie slow motion, the bear began to lunge and she positioned the Winchester against her shoulder and aimed. As the bear emerged onto the road, her finger found the trigger and, pulse thudding in her ears so hard she was shaking with the force of it, she squeezed. Light and smoke exploded from the steel barrel. The gun kicked hard against her shoulder and leaped out of her hands. The bear roared again and slapped at his left arm.

Like an indignant human, the creature gazed down at his fur, saw the blood, and attacked. Betsy fumbled for the gun, but her right arm was numb and didn't move as fast as she wanted it to. Morris chose that moment to leap into a full gallop. The buggy jerked, she lost her balance and tumbled right off the floor, rolling head over skirts in midair. For the brief instant she was upside down, with her petticoats spilling over her face and the ground rushing up to meet her, she caught sight of her fork shimmering in the bright sunshine.

It was an odd thing to notice, she thought in the last few seconds she had left to live. The bear's enormous hairy feet were pounding toward her and her thoughts flashed forward in time. If she somehow lived to tell this tale to her dear friends, whom she was to meet this afternoon for tea, she could imagine how they would laugh hysterically about the bear's feet. It would sure make a funny story, how she was almost eaten by a bear while eating her lunch—

The ground stuck her hard in the back and seemed to jar some sense into her. Her body impacted next. Pain thudded through her. Air left her lungs in a whoosh. Suddenly a shadow rose over her and she squeezed her eyes shut. She no longer had hold of her gun. She was defenseless and this was it—this was death. She didn't want to see the bear's terrifying teeth and lethal jaw opening wide to take a bite of her. Fear turned her blood to ice and there was nothing she could do. There was no way to stop him—

A gunshot cannoned above the pounding sound in her ears. The bear roared a final time before the earth quaked around her. Betsy opened one eye and realized the bear, with blood oozing from a bullet wound between his eyes, was lying right beside her. Another creature was towering over both of them, casting them in his significant shadow.

For a moment Betsy wondered if it was another bear, for that was the impression he gave—of raw lethal power and wild fury. But bears didn't wear leather boots and denims or carry a polished rifle.

Duncan Hennessey stared down at her with a grimace so terrifying he made the charging bear seem friendly. She tried to drag air into her spasming lungs and failed. As she coughed and gasped, she looked at the dead bear with longing.

She would have much rather dealt with that beast than the one towering over her, loaded gun in one hand and eyes black with rage.

Chapter Two

Duncan noticed the fork and the strawberries gleaming bright red in the middle of the grassy road and took in the scent of fried, crispy salt pork. Women. Most of them didn't have a drop of common sense. Not that he cared.

He'd done the right thing in coming to her rescue, but it only made him more annoyed. He was doing fine alone. It was other people that brought misery. Today, he'd been content enough to work on his winter supply of wood. But a woman comes along and, by getting herself nearly killed, forces him to become involved.

He hadn't run full-speed through the forest because he'd been concerned about her. Nope. He simply couldn't let a pretty woman get hurt, because she was bound to be missed and someone would come looking for her and blame him for whatever happened.

Really. He was just acting out of his own best interests and not some noble code to protect the weaker. He didn't care about her at all, even if her big blue eyes were wide with fear and her softly ample bosom rose and fell as she gasped for air. He steeled his feelings against her, because it was the only thing he could do. Women came with a cost. He'd paid with his life, his future and his family.

It had been too much.

She was safe now. What he ought to do was leave her heaving for breath in the road and let her find her horse on her own. Maybe that would teach her a lesson, he reasoned. What he really wanted was to get away from her before any misunderstandings occurred. You could just never tell what a woman was plotting. Even with something as innocent as this.

He pushed the panic rising within him away and headed for the downed bear. Fine, a bear had attacked her, but even this could get twisted around. All anyone might see was a horse and empty buggy fleeing the forest, the pretty young woman missing, and it would start all over again.

The images raced through his mind like a river at flood stage, speeding and fingering into little eddies so that more memories came to life. The noise of the crowds, the jeers of hatred, the cold metal encircling his wrists and the final clank as the marshal closed them.

He could feel the agony in his mother's broken heart and, in bleak devastation, felt as lost as the darkness in the cell's blackest corners. The rank odors of the windowless holding cell filled his nose, where he could not sleep because he couldn't see the sky. He'd lain awake waiting for the night to pass.

Waiting to see if they would hang him come morning.

No, that wasn't going to happen again. Never again. Rage made him as hard and as cruel as the mountains behind him. He refused to touch the woman. Her skirts were askew and her bare knee was showing. He made sure he kept his distance as he knelt so they were eye level. Her porcelain features crinkled as she fought to breathe. She looked at him with the question clear on her face. *Help me?*

Only so much, lady. He checked to make sure the bear was good and truly dead. No pulse beat in his throat and his chest was as still as the earth. Good. Now he could think about what to do with the woman. "Just relax. Try to breathe in slow. You're gonna be just fine."

Her gaze latched on to his, and he felt the impact as if she'd reached out with her soft dainty hands and grabbed hold of his throat. More panic zipped through his system as if he'd been struck by lightning. He felt her fear, and he understood. She'd had a pretty good scare. That could unsettle a person.

He'd done time as a soldier in the Great War between the states and had come across enough wounded there, in prison and in these mountains that he knew by looking she wasn't hurt. Just scared. Fear could be a living thing, he knew, seizing up a person.

"C'mon now, you just got the wind knocked out of you." He simply needed to get her thinking about something besides the dead bear beside her. "What did you think you were doing, eating in these woods? It's feeding time for the bears. You know they hibernate, right?"

The fear glazing her eyes was fading. Air rasped into her lungs.

Being angry with her was working, so he kept on going. "Bears eat a lot before they hibernate. That means they are hungry. Any person with a speck of sense knows to stay away from hungry bears. But not you. You open up a salt pork sandwich and strawberries. *Strawberries.*"

He hated to think what would have happened if he hadn't gone against his principles and come running when he'd heard her gunshot.

She was breathing nearly regular now and the color was back in her face. He fought the urge to help her up and to treat the cut bleeding on her hand. It was the same protective instinct that had gotten him in trouble long ago, so he straightened and began to back away until he'd put a few more yards between them.

Now what should he do? Her horse and vehicle were gone, and there was no telling where he'd find them. She was female, and they were alone together. He didn't like her, he didn't trust her and he didn't want her anywhere near him.

He couldn't leave her alone.

She was a little thing. He'd never studied her this close before. A tiny blanket of freckles lay on her nose and cheeks. Her eyelashes were thick and dark, and there was something so vulnerable in the way she sat up and wiped the grass seeds out of her hair with a shaking hand.

Something moved deep down within the iron weight that had replaced his heart. It wasn't a feeling—he didn't have feelings. He'd found no need for them, but he couldn't rightly say what hurt where his heart used to be.

It was probably indigestion. That's what he got for running hard through the forest right after his noon meal.

The problem was still before him. The woman. What should he do with her? "Can you stand?"

"I think so." She smoothed her skirts as if gathering up her strength, but she didn't get on her feet.

Fine, he'd carry her, saddle up a horse and make sure she was able to sit in the saddle—

Branches broke with a snap-snap in the woods behind him. The woman's eyes flashed wide and utter fear twisted on her lovely face. Duncan pivoted, hauled his rifle up by the stock, but the big black bear was moving fast.

Too fast.

He got off a shot—missed the heart—and cocked, but that was all before the bear pushed away the smoking rifle barrel with the mighty swipe of one sharp claw.

Oh, hell. Duncan watched his favorite rifle crack apart and fall in two pieces to the rocky ground. Good thing he was prepared. He drew so fast, he got off a shot, but two bullets in the chest didn't stop this bear. He charged, and both foot-wide paws scraped deep into Duncan's shoulders.

Claws sliced him like a dozen razor blades. He was a dead man. Duncan tried to fight, but the bear was twice as strong and clawed through both shoulder muscles and downward, breaking ribs. Duncan fell to his knees as the bear knocked him to the ground and bent to sink his teeth into Duncan's neck.

It's over. Just like that. Duncan met the bear head-on, fighting even as the animal's jaws parted for the death bite. He saw the woman out of the corner of his eye. She had climbed to her feet and was shouting and throwing rocks at the big animal, but the hunks of granite didn't harm the bear. Or stop him. Still, Duncan appreciated the effort as his left hand groped along the top of his boot.

The first prick of incisor drilled into Duncan's throat, but his fingers closed around the knife handle. He was dying, fine, but he'd take the bear with him. He'd make sure the pretty laundry lady with her sunshine and freckles would live.

With a roar, Duncan slid his bowie knife into the bastard's ribs. He ignored the spray of blood as he twisted and turned the blade deep. He felt death come in a swift black wave that drained the light from his eyes and the strength from his body. He was falling. Vaguely he felt the brutal impact of hitting the rocky ground, knew blood was gushing out from his neck and chest, but the bear was dead. That was all that mattered.

He was drifting like a dying leaf on the wind. Her voice was the last thing he heard. She was speaking his name, calling to him, but he was already floating away.

When he looked down, he saw her huddled in the road, flanked by two dead bears, cradling a bloody man with his head on her lap. Her hair had tumbled free and her dainty yellow dress was stained crimson.

It was the sound of her tears that drilled deep into his steeled soul.

She was crying for him.

Betsy held on to him. She didn't know what else to do. Blood was everywhere and her nightmare was happening all over again. Times she'd rather forget rolled forward and she couldn't squeeze off the rush of memories. Years ago she'd held another dying man in her lap just like this and watched the blood drain out of him. The doctor had worked frantically but couldn't save her husband.

How on earth could she hope to save Mr. Hennessey? Despair overwhelmed her. Trembling, she wiped blood from his face. His was a strong face, with high and sharp cheekbones and a profile like the Rocky Mountains that soared so strong and unfailing into the cloudy sky. But Duncan Hennessey was not made of granite, no, he was as vulnerable as any human. No growling demeanor and intentional rudeness could make him more immune to death.

Blood. There was so much of it streaming from the open tears in his flesh. Panic threatened to overtake her, but she couldn't let it win. She couldn't sit here, holding his head and fighting off a case of the vapors when she had to try to save him. She had to think. She had to remember what the doctor had done for Charlie.

She had to stop the bleeding, she knew that. But how? There were so many wounds, and the buggy was long gone. All she had were her petticoats, so she yanked them off and tore at the fabric. As fast as she could, she bunched wads of muslin into the wounds. The white material quickly wicked up the blood, turning red even as she pushed more into place.

Okay, that wasn't going to work. Her fingers felt clumsy as she pulled her little sewing pack from her pocket. The needle was small, but she had enough thread to sew the worst wound.

She pressed her hand against the curve where shoulder met neck and the bleeding slowed. She broke off a length of thread with her teeth, working quickly. She couldn't let him die. She wouldn't. But she knew it was hopeless as she licked the end of the thread to stiffen it. She could feel his pulse quicken as she threaded the needle.

Crimson continued to pool on the earth beneath him, staining them both, making it impossible to see as she probed the gaping wound. Her stomach went weak and her knees to water at the sight of torn muscle and exposed bone. As if she were basting a collar, she nudged the edges of jagged skin together, fitting them as a seam and took one stitch deep. Then another.

Her heart beat as fast as his. A creature in the shadows howled. She couldn't see it through the dense evergreens, but she could feel it. A wolf pacing and waiting for the right moment to strike.

She'd stopped the most profusely bleeding wounds. Encouraged, she kept going. He lay as if dead, but he was still breathing. It wasn't enough. He was going to die, just as Charlie did. This time there was no doctor nearby. There was no one to help. Shelter was over a third of a mile through the woods where the brisk winds were quickly spreading the scent of fresh spilled blood.

If meat and strawberries had brought a hungry bear and his mate, then what would this bring?

Fear shivered through her. The forest had gone quiet and it felt as if the trees had eyes. Had every predator within a five-mile radius come to hunt?

Mr. Hennessey lay as limp as a rag doll, all six-feet-plus of him. The hue had washed out of his face and he looked ashen and lifeless. His chest barely rose with each breath. His pulse fluttered wildly in the base of his throat.

Death. It hovered close, waiting for him. Betsy knew. She had felt it before. She'd been there when it had stolen her husband away.

But this man, he had no woman to mourn him. He lived alone. If he were to die, then how sad that was. With no one to miss him, then it would be as if his life never was. He didn't deserve that. Nobody did. She brushed her fingertips along the stubbled curve of his jaw. She stared into the shadows that were growing darker as the sun sank in the sky. The silence seemed to grow and lengthen. The small animals of the forest were hiding from the hungry creatures that watched and waited.

She had to prepare for the worst. She retrieved the handgun from where it had landed in the tall grass and checked the chambers. Five shots were left. She closed the chamber and cocked it.

Thank goodness she'd grown up with four brothers. She'd been around guns all her life. She took some comfort in that. The weapon was ready to fire and she was confident she could use it. If only she felt as confident with her aiming ability.

"Don't worry." She let her hand brush across his hairline and along his temple. She hoped if he was somehow aware of what was happening, that she could give him some comfort. "I promise, whatever happens, I'll stay right by your side."

There was no answer. She didn't expect one.

Because the sun was slipping behind the tall trees,

it felt as if the day were almost over. Long shadows crept across the ground, chasing back the scant amount of sunlight. The wild sunflowers with their petal faces began to bow.

It was as if the entire mountainside waited.

She had to move him, but memories haunted her—of the doctor and Charlie's brother moving him from the barnyard to the house. That's when the wounds had broken open again and there'd been no stanching the blood loss. Charlie had been dead less than five minutes later.

She thought she spotted a movement in the shadows. The glint of luminous yellow eyes behind a fern leaf, and then only shadows.

She had a small length of thread left. She'd work until it was gone and then she'd have to move him.

He didn't know how it happened, but he was back in the quarry. The sun blistered his skin and burned through flesh and bone until he was on fire from the inside out. His eyes stung from the salty sweat pouring down his face and pain was a living enemy that could not be killed. The places where his flesh gaped open from the lash of the foreman's whip throbbed fiercely. He was beyond exhaustion and thirst. Hunger and hope.

He heaved the rock from the ground into the wagon behind him again and again. Minute after minute, hour after hour without end. The sun was motionless in the cloud-streaked sky.

It was his second day as a guest of Montana territory. His second day serving time. The prison clothes were scratchy and too tight at the shoulders. His stomach twisted in nausea from the morning's gruel. Although nearly ten hours had passed since he'd eaten, his breakfast remained a sour lump in his gut.

He left bloody prints on the twenty-pound boulder he heaved into the wagon. As he stepped back, his chains jangled and tore at the raw flesh above his ankles. The boulder, gaining momentum, rolled over the pile, bounced off the railing on the other side and sailed over the edge.

The quarry silenced. Duncan read the faces of the men surrounding him, chained as he was, and saw the knowledge of what was to come. He was not surprised by the piercing sting of the bullwhip or the burst of pain spraying across his shoulders. He stumbled beneath the force of the next blow; sagged against the wagon, clinging to the rail boards as the whip snaked and hissed and sliced.

"Maybe that'll teach ya," a hate-filled voice growled out. "Now git back to work."

His vision was hazed. Dark spots swirled before his eyes and shock rolled through his body. He fought nausea and dizziness to kneel and heft another boulder into the wagon.

Across the rails, there was a hard thud. The boulder that had fallen was back in the pile, as it should have been, lifted into place by a man who was also bleeding. Duncan realized that he'd not been the only one punished for his mistake.

A week ago at this time of day, he'd been getting ready to close up his shop. He'd have been thinking ahead to getting supper over at the hotel—it was usually fried chicken on Fridays with fluffy biscuits and fresh buttered peas and mashed potatoes. As he did every evening, he would have followed the meal with coffee and a slice of pie and, content with his life, he would have settled down at his lathe to work before bedtime.

It seemed impossible that he'd lived that life, that it had ever been real. Now it seemed like a dream, Duncan thought hours later, when twilight fell. His old life was as if it had never been.

At the workday's end, when the last light was wrung from the sky and it was nearly ten o'clock, Duncan stumbled along the path through the quarry and into the prison yard, where he lined up among the other men waiting to enter the dining hall. How was he going to eat feeling the way he did?

"Hey, you." It was the man who'd returned the fallen boulder to the wagon. The whip's lash across his forehead had clotted and left a rough black-red streak between his eyes.

Duncan didn't see the first blow. It had come from another direction. The second punch had his knees knocking and he fisted his hands, but it was eleven men to his one, and he didn't have a chance. He choked on blood as he fought off one blow after another until he caught a right hook beneath his jaw and landed face-first in the dirt. A kick struck him in the gut. The beating continued until the line moved forward, and he was left to huddle, bleeding and vomiting.

The young man he'd been had died in the dark prison yard that evening, wearing prisoner's garb and a convict's ankle cuff. The man who'd risen from the ground and wiped the blood from his eyes was someone else. There'd been no softness or emotion in the cold-eyed figure that took his place in line. Who'd turned his back on the small glimpse of sky above the high walls.

Like a dead man, he'd had no feelings, no dreams, no needs.

He was made not of flesh and bone, but of iron and will.

It was that iron will that remained as the pain changed and he fought to open his eyes. It was twilight. He was bloody and hurting. But he was not trapped in the nightmare.

He was in a forest, gazing up at a woman. Her features were blurred because he couldn't see clearly. He hurt everywhere, as if he'd been lit on fire, but that didn't bother him nearly as much as the woman. Who was she?

"Don't you dare die on me, do you hear? Not that men ever listen to a woman, no, they wouldn't dream of doing that, but don't let me down, Mr. Hennessey. Stay alive for me, all right?"

Lustrous curls tumbled around her face, tangled and wild, and her sweet heart-shaped face was familiar. Worry crinkled the corners of her eyes and emphasized the dimple in the center of her delicate chin. She was a petite thing, and she smelled good. Like sunshine and clover and those little yellow flowers that used to grow on the fence in his mother's backyard.

Pain scoured his chest. His thoughts cleared and he knew where he was. The dark shadows were his trees and it was his laundry lady kneeling over him with her riot of dark gold curls bouncing everywhere, thick and lustrous and rippling from the wind's touch.

Another wave of pain crashed through him. He was here, in the present, the past vanishing like fog.

Her eyes, so blue and gentle, gleamed with an unspoken kindness. "Oh, thank Heaven. I knew you were too ornery to die on me."

But the way she said it wasn't harsh. No, it was tender, as if she didn't think he was ornery at all. And he was. All he could think about was how he despised women like her, so delicate and soft and sheltered. She wanted something. All women wanted something. A woman like that had ruined him. Maybe it was bitterness, or maybe it was just his broken spirit that made him believe a woman could be no other way.

"What do you want?" he snarled as she whipped out a needle and stuck it into his neck. "I don't have a lot of money."

"Money? I might charge you a fee for doing your washing and ironing and mending, Mr. Hennessey, but I'm not about to bill you for patching you up. Not when you saved my life as you did." She tugged the thread through his skin, quick and tight.

Agony drilled through him. He lifted his head and tried to get up, but his body wouldn't move. He was wet with his own sweat and blood, and he began trembling. She leaned over him, giving him a perfect view of her white chemise. Lace edged the top where the soft creamy curves of her full breasts strained at the fabric.

Panic overrode pain. He was alone with a woman in her underclothes. That couldn't be good. Memories rushed into his mind and he was too weak to stop them. Memories of another woman in her lace-edged chemise, memories of a pack of men shouting and beating down his door. The splinter of wood breaking. The rage of the crowd as it crashed through his shop—

"No!" He heaved to the side, but his body felt distant and wooden. His strength was gone. Gone. No, that wasn't right. He had to move, he had to get away from her—

"Wait, oh, no! You're tearing up my work. Please, Mr. Hennessey." Her cool hands grabbed at him and pushed him back down. Her face hovered over him, full of concern, like an angel of mercy. He didn't believe in mercy. "Please, you have to let me do this. You have to. I can't watch another man die. So you have to let me help you. That's all I want to do."

"I don't want your help. Get away from me."

"You'd rather bleed to death, is that it?"

"Yeah, now get off me."

"No. I'm going to save you whether you like it or not." She rose over him and sat on his waist. Silver tears filled her eyes but they didn't fall, and he could only stare.

Were those genuine? He remembered how it had seemed he was looking down on her and she'd been crying over him. He could see the faint tracks on her cheeks.

She meant to help him, he could read that plain enough on her face. But she would bring him harm, just the same. Whatever it cost him, he had to get up, he had to find her horse and buggy and send her on her way. She'd bound him with her dress and petticoats, and while any fool could see the yellow gingham wrapped around his wounds, it didn't change the fact that she was alone with him—in her undergarments. And with his past—

He had to get up. He tried. He really did. His left arm moved and his left hand scrabbled along until he seized on something. He turned toward it. The low branch of a tree. It looked sturdy enough. He pulled, dragging his body along the gritty earth. Rocks jabbed into his spine, but he was moving. Something hard slid off his chest and poked him in his ribs.

His Colt .45. Relief made him forget about the woman trying to hold him down, talking a mile a minute as she kept on stitching. He pulled on the tree branch with all his might. The tree shook, the limb groaned as if on the breaking point, but he was sitting up. Now if he could just stand—

"No, hold still, I have to knot it." Her words came in and out, fading along with his vision.

Duncan fought the blackness. Breathing hard, as if he'd worked a sixteen-hour shift in the quarry. He fought to stand. And then he saw movement in the shadows. A wolf leaped through the trees.

He let go of the branch and grabbed the Colt. Missed. His reflexes were too slow and his hand was no longer working.

There was a shot, a flash of fire, and the last thing he remembered was his laundry woman kneeling beside him, protecting him with her body, as she fired off a second round.

The darkness stole everything—his sight, his hearing, his thoughts, and even the pain. There was nothing but blackness taking him down like deep water.

But he wasn't alone. He felt soft fingertips brush his brow. It was the woman.

Chapter Three

It was hard to look at this unconscious man and to not remember another. Betsy let the swell of sadness fill her up. Time had healed her grief, but she'd never forgotten. When Charlie had died, it had been a moonless night like this, too, and silent, as if the entire world had lain in wait for him to pass. She'd been just as helpless then.

Like Charlie, Duncan Hennessey had lost too much blood. He'd fought her, breaking open his worst wound. Getting him down the rocky road and shooing off the coyotes that were brazenly following them had drained every ounce of her optimism. She'd had to finally fashion a torch out of a branch and keep it lit to ward off the more dangerous predators.

It had worked, and now the stout log walls of his house protected them. But the animals were outside the door. Even with a torch, she didn't dare head out into the night to fetch more water. She wrung the washcloth from the basin at her side and carefully cleansed the dried blood from his chest. His pulse thudded too fast at the hollow in his throat and his breathing was shallow.

He wasn't nearly as disagreeable unconscious. He was a big man, over six feet, and his build was strong. Even slack, muscles were visible beneath his sun-bronzed skin. He radiated pure masculine strength, as if it came not only from his physical form but also from his spirit.

His skin was hot. The male scent of him—salty and woodsy—made her remember what it was like to be married. To share intimacy and morning cups of coffee and quiet evenings, of the immeasurable emotional bond that bound a man and wife. She hadn't minded these years spent alone. That didn't mean she liked it. Only that she hadn't found a man who she could laugh with. One who seemed to fit with her.

The lantern light flickered. The oil was low. She should get up and search through his cupboards for more, but she didn't want to leave him. Not unless she had to. He was dying, she knew it. She feared nothing could stop it. And it was her fault. He'd been protecting her.

He moaned low in his throat, troubled by dreams. Was a fever setting in? She leaned her cheek against his brow. He did feel warm, but not too warm. Yet. The pungent odor of boiling onions mixed with the nettles she had stewing on his stove—both smelled nearly done, she figured. Soon she would have to go check on them and see. She'd search for the oil can then.

"In the meantime, just rest."

The flame writhed and swelled, and the strange orange light swept over the hard crags of his face and the vulnerable underside of his jaw. The shadows seemed to cling to him, as if he belonged to the night. As if there were only the shadow of him remaining.

She finished washing the blood from his chest and wondered, Did she finish stitching the lesser wounds? The horrible gashes spread nearly a foot and a half from his chest to his shoulder. Several were still seeping, but she feared by removing the bandaging, she would break open the clotted places.

He grew still. Was he breathing? Was his heart beating? Fear quickened through her veins as the long second stretched out and then his chest rose faintly, dragging in a ragged breath.

Thank goodness. Just continue breathing, all right? She couldn't help stroking the iron curve of his face. The rough texture of several days' growth abraded her fingertips. He was dreaming. His eyes were moving beneath his lids, and his mouth tightened. The hard thin lips that seemed to have been in a permanent frown twisted, not in anger but in agony.

The flame in the glass chimney flared with one last effort before the brightness waned and plunged the cabin into darkness.

Outside the thick walls, a wolf howled. Another answered. So close, she could hear the scrape of paws outside the window. Betsy did not consider it a good sign for the long night ahead. There was no way the predators could find their way inside, but still, it unsettled her to be in a wild land where only the strong and the cruel survived. What benefit did Mr. Hennessey—or any of the mountain men—see in living so far from civilization?

Shivering, and not with cold, she hurried to the

warm stove where her home remedies simmered and seasoned. She knew there was a second lantern on the shelf next to the stove. As she struck a match, she heard a thump on the roof overhead and the scrape of claws digging into the wood shingles. A cougar.

The match flared, light glowed, and Betsy quickly lit the cold wick. Bright lemony rays pushed back the wall of darkness, but her fears remained. It was as if death were outside, looking for a way in.

Betsy knew all too well that was one predator no one could lock out.

Duncan saw the light as if from far away. A blurred image that hovered at the edge of consciousness. He felt weighted, as if the air had become heavier than he was and pressed down on him with a mighty force. He could not move. His mouth hurt with thirst. His tongue felt swollen and sandy. The acrid scent of blood filled the air and a noise rushed through the darkness. Something he couldn't place.

Was he dreaming? Or awake? He didn't know. Either way, it was memory that swept him backward to the crash of a door breaking open, the frame cracking into pieces. The drum of an enraged mob pulsed and shouted into his workroom. The hum of the lathe and the sharp, pleasant scent of walnut wood faded with the angry shouts and sweating men, the odor of whiskey strong on them.

"There he is!" Eldon Green's baritone boomed deep with hatred. "Let's string him up, boys."

"Hanging is too good for him!" his brother Lindon shouted.

Duncan couldn't move for a moment. He stared

without believing what his eyes were seeing as men he called friends charged at him. Lindon held a rope coiled in one hand, a noose dangling at its end.

Shock numbed him as the table leg he'd been working on whispered to a stop, his chisel tumbling from his hand.

Pain sliced through his chest and he realized it was the noose closing around his neck. He grabbed it with both hands, desperate, panic roaring through him. He had to get it off. This was wrong. All wrong. Why were they doing this?

"Shh." A low gentle sound tried to chase away the bad dream, which was no illusion but his life. A memory the cool brush of a cloth soothed into nonexistence.

He opened his eyes. He was in his cabin. In his bed. Staring at the circle of light on the open timbers of the ceiling, where lantern light gleamed. Pain began like a bullet, pointed and deep, then streaked outward. He took a shivery breath.

He already knew it was her. The tug of skin, the drag of thread through raw, ruined flesh. His fists clenched and his teeth ground together. There she was at the edges of his blurred vision, her hair falling over her shoulders and the white lace at her chemise. Her creamy skin looked as soft as silk and her sweet summer scent pounded in his head.

He heard the chink of a glass bottle and the glug-glug of liquid pouring. Whiskey. The sharp scent brought back the images of the memory as the noose burned into his throat, choking him as the end of the rope was tossed over the center beam and pulled. Some nightmares were real, and he was looking at another one.

It was night—his cabin was pitch-black. He was alone with her. There were signs of no one else in the room. Who else would be here? And she was in her underclothes, wearing one of his flannel shirts that, unbuttoned, slipped off her shoulders.

He tried to lift his head off the pillow. He couldn't. His limbs felt as heavy and dull as lead. Weakness washed through his veins. He was too weak to move. Too weak to protect himself. Too weak to put Miss Laundry Lady on his horse and make her leave.

"I was beginning to worry that you would never wake up." She chatted in that friendly way she had.

The way that he despised—because they weren't friends. He didn't want to be friends. He wanted to be left alone. Horror churned up inside him until he could taste the sourness of it filling his mouth. "Just go."

"And leave you like this? Not for anything." She seemed to float over him, but then he realized it was the light dancing on the wick. The golden glow lapped at her luminous skin and bronzed her shimmering hair. "I owe you my life. And I'm the kind of woman who pays her debts."

"Git. Shoo."

"Go ahead and growl. You don't scare me a bit." Her kindness warmed her soft words and added extra beauty to her serene face. She held a tin cup to his lips. "This will help with the pain."

Whiskey fumes nearly had him coughing. His chest wheezed out and puffed in air, and agony drained him. He couldn't speak. He couldn't push her away. He couldn't move.

Shame filled him to the brim with darkness. He

managed to turn his head away to stare into the shadowed room. He didn't have the strength to do more than breathe. He was alone with a woman he couldn't trust.

He'd rather bleed to death than let her touch him, and the truth was, he couldn't stop her from it.

"You've lost a lot of blood." She paused as, with a clunk of tin, she set the cup aside. "I've sewed up the worst of the gashes, but the truth is, you're still bleeding. I'm afraid this is going to hurt quite a bit, but I'll be as quick as I can. And as careful."

He didn't acknowledge her. He had his pride.

The first stitch hurt no worse than he was already hurting. He took it—he had no choice. She leaned forward and as she worked, he could feel her nearness like a breeze against his skin. The satiny tips of her curls danced and skipped over his arm and abdomen. Out of the corner of his eyes he could see the fullness of her breasts.

This was wrong. All of it. His vision blurred into darkness and back again. He tried again to tell her to leave him be, that dying alone was better than this disgrace, but he couldn't form the words. His lips were too numb to speak.

"That's it. I'm almost done with this one. That bear sure got you good." Her voice was like poetry, like the sweeping cadence of Shakespeare's sonnets. "I'm so glad you're still with me. I'll have you patched up, and then I'll make a good hot soup. My ma says there's nothing a good bowl of soup can't cure."

Great. Just his luck to be trapped with a talker. He liked his women silent—in fact, he liked his women to be absent. Was there any way to be rid of her?

A horse's whinny pierced the darkness and even though the thick walls muffled the sound, he knew it was not one of his. He withered at the faint clomp of steeled shoes on the hard packed earth outside his front door. A light flared in the window, bobbing up and then away.

"What the—" The laundry lady set aside her needle and thread and the bed rope groaned as she stood. Her slender shadow fell over him.

With an ear-splitting crack, the door broke open, wood splinters flying into the air as wraiths and ghosts emerged from the night. Eerie dark shapes that became men as the light touched them. Wide-shouldered angry men, with rifles in hand and a lantern shining suddenly into his eyes. Onto the bed. Where Betsy Hunter stood, her hair tangled, her undershirt and skirt covered with spots of blood.

He knew what was going to happen next. He'd been surly and rude and horrible to this prim and sheltered woman, and now he was going to pay for it. He knew how this was going to go.

His mind leaped forward and he saw what was to come in a flash, but it was really the past. The murderous rage, the shouted accusations, the noose closing off his air. He would lose everything. His life, his home, his work, his freedom.

He remembered Ginetta Green's tears as she'd spoken to the sheriff and how Duncan had had hope then, hope that reason would rule and it was all a big mistake. What else could it have been? He'd never hurt Ginetta. He'd never hurt anyone. Ginetta had used him, she'd lied about him, and she'd betrayed him for reasons he would never know.

Betsy Hunter stood in the shadows, radiant as a midnight star in a moonless sky, but he was not fooled. Not by a woman's beauty. Not by her seeming goodness. Not by her kindness. She wanted something. What? How was she going to use this to her advantage?

Duncan saw the barred door close on his future once more. Her rescuer with his search party stormed through the dark main room. Beefy hands closed around his throat and Duncan knew the sting of a woman's betrayal twice in his life.

At the edges of his vision he saw her. Perky Betsy Hunter, ready to condemn him. No one was going to believe him, a man convicted of rape. Defeat curled around his soul and from a distance he heard the men shouting, the flare of lantern light on a rifle barrel as it aimed directly between his eyes. He felt stitches at his neck tear, felt the hot rush of blood.

"No!" Suddenly she was there, her calm touch against his face, she was splaying the flat of her free hand against his wound. "What is wrong with you, Joshua? Put him down before you kill him."

"That's the idea."

"Stop it. Didn't you see the bears dead in the road?" Men. She would never understand them. She'd grown up in a houseful of brothers, she'd been married, and all the time in the presence of the species she could never figure out why they were so downright bullheaded and pushy and all male temper. "What's wrong with you? I said, put him down."

Her oldest brother kept right on choking the dying man. Duncan might be the bigger of the two, but he'd lost more blood than Charlie had, at least it seemed that way, and she couldn't bear it, she simply couldn't. "James! You get over here and help me. His stitches are torn. Isn't that just like a man to rip out half an evening's work."

Joshua gaped down at her, some of the wild male protective rage leaving him. A small glint of intelligence came back into his eyes. "But he hurt you. Don't try and defend him."

"He saved me. Think, would you? Look at the wounds. Doesn't that look strangely as if a bear clawed him?"

Betsy gave her brother a kick in the shins, and grabbed her other brother by the wrist. "That's no way to treat the man who nearly died for me. Ease him down gently… That's right."

Her heart was breaking, that was it. It was a lost battle from the start, she knew that, but now all her work was nearly undone and fresh blood wet his chest.

The image of him standing tall against the great black bear—no man fought one of those creatures and lived to tell about it—he'd known he was forfeiting his life from the start. From the moment he must have heard her gunshot. And yet he'd come anyway, to save her.

His hand flailed, that's how weak he was. His big fingers were cold as they closed over hers. "T-thank you." He coughed, blood staining his bottom lip. "For the truth."

Whatever could he mean? She watched his eyelids flicker. As silence filled the room, it seemed as if his life force was disappearing.

"You're my very own hero," she whispered in his

ear. "You can't leave me now, when I've only found you."

But his breath rattled and his fingers went slack.

In the silence, Betsy waited for his chest to rise with his next breath. It didn't, but she kept waiting.

"Come away from him now." Joshua's hand settled on her shoulder, a comforting weight in the darkness broken only by the lantern hung on a nail over Duncan's bed. "You've done all you can."

"It isn't enough." It could never be enough. She was banged up and bruised and bandaged, and without her favorite dress, but it was nothing—nothing—at all. The bear attack had been terrifying—beyond terrifying.

Now, safe in the cabin with her brothers at her side, the shock had worn off and horror clawed at her soul. The images of the huge man battling an enemy at least twice his strength tormented her. Images of how the predators gathered, drawn by the scent of spilled blood. Duncan, his life force rushing out of him and pooling on the dusty wheel tracks. Duncan, so still that death hovered in the room above him like an invisible smoke cloud, draining the brightness from the lantern and making the night seem more hopeless.

She could have died, and in terrible pain. She'd seen the damage on Duncan's neck and chest and shoulders. He'd saved her from that fate and chose it for himself. She'd never met a braver man. What did a person do for someone who had not only saved her life, but also sacrificed his?

Thanks was not nearly enough. She'd made a promise that she wouldn't leave him—the very least she could do was to keep her vow. No man should die alone, without someone to care.

"The doctor will stay with him." Joshua, her sensible big brother, presented her with his coat. "We need to get you home. You can't stay the night here, Bets. You have to think of your reputation."

"I'm thinking of my honor."

"Folks won't understand. You know how some people can get. Quick to judge and quicker to condemn. I don't want you to be hurt, Bets."

"You are the best brother a girl could have." She didn't take his coat. She squeezed his hand that remained on her shoulder, a comforting presence.

For as long as she could remember, Joshua had watched over her and protected her, and she loved him for it, but sometimes the right choice wasn't the easiest one. Some folks might hear about her staying the night with a mountain man. Then they would know what Duncan Hennessey did to defend her. They would have to see how noble he was.

It was that simple. How could this be mistaken for anything else?

"Go home, if you have a mind to." She gently waved away the offer of his coat. "And thank you, for fetching the doctor."

"I can't leave you here."

"You have responsibilities to tend to. Go home, get some sleep and see to them. I'll be fine."

"Mother would box my ears if I did."

"Mother isn't tall enough to reach your ears." It was an old familiar joke, grown fond through the years, of how their tiny Irish mother had birthed such a collection of fine, strapping and tall sons. All of her children had looked down on her since they were eleven years old, including Betsy. "This is something I must do."

"And how am I supposed to leave you?" Joshua straightened, losing the argument. For all his deep booming voice and big hulking presence, he was really not so fierce at heart. "I can see you owe this man the courtesy, but surely he has family."

"I don't see any evidence of it, do you?" She gestured at the bare walls and empty tables. Not a single tintype or photograph anywhere. No hints of birthday or Christmas gifts from a mother or sister. "Do you know what would help? Send Liam tomorrow with a change of clothes. I can't ride back to town wearing naught but my drawers and Mr. Hennessey's flannel jacket."

"You'd cause a scandal, that's for sure." As if relenting, Joshua ruffled the top of her hair, as he always used to do when she was little. "I'll be back. Let me know if you need anything. You know I'll be ready to help with any…arrangements." His gaze traveled to the bed.

He meant for the man's burial. Betsy took a shaky breath. Joshua was only being practical, it was his way. But she couldn't give up hope. Not as long as Mr. Hennessey drew one breath and another. It seemed an eternity between them, but her tough savior was still alive and so there was hope.

"You'd best go on with your brother, ma'am," Doc Haskins told her as he packed his stethoscope into his medical bag. "I'll stay on here until the end. It won't be much longer now."

"No, I will stay with him." Sadness choked her. She said nothing more. There was nothing left to do but to hope her presence gave him some comfort. He'd never seemed to like her much. Well—to the point—he'd been extremely clear how much he didn't want to be anywhere near her. But deep down, she didn't believe him. Why would a man who hated her trade his life for hers?

Already grieving him, knowing that even her most fervent, optimistic thought could not spare him from the inevitable. She could feel it, too, how still his big body was, taking up so much room on the bed. And now, the space between breaths seemed a longer eternity. The doctor was packing up the rest of his things. It would not be long now.

She lifted his hand, lying so still at his side, onto her thigh and covered it with her fingers. Felt how cool he'd become. She moved away to find another blanket. She found a lined buffalo robe and added that to the top of his bed, smoothing it with care. When she returned to her chair to sit and took his hand in hers again, she was surprised when his fingers gripped hers. Strong. With need.

Something broke apart deep in her chest, like a shattering pain she'd felt once when she'd broken her wrist when she was eight. It was like that now, sharp and jagged pain centered so deep within her, it hurt to breathe.

There, where it had been as if dark, a small warmth glowed.

Chapter Four

It was shadow land. Duncan did not know if he dreamed or if he lived, but he could hear a soft sound. Low and bright, like the solemn call of a sweet bell, but it was a woman's voice. His mother's? He knew that wasn't right even as he thought it.

No, his mother's singing was deeper, with a lower note, the rhythmic roll of her native tongue like thunder and wind, rain and rivers running. Those were the sounds of his childhood and those memories returned with a stinging clarity. Rich green grass and hot sunshine and dry and dusty earth between his bare toes, and his mother singing while she worked.

It was the melody he'd woken to in the dark hole of prison, where for an instant he was caught in dream and happiness. Then the dream would break into wisps like smoke, blowing away to the real nightmare of the dank cave of his cell where mice skittered and bugs crawled.

He did not awake there. He could not seem to wake at all. The shadows held him, and there was no pain. But that voice—it was captivating. It held him as if the

cuff and chain were once again tight on his ankle. There
were no words, this was not singing, but a humming
cheerfulness, and it glittered inside him like sunshine
through rain. A melody that rose and fell and lured him
back to the darkness of his life.

He did not want to go back. Here, in the shadows,
there was no grief. Loneliness didn't stick in his soul
like a sharp rock, jabbing deeper and deeper with every
step. Here, the bitterness seemed far away and he knew,
if he simply let go, he would travel to what his grandfather had called happy hunting grounds, his father
heaven, and his mother simply home.

His mother. Would he see her there? Was she waiting beyond the threshold? The thought of seeing her
again made joy crackle inside him. Roaring and growing like a fire in dry grass.

But the humming melody called to him, too. Made
him yearn with the heart of a man. He knew it was her,
the woman and her corkscrew curls and her generous
smile and kindness. He would not like her. He would
not want her. He no longer believed in the good of any
woman, and yet he followed the sound of her voice, innocent and sensual at once.

Pain slammed into him like an avalanche of
snow…and he was falling. Then there was her. Standing over him like an angel in morning light, and her
clear alto. It was a tune he didn't know, and the brisk
dawn's sunshine was suddenly too bright. His eyes
stung and he couldn't seem to focus. Maybe it was the
pain leaving him breathless, as if he'd been crushed at
the bottom of that avalanche.

But it was strangely all right. For she was here, her

hand in his, holding on to him, pulling him back, even as oblivion claimed him, it was only sleep.

Betsy knelt at the edge of the hand-dug well. The board frame bit into her knees as she unhooked the bucket. Cool, clear water sloshed over the side of the pail and onto her clothes.

Every inch of her seemed to ache, or maybe that was just sorrow brimming over the rim of her heart. Through the golden streaks of the sun rising at the edge of the forest, she watched the doc's buggy bounce down the road. The stand of evergreens closed around him and she was alone.

The doctor's prognosis echoed in her thoughts. *I've seen this type of lingering before. He'll not awaken. No man loses that much blood and lives. Remember Charlie.*

Remember Charlie? She'd never forget. She hurt as if the doctor had reached out and slapped her, and she thought of the injured man still breathing, still living, and refused to give up hope. For without it, what good would life be? Without it, how could any good at all come out of this? He'd tried to awaken earlier, she was certain of it.

Perhaps it was the doctor's job to be so practical, but he'd been drowsing when Hennessey had stirred. It had been slight, but there.

Cool water sloshed over the rim and onto her again as she unhooked the bucket from the rope. Exhaustion made her muscles feel heavy as she stood. Overhead an army of birds twittered and chirped and flitted from tree to tree, and the noise they made was as loud as the train rumbling through town. A body certainly wouldn't need a clock living out here.

On her way back to the cabin she felt…well, watched. The nape of her neck prickled, but there were no obvious signs of danger. Goodness, how could there be with the breeze pleasant through the drying grasses and the tall trees waltzing with their branches outstretched and the sunshine warm and friendly? The splashes from the water bucket sprinkled across her bare feet and plopped onto the soft earth.

There, in the loose dust in the path, were tracks. As clear as her own footprints heading to the well, but those imprints hadn't been there when she'd gone to fetch water.

She looked around carefully and shivered. Was it her imagination or did the wind have a mean edge to it? Nothing knelt behind the woodpile, not that she could see, or crept through the unmown grasses.

The giant cat tracks ambled along the road, as if the cougar had been heading to town and following the doctor's buggy. Maybe the animal had continued on. Maybe not. Maybe it was watching her from the thicket of the crowded evergreens—and getting hungry.

She certainly had no notion of being any creature's breakfast! Heaven on earth! She'd been out this way on her deliveries once a week for several years now. Before yesterday, the most wildlife she'd seen in these woods had been a few grazing deer. She picked up her pace and sprinted up the porch steps. With the stout wall to her back she felt safer as she looked back, at the fresh tracks—they looked just like her little kitty's paw prints back home except each imprint was as big as her foot. She didn't feel safe until she shut the door behind her.

"W-water."

"Mr. Hennessey?" She nearly dropped the bucket in shock. Coming to her senses, she set it on the nearby table and was at his side without remembering crossing the room. His eyes were open and in them she read the agony he was in. "Oh, it's so good to see you."

His hard mouth curled into a frown. "Water."

"Oh! Of course. I can't believe it, but I wouldn't give up hope for you. The doctor was less than encouraging, but I knew." She was babbling, and she couldn't stop the happiness from bubbling up. "You're going to be fine. I know it. I'm so glad. You were so heroic, coming to my rescue as you did." Her fingertips reached out—she simply couldn't help it.

Emotion overwhelmed her and tears blurred her vision as she stroked the side of his face. Stubbled with prickly whiskers, it felt so good and right just to feel the very manly texture of several days' growth. Her chest clenched tight with an odd longing. It wasn't sexual—she'd tried very hard not to notice the incredibly perfect chest of his and more, much more.

It was something else, something amazing. Her very being seemed to quicken and that warmth new in her chest seemed bigger. It hurt, strangely, and she didn't know what to say. How to tell him she knew he was weak and he would be bedridden for a long while, but she wouldn't let him down.

He'd saved her, and she intended to save him right back.

"W-water," he snarled.

At least he had the strength to snarl. That had to be a good indication, right? She smiled at him because nothing could dim her gratitude. She raced to the table and stole a tin cup from the shelf overhead. Her fingers were trembling, she spilled water everywhere, but she didn't spill a drop when she eased down beside him on the wide feather bed and held the rim to his cracked lips.

He groaned with pleasure as the cool goodness ran across his bottom lip and over his tongue. He swallowed with difficulty and grimaced in agony at the pain it must have caused.

"Oh, I am so pleased," she told him, holding the cup to his mouth again. "It is not every day a woman gets her very own hero."

Hero? Hardly. Duncan growled and, although he'd only swallowed twice, it had exhausted him. He lay panting, eyes tearing, his entire body vibrating with unbearable pain and he remembered her humming. He remembered her at his side and how she'd told the truth.

This morning her eyes were red-rimmed and she was pale with strain. She was wearing his shirt and a pair of his trousers tied with a rope at her waist. The clothes engulfed her, but nothing could dim the sincerity as she eased over him, careful of his wounds and laid her head over his heart.

A sharper pain than he'd ever known bore through his chest. It was an odd thing, to feel tenderness for this strangely emotional woman who'd been honest. And the way she held him seemed just as honest as when the men had come and he'd thought, confusing the present with the past, that he was going to be wrongly accused again.

The sweet scent of honeysuckle filled his head and he wished he could move his arm. Because if he could, he'd lay his hand over her head and wind his fingers through her soft hair. He'd press her close and hold on tight, because she was surely a dream. Surely.

But too soon the outside door swung open and eye-stinging light filled the room. It was more people—he saw the swish of a woman's skirts and heard the low murmur of a man's voice—the same one from before. And she was leaving him, lifting her head and straightening it.

Longing pierced him, but it was impossible because he didn't need or long for anything or anyone. Especially not a pretty and proper town lady who was everything he'd come to distrust. She stood. Her weight lifted from the mattress and he was alone. His chest ached with emotion, but it was impossible to know what emotion he was feeling.

He'd given up on feelings long ago.

"Granny!" It was Betsy's voice, rising with excitement, moving away from him. "What are you doing here? I don't understand. And Mama—"

"What were you thinking? Spending a night all alone with a mountain man. With any man!"

It was a mother's scolding voice and through his foggy vision, he saw two women. One a matronly figure decked out in an enormous hat with a fake flower that bobbed with the movements of her head, which she nodded to emphasize nearly every other word.

Clearly, Betsy's mother. Her ample figure suggested a life of being well fed and her brown dress looked to be of the finest material. He recognized the mother-of-pearl buttons that marched from her chin to her toes and the disdainful frown that withered her otherwise pleasant face.

She glared at him as if she smelled a skunk. That's all it took and he knew what Betsy's mother saw. She was a lady of means, probably the type that liked everything in its place including people in the slots where they belonged.

And she was right. Her daughter should keep a far distance from him. The stink of prison felt as if it had been ground into his skin and deeper. It had changed him. Tainted him.

Mrs. Prim and Proper shook her head from side to side as she studied him, the flower on her bonnet swaying to and fro.

He focused on that.

It was safer. Easier.

He wished for the strength to let it mean nothing. Nothing at all as the three women—daughter, mother and grandmother—gazed over him. He saw compassion in the elderly woman's eyes and he knew. She knew. Shame rolled over him like a flooding river and the tide of it drowned out everything he'd worked to become. Washing away all the good he'd ever done, and he felt more naked than if he'd worn no clothes at all. And worse, he saw her pity.

"Come, my sweet Bets." The elderly woman turned her back to him and grabbed hold of Betsy's slender arm and pulled her from his side. "You have worked all night, and I am here now. Go with your mama and your brother, and I will tend the mountain man."

Yeah, he knew they'd take her from him. They

should. His heart was steel again. His soul impenetrable. Strong again, he let no weak emotion live within him. He watched as her brother took her other arm.

"Come now, Bets," the brother was saying, not placating, but with real caring. "You have your reputation. The doctor promised me he'd stay with you and he broke his word."

"Joshua, he had other patients waiting for him. Please, there is no need to be so angry. How could my reputation possibly be damaged? Goodness, anyone would do the same if they were me."

"Then think of your health, dear." Granny slipped a thick shawl over Betsy's shoulders, the fine wool wrapped her from chin to ankle. "That will do for now, until we get you home. You've been up all night, haven't you? And with the weather turning, you'll likely catch cold and fall ill. You let your mama take you home and spoil you."

"Gran, I don't need to be spoiled. I caused this man's injuries."

"Not you, dear, but the bear."

"Bears." It was important that Granny—that everyone—understood. "I have to make this right. I can't leave him. He's too weak to fend for himself, and there are no neighbors close. No one to come if he should need help."

"There's me." The gleam in Granny's green eyes said more.

Betsy understood. Mama was so…well, overbearing. She looked at Mr. Hennessey and saw a mountain man who was of no worth. For, as Mama said, what gave a man more worth than a good-paying job and the sense of responsibility to show up for it every day?

All anyone had to do was to glance around the dim one-room cabin to realize Mr. Hennessey wasn't a wealthy man. But he was a worthy one. That was something Granny had to understand.

"I will tend him as well as you would do." Granny pressed a kiss to Betsy's cheek and secured the shawl pin beneath her chin. "Now, don't worry, my sweet girl. This is for the best."

"No, I don't think—" She peered over her shoulder at the man who was more shadow than substance, lost in the dark corner where the light did not seem to reach. Her heart wrenched hard, bringing with it a suffocating pain. "He needs me."

"He needs care, and I will give it to him." Firmly, although there was no mistaking the love warming her stern ways, Granny turned her around and gave her a shove toward the door.

Exhausted and weak—she hadn't eaten nor drank— her feet seemed to trip forward and she wound up in her brother's firm grip. No, this was wrong. She needed to stay. She had to. "Please, Joshua. I can rest here and eat. That way I can be close—"

"You will do better in your own bed, and he has all he needs."

Joshua lifted her into his arms, as if she were a child, and it was tenderness that gentled the fierce frown that made him look nearly as intimidating as Mr. Hennessey at his worst.

"No, please, you have to let me—"

"You are what matters to us. Come, let us take care of you. When you are stronger and rested, we'll talk about you coming back."

It sounded reasonable. Even sensible. She was light-headed, she realized, from lack of food. Maybe that's why she was acting the way she was, as if everything was more intense than usual. Maybe that's why it felt as if she were breaking from the inside out, as if something vital were being wrenched from her innermost being.

She strained to look over her brother's shoulder as he carried her through the threshold, turning sideways so her dangling feet wouldn't smack against the door frame. She saw that Duncan was awake, twisting his head on the pillow, watching her leave. Struggling to keep her in his sight, although he was too weak to do more. His shadowed face was furrowed, his eyes intensely following her progress away from him, and it was almost as if he couldn't take her leaving.

As if he didn't want her to go.

Their gazes met and the impact was cataclysmic. As if the moon exploded and the earth cracked into pieces and the sun burned into the greatest darkness. She felt as if her will had helped him through the night. She had made a difference, even a little, and she didn't want to let him go. Didn't want to stop hoping.

"Joshua, please, I have to stay."

But he whisked her onto the porch and the well-built log walls stood between her and Duncan. She tried to push out of her brother's arms, but it was as if she'd used up all her strength like kerosene in a lamp and it was gone. Tears blistered her eyes and she couldn't see as he laid her in the back seat of the family's surrey.

Joshua covered her with a wool blanket and kindly told her to rest, this was for the best, to trust him, but she felt betrayed.

How could her family do this to her?

The surrey jolted as the family horses leaped into a brisk trot, and on the leather-springed seat, she bounced and bumped and watched the cabin grow smaller. Her cheeks were wet and she felt as if she'd been the one clawed apart by a bear. It was wrong to leave him like that. When she'd promised him, she'd *promised* him, that she'd stay by his side.

Inside where Duncan Hennessey still fought to live. He'd made it to a new day and surprised the doctor, but he was too weak to lift his head from the pillow. Far too wounded to care for himself. Granny was magic— her home remedies legendary, and Betsy trusted her with all of her heart.

But I should be there, too. A vow was a vow, and when she made one, she kept it. Duncan needed her. It had been so long since someone had truly needed her. She knew Granny would go about tending him. Gently cleaning off the poultice Betsy had boiled up in the night, and the doctor had applied over the red swollen gashes of flesh held together by her hurried stitches.

Granny would bathe him while she steeped her special willow-bark tea and simmered chicken broth and herbs on the battered potbellied stove. She'd do her best to care for him with the same loving warmth she gave everyone. Duncan couldn't be in better hands.

But she wanted to be the one to hold the cup to his lips. To sit by his side and comfort him, so he would not be alone. She knew, without knowing how she knew, that had she been injured instead, he would have moved heaven and earth to take care of her.

Mama perched on the front seat beside Joshua, who

was driving the team through the eerily dusky woods where the shafts of the rising sun did not seem to penetrate. The dry grasses rasped. The limbs overhead groaned. Remembering, Betsy closed her eyes. She'd give anything to have Duncan as he was when she'd first arrived yesterday, growling and caustic and hostile. His horrid demeanor was starting to seem less beastly to her.

"Good, she's asleep." Mama's voice cut fearlessly through the shadows. "We got her out of there just in time. No one knows she was alone with him."

"The doc does. And the mountain man, of course."

"They can be managed. What matters is our dear Betsy. She's a fine girl, but you know how people are. They can be cruel, if they have the slightest reason, and I won't have Betsy hurt."

"I won't allow it, Ma. You know that." Joshua sounded fierce. "Since Pa's passing, I'm the head of the household and I will protect my sister with everything in me. There will be no damage done. I'll see to it."

As if a person's reputation—simply what other people thought—could be weighed against a man's life. Betsy was too weary to argue and she knew the pointlessness of it. When Mama made up her mind, it would take an army more formidable than any on this earth to sway her from her course. She wanted to be angry with them, but how could she? They were acting out of love for her. Misguided, yes, but goodness, they loved her. She knew that. Her parents and her brothers had always wanted what was best for her.

Taking her from the mountain man was important to them, and she was too weak and weary to fight.

Granny was there, seeing that Duncan lived. *I can trust Gran, I know I can.*

As the surrey jostled down the mountain road and into the bright expanse of prairie, the morning sun turned the insides of her eyelids orange. She screwed her eyes shut tight, but the brightness remained. All around her was life. The twittering larks and the cheerful robins and jackrabbits darting out of the road. Gophers popping out of their holes to stand on their back feet to watch the passing vehicle. Their gossipy chatter carried their excitement on the wind.

All of these things she always took such delight in. But on this new day, she felt as if a part of her had been irrevocably lost. It was foolish to think so much about a man who probably never wanted to see her again. But she felt as if a link of some kind had been forged between them and, like the sun to the earth, it remained.

Who knew what held the sun in the sky? It was the same with her heart. She did not love Duncan Hennessey. She did not like him. She knew he was an unpleasant loner who seemed to hate her.

But true need and sorrow had flashed in his eyes. It had been real, for she felt it still. A hard dark shell blotting out the light of day. As though a shadow had fallen permanently across the sun's face, and nothing would ever seem as bright or as warm again.

Chapter Five

The side gate squeaked open, and Betsy leaned over the wooden rail on the back porch and squinted through the bright afternoon sun. She predicted it was Mother and resisted the urge to run into the house, bar the door and hide down in the cellar until her mother gave up and went away.

The only problem with that wish was the fact that Lucille Gable never gave up until she got what she wanted, so there was no point in hiding. Not that Betsy was someone who ran from her problems instead of facing them, it was just the hope of escape that was tempting.

Remembering how her mother had taken charge once they'd reached the edge of town, giving Joshua orders and escorting Betsy into the house and putting her to bed. She'd lain there to please Ma, but she hadn't been able to sleep. Her mother had stayed, and she'd never seen her mother more determined. They'd argued, and Ma had charged off in a huff.

Betsy was certain her mother would return with renewed determination. Her stomach tightened. She loved her mother. She didn't want to fight. But she couldn't give up her life and her freedom, either. She loved this little home she rented. She even enjoyed being a laundress. It was better than living in her mother's house as if she was still twelve and her doting and well-meaning Ma would spoil her and suffocate her and, well…she'd be as good as jailed.

Dreading a certain confrontation, Betsy tucked the needle into the trousers' waistband, set it aside and tried to figure out how to manage it better this time.

But it wasn't the imposing form of Lucille Gable that came around the corner of the house, but one of her dearest lifelong friends. Rayna Ludgrin Lindsay, glowing with her pregnancy, barely noticeable behind the gathers of her full skirt, nearly stumbled in her relief.

"Good afternoon!" Betsy had never been so glad.

"Oh, there you are! Your mother had me believing you were knocking on death's door, but look at you. You're in one piece. You're safe. You're not harmed?"

"Heavens no. I've lost one good night's sleep, and that's not so terribly serious. You know how my mother can be." Betsy eased her steaming cup onto the flat of the porch rail. "I'm just sorry I missed getting together with everyone. And I was supposed to bring dessert."

"I know. To think the lengths you will go to get out of baking." Rayna, with a small basket on her arm, swept up the porch steps. "I'm glad you're safe and sound. You have no idea how Mariah and Katelyn and I worried."

"And all for nothing." There was so much she could

say, but she was ashamed to have come out of the ordeal with nothing more than a few bruises and scratches. "What about you? How are you feeling?"

"I hate to speak too soon but, knock on wood, I think my morning sickness is finally over." Rayna set the basket she carried on the seat of the empty chair and wrapped Betsy in an exuberant hug. "It is so good to see you."

"Me, too." Warmth coiled tight in Betsy's chest, making it hard to breathe. To think all this—her life, her friends, her pleasant days—could have vanished in a blink of an eye. She held on extra tight for a moment longer, grateful.

Rayna stepped back, her voice choked. "Oh, we were so scared when you didn't show up. And then, when your horse came in with a lather, with broken traces and his reins dangling and no buggy, why, we all feared the worst."

Betsy saw the genuine fear in her friend's blue gaze. "I hate that anyone became so worried over me. I didn't look beyond taking care of Mr. Hennessey. Rayna, he was incredible."

"I heard what he did. Your brother told my husband last night."

And that's why Rayna was here bright and early with muffins and her comforting presence. "Any spare good wishes and prayers you have, please send them his way. I don't even know how he's doing."

"Your grandmother's taking care of him, isn't she? Hasn't she sent word with one of your brothers?"

"I don't know because Mother thinks hearing anything about Mr. Hennessey will overset me. I just wish—" She couldn't rid her mind of the images of him lying there in bed, his unblinking gaze like a lasso trying to pull her back. "I should have stayed with him."

"But what about your reputation?" Rayna asked quietly, so different than her family's boisterous concern. "What about your safety?"

"No, he'd never—"

"You don't know him. You were alone with him out there in the wilderness. The few folks who know about him say he's no gentleman."

"No. He certainly isn't." She couldn't imagine Duncan Hennessey in a jacket and tie. She couldn't picture him as the local banker. Duncan Hennessey was everything that ought to be bad in a man—except he wasn't a bad man. She'd never thought so. "There have been plenty of respected men in this town who have been less than gentlemanly since I've been widowed. You know how it can be."

"I do." Rayna, after her first husband's sudden death, had had her share of troubles from a neighbor. So it was with honest empathy she said, "You enjoy your independence from your family. Staying with them after Charlie died was one thing. But it's been, what, five years?"

Betsy nodded. She missed so many things about Charlie and being married to him, but time had dulled the ravaged edges of her grief. When she looked back, it was the good memories she felt. Their happy times together as man and wife, and there were so many. "I know what I'm doing, Rayna. This makes me happy. You don't agree with my mother, do you?"

Rayna looked stricken. "No! Of course not. But there

are bad men out there. We like to pretend that's not true, but it is. And you can't always tell. A man who behaves decently in public, in private may be completely different."

"I can take care of myself. It wasn't the man I had problems with. It was the bear! Goodness." There she was, thinking of him again. And not just thinking—picturing him. The hard plane of his chest, the horrible wounds, the way he'd acted as if being touched by her—and having her sew up his wounds—was the worst insult.

She yanked open the pink mesh screen door and led the way into the kitchen. "Mr. Hennessey would have rather bled to death than let me close enough to touch him. The bear, however, came at me with his big shaggy paws and salivating at the sight of my strawberry pie, I tell you. My family should be on a campaign to keep me away from bears, not from people paying me good money to wash and iron their clothes."

"We all love you so much. What would we do if anything happened to you?"

Betsy plucked the whistling kettle from the stove. "That goes for you, too. Now go sit down and put up your feet."

"I'm pregnant, not sick. I'm perfectly fine."

"So I worry. What would I do if anything happened to *you?*"

Understanding softened Rayna's lovely face. "You're trying to change the subject."

"Yes, I am." She poured steaming water into the delicate china pot. "Go outside, sit down and rest. We will pretend that you are trying to set me straight, so after you leave here, you can tell my mother that you tried your best."

Rayna opened her mouth as if to protest, but then her lovely face softened. "If that's what you want."

"It is."

"Then don't forget plates for the muffins I brought."

"Would those be your magic muffins? The best blueberry muffins in five counties?"

"It was four, and I took second place at the fair the following year. I wonder who took first?" As if she didn't know the answer, Rayna shouldered open the screen door and the hinges rasped pleasantly as they laughed together.

The door slapped shut, leaving Betsy alone with her memories. Okay, so she'd won first place with her strawberry cobbler, but she'd never been able to match Rayna when it came to muffins.

As she set the teapot on her pretty silver tray that Mariah had given her for a wedding gift when they were all so young, just out of public school, she was grateful for this life she'd been given. Look at the friends and family who cared about her and fussed after her and mattered deeply to her. She'd had her sorrows and heartbreaks like anyone else, but she had so much.

When some people had so little.

Duncan Hennessey. She owed him a debt she could never repay. It was natural that she'd think of him. Natural that she couldn't stop. As the warmth of an Indian summer's sun sifted through the cottonwoods and the leaves sang in the warm breeze, she set the tray on the small table between the two porch chairs.

All the while they chatted of small everyday things, and as they enjoyed the flavorful muffins and the comforting goodness of freshly steeped English tea, Duncan remained in her thoughts.

It was as if an invisible rope connected her to him and tugged at her heart. At her conscience.

Was he in much pain or had the doctor's laudanum helped? Was he gaining strength or slipping away? Did he awake to bright sunshine streaming through his windows and realize she wasn't beside him? That she'd broken her word?

Or was he simply relieved she was gone?

"There now, swallow this." It was a woman's voice, but not the laundry lady's.

He was still groggy, lost in the cloudy haze of a deep dreamless sleep, but he knew he was home. That he was in his bed. That pain raked from his back over his shoulder and throat to his chest. The only good thing about pain was that it let a man know he was alive. Some days, that was a victory.

Light seared his eyes and he could make out a woman's silhouette. Curly hair and the scent of lavender, not honeysuckle. Before he could think on that, a wave of bitterness filled his nose. The cool edge of a spoon cut against his lower lip. Wetness spilled across his tongue. He'd never tasted anything so horrid. He choked, coughed, and what tasted like skunk spray remained thick on his tongue.

What was that and who in the hell was trying to kill him? He shoved at the spoon. "Get that damn stuff away from me."

"Fine. So you want to be a tough man, go right ahead. I won't stop you."

For a brief moment, he heard Betsy Hunter's cheerful voice, as light and weightless as the larks in the meadows, but the light shifted as the wind teased the boughs of the trees outside the window, and he saw Betsy's profile become someone else's. Someone with the same sloping button nose and rosebud mouth and dainty chin. Those thick locks of corkscrew curls gained the tarnished elegance of silver, and it was an elderly lady who smiled down at him with Betsy's irresistible smile.

Not that her smile affected him, because he was immune. Immovable when it came to the charms of womankind.

"I suppose you'd like a bit of water to wash that nasty taste off your tongue?" Her eyes were Irish green, where Betsy's were blue, and wreathed by smile lines etched deep into her papery skin. "Go ahead and be gruff about it. The likes of you don't frighten me a bit."

Apparently not only the curls and the smile were inherited, but that aggravating lightheartedness.

Shit, but he hurt. He had no more strength than a baby, and it was shameful and unmanly and weak—he hated weakness. He strained every muscle in his tortured body, but he couldn't lift his head off the pillow. Shame burned in his eyes and smoldered in his chest and he had to look away as the tiny, fragile old lady handily lifted his head for him and held a cup to his mouth.

He swallowed and the tendons and muscles in his neck and throat resisted. Pain grew like a fire, crackling and consuming ever higher, and the moment his head hit the pillow, he screwed his eyes shut and cursed all women. If it wasn't for a woman, he would be outside chopping wood, splitting and stacking and enjoying his peace and quiet.

That was all blown to hell. He was just glad that awful medicine was fading from his tongue. Maybe it was some powerful sleeping draught the doc left, and he'd be lucky enough to sleep long and deep and when he opened his eyes, he'd be alone. There'd be no women anywhere within fifteen miles. Just the way he liked it.

"Oh, you can't fool me, mister, you're still awake. Open up now, like a good patient."

He slitted one eye. The lady was still here, amiable and chipper and as merry as the larks singing outside the window, holding a loaded spoon as if it would cure him of all his ills. "I've had enough of your medicine. Go away."

"O-oh, you are a testy one. Betsy warned me you had a gruff manner, but fortunately for you, I married the roughest log skinner this side of the Mississippi. Growl all you want. I mean to get this soup in you, and I will."

He wasn't troubled by the tiny woman's announcement. No one made him do anything he didn't want to do. But what really troubled him— "You mean, that was *soup?*"

"My own mother's recipe. Does the trick, don't you worry. After a bowl of that, you'll feel as right as rain."

"After a bowl of that, I'll be dead. I don't eat poison."

"It's just what you need. Trust me. I haven't been around for seventy years without learning a thing or two." Those green eyes twinkled in the same glittering way Betsy's did.

If it was soup, it was the least appetizing he'd ever eaten. The vile liquid slipped over his lip and clung to his tongue like a leech and didn't let go. His stomach rolled, his vision blurred. He swallowed until he couldn't. Until he was too exhausted and greedy sleep snatched him into darkness before he could try to look for Betsy in the room.

Alone, in the dark sanctuary of sleep, he dreamed of lying with his head in her lap and listening to the sound of her tears calling him back and keeping him here.

"Return the gelding when you get a chance." Rayna leaned down from the buggy seat as far as she dared. "I'll be all right driving with one for as long as you need him."

"Only until Morris has regained his composure." Betsy held tight to the big gray gelding's reins as Rayna pulled away. The horse nickered, and it was a lonely sound. No doubt he was probably wondering why he was being left behind.

Rayna's buggy kicked up dust that rose in thick chalky clouds and although Betsy couldn't see it, she knew Rayna was waving farewell, and so she waved, too.

The gelding nickered again, this time a little more desperate.

"I'll be good to you, I promise, you handsome boy."

She stroked his velvety nose and laughed as his nostrils flared, scenting her. "You know me. I've seen Rayna at least once a week for as long as you've been driving her vehicles. Goodness. I'll give you back, don't worry."

The gelding did not seem comforted. He studied her with his intelligent brown eyes and snorted dismissively, as if to say he seemed to think he had a great deal to worry about.

"Goodness, it's just a little twenty-mile ride. Nothing to worry about. You can make it before dark falls without a problem." She took the cheek strap firmly in hand, to use the bit as leverage should the gelding decide to take off after his mistress and horse mate. But he came along when coaxed.

Morris, still traumatized by the bear, was huddled in his corner box stall, shivering even though he wore a heavy winter blanket. She comforted him, fed him his evening meal of hay, oats and mash, and watered him well. He nickered low to the gelding she'd tied in the shade outside the stable door. If horses had language, then whatever he said seemed to have made the big gray nervous.

"Like it or not, we're going."

She had no choice. It was a matter of conscience. With care, she hitched the animal to her old cart. The vehicle had grown dusty and the wheel spokes crisscrossed with cobwebs. The wood grayed with age showed the dents of Charlie's hammer—it had been one of his first projects after they'd been married. And the happiness of that time came back to her as it always did, making her throat ache with the sweetness.

It was a feeling she carried with her like a weight on her heart as she organized her sacks of freshly laundered clothes—she was a day behind, but she intended to make up for that. Joshua had promised to make her pickups for her, and her delivery route should take her within five miles of Duncan's cabin.

"Where do you think you're going?" Joshua's ire boomed like winter thunder—cold, formidable and final.

Good thing she was used to his dominating ways. She closed the door behind her and hooked the screen door shut. "Deliveries."

"I thought this would make you see reason. It's not safe."

"I'll be careful not to eat while I'm in the forest. One thing you can say about me is that when I make a mistake, I learn from it. I never make the same one again. Just different ones." She wedged the Lofton brothers' rucksack against the cart's rickety tailgate and gave it a shove. It didn't fall out. "What are you doing over here? Checking up on me?"

"What will it take for you to give up this menial service you're doing and come live at the family house?"

"Are you happy there?"

"Sure."

"You don't look happy. That's why you're so difficult. A man your age needs a wife and a family."

"No." The thunder returned, harsh with a dark emotion that was harder to name.

Whatever it was, whatever had happened to turn her brother against finding love and marriage, made his eyes sadden. He looked away, his brow furrowing deep until his despair felt as tangible as the wind.

Gently, because she loved her big brother and because she knew what sorrow it was to live on with a broken heart, she laid her hand on his. "Then help me, please, or I will go alone."

"You know I can't allow that. I have to protect you, and that means your reputation. You were alone with him."

"My reputation has survived just fine for the last few years I've been riding out to deliver his laundry. I wash the underdrawers of about…what, a third of the men in this county? I find that much more personal—"

"Betsy!" Joshua's face twisted as if he was too angry or shocked to know what to say.

"Much more personal," she repeated for emphasis, "than tending a man with life-threatening wounds. You saw how badly he was injured. A reasonable person would see right away how it would have been impossible for my reputation to be ruined in any way."

"People aren't always reasonable." Joshua sounded exasperated, but he wasn't. She knew he'd lost faith in too many people, been hurt too many times. He thought he could predict what was going to happen—folks would get to talking, some folks with nothing more constructive to do. The gossip would grow and she would lose not only the little business she loved but any chances to marry well.

He couldn't watch over her forever. If this incident had shown him anything, it was that you never knew when your time would be up on this earth. He could have lost her yesterday. Betsy, his sweet and funny little sister. He could have been picking out a casket for her and making funeral arrangements today. The last acts of love he would have ever been able to do for her.

He wasn't, and that put him in a bind. He was grateful the mountain man had come to Betsy's aid. He was sad the man was injured. Might even be dead by now, for the doc hadn't been hopeful. But he couldn't risk his little sister, grown woman though she was, traipsing off into the mountains. Not again. Not after this.

He'd take her to the cabin. He'd let her say her piece, say goodbye, and it would be over. Whether Hennessey lived or died would not change the outcome. His sister would not be driving alone into that forest again.

Chapter Six

There was a reason her dear Charlie had often called her the most stubborn woman on the face of the earth, mostly while he'd been storming away with his boots smacking the wood floor in cadence with the rising steam of his temper.

She *was* stubborn. Sometimes it was a flaw, to be sure. A person shouldn't always be stubborn. It was important to know when to give in, but in her experience, not often. Working hard, digging in her heels and refusing to give up was one of the only ways she knew to get what she truly wanted. That was no bad thing. Her stubbornness had a boon side, too.

When a fire had caught in the hearth, she'd worked so hard and furious, she didn't give up until she'd beaten every flame and spark from the roof and chimney column. If she'd been one to give up easily, then their house would have burned to the ground, and perhaps she and Charlie right along with it.

When the crops were nearly lost to grasshoppers, she worked at her husband's side to beat off the plague of those creatures, through an entire two days and nights and into the third day. When everyone else on the neighboring ranches gave in, she would not. Theirs had been the only ranch with a cash crop come harvest.

If nothing else, all those events just served as practice. Her stubbornness was as strong as ever, maybe stronger. Nothing was going to stop her from seeing Duncan. Not today. Joshua had come along, and he wasn't happy, but he had to understand. She owed the mountain man, and Betsy Hunter was not one to shirk her obligations.

"We can turn around," Joshua said, as if he expected her to be reasonable and give in. "It's not too late. You can't want to drive down that road after you were terrorized."

"I am wise enough not to eat strawberry pie this time."

"It's dangerous country."

"Life is dangerous. That doesn't mean we shouldn't live it. Don't worry, big brother." She laid her hand on his dependable rock-solid arm. "Keep driving. I won't start getting the vapors, as Mama is prone to do."

That only made Joshua frown, his entire granite face grimacing with cold fury. He had a lot of burden on those invincible shoulders of his, she knew, taking care of the ranch and the brothers, keeping Mama cared for and comforted, for Papa's death, soon after Charlie's, had been a hard blow that had devastated them all. Joshua took his responsibilities seriously, but his heart was pure gold and she was counting that he wouldn't disappoint her.

"I don't understand you. I never have." He growled, but it was a surface anger only.

She knew his fury did not go deep. So she was gentle with him as she gave his forearm a sisterly squeeze of affection. "There hasn't been a male brain in existence that can understand a woman's humors. I'm simply grateful you decided to come with me."

"Because I was hoping to talk some sense into you and turn around before—" He ground his teeth.

Whew, he truly was angrier than she'd reckoned. Probably because she hadn't come around to his sensible way of thinking. She couldn't begin to measure the respect and affection she had for him. He didn't understand because he was too busy protecting her, as he'd promised Charlie and their father before they'd both passed from this earth. Too determined to keep her safe to recognize that had the tables been turned, he'd feel the same way she did.

Joshua pulled back on the reins, slowing down as the long shadows of the forest fell into their path and it seemed as if there was something sinister in the shadows luring them closer. The surrey was hardly moving, but it was creeping toward the thick shadows where the sun had already sunk behind the great peaks beyond, turning late afternoon into a cheerless twilight.

Her blood cooled in her veins. Fear. She could feel it creep from the inside out until her skin prickled. Danger seemed to lurk in every shadow. Every sweep of a bough in the rising wind seemed to be a predator springing.

This is no different than before. She set her chin, her stubbornness at full steam. One time out of all the trips she'd come this way. Once there had been danger, and perhaps, as the mountain man suggested, it had been more her fault than not.

Well then she had nothing to fear, did she? When Joshua had purposefully slowed the horse to a near standstill, she didn't know what to say. Her poor, over-protective brother, he simply would never understand her. She needed to do this, and he was doing everything in his power to pretend to help when he was really try-ing to do the opposite.

Well, she'd show him! She wiggled the whip in its socket with the toe of her boot. The sudden lashing, al-though harmless, convinced the horse to surge ahead. Perfect.

"Whoa!" Joshua yanked on the reins, nearly com-ing out of the seat as he looked behind them and around. "We'd best turn around, Bets. Look, the horses are spooked."

"And it was me who did it!" She couldn't help laughing, not that she was in a merry mood. No, she was far from it. But to think her brother so readily ex-pected doom. "I've been traveling this road for some time. Here, give me the reins."

"I'll handle them myself." He sniffed at her, his face lined harshly with disapproval. Joshua was far too seri-ous for his own well-being. "You could get hurt."

"True, seeing as I've never been one to drive my own team!" She couldn't believe him, although she feared he needed her compassion more than her ire. Poor Joshua, he tried so hard. "I'll be good. Go on, keep driv-ing. I won't try to take over."

"How you test me, little sister." Grim, he stared straight ahead, on guard and fierce-seeming as the light was blotted from the sky and the long tree shadows swallowed them.

"We all have our trials."

He gave a huff of irritation. He was so fun to tease, she simply had to exert all her willpower to keep from tormenting him further. She sat quietly through the long twilight where she saw ghosts of memory—the charging bulk of a bear, Duncan Hennessey standing tall and the sobering image of holding him in her arms.

The darkness broke and the waning afternoon sun bled color through the tops of the trees and cast blue-gray shadows on the path to the log house nestled in a spot of sunshine, the stable and outbuildings huddled close by. There were no signs of life—no face looking from the open window, no curling smoke from the stovepipe, no front door swinging open in greeting.

Just silence that felt as thick as an autumn's fog.

He can't have passed yet, Betsy assured herself as the horses slid into a slow walk as they curved along the dusty path. There was the woodpile, half chopped, where Duncan had been splitting the enormous logs that lay neatly stacked next to the abandoned ax and wedge. The place had an abandoned feeling to it already.

Granny's rail-thin figure filled the doorframe. Her silvered hair was tumbling from its tight knot and dark circles marred her nearly flawless face. Sadness had taken the sparkle from her eyes.

The tiny hope Betsy had nurtured began to flicker like a single candle flame in a heartless wind. As the wagon jerked to a halt, she braced herself so the bad news would not come as such a shock. It could not be surprising, since she'd seen the wounds with her own eyes. Yet she'd so stubbornly hoped—

"He's drifted off." Grief wreathed Adelaide Gable's porcelain face. "You'd best be quiet, love."

Out of respect for the dead. Of course. She felt as dark as a winter night, when bitter blizzards raged. Ice crackled through her blood and into her limbs, making it hard to climb down from the comfortable surrey. Harder still to pull her way up the simple wooden steps and into Granny's arms.

"There, there." Adelaide Gable was a hard woman who packed a Colt .45 on her hip, but her hugs were as sweet as spring's wild violets. "You come in now and say your goodbyes to him. That man is no greenhorn, he's survived in these harsh mountains for years. When he came to fight for you, my sweet Bets, he knew what he was doing."

"How can I live with that?" As much as she wanted to stay safe in her grandmother's arms, she stepped back. There was no true comfort for the guilt clawing through her like a hawk's talons. "Duncan was right. This was utterly my fault. I was hungry and I just didn't think."

"There is one silver thread in this. You'll never forget to save your meals until you are out of the wilderness, will you?"

"Heavens no, and, Granny, that is no silver thread. How could any good come from this?" She straightened her shoulders, tapped into her reserves of courage and made her way to the bed where her savior lay so motionless. He lay as if dead, but when she scooted onto the chair at his bedside and took his big scarred hand in hers, it was warm and supple.

So shallow was his breath that she could not see it.

So weak his pulse, she could not feel it when she reached for his hand. Was he suffering? she wondered, breaking a little more inside. Or was he beyond pain? Would a man as disagreeable and as wounded find peace in heaven?

Or would he be banned to Dante's purgatory? She could imagine him there, for perhaps he would be happier in the shadow lands than he would with wings in a happy and peaceful heaven. He lay with a frown dug into his face, perhaps that was his natural expression. Purgatory, definitely.

His hand in hers was heavy. So big and rough. She stroked her thumb over his wide knuckles. His fingers were broad and looked as powerful as if hewn from steel. When she turned his hand over, his broad palm was coarse with thick calluses. Remembering him shirtless, swinging the ax as he'd chopped wood, his muscles had bunched and rippled beneath his bronzed skin. Whatever this man was, Granny was right. He worked hard.

Tenderness glowed like a lamp's flame given more oil to burn on a long wick. It was a painful experience, the way her chest felt as if it were burning. His hand in hers began to tingle and a strange tug and pull deep in her soul made her wonder. What would have been between them if he'd lived?

It seemed to her his skin grew cooler. His high, proud cheekbones jutted through his sun-browned skin as if it had become paper-thin.

She pressed a kiss in the center of his palm. He tasted salty. The flame within her writhed and fought to burn like upon a too-short wick. There was no way to hold on to him, so she let him go.

Cradling his hand in both of hers, she leaned close to whisper. "Thank you. It is so little for such a great deed. You are my only hero."

There was nothing. No sound. No movement. She felt Granny's presence behind her. "It's done now, little chickadee. Leave me to tend his body, and go with your brother."

"I ought to at least arrange for his burial."

"That is for your brother to do. It would not be fitting." Her grandmother knelt, wisdom alight in her Irish green eyes, and a surprising understanding. "I see how you feel, but it is too late for him. Do not grieve too hard."

"How can I not?" She memorized the craggy beauty of his face. The pure black hair. The proud ridge of his nose. The surprising softness in his usually hard unforgiving mouth.

"Thank you," she told him. "It is so little to say, I know. But I will never forget you. I will never forget."

Sorrow crushed her. She cried until there were no more tears left. When she let her brother lead her to the surrey, night had fallen. There was no moon to light the sky and no stars twinkling to dust the lustrous black world; only a wolf's howl in the night of defeat.

Joshua gripped his loaded rifle and, nosing the horse home, sent them into a fast trot. The cabin merged with the darkness. Even when she glanced backward as the surrey bumped around the curve in the road, it was lost.

As if forever.

It was a sound that woke him, but the sunshine in the window was gone, the elderly lady had nodded off in the chair beside the bed and no light burned to let him see her by. He listened for her breathing—she might have made a bed on the sofa.

But there were only two people breathing—the older lady and him.

Disappointment choked him and he struggled to sit. He felt the pull and tug of his stitches sewn tight as he moved—he remembered Betsy struggling with her needle as he'd fought her off.

He remembered her pleasant touch to his brow, her words warm against his ear and the sizzling heat of her kiss on his palm. Had he dreamed it? There was no sign of her, but as he'd dreamed he recalled how the air had shivered with an uncommon vibrancy whenever she was near.

He had an iron will. A man could not survive hard labor in the toughest territorial prison this side of Texas and be made of something less than steel. He'd hunted in the old ways of his grandfather, he'd fought in the War Between the States. He'd survived what should have killed him. If not even a great black bear could, then what?

He'd endured betrayal and injustice. Anguish and a banished life.

Sometimes he wondered if he lived at all. His heart had died long ago; his spirit had been blotted out with the dark of an endless winter night.

Until her kiss on his palm. He'd dreamed it—it could be nothing else but a dream. But awake he could sense the change in the air. She had brought lightness into this night-black cave. Her bright scents of sunshine and little yellow flowers lingered.

If he concentrated hard enough, he could conjure the image of her beside him, her head bent, her soft face leaning toward him. His palm burned with a strange life.

Oh, if he were man enough with a clear past and a whole heart. But he was not. He could not have her. He could never look upon her again. She was like freedom to a man robbed of it. She was the chance at life to a man who'd died in every way that mattered. She was beauty he did not believe in.

"Oh, so you live." There was no pleasure in the old woman's words as the chair creaked and the strong scent of sulfur stung the air. A match snapped to life, flame igniting the battered lantern on the floor. Sinuous orange light twisted across the crone's face. "I had hoped that would be the end of you."

"A man already dead cannot die again."

"True." Her thin mouth pursed, bracketed by lines made deeper by the shadows. "I know who you are. What you are."

"You sent her away."

"Betsy?" The crone's smile was a dark one. "I did. You are as good as dead to her."

"Then you told her."

"You're a monster. There's no other word for you, and in my opinion, the law was too soft. It's all the bleeding hearts that think a monster ought to have more rights than the poor innocent young woman you destroyed."

"I didn't—"

"Oh, don't you play that hand with me. I'm wise to men like you. I know what you are. I say ten years wasn't near enough for what you did. I would have let

you hang, and that would have been too good for you."
Adelaide Gable had known sorrows her own mother
would not acknowledge, and it was all she could do not
to be rash and go against her own beliefs. "It would
have been simple to let you die. Just to have let your
wounds seep until they festered. Let gangrene take you,
and believe you me, that's a bad way to die."

Duncan squeezed his eyes shut, forcing away the
memories and the smell that over twenty years later still
made his guts fist with nausea. He could taste the bile
building, feel the quiver of his diaphragm.

"Betsy is a good girl. The best. She's the apple of
my eye, I'll tell you that, and everyone who knows her
loves her. You—" Her finger stabbed like a bone against
the center of his chest where the last claw marks ended.

Fire consumed him and between the pain and the
memory, he felt his abdomen clench. He would not
vomit. He refused to give the old woman satisfaction.

"You want her. I can see it."

"N-no." It wasn't like that. The old woman would
never understand. Ever. The tiny glimpse of brightness
Betsy had somehow left began to fizzle like a candle
in a cold, hard wind. He wasn't strong enough to hold
the wind back and to protect the flame. He'd never hurt
Betsy, he would never hurt any woman, but Betsy, she
was like the noon sun, bold enough to warm the world.

"I can only thank the heavens above you didn't try
to hurt her before this—"

"I d-didn't—"

"She thinks you're dead, and you listen up. If you
want to live, you'll leave it that way. There's no reason
for her to come out here. Not to pick up and launder a

dead man's shirts. Do you hear me, you beast? If you know what's good for you, you'll stay dead."

He wanted to hate the old woman, like a demon shivering in shadows and hellish light, her narrow face taut so that she looked to be all but eyes, teeth and bone. His mouth was filling, his body trembling, he could feel the violence gathering in his fisted stomach.

"But if you don't, on my grave, I'll tell her everything. Is that what you want?"

Betsy would look at him with hate in her eyes, like this woman, her grandmother, someone she trusted. Someone she'd believe without question. He remembered the sound of her tears, he remember her words, *Thank you. It is so little for such a great deed. You are my only hero.* No one had ever said such things to him. It hadn't mattered how he'd treated her, shame filled him at the memory. He'd only been trying to drive her off, to keep himself safe, but all he'd done was be cruel to a truly good woman.

No matter how vicious he was to her, she was irrepressibly cheerful, and he hated it and nothing, nothing would stop the agony of seeing Betsy, who'd held him in her lap and cried, pushing him away. Repulsed. Hate-filled. Seeing nothing but a monster.

Oh, no. The force was gathering inside him. Pain, worse than any he'd known, blackened his soul, roaring up from the bottom of his spirit, tearing through his body, filling his mind. The realization made sweat break out anew. He'd never see Betsy again. Never need to hide out in the forest or in his workshop during her weekly visit. No more grumbling. No more abrasive fury. No more sunshine yellow dresses and charming smiles.

Bile flooded his mouth, his abdomen jerked, his head lashed and physical pain made his eyes fail. There was only blackness and burning fire and desolation as he became sick, turning his agonized body to the side of the bed. Shame filled him.

Drained him.

Betsy wished she could stop crying. It made no sense to weep for a perfectly not-nice man. No, no one with a lick of common sense would be choking on sorrow at the thought of never again seeing the scowling, growling and vicious-mannered mountain man. But all she could think about was how vulnerable he'd looked in death, and sorrow clawed through her like an eagle's lethal talons.

He wasn't such a bad man. No, not at all. For all the times she'd dreaded driving into the far-reaching cloud of his hate that hovered over the forest like a fog, she would give anything to have him alive. Alive to scowl at her and to spit and hiss like a cornered mountain lion whenever she arrived a bit too early or late with the laundry delivery and caught him by surprise. Or like last time, when he hadn't even been expecting her. He'd come to her aid like a real hero. She pushed her face into her hands, sobbing, more agony shredding her until she was like a spider's web blowing in the wind, unwinding.

The gentle sounds of the night did not calm her. She let the tears fall and they kept rising through her in hot, twisting sorrow as the moonlight washed through the open window to gleam like a pearl on the lacy curtains and paint the intricate pattern of the lace onto the polished wood floor. The warm wind puffed through the mesh screen and brought with it the smell of ripe apples from the orchard and honeysuckle sweetness from the trellis where the vines clung to the sides of the house. The near silent glide of an owl cut through the moonlight and flickered a total brief darkness onto the window.

"Don't grieve him overly much," Joshua had told her when he'd seen her safely home. "He was no good. An outcast. He lived far away from decent people for a reason."

Oh, how wrongly Joshua assumed. He saw only the outside Duncan Hennessey. Her least favorite customer was everything unpleasant, but she'd seen inside him to the man she'd always suspected was there. A great wounded man who would give his own life to defend a woman he didn't even like.

That was rare indeed.

She wanted to say that it was admiration and gratitude that had her crying so that tears turned to sobs that turned into a place where there were no tears. She wrapped her arms around her waist, hurting inside with the same intensity she'd felt when Charlie had died, trying to deny the simple truth. Why her heart recognized Duncan Hennessey, she didn't know.

All she knew for certain was that something had changed deep within her. That no matter what anyone said, she would always see the good in the mountain man who'd saved her. Who'd made her spirit stir.

Chapter Seven

Betsy tried to pretend the bright afternoon sun did not scrape against her sand-rough eyes, which were sore from the past few nights' crying and from too little sleep. She couldn't help it, she was grieving the mountain man, and as she studied her long-time friends since their early days in the public grade school, she wasn't certain they would approve.

Rayna Lindsay with her expectant mother's glow as she moved with grace from table to counter, and dug for the hot pads always hidden in the back of the top drawer. Not that they were exactly hiding there, but through all the opening and closing of the drawer and the contents sliding around, and after she'd gotten done rummaging for whatever she was looking for, they always inexplicably slid to the back.

Mariah Gray had started the laundry business when her father died. Then she'd gotten married and sold it to Betsy and rented her the house, too. Mariah, a take-charge kind of woman, took it upon herself to grab enough plates from the sideboard. "You still look worse for the wear, Betsy. Sit. Relax. You look so fragile."

"I should say so!" Rayna stepped around a bag of laundry to lift the boiling coffeepot from the stove. The heat it gave off made it much too scorching to sit in the kitchen, so she carried the pot between the rows of bagged garments that lined the inside of the kitchen to the door.

The screen hinges squealed as she shouldered the door open and paused to tsk. "Betsy, I can't think of what a harrowing ordeal that must have been. And to think you came away from a bear attack with little more than a few scrapes."

"And easily mended." She held up her hand. Already the skin was healing over, red and tender but healing well beneath the bandage. "My mother forbade me to work. She was terrified I'd get a festering from my hand being in wash water all day and they'd have to cut my arm off to save me from gangrene."

"Your mother has an imagination." Rayna politely said the only thing she could before twisting out of sight, leaving the screen to bang shut behind her.

"An imagination, ha!" Mariah scooped up forks to go along with the dessert plates and spoons for the coffee. "Your mother is so headstrong, she makes me look like a wish-wash. I'm proud of you for sticking to your guns. You are doing a great business. I've heard nothing but compliments."

"Goodness, I sure try, but it isn't easy." She'd gotten behind after the buggy wreck. The vehicle had been towed to the livery but there was no telling if it could be salvaged.

Her kitchen was crammed with ironed laundry freshly folded, stacks of stiff, dried garments yet to be sprinkled and ironed, and the huge bags of laundry she'd picked up just this morning, blocked the lean-to door. Her friends had come, since she'd missed their usual weekly afternoon gathering, and this time it was her turn to host. She'd been glad enough that she'd been able to whip up a cake in time.

"Joshua is insisting on driving me everywhere. He's a cautious driver and it took forever to come back from the west plains. He's going to put me out of business." She lifted the pedestal cake plate, carefully holding it steady—it was such a lovely thing—and let Mariah hold the screen door for her.

"Do you think it's intentional?"

"I know it is." Betsy waited while Rayna moved aside the coffee cups to make just enough room on the small coffee table for the cake plate.

It looked so pretty next to her china. A gift from Charlie she would always cherish, the pattern of butterflies soaring above cheerful sprays of flowers was just right. She reached for a cup now, slipping into the wooden rocker and cradling the scorching hot cup, not caring that it stung her fingers. Not caring at all.

The blue and yellow butterflies reminded her always that life went on, from caterpillar to cocoon to butterfly, and then on to the next life, which had to be more beautiful yet.

It was hope, and she clung to it, for Charlie's sake and now for Duncan Hennessey's.

Rayna stirred sugar into her cup and pushed the delicate sugar bowl across the little table to Betsy. "Joshua is a big brother. Of course he's going to protect his baby sister, even if she is over thirty years old."

"And widowed, self-sufficient, independent and a businesswoman to boot!"

"Oh, I can see you're frustrated." Rayna sympathized and began to cut the cake. "All I can offer you is a slice of your own cake. It's temporary, but it is comfort."

"Angel food cake. It is comforting. So sweet and light and spongy." Like hope. Betsy sighed. She thought of the man she'd left still and lifeless in the mountain cabin. She felt drained of hope. Nothing seemed to make sense like it did before. "My family worries and frets, but the truth is, I'm a grown woman. If I were married with a family of my own, like James, then no one would be knocking down the fence to see what I'm up to."

"Does your mother still want you to give up the business and move in with her?" Mariah took the sugar bowl, dumped three teaspoons into Betsy's cup.

"You know she does. I love my mother, but I can't live with her."

"A saint couldn't live with your mother." Mariah meant it in a kind way, but the truth was the truth.

Mother *was* difficult, there was no denying it. "I haven't been able to live with her since I was fifteen. She's bossy and wrong at least half of the time. When I lived with her after Charlie's death, you remember how I was. As crazy as a loon."

"We remember."

"Ten times a day it was 'Betsy, a decent lady does not let her ears show.' 'It's not eighteen thirty-two,

Mother!' 'Betsy, a decent woman doesn't sit with her knees gaping.' 'Mother, my knees are half an inch apart, not three feet and gaping while wearing no drawers in the middle of Pearl's House of the Red Curtains.'"

"Or simply on the bench outside the mercantile," Rayna added dryly, and they all burst into laughter.

"She went on like that all the live-long day. Without end. The woman was like to drive me mad. Until finally I reached the point that if I'd stayed much longer, I'd have gone running screaming down Main Street with my skirt over my head and my drawers showing. And here Mama was worried about my knees!"

Rayna laughed so hard she had to put down the cup. "That would have ruined your reputation for sure."

"Yep. Everyone would have said, 'Forget it, take Betsy Gable Hunter off the marriageable widow list!'"

"But everybody knows your mother," Mariah pointed out. "You still may have saved some of your reputation. You know, tarnished, but still marriageable."

Betsy sighed, no longer laughing. "Yeah, everyone knows Lucille Gable is a proper woman, but she pecks like a vulture."

"She means well, at least you have that. My mother didn't," Mariah sighed.

Reminding Betsy how fortunate she was. "Exactly. My mama would crawl to China on her hands and knees if it would make me happy, but she is headstrong and I love her much better when we are under separate roofs."

It was the way her family was. All of them. From the aunts and uncles, grandparents and cousins. Nosy, every last one of them. Always getting involved in one another's concerns. But at least it was done out of love. It was just one of those facts of life that love wasn't always soft and mushy and gooey. Real love took grit, and it wasn't easy to love someone no matter what in spite of their imperfections, but that was one of life's challenges.

And the good part was that her family loved her the same in return, even if she was independent-minded and stubborn. Boy, could she be stubborn and sentimental. Lord, was she!

That overwhelming sentiment began to build up when she looked at the fluffy angel cake topped with powdered sugar and drizzled with strawberry syrup.

It was the strawberries that reminded her. *Oh, Duncan.* Her heart cracked wide open. She opened her mouth and it all came out. All of it. The way she'd thought it was him attacking her initially before the bear emerged from the thick foliage. How he'd come to her rescue only to be mortally wounded, protecting her. Always protecting her, even in his death.

"And he passed away, about the time I got there the other night." She pushed the cake aside and sipped the coffee, rich and bitter; it was comforting, simply breathing in the smell of it. To let the warm liquid seep into her stomach and spread through her middle.

"How heroic." Rayna looked thoughtful as she reached for her piece of cake, which she'd set aside to listen to the long tale. "Not many men would behave so gallantly. That's how I knew my Daniel was a worthy man. His noble honor. It sounds as if your mountain man had a great spirit, too."

"I'm sure many wouldn't agree," she teased, just a little, to hide what she felt too shy to say. "He was very embittered. I think he had a great sadness in his life."

"His family was murdered, his mother, her husband and two daughters. Burned alive in their house." Mariah shivered. "Horrendous, what some people are capable of."

"You mean, someone did that on purpose?"

Mariah nodded. "No one was ever found guilty of murdering those poor people. Can you imagine, finding your family tortured and killed?"

Well, no wonder. She knew he'd endured a terrible tragedy, but to be left alone in the world, by means of injustice. She couldn't blame him a bit for his anger. What was sad, though, was that no one had been left to soften his grief. To make gentle his world.

"…but that's about all I know. It happened to the south, near Great Falls. I remember my father talking about it but I can't recall any of the details."

Mariah had laundered Duncan's shirts for many years. Before Betsy had taken over, of course. As if she were trying to remember every important detail of her time delivering his shirts, Mariah forgot her fork was suspended in midair with a bite of delicious cake.

She looked very distant for a moment. "I was never sure about Mr. Hennessey, but I tell you, he amused me. He was so taciturn. So caustic. Actually, sometimes he was really funny. He'd say something like 'Not so much starch next time, I'm no preacher.' And I'd drive away before it hit me, the image of dour Mr. Hennessey in a stiff white collar and coat, preaching up a Sunday sermon. I can't imagine how well that would go over, unless he deleted some of his especially vulgar swear-words."

"I have increased my vocabulary because of him." The tattered shreds of her heart throbbed with sorrow. "My brothers are always so gentle around me, and so was dear Charlie, that I had no notion of what Mr. Hennessey would be shouting whenever I'd drive up and startle him and he'd swing his hammer and hit his finger. I didn't know words like those existed. I had to make James tell me what they meant.

"Boy, was Duncan hard to surprise, but once, when he was pulling honey from a hive and obviously concentrating very hard, I rounded the corner quite a bit earlier than usual and you know how my old wagon rattled louder than a stampeding herd of cattle? He didn't hear me until I was almost upon him and he started, jumped and got stung. He was swatting and jumping and cursing and wouldn't let go of the honey.

"About any other man would look like a fool, but he did it with great dignity. And, somehow, he charmed the bees because they stopped stinging him and started swarming again. Very impressive. But I'll never forget the look of horror on his face when he saw me coming down his road. From his perspective he probably preferred the bee stings, and it wasn't the bees he was cursing."

Betsy swallowed hard. "He was everything opposed to what a perfect gentleman ought to be and yet I preferred him."

"At least he was never two-faced. He said what he meant. You can't say that about a lot of men."

Rayna seemed thoughtful as she reached for the coffeepot. "Betsy, I think you owe this Mr. Hennessey a great debt. When is his funeral service?"

She didn't know. "I don't know if there even is one. I only know of Mariah and I who even knew he lived out there."

"Surely he needed supplies for the winter," Rayna persisted, filling each cup with care. "Someone must know him."

"I don't know if he ever came to town." Betsy reached for the sugar bowl.

"No," Mariah said thoughtfully. "I know he came to town a few times a year. To trade in his furs for staples, of course. But also to put his woodwork on consignment."

Betsy forgot her fingers were holding the spoon and it slipped into the bowl. She left it, coffee drips and all, her mind skidding to a dead halt. "What kind of woodwork? Like whittling?"

"No. He makes furniture for the furniture store on Second Street."

What kind of furniture? Betsy was dying to know. It was wrong, this interest in him. He was gone. Dead. Probably buried by now. But Rayna's words troubled her greatly. She might be one of the few people who even knew him. Maybe that accounted for the strange way she felt moved inside…not sexually, goodness, she hadn't thought that way for years, but in her heart. As if something had changed between them on the night of so much death.

On her way out of town, she'd convince Joshua to take her along Second and she would see for herself. She couldn't say why she felt compelled to do so. Only that she did.

The afternoon sky felt changed, although the sunshine was lovely.

Mariah felt it, too. "Looks like we'll be in for some rain."

The furniture was beautiful. She knew it was his without explanation. Bold pieces, masculine and strong. As stalwart and as breathtaking as the mountains where he'd lived. As the man had been.

I never knew. She pressed her hand against the window glass, the sounds and smells and heat of the brilliant Indian summer's day faded to nothing. Nothing but the beat of her heart, the tug of her soul. They were chairs made for sitting on a porch. A pair of deep-backed, low-slung seats made out of rich cherry gleamed like sleek marble.

It's so beautiful. Her fingertips itched, anxious to slip along the polished armrests. To admire the crafted slats fit perfectly together. To trace the carved trail of climbing roses up the leg, along the back and across to the other side.

How could fierce and rugged Duncan Hennessey be the same man who put blade to wood and created something so fine and delicate it was hardly visible through the pane of glass?

"Bets!" It was Joshua, impatient with her again. Did he not have a ranch to run?

She ignored him, drawn back to the matching side table, equally exquisite. How comfortable those chairs would be, with cheerful yellow cushions, and it would look perfect on her back porch, where she so loved to spend a few moments of an afternoon. Dragging her kitchen chairs in and out of the house was cumbersome. But to have something more permanent…

You can't afford it, Betsy Ellen! Don't even reach for the door handle. Her hand seemed to be moving of its own will and the knob was sun-warmed brass against her palm. With a tug and the jingle of an overhead bell, she found herself inside the store. She caught a flash of the image of Joshua reflected in the door as it closed. His outrage contorted his chiseled face, and then she saw it. All of it.

There were more. Many more pieces than she could have imagined. No, there was no way one man could have done all this. She imagined a factory back East where men would work patiently for months to churn out such breathless pieces. She must have been wrong. It was wishful thinking, was all. Wishing she could have something to remember him by.

The tap of expensive boots on the polished floor behind her should have been a warning, if she'd paid enough attention. But no, she was too busy recoiling from the disappointment she'd created herself by wrongly believing this was Duncan's work. Instead of pivoting right out the door and escaping his clutches, she didn't move fast enough to elude the man who scraped to a stop behind her.

"Betsy, this is the most fortuitous occasion. I'd heard of your ordeal. And to think there's not a scratch on you, or so it would appear."

She grimaced, dug deep for enough courage and faced her nemesis. Ray Hopps, resplendent as always with his black coat and perfectly ironed trousers. He wore a white shirt and vest and a black string tie. His thinning blond hair was combed back at a jaunty angle. Perhaps he thought it made him debonair and attractive to desperate women.

But she was not that desperate for a man. In fact, there was only one reason she could think to even marry a man again, and that was for love. She sincerely doubted she'd ever feel more than mild repulsion for Ray Hopps, who blushed furiously as he brushed nonexistent lint off his jacket.

It was situations such as these where she admired her mother. No-nonsense Lucille would have had no problem managing any man. She simply would have spoken her mind, and Betsy wondered what the store owner would do if she simply said what she was thinking, "You have a better chance of getting a wrinkle in your knickers than me taking a spark to you." It was Ray Hopps's luck that she wasn't her mother.

Instead she looked past him, making it clear she was not interested in him again. It was the bane of being a young widow in a territory where unmarried men outnumbered unmarried women by at least five to one.

She tried to be sympathetic with poor Ray. He'd never snare a wife when he wore such ironed garments that seemed to hint at a man with rigid standards. The creases down the front of his trousers were as perfect as a surveyor's property line. She knew, because she was the one who ironed his garments weekly—and he was very picky when it came to the perfection of his ironed clothes.

Oh, he was waiting for an answer. What had he asked her about? That's right. Her "ordeal," as her mother had dubbed it. "I'm fine, thank you, but my buggy was damaged and I'm an entire day behind on my work schedule. I am supposed to be delivering your laundry this afternoon, but I intend to come tomorrow morning, early, if that's acceptable?"

"My, Betsy. Of course. If you'd rather, you could make it later in the day." He laid his long fragile hand against his heart, dramatic, but he hadn't been raised in Montana. Maybe he thought it was a dashing gesture. She tried not to fault him his foppish manner. "If you preferred, you could make your delivery the last of your day, on your way back into town, and I know my mother would be pleased to have you to supper. She is quite fond of you."

"Well, I do take care to starch her crinolines and mend the tucks in the seams of her corsets without charge."

Ray's face bloomed bright red. "I'm sure my mother appreciates that greatly."

"I'm so glad. She's been a wonderful client and I do want her to be happy." Betsy knew she'd derailed Ray's wooing and cast her gaze around the cramped, overly warm store.

There were gleaming oak tables and sideboards and heavy horsehair sofas and rich tapestry rugs of jeweled colors. Nothing that looked as if it had been made by a caustic mountain man. *It looks as if you raised your hopes for no good reason.* It seemed like such a small thing, to want to see his furniture, what was she going to do had she found it? Buy it? She was scraping a living together. Barely.

But she turned to the still-blushing storekeeper and

the question rose up as if she were destined to ask it and there was no way to stop the rush of words. "Perhaps you could tell me if you have any furniture from a local craftsman."

"Why, these pieces right here. Lovely, don't you think?" He gestured to the stunning cherrywood porch set and to the gleaning oak pieces. "We are unusually lucky to have such a skilled furniture maker in our midst. He lives in the county."

Don't get your hopes up. It could be another craftsman. The blood pounded in her ears and she heard herself say as if from a great distance. "Up near the Rocky Mountain Front?"

"Why, you must have heard of him. He's anonymous. To tell you the truth, he wants it that way and that's how we prefer it, too." A shadow passed over his elongated face. Narrow, thin features squinted, as something seemed to occur to him. "You don't happen to be looking to purchase these pieces, do you?"

"Yes, I am." Her obviously wicked, less than sensible side must not see the folly of buying expensive furniture she couldn't begin to afford. But did that halt her rash behavior? Of course not. "I would have to have the pieces lain away."

"Oh, I think Mother and I could trust you to make payments." Ray, as if happy to be of service, puffed out his narrow chest like a robin after gobbling the biggest worm in the garden. "Of course, we don't often accept payments, but we are all too happy to make exceptions for our special customers."

He slipped his fingertips into the shallow side pockets of his vest and looked very pleased with himself.

Say no, the sensible side of her urged. He will only see it as an opportunity to push for more than a proper chaperoned supper to something more suitable to a courting man—like a Sunday drive. If she agreed to his payment suggestion, then she would be in his debt for as long as she made those payments open to his advances.

There was nothing visibly wrong with Ray Hopps. In fact, if she did not launder his clothing she would have found him to be pompous, but perfectly decent and kind. She knew he was very generous with his donations to both the school's yearly fund-raising and her Ladies' Reading Society's campaign to raise funds for a lending library.

Except for the fact that she'd found in his vest pocket upon several occasions small match tins from the brothel on the far side of town, she would find no real fault with him whatsoever.

Sadly, she would not let a man court her who frequented such establishments.

"Perhaps you could give me a monthly sum on the porch chairs in the window. And, oh," she breathed in wonder as she turned to the display corner and saw the most beautiful bedroom set.

The high poster bed was hewn of gleaming dark oak and carved painstakingly so that the legs of the bed frame were roots of the climbing rose's stems rising up to the ceiling where graceful buds opened and dew rested on dainty leaves.

How could the man who'd wrestled a great black bear and won have made something like this? The man she'd held dying in her arms, the one who'd panicked in her presence, the one who'd lain motionless in near death—he had been the woodworker who'd done this. His soul had stirred hers.

This was why. Her eyes stung as she let her fingers caress the smooth varnished leaves and flowers budding across the headboard, etched and cut as if the hard unyielding wood had been bought silk. How many hours had he labored with tremendous patience and care?

I have to have this. Absolutely. She would give up anything to own it, not because it was beautiful, but because when she felt the warm wood solid against her hand, her soul stirred again.

And again.

"Uh, Mrs. Hunter. Can I call you Betsy?"

It felt odd to see how this man failed to move her in any possible way. Duncan Hennessey was gone, and she'd said goodbye to him. She'd thanked him. But seeing the exquisite loveliness he'd made with his rough, broad hands made her all the more certain she'd met the real Duncan Hennessey.

"No, you may not." She cleared the ragged emotion trembling in her voice, but nothing would shake the aching deep within. "Mrs. Hunter is fine. When can you deliver?"

"Perhaps after supper tonight, if you'd care to grace our dinner table with your presence?"

So much hope in his invitation. It had nothing to do with selling furniture and everything to do with another man offering her something she could not stomach. Settling for the average. Not when marriage was so important and the love that ought to support it.

"That is a very tempting invitation, for I know you

mean it sincerely, but no, I am content to dine alone in my own kitchen. Will your delivery men perhaps be available tomorrow?"

Ray Hopps's chest deflated, but it was with dignity that he led the way to his pristine, polished desk. "Of course. What time would be convenient for you?"

They made arrangements, and she could feel Joshua glowering at her through the thick outside walls.

He could wait. He was the one insisting on escorting her on her boring delivery route through town and across the prairie. She took one more look at the bed and the matching bureau and drawers and side tables. Such a bed was meant for a bride, for a wedding night joining a man and woman in true love.

Why did she feel as if she'd spend the rest of her life alone in that bed, wondering what it would have been like to be loved intimately by Duncan Hennessey? To know the spice of his kiss and the wild tenderness of his passion?

She wanted to tell herself it was only a woman's needs making her wonder, but she knew better. Having been a happy wife and a lonely widow, she knew her soul's match when she found it. For she'd felt this way only once before.

Was it rare to find more than one soul mate in a lifetime?

Afraid she knew the answer, she signed Ray's paperwork, not even noticing the purchase price that would only make her panic. The instant she stepped foot outside the door, the sky broke wide open and cold bitter rain pounded over her.

It felt as if the heavens had answered.

Chapter Eight

It felt as if autumn were holding off, giving way to the bolder demands of the summer sun. Any number of slow weeks had crept by, with each day more agonizing than the last.

Duncan cursed the heat that baked him from the inside out. Seeing to his basic daily needs of washing and eating, or tending the livestock, left him wrung out by midday. He slumped, panting and weak as a trickle of water trying to head uphill.

The deer and elk had disappeared from the mountainside when the dry season hit, and they had not yet returned. That told him the autumn would be long and the unforgiving sun would dominate the days left before frost crisped on the wild grasses. Before the bears curled in their dens and the herd animals returned.

There was a chance he'd have time enough to reach town before the blizzard snows trapped him in. His woodpile lay as he'd left it, scattered, and with endless hours of splitting and stacking needing to be done. It would have to wait until next spring. He was not strong enough to wield an ax and even if he was, there was barely time for the wood to season for adequate winter burning.

No, somehow he'd have to buy coal and haul it here. When he had no strength to hitch up the horses. He was too weak to sit aboard a bouncing wagon for twenty miles in one direction. He could never unload the coal when he returned.

The crone's bitter farewell mocked him now, like the echoing caw of the crows that scavenged along the mountainsides. "You live, and I saw to it. But no more. If you survive beyond this point is your lookout. Either way, you are nothing but a dead man. Step foot in town or approach my granddaughter in any way, and you will discover firsthand the fury of a woman protecting her own."

The tough old bird had spit at his feet and left him, barely able to sit.

He could not blame her. When Betsy was his to protect, he'd been deadly. The memory of the fierce wildness within him, the murderous need to keep her safe, had made him feel twelve feet tall. The lessons learned during two years serving in the Union army's infantry had surged through him, and he'd been that soldier again, fighting for what he held dear.

No, he did not think a pampered sunbeam of a woman was dear. And he would say that over and over until he believed it. Until it was true.

Hell blazes, his head was killing him. It had throbbed with a dull pounding at the temples and across his forehead ever since he'd been hurt. He hadn't hit his head, he didn't know why it hurt, or why the cursed thirstiness never seemed to leave him, no matter how much he drank. All he knew was that the snows would come, regardless of the sun shining as if it were midsummer. These were the Montana Rockies, some of the toughest winters anywhere, and he had to be prepared.

He had to figure out a way to get his strength back.

Maybe it was his headache, but it seemed the sound of the forest changed. With his luck, it was the wolves that seemed to hover around his land by day and circle his cabin by night. Maybe those animals knew his future more than he did. As did the vultures that would check in on him from time to time, spiraling in the cloudless sky overhead as if in foreboding.

His grandfather would have turned to the Old Ways, the Traditions of their People. Duncan couldn't imagine Grandfather would see any good news in a bunch of waiting vultures. Or the way birds startled from their daily work to perch in treetops, safely out of harm's way.

The wind rustled the tinder-dry grasses and they rattled like dried bones. He could have sworn there was a whistle coming from the road. And yet, no one had traveled down that overgrown path that served as a road for what had to be a month, maybe more. The old crone was gone and there was no one who cared enough to visit. His extended family, who did care, he'd pushed away long ago.

The wind's rustle became the whispering *squeak-squeeaak* of a buggy wheel. No, it couldn't be. He had to be hearing things, wishful thinking of a lonely man. The squeaking grew stronger and louder until the drum of a horse's hooves accompanied it and there, breaking from the overgrown branches, was a chestnut gelding and the front dash of a fancy black buggy.

With the top up to block the beat of the sun, it was impossible to see the figure who held the thick leather reins, but he could see her hands, which were extended enough so that the shade didn't hide them. He recognized small dainty gloves of tan kid leather and the yellow curve of a sunbonnet's brim.

I have to be dreaming. He blinked, but she was still there, close enough to see how the gelding's skin twitched in fear. Near enough that Duncan could make out her silhouette beneath the canopy top. Betsy Hunter, her jaw slack, leaning forward so that the sun found her, and kissed the soft golden skin of her face.

This has to be a dream, he thought, desperate, already looking for the brothers to come riding up behind her, shotguns at the ready, sent by the granny who'd threatened to ruin his life if he ever saw Betsy again. If she ever found out he was alive—

"Oh, God, I don't believe this." The buggy hadn't stopped but she flew out of it, her skirts billowing. A glimpse of snowy-white petticoat flashed beneath the butter-colored skirts. Her black shoes, perfectly polished, hit the earth, dried to powder, and dust flew like flour. "You're alive. What are you doing here? Oh, my God."

She was running, not noticing that her gelding had veered off the overgrown driveway and was circling back the way it had come.

Panic ripped through him, like a bandage from a wound, opening it anew. He tried to scramble to his feet, to get as much distance from her as he could, but she went down on her knees on the bottom step and her face fell to his knees.

He recoiled as if she were poison seeping through his trousers and into his skin, but she had a tight hold on him, her arms clasping his legs tight, and the fear faded. His self-lies silenced. He could pretend all he wanted but she was dear and he couldn't say why.

From his angle he saw the back of her head, covered in the matching light yellow of her dress, and the hint of golden brown hair escaping from the pins in gossamer wisps at her nape. Her neck was a slender column so small, the width of it could fit in his palm, and the bumps of her vertebrae and the arrow of her hairline showed how small and vulnerable she was.

She was petite as a fairy, and he didn't know what devil possessed him but he ached to press a kiss right there, at the nape of her neck where the collar of her dress began. And mocked him by hiding away her satin-warm skin and everything that dress covered.

Her breasts had flattened against his shins and he could feel their heat, the soft mesmerizing fullness that a man in his position really oughtn't to be thinking about. He wanted to blame it on his weakened condition, but there was no excuse for the yank on his heart as she lifted her face, streaming with tears, and laid a hand against his jaw.

So small and slender, but the wave of caring he felt left him paralyzed. He knew he had to push her away, demand she leave, scare her enough so that she would never return to these woods and the dangerous man he'd become.

The man he used to be, who'd lain dormant and patient, still knew how to wish. How to feel. It came to him in a flash, how she'd sat at his bedside and he'd known, upon awakening, she'd been there. This is how he knew. The way his spirit rested, as if it had been searching endlessly all his life and, weary, was home at last.

But he was no longer the craftsman who loved to carve and etch and sand a curve until it was just right. No longer a man who saw poetry in the world. Nor beauty.

He was no longer a man with a heart left, so he could not love.

But if he could, then it would be Betsy. In a different world, perhaps.

"Oh, they told me you were dead. I was right at your side, I couldn't feel your heartbeat. You didn't seem to be breathing and I'd thought you'd just passed into the hereafter."

"I remember."

"But you weren't awake."

"No." But my soul was. He grimaced and wanted to laugh out loud at his stupidity. What was wrong with him that he was sitting here mooning over some woman who'd brought him nothing but pain? Hadn't he been destroyed enough times over a pretty little woman? "What are you doing here if you thought I was dead? You didn't come to pick up my laundry."

"No, but I gained a new client out this way, south a bit, toward the Big Bear Mountains."

"You call that nearby?"

The bite in his combative tone made her realize what

she was doing. She was wound around him as if they were lovers. She pulled back, and it was like taking a step into darkness. The wind was as warm, she knew, but to her skin it was cooler than it had been a moment ago. She studied the hard, chiseled features of the man before her and she saw a man suffering.

He'd lost too much weight, so that his cheekbones seemed to hold out his skin, and his jaw was rough and covered with an untrimmed beard. His black eyes had sunk deeper into his skull, and on any other man it would have been ugly.

Duncan Hennessey looked compelling. There was no other way to describe the fire crackling in his black irises and the proud granite set of his chin. Like the warriors who used to ride their ponies bareback and without bit or reins, his spirit shone through. Vibrant. Unyielding. Unconquerable.

I cannot believe he is here. She dared not touch him again, but she ached to pull him into her arms. For all his ferocity, he was turning ashen. The reason she'd come forgotten, she straightened and took his arm.

"You need care. How long have you been on your own out here? And why did Granny leave you here? Why did she say you were gone?"

Duncan did not answer as he searched her with his brutal gaze. How his eyes seemed to bore past her skin to her very being was something she couldn't explain, but she felt it like a bruise deep inside. She wilted like a flower too long in a hot sun, without relief or water, as she watched the change come over him. As powerful as a storm from the south, rising faster than a horse could run, turning darker and more dangerous. Until she could feel the zing of the earth waiting for the lightning's touch.

His mouth twisted and there was no artist in the beast that shoved her away and stumbled to his feet. Like the bear he'd defeated, he rose over her, all hulking power and mighty rage. "Get out of here. What do you think you're doing? You don't fool me. You're not bringing ruination to my door, no way in hell. You turn around and get outta here."

"What on earth are you talking about?" She toppled back, her heel catching on a rock, and she lost her balance. Pain winged up her ankle, but her good, tight shoes protected her from twisting it any further and she tripped sideways, as if fate had wanted her at a safer distance.

Hate. She felt the emotion roll over her like smoke. He hated her? Her mind wasn't working, she couldn't move beyond the notion that he hadn't died at all. Then why had Granny said he was gone? Why had Joshua said he'd paid for a decent casket and buried him here, on his land?

She trusted them beyond all things, she couldn't reconcile the fact that they had to have lied to her, when neither Joshua nor Adelaide Gable were ones to make up falsehoods. Why had they done this? Had Granny only thought he was dead?

Well, that didn't make sense because Joshua clearly hadn't buried him.

Had they left Duncan mortally wounded to fend for himself as best he could? Outrage left her paralyzed as she watched the wounded man stumble up the stairs, catch his toe on the lip of the top step and go down like he'd been sucker punched. He hit the porch with a thud that sounded like a woodpile clattering down and lay there, motionless except for the rapid rise and fall of his rib cage and the jagged rasping of his strained breathing.

"Duncan!"

She dropped to her knees beside him, but he was already shoving at her, the flat of his hand at her knee and thigh, pushing her like a bucket across a floor. Making it clear. This connection she felt with him was like a one-way train track.

He averted his face, as if he thought so little of her, as if he couldn't tolerate the sight of her. He had to know she cared for him, and as weak as he was, he was bandaged at his neck, still, for she could see the white muslin poking up from his undershirt collar. He wanted nothing to do with her, even to accept help from her.

She thought of Ray Hopps and how she'd deftly done the same thing, putting him in his place, letting him know she was simply not interested.

Oh. She sat there for a moment, letting the realization sink in.

As if in great pain, Duncan limped through the open doorway and she watched in disbelief as he disappeared, hunched and ambling, into the deep shadows inside the cabin. With her mind spinning, her emotions in shock, she felt the tears on her cheeks at the image of the once proud, once mighty giant of a man gravely wounded, still.

The image of him lingered, of how his right arm had shook with effort and weakness as he'd fought his way back onto his feet. And how he moved as if broken, protecting his side and one arm and favoring his leg, made it undeniable how injured he'd been. He was suffering and she was not.

"But I don't understand." She followed him through the open door and into the deep shadows of the main room that smelled stale and was illuminated only by the faint glow from the sunlight curling around the edges of the heavy window shades.

Furniture hulked like monsters in the corners and the kitchen felt as if ghosts hovered over tabletops and counters. An odd chill misted around the rooms, as if Death were watching and waiting.

The ghosts became piles of dishes left undone. Clods of dirt from Duncan's boots crunched and powdered beneath her step. She could smell the dust and stale air. "Granny was here. Why did she think you'd died? Is that why she left you?"

"Sure, that's what she did. She thought I was dead." Sarcasm dripped like fester from a wound as he disappeared into the back of the cabin. "I was damn lucky she didn't put me in a coffin and bury me."

"What are you saying? We all thought you've been dead. I've been mourning you."

"Sure you have. Your family's still wearing black, huh?"

"No, but Joshua said… He said…"

"What did he say?" Duncan wished to hell he could keep the hate from his voice. The hatred and anger and disillusionment that no matter where he lived, no matter what he did, human beings were the scourge of the earth, how God could ever have given them life was a real puzzle.

It was not simply the matter of the settlers and the natives, the Union and the Confederates, the right and the wrong. Where there was no reason and no sense, some folks went right ahead and did as they pleased. Destroying others and taking pleasure that they'd gotten away with it.

"I bet your brother managed to shed a tear of pity after lying about what a Good Samaritan he was to pay for a good coffin for my worthless hide to rot in."

"No, he wouldn't do that. He wouldn't lie."

"Is that what he told you? Am I right?" Yeah, it was about what he'd figured. "Well, I'm alive, right? So obviously he lied. What do you think I did? Come back to life, break out of a coffin and dig my way to the surface?"

Her eyes rounded, mortified and shocked. Her bottom lip began to tremble and shock and disbelief rolled off of her like radiant heat from a potbellied stove and he refused to feel pity for her. He refused to soften the vile truth of what her loved ones, so good and honest on the outside, had so easily done.

"Your grandmother and your brother both threatened to ruin my life if I ever showed up in town alive, so that you would find out." He was driven by an old rage that had less to do with that vicious but understandably protective old woman and more to do with bitterness that was obliterating him from the inside out. A bitterness that wanted to deny the honest shock as Betsy Hunter turned and walked out of his life.

Yeah, keep on walking, he thought, letting the acid within him take over. Drained, his knees gave out and he slid onto the edge of the mattress. Too feeble to manage his boots, he simply lay back and let his legs dangle.

His head cracked like thunder resounding through his skull. His guts knotted, making him taste bile. The bed began to rotate, or that's how it seemed. Even when he closed his eyes, the spinning remained, and he was whirling faster and faster as the darkness took him.

She was gone, good riddance. So what if he hadn't spotted a speck of an apology on her face? It didn't matter to him one whit if she didn't believe him. Sure, she'd walked away. It was exactly what he'd expected. He'd saved her, and she was just like any woman he'd ever met, except for the rare few, who were out for their own gain. Careless and self-concerned, all those skirts wanted was a man to fulfill their shallow whims. Why would Betsy be any different?

Blackness surged upward like a tide washing away the places within him he could still feel until it was only a dark, drowning hatred no different than the years after he'd returned from prison. The injured muscles in his neck, shoulders, arm and chest thrummed from overuse.

Hell, I hurt. He squeezed his eyes shut, trying not to acknowledge the twitching pain, sharp like a blade and as crackling like lightning as the nerves vibrated up and down the length of his injuries.

What he needed was a few hours' rest. Then he'd be strong enough to break open a can of beans and stumble back to bed. If only he could get the pain to stop, the nerve endings from snapping, the beat inside his head to cease.

He didn't hear her as much as he sensed her. Felt her

from the length of the cabin away. Even though she moved with hardly more than a whisper-soft pad of her shoes on the puncheon floors and the leaves-in-wind sound of her skirts, he perceived her nearness like the softest of touches.

As she hesitated at the foot of the bed, towering over him, her breathing in time with his own, he wondered what she'd come to say. If she was gathering her nerve to tell him to go to hell, to condemn him for lying about her loved ones. Then, he wagered, she'd proceed to tell him how worthless of a man he was. No job, no impressive house, no high-stepping horses. He was just a half-breed, more garbage than man.

Yeah, he'd heard it all before and worse. So much worse.

He heard the rustle of fabric, the hush as she laid something on the bed beside him and the scrape of her heel as she spun. The swish of her startched petticoats as she walked away, leaving him, shutting the door firmly behind her as she went.

His head screamed with pain, but he opened his eyes anyway. Waited until they'd adjusted to the after-midnight darkness in the room.

She'd laid three roses on his bed.

Flowers she must have brought for his grave.

The grave that didn't exist.

Chapter Nine

"Betsy! Hell, I've been worried about you."

Joshua was sitting on her front steps, his hat in his hands, looking not the least bit guilty. And after how he'd behaved! "I do not need a babysitter, thank you."

"Aren't you in a snit."

"Actually, I feel downright uncivil."

"You? You're never uncivil. You always are and always have been my own sweet Bets."

His nickname for her, when he was three and she an infant had amused their parents greatly, and the nickname had stuck. It was an endearment she'd known all her life, one that expressed affection between her and Joshua; they'd always had a strong bond. But she stared at her big, bold, powerful brother and saw a man who looked invincible, not in the same way as Duncan did, but Joshua was every inch a capable man.

She'd always been so proud he was her brother, as she was of all her younger siblings.

Surely the Joshua Gable I know and love would not have deceived me. She hopped down from the buggy, refusing his hand to help her and led Morris by the bridle's cheek strap through the side gate to the stable out back.

Clearly, Joshua had deceived her. Calmly, so he would not suspect, she tossed the question over her shoulder. "I was delivering out near the Rocky Mountain Front, you know—my new client down at the base of the Big Bear Range?"

"Oh, that's right." Smoothly, as if there was nothing amiss, at least not in his world, he bounded ahead to haul open the heavy double doors and began releasing the harness buckles the instant Morris stopped moving.

"It reminded me of that poor mountain man. He was always gruff, but he tipped so well. I miss the income." And she waited.

Perfectly timed, as if he'd counted to five, Joshua released the traces and rose, working easily with the leather harness. The honest and salt-of-the-earth man he appeared to be.

"Are you hurting, Bets? I can always lend you money. Better yet, you should come live with Mother. She's lonely and you know she'd love having you."

"Lonely? How can she be with every one of us but me and James living with her?"

"We're a big family. She's used to all of us."

Hmm. Interesting. She knew he would turn the conversation to his advantage, always gently pushing her to give up her independence. This home that was hers alone. "It's been—what?—a month, since the poor man died. I had never asked if you'd seen to a headstone for his grave."

"I had not thought of it, since he has no relatives."

"My friend Katelyn's husband's surname is Hennessey. I wonder if they are related."

"I doubt it. If that recluse would have had family, surely he would not have lived alone in the wild."

He is not himself, she realized as he led Morris to the corner stall, so nice and boxy and filled with fresh straw. The dried stalks rustled and whispered as the gelding ambled to the feed trough and began crunching on his oats. Morris's ears were swiveling and alert, and he kept a good close eye on Joshua.

See? Morris sensed it, too. Joshua was tense beneath the smooth motions as he shook out the thick leather harness and hung it to air with the ease of a rancher who had done the same act several times a day for the last decade.

Joshua was not making eye contact. That was it. That was what seemed different as he hefted the shoulder collar and lifted it onto the storage frame.

"Still," she persisted, "I would rest easier knowing the man had at least a properly marked grave. Would you see to it?"

"Yes, but why all this curiosity?"

There was suspicion in his eyes as jeweled as her own. Well, he ought to be suspicious! He was lying to her. Duncan Hennessey had been one-hundred-percent correct. How could this man have the same blood flowing in his veins and act as if he were not being duplicitous?

Joshua waited, the stable work done, his rugged hands fisted on his hips. He looked like a general in command of his troops, and she burned with anger, as hot and bright and cruel as the midday sun during a two-month-long drought.

He was bossy and he'd always been that way. His heart was in the right place, she knew, but she thought about how difficult it must have been for Duncan. "I'm not curious. I'm simply thankful. I don't want to forget or take for granted what he—"

"For God's sake, the mountain man was an outcast from society. I don't know why we all didn't put a stop to this foolishness of yours before this. Mama is worried about you. Granny is worried about you. I have enough responsibilities without having to be half-sick with fear that something is going to happen to you."

"Like washing a mountain man's shirts?"

"He was dangerous. What if he'd decided to hurt you? You could never have defended yourself against his advances, even with that old rifle of Charlie's. Hell, he fought a black bear and lived long enough to tell about it. With that kind of savagery, how could you ever be safe?"

"Because he hates people, Joshua. He never got close enough to me. He wasn't interested in me. I believe he harbored great distrust for women. I'd always wondered if a woman had broken his heart badly."

"See? There you go! This is the reason I'm here come to check on you instead of putting up my feet and relaxing after working in the fields until sunup."

Thank goodness the Indian summer had been long enough for Joshua to get a rare fourth cutting of the grasses for hay. It had necessitated his stay on the family property so she could return to driving alone. "Nothing has happened yet. Nothing will happen."

"Not now." His eyes narrowed. "Did you drive out there? Is that why you're late?"

"I'm late because I stopped by Mariah's on the way home. She'd invited me out to discuss a few things for the next fund-raiser. You know we're both in charge of the next lending library supper."

"Oh." He visibly relaxed.

Liar, she wanted to rail at him, and whack him hard alongside his head so that maybe whatever rock was loose in there would jar back into place and he wouldn't be a jackass. "You'll see about the headstone?"

"I promise." In a big-brother way, he cupped her chin. "We all love our dear sister so much. Stop making us worry."

"As much as I love you right back, you can't control my life, Joshua."

"I'm not trying to control you, Bets. Just protect. You could always remarry. You've been without Charlie for a long time. There are so many good men in this county, solid, working men. You could get married."

"I will when I want to."

She shoved bags of dirty laundry into his powerful arms. She might as well take advantage of having him here, since he was giving her a royal headache. But at least she knew why. He'd done such a terrible thing. Out of a misplaced sense of love. And a man had suffered because of it.

Oh, it made her furious as she filled her arms, juggling the bags so she could see her way to the door. Furious and frustrated. How lucky she was to be so loved by so many people.

So many overprotective, overbearing, impossible liars!

"When you want to? What kind of arbitrary attitude

is that?" He hurried to catch up with her, but she was in a good steam, marching so fast he had to work to keep up. "Bets, I'm making you mad, I can see it."

"Mad? No, I wouldn't call this mad. Outraged. Furious. Ready to cover you in hot honey, stake you in the middle of the plains and let the ants and bees and bears do what they will with you."

"Whoa, you really are mad."

Men were brilliant, truly. She smacked open the side gate and stomped along the stones and up the steps and into her very own house.

"You," she announced in a voice that even he could comprehend. "You are not welcome here."

Genuine hurt washed over his face. He wasn't bad; he was just a man.

The rage dribbled out of her, becoming smaller as she shut the door instead of slamming it, realizing she'd dropped the six bags she'd juggled at her feet and had a hard time stepping over them.

Joshua was still out there, she could see him through the kitchen window, holding the stuffed pillowcases and rucksacks full of other people's laundry.

He looked confused, continuing to stare at the door as if he'd either imagined her tirade or expected her to feel bad, which was what she was doing, and open the door. To apologize and invite him in so he could railroad her and boss her and interfere. He meant well, but he didn't understand. This was her life. Hers alone.

She wasn't about to let him in and apologize, which is exactly what she always did every time she lost her patience with anyone in her family. They loved her, she knew, because she loved them. But she was a grown woman and what she wanted wasn't simple. Did he think she treasured listening to her movements echo in the evenings when the shadows lengthened? When she'd used to spend lovely evenings like this with Charlie.

After the supper dishes were done, she and Charlie, exhausted from work and dealing with problems and crises and debts, would enjoy cool tea on the back porch side by side, stealing those few minutes, sometimes as much as two whole hours, just basking in one another's company.

Listening to the beauty around them, the birds on their last-chance hunt for bugs and worms before nightfall. The cat curled up on the cool shade. Charlie's hand warm and reassuring around hers. Knowing that whether they read or talked or simply sat in silence, they were content to be together.

And come bedtime they would go upstairs together in their little house on the high plains north of town and make love, the sweetest way to end a day spent in paradise—because what else could it be to have the privilege of spending a day with the one you loved?

She'd do anything to bring those days back, to have one more evening and one more night in Charlie's arms. It was a sad fact of life that a person couldn't go back, only forward.

Did Joshua or anyone in her family really want her to marry someone like Ray Hopps? Someone who seemed hard-working and pleasant enough, except for the secret brothel habit, but he was not a man she would want to sit next to every evening in the long shadows and soft golden and often rosy glow of twilight. Fulfilled and happy and so much in love, it hurt.

No, she wasn't about to try to imagine a man like Ray Hopps on her back porch, sitting at his side, holding his hand as night fell. She wasn't about to settle for almost good, when she'd had the best love life had to offer.

She might be alone, she might be washing other people's worn clothing, but she wasn't beside a man she'd wished would fulfill her simply by meeting her gaze across the room.

Simply by holding her hand.

She surveyed the laundry bags she'd dumped on the floor. She grabbed up the Landers's laundry. Pulled out a small garbage pail and began sorting. Whites, colors, intimates, sheets. She checked every pocket and found a nickel, which she would return taped to the weekly bill, a wadded-up handkerchief, which she held by the corner and tossed into the white pile, and a familiar match tin from the Red Curtain. It was apparently the brothel of choice among many of the county's male citizens.

"Betsy?"

Goodness, was he still out there? She leaned across the table, straining to see if he was still standing where she'd left him

Yep. He even still held the laundry bags.

"I'm not apologizing to you," she said after she'd opened the window to let in the cooler twilight air. "Go home and think about what you've done."

"What did I do? Wait, is this about the talk I had with Ray Hopps?"

"What talk?"

"I just assumed you might be sweet on him, since you bought that furniture you couldn't afford—"

"Stop assuming." Suddenly the pieces fell into place to make a whole realization that made her even madder. "You want me to marry Ray."

"He'd be a good husband, no doubt about it. He's very successful with that store of his."

"It's his father's store."

"Well, he's a good partner, then. C'mon, Bets, let me in."

"No."

"Can I at least put down these bags?"

"Sure. Leave 'em against the door. 'Bye." She shut the window, her hands shaking, trying to keep from losing her temper. Yelling at him wasn't going to mend the wrong he'd done.

He'd done it for the right reasons, she knew, but he'd left a wounded man to fend for himself. And Granny, too. Why?

Because they, of the marriage-minded, didn't think Duncan Hennessey, loner and terse mountain man, was in any way good enough for their little Bets.

When in truth, she thought he was the only one.

Duncan awoke to sunlight. Bright blocks of it angling into the room as if Rembrandt had painted it, bold and vibrant and holy. He couldn't remember if he'd left the shades up to let in the cooler night air. He couldn't remember much of anything.

Except for her.

The new depth of bitterness he'd achieved had

drained all his strength. He was still on his back, with his boots on and his feet in them, on the floor. The only stroke of luck was that she'd closed the front door behind her, as if to say she wasn't coming back.

Of course she wasn't. She didn't believe what he'd said, and as for the old woman and the jackass brother of hers, he was surprised they hadn't come with the dawn, with a lynch mob and a coil of rope.

At least Betsy wasn't the kind of woman who'd outright lie. He saw that now, how horror-struck she'd been when he'd told her what her loved ones had done. Lying seemed to be a huge sin in her eyes, for the way she'd been affected.

Not that she minded much about him, about the fact that they'd left him to die…or so they'd hoped.

It was time to be moving on. If he could sit up. He strained, he groaned, he tried leveling his body up with his good arm. Nothing.

He gave up, panting and sweating. Looked as if he'd be here for a while, staring up at the open beams in the ceiling he'd built from logs he'd cut down and skinned. The thought of starting over somewhere else—again— had the bile rising in his throat.

A sound rasped from the other room. It wasn't a normal sound, not the wind at the eaves or the low fir bough scraping against the corner of the house. It wasn't a cougar crossing the roof. It wasn't a moose rubbing his great horns on a tree outside. It wasn't a mouse digging in the pantry—although that's what it sounded like.

Except mice didn't make shoe falls or have petticoats that rustled like a spring breeze.

The old woman. She was back. He'd slept through her arrival, but she'd come as she'd promised. To make good on her threat. She was here to defend her granddaughter, and he hated her for it, and envied Betsy.

Although she cared so little for him, enough to walk away when she knew he was alive. Enough to have let her brother take her away in the first place, he felt a singular force when he was in her presence.

It was as if she were near. Simply thinking of her made the place new and tender in his heart move as if a current directed it. Like the rush of a river's stream. Like the lap of a mountain lake's tide. Like the moon drawn from horizon to horizon across a star-spangled sky.

The old woman was coming. Her step, light and delicate, tapped steadily in his direction until she cut through the brightness spilling through the window and he felt her shadow fall across him.

He waited. He was in no hurry to talk to her. He didn't want to hear what she had to say at all. So by now Betsy Hunter knew the truth about him. Fine. She wasn't here for him to see the disgust on her face. The hatred. How he'd go from hero to liar to rapist in her opinion.

He turned his heart to steel. His soul to cold iron.

Finally, the old woman spoke. "I would have removed your boots so you were more comfortable, but I didn't want to disturb you."

It was not the crone's voice.

He listened to the warm cadence of Betsy's voice, the gentle resonance of her, and he was sure that he was trapped in some cruel level of Dante's purgatory, where he would be forever haunted with dreams for the woman he longed for and could never have.

He squinted through one eyelid. The sun glowed around her, as if she were made of the same light. Good and strong and pure. Brilliant enough to change the world from night to day.

"Here, let's get you sitting up."

His head was ringing, his body boneless. He saw her coming and panicked. Her small, dainty hands curling around his good elbow, her other grasping him carefully around the chest. The scent of her hair was like a spring garden and he breathed her in. Her sweetness filled him until he had to turn away or she would know.

He did his best to move on his own, accepting little help from her as he dragged his seemingly wooden body along the mattress to collapse, exhausted, on the pillows. The softness felt good, so damn good, and that was why his chest gave a hitch of gratitude. To be lying properly in bed against a pile of pillows.

Sitting up, his head didn't drum as much. He let his head roll to one side and he stared at the walls. The careful chinking he'd spent weeks on when he was building this place. The logs had matured to a rich dark honey and the thought of building another cabin had him angry all over again.

This time he'd build something he didn't care about. Something like those tiny shanties that pockmarked the prairie. They looked more like piano boxes than houses. They were simply one half of a little house, with the slant of roof going in one direction only to encourage the winter's barrage of snow to not accumulate. And the shanty itself nothing more than the length of the boards it took to make it. Eight feet by ten feet. Some were larger.

Yeah, that's what he'd do. Slap something together that would be good enough for the coming winter, wherever it was he settled, and when it came time to pack up and leave, it wasn't something he'd miss.

That is, if the Hunter family decided to chase him off instead of bringing vigilante justice. Not that he'd touched Betsy, but the thought that he could would be enough to drive them into a frenzy. Fear changed people. He'd seen it.

Whatever was coming, he had to be prepared.

"Here, let me help you to get comfortable."

As she leaned over him, escaped curls from her hair knot bounced against his cheek and caught on his scruffy beard.

Hell, she was nice. He held on tight—he would not give in to this flooding river of wanting that seemed to take over. He was a strong-willed man, and still it overwhelmed him. The beat of his heart sounded tinny in his ears. His blood like hot springs bubbling up from the earth.

His groin, as weak as he was, hitched as he inhaled her scent. As he felt the subtle heat of her skin. It took every ounce of his warrior's will not to lift his arms the few inches separating them, pull her down to his chest and leave the troubles of the world behind—for a while—and lose himself in her.

No other woman had affected him this way. She melted his will like steel in a forge and he wanted to curse her for it. But like the pure beam of light she was, she didn't have any inkling of his thoughts as she plumped his pillows and moved away to tug off his boots.

He wouldn't look at her. He could never cast his gaze upon her again without tasting this hunger. Wanting to spend his passion in the warm comforting heat of her body. Holding her so tight, it felt as if they could never be apart again, even after they pulled apart.

He wanted her with a fire he'd never felt burning before. It was greedy and selfish and consuming. He feared it because it was not lust. No, the emotions went deeper than that.

"Here, I brought you coffee." The mattress dipped on her side and he felt the distinct curve of her hip and upper thigh fit against his side. "I don't know about you, but if I don't have a cup of coffee first thing in the morning, just to sit and sip and soak in the beautiful dawn, then my day turns out to be a load of horse dooey. Every time."

"Horse dooey?" He'd never heard that term before. But why was he surprised? She didn't look like a woman who'd ever said the word "crap," much less the more colorful terms he could think of.

No, Betsy was…amazing, his heart wanted to say, but the hard cold truth was he had no business thinking anything about Betsy Hunter. She obviously hadn't been told what he'd done. Who he was. Or she wouldn't be anywhere near him or lifting a battered tin mug to his lips.

"Careful, it's hot."

She was close enough to kiss. He couldn't help thinking it. Her face hovered close to his and he could see that her skin was creamy and her freckles lay like tiny dainty snowflakes across her nose.

He wanted to kiss each freckle. To nibble the dimples that accented her smile. He wanted to run his hand down the graceful arch of her neck and tug at the prim buttons at her collar.

He'd bet all he had that Betsy Hunter was anything but prim.

The vibrant taste of coffee spilled across his tongue and he savored it. Hell, that was good. She sweetened it, he liked a couple spoonfuls of sugar, and that surprised him because he didn't keep sugar in his pantry. He didn't need it. He didn't bother to buy extras that had stopped mattering long ago. But the sugary taste was welcome.

"There, it's not so full. Do you want to hold it? Or I could put the cup down on the table?"

"I'll hold it."

"Good. I'll be right back." She hustled away, skirts swishing, shoes tapping.

The sunlight seemed to follow her as she disappeared from his sight.

That's when he noticed she'd moved the roses she'd brought to the night table, where they leaned to one side in his army field cup of water. The yellow buds had opened and the delicate inner petals unfurled like hope in a place where hope could never be.

He heard the clang of a pan and realized the cabin was so hot because the kitchen stove was lit. The sizzle told him she was frying meat—sausage patties by the smell of it. His stomach growled like a furious bear. He was so hungry for real food that his mouth wouldn't stop watering even as he drank the coffee until the mug was empty.

She returned with a plate heaped with food. He knew he ought to shout at her and frighten her away, but she'd turned his will to "dooey," as she would say, and he hadn't had real food since the bear attack.

"I'll fetch more coffee, too," she said, dragging a pillow over his lap to set the plate on. It made a rickety table, but it was enough to hold the plate level as he grabbed the fork, stabbed a slab of greasy, spicy sausage and shoved it into his mouth.

Damn, but it was good. Sunny-side up eggs, fried potatoes and three flakey biscuits with butter dripping from the center cut. He hadn't eaten like this since he'd lived at home. Since he was a real man with a real life just like anyone else. He'd have eaten anything—as evidenced by the stack of empty cans tossed in the kitchen—but this, it was too much, too good to be true.

He wanted to savor it, to enjoy the tastes and textures. Betsy was an amazing cook. The potatoes were buttery and peppery, with something else he couldn't name, but he couldn't eat them fast enough. The eggs were perfect, just a little runny, mostly soft and the whites fluffy.

And the biscuits… Lord, he'd gladly go to prison for another ten years just to have more of the moist, rich, buttery flavor.

She poured the coffee, draining the pot. He watched out of the corner of his eye as he polished his plate clean. She stirred sugar in his coffee, took the plate and disappeared into the other room. He heard the splash of water, the clink of dishes, and then she returned.

Every place within him burned—not with the fire of anger or the inferno of lust, but a heat that was altogether more powerful.

"I've cleaned your kitchen and left a basket on the table. It's enough food for your lunch and supper."

She reached for her sunbonnet, a thoroughly female motion of shaking out the hat and pulling it in place over her lush dark hair. The blue bonnet framed her face, bringing out the jeweled sparkle in her eyes and the pink of her rosebud mouth.

The mouth he hungered to taste.

"I have to hurry. I have to get home before anyone notices I'm gone, and then I have my washing and ironing and deliveries. But I'll be back tomorrow morning, I promise."

She paused at the door. "Is there anything you want me to bring back with me? Oh, and I've already watered and fed your horses, so don't worry. Just rest and heal."

His throat ached. She flickered her fingertips in that endearing wave, the one he told himself to hate, and then she was gone, humming as she closed the door, her voice growing faint as she called out to Morris, who must be her horse. Who would name a horse Morris, the poor creature.

Duncan listened to the rattle of her buggy and the squeak of her wheel, which was getting worse, until there was only silence and sunshine spilling into his cabin.

As if trying to fool him into believing there were nothing but blue skies ahead.

Chapter Ten

Why was it the man looked like an archangel while asleep? Betsy resisted the urge to brush the tangle of black hair away from the hard angle of his face so she could admire him better. His features were hard, but the muscles beneath the bronzed skin were relaxed. Not exactly soft, his face could never be mistaken for that, but the bitterness was gone along with the anger and the ferocity. What remained carved in his features and etched in the grooves and character lines on his face astounded her.

Nobility. Strength. Integrity.

Vastly different from the man who burned with so much hatred that the fury emanating from him would make the fires of hell seem tepid by comparison.

It didn't look to her as if he'd moved since this time yesterday, but the basket on the table was empty. Good. She couldn't resist laying her hand on his brow. Not overly warm—just warm from sleep, not from fever. He made a low noise in his throat, not exactly a moan but definitely a sound as if he'd liked being touched and pressed against her.

Her heart gave a little sigh. Why on earth she felt affection for this difficult bear of a man, she wished she knew. He couldn't seem to stand her when he was awake. The total sum of their interactions had been, in large part, him trying to escape her or telling her to keep away. No, he definitely didn't feel this floating awareness, like a summer's cloud sailing along. But she'd been in deep love before and it was not so long ago that she didn't remember how it started.

Just like this.

What she didn't know was what to do if the man didn't feel the same way. With Charlie, it had been evident from the start the way their souls stirred when they were together that they were destined to marry. To spend a happy loving life together.

And they had.

The problem was that she thought her marriage to be so special and rare, the bond she and Charlie had, that finding that again would be impossible. Didn't a soul mate imply there was only one match? That as soul mates, there could never be anyone better for the other?

And what happened to Charlie, waiting for her in heaven, when she was falling in love with someone else? These things troubled her greatly. It was a sign she was thinking too much. The one thing she knew for sure was that she never had to worry about replacing Charlie. Duncan Hennessey hated her. It was that simple.

And that sad.

She withdrew her hand to lay her palm against the center of her chest, between her breasts, where she hurt as if a serrated blade had sunk deep behind the bones. When she ought to be getting something accomplished, she was sitting idle, watching him sleep. Staring at the way his mouth, a hard, terse frown by day, had transformed into a pliable, soft-arched upper lip, with a pronounced dip that made her want to lay her lips on his, and a bottom lip that was made to bring pleasure to a woman.

Not that she should be considering his mouth whatsoever. Or his kiss. Or wondering how his lips would feel grazing over her bare flesh....

Whoa, right there. She'd certainly missed the marriage bed, but that was no reason to let her mind wander in that direction. Because Duncan wasn't just male, he was a man. In every possible meaning of the word. His frame was big, his muscles corded. His abdomen flat, his arms, while relaxed, showed the cords of muscle and sinew. A lesser man would not have survived his injuries, but even those were healing. Beneath the edge of the bandage she saw the red tender places of new skin.

His hands were big like the rest of him, and so were his feet. Big, thick toes. Before she started wondering if he was like-size anywhere else, she bounced off the bed and made herself gather up the pile of clothing tossed in the corner, stuffed it into his rucksack and went outside to load it into her buggy.

On her return trip she carried in the second basket, heavy with food. She saw him stumbling up from the bed. His long hair tangled, his clothes twisted and wrinkled. He wasn't exactly gray, which was an improvement over yesterday. A harsh spark flashed in his dark gaze and his jaw tensed. A muscle twisted along his jaw.

She perched on the top step. She could set her chin, too. She could make a fierce challenge with her eyes. "Are you going to slam the door and send me packing?"

"Tempting."

"In your weakened state, you never know. I might be able to push you around."

His left brow arched. Did she really think she could ever push him around? "I could just take your basket, shut the door and lock you out."

"You could try it, but then I wouldn't bring you more food." A furrow dug between her eyes, above the bridge of her nose, and it was adorable how she pulled her eyes into a frown as she thought. He had her wondering, he knew, if he was teasing or serious.

He should take her basket, snarl the meanest words he could think of and send her on her way for good. That was the only solution. She couldn't keep coming out here. Her family was bound to figure it out and they wouldn't approve. It was only a matter of time before she knew the truth. He should end it now.

Besides, associating with women like her was against his principles.

So what did he do? Did he snarl and shout and terrify her? No, he didn't do that. It was an impulse, he blamed himself for later, an impulse of a man living too long alone. He did the only thing he could, ravaged as he was. Knowing how he looked to her in clothes he didn't know how long he'd been wearing, unwashed and unkempt. He couldn't even stand up straight.

He had no business opening the door wide. "I don't

have the patience to argue with you today. Maybe to-morrow."

"How gracious of you. I knew you were gentle as a kitten. Why else would you roar so loudly?" She could tease, too, and watched the indignation streak across his face. Gone were the glimpses of the noble Duncan—the real Duncan.

His features hardened. Sharpened. "You mistake me for someone else. Don't tell me you read a lot of those dime novels."

"I do. I am a great fan of the romantic novel." With a sigh, Betsy stormed her way inside, knowing it was the food he wanted. But goodness, she intended to feed him until he was well.

She stumbled her way in the dim light; the sun seemed to have disappeared. The kitchen echoed with shadows—not just emptiness. It felt to her as if a great sorrow hung in the air like cobwebs in the corners, needing to be chased out.

Remembering what Mariah had said of Duncan's parents, she understood him more. Home is a sad place when the people you love are gone forever.

She set the basket on the table next to the first one she'd brought in. Leaving Duncan to paw through the contents, she went straight to the shades, drew them up and sighed at the soft light shining through. Clouds were crowding together at the rugged faces of the mountains spearing up through the green forest, so close, Betsy had to tilt her head back to see, but their peaks were hidden.

"What are you doing?" Duncan scowled at her as he opened a canning jar with his bare hand—one twist was all it took.

And she had to beat them open. Hmm. She ignored how he dug a peach slice out of its syrup with his fingers and popped it into his mouth. It was tempting to comment on his manners, even to rummage around in the dishes she'd left to drain on the board after washing them for a fork for him to use.

Tempting, but she was grateful to see Duncan's appetite improved. He'd gotten some good rest, maybe even some deep sleep, and his face wasn't as hollowed.

How, she thought angrily, could Granny and Joshua have left him out here to fend for himself? She couldn't get over that. She'd seen how helpless he'd been…and because of her.

For her.

Duncan sank into the closest chair, trying to hide how his knees were quaking. The soft daylight caressed the side of his face and she realized he'd shaved. The lean cut of his cheeks and the golden bronze of his skin combined with the way the hushed light shrouded him, she realized why he appeared noble, when he wasn't scowling. His heritage. He had to have some native blood in him.

He opened a wrapped loaf and made a choked sound. "Apple bread?"

"And I put apple butter in there, too. My first batch of the summer. Oh, it's sweet. That's for later in the day… No, I put breakfast in there, keep digging."

"You brought all this for me?" He looked from the crock of raisin-oatmeal cookies to the wrapped fried slices of bacon, and the honey-cured ham and the boiled eggs and more of the biscuits. A ball of butter. A jar of fresh milk, still warm from a cow.

There were slices of bread and he realized she'd made him sandwiches for lunch. Thick slabs of roast beef and juicy red slices of tomato—how long had it been since he'd had a tomato? And homemade pickles and relish and mustard. And for supper, a wrapped half chicken, coated, spiced and fried. A bowl of potato salad and another of baked beans.

"There's enough for days."

"That's the notion. I can't drive out here every day. That should see you through to midweek, don't you think?"

"I can't believe this." His head was pounding, he wasn't thinking clearly. He wasn't thinking at all. His stomach was growling and she was here, setting a clean plate before him, from the drainer full of the dishes she'd done yesterday.

She set a knife and fork on the table and poured him a glass of milk. "I'll have this heated up, if you want to wait."

"This is fine."

She set out a good portion of the bacon strips and the ham slices. Broke and peeled three eggs. He buttered a biscuit and ate it in two bites. He was ravenous. He drained the glass of milk and she filled it again and while he ate she set out half the remaining peaches in a small bowl and lit a fire in the stove. He smelled fresh coffee grounds.

"A good appetite is a good sign." Betsy measured out the dark grounds and pumped fresh water to boil it with. "I can only hope it's a proportional thing. The hungrier you are, the better you must be getting."

"I have to get on with my work. Don't tell me what

day it is today. I don't want to know how much time I've lost."

"Work time?"

"Yeah. I had the winter's fuel to get in, but I'm not gonna be able to do that. Look out the window."

The daylight was thinning, and from where he sat behind the shaded end window, he could see out the smaller one where she stood, outlined by the gentle haze as the storm clouds gathered, moving swiftly, merging to form one giant darkening mass. The mountains had disappeared, leaving wisps of clouds to devour the tops of the pines and firs marching up the mountain slopes and out of sight.

"You'd best get going if you want to keep ahead of the storm. It'll be a cold one."

"How do you know?"

"See the low bottom clouds streaming through the trees?"

She turned her attention to the window, where the world continued to darken in degrees of gray. The sky blackened. A sudden wind blasted the north side of the house, driving the trees to bow before it and rattling the glass in their frames.

Duncan loved a good storm and he was not one to miss the first of the season. But he couldn't look beyond her. Beyond Betsy like a summer garden with her calico dress of sky-blue sprinkled with a thousand tiny flowers. Pink rosebuds. Yellow marigolds. Tiny green leaves.

She's so beautiful. Her hair was down, tumbling like magic over her shoulders and breasts. The tangled thickness was drawn back to her nape and secured with a broad pearl pin.

He wanted to unsnap the barrette and watch her thick locks bounce and shimmer. He wanted to dig his fingers into her silken hair and hold her hard to his kiss. To a kiss that would make the proper Miss Hunter burn the way he was burning. From the inside out, half-blind with a want that he didn't understand.

He understood lust. He understood want. This, it was more.

It was something he could never have.

So it was right to want to send her away. "That's snow."

"Is it? It's beautiful the way it falls at such a distance. Like magic."

He'd seen it hundreds of times, but he was a man to appreciate beauty. If it was his to appreciate. And Betsy with her sensuous hair and her lovely spirit and the way she made him want… No, the best thing to do was to send her on her way.

"The snow is coming. Do you see it?"

"Oh." Her eyes widened. "You mean it's going to be here pretty soon?"

"Yeah." He regretted the change.

"What do you mean?"

"The winds are blowing down the mountain. This way." He pushed onto his feet. Then he pushed until he was standing straight. "The low bellies of the clouds are slipping lower. See the foggy stuff? That's snow. It's moving fast. C'mon. I'm not moving very quick yet, but I can help you get on your way."

"I'll do it. You shouldn't be lifting anything heavy like a shoulder harness." Betsy had never seen anything so beautiful as the view from the window in this dark little house. It was like glimpsing a paradise that was serene and majestic.

The solemn evergreens marched up the steep mountainside, their tops bent with their effort. The haze of snow and cloud mixing shades of white against the bruised sky. "How can you look at this every day and not be in a better mood?"

"What did you say?"

"You heard me." He couldn't fool her with his Mr. Curmudgeon routine. Not anymore. Not ever again.

Not that she was going to argue with him about it. He needed to conserve his strength and anyone who wished to argue with her had to be ready for a long, hard row. She needed to get out of the mountains before the wall of snow decided to trap her here.

She unhooked her coat from the wall hook in the living room, poking her head around the corner where he sat. His hands dwarfed the coffee cup he cradled as he stared out the window at the wall of white that was moving so fast, it looked as if it were coming straight for the cabin—

The storm hit the kitchen wall with the force of a hungry tornado and the speed of a runaway train. The windows rattled. The house rocked. The floor beneath her rumbled. The daylight faded as utterly as if it had been a lamp's flame to extinguish. Darkness made brooding shadows of the furniture and stove and the man seated at the table.

Ice pellets scoured the thick logs and struck like bullets against the windows. What kind of blizzard was this? She'd lived on the high Montana plains her entire life. She knew what a blizzard was—what other kind of snowstorm was there on the desolate prairie where winds swept down from the northern mountains with enough force to blow over shanties?

But this. This was like an apocalypse. Like the storms at the end of the world. No horse could outrun it. No human or animal stood a chance exposed to it. The crack of ancient trees breaking echoed like cannon fire above the howling rage of the killing winds. How was she going to get home now?

The acrid scent of sulfur scorched the air and the single candle flame danced and struggled against the encroaching darkness. The timid light caressed the planes and lines of Duncan's hard-set features. There was no missing the harsh frown drawing deep lines around his mouth.

He wasn't pleased with the turn of events? He was, at least, home. She had dinner at her mother's, as was the custom every Sunday afternoon, and she was to bring the baked beans and strawberry cobbler.

Which were sitting wrapped and waiting on her kitchen counter. What was Mama going to say about this? "You could have told me when you said I'd better start heading home while I could, that you meant racing as fast as Morris could go. And still being caught in it."

"I haven't seen one move in that fast in a long while." He lit a battered tin lamp and the reflector cast the steady light into a bright glow that only better illuminated the cruel slash of his mouth. "What are we going to do now?"

"I obviously can't drive home."

"Yep." Smoke puffed out the seam in the stove door,

driven down by the wind. The damper must be wide open, and that was a problem. Pain wedged through his ribs as he leaned forward.

But she was already there, Miss Spring Garden, as she knelt and pushed in the knob. Whispering to herself, "It's hot. O-oh, good one, Bets," she sprang up to plunge her fingertips into the bucket beneath the hand pump.

Why can't I stop wanting her? Duncan wanted to curse the fates that had brought the storm down the mountain. The interfering Great Spirits that seemed to have offered him the chance to an untold dream.

And that dream dabbed her dainty fingers on her flowery skirt and went about pulling open drawers in search of what, he didn't know. He only knew that he seemed entranced by the soft curves of her breasts. They were full and ripe enough to fill his hands with plenty to spare. The soft curves jostled ever so slightly as she withdrew a dish towel, saw how it wasn't clean and pulled out more until one met her exacting standards.

"Do you want some?"

Her question made his jaw drop before he realized she was unaware of where his gaze seemed to be glued. Embarrassment seared his face as he looked hard at the edge of the table where the pool of the lamplight could not touch. He traced his forefinger along the carved edging he'd etched.

She was still waiting with an empty cup in one hand and the steaming ironstone pot in the other. "Well?"

He didn't trust his voice, so he nodded. All he knew was that he hungered to lay his head between the valley of her breasts, to breathe in their woman's fragrance of salty skin and sweet, scented lotion and heat.

He longed to know the feel of her fingers cradling his head, and wondered if she would hold him to her plump rosy nipple and let him suckle until she moaned and arched against him. Or was her passion the quiet kind, of big glowing eyes and soft sighs and laying back to surrender her body to her man's lustful will.

No, he couldn't imagine Betsy surrendering, quiet or otherwise. She poured his cup with a flourish. She apparently never did anything the way any normal person would. She withdrew a small covered bowl from the second basket and nudged it toward him.

"Sugar," was her explanation before she went in search of a second clean cup.

He was loath to lift the lid because he knew he'd find the fancy white sugar, expensive as could be. Had she dipped into her special sugar kept for company and special occasions? Or was this the way she lived, used to white sugar for her coffee? Fringe on the roof of her buggy. Tassels on her fine leather shoes.

Beneath her pretty flowery dress, he'd wager his year's consignment income that she wore fancy lace undergarments. And her skin would feel like warmed satin when he touched her. When he laid her out on his bed and stripped off her lace and silk and kissed his way from lips to her generous breasts spilling into his hands, to her softly curved stomach. He bet that she would moan for him and enjoy the sensation just as she made a low hmm in her throat, as she tasted her cup of sweetened coffee.

Yep. He had just as much of a chance making love

to Miss Betsy as he did being named honorary son to her family.

She took the chair across the table from him and wrapped her hands around the cup's warmth. "How long do you think the snow is going to be like this?"

"Hard to say."

"Okay, then give me a good guess. It blew in fast, so it should blow out fast, right?"

"Who knows? I've seen storms like this last two hours."

"Oh, what a relief." Her lush mouth parted as she sipped.

Duncan envied the cup. What would it be like to have her agile, sensual mouth softly opening around his bottom lip? Would she let her eyelids drift shut and savor him? Could he make her sigh deep in her throat, the way she did after she swallowed the rich, sweet coffee?

Shameful desire roared through him like the blizzard through the mountainside. Obliterating everything until there was only the wild need of a man so lonely, so in need of human touch and physical and emotional bonding, that he would throw away his life and risk more, just to hold Betsy in his arms. To take her to his bed for one night.

Just one.

But he'd learned his past lessons well. He knew exactly how Betsy's family would respond to his seduction of their precious girl. He had no interest in bedding a virgin. Worse, a woman from town with her tassels and satin ribbons and lace. Those women were nothing but trouble. *Nothing.*

So why did his blood remain hot and pulsing through his veins? Why, when he was injured and in a weakened condition, did his groin ache with need and his trousers grow tighter?

"I may as well get busy while I'm here." She set her half-empty cup on the table and glanced around with purpose. "I think I can get quite a bit done."

"You're going to do my laundry here?"

"Oh, no." She could have been an Irish fairy for the way her sapphire gaze shimmered with mischief. "You saved my life, Duncan Hennessey, and for that you will have my eternal gratitude."

"Hell, give me anything but that. Gratitude." As if he hated her, he grimaced harshly and stared into the gray mass of the cruel storm. "You're here for the duration of the storm. We both know it. There's no way to change it."

"My, you sound pleased."

"Just stating the facts. I don't like 'em. If I had my way, you'd be home where you belong. Bothering some other undeserving man." He snarled out the words so there would be no mistake. She couldn't think it was fine to just drive up and invite herself in as if they were friends.

He didn't want her friendship. He didn't want anything to do with her. He had to hate her, because if he didn't, then the consequences would be too grave to endure.

He'd had enough devastation in his life. Lost too many people he'd loved. Seen too much ugliness and evil in the hearts of both women and men to begin to trust another human being. Another woman. Another chance for happiness.

No, all he had to do was to look at Betsy Hunter. She wasn't a spinster yet, she may be unmarried but she was heart-stoppingly beautiful. And charming. And funny. And alluring. And *everything*.

Everything he could not have. Everything he could not trust.

He *would* hate her, and he would invent reasons if he had to, until the sight of her stopped the heat in his blood. Until the thought of her had him snarling so fierce and mean that she'd run out of his cabin the instant the blizzard stopped.

He would hate her. Even if it destroyed what remained of his soul.

Chapter Eleven

He's been horribly hurt, Betsy reminded herself as she tapped the excess soapy water from the bucket. But even her sympathy was wearing thin. He wanted to push her away. He wanted to hurt her.

And now he appeared even more miserable staring at the fire writhing in the stone-crafted fireplace. A frown pulled his hard mouth into an unforgiving line that said, *Don't tempt me.*

His words carved at her like a whittler's knife while she scrubbed the brush along the beautiful polish of the wooden floors. She'd never seen puncheon flooring, although she'd heard of it, and how Duncan had managed to perfectly split an ancient pine in two and sand it to perfection was a mystery.

The trees must have been enormous, judging by the widths of the halves that each stretched a good eight to twelve feet, and had been laid in such a way to emphasize the marbled beauty of the grain. The tough varnish protected the soft wood and gave it a honeyed gleam.

"You don't have to scrub the floor just because you're unhappy about being trapped here with me."

"I didn't say I was unhappy."

"What else could you be?"

That was a very good question. Anyone could see he was expending a lot of effort to make her miserable. Betsy's chest tightened with too many emotions to name. Sympathy, yes. Concern, yes. Affection? She sighed, returning her attention to the floor. Scrubbing hard, she felt the blaze of his attention. Did that kind of emotional power come naturally?

Or did he have to work at it? His fury felt larger than the winds battering the cabin. He might fool everyone else into thinking he was a fierce bear of a man by this concentrated effort of disagreeable behavior.

But she wasn't fooled. "I'm very grateful to be here."

"You're not impressing me by scrubbing my floor."

"Good. I wouldn't want to do that." She couldn't imagine what it would take to wipe that grimace off his face.

He must not have liked her answer because he kept staring at her, like a cougar watching its prey. And she had the distinct impression that he was trying to figure out the next step in his attack.

That was probably what he was going to try to do. When Mariah had told her about what happened to Duncan's family, it only proved her assumptions about him had been right all along. He'd survived a terrible tragedy, the kind of heartbreak that cut a man to the soul.

How could anyone overcome losing his entire family? With the taste of loss she'd had, she couldn't truly imagine. Charlie had been her world, but she hadn't been alone. Her family was overprotective and bossy, it was hard to deny, but they were also loving and caring to a fault.

But Duncan clearly had no one. Or if he had, he'd pushed them away.

So, Duncan, do your worst. He could snarl, hiss, swear and insult her all he wanted. Fine. She was grateful he was alive to do so. And until he was fully recovered, she intended to do all she could for him. If he didn't like it and if he would rather be alone with his growly self and even if he didn't want her in his presence, that was simply his burden to endure. He was stuck with her and not only because of the storm.

Because when she stopped to dunk the brush into the soapy water, she could feel a flutter in her deepest being.

Maybe Duncan Hennessey had saved her in a more important way. And he didn't even know it.

"I don't care if my floor is filthy. I don't care if rats think my floor is filthy. Stop doing that."

"No." She was nearly done anyway. She attacked the last section of the kitchen floor—of course, there was the rest of the cabin. But she had a plan to clean room by room and to get everything in perfect order for Duncan. So it was simple to say no.

His baritone boomed like a dynamite explosion and made the deafening blizzard's howl seem tranquil. "Did you tell me no? In my own house?"

"Boy, you are honestly giving extra effort to your beastly manners, aren't you?" She crawled back through the threshold, dragging the bucket with her. "I know that usually terrifies most people, but I've been around you enough not to be perturbed by it."

"Perturbed?"

"Yes. You know what it means, don't you?"

Duncan saw red and he let his teeth clench together with a loud clack and hissed out the steam of his rage. "That's it. Stop your infernal cleaning right this moment. I told you, I don't care. This isn't impressing me."

"I heard you the first time. Besides, I doubt very much if anyone ever could impress you. You seem to have very low expectations."

His dark brows pulled together as he rose up from the chair where he'd collapsed near the fireplace. And for an instant he resembled the great black bear that had nearly taken his life. The darkness in the room seemed to grab at him and she could see only the piercing hatred of his unfeeling black eyes.

"What have you seen in the world, little miss? What do you know about men? You live safe and protected with your family doting on you. The worst thing that ever happened to you was eating strawberries in a forest in September. You don't know what cruelty a man is capable of. Or a woman. Especially a woman."

"Your insults are not going to work. Just so you are aware. I'm headstrong enough to resist words."

She doesn't understand, Duncan thought. She was everything he'd ever wanted and never thought he could find. She was beautiful and smart.

In a different world, if he was a different man, the Duncan Hennessey who had his own furniture shop, then maybe. Maybe, when he'd been a man who'd spent his days quietly at the lathe and the blade, gluing and pressing and patiently sanding. The man who went to his mother's for supper on Sundays when his shop was closed, *that* innocent young man would have fallen irrevocably in love with Miss Betsy Hunter.

He was no longer that man. And he could not pretend he was. Could not dare admit that the reverberation of emotion sitting dead-center in his chest was love.

No, because a woman like her could never love him. And no amount of her scrubbing his floor was going to change that. He figured her family was going to find out she'd been alone with him, and they would assume the worst. That's what folks tended to do.

He doubted her family would demand a shotgun wedding to salvage her reputation. Thinking about everything that could happen…that made the old panic overtake him. He fought it until he was as unfeeling as the granite stones that broke from the great faces of the mountains and rolled downward, fracturing apart as they tumbled.

Breaking and breaking again, and there was no outcry, no roar or cursing. After the pieces had finally stopped, there was merely silence. A rock could feel nothing.

Nor could he.

"There. That room is done."

She plopped the brush into the bucket with a splash. When she stood, her dress shivered around her slender curves, full and soft in all the right places and she moved like a metaphor in a poem, like snow on a calm morning, and his pulse beat with desire. To pull her into his arms, fold her snug against his chest and breathe in the warm scent of her.

Why was he doing this? He was only hurting himself. He tried to will the longing from his blood, but his soul kept throbbing. *I want you. I want you so much.*

And I cannot have you. He gritted his teeth, ground his jaw and closed his eyes, but he could still see her. The last image of her twisted at the waist, stretching out her back. The extension from side to side emphasizing the curves of her breasts, soft and full and made to fill his hand.

And if that wasn't enough to drive him out the door and into the blizzard to cool down the tightening thrum of his noticeable erection, her skirt clung to her hips and backside. She had a sassy little fanny to match the rest of her and there was nothing he wanted more than to keep her.

You have to stop thinking like this. It was killing him. He twisted away so she could not see the agony on his face. He could hear her sigh of relief. She must have stopped stretching out her tight muscles, and the clink of the bucket as she hiked it up and, finally the swish and tap of her was a thoroughly feminine sound that made him want to turn and follow her.

To reach for what he wanted more than anything.

She clanged and clattered around in the kitchen, humming a tune he didn't know, but the alto of her voice lilted above the roaring storm. His skin prickled into little bumps, as if cold, but he wasn't. His blood had heated up hot enough to melt steel, and he could feel his will buckling, like a horseshoe laid to the smithy's fires.

You should have never allowed her to step foot in this door. He cursed himself for his own stupidity, raking his hand through his hair and breathing with the effort. He hauled his uncooperative body up from the chair and limped to the door.

She was still humming and making noise in the kitchen. It sounded as if she were pumping water. Good luck, he wanted to tell her, since the temperature was rapidly dropping. If the water froze, what difference would it make to him?

He wanted her to stop cleaning. Stop this effort to show him how well she could clean. No woman had enough integrity to do so much free work without wanting something in return.

Yeah, he knew women, he thought bitterly as he laid a hand on his fur coat. The question was, What did Miss Betsy Hunter want? She emerged from the kitchen, her apron at her waist. She'd apparently found his broom and started sweeping up the month or so's accumulation of dust, dirt and anything else that had hit the floorboards with the determination of an army general close to victory.

"I cleaned the chamber pot, so you don't need to go outside."

"Lady, I wouldn't piss in a pot that you'd scrubbed. Damn this hell-blasted storm!" He retreated into rage again, stuffed his injured arm into the sleeve and then his good one, moving as fast as he could, working the buttons, remembering she'd taken his boots off.

"Shit!" He did his best to storm across the wide room, but the pain was mounting. He'd been up too much, done too much, and he couldn't boom through the house like he wanted to. Every time he stomped on his bad leg, agony shot in white-hot streaks along his leg and up through his abdomen all the way to his pounding head.

But he didn't let that stop him, not when he had a point to make. He didn't want her. And since his steel will was bending, he was going to make damn sure the pretty little miss wouldn't want to be in the same room with him. That was the best way to ensure, if his good sense failed, that they wouldn't end up in his bed together.

Because he wanted her with a force that was blinding him. So it was up to her to hate him so much there was no possible way she'd look at him with those big doe eyes and smile with her lush beautiful mouth he wanted to kiss. He had to make sure she'd recoil in disgust because all he wanted to do was to feel her luscious mouth on every inch of him—

Damn it! Stop thinking like that. He had no control, it was completely gone, and it enraged him even more.

In a full temper he bent to grab hold of a boot; he didn't give a crap about his wounds or the fact that when he bent over to yank on his shoes, pain flashed black across his vision. He dragged in a moan and fought to keep it silent.

"What is the matter with you?"

She was there, all softness and light, her skirt swirling around her lean hips, curved just right, touched by the firelight as she knelt before him, uncurled his fingers from the boot's heel. It was concern on her face, and he knew she was only worried about her last chance for marriage.

At least, that's what he told himself as he tried to steal the boot back, but the damnable woman held it out of his reach. "It's my boot. Give it."

"What are you going to do, go out in this storm?" She wasn't in a bad mood at all, she was so hellfire cheerful. The mahogany curls framed her lovely oval face, and the bright sapphire of her eyes made her seem the dearest woman he'd ever come across.

All he had to do was to lean forward two feet—twenty-four inches, that was all—and he could capture her lush mouth with his. Find out if she tasted like dew on a morning's garden and if her kiss was as luxurious as a rose's velvety petal.

What was he doing? Stop it, you cannot have her. He reined in his desire, stopped his thoughts and launched forward, bullying the boot from her surprisingly strong grip. The not-so-delicate Betsy Hunter snatched the boot right back and flung it across the room.

"You're not going out. I'll go bring in more wood."

As if he were completely as crazy as a loon and she was the sane one, she shook her head at him in a scolding way, bouncing up, pure fire and charm, and he felt his will liquefy as she swished away.

Leaving him breathless and weak, pulling away every thought from his head. He couldn't even think to stop her and by the time his mind started working she'd wrapped up and was unlatching the door.

That damnable woman! He was on his feet as the wind caught the door and ripped it from her hands, the blizzard punching in, stealing Betsy from his sight. That woman was going to be the death of him one way or another, that was for damn sure.

Swearing with every step, he raced headlong into the whiteout that blew out the lamp and brought down darkness and ice. There was nothing but wind pushing him back and he fought it, reaching out, finding only darkness and stinging snow, and suddenly there she was, a soft shelter against his chest.

He held her there with his injured arm and caught the edge of the door with his good one and growled, bucking the wild storm that felt strong enough to topple them both.

With every drop of his strength, he wrestled the door closed. Snow fell to the ground. The winds disappeared and there was silence and darkness and only the impotent flare of the fire in the frigid room.

"Oops." Betsy resembled a snowbank more than a fancy town lady, but the shrug of her slim shoulders sent an avalanche of ice from her face and neck, revealing her delicate bobbin of a chin.

Oops? What kind of an answer was that? "You could have killed yourself!"

"Well, not *killed,* but perhaps a little frostbite on my nose, anyway!"

She didn't look the least bit repentant. "Well, that didn't solve anything. You open the door, if you will, and I'll go outside—"

"You're not going outside!" She had no common sense. It only went to show she was just as he figured she'd be—a pampered, sheltered princess—and it made him even madder because he wanted her to be different—and couldn't face it if she was it.

She needed someone to take care of her; her old crone of a grandmother and her ass of a brother weren't here to do it, and he hated to be stuck with the job.

He didn't want a woman. He didn't want to feel hot and hungry with need every time he was around her. "What are you gonna do? Carry in one stick of wood at a time?"

"No, I mean, why did you say it like that? As if I weren't perfectly capable of carrying more than that?"

"Because look at you!" He couldn't stand the way she stood there so serenely, not understanding at all. "You'll freeze to death, and then I'll have to explain how I let a little woman like you go out into the blizzard and freeze to death. Believe me, your family isn't going to be too kind if I let that happen."

"My family. They can be difficult, but I love 'em." She sighed, blowing at a spiraling strand of hair that had frozen to her nose…and remained. Ice crackled as she tried to blink her eyelashes.

"Hold still." He took her by the shoulder and used his sleeve cuffs, as ice-driven as they were, to brush the snow frozen to her lashes and eyebrows. To rub away the layer disguising her face.

It was strange, Betsy thought, to watch him go from yelling barbarian to gentle man. For the moment he was tame, and she watched him through her lashes, not daring to move, feeling the hard, possessive grip on her shoulder—and the answering curl in her heart.

He was lost in the dark, hardly more than a shadow, but she could feel every inch of him as if she saw him. Felt him with the awareness of one soul mate recognizing its other.

How often does a gift like this come along? Her

throat closed up tight and she struggled for breath, but he kept stroking the fraying cuff on his sleeve—she'd have to remember to mend that—over the bridge of her nose, rubbing as if to scrape away every particle of snow.

She'd clamped her teeth together to keep them from chattering and a knot of cold cinched round her middle and yet she was warming, melting like ice in the sun, and it was his doing. The air in the cabin was slowly warming, but their breaths rose in foggy clouds.

A powerful heat seemed to flow from his hand on her shoulder straight into her spirit, into the deepest part of her. How was that possible?

She watched in fascination as an entirely new Duncan, one neither beast nor savage nor fierce mountain man, quirked the corner of his mouth into a real smile. "That's a freckle. I guess that isn't gonna come off."

She fell—just like that. Between one breath and the other, between one beat of her heart and the next. A love so strong surged through her, more silent than the blizzard that had blustered through the cabin, but tenfold more powerful. She saw him in the darkness—the real Duncan Hennessey—a tender soul who nudged her to his snowy chest, so wide and strong, and enfolded her against him.

Her cheek lay on his sternum and beneath it the fast pulse of his heart. Too fast for a man not affected. For a man not in love.

She knew, for it matched the rapid flutter of her own.

He looked down at her, meeting her gaze, and it was as if he'd penetrated her, although it made no sense, did it? She felt the connection and it was as if they were lovers, joined in that rare, amazing intimacy, and her heart fell wide open. Oh, why do I love him so much?

He cleared his throat and she could feel the rough edges of his emotions surging through her as he cupped her face in his broad palm. "I don't want you going out into the storm. Do you understand?"

She heard what he didn't say, knew it with certainty as if his thoughts had somehow entered her mind, too. What would he do if she became blown off course and lost in the forest?

Pain worse than he'd ever known coursed through him and he felt ten feet tall, ready to tear the world apart if he had to, to keep her safe. He didn't want her cold or lost or afraid. He didn't want her struggling against an impossible wind.

He wanted to keep her warm and safe forever.

Then it happened, the most amazing thing of all. He bent to her, as the inches separating them shrank and her pulse fluttered with his. Her breath caught at the same exact moment. Neither blinked. Neither broke their gazes.

Already as if joined, it was no surprise when his mouth captured hers in a brief, thrilling taste. The caress of his rougher, firmer lips fitting over hers and gently sucked.

On a sigh, she surrendered, parting her lips for a deeper kiss, to give him anything he wanted because she was already his. But he didn't invade with his tongue and he didn't take what she was offering.

Instead he kissed her again, tenderly, dragging it out as if he could not stand for it to end. Then he pulled away, kissed the tip of her nose and held her as if she were the most precious thing in the world to him.

Because she was.

Duncan held her until she stopped trembling, from cold or passion, it didn't matter. The fire was flickering down, the cabin was chilly, and he could not seem to let her go.

In his entire life he'd never felt like this, as if his heart were on the outside of his chest instead of inside. Exposed. Vulnerable. Maybe, for this one moment in the dark, it was all right to taste her kiss one more time.

And to treasure the knowledge that kissing her was sweeter than morning dew on roses, than dawn on the craggy peaks of the Rockies, than any single thing he'd ever known before.

Or ever would again.

Chapter Twelve

Even hours later, the kiss remained an unspoken tension between them. Not mentioned, but felt. An invisible cloud of smoke that seemed to choke the air and make Duncan seem distant, when he was only on the other side of the kitchen stove.

The wood he'd brought in was nearly gone to feed the greedy fire, and the main room had proved impossible to reheat in the rapidly dropping temperatures as evening came. They'd retreated to the kitchen where, with the door closed, the potbellied stove could burn more efficiently, but it didn't seem to be driving out the cold.

In fact the chill seemed to creep like a thousand cold, black hairy spiders through the minute cracks in the solid wood floors and beneath the bear fur blanket. And under her petticoats to bite her skin.

If she were this cold, then how frozen must Duncan feel? He'd braved the vicious winds and lethal temperatures to bring in the wood that was by now almost gone. And because he'd refused to say a word to her other than "Stay by the stove, don't you move!" it was hard to know how he was truly doing. Although the way he sat with jaw clamped and trembling beneath his fur seemed pretty clear.

He was colder than she was, and soon he would have to face that wind again.

The fierce set of his face told her she should not volunteer to go out into the storm again. He was not in a good mood.

No, that was an understatement. Duncan exuded such a powerful rage that one glare could send a pair of grizzlies running in the other direction.

That's how he looked at her—the woman he'd deliberately kissed. The tingling thrill of it remained on her lips like a fiery brand. Never had she been kissed like that. And how did it affect him? It made him glare at her with distaste and anger.

It's a good thing I've kept my real feelings to myself. She felt shame roll through her and she stared at the shadowed wall, the chinking stripe between the logs was perfect—she turned her attention to that instead of on the man a few scant feet away. Maybe she could forget the sinking disappointment weighing her down and the shame that she'd let him so easily kiss her when it wasn't about love. It wasn't out of affection. When it was something he regretted an instant later.

She rubbed her face with her hands, as if she could rub away the tears building behind her eyes. Her throat ached and she was glad he refused to speak with her for the only reason that the emotion aching in her throat would give her away. She was in love with him. And he wasn't in love with her. He didn't even like her. In fact, he seemed to detest her even more that she'd allowed that kiss.

Her mother's scolding echoed in her head, words she'd heard a thousand times before while growing up. *Give a man a reason to disrespect you, and he will. A decent man will be disgusted by a forward woman.*

Apparently, Duncan was a very decent man because he refused to look at her or even in her direction. And his sneer…

Her stomach tumbled and shame filled the void where it used to be. She was miserable as she wrapped her arms around her knees and shivered, growing ever colder beneath the thick, flannel-lined fur. Did he think she'd been hoping for a kiss? For more? That she was the kind of woman who gave her affections easily, as if they were nothing?

Why was his opinion of her so deeply important? Because his kiss burned on her mouth as powerful as if it hadn't been three long hours ago? She let her head roll forward and rested her forehead against her knees. If she closed her eyes she could still feel the intoxicating caress of his surprisingly gentle mouth on hers and the surge of his tough tenderness that rolled from him into her.

So much tenderness. She sighed, wanting and wishing for a second kiss just like it. To close her eyes, surrender and know true love again.

Except it wasn't true love for him.

She felt him move before the rustling sounds and the groan of pain told her he'd stood. Awareness sparked through her like sunlight through a creek and nothing could stop it, nothing could dim it. Not even her will as she tried to still her heart. Silence her feelings. She told herself over and over again, He doesn't want you, Bets, not that way, but there was no other way she would be with a man.

The hinges of the old potbellied cookstove groaned and the flames flared, licking dangerously around the top edges of the door, as if trying to escape. She lifted her face and the blast of heat tightened the skin on her cheeks, and she welcomed it. Her face felt hot, but the rest of her shivered.

"There." Duncan broke the silence between them after he'd used the last of the wood, filling the stove full. He brushed the bark from his sleeves, lumbering away from her.

He stopped at the door to jam one arm into his fur coat. "Stay by the fire until I return. I don't want you near the door. I won't be able to see. You understand?"

It wasn't his tone, which was brusque, but the harsh glaze to his black eyes that warned her his temper was on a short wick. So she nodded, not trusting her voice, shuttering her heart so he couldn't see the truth. *Why do I love him so hard it hurts?*

There was no answer as the wind and dark stole him from her sight.

She tried to imagine what Mama would think of him. Lucille Gable would take one look around this dark cabin, give Duncan a doubtful arch of her left brow and say, "You could do much, much better than this." For it had been something her mother had said numerous times before.

No one—not even Charlie—had been good enough

for Lucille's only daughter. *Why not that nice banker? He's a widower and there's no one more respected in the county.*

That was something Mama liked to say, too.

Betsy felt the cold blast of arctic fury as the door slammed open, the sounds of Duncan struggling to dump wood on the floor lost in the deafening noise. Then suddenly the driving ice bits fell, the air cleared and there was only the sweep of inches-thick snow settling to rest on the floorboards and on the armful of wood tossed out of the way of the door.

Somewhere in the dark reaches of the far room, a musical bong counted off the hours, a dulcet soothing chime that surprised her. Duncan seemed the type that would have an abrasive, booming clang. Not something so musical it made her yearn for her piano back home.

It could have been the first strains of a Brahms or Bach concerto—but the bells silenced at the second chord. It wasn't anywhere near two o'clock. The wind raged like a snarling beast outside, ever louder and harder than before.

It had to be noon. What she should be is back home by now and arriving at her mother's house, no one the wiser for her quick jaunt up into the mountains. This dang storm! It was the only reason she wasn't driving Morris up her family's long curving drive and into the shade of the magnolias.

Sundays at her mother's was a big event. Her brothers would already be there. Betsy closed her eyes and knew that at this exact moment, because Mama lived on a rigid schedule, that she would be in the kitchen, bustling around, ordering Anya the maid to hurry with the pie crust.

About this time Betsy would walk through the doors of her childhood home, into all the warm memories of her life growing up. Upon seeing her, Mama would drop whatever she'd been preparing, wipe her fingers on her apron swathed around her fashionably plump waist and march like a general across the sunny kitchen.

"Oh, it's my Bets, come home. It's about time! You're late, as always." Mama would wrap her in a wonderful hug, scolding even as she pressed a kiss to Betsy's cheek. "Come, tell me all about it and peel the potatoes for me."

The wisps of memory tore apart as the door banged open, more snow and wood and wind exploded through the dark cavern of the door and then as suddenly closed. Alone in the impossibly colder room, Betsy's stomach rumbled. It was early, but there was no better way to warm up than to eat some nice hot food. Duncan told her not to move, but that was because he wanted her to stay out of his way.

Maybe once he got a nice steaming cup of coffee— no, she'd best make him some soothing tea. If she got to work now, she'd have something hot for him when he returned, since he was seven times more headstrong than her mother and meaner than a wounded bear by insisting he'd be the one to risk the storm.

Surely it couldn't last much longer. Usually, back home on the plains, a mere twenty-two miles away, the more violent the storm, the shorter its duration. Maybe by the time she'd washed and wiped their supper dishes, she'd be able to head home. Although what about the buggy? There was no way those wheels could work in any real depth of snow.

She filled the teakettle and set it on the stove to heat. Perhaps she'd simply ride Morris barebacked home. Not that she knew how to ride on a horse—Mama was adamantly against anything that involved a female parting her thighs in any way.

But surely Morris would be accommodating, he was such a sweet old fellow. She couldn't imagine him objecting since he truly hated traveling up the mountain now that they'd been attacked. Likely as not, he'd be ecstatic to be heading home.

The door swung open and the driving gale pierced through her layers of cotton and muslin as if they weren't there. As if she were standing naked in the kitchen. A chill crawled inside her, curled up and took root in her abdomen. Teeth chattering, she held out her hands but could not feel the stove's heat.

She saw in the weak flicker of the single lantern's light Duncan's furious face and his mouth growling words she could not hear over the blizzard. He pointed one fur-gloved hand at her place where the blanket lay abandoned and spit out an obvious curse word. The slam of the door made the wild storm seem meek.

He's mad. It was hardly a new concern. He'd been angry and cursing since the day she'd met him, so what did it matter now?

When he returned, he could shout all he wanted. She hardly cared. She was hungry and she was going to eat. And, with any luck, get enough food inside him to warm him up, since he was cold on her behalf. She was not the wisest woman to care so much, but she'd always placed more importance on heart than intelligence.

By the time he'd fought the door closed for a final time, she had beans heating in the tiny oven, the tea steeping and the sandwiches warming on the stovetop, along with the jars of pickles, relish and mustard that were trying to freeze. Wrapped in a damp cloth, it took no time at all for the bottoms of the jars to warm. And as Duncan shook off the layers of ice and crackling snow from his wraps, she deftly popped open the lids and set them aside to hand him a steaming tin cup.

The cup looked miniature cradled in his huge hands. Hands scarred and rough. Hands that looked capable of great violence and great strength.

And incredible tenderness. Betsy swallowed, trying to will away a rising desire she couldn't give in to. It would only lead to heartbreak. See how he wasn't even looking at her? He didn't thank her. Somehow he was grimacing at her while he was slurping down the hot tea, certainly no easy accomplishment.

And here she was hoping…for what? She turned away before he could see the blush on her face, hot and scalding even in the frigid air. Her breath rose in great foggy clouds as she flipped the sandwich over, checked to make sure the meat was warm and no longer partly frozen, and then, satisfied, slipped several slices of tomatoes between the meat and the bread and handed him a plate piled high.

He crooked one brow, as if in a silent question, but did not speak. He did not look at her. He seemed more a part of the shadows and the storm. As if irrevocably lost. He retreated and the darkness seemed to thicken as it did in the desolate hours after midnight until she could not discern him at all.

Lonesome in the light of a single flame, Betsy turned the wick higher but the lantern did not shine more brightly. The blackness seemed to devour it until there was only the faintest of golden light struggling to burn.

His voice, when he spoke, sounded as merciless as a snarling wolf. "I'm not fooled."

"Fooled?" The man was harder to understand than if he were speaking a completely different language. He might as well be speaking in his ancestor's language. She had no notion, no notion at all, what he meant.

She spooned the steaming beans from the crock into a chipped bowl. "Duncan, you're going to have to explain. I'm too tired, cold and starving to try to figure out your meaning."

"I suppose the helpless, can't-understand-anything act works with other men."

"What other men? You mean, my laundry customers?"

"Customers? Is that what you call them?"

The booming insinuation in his voice made it sound as if…as if… Fury snapped her to attention, searching for any sign of him in the nearly hopeless dark. "Why do you say it like that? As if I'm not a proper businesswoman making a living laundering shirts!"

"Well, I wasn't talking about that…not exactly." He jerked the bowl from her hands, as if he stood directly before her.

She could not see him, only feel the cold radiating off him. Not only the ice from the storm but that which was his heart. It was a shocking thing, to feel something so barren. Sympathy welled up in her so fiercely, she wanted to wrap her arms tight around him and hold him until he'd thawed, until he was no longer bereft.

And yet she knew he would not want that from her. He did not want her. Already there was the faintest whisper of a footstep far in the corner of the room, where the blackness was deepest.

Aching for him without knowing why, she filled a bowl for herself. Cupped her hands around the warm stoneware and, stomach growling, eased to the floor where her blanket lay crumpled, no defense against the creeping cold.

"I mean, a woman like you. Of a certain age." His accusation came flat, emotionless and cruel. "Your laundry business must be a good way to meet eligible bachelors. Widowers. Men you could marry."

"Whatever has given you that notion?" She pretended his words didn't hurt at all. "You sound as if you've been speaking to my mama."

"I've never met your mother, but I know a lot about you women." He spooned the rich syrupy beans into his mouth, ignoring her.

Savoring the exquisite taste of sweet molasses and beans done to perfection, breaking apart on his tongue. A tang of what had to be a homemade sauce of some kind and the salty goodness of real bacon. Not salt pork, which was cheaper.

Yep, she sure went all-out to impress him. To show him what a good wife she would be. "There was a spinster who owned your business a few years ago. She married one of her customers, did she not?"

"Well, not exactly. Mariah is a dear friend of mine,

and when a man who'd wanted to court her when she was young became widowed, he proposed to her. It had nothing to do with her trapping him... Wait a moment." She stood against the light like a wraith, trapped between this world and the next.

The sparse light played on the pleats of her skirt and she looked as though she floated instead of walked toward him and into the darkness. He could barely make out her silhouette, but there was no mistaking the hard line of her shoulders and the hot rage steaming from her like heat from a teapot.

He was in no mood to be yelled at by some opinionated woman. "I wish you luck, Miss Hunter, in finding that husband you're posturing for, but I will swear on my grave that husband will never be me. So keep your distance, stop your infernal cleaning and cooking and stay the hell away from me. Got that?"

And he left, taking the last of the beans with him. Stepping over the empty plates and past her rigid shape in the dark. Stalking despite the exhaustion and pain and heartsickness into the frigid front room, where the blizzard had frozen the room so solidly, a crust of ice crackled on the floorboards beneath his feet.

By the time he heard the intake of her first sob, his heart was granite. His soul, marble. He closed his eyes and covered his ears against the sound. The beans forgotten, the delicious food she'd prepared an indigestible lump in his gut.

He'd never done anything so rotten in his life. Hurting women went against everything he believed in, everything he'd been taught, but there was no other way to save them. No other way to make certain he did not give in to his baser impulses and his burning need to hold her and wind up covering her body with his, end up loving her with everything within him, of ruining her reputation, of bringing endless shame upon them both.

I'm so sorry, Betsy.

As she exhaled the sob, the sound thin and vibrating, he became less like a stone and more like the dark. The cold enveloped him and he could feel the icy sting upon his face—but that was it. He could feel no more as he became nothing at all.

The second sob rang more strangled. It had a strange tone to it. Not exactly anguish… He listened hard, but could not hear her as the winds crescendoed.

It was just as well. He'd survived enough heartbreak without listening to hers, too. Even if he caused it.

That made him a bastard and worse. The thought of hurting sunny, cheerful Betsy, with her jeweled eyes and dazzling brightness… He hated himself. Unable to stand it, he buried his face in his hands.

It was as if the cold couldn't touch him. It was as if he wasn't alive. As if he were no longer made of flesh and blood and bone. No longer mortal. No longer a man.

How could a man be anything real, when all hope had fled?

Betsy wiped the dampness from her eyes before her eyelashes froze. Goodness, was that all that was troubling him? He thought she was trying to entice him into marrying her? Ha! Wait until she told her friends this one. They'd be laughing for months….

And then she realized, as the lantern flickered and the

low flame died, that there was nothing amusing about a man with so little heart. And even less faith in humanity.

What had seemed ludicrous dried up and broke into dusty, blown-away pieces. He thought she wanted to marry him? That she was using her business to meet eligible men? Did he think her cleaning and cooking and her care for him had such a petty motivation?

He couldn't see the truth, she realized. The truth that she was grateful to him. That she wanted to do something, however small, to thank him for his noble deeds. His acts of bravery. To let him know that her respect for him would never falter, even if all she had to offer him were baked beans and a sandwich.

Wasn't it the thought that counted?

And Duncan, alone in the freezing dark, so determined not to be fooled by a woman trying to trap any poor man into matrimony. *What did someone do to you?*

She finished wiping her eyes, felt through the drawers with care in case she came across a sharp knife, and found a candlestick. The smooth wax and the trimmed wick told her there was a holder somewhere around, although she had to use a match from the tin beside the stove to light the taper. Then she searched with the flickering candle in hand until she found the plain glass base not in the same drawer but tossed in the back of the pot cupboard.

Fortunately in her search she ran across the kerosene can. The fuel echoed in the tin, and it sounded suspiciously as if there was very little left. She set it aside to deal with later, after she'd set Duncan straight.

With the buffalo fur draped over her shoulders, she filled the last clean cup, stirred in a generous teaspoon of honey and, heedless of the danger, crossed the threshold and into a darkness so stark, it was like death.

Chapter Thirteen

"Duncan?"

She'd already predicted he wouldn't answer her. But did he have to be so difficult? So stubborn? It was a good thing she was used to people like that.

And besides, there wasn't a creature on this earth she couldn't eventually charm. Although, she sensed it might take all her strength and will to lure Duncan from his dark, icy prison.

"I brought you some more tea. It's scalding hot. I put in extra honey."

There came a scrape from the far corner, as if his boot heels grated on the varnished floor. Was he near the bed?

"Put it on the night table."

He sounded eerily hollow, as if a ghost spoke, and yet Betsy knew how it felt to be hollowed out like a log made into a canoe. Hollow and empty and torn wide open. As if everything important within had been scraped and lashed away.

She did as he requested, feeling her way across the

room. She stubbed her right big toe on the foot of the couch. Hit her knee on the wooden bed frame and felt with careful fingers along the carved edge of the night table for a safe place to rest the cup.

Except the carving…it was intricate and masculine. She could tell as her fingertips traced the pattern that it wasn't the same as the bed set in her modest upstairs room. But it was similar enough that she had to see it.

She released the cup safely in the center and dug into her skirt pocket for the little match tin. But it wasn't in her right pocket, so she plunged her hand into her left.

"Are you still here?" he barked. "Go. Leave me."

"What, is a big strong man like you afraid I'll try to trick you into proposing?"

"Yeah."

"Trust me, you're in no danger."

"You mean, you aren't a desperate spinster who'd do anything for a husband. Hell, you look like one to me."

"Me? I look like a spinster? Goodness, thank you for the compliment." Really, she thought, rolling her eyes. She found the tin in her apron pocket and struck a match.

A brief light flared, and in the moment it fought for life, it illuminated only the angles and planes of a face that looked more gargoyle than human, more snarling predator than man. The deep grooves etched around his mouth gave the illusion of jowls opening in the moment before an attack, and the flame sputtered out, as if terrified by the sight.

She did not turn and bolt. No, she struck another match and lit the bedside lantern. A soothing brightness cast a soft circle over the table, ebbing to where Duncan sat as motionless as stone on the edge of his unmade bed. "Thank you so kindly for that lovely compliment. Every woman who'd celebrated her thirtieth birthday likes to be told she looks like a spinster. And a desperate one at that."

"It's the plain truth. I know what you are."

"Do you, now?" Betsy didn't grow up with five brothers and stay happily married by not understanding that men were unintelligible.

It was a given fact that a woman simply had to accept or the confusion of it all would drive her mad. Men and their illogical brains required infinite patience…and a little artfulness. So she knelt to study the masculine and bold carving of river rocks so exquisite she couldn't believe this stubborn mountain of a man could have that much poetry in him.

She cast her smile wider, so her dimples showed. She was bound and determined to wipe the bitter pain from his tortured face…but how? "This is beautiful. The furniture."

His gaze blackened. "I'm going to say it again. I'm not going to marry you."

Apparently he thought it was very important that she understand this. She could feel his agony. She laid her hand on his granite-hard knee and felt him flinch at her woman's touch. Saw the distrust well up through the bleakness.

Gently she said, so he would finally believe her, "We're in agreement, Duncan. Don't worry. I don't want to marry you."

"Agghh!" He shot off the bed, pretty fast for an injured man. Maybe that was proof of how het up he was.

Lost in the reaches of the room, and any noise he made obscured by the screaming storm outside, Betsy would have sworn she was alone if she didn't know any better. When she spoke, she wasn't even certain if he was listening. "Why do you think I want to marry you?"

"What woman isn't trying to trap a husband? Get him to pay her bills and provide a house for her to clean. *What?* Why are you looking so shocked? Isn't that the damn truth?"

"What have I ever done to suggest I'm that horrible of a person?"

"You came. You—you *cleaned.* You didn't leave when I told you to."

"I came because all that time you were here alone and injured, I thought you were dead. I can never pay you back, ever, for what you did in the forest. So I am doing what I can while you're recovering from the wounds you incurred on my behalf!"

"You cooked! Baskets of food."

"So you wouldn't have to fend for yourself. You know that's true. If you'd settle down enough to feel what's beneath your very offensive anger, you'd see—"

"*Offensive?* It's not offensive! It's justified!" Red exploded behind his eyes and he slumped against the wall, too weak to stomp out of the room like he wanted, and he gave thanks for the shadows that hid the truth. Summoning up the loudest, most vicious tone he could manage, he roared like a mountain lion. "You shove your way in here. Manipulate to spend the night in my cabin—"

"Manipulate? O-oh, it's true! I have powers over the weather and I made the blizzard come down the mountain so fast, that I had to stay or be frozen to death on the road back home."

"You damnable woman!" The red behind his eyes exploded into a swirl of heat and hot, searing white. "Don't make a jest of this! I'm not about to let you tempt me. Get this straight—you stay far away from me. Now. Do it. Go into the kitchen and stay there. You'll keep your virginity, do you hear?"

"Do you often mistake a woman for a dog? Or for a bridled horse?"

"Is there no end to your sass? No wonder you've never married! Any man with a lick of sense would run as fast as he could in the opposite direction. Which I wish I could do right now."

"Me, too, because you're so pleasant. And for your information, just so you know, in case you're trying to trap a woman into marriage so she'll cook and clean for you? Stay away from me. Don't tempt me. And what else did you say?"

Framed by the soft glow of the lamplight, she cocked her head to one side as she thought, causing the thick, long riot of abundant hair to bounce enticingly over her full breasts and along the curve of her tiny waist. "Oh, I remember. Don't worry. You'll keep your virginity."

"This is no joke!"

"I see that." Calm, so annoyingly calm, she flashed him a gentle smile with dimples and charm, and made his toes curl and his soul stir.

Desire surged through his blood and he was rock-hard. Damn it, aroused was the last state he could risk being in. How could she affect him this way when he was roiling with rage and wished to hell that he'd never met her?

Because he wanted nothing more than to wrap her in his arms. To kiss her until she made low moans in her throat, until she was soft and wet and accommodating beneath him. And then he could push his way inside her tightness, love her until they were both spent, hold on to her forever so the world and its cruelty and sorrow stayed forgotten.

He felt ready to shatter into small, irretrievable pieces with wanting her. To feel her kisses, to surrender to her gentleness, he would give anything. Do anything. He wanted her so much.

Her touch came out of the dark, as if from a dream. So magical he thought he was imagining it and he straightened, inviting her silently closer. She came behind him, her fingertips exquisite brushes of heat along the outer curve of his shoulder.

"Do not worry, Duncan. I'm not trying to trick you into anything." When she should have been furious with him, for the way he was treating her, she was kind. Her voice warm when it should have been hateful. "I am no spinster or virgin. I've been married and widowed."

"No. I don't believe it."

"Too bad, for it's true. I have my own house, I run my own business, I'm happy. I have no need to bring heartache upon my life by marrying for any other reason than true love."

True love? He scoffed. Acid flooded his mouth, tasted sour on his tongue. Unrelenting on his soul. "There is no such thing."

"You're wrong."

"There's no way you can be a widow."

"Why not? Because I'm not in my later years?"

Because you're so beautiful. The words caught in his throat, unspoken. Words he could never say. Because she was lovelier than anyone he'd ever known. Because love and trust, even for one moment, brought with them consequences he could never endure again. Because once the storm was ended, there would be consequences enough without his ever laying a hand on her. Without another singular kiss.

"I'm a widow. Not out of choice, mind you, so don't even try to pick a worse fight with me, because I will not fight you, Duncan." Gentle her words, alluring her voice, warm her heart.

How was he going to resist her now? He swallowed hard against the emotion in his throat but found he could not speak. He was trapped in silence and darkness and ice while her petticoats whispered like a temperate spring breeze. And he squeezed shut his eyes and turned his chest to impenetrable steel. And what good did it do?

She was still here, her hand on his shoulder, her spirit a gentle presence against his.

"Charlie was my true love. Maybe my only love. I don't know. I suspect there is only one great love meant for each of us. That somewhere in this world is our true match. I found mine, and when you think about it, it must be rare, in all the places of this world, of all the people alive and dead and yet to be born, I found my perfect soul mate."

"Sure. Whatever you say."

His bitterness gathered around them like the blizzard that swarmed the cabin. Closing them off, blocking out all light and hope. As barren as a vast glacier field.

What did she do to you? Betsy knew there had been someone he'd loved once, long ago. But what could break a man's heart so that, instead of beating despite the breaking, it was as if the very core of him had been obliterated. She could feel the edges of the abyss and the hopelessness that plunged into his soul.

How could anyone—man or woman, strong or weak—live with this mortal wound? She knew darn well he wanted to be alone, and she knew why. Because being alone was safe. Being alone meant you didn't have to hand over what remained of your heart. Being alone meant you never had to trust again. Hurt again. Lose again.

Alone meant that the worst thing that could happen was nothing. Nothing at all. Sometimes, that was the wisest, safest choice.

But not today.

When she should have left him be in peace, she placed her hand on his chest and, fingers splayed, felt the dependable, mighty thud of his heart.

And it was as if she could feel the devastation. Feel the agony that twisted through him at her touch. He didn't move. She was aware as his every muscle stiffened.

It was as if he'd shielded himself behind an iron wall. And although she was close enough to feel his warm breath across her cheek and the rhythm of his life force against her palm, the essential part of him seemed to be hundreds of miles away.

Please, let me help you.

If nothing else, she wanted to do this for him. He did not love her, this she knew and even understood, but she could not leave when the blizzard was done knowing she had made his existence more painful.

That beyond his physical wounds, which she could never be sorry enough for, there lay a wound of his spirit. It was as if being close with her and having her in his house reminded him of a time in his life that had been like an autumn's first hard frost, killing all green things struggling to grow.

It was the very least she could do for this man who was so great.

"Never think that I'm going to make something of my entrapment here, all right?" Gentle she spoke, so he would listen and hear her meaning. So he would turn toward her and, like a wounded animal in the wilderness, let her close enough to save him.

"Why should I trust anything you say? You're a woman. The only thing a woman can give a man is pain."

"I suppose there are women who might try such a thing, such a horrible thing, but I am not cut from that poor quality of cloth. I married Charlie because there was no other choice to make."

"Oh, he had money, did he?"

"No. He was poor. That was why my family objected to his courting me."

"I've met your family. I can't imagine how you ever trapped him into marrying you. Unless it was with sex."

"Oh, Duncan." Her laughter rippled as alluring as a high mountain creek.

She wasn't angry or amused or mocking, and it shamed him. His chest swelled and there was no room for anything but his bitterness. He hung on to it with all his might. It was the only thing protecting him from the world. The only thing saving him from giving in to needs too long denied and reaching for daylight—for her.

"Hasn't that happened to you? The startling telegraph of connection that just fills you up and turns you inside out?"

Yes. Once. With you. Duncan wrenched away from her touch, turning so that, although she was nothing more than a silhouette in the storm-dark room, she couldn't see inside him. So that the arc of connection that seemed to flow from him to her would stop.

Forever. He had to stop it now. Panic rose up and he could feel her turning with him, moving in the dark, as if they were waltzing in the light, heart to heart, moving in synchrony and all he wanted, all he needed, was to break away and be alone. He could not stand to have her so close. So near.

But did she understand the hint? No. Duncan kept moving and she kept following, her hand always touching him, lighting on his shoulder. And he shrugged that away, and she touched down on the middle of his spine. Like lightning through an unwilling sky, that's how she sparkled through him, a harsh piercing of light that was blinding.

And still, she kept speaking. "A real love, a real marriage, is struggling to make life better for the person you love."

"That's just how women do it." He ground the words out, crumbling. Hell, he was like a granite rock disintegrating. "They say all the right words. Do all the things meant to fool a man into thinking…"

He choked back the rest of the memories too bleak to examine. Images that whirled like black wraiths before his eyes. "Women know just what to do to make you think how wonderful they are. So sweet and dainty and feminine and loving until your heart is caught like a fish on a line and you don't even know enough to escape until you're out of the water. Struggling to breathe. Seeing the glint of the knife before it slices you wide open. So when I say, 'Get away from me,' I mean *get away from me*."

Her hand flew off his back as if he'd slapped it away. He waited, panting, as she stepped away and disappeared into the darkness.

She fled, staying out of the reach of the only lamp. Her rustling skirts faintly marked her progress across the room and into the kitchen, where she remained, a light in his darkness he could not extinguish.

Or ignore.

Silence. How loud it seemed when her ears were no longer filled with the savage sounds of the storm. The blizzard had blown out but snow obliterated the windows in the kitchen, so she could not see out to be certain if it was safe to venture home.

Well, I can't stay here all night. Her mother would be worked up into a flurry, wondering why her daughter hadn't arrived for the noon meal as promised and why, when she sent one of the brothers, which she would predictably do, the house in town would be empty, as well. Betsy added more wood to the fire. There was no doubt her family would be hunting her down, and how was she going to confront them about Duncan?

Women know just what to do to make you think how wonderful they are. So sweet and dainty and feminine and loving until your heart is caught like a fish on a line. She remembered how combative he'd been and how silent in the hour or so since. Her rifle-toting grandmother and her overprotective brothers had said something horrible to him.

But what? And if they'd told him he wasn't good enough for her—wasn't that all they seemed to do, try to find her eligible men to marry or to eliminate the unsuitables?

How dare they decide that for her? How dare they hurt the one man who'd made her wish? The one man who'd made her feel again in all the long, lonely years of her widowhood?

A floorboard creaked and there he was, slicing through the shadows as if he were part of them. Hardly discernable as he grabbed his coat from the hook by the back door. Ice broke from the fur to tinkle to the floor. His boots crushed the ice slivers as he came near, into the small glow of light.

"Why do you have the lamp turned so low?"

She tried not to jump at his hard words and how they reverberated in the room. "That's the last of the kerosene, unless you have an unopened tin somewhere."

"No."

"We have wood enough for a spell. Let me warm your wraps before you put them on."

"Damn it, woman, stop meddling." He eased into the coat, still frozen nearly stiff from his earlier trip outside.

He truly did not seem as if he could tolerate her presence. Had she been wrong to push him? To try to let him know that he may not feel that special twinkling lightning strike for her, but some woman in the future, perhaps. His future need not always be lonely. If she could save him from his hopelessness, then maybe she could repay how he'd saved her.

"I think the snow is—"

Too late. He yanked open the door before she could finish her sentence and she had the distinct feeling he would refuse to listen to her anyhow. Snow glistened from the bottom of the threshold to the top. Snow packed so solidly, it was not going to be easy to move.

Without a word to explain, he slammed the door closed and stomped through the cabin. The other door opened and slammed, leaving behind an empty sound.

Maybe it was time to go. Betsy stood, bringing the blanket with her. Should she try to leave for home? She padded through the darkness to the mantel clock and squinted—it was nearly five o'clock. It seemed like midnight, for it was so dark she couldn't see through the window. Her face reflected darkly back at her and the wilderness outside was one enormous hush, as if nature were holding back for an even more dangerous act.

I definitely ought to go while I can. She thought of Duncan so quick to be rid of her. He'd probably reached the stable and was preparing her horse at this very moment. She thought of the chores left to be done—the supper meal to warm for him, a new pot of tea to steep for when he came in, the main room to clean and dust and mop. The laundry she meant to gather to take with her.

Before she could take another step, thunder exploded so hard the entire cabin seemed to lift up and drop. The floorboards heaved. The walls moaned. The timbers overhead groaned as if alive. The thunder came not from the sky, but from the mountains behind them.

She heard the roar of the snow, the crack of ancient trees snapping like toothpicks and the ring of wind and fury. The cabin seemed to explode and she dropped to her knees. Something hard struck her against the back, pinning her to the floor, but it was only the safe end of a rack of antlers that must have been mounted on the wall above.

She moved it safely aside as the cabin continued to buck. *Duncan.* He was outside in this. What if he were swept away? The cabin bucked and jostled, and around her, the world broke apart.

Glass shattered and she didn't see the tree coming until it was too late. Until the limb slapped her across the jaw. She felt the sting and then a greater pain. Like a sledgehammer pounding against her head. And then there was nothing.

Nothing at all.

Chapter Fourteen

Safe in the hayloft tucked in the steeple of the stout log stable, Duncan witnessed the avalanche explode down the mountainside.

While no star glistened from the black sky, the night had hues of its own. Shades of shadow and night that made his sensitive eyes pick out the polish of the hard-packed snow, the somber specters of the giant evergreens and the unforgiving peaks of the rugged Rocky Mountains.

The avalanche was not a big one—he'd built his stockade tight to direct the deadly power of the snow around the house and stable. But it was the first of the season and brought with it the crack of trees weakened by age or conditions through the temperate summer.

So when he heard the gunshot-like report of a tree shattering, he figured, by the ear-ringing loudness, it was an ancient cedar, the kind large enough to take other trees with it when it rolled with the lethal force of the snow.

Right for the house.

He saw the dark length of the giant tree, rolling and

breaking apart as though it were a mere stick. He watched the supple top of the tree snap and crash into the blockade barrier protecting the house. It was a hard blow, and he was surprised the huge tree took a small portion of the logs imbedded into the earth with it and crashed into the house.

Betsy. Betsy was in there. And if she'd been any-where in the front room... Duncan couldn't see the damage from where he stood, but he couldn't get the ringing tinkle of breaking glass out of his mind. And how he heard such a delicate sound over the savage roar of snow and broken trees, he could not explain.

Or maybe because his entire being was focused, not on the destruction to his house, but on the woman in-side. The woman in his protection, because that was the only reason he cared. If something happened to her, then worse would happen to him.

He would not allow for any other reason or any other emotion as he stood helpless to hold back the destruc-tion as the cascade thundered by. His eyes strained to see anything more in the utter bleakness and there was nothing but the lump of shadow that was the house and what looked to be a gigantic cedar, as large around as a locomotive, butting into it, held there by the force of the avalanche.

She's all right, he told himself. She's probably safe in the kitchen where it was relatively warmer. It was senseless to be worried. She was fine. Simply fine.

Then why could he not feel the buzz of awareness in his soul? The one Betsy put there? The place that felt like spring to his tired old spirit. What had happened to her? Betsy, you stayed in the kitchen, didn't you?

And he knew she hadn't. She would have wanted to leave right away. He'd treated her abysmally and of course she'd want to flee as fast as she could the instant she could. Sick fear gripped his stomach and stayed holding on. He wondered what the horse sensed, the gelding seemed deeply attached to his mistress. *Yeah, fella, I know just how you feel.*

The night clung like death to the world where there were no stars, no moon and not a single light anywhere. Nothing but shades and shadows and the quiet roll as the last of the high country snow crumbled from somewhere far above on the peaks and silenced.

The wilderness rang with it. As if the trees were alive and stood in wait, not quite daring to release their held breaths. No creatures stalked the forest, no hawks or owls hunted the skies. Nothing moved as the mountainside remained hushed. Was the danger past?

Duncan didn't care. He was already out the door and crossing the pathway between the stable and the house. Let the snow come, nothing was going to stop him from reaching his Betsy. He kept one ear cocked for the half second of notice he would get if there was a second avalanche, but the mountain waited until he was safely in the door.

"Betsy?"

He could smell the desolation and the fresh scent of broken tree bark and inner fiber. The feel of danger in the air. The ice crunched beneath his boots as he followed the hush to where the tree had angled in, broken trunk first, thrust through the main window and into the front room.

Furniture was knocked aside. Books, open and ragged, had tumbled from their shelves, and glass from the lantern crunched beneath his feet. He could smell the faint acrid scent of smoke.

It was sheer luck that the snow and wind must have dowsed the flame.

"Betsy!" He bellowed her name, but she didn't come running, as she would have done had she been in the kitchen. That had him dropping to his knees, frantically feeling through the destruction.

He couldn't feel her. His heart was silent. He had to find her. He had to—

He felt the softness of cotton against his fingertips, lost beneath the hard wedge of a thick lower bough. He found her motionless beneath the flanged branches with the weight of the tree pinning her to the ground. Was she breathing?

But no, he would know if she were gone. There remained in the center of his soul a small light burning.

Hope lived, after all.

Hope.

The sweetness of it rushed through him as her fingers tightened around his. She was alive. She could move.

Hell, he was grateful for that. He closed his mind against the possibilities of severe wounds—he couldn't tolerate the chance of it.

He splayed his palm gently against the side of her face, her dear, beloved face. "Lie still, my darling. I'm going to lift this damn tree off you, okay?"

She moaned and he went hard with fear. Then hot with rage. How dare this damned tree hurt her?

Irrational rage pumped through him and in an instant

he'd hefted the treetop's weight from her fragile form and protected her with his body from the limbs as he hurled it up, through the window, jamming it back the way it had come as hard as he could. He ignored the pain, ignored everything.

"Duncan?"

He could hardly hear her over the roar coursing through him, but he forced a deep breath into his lungs and left the tree where it protruded through the window—he'd have to wrestle it out from the outside. Later.

What mattered at this moment was this woman. Only this woman.

He went to her gently, kneeling at her side to support her head. "You shouldn't move. Shh. Tell me what hurts."

"My pride is all."

"No, you took quite a blow." His fingers skimmed over her. Her hair was wet…but not sticky from blood. He sniffed and couldn't scent it. He'd fought in the Civil War, so he knew something about injuries. Still, that didn't mean she wasn't injured in other ways— "Lie still, damn it!"

"I'm fine. I merely took a branch upside the head. It smarted, but I don't think—"

"Where?"

She flinched. What was he so angry with her for this time? Did the man have any other emotions than either stoic or enraged? "Right here in front of my temple."

"Let me see—" He swore and rose away. "Stay there. Don't move. Do you hear me?"

"I haven't gone deaf, so you don't need to yell as if I have."

"Hellfire! What did I do to bring you to my door?" He swore more viciously, using words she'd never heard before—if indeed they were words.

She wasn't about to be bossed around by any man so she sat up—and her head swam. She hadn't been hit hard, but it had been enough.

She hissed through her teeth—heavens, did that hurt!—and tenderly felt the sore spot with her fingertips. The raised bump was unmistakable.

So was Duncan's temper. She didn't blame him. He hadn't asked for any of this—not one thing, except to have his clean laundry delivered weekly and his dirties washed and ironed, and all for a very generous fee.

He was her best customer, and look what she'd brought down on him. He'd had to wrestle bears, deal with her family and now was stuck through both a blizzard and an avalanche. She didn't blame him one bit, no, but she was relieved to see him moving around, stiff but still moving.

How had he lifted that tree without tearing open his wounds? Well, it had been over a month, perhaps he was healing better than she imagined.

Light accompanied him on his return from the kitchen. The meager flame danced over the wreck of the room and over the harsh lines carved deep in Duncan's masked face. He looked as distant as the granite peaks of the unforgiving mountains behind his house.

Yet, as he knelt to study her forehead, his nearness made her skin prickle. Her entire being opened like a new spring flower to dawn's light.

"Do you see one or two of me?"

Not even his acrid tone could stop the flow of what felt like warmed honey through her veins. "Just one."

"And that's more than enough, huh? You're not bleeding. You're bound to get a bruise, but it's a small bump. How about your fingers? Can you wiggle them? Your toes?"

He moved to her feet, as caring as a doctor, his hand lighting on her calf. His touch was intimate, even through the layers of stockings and petticoats and skirt.

He unlaced her shoes and removed them, taking care. "Let me see."

"I'm fine."

"Move them." The deep creases gouged into his face eased when he saw her toes bend and flex. When he spoke, his voice came out ragged and strained. "Oh, thank God. How about your abdomen? Does it hurt to breathe?"

"I told you. I'm fine." Her voice came ragged, too. He was acting as if…as if he had some affection for her. But how could that possibly be?

"Are you sure?" He pressed the heel of his hand gently against the curve of her belly. "Any tenderness?"

She moved her head and her dark curls shook and bounced. He picked a broken cedar needle from her hair. The weak light caressed her creamy throat and face, bringing out the luster of her inner being.

She was beyond beauty. She was everything he held dear—the only thing. And, God help him, he could not stop the sob of gratitude that shattered him as his head fell forward onto her lap.

Her skirts were soft and her thighs firm, and he gritted his teeth, holding back the burning gratitude that made his eyes smart. If anything had happened to her, he wouldn't have been able to go on. He couldn't lie to himself. He couldn't do it anymore.

He knew he was acting like a fool, like a man in love with an enchanting woman he could never deserve, but the steel within him was not so strong, after all. Not if one small woman could bring him here, to his knees.

"Oh, Duncan. I was terrified for you, too." Her fingertips feathered through his hair and it took a moment for her meaning to penetrate the wave of emotion drowning him.

He straightened, seeing the most amazing emotion alight in her eyes so blue, on her face so dear. For him. Her love for him.

He swallowed, not trusting his voice. There were no words, anyway, no mere pittance of sounds and syllables that would begin to illustrate to her the depth of his feelings.

Like the snow that had broken away with such force from the granite peaks of the mountains above, his love for her cascaded through him. Obliterating all his barriers and defenses, breaking him until he was like that tree laid open and revealed, and he didn't care; he covered her mouth with his without thought or intention.

Suddenly her lips were against his, a gentle caressing so exquisite he choked on his own air, cradling her jaw so he could kiss her again, plunge into her mouth and taste her sweetness.

Feeling the race of her heartbeat against his and how she was kissing him in return, her hands winding into his thick hair, and she was pulling him along as she lay back in the snow and broken branches and he came with her, his rock-hard shaft caught between them.

Lost, there was no control, no logic, no ounce of common sense. He cupped her breast with his free hand and she moaned, surrendering beneath him, compliant and supple, and he knew without asking what she wanted.

He took the time to unbuckle his belt, unbutton his trousers and, hands trembling, smooth her skirts and petticoats up over her hips. Her creamy thighs were trembling, too, and she watched him with huge eyes, saucer-wide with emotion.

No woman had ever gazed upon him that way. No woman had given him that slow, secret smile as she reached down to untie the waist of her drawers.

There was no need for words as he covered her. The lightning shock of his hardness against her ready heat jolted through him and into her.

He did not trust himself to speak, as she reached with both hands to pull him down to her kiss, down into the resisting heat of her body, as she opened to him, the wind storming through the night outside, battering the small house, but it could not touch them.

It could not stop the beauty of this as Betsy wrapped her thighs around his hips, to keep him inside her.

They moved together, more than lovers in the night, lost in their own storm. In the ancient tempest of man and woman joined.

When it was over, he held her while the last waves of her pleasure ebbed through her. Then, holding her so they remained as one, he lifted her, carefully because he was still recovering, and carried her into the warmer kitchen.

Where, in the dark, he loved her all over again. With everything he had. With all the tenderness within him he didn't know was there. Until he lost himself, his past, his pain, his sorrow, and there was only her. No past. No present. No dawn when she would have to go home.

Only now. Buried within her tight heat. Surrendering to her gentle passion. He would not think of what was to come.

Only now. And only this woman he treasured most, who was honestly and sweetly loving *him*.

Betsy wished she could hold him forever. The blankets could only provide so much protection and somewhere along the way they'd lost all their clothes.

The furs felt luxurious against her skin, almost as good as Duncan. She rubbed her knee against the down of his thigh and he growled low in his throat, tightening his arms around her.

Snug against his chest, content, lulled by the cadence of his breathing, she tried to hide her smile and couldn't. She hadn't been this happy in so long and it made her realize how empty her days had been. How lost the years since Charlie's death.

She had found purpose enough for her life; she had family and friends and activities that filled her days. But her heart…

She'd found her heart again.

Ever grateful, she pressed a kiss to his warm, textured skin and hugged him with her whole body. He was a warm, delicious weight, his shaft heavy inside her.

She liked how he moaned, this Duncan who was tender as he pressed a kiss to her forehead. She tipped her mouth to meet his and he kissed her like a man who means it. He growled low in his throat as he curved his hand around her hip and tilted her to slide more deeply within her.

Thrilling pleasure shot through her, but as wondrous as it was, it paled against the emotional pleasure of being with him.

He was a powerful tenderness as he caressed her breasts. Kissed the tip of her nose, each freckle that marked her cheeks and the small dimple in her chin.

She shivered, soul-deep, for being with him like this, it felt right, as if it been fated long ago. She traced her fingertips along the muscled length of his back, enjoying the solid male feel of him.

Exploring how his spine dipped between the lengths of definite muscles. Discovering that when she tickled the small of his back, he tried to hide his reaction and turned a laugh into a growl and he was hard again, moving deeper still, his gaze penetrating hers.

Hilt-deep, he froze, holding her there on the flare of his shaft, and he knew it would make her shiver with pleasure.

"You like that, huh?" Duncan asked, although he'd already tortured her like this before. He leveled his weight on his elbows and slipped both big hands beneath her head and cradled her, this woman he loved. He loved how she blushed. He liked how she locked her ankles tight around him as if she never intended to let go.

Hell, he could not think of the dawn to come. Not yet. He brushed the tip of his nose to hers and her smile grew. Dazzled, he was helpless as she moved to rock against him, her body supple, her fingers sliding along his chest and cradling his face.

He matched her pace, rolling against her. He was rewarded by a low purr of pleasure and her tantalizing kiss.

"Oh, Duncan," she sighed, clinging to him, this precious and beautiful creature; and he loved her, and, helpless, he moved to her demands, her quiet mews of pleasure and the quickening of her inner muscles hugging him too tight.

He could not find words to speak of the depth of love he felt for her. He did not know how to measure anything so large. He never knew a man could feel this for a woman. Beyond devotion and affection and faith.

Nothing else in his life would ever mean so much, and nothing ever had.

Every breath he took, every thing he did and every word he said would be, from this moment forth, for her.

"Oh, yes." Sheer love glowed in her eyes as she began to arch.

Her gaze never left his as her release washed through her and he felt the first shuddering wave rippling through her and into him.

"Oh, oh, I love you so much," she whispered, her words broken by the second and the third current of her climax.

"What did you say?" He had to hear it again, to be sure. To be absolutely certain he wasn't imagining those rare words.

"I love you."

She smiled and held him tight while he came. Found, when he should have been lost. Whole, when he should have remained broken.

Healed, when he thought nothing or no one could save him.

Chapter Fifteen

Was there a way to hold back the dawn? Betsy couldn't think of one as she lay in the warmth of Duncan's arms, snug against him. Their legs entwined, they were naked and satisfied.

Oh, she'd missed this part of marriage, not that it was the most important part, but the intimacy, the closeness, the sharing…and yes, the passion. How lucky she was to find this bond again. She'd all but given up hope. Love was too important to settle for anything less, and this man…

Oh, this man. Her grin broadened and she could feel the stretch of it on her face.

She could feel him stir awake. The ripple of awareness, the intake of his breath, the realization it was her he held. And how his big masculine body burned against hers. He nuzzled her hair. "I thought I was dreaming for a moment."

"Hmm, if this is a dream, then it's the best one I've ever had."

"Me, too." He leaned back, fixing a hand on her

fanny to bring her with him as he stretched out. His arousal was obvious and quite substantial.

She couldn't help the smile that widened until her entire face hurt. Joy shone inside her like first light and she gave him access to her breasts and kissed his forehead and he suckled and pleased her.

"Are the birds loud enough for you?" He peered over the crest of her bare bosom.

He was substance in the prelight shadows and she welcomed him into her body. Sighed as his thickness stretched her. "Are they this loud every morning?"

"I don't know. I can't seem to pay attention to them."

"I wonder why?" She liked that he chuckled, that in the dark he was revealed. A tender, gentle giant of a man.

Love so pure left her breathless as they moved together, his hand firm on her hip to guide her. Whatever this connection was between them, it was more than sex, more than passion.

Her heart felt wide open, her entire being shimmered and never had anyone mattered to her so much. He buried his face in her shoulder, clutching her as his big body stiffened, driving into her as deep as he could go, so deep she swore their souls touched.

As joy spiraled through her and she came, crying out his name, the first golden rays of light broke through the shades drawn at the window and she saw him illuminated.

The grave, honest love in his eyes was unmistakable as he brushed the tangled curls from her face. She was his now, they both knew it, and she could not bear to part from him. She pressed her face against his throat, one last effort to hold back the day from coming, but it was coming anyway.

Duncan pulled out of her and in the intimate morning shadows, regret lined his face. He moved slowly, climbing out from beneath the thick furs and into the frigid air where his breath rose in great clouds and his skin goose-fleshed. He hurried into his clothes, pulling on layer after layer.

Sadness filled her up until she couldn't speak.

"Stay in the blankets until the room warms up a little." He'd fed the fire through the night, and he filled it full, leaving the damper and the oven door open to encourage hot flames. "I'll tend the horses."

He meant harness her dear Morris. She could only nod and hide her face in the furs. She waited until the back door clicked shut—apparently the snowdrift had shifted and he was able to leave. The twilight shadows lengthened, as if pushing back the dark.

Outside the shrill cacophony of more birds than she could name or count chattered and squealed and whistled and sang in great disharmony. The sound was so loud, it was as if every winged creature in existence had perched in the trees just outside the back door.

Dawn was arriving in new bits of color. Or the first hues of purple and magenta giving way to a rosy light. The birds silenced. The world became multicolored again as golden new light spilled through the windows, bringing with it the reality of the outside world.

Her family would be looking for her. Probably organizing a search party—no, a lynching party if they'd known what she'd been willingly doing with the highly inappropriate, for her, mountain man. That, of course, would undoubtedly be her mother's opinion. But Mother would simply have to alter her opinion, for the impossible had happened.

If only I could stay. She glanced around the kitchen and saw it for the first time. She gathered the furs around her, holding them tight to keep in her body's heat, and released the shutters.

Once the main window was uncovered, she saw that the high drifts had been blown away in the night. Light slashed through the hand-carved windowpanes and into the room. The gentle light warmed the honey log walls and shone on the floor. She noticed the table first, shimmering varnish pine of a heavy masculine design. Simple and striking and matching the chairs tucked neatly into place. When Duncan had been up to feed the fire, he must have picked up some of the mess.

What surprised her were the books. Tucked beneath the window seat were two shelves of leather-bound volumes. Shakespeare and Chaucer. Dickens and Jules Verne. Hawthorne and Twain. She eased onto the wooden seat and, trembling with the chill in the room, looked through the brand-new volume of Twain's latest, *The Prince and the Pauper.* She'd been saving up to buy this very book before she'd bought furniture instead.

It was so easy to dream. Dreaming was something she hadn't dared to do, and now it came so readily. How pleasant it might be to sit here on a winter's morning, when there was little work needing to be done, with the breakfast dishes finished and a second pot of coffee set to boil, and read.

She could make pillows and cushions and this would

be a beautiful place to spend hours, soaking up the sunshine and reading. And, when she stopped to fill her and Duncan's coffee cups, to look at the view. The mountainside sloping past the house was littered with chunks of rock and broken boughs, but the scenery was breathtaking. Regal forests and somber mountain peaks painted with the bronzed light.

What perfect happiness there could be to spend her life here, with Duncan. Her eyes burned and she rubbed at her tears. Mama was always saying she was too prone to extremes of emotion, but she was like the sun. Shining so brightly, she could not keep it all in.

She'd been well loved, her body felt that thrilling exhaustion and the awareness of where he'd been lodged deep within her remained.

She felt him before she heard his boots on the hard packed snow. She knew before he pushed through the door that he was already searching the room for her. He still limped and favored his wounded side. Even more as he dropped into the chair nearest to her.

Sadness made his eyes black. "I put my runners on your buggy. I hope you aren't mad, but there's no other way to get you home."

"Thank you." She carefully closed the crisp volume. "Have you read this yet?"

"As soon as I brought it home. I had to order it from town."

"From the mercantile? It's hard to convince the McIntyres to order a book without payment up front. I had been saving up to do the same."

"You like Mark Twain?"

"I do." She swallowed, as if it were painful to talk.

Yep, I know just how that feels. Duncan cleared the thickness from his throat. Betsy had already knelt to replace the volume where she'd taken it from the shelf, and he covered her hand, stopping her. "Why don't you borrow it?"

"Oh, it's too costly to borrow. I couldn't afford to replace it if anything happened to it."

Duncan had to stop for a moment to study her. Was she truly being sincere? He thought of Ginetta, the young woman who'd destroyed his life with a lie. He'd been enamored of her and she'd used that knowledge to manipulate him and the circumstances. She was the type of woman he thought only existed. The kind out for gain and advantage and nothing more.

But Betsy, after a night of passion, was assuming nothing. Was asking for nothing. Was not the kind of woman who borrowed routinely, not by the worry pinched into the adorable creases in the corners of her eyes. The old bitterness was still there, and he had to fight it back, had to bite his tongue to keep from saying that she was acting that way simply to hide the fact that she wanted the book. But he knew it wasn't true.

The Betsy he'd held in his arms, the woman who'd given him her love freely, was the same one stubbornly replacing the book with a smile. The fur wrapped tightly around her began to slip off her shoulder, revealing the fragile line of her collarbone and the curve of her neck where he'd kissed and stroked countless times through the night.

Love pulled him down and he was suddenly with her, handing her the volume. Hell, it was only a book and, right now, to keep her here, he would give her anything. Everything. If only she could remain his for a while longer.

"Keep it," he urged, because he could not ask her to stay.

Because he had to let her go.

"I'll borrow it. And I'll be so careful, I swear it."

"No. It's yours." He brushed her lush mouth with his and drank in her passionate taste. He loved how she sighed against his lips. How her spine arched and she surrendered, and they were both breathing faster.

"My family is going to be worried about me."

"I know." There would be consequences for loving Betsy. He was ready for them. Duncan held back all the things he wanted to tell her—about how wonderful she was, how he wanted to keep her right here with him forever and how she'd saved him.

But she was no longer his. The sun was rising, her horse was harnessed and her buggy awaited her. She had a life and a family. She did not need him.

And from this moment on, he could not need her. He gathered up her clothes for her and, while she shivered into them, adjusted the stove, put on some coffee. Hiding the pain from his healing injuries.

Hiding the pain in his soul.

A man with a future to offer would let her know how much she meant to him. But he had nothing, and he could not know what consequences were to come from loving his Betsy. But whatever trouble came his way, he would bear it gladly. If he never saw her again, if he never had the privilege of holding her through the night, or of being together in the most intimate way, then it would be a great sorrow.

But he would never regret her.

At last, when she was dressed and bound up in her coat and muffler and scarf, he poured the steaming coffee into his thickest cork jug, a drink to warm her on her long, icy ride home. There was nothing left to do but to tell her goodbye. And he could not.

So she wouldn't know how it shattered him, how he wasn't made of steel in truth, he simply walked away. Brought her horse and buggy, mounted on the sled runners, to the door and held the gelding's bridle while she climbed aboard. Since she didn't have a blanket, he wrapped her snug in one of the furs. Not looking at her. Not daring to speak.

"Thank you."

He didn't answer her. He handed her the thick reins, holding the straps so she could easily place them through her fingers.

"Oh! I forgot your laundry."

His jaw worked. He shook his head and deliberately looked away toward what remained of the road that wound through the forest and down the hillside and far away from his cabin.

She saw what secret hid in his heart, for it was the same within hers. Encouraged, she pressed a kiss to his gloved hand, wishing more than anything she could stay. And knowing she had obligations and a day of work ahead of her.

"I love you." She let those brave words into the air, knowing he needed to hear them.

He smiled, no longer the bear of a man she'd mistaken him for. "If you don't come back, I'll understand."

It wasn't possible that there would ever be the chance to keep her as his, but he was merely a man and he had one thing he hadn't had in over half his lifetime: hope. He had hope.

"Hungry bears couldn't keep me away." She smiled.

And it was his future he saw.

When she drove down the road and out of his sight, it was his heart that went with her and his soul, which would never be his again.

Betsy had been worried during the long ride home. Anxious over leaving Duncan behind to fend for himself. Half-sick over the expectation that Mama would be waiting for her with news of the search party looking for her broken and wrecked buggy.

Her only consolation was that the snow remained deep and hard-packed all the way into town. The blizzard may have come here, too, and if that were the case, then of course she wouldn't have shown up for Sunday dinner.

And maybe Mama would have no notion of where Betsy had spent the night. It was unlikely, but a girl had to hold on to whatever hope she had.

When she saw her mother's imposing surrey, also on runners parked in the lee of the small stable, she knew there was no escape. Mama would be waiting for her inside the house and she'd immediately see that no morning fire had been lit. The bed had not been slept in. That she—Elisabeth Gable Hunter—had spent the night experiencing passion with a man her mother would never accept.

And what a passion it was. Betsy sighed, savoring

the glow shining through her body. The wisps of memories from last night remained and her body felt forever marked. Claimed. As she pulled Morris to a halt in front of the stable door, she stood and was reminded of places where she was deliciously sore.

There, where Duncan had been inside her, she still felt textured by his seed. And it was an amazing, intimate sensation, remembering well how he'd emptied into her more times than she'd thought to count.

Not that anything would come of it. That made her sadder still. She and Charlie had never been blessed with children. And there was no reason to believe that events might turn out differently with another man. No, it was a hope she couldn't let in, for it was one that would only lead to disappointment.

Yet somewhere deep within her spirit she harbored that tiny wish. The image of a child of Duncan's for her to hold. With his beautiful bronze complexion and eyes dark like the night—

"Elisabeth! There. You. Are." Mama marched around the corner of the house, her skirts flying, her mouth pursed into a furious line and looking more like a battlefield general than one of the most respected women in town. "I. Was. Worried."

"Goodness, there was no reason to be." Ducking so as to keep her face hidden, for her mother was an excellent face reader, Betsy industriously worked the buckles of Morris's harness. "Wasn't the storm something?"

"I sent Joshua over to make certain you had enough dry wood and he said you were not here." Out of breath, with both rage and the effort of moving too quickly with a too tight corset, Mama was barely able to manage her usually imposing, "Humph!"

"I am perfectly capable of bringing in enough coal to keep the house warm. Did everyone make it over for dinner yesterday?" She was not trying to deceive her mother, for if Mama continued to demand the truth, Betsy was not one to foster lies. However, if Mama happened to become distracted and forgot to keep pestering…that was a different matter entirely. "How are James and his new wife?"

"Miserable." The strategy worked, for Mama wrapped her arms around her middle, scowled as if she'd gotten a particularly strong whiff of the soiled straw pile. "I told him he'd be absolutely wretched if he married her, but would he listen to his own mother who loves him more than her very life? No, of course not! He's a man. Men don't listen to anyone. They think they know everything, but they don't. And now he's sorry!"

It was better that Mama went on about James's wife than about Duncan Hennessey. If her mother went into a conniption over the admittedly selfish Eileen, then Betsy hated to think how Mama would react if she found out her only daughter had just crawled from a mountain man's bed and still had the scent of him on her.

Besides, there were matters to sort out. The fact that her family had left Duncan injured and alone made her quite angry. She yanked the last buckle loose, startling Morris, and she had to reassure him before she could lift off the heavy shoulder harness. "What did Eileen do this time?"

"Do! She came into my kitchen yesterday afternoon, as pompous as you please, and gave orders to my servant. Mine! *I* pay her wages. *I* provide room and board. Then that woman had the audacity to ask for Anya's help this Wednesday for a ladies' luncheon she's hosting. That woman presumes far too much!"

"I don't even ask to borrow Anya."

"That's what I said! Look to my dear little Bets for a fine example in a young lady—"

"Mama, I'm no longer so young."

"You are lovely, my sweet, and that woman could use a few lessons from you!"

Thinking of her behavior last night, Betsy bit her bottom lip to keep from laughing out loud. "Yes, Mama. Would you like to come in? I'm afraid I have a lot of work awaiting me this morning. Monday is my busiest workday."

"I have no desire to sit and watch my only daughter work her fingers to the bone scrubbing other people's drawers!"

Dramatic was one word to describe Mama. The other was deeply loving. The only way to handle the combination was to be tolerant. Her mother meant well, regardless if her actions brought the opposite result. "I scrub shirts and trousers, too. And sheets. Towels. Dishcloths. All sorts of things besides people's undergarments."

"What am I to do with you?" Mama gave her muffler a hard yank to tighten it around her throat. "The first snowfall of the season and it was a blizzard! I had visions that you had become lost in the storm and blown off course and had frozen to death somewhere on the desolate prairie. And when Joshua said you were not at home this morning! Oh, Bets, you must stop driving all over tarnation or it will give me heart palpitations."

"I know you worry, Mama. But I worry about you, too." She pressed a kiss to her mother's cheek. There had to be a way to break the news gently, that she was in love again. It would be very difficult for Lucille Gable to accept, Betsy knew. But the silver lining was that James's Eileen might not seem so bad after acquiring a rugged mountain man for a son-in-law.

Her poor, well-meaning mother. "I've got to get scrubbing, Mama, but thank you for coming over. Are you certain you couldn't do with some hot tea? I bought the kind you like."

"You're my good sweet girl, but I'd best get back home so that woman doesn't try to steal away my housekeeper!" With a wave, Mama was off, climbing into her surrey, whistling to the team and speeding out of sight.

Whew. Close call. Betsy couldn't begin to imagine what Mama would do if she'd discovered the truth. As for how Granny and Joshua would react—well, she still had them to deal with. Later, she thought as she rubbed Morris down and forked extra straw into his stall for comfort.

"Where were you?" Joshua was dismounting from his fine black gelding, his gaze as righteous as a hanging judge's. He was a big man and could be intimidating when he wanted to be. "And those aren't your runners. I know because I came over this morning to put them on your buggy box for you."

"That was thoughtful of you, Josh, but as you can see, I've got it managed." Betsy leveled her oldest brother with a hard stare. He was no villain, but he behaved that way. No doubt out of some overprotective-loving-brother motive, but she had to wrestle down her temper as she unlocked her door. "I have work to do, but you're welcome to come in if you want."

"That's not exactly a welcoming invitation."

"Sorry." She was through the door and sending silent suggestions—Don't come in, Joshua, go home—but his boots knelled on the steps.

As she peeled off her wraps, she could see him through the window. He was shoveling off the snow that had accumulated on the porch and on the steps. Red rage flared before her eyes, blinding her, and she shook the ice from the damp morning air from her coat and muffler and hung them on the pegs by the stove to dry.

A fire was already crackling in the stove. Judging by the looks of things, it had been going for some time. How early had Joshua come over and let himself into her house? He would have known, if it had been early enough, that she hadn't spent the night upstairs. She needed time to get control of her emotions. How she handled this situation had long-reaching effects on all the people she loved.

Especially for Duncan. Duncan, who had experienced cruelty from her family already.

There was no question in her heart. He was the man she intended to spend the rest of her life loving. He was already a part of her, as if a part of him had remained inside her, and her spirit was no longer hers alone. She thought of him, wondering what he was doing right now. Had he enjoyed some of the breakfast out of the baskets she'd packed for him? Had he already been fixing the damage the avalanche had done to the front room of his cabin?

She worried that he was working too hard. Although every movement brought him great pain, he hadn't complained. He had done his best to pretend he wasn't wounded at all.

She'd return the first chance she got. He needed a woman to take care of him, to soften his life, to let him know what a fine man he was. But there was Joshua, opening her door and stomping the snow off his boots before stepping onto her kitchen floor—Mama had trained him well.

He took off his hat and hung it on the coat tree next to the door. "I don't suppose you've got coffee going?"

"I'm measuring the grounds right now." She finished her work, keeping her back to him. The silence thickened between them, so the sound of his boots crossing to the table rang like cannon fire.

"So do you want to tell me where you were last night?"

She grabbed a loaf of cinnamon bread from the pantry and sliced it. "I didn't know it's your business."

"Damn it! I've never known you to act like a loose woman! What's gotten into you, Bets?"

"I'm not ready to discuss this right now." She slipped the slices onto the top oven rack to toast and then reached to slip the frozen-solid butter ball into the heat to thaw.

"You are going to talk about this!" Joshua's anger

crackled louder than the flames inside the stove, but he was worried for her. "Maybe I know. You had a close brush with death when that bear came after you and now you need to feel alive. Sometimes that happens. But don't do something you'll regret. If word gets 'round of what you're doing—"

"What am I doing?"

"You had to sleep somewhere last night. I was here before dawn and I saw you weren't here. You hadn't been in your bed all night, but you're looking satisfied and chipper this morning. Fine, you had your night of passion, but it's over and no more. You don't want folks disrespecting you or trading gossip about how loose your morals are. It will hurt your business, I can promise you that."

"I thought you hated my business. That you'd like nothing more than for me to fail and have to move back in with you and Mama so that all of you can keep a better eye on me." She slammed the clean plates onto the table with enough force to crack them. "And clean up your thoughts. I wasn't out having passion, as you call it. I'm not wanting to throw caution to the wind because I came face-to-face with my own mortality."

"Then would you tell me what the hell is wrong with you? That way I can stop worrying myself sick that someone is going to hurt you or rob you or mug you or rape you or something." He jabbed his fingers through his hair, distraught, pain twisting his handsome face until he looked like a hung criminal.

"Oh, Josh, stop. Please. I'm all grown up. I don't need you to be a big brother to me anymore." She wrapped her arms around him from behind, she couldn't help giving him a hug when she ought to be smacking him alongside the head with her fly swatter. "I'd much rather have you as my friend. Not my protector."

"Oh, you're going to be the death of me." He shook his head, refusing the weakness of normal human emotion. "Tell me this isn't what I think. That I'm not going to have to grab my shotgun and force whatever lowlife had his way with you to marry you."

"He's not a lowlife and it's not like that. I'm in love." She hurried away to rescue the toast and butter, careful to keep her back turned.

The new affection was tender and the relationship with Duncan precious. She needed to protect him, until she was certain her family would accept him. And they would, she knew, if she asked them to. But for now, he was all hers. To cherish and honor and love.

"Is this man you're smitten with going to propose?" Joshua fetched the cups from the shelf and stood next to her at the counter. His presence was comforting, his tone caring. "I'm not about to let anyone break my sister's heart."

"Oh, stop. He's in love with me, too. I've been a widow for a long time, and you know how sad I've been."

"That's why we've been wanting you to settle down."

"I will. Just let me have my privacy, Joshua. Please. After years of sorrow, I've found someone to fill my heart again. Someone I can't stop thinking about. A wonderful man who I want to be with more than anything. Please, don't spoil this. It's like magic. It's so rare, and I just want to enjoy it."

"You mean enjoy sex without benefit of marriage? That's it, I'm gonna hunt down this fellow and make it clear. It's a wedding or his funeral—"

"Josh!" She kicked him in the ankle to get his attention and ignored his protest of pain. "This is the real thing. Be happy for me, because I never thought I would be again."

"Are you? Happy?" His gaze searched hers and, for all his faults, he wanted the best for her.

She could read it so clearly. "I'm blissful. Now sit down and eat while I get started on my work. And tell me what happened with Eileen. Did she really ask for Mama's housekeeper?"

Her big brother relented, gave her a smacking kiss on the forehead, and took the plate stacked high with sweet, spiced bread. He began the tale of yesterday's drama while she put her wash water on to boil.

She tried to listen, she really did, but her thoughts kept drifting back to the man who'd left his mark on her. Who had claimed her, whether he knew it or not, for the rest of her life.

She couldn't wait to see him again.

Chapter Sixteen

Duncan hoped he'd never see her again.

And, as the days passed, it looked as though he might get his wish. There was no sign of Betsy. He'd watched the clearing and imagined the sight of her coming around the bend until he thought she was coming. But when he blinked, the image in his mind was gone and there was only the lonely forest and empty road.

It was for the best that she'd forgotten him. It was what he wanted. This is what he told himself as he went about his work. What had happened between them had been plain wrong—even if she'd accepted him with the same emotional and physical hunger that had him lifting her skirt.

Women, even someone with as much integrity as Betsy, were emotional beings. He was prepared for her to regret what they'd shared. He expected that she'd see making love with him as a mistake.

Too much disaster could come from it—her family discovering she'd come to him, her reputation would be ruined, she'd probably lose her laundry business and there was always the possibility of a pregnancy. He'd marry her, of course, he'd give anything to have the right to call her his own, but...no, she hadn't come.

She would not come.

He accepted it. It was for the best. It was what he wanted—and if he said that enough times to himself then he was bound to start believing it. Eventually the memory of her smile would fade. The rare joy of making love to her would disappear. The punch of devotion in his chest would lose its power.

He might even forget how it felt to hold her against him in the night, their bodies entwined, her soft curves and silken hair on his chest and her magic as she'd surrendered to him....

He didn't have to close his eyes to remember how she'd opened her soul to him as the dawn came and merciless orgasm gripped her so hard she'd cried out his name. Her fingers digging into him, her heat tightening around him, demanding his release.

And he'd spilled into her, unable to hold back, and she'd smiled, a slow, satisfying grin that he could still see although he'd awoken alone for several mornings in a row now.

Although he stood in broad daylight with the snow melting in a song of cheer, and he leaned the ax he'd been using to plane a smooth windowsill to replace the one broken by the rogue tree.

Betsy. His entire being cried out for her. He died a little more each day, trying to forget her. Trying to pretend it didn't matter that she'd changed her mind. Maybe even regretted giving herself so freely.

Letting the old bitterness wrap around him like a comfortable, familiar coat, he went back to work. Eventually he'd be able to whittle the pretty dark-haired beauty from his memories.

Yeah, maybe when he was a hundred years old.

Pretending it didn't matter, pretending he wasn't hurt, he grabbed the wooden handle and sunk the ax into the wet meat of the fallen cedar.

She'd been keeping an eye on the snow clouds all the way from her last delivery west of town, but the closer she came toward the stunning wall of the Rocky Mountains, the more uncertain she became. The early snow had melted and she was back to her squeaking buggy wheels, but she didn't trust the leaden clouds massing along the northern sky.

It wouldn't be fair to have to turn around for fear of a blizzard and miss her first chance this week to see Duncan.

Morris sensed the danger, too, or, as likely dreaded the trip through the dark forest where they'd come across so much peril, so she talked low to him, soothing him as she always did while the prairie fell away and the mountain rose up to meet them.

She'd struggled hard over how to handle her family. She'd kept her distance from them, unable to forgive them for their lies and their cruelty. She knew why they'd done it, but she'd never felt so alone as after she'd returned from the mountains. The man she loved was far away, her workload had doubled with temporary laundry work one of the boarding houses had needed when an employee fell ill, and keeping away from her family meant she was lonelier than she'd been since she'd been newly widowed.

Anticipation thrummed through her, keeping her quite warm, so she didn't notice the sting of the icy wind. Tiny flakes of snow crystallized in midair and caught on her nose and eyelashes as the road began to steepen. Duncan was just beyond the trees.

Had he been missing her? Had he spent his days and his nights remembering their time together? The closeness they'd shared? She seemed starved for the sight of him and the moment Morris broke through the forest and into the clearing, she cast around for signs of him.

Nothing. Nothing at all.

A hard crust of snow covered everything, the place where he'd chopped wood that fateful day was wiped away…by the avalanche and he'd not cut more trees for fuel. Perhaps, with his wounds still tender and newly healed, he would not be able to use an ax. But that wasn't all that was amiss.

There was a vacant feeling to the place. As if it had been abandoned. The stable was closed up tight. The house was dark. No smoke curled from either the chimney or stovepipe.

Had he fled? Surely he hadn't packed up and moved away because of what they'd done? What if Joshua had figured it out and had threatened Duncan….

Or heaven forbid, what if Mama had learned of her affair and had come to give him a piece of her mind? The mere thought sent chills through her.

It was not fair. She needed to speak to her love, so he would know. He would understand. She wanted to protect this new love she felt, not subject him too soon to her meddling and messy family.

"Duncan?" She climbed down, tossing the reins over the dash and leaving Morris standing in the cool sun. Her breath rose in great white clouds as she hiked up the steps. A layer of snow crunched beneath her feet. He hadn't shoveled the stairs for whatever reason. She knocked on the door.

No answer.

What if he was gone for good? Her entire being recoiled at the thought. No, she thought fervently, he wouldn't have vanished. Not without saying goodbye. Not unless he regretted what they'd done—

The door snapped open without warning and there he was, his face inscrutable as he towered over her. Her heart soared. It was so good to see him. To let her gaze wander over the craggy features of his handsome face and to take delight in his surprised scowl.

He looked stronger, as if the regular meals she'd left him had helped. But then love was the greatest cure of all.

Joy exploded and she wrapped her arms around his neck, holding him tight, savoring the hard masculine feel of his iron chest and steeled arms folding her close. "Oh, I missed you! It feels like forever since I've seen you!"

"W-what are you doing here?"

"Don't sound so surprised. I told you I'd be back as soon as I could. I got an extra job that kept me busy, but that's over now." She didn't let go of him. She continued to hold him tight, it was as if she'd never let him go.

Duncan's throat thickened. All the angry words he'd been storing up over the days were trapped there, below his Adam's apple, and he couldn't seem to force them up. He should be angry with her. He ought to send her away. He could list several sensible reasons why it would be better for both of them if she knew the truth right now. So she'd leave and never come back.

He cleared his throat, ready to end this for good. When she released her hold on his neck, framed his face with her soft, small hands and gazed up at him with light sparkling so pure in her eyes, he forgot to breathe. His heart forgot to beat. His soul stilled. How could it be possible that she felt that depth of emotion for him?

"Did you miss me, too?"

He knew how vulnerable she felt. It would be so much easier on him to lie and say no. To lie and send her back the way she came. He could not do it. He fought to keep control of his heart as he nodded once. And felt the relief shiver through her.

Her sweet mouth went tender. Her lips covered his and he drank her in, holding her so tight that if he could just pull her close enough, he could keep her with him forever. His lonely soul ached in her presence and he kissed her with all the tenderness he was capable of. With all the love he didn't know was in him.

She did this to him. Made him feel. Forced him to come alive, and he breathed in the rose scent of her hair. Ran his fingertips over her petal-soft skin. Hated that he could never peel off her clothes and love her until she was crying out his name. Clinging to him, one with him.

How could he do the right thing by her and turn her away?

"You're looking so much stronger." She teased her fingertips across his chest. "You're feeling better?"

"Remarkably."

"Good. I brought another food basket, so I know you're eating right. And your book. Thank you so much for lending it to me."

There was no stopping the sun and there was no stopping her. He shouldn't let her in. He already knew how this would end. Not even Betsy, as wonderful as she was, would understand.

No, it was a given. Her family would find out she'd been coming to him. All anyone would need to do was to gaze upon Betsy and know they'd been lovers.

All hell would break lose. Her grandmother would make good on her promise. Betsy would learn the truth and despise him. She would hate that she'd ever trusted him with her heart.

Tell her now. He knew it was the right thing to do. Stand firm, be honest. Let her know there could never be a future. There would be no proposal. No wedding ring or vows. No happily-ever-after spent in this house as man and wife.

It was what she wanted. What she believed could be. He didn't have to be able to feel her emotions to know. It was there on her face, the hope of someone who'd given up. Only to be given that final, perfect chance.

"Oh, you fixed the window. It's beautiful!" She turned in a circle in the middle of the room, cleaned and put to rights, the outside window and wall repaired.

He hadn't replaced the shades and weak sunlight streamed through the panes to caress her springing coils of thick hair and burnish gently the curve of her face. Her yellow wool skirt flared and swirled around her slim ankles and he caught her by the wrist, halting her before she could spin another circle. Framed by the sunlight and the silent forest through the large window.

A perfect picture his heart would never forget.

"Oh, I was hoping you'd want a little closeness." A mischievous grin shaped her perfect mouth. Trouble lit in her eyes as blue as forever.

Closeness? Hell, he wanted to get as close to her as he possibly could. He wanted to please and pleasure her until he couldn't take any more. He wanted to make her love him enough so that nothing—not her family and not the truth of his past—could ever rip her away from him.

What kind of love would be strong enough for that?

Nothing could be, he realized with a sinking heart. She may have come back to him, but he had to be a strong enough man to let her go.

"I've never seen this room in full light. The windows were always shuttered. You did all this?"

He lifted one big shoulder in a casual shrug.

She wasn't fooled. She'd never seen anything so lovely in her life. From the scene carved into the massive mantel, the theme continued in the high-backed sofa and the matching chairs, the low tables and the coffee table, and again in the bedstead and the heavy wardrobe and bureau.

From the shelves to the molding to the trim at the windows. Stunning work of hard and soft woods combined and carved to depict an entire forest scene. Of creek and meadow. Grazing deer and hunting wolf. Of mountain peaks and deep, still mountain lakes.

"I like to work with wood," he explained.

He was an artist. Betsy could find no other word to describe what she saw. The furniture she'd bought was lovely, but this… "How can it be that someone of this amazing skill isn't selling his furniture in one of the bigger cities? Why? You're so gifted."

"No. It's not a gift, it's a hobby." He turned away, wishing there were shadows in the room to retreat to, but the shade had been damaged by the tree and he'd had no time to order another from town.

The sunlight faded as a cloud must have moved across the sun, but there was still the lovely day's light that allowed no truths to remain hidden.

"But you could sell your furniture…oh, I don't know, to important people, and make a lot of money."

"I had that dream once, but it was not meant for me." Sorrow filled him and he lifted the baskets, filled with the dishes of hers that he'd washed and the cloths he'd neatly folded. "Thank you. The meals came in handy."

"You seem to be moving better now, and better able to take care of yourself. I know you've probably cooked your own meals for a long time, but I couldn't help fussing. And no, not because I want to impress you. But because I love you. If there's any way I can make your life better, then that's what I want to do."

Not even his hard-won cynicism could stand up to Betsy Hunter's dazzling sincerity. Doubting her would be equal to doubting that the sun could shine. It shone, not for its own selfish reasons, but to give warmth and light to the world. How could he not love her so much? Every moment that passed, he loved her more.

Why would fate be so cruel as to give him this chance for happiness, when it was not possible?

"Forgive me." She came to him like the snow to the mountain, inevitable and natural. As if there were no other choice than for her to step into his arms. "I didn't mean to sound pushy. You're not the kind of man who likes living in town. I seem to remember you saying something about that once."

"It's true. Living in town brings with it...bad memories."

They had to be very bad. Betsy hurt for him as she held the door open for him. As she watched him hop down the steps with barely a trace of his limp and amble across the yard to set the baskets snugly in her buggy's boot, she couldn't help remembering all Mariah had told her about Duncan's family.

"I only meant to compliment your work," she said when he returned. "I've never seen anything so amazing."

"It's just wood. I whittle."

"Well, I love it. I didn't realize you could see me coming." She gestured to the wide window he'd repaired that offered a sweeping view of the forest sloping downward to the prairie that stretched forever and in the far, far distance, mountains she didn't even know the name of. "That's how you knew when to skedaddle."

"Guilty. I do find that view useful when I'm expecting a certain woman."

"Because you wanted to avoid me."

"Yes. Because what chance does a man like me have with a woman as lovely and as good as you?"

Her heart tumbled, and if it were possible to fall in love with him again, she did. "Even when my family left you here alone? I don't think I can ever forgive them, and yet you had no problem forgiving me."

"You would have stayed, I know. But they wouldn't let you. And your grandmother was right." It was now or never, and Duncan was a man who did not skirt, who did not crumble. "I have a past I'm not proud of."

"You're such a good man. What possible bad thing could you have done?" She had no notion how her words were killing him, driving deep like tiny blades into his vital organs. "I promise that when my family comes to know you the way I do, they are going to see how horrible they'd behaved. It was plain wrong, leaving you out here. I can only imagine what they told you."

"Something about how beloved and precious you were to them. I didn't understand it at the time, but since I'm starting to develop a slight fondness for you, I guess I see their meaning."

"You're not angry with them? I surely am. Furious. I can't trust myself to talk to them without losing my temper. Do you know they make a habit of this…this meddling, and they always will. You said you were in love with me, well, they are likely to be the test of it."

"I cannot blame them, because I have come to see their point."

"What point?"

She didn't know, he realized, that it was impossible not to love her. He'd wanted to hate that meddling grandmother of hers and that overbearing brother, but if the situation were reversed, he would do more than lie and issue threats to keep Betsy safe. Even before he realized he was in love with her, he'd been willing to die to protect her.

"So if they come here and raise a fuss about all this," she went on, trying to heft a full basket from the buggy's crammed boot. "Ignore them. Please. They mean well, which is their saving grace."

He reached around her, and it was intimate the way she turned toward him to brush her lips against his cheek. "Maybe they have a damn good reason for wanting me to keep my distance."

"They are like this with everyone they don't think is good enough for me. Mama would prefer I married a wealthier man this time around. My grandmother thinks that is the best suggestion she's ever heard. And Joshua… I hope he understands."

"He understands just fine. I'm not good enough for you."

"And why do you think that? Unless you've decided that you don't want to see where this bond between us leads?" *Please, don't say it's over.* Betsy ached with the words, putting her entire heart into them.

Her worst fears were confirmed as Duncan turned his back to her, his arm muscles bulging against his long-sleeved, insulated shirt as he hesitated, as if debating her words.

Then he put the basket in the compartment where he'd gotten it and walked away. Leaving her standing alone by the buggy.

Was it something a member of her family had said to him? Or was it that he was afraid, because she mentioned marriage, that she was angling for a proposal, just as he'd initially feared?

She found him in the kitchen, the lovely room framing the stunning mountain and forest views. His back stayed to her as he opened a case of bullets and began counting them out onto the table.

"I didn't realize what I was saying." She felt as helpless as she had the day the bear had charged from the forest's shadows. Except the man before her exuded a cold emotion she didn't understand, but whatever it was, she'd done this to him. She'd made him walk away.

She had to fix this if she could. "I shouldn't have mentioned getting married at all. The truth is, as much as I've come to love you, I would never want to marry anyone who doesn't want me. Do you understand?"

"Is that why your brother didn't show up with a shotgun the morning after we…" He grabbed his Winchester, snapped it open and slid in the first cartridge. "They didn't know you spent the night here."

"I didn't think it was any of their concern. I've been married and widowed. I worked side-by-side with my husband to make a successful farm, and now I work hard at my own business. I love my family, but they don't dictate my life. I'm wise enough to know a good man when I see him."

He couldn't be beguiled by her words; at the same time he wanted to be. "You're just saying that because you want another husband."

"Yes. I want you." She pulled the rifle out of his grip and set it on the counter. Then pushed the bullet cartridges out of the way. She eased her fanny onto the table so that she had his complete attention. "Now I just have to convince you to want me."

"You don't know who I am."

"You are the man I love." She wrapped her arms around him and breathed him in. His integrity. His honor. "There is nothing that could ever make me stop loving you. Please, love me in return. Just love me."

"You seem so sure."

"I am." She kissed the center of his chest. Like a promise meant to be kept, she kissed an inch lower. And then another inch. Tugging at his buttons to get at his bare flesh.

His groin tightened. Desire thrummed through him as quick as a whip's lash. Love so pure made him catch her mouth with his, lay her back on the table. *I would give anything for you.* He took her hand in his and kissed the backs of her knuckles. It was wrong to take this any further. But how did he tell her the truth?

"You don't know me at all." He choked on the words.

"I know what matters. If it's real love, Duncan, then it can't break. Then nothing will destroy it. Trust me." She caught hold of his belt and worked the buckle loose.

He was lost the instant she curled her hand around his arousal. He loved her with enough power that it made him trust that she meant what she said. That she meant it when she guided him into her tight heat and whispered in his ear. "I love you more than anything. No matter what. Is that how you love me, too?"

"Yes." His voice broke as he covered her mouth. He kissed her with all the gentleness in his soul.

She loved him no matter what, she'd said. As they clung to each other, lost in their love, he found hope. Because if this wasn't worth fighting for, then nothing was.

Chapter Seventeen

Betsy hurried down the hallway, her steps echoing in the emptiness. The meeting had started without her. Not that she minded being late, but everyone was going to watch her slip in late—there was no way around it. Mama would notice.

What was her mother going to say? Betsy paused, cold with dread, outside the door to the church's auxiliary room. Her hand remained in midair as she contemplated the wisdom of leaving her lover and speeding straight here without benefit of even a mirror.

She could have sex hair, the curse of her long bouncing locks. They were untamed enough as it was, but add ecstasy and a couple of climaxes and not even her best bonnet—which she was wearing—could cover the disaster. I'd better take a trip to the necessary room, she thought. Some generous patron had donated a wall mirror.

The instant she spied her reflection in the polished looking glass, she was very glad she'd thought to check her appearance before waltzing into the crowded room full of proper and prim church-going ladies.

Heavens, I look like a well-loved woman, and I'm not a married woman. Her cheeks glowed a very bright pink, flushed from the three orgasms Duncan had generously given her. Her curls were a tangled mess from how his fingers had wound through her hair.

Her soul sighed, remembering how he'd cradled her head while they'd made love. And he'd thrust his wonderful thickness into her, gazing into her eyes the whole while. She'd come, pulling him down into orgasm with her, and still, he had not looked away.

I love that man. Her heart sang with the power of it. How was she going to walk into that room and pretend as if nothing extraordinary had happened? How was she going to act normal, speak sensibly, and give a whit about the upcoming funding when she wanted to be alone? She wanted to savor every image, every sensation, every word Duncan had said, and every loving act he'd committed this afternoon.

Most of all, she wanted to cherish the sweet intimacy that lingered in her body and in her soul from being joined with him. Maybe she ought to go home and cry off the meeting entirely. She'd been out on deliveries, it was a legitimate excuse she could stretch into a little white lie so that she could keep Duncan all to herself for a little while longer.

Mama was going to throw a conniption. Joshua was going to get his gun. The rest of her brothers would hunt down the preacher. And all she wanted was to enjoy every step of this lovely courtship. Because that's what this was. Duncan was courting her. He'd promised to come by her house for supper.

Duncan. In town. Eating in her house. He had to be seriously in love with her to agree to that.

"Betsy?" came Rayna's voice from outside the door. "Is that you in there?"

"Guilty." Betsy unlatched the narrow door. "How did you know? How are you?"

"Needing in here. The bane of every expecting woman." Not unhappy at all, Rayna stroked her tummy hidden beneath the full gathers of her skirt. "I couldn't catch up with you in the hall. Are you all right? You look warm. You're not feeling well. It's the change of weather."

"No, not the weather." Betsy knew she shouldn't say one word. She loved her friends, but secrets didn't stay secret for long, and… Oh, she couldn't help it! She was bursting to tell. "I was seeing a certain gentleman and—"

"What gentleman? Oh!" Rayna's eyes went wide with shock. "You look like a well-pleasured woman. You haven't been…"

Betsy blushed rosily and nodded. "Please, don't tell anyone."

"This is too good to keep to myself! Wait—I've got to go!" Rayna hurried into the water closet and closed the door behind her. "Are you going to tell me which gentleman?"

"My family hates him."

"That doesn't narrow it down much." Even though she spoke quietly, Rayna's voice echoed in the small room.

Betsy splashed cool water onto her cheeks, but to no

avail. Her face wasn't quite so bright but her eyes glinted with the greatest of happiness. Looking at her swollen lips from hours of Duncan's tender kissing, she realized there was no way to hide the fact that she was dangerously in love. With a man who loved her in return.

What had she asked him? *I love you more than anything. Is that how you love me, too?*

Yes, he'd said, his voice breaking, his hands sliding down her hips and beneath her skirt and—

Her face flamed remembering how he loved her so thoroughly, she'd been changed. She would forever be a part of him.

Betsy frowned in the mirror and splashed more cool water on her cheeks. If she kept remembering making love with him, then she'd never appear demure enough to join the Ladies' Aid weekly meeting.

The door opened and Rayna emerged to wash her hands and splash her face. "That feels good. I suppose it will help me more than you. After all, I haven't just come from my lover's bed. You are a shady type of woman, Betsy, and I'm afraid I can't associate with you any longer."

"I know. I lost all self-respect. I guess that's what happens when a widow goes too long without remarrying."

"It was bound to happen. Sad, but true. So are you going to tell me which gentleman you've chosen? Wait, it's not that furniture store owner, is it? What's his name? Hipps?"

"Hopps. He's on Mama's list of desirable son-in-laws—"

A knock rapped on the outer door and there was Mariah, shaking her head. "I could hear you two through the wall. You'd better not say you're frolicking with Roy Hopps—"

"It's Ray, not Roy and no, it's not him." Betsy shivered. "Never him."

"I used to find incriminating items in his trouser pockets!" Mariah, who'd started the laundry business over a decade ago, obviously had found the same match tins.

"It's not him." She took a deep breath, debating. Oh, she couldn't keep a secret like this from her best friends. But she had to protect this new tender romance. She wasn't ready to share it just yet. But soon. "He's coming to supper tonight. I was out on deliveries and got carried away when I saw him—"

"You mean, when you behaved like a trollop." With a wink, Mariah made a point of looking in both directions down the hall before stepping into the tiny room and closing the door. "He's a customer, isn't he? That's why you've been able to get away with this romance. You're out delivering and picking up laundry and so you have time to dally."

"Tell us," Rayna prodded, releasing several hairpins from Betsy's tangled hair. "Or we can go through your customer list until we guess the right one."

"Oh, I don't know. My family isn't ready to know about this. Not yet." Betsy didn't know what to call the confusing tangle of emotions that felt more like rage…and then sadness. She knew that when the time came, she would need to make a decision between her overbearing family and Duncan. She already knew what that choice would be.

Mariah, efficient as always, grabbed the comb from Betsy's open reticule. "I'd wish you luck, but I know you don't need it. I can see how happy you are."

"I haven't been this happy for so long. I'd almost forgotten what it was like." Betsy knew her friends understood.

Mariah had been a spinster for many painful years caring for her father, and then alone for more years after his death. The right man had transformed her life, and where Mariah had been a quiet, prim spinster, she was now a wife and mother. She smiled. She laughed.

She blushed, as she was doing now. "I can see by the satisfied grin on your face, that you've been…how shall I put this delicately? Testing out your marital candidate?"

"Well, the passionate relationship between a man and wife is extremely important." Betsy felt her face heating, but she didn't care. She knew, unlike her family or the other women in town, her friends would understand.

"Very important." Rayna flushed as she set the hairpins aside and stroked her swollen tummy. "I didn't get this way by accident, but from a lot of practice."

"I miss a lot of things about being married. The emotional bond, you know, when you look across the room and your eyes meet and you know him so well, you know what he's thinking. I miss the companionable evenings and I do miss the passion. Very much."

Betsy didn't know how to speak of the emotions that ran so deep and vast beneath the surface. "I'm just doing my best to be sensible and I'm failing miserably. I just want him."

"I think it's wise. To test out your future husband to make sure he is up to your standards." Mariah bit her bottom lip to keep from laughing, but her eyes were merry as she confessed, "Wifely duties are a very serious matter. You need to know that you will be well satisfied with your husband. Look at all the practice we married women are getting."

Rayna blushed rosily. "Love is a very, uh, thrilling condition."

Mariah's grin spread across her face until she glowed. "Yes, it certainly is, and I seem to have fallen victim to the same malady as Rayna. And all from too much practice being a good and passionate wife."

As Mariah's announcement sank in, a brief, rare silence fell between them. Then Rayna laughed.

"You're expecting?" Betsy couldn't help the flow of happiness for her friend…and it gave her a little hope for herself.

There was no telling what could happen in the future. Five years ago, Mariah had been a spinster living in the same house Betsy was renting, running the laundry business, and alone. Without a husband. A family. Children. And now she was a mother of three, and expecting another child.

Was it too much to hope for a similar kind of future?

The conversation turned to Mariah, to when she was due, and all the excitement that went with such talk. When Betsy's hair was finally tamed and demure, the three of them ambled down the hall, falling quiet outside the auxiliary room's main door. Mama was in that room and she was as sharp-eyed as a hungry eagle.

"Are you sure I look normal?" she whispered.

"There's no way to hide the glow of a woman in love." Rayna leaned close to answer. "Whoever he is, your mother isn't going to approve. But don't let that stop you, all right? Life is too short to spend it alone, not if you've found your heart's match. Don't waste any time, just enjoy the rare gift of love come a second time."

If anyone understood, it was Rayna, who'd buried a husband and mourned him. And found happiness again. Betsy pitched her voice low as she stood behind Mariah, who was opening the door. "It seems too good to be true. There are so many obstacles."

"True love finds a way. Believe."

Rayna's promise remained even after they slipped into their seats behind the long cloth-covered tables. Her words remained strong in Betsy's mind as the meeting progressed and her mother, seated across the room, studied her with knowing eyes.

Betsy hadn't been gone more than a few hours and as the afternoon shadows grew long through the trees, Duncan could no longer pretend he didn't miss her. It was as if she'd taken all the life in him with her and he was an empty shell.

He missed her laughter. He missed her sunny presence. He wished he could keep her here on his silent mountain forever. It was amazing how one vain woman's lie had irrevocably changed his life. Brought him the taste of severe injustice and taught him the brutality and the hurt that lurked within the human spirit.

That was why he was here. Not because he was hiding. But because he'd lost hope entirely. What good could ever come out of a world plagued by that brand of evil?

His grandfather had often said there is justice, it is not swift but it is evenhanded in the end. Through his haze of grief and killing bitterness, he'd retreated.

He would rather live among the wild animals, among predators that hunted and devoured one another, because it made sense. They were protecting their young, their territory or they were hungry. But people…

People were not so logical. He'd had enough of people who enjoyed the harm they caused. The destruction and devastation and death, and all because they could do it. He wanted nothing to do with civilization. With laws and rules and people who said one thing and did another.

And then the Great Spirit had brought him Betsy. There wasn't an ounce of malice in her. She was like the warm winter sun on his face, burning bright and clear regardless of the crusted snow on the ground. The clouds massed and fought, but still the sun found a way to shine through, in thick heavenly rays that could not be conquered.

She'd accepted him. She'd saved him. She'd reminded him what it was like to be alive. Her soft woman's scent remained on his skin, and breathing in the faintest scent made his groin tighten and his soul stir. He'd tried to tell her that her family was never going to allow this, but she hadn't cared.

She'd made her own decision, he realized, and made love to him. Making it clear, as she'd laid back on the table and guided him into her heat, that she'd chosen.

Incredibly, she wanted him. They'd moved together, creating something much more than passion and as he'd watched and felt pleasure roll through her in tight waves, he hadn't been able to tell her the truth.

He'd had more than enough opportunities. Before he'd made love with her, after he'd made love with her. The entire time she'd sparkled in his arms and she'd served them lunch from her big basket, and while he'd been kissing her goodbye, he could have said the words. But for some reason, saying "I was convicted of rape and sent to prison for ten years," didn't roll easily off his tongue.

He was a hard man—hard, but honest. For whatever reason fate had given him a great chance. And he wanted to tell her. He intended to tell her. Hell, he'd started to tell her why her family objected to him so vehemently. But when he'd gazed into her trusting eyes and read the love for him twinkling there, as bright and everlasting as the brightest stars in the sky, he just couldn't make himself say the words he'd known would drive her away for good.

He never wanted to change the way she lit up inside whenever she looked at him. She touched him with immense trust, and she treated him like a man without his godforsaken past.

If Grandfather had lived, the wise old man would have said that the ancestors had been watching over him during those bitter years in prison. Now they had chosen to balance that great wrong. To make right the injustice. To give him back the family that he lost.

While he worked stacking the wood he'd salvaged and cut from the rogue avalanche, he thought. And as he thought, it became clearer. He had two choices. To take what time he could with her and accept that it would end when she found out about his past—which she surely would the instant her overbearing family figured out where she was spending her spare time.

Or he could tell her and hope she would understand. That, as impossible as it was, she would be the one person who could look past the lies and see the man he was. The man he'd always been.

Yes, it was strange how one woman could change everything. Maybe Grandfather had been right. One horrid woman had ruined him. One lovely woman had saved him. It was evenhanded. It was the chance to make right the wrongs of the past. And while it could not be undone, the wound to his spirit could be healed.

He was Duncan Hennessey, Standing Tall, son of Summer Rose, grandson of Gray Wolf. And he would fight for this woman he loved.

He could almost feel his mother's approval as the finest snowflakes kissed his cheek. He could hear his grandfather's voice in the thunder overhead.

And he was made whole.

"Yoo-hoo! Betsy!" Mama may think her false cheer appeared to be genuine.

Betsy wasn't fooled. She'd watched the calculations and the questions pass across her mother's face throughout the meeting that had gone overlong. If Mama noticed anything incriminating, well then good, because she had a few things on her mind to tell Mama.

She waved to her friends, letting them know she was ready. She'd had time to think on the way back to town and then to consider Rayna's words through the nearly two-hour meeting. She accepted her friends' good-luck wishes, but since they didn't know whom she'd been with this afternoon, they couldn't know just how much luck she needed.

No, not luck. It didn't matter how this turned out, if Mama approved or not. Rayna was right. A second chance at finding a good man to love, and who loved her in return, was a rare gift. One she wasn't about to turn away. If she ended up marrying Duncan, then that was up to the two of them to find out. Not for her family to influence.

Or anyone else.

Night was falling, half the stores were closed, their windows dark on Main Street, and it was hard to see the expression on her mother's face. So she had no clue as to how to start the conversation.

Mama took care of that for her. "You. Were. Late. I worried."

"I was perfectly safe."

"I didn't know that! I sat there listening to Harriet Willington go on about how chocolate cakes and cookies were the highest and best-selling items at the last three bake sales, and was I listening? No, I was not! I was trying not to imagine the horrible things that could be happening to my only daughter."

"Nothing happened, Mama."

"I didn't know that. You're driving farther and farther out on your deliveries. Thank the heavens above you're no longer traveling up into those mountains!"

"I have been traveling up into the mountains. To pay my respects to Mr. Hennessey."

"Alone! The least you can do is have one of the boys go with you."

"Mama, the boys are all grown men with lives of their own. Besides, I owe Mr. Hennessey my life. Remember? Since he died saving me from not one but two bears?"

Mama sagged a little, unusual for the always-confident woman. A hand fluttered to her throat. "I have no malice toward that man, that is for sure. I can think of plenty of men who would run from a bear instead of fight to protect a lady. And for that, I am grateful because you are alive and unharmed. It was no small sacrifice he made."

"You sound as if you speak from your heart, Mama."

"You know by now I always do." Lucille Gable was no sentimental sop, but she couldn't hide the emotion making her voice sound thick and her vision blurry. "This has only shown us you must take care. Perhaps you should keep the nearer customers and let some other person take the risks of driving from here to tarnation and back, for what would we all do without our dear Bets?"

"I'm not five years old, Mama. You have noticed, right?"

"You will always be my little baby girl. Now, come to supper tonight. I know you've got to be lonely, so I've invited nice Mr. Landers to join us—"

"I'm not interested in Mr. Landers." Poor Mama, she meant well.

But there was no chance Mama could know that the bachelor she'd invited to supper was having an affair with a married woman in the next town. Betsy had found a love letter from the unscrupulous woman in his pocket, and she'd done her best not to read more than the first few lines. "I have someone I would love to bring to supper sometime."

"A man?" Mama royally thanked the family's driver for offering her a hand up into the back seat of the fringed surrey. "Oh, praise the heavens! At last! It's Mr. Rutgers from the bank, isn't it? Oh, I know he has immense respect for you."

Mr. Rutgers from the bank had a gambling problem—she'd found the IOUs in the breast pocket of one of his best jackets. "No. He's a customer of mine. That's how I came to know him. He saved my life, as it turned out, the mountains are very perilous. I am in love with him and it seems he feels the same way."

"More danger! You will be the death of me. That's it. Marry this man, settle down in the carriage house on our property and then I shan't have to spend my days worrying and worrying."

"He is not a banker or a lawyer or a businessman, but I want you to like him."

"I put up with Charlie." Lucille opened her mouth, considering staging an argument, then seemed to think better of it. In the lantern light swinging from the surrey frame, there was only concern and no deception on her face as she seemed to soften for an uncharacteristic moment. "I would give anything to see my little girl smile again, not a little smile, but big and beaming, the way you used to. Charlie was not my choice, but he made you happy."

"Happy is what matters, Mama. It's a rare gift, to truly be happy in a marriage."

"Yes, I had that gift once. I desperately want it for you. So if you must choose another working man, please, don't even tell me if he's another farmer! I will keep my mouth shut and tolerate him. But only for your happiness."

"Better than you did for Charlie?"

"I didn't say I would like him. I didn't say I would speak with him. I said I would tolerate him." Mama smiled. "Just be happy, my good girl. And next time you come from this man's bed, make sure you stop smiling so wide. Because you've got half the Ladies' Aid wondering what you were up to."

"No good, as usual."

Mama shook her head, ordered the driver to depart, and blew Betsy a kiss. "Tomorrow night for supper. Be there or I will hunt you down."

"But—" There was no use arguing. Her mother had turned her attention elsewhere intentionally, so her royal edict would be obeyed instead of argued with.

Her mother! It was hard not to love a woman who cared so deeply about you, but Betsy could only rub at the tension gathering at the back of her neck. The first step had been made, and Mama didn't seem too opposed to meeting Duncan. She didn't know that he was still alive. So that meant—

A man on foot led his gelding by the reins from the shadowed alley that stretched behind the church. The hitching area was empty, except for her horse and buggy. Most of the members of the Ladies' Aid had hurried off to their homes, where supper and children and husbands waited.

Alone with a stranger in the gathering dark. Her

palms turned cold as the stranger stopped between her and her horse and buggy, a tall, square powerhouse of a man that looked strangely familiar. "Duncan? What are you doing here? I thought you hated to come to town."

"I do. I came to talk to you." He didn't look happy. No, he seemed as grim as the night, as cold as the bitter flakes drifting down from a frozen sky.

That didn't bode well, she realized, as he kept his distance, this man she had intimately loved only a few hours before.

Inside she felt as desolate as the night as she worked the reins loose from the iron bar at the hitching post. "My house isn't far away."

He didn't answer. In fact, he'd become one with the dark shadows, and it was as if he were already gone. As if he'd finally turned into shadow and night and there was nothing she could do to draw him back to her.

Chapter Eighteen

"What do you want to talk about, that you'd come all this way? And while it's snowing?" She was like the snow, fragile and delicate and white, so achingly white. In the colorless world of nightfall, her light-gray coat glowed like platinum and her matching hood framed her angel's face like a halo.

It made him ache to look at her, this woman he loved, the woman he'd possessed and claimed with his body and his soul. The one female he'd trusted above all else.

Her words came back to him, a comfort he clung to like a child's favorite blanket, his only reassurance on this cold night where decent people had scurried from his path. He doubted they knew anything about him, only that he was different. An outsider. An outcast.

He feared it wasn't his bitterness as much as the tarnish of prison that he could never wear off. *If it's real love, it can't break.* That's what she'd said. That's what she'd told him. That she would love him no matter what.

Now was the test. The time to know if her love was real. Or if any love, no matter how true and rare, could stand this test without shattering.

He feared he already knew how this would go, but when there was a war and his country needed him, he fought for the Union. When his mother found herself homeless and abandoned by her first white husband, he'd settled down, started a business and taken care of her.

When a spoiled little rich girl had lied, he hadn't run. He'd faced the vigilante's justice and then a trial with a jury who'd already made up their minds. He'd served time and he'd been released.

He was no coward, no quitter, no fop that would rather run than fight.

Even if that fight would cost him Betsy's love.

She twinkled like the stars in the heavens. How could it be that no other man had snatched her up and made her his wife? How could it be possible that this amazing creature brightened in his presence? That she looked to him with love and trust and came to him with her hands out, ready to take his. Expectation lighting her up.

It was all going to end. He knew it.

He should say the words. Just spit it out. It didn't have to be pretty. It didn't have to be nice. It just had to be honest. The truth, plain and simple.

No embellishment, no explanations, just the stark facts. And then he'd better prepare for her to hate him. To shudder at the thought of letting a man like him touch her intimately, love her tenderly, and dream of cherishing her forever.

"That was your mother?" he found himself saying instead. Coward, he wanted to call himself, but how could any man, regardless of how strong, knowingly say anything that would cause her pain?

"How long were you watching? It was odd that I didn't know you were there. You are…so distant. I can feel you, isn't that strange?"

"No, because I can feel you, too."

"I can't now."

"No." How could he tell her he'd made himself as frozen as the night. As empty. As dark. "I would not be a man, or what a man ought to be, if I don't tell you the truth."

"What truth?" Her hands found his and her touch was as startling as lightning from a clear blue sky. As snow in June. As a twister pointing from the clouds to the sky and touching down without warning.

He was not so well shielded, after all. "I'm not a little in love with you."

"You're not?" Her brow wrinkled.

He leaned his forehead to hers, an intimate connection, tender as she gazed into his eyes and the worry lines fell away. He searched for the right words, words for feelings he could not describe or name. Only wish he didn't feel.

"And I'm not just a lot in love with you."

"Me, either." As if she understood, her lush mouth curved into an inviting grin. "You are a gift. You know that, don't you? When I never thought I would ever feel this way again, I found you. A man I love more than anything. I didn't know it was possible to love someone so much."

Hell, she was killing him. As if shot in the gut and mortally bleeding, his knees turned to water and it was all he could do to stay standing. To force the confession from his soul. "Yes."

It was only one word, but her breath caught like a sob and her fingertips brushed his chin, pulling him to her kiss.

He hungered for her. Not out of lust, it went far deeper than that. It was love overwhelming him, flooding him with a fierce need to make her his again and again. To hold her tight while he could. Before she knew the real Duncan Hennessey, past and scars and all, and could not accept him.

He'd seen her mother. One of those proper society matrons who judged no one ever to be good enough. She was the kind of woman who'd been the most hateful to him those long years ago. In another town, in another time, but he would never forget the outraged mothers who'd wanted him hung and only after a good beating for daring to harm a judge's daughter.

And not only because of the rape; those women had made it seem doubly worse that he was a half-breed, a man without social or financial clout. A working man with nothing but a storefront and a savings account at the town bank.

Betsy's mother was the kind of woman who condemned without mercy and if she knew of his past, there was no way Betsy would be standing before him alone and unguarded by all of her brothers and half the town.

"You've ridden all that way and you've got to be freezing. Your hands are ice." She kissed his knuckles, her lips caressing and nibbling and sucking.

All proper woman, but warmhearted and passionate, too. He swallowed, trying not to remember exactly how passionate, how tenderly she'd shown him how much she loved him, for remembering would only make it harder.

"Do you want to come home with me? You can warm up by the fire in the parlor and I'll warm up some stew and cornbread."

"What I have to say won't take long."

"Something *is* wrong, and I have a suspicion I know what." She could feel the hurt rolling off him like vapor from an icy pond and she wasn't about to leave him alone. Mama might be innocent of the cruelty her family had shown him, but that didn't mean Joshua hadn't decided to intervene.

Well, she knew exactly how to handle him. As for Duncan, he was like a warrior of old: powerful and silent and invincible.

A real man, who'd stolen every last bit of her heart.

"Come home with me."

"Home with you? Alone?" There were houses lined up in orderly rows, their windows golden rectangles, and they seemed so close. He felt so closed in.

But it wasn't the structures or the town. It was him, twisted up until his skin felt so tight he was ready to pop right out of it. He'd felt like this while he waited for the jury's verdict. It had taken them exactly forty-five minutes to declare him guilty. Despite his alibi, despite the discrepancies in the young lady's story. Truth didn't matter, he'd learned that the hard way.

What had Betsy said to him? *You're such a good man. What possible bad thing could you have done?*

Words that had given him faith to hold her hand in his and to know there was nothing he would ever do to hurt her.

She had to know the truth about him. He didn't want it coming from her overbearing brother or that fierce granny of hers. She deserved to hear the story from him, and the freedom and time to decide for herself what she believed. If the words she'd said were ones she meant.

And if not…

Then at least they both knew. They could end it here, before they became more involved and before it was even harder to walk away. To minimize the pain and the heartbreak.

"No, I don't want to be alone with you. This is fine. There's no one around and this won't take long."

"You are starting to scare me. What's happened?" Her hand stroked his chest, as if he were a cat to calm. In the shadows, silhouetted by the streets of houses, he could see the round worry of her eyes. "Did you hear what my mother said?"

"No, this isn't about your mother, but it is about your family. There's no other way to do this, and I know it's going to hurt you. And I'm sorry."

"Are you ending this? Please, don't tell me that. I meant what I said this afternoon and I thought you did, too."

He could feel how he'd hurt her, and it was killing him. There was no way he could let her think he didn't love her. "Being with you is the very best thing that has happened in my life. I can't tell you—"

There were no words, only actions, and so he kissed her one last sweet time. The brush of their lips, the mix of their very breaths, the sweep of their souls was like touching heaven. He savored her as long as he could. Love beat in his heart as he broke away.

"Remember how I told you that I have a past I'm not proud of?" He stroked her chin with the pad of his thumb, doing anything to touch her, to remain connected to her.

She leaned into his caress, feeling the connection, too. "And I said what possible bad thing could you have done?"

The way she said it was as if she saw the real Duncan Hennessey, the man he'd always been. It was a heartening experience to have someone so good, someone who cared truly for him and saw the truth in him.

But would her opinion hold when she knew more?

Please, don't fail me, he pleaded as he took a breath. "You hardly know anything about me. About what I've done. A while back I spent ten years in the territorial prison."

There. He'd said it. He wasn't waiting around to see the look of horror on her face. He already knew how she would recoil. It was predictable. What woman on earth would want a man like him? He was hard. He was obstinate. He was cold. A convicted felon, a rapist, had no chance of a normal life. None at all.

He didn't blame her one bit for the shock dragging down her jaw. For the way she stammered, unable to speak, too confused by what he'd said.

"I don't understand." She shook her head, but it didn't clear it of the thunder crashing through her ears so loud, she couldn't think. Only it wasn't thunder, it was her pulse and she couldn't seem to take in enough breath. "Y-you were in prison?"

"Yep. I was sentenced and sent to the hard labor camp up near Deer Lodge. The quarry, where I worked from sunup to sundown every day for ten hellish years. I paid my debt, and I don't intend to go back."

Jail. Ten years of hard labor. It didn't make sense. She couldn't get her mind to think. She'd expected him to have overheard what her mother said, about the banker and tolerating whomever it was Mama had chosen.

But not this. She hadn't expected him to say this. "Prison?"

"Yes. I'm a convict."

She said nothing more, and that said everything. He couldn't wait for the shock to wear off and her disgust to sink in, so before she could say anything that would break him, he walked away.

She didn't call out for him.

He didn't expect her to. He kept going, leading his gelding down the shadowed road, his boots crunching in the accumulating snow, until he reached the main street. Looking back, she was still standing in the lot next to her buggy. Snow crowned her. Made her shimmer like an angel in the background light from all the windows up and down the street.

You disappointed me, Betsy. His soul throbbed with a pain that felt worse than defeat. More encompassing than sorrow. He'd lost his future; he'd lost more.

He'd never hold her again. Never bask in the cheer of her smile. He'd never know what it would be to call her his wife. To hold her in his arms at night while they drifted off to sleep. Never know what it was like to be loved, truly loved.

It was a pretty high price to pay, and to keep paying. But she'd behaved about the way he'd expected. She was a proper town lady. Her mother had appeared to be a matron of society in her finely tailored clothes and expensive surrey and with her personal driver. Betsy Hunter was a rich woman's daughter, and women like that didn't marry men like him. Loners. Outcasts. Convicts.

It was a good thing he was made of steel. Nothing could hurt him. Not anymore.

He mounted up, nosed the gelding into the frigid wind and rode through the snow and the night where no moon lit his path. Where no stars shone on the polished nightscape.

It was a dark night, cold and mean. He rode until he was like the night, desolate, and without a speck of hope to save him.

Chapter Nineteen

The dense shadows of nightfall were made longer by the snow falling around her, cold pieces of ice she could not feel. She could not move. She could not think. She watched as Duncan walked away, back straight, without looking back. His confession reverberated in her mind over and over again. *I spent ten years in the territorial prison.*

Prison? He was in prison? She simply could not believe it, and yet he'd been very clear. Prison. How could that be? He radiated strength and integrity. While she'd never known a convict before, she knew Duncan. She'd felt his heart, touched his soul. If she closed her eyes and became very still she could feel his emotions, as if they were her own. All she felt was one big black glacier of pain and misery.

He was trying to drive her away, just as he'd done all along. And this was why. He didn't believe she could ever look beyond his past. And who could?

A criminal. No, she couldn't see it. Maybe she didn't want to see it. But no matter how hard she tried, she could not imagine him doing something so wrong or illegal. Not the same man who made such beautiful furniture. Nor the man who kept volumes of English poetry in his log cabin. Certainly not the man who had opened up to her and loved her with devoted tenderness.

It wasn't only that she couldn't imagine Duncan a criminal; it was that he had the heart of a poet and the soul of an artist, despite the growling and snarling and the solitary life in the wilderness.

He'd lost his family. He'd lost ten years of his life. The question was, why?

She could not love a bad man. Could she?

He'd gone. There was no one to ask but the snow tumbling down everywhere, making the world feel more cold and heartless as she climbed into her buggy.

All the way home, his confession troubled her. All the while unhitching the buggy and stabling Morris, she felt as frozen as the winter landscape. Her heart ached from disbelief, shock or disappointment, she couldn't say. Only that the house looked so dark as she latched the stable door behind her and trudged through the yard.

The hinges on the garden gate gave a mournful squeal and she had to give it a hard shove to knock aside the wet snow that had accumulated so she could squeeze past. If a storm wasn't blowing in to stay and there had still been even a drop of daylight to see by, she'd have headed out of town as fast as Morris could go. She would have hunted down Duncan and demanded the answers to her questions. What had he done? How could the man she loved be a convicted criminal?

She'd felt his heart. She'd touched his spirit and she *knew.* Whatever it was didn't matter. Whatever he'd done had happened a long time ago, obviously. It suddenly all made sense, how he kept away from people, how he'd found contentment living on the mountainside. How he kept everyone at a far distance.

Whatever he'd been as a much younger man, he had changed. Whatever had happened, maybe it was what Mariah had said, how he'd lost his family and that had changed him for the better. The Duncan Hennessey she knew was a hardworking and honest man who made beautiful furniture, wasn't afraid of hungry and wounded bears and who read Shakespeare during the long cold evenings in his home.

That was the Duncan she loved and trusted. This Duncan had spoken with shame of his past. He feared it would drive her away—and it probably should. Heaven knew that if Mama ever got wind of this information, she'd have a conniption that would be the talk of the town for the next twenty years.

Well, she doesn't have to know. No one does. Duncan had paid for his crime. He obviously had become a good, strong man and maybe that spoke even better of him. Perhaps that showed that he'd overcome great mistakes and circumstances, and while he might be bitter, he was a man who could love and protect and, when he touched her, there was only tenderness in his hands, in his voice, in his warrior's soul.

Duncan had expected her to reject him, she could see that now. And he was wrong.

Love still burned for him, more brightly than ever. She needed to tell that to Duncan. She'd have to wait until morning to see him, and she didn't know how she was going to even pretend to sleep. Not when she could feel his pain. Not when she knew he was hurting, believing he was alone in the world.

He wasn't. He wouldn't be, not ever again.

Determined, she trudged through the snow toward her dark house. In the thick blackness the snow cast a ghostly glow to the roof and eaves and the rails of the porch where the precipitation clung. A man's shadow huddled on one of the chairs she'd bought in the furniture store. A prickling crawled down her nape and beneath her collar and a cold uneasiness sharpened her senses. It wasn't Duncan. Whoever it was he remained as still as stone, and in the dark she couldn't see his face, but she recognize the tang of pipe smoke lingering in the air and the hunch of wide shoulders.

"Joshua?"

He didn't move. He sat as still as ever. Something was wrong. Terribly wrong. Panic shot through her. And launched her up the steps. "Is Mama all right? Granny? She's not sick, is she—"

"No." His answer came like a single echo of thunder. "Ma said something interesting when I ran into her at the mercantile."

Oh, here it comes. Betsy braced herself for her brother's fury because in truth, he was going to get a little bit of hers in return. "All of my life, I've looked up to you, Joshua Monroe Gable. You've been my big brother. My confidant. My comfort when I lost Charlie. And my very first laundry customer."

He slowly rose, unfolding his over-six-foot frame

from the shadows. "Don't you find fault with me, I know that's where you're going—"

"Damn right I am!" She didn't care if she interrupted him or that he was twice her size, she kept coming, ready to knock him off the porch if that's what it took. "You left him there to fend for himself. When he was too wounded to do more than breathe! You left him!"

"Do you see why I did? I knew this would happen! That you'd develop this heroic view of him and he's nothing but a common—"

"Don't you dare say it! He's served time, I know, he told me. But he saved me, and not just from the bear. You and Granny had no right to abandon him—" She wanted to grab her porch broom, the old one she used for sweeping the snow off the steps and whack him with it, not to hurt him, but to knock some sense into him. "It was wrong what you did, and you had no right. He could have died. He certainly suffered—"

"That would be too good for the likes of him. Suffering! Ha!" Dark rage poured off Joshua and, as if he'd guessed her desire, he grabbed the broom by the battered handle and marched past her, his boots slamming into the boards, punctuating his fury. "He's a rapist! Did he tell you that?"

"What?"

"A rapist. According to Granny, who'd been visiting her sister at the time, it was all over the local papers down south. He'd helped himself to a pretty young lady, a judge's daughter, and the law showed him no mercy, just as he deserved. They ought to have hung him, a monster like that, but they sent him to prison over at Deer Lodge."

"The hard-labor prison?"

"Not hard enough. He served his time, they let him out when he ought to be caged like the animal he is. And to think you'd been driving out to deliver his laundry. Think what could have happened! What he could have done to you! Do you see now why we did it?"

Her knees gave out and she sank weakly onto the nearby chair. The chair Duncan had made with his big, gentle hands. Gentle hands she'd experienced on nearly every inch of her body. The tender caresses, the knowing strokes and the loving touches.

No, it can't be true.

"All the times you could have been assaulted, and we didn't even know the danger. To think he could have hurt you and worse, and we might never have known what had become of you. You can never see him again. You see now why you must stay away from him?" Joshua savagely swiped the top step with the broom and the wooden part that held the bristles flew off the handle.

"It's broken. You have to be careful with it."

"Then buy a new one that works!" Joshua's temper was burgeoning as he stormed down the steps, grabbed the broken part from the snow and bent to twist it back onto the wooden handle. "Damn it, I'll buy you one myself."

He tossed both the bristles and the handle into the dark reaches of the yard. "I need to hear the words, Betsy. Tell me you won't go anywhere near that man. I couldn't live with myself if I let something happen to you."

"Oh, Joshua. The very worst thing has happened—

No, he didn't touch me." She stood, trembling with shock, but she was not weak. No, she was not afraid or heartbroken or confused. It was all very clear. "Did you tell this to Mama?"

"Tell her? Hell, no, it would have sent her into the vapors. We all love you. We want what's best for you."

"I know you do." She pressed a kiss to his cheek, her poor, misdirected brother. "But I'm not a little girl. I'm thirty years old. I can take care of myself. Go home, and don't tell anyone about this."

"You're one of those softhearted types, Betsy. You're not going to go see him, right? You understand how serious this is? He's a monster, and there's no way I'm ever going to let him hurt you."

"Don't worry, Josh." She stepped away, lost in the night, overcome by the truth.

She saw it all so clearly, what had happened. That Duncan had come to her tonight with his confession, and it shone in an entirely new light. All that he hadn't said weighed on her now as she leaned against the railing, snow wetting through her coat, but she didn't care.

"There is no more danger," she told him. "There is no need to worry. Just leave me alone."

"You cared about him?" Joshua sounded incredulous.

"No, I was in love with him." There was no possible way her brother could understand. He'd never been in true love, the kind that came not from the physical, but from the soul. So he could not understand what she'd lost.

She put her face in her hands and wept. Wept for the man who'd walked away from her. Grieved for what could never be.

Chapter Twenty

It was a sloppy and nasty mess. Duncan wiped his rain-drenched hair off his forehead and positioned the wood chunk with the awl. Last night's snow had turned to rain and until winter set in for good, the yard would be mud. The snow melting on the roof was going to keep sliding down in dangerous chunks he would have to watch out for, and everywhere sang the musical drip of water. Off the trees, off the stable, plopping into the mud puddles and the stream made by so much runoff gurgling everywhere.

He'd had a bad night. He hadn't been able to sleep at all. He'd woken to a dismal day and worked in the downpour since sunup, not that he could have seen the sun then or for a single moment since.

He hefted the sledgehammer to his shoulder and, summoning up all the strength he possessed, swung. The iron head rammed the awl into the wood grain, tearing the heavy wood chunk into two smaller parts. Smaller, in that it would take several dozen swings of the ax to split the hunk into manageable sizes for the stove.

Puffing in the cool damp air, he bent to kick the pieces out of the way for splitting later and dragged another log into position. That's when he heard it. The faint *squeak, squeak, squeak* of a buggy wheel. Of Betsy's buggy wheel.

She ought to get that thing fixed and oiled.

He turned his back to her. He had better things to do than to listen to her tirade. Yeah, he already knew why she was here. She'd come to give him a piece of her mind for deceiving her. For being a criminal. For a man like him daring to touch a good woman like her.

Hell, he agreed with her. Her silence had said everything last night. Her shock had cut him to the quick.

So much for unconditional love.

Bitterness filled him up like fouled, black water, and he turned away. Tried hard to find some reason to hate her, because hate was a good shield. Anger was one, too. Except, how could he be mad at her? How could he hate the sunshine of a woman who'd healed him?

She'd come to say her piece, he knew women had a knack for doing that, but the truth was, something within him had changed. The bleak suffocating pain that had haunted him for half his adult life was gone.

He'd found the man he used to be before prison and discovering his mother's grave. A man who was more than bitterness, more than what circumstances had made him. He stood taller now. No matter how others looked at him or what they called him, he knew the truth down deep in his soul. It was time he let go of that great wound. He knew he was no criminal. He was no rapist. He could not be broken.

The squeaking sound approached and he kept his back to her. He didn't need to look at her. It was over. There was no sense in stirring up longing he could never satisfy and love he could never express. He sent the sledgehammer into the awl and the steeled wedge cracked open the enormous log. Rain sluiced down the back of his neck and wet his shirt from the inside as well as the outside.

He didn't turn when the buggy stopped squealing and he could sense the radiant light of her presence. He just bit out while he kept on working. "What do you want? I hope to hell you didn't come for my laundry."

"Uh, no. It's not my usual delivery day."

He retrieved the awl and positioned it, tapping it into the center of the log round where sap seeped like blood. He kept his heart hard and his eye on the wedge of steel and he pulled back the hammer. "I have no time to listen to a woman's idle chatter. I'm firing you as my laundry lady. Get outta here."

With all the agony of his broken heart, he heaved the sledgehammer through the air and onto the target. Metal screamed and wood ripped apart. Huffing, he didn't look at her. He erased her from his thoughts, from him senses and from his memory.

"Well, I refuse to be fired."

"Too bad." He remembered to count to ten, but all he could see was red. Anger built in his head like steam in an engine, roiling ever hotter. "How much do I owe you?"

"You always pay ahead. You know that."

"So then what's keeping you?" He didn't bother to wait for her reply. "I've got work to do."

He heard her sharp intake of breath. He'd hurt her. He wasn't proud of it. In fact, agony ripped through his belly as he did what he had to do.

But he was no longer a dead man who was still walking. He was achingly alive and it was all Betsy's fault. She'd done this to him, and like a bear out of hibernation, he could feel the cold, feel the pain and emptiness that his life had been. He tossed down the ax, sending the dangerous edge deep into the earth, and marched away. When everything within him screamed for him to go to her, he forced his feet to carry him in the opposite direction.

"Wait, Duncan! I brought a peace offering." When she should have been furious with him, when her lovely voice ought to have been dripping with contempt, her words carried a hint of humor.

Humor? That didn't make any sense. Puzzled, he turned and there she was, holding a strawberry pie. The golden crust oozed the sweet fruit through the flowers cut into the covering.

"Do you have to put flowers on everything?" he growled.

"I don't know how to cut a bear into pastry, or I would have done that in honor of your charming personality." Her chin thrust up and there was a challenge in her beautiful eyes, not hatred. Her mouth was lush and bow-shaped, as if anticipating his kiss, not pulled down into a grimace of loathing.

She was everything he loved, everything he desired and everything he'd hungered for through years too lonely to describe or to think about. "Why are you bringing a peace offering?"

"Because of how I treated you yesterday when you came to me. When you came to tell me about your past." She set the pie back in the buggy and wiped her hands on her skirt and she came to him.

A roar filled his ears and he felt as if he were shattering from the inside out. "I don't understand. Why are you here?"

"I brought a strawberry pie. It's probably not equal to the way I behaved yesterday, but I was simply so surprised. And then, after speaking with Joshua, I knew why."

His head bowed forward and he stood back straight, arms at his sides, legs braced, looking like a man who knew he'd lost everything and still, if nothing else, had the pride to stand upright. "I don't want your pie."

"In a way, my strawberry pie started this. I thought it would be appropriate."

"To end it?" He scoffed, and it was a bitter sound.

But it didn't ring true. His pain fractured through her and she dared to lay her hand on the center of his back. She felt the snap and crackle of attraction and the stir of her soul. This man was the one she would love and take good care of for the rest of her life.

"No, I told you this is a peace offering. Because I need to ask you to forgive me. I should have said to you then, Duncan, 'that doesn't make sense.' How could a man like you, so noble and true, have done anything to land you in a hard-labor prison?"

He remained like granite. As still as the mountains in winter and silent beneath sheets of glacial ice. He didn't even appear to be breathing.

"But when Joshua said you'd been convicted of rape, I knew for absolute certain."

He squeezed his eyes so tight they hurt. He didn't have to listen; he simply had to appear to be listening. Let her say her piece, take her pie and leave forever.

But her hand on his back made it impossible to stay as cold as stone. His spirit turned to her like the earth to the sun and he waited for her hateful words because he deserved them.

He should have told her from the start. Then they never would have fallen in love and became lovers and he wouldn't be standing here, with everything that ever mattered in his life crumbled to bits for the second time—no, the third time in his life.

"There is no way you could have done anything so terrible."

Hope lurched in his chest even as he knew he had to have imagined what she'd said. Everyone save for his mother had taken one look at him and judged him to be guilty.

"I know the man you are."

She swirled around him, her skirts brushing his ankles as she wrapped her arms around him and laid her cheek upon his chest. Her tangled curls bounced and shimmered and he went rigid, not believing. He simply couldn't believe.

"You were innocent. You would never hurt a woman, and I know because you were willing to give your life for mine, the laundry lady you detested— I noticed you didn't like me so much at first."

"You've got that wrong," he ground out, not believing this could be real, but wrapping his arms around her tight anyway. "I loved you from the very first moment I saw you in that frilly buggy of yours and you wearing a yellow bonnet and yellow dress. And I knew in a million lifetimes that I could never have you. Ever."

"You have me now and forever."

"You believe me."

"I'll always believe in you, my hero, my love."

She rose up on tiptoes, offering her kiss, and he came to her, slanting his lips over hers. Tenderly opening her mouth with his tongue to slide in deep and slow.

She broke away, her gaze searching his face, and when she spoke, it was the truth he heard, truth he could put faith in. "You and I have been alone countless times, and you worked so hard to drive me away. When we were lovers, from the first moment you touched me, I was astounded by your tenderness. Your gentleness. You have a poet's soul, my rugged rocky mountain man. I know. Because I can feel you inside my heart."

"I love you." Overcome, he held on tight to this woman who was his very life. "Marry me. Be my wife."

"I was hoping you would ask. I would love to marry you."

"But what about your family? They can't approve of me."

"I can take care of my family. You are the rarest of gifts and they'll come to love you as I do, or I'll hurt them." She winked, but her words of faith and loyalty and love left him in disbelief.

But this was real, as rare and perfect as a dream come true. Overcome, he buried his face in her hair.

Blinding joy burned within him. As the rain pounded down ever harder, the cool, cleansing drops seemed strong enough to wash away the past. To erode the years of bitterness and sadness.

Grandfather would think it fitting, Duncan thought, that one woman of pure goodness had given him a new life. One of hope and love and family. Duncan Hennessey, loner and mountain man, was no longer alone.

He thought he felt his grandfather's approval in the cold hand of the wind that seemed to push them in the direction of the house. Betsy grabbed the pie, he opened the door, and they were inside the sheltered warmth with the view of forest and mountains surrounding them. Fire snapped in the hearth as they shivered together.

As he pulled her down onto the bear rug before the warm flames, he kissed her long and deep. He was no poet, he did not have the words to tell her how dear she was to him. That she shone like a light that blinded him to all else, and from her long hair to her enchanting sweetness to her ardent passion, he adored and loved her. No, love was too small of a word for what he felt for her.

If he could spend his life with her, waken beside her every morning and spend the golden moments of each day with her, then the wrongs of his past were worth it. Because every step of sadness had brought him to her. To the magic of true love that nothing could break. Nothing.

He had no words for his feelings, so he kissed her again with all his heart, so she could feel it. So she could feel his steadfast love for her, the woman who had changed his life.

Epilogue

Later that evening

Betsy didn't bother to knock on the back door of her childhood home, mostly because she recognized Joshua in the window, straining to see through the evening shadows the tall mountain of a man leading a trembling Morris to the stable. Duncan would be kept busy putting up the horse for a few minutes, and that was about the time she needed to make her point.

The moment she pushed open the door, the warmth and aroma of the kitchen wrapped around her like a warm blanket. Thousands of memories of her childhood rolled through her, of Mama in the kitchen and of Pa coming home from work at the bank. Of her brothers scraped or bleeding or sporting a broken arm or two, since growing boys would be boys.

This was the kind of home she and Duncan would have one day, one filled with memories of decades. A home she and Duncan could grow old in together, in their hideaway cabin in the forest. Where their children and grandchildren could visit, boldly walking in the door without knocking, for they were coming home.

Mama was whipping potatoes in a giant kettle and asking Anya to check on the buttermilk biscuits that ought to be done. The moment Mama spotted her only daughter, the happiness lit her up like sunshine in December. "It's about time, young lady. And twenty-two minutes late! I was about to send the boys out for you. Come make your mother happy and give me a kiss."

"As soon as I'm done talking with my lovely brother Joshua." Betsy unhooked her hood, focusing her attention on Joshua.

He didn't even have the grace to look repentant. He was working up a good mad by the looks of it. His mouth was twisted into a premature frown and the tendons stood out in his thick neck. His eyes spit fire as he took her by the wrist and pulled her into the dining room, where crystal and china glinted in the lamplight. "How dare you bring that man here to our mother's house?"

"Easy. He's proposed and I've accepted. Isn't that wonderful news? We're going to announce it at dinner, so don't spoil the surprise for Mama."

The muscles in Joshua's jaw spasmed and a tick beat right along with his pulse. "Have. You. Lost. Your. *Mind?*"

"No. Duncan was falsely accused, and if you don't believe me, I don't care. That is how you will treat him. He is a wonderful man to me and I love him. I'm warning you, Joshua, don't ruin this chance I have for happiness. Love comes around rare enough in life the first time. Mama has said she'll accept him, and I expect you to do the same." She pitched her voice a little louder, in the direction of the archway into the parlor. "And you, as well, Granny."

"Ha! That will be the day." The older woman creaked out of the chair, troubled by her rheumatism that strangely came on strong whenever it was convenient for her. "I'm just a poor, sick old lady, and—"

"Too bad. I cannot forgive what you did to Duncan, leaving him when he was so wounded, but I think I will be able to forgive you if you treat him with the respect that is due my husband for all the happy years of our marriage to come."

"He's already had a bad influence on you." Joshua's jaw was clenched so tight it was amazing he could squeeze out any words at all. "I intend to set this straight."

"No, you will not. As far as I know, you two are the only ones who have realized Duncan's history, or at least been mean enough to bring up a very painful event in his life. You will remain silent, both of you, and never tell another living soul. Because he is not the only one in this house with secrets."

Joshua went pale. "What do you mean?"

"I have been washing your clothes for a long while now. And yours, too, Granny. It's amazing what an innocent laundry lady comes across while checking the pockets of the garments before she washes them. All I'm going to say is this: if you want your secrets kept, then you'll keep Duncan's."

"I have no secrets!" Joshua turned as red as a boiled beet.

"Oh, of course not. Let me just go tell Mama—"

"All right." He stomped out, clearly not happy, pushing his way around the table to the refuge of the parlor's hearth.

"I suppose you don't have any secrets, either, right, Granny?"

Grandmother Gable took a long cool look at the big man who'd just came in from the cold. Duncan Hennessey was all man, handsome and strong and noble, and there was no mistaking it. Or the love that warmed his dark gaze when he looked upon his lady love.

"He's at least good-looking," Granny conceded. "A man is such trouble and a bane to a woman's existence, he ought to at least be pleasing to the eye."

"I'll take that as a congratulations on my upcoming wedding. Thanks, Granny." Betsy pressed a kiss to her tough old grandma's cheek. "You'll like him, once you get to know him. I promise."

The old woman grumbled something beneath her breath and reached into her skirt pocket for her tobacco.

Duncan. His gaze collided with hers across the length of the kitchen, where kettles boiled and biscuits steamed and the gravy bubbled up, causing Mama to come rushing to the servant's aid. James and his wife had arrived, and Jordan was ambling down the stairs, yawning and groggy from his nap, the lazy bum, and joy filled her up like water in a cup, spilling over and over without end.

She walked into Duncan's arms, this man she would forever love, and wasn't surprised at all to feel their hearts were beating in synchrony. They took in breath at the same moment.

"We're going to live happily ever after now," she told him. "All you have to do is believe."

"I already do." He took her hand and sealed his words with an everlasting kiss.

* * * * *

He was right behind her. Vision gave her a particular feel as a hand reached for her hair. She shook her head sharply. The hand missed. When it came again she ducked and it grabbed empty air.

Deep in a flickering foresight, she saw him move, right before he did. She sidestepped. He lunged. She stopped suddenly, and turned in place. He stumbled past.

He froze where he stood, looking at her. He understood now, she could see from his expression. As he was considering what to do next, vision told her to go, and she did, turning to run, glancing back as she stumbled ahead on the road.

He took the bow off his back. A moment later she felt a pressure, a craving to stop, to step to the right, to brush a particular tree trunk as she passed, so she did. An arrow hissed by her ear, sinking into the ground beyond.

She launched away from the tree, a sprint forward, dodging bushes, running as fast as she could.

An arrow through the air, a finger width from her neck.

Suddenly she felt light-headed, giddy. The future knew where he would aim better than he did, and the future was hers. She sprinted past trees, bushes, mind jumping between now and a heartbeat ahead.

He was following, but he had to slow to put an arrow to his bow, take aim, and shoot, and he fell behind as she ran.

The pressure again. She stepped to the left, heard the arrow sink into a nearby tree.

Then something shifted. The next moment narrowed to a pinpoint, and the dark wall returned. Two options unfolded: an arrow through her ribs, or a fall to the ground.

She let herself fall . . .

The Seer

Sonia Orin Lyris

THE SEER

Copyright © 2016 by Sonia Orin Lyris

A Baen Books

Baen Publishing Enterprises
P.O. Box 1403
Riverdale, NY 10471
www.baen.com

ISBN: 978-1-4814-8237-0

Cover art by Sam Kennedy
Map by Randy Asplund

First Baen mass market paperback printing, February 2017

Distributed by Simon & Schuster
1230 Avenue of the Americas
New York, NY 10020

Library of Congress Cataloging-in-Publication Data:
    2015039679

Printed in the United States of America

10 9 8 7 6 5 4 3 2 1

Dedication
✠ ✠ ✠
For Devin

The Seer

Chapter One

The tall man dropped five silver falcons onto the rough wooden table. The coins clinked against each other, silver faces bright in the light of the single candle that Dirina had just sparked to flame.

"I want answers," he said.

Her hand went toward the coins as if of its own volition. She pulled it back, tucked it under the blanket wrapped tight around her shoulders.

If he wanted answers, he wanted Amarta, asleep with the baby in the small back room of the shack.

Her gaze went to the bright coins. Three were bird-side up; the king's profile was on the other two. A good omen?

His large palm came down flat, covering the silver, breaking her focus. She looked up at his bearded face and met his dark eyes.

"Now."

Now was moments after being woken by his pounding that shook the entire structure, dragging Dirina awake and

1

off the cot where her sister and baby miraculously slept on.

Her gaze went to his hand, then back to his face, trying to make sense of this.

His expression told her nothing, but his cloak and coins and smell of horse said plenty. That her sister's reputation had spread, again, far beyond this small mountain village to which they had come only last spring, before the baby was born. Where they were still welcome, if barely.

Were there really five falcons under his hand? Maybe she had imagined them.

She would tell him no. Come back tomorrow. When Amarta was rested. When Dirina could see him clearly in the daylight.

"Your pardon, ser," she said, ducking her head. "She is asleep. She's only a child. She—"

He picked up his hand, revealing the five coins again. For a moment her mouth moved silently.

"She's only—"

"Asleep. A child. I heard you. Get her in here."

Outside the wind picked up, blowing a roar through the trees, scraping branches against the roof, hissing through shutters that never closed properly, sneaking under the door that had to be bolted to stay shut in high winds.

Five falcons.

But Amarta was exhausted. She had foreseen three times today already. Next week's weather, when the goat would birth, how many kids, the arrival of trade wagons. So, today, they had eaten.

Dirina liked eating. Feeding the baby from her own body always left her so very hungry. She always wanted more food.

Also, rent was due, the roof needed patching, and the stove ate peat voraciously.

Five falcons. She ached to touch them.

The candle flickered wildly in a puff of air. On the walls, shadows danced with the flame's motion.

"I'm sorry, ser," she said, pulling her hand back again. "She's too tired. She can be ready in the morning. At first light. Then she would be happy to answer—"

Her breath caught at his look. He scared her, this large stranger whose face she couldn't read, who had five falcons to spend on a child's divination in the middle of the night.

Even his clothes were odd. Loose, as if he had so much material he didn't know what to do with it. Some kind of wool, fine and thick. She wondered what it felt like.

He made a noise. Sharp, displeased. Taking hold of a nearby stool, he pulled it to the table and sat. It creaked a little.

"One of us is going to go back there and get her. She might prefer it be you."

Dirina's stomach tightened. She looked for the oak stick she kept in the corner, alarmed to not see it. There it was; it had slipped to the dirt floor. When she looked back at him, he was watching her.

This man had needed to bend to come inside. His loose clothes did not hide his bulk.

She should never have let him in.

Again his hand went for the falcons, and for a wretched moment she thought he might take them away. Instead he dropped another silver coin onto the pile.

Then another.

A beautiful, terrible sound.

"A moment," Dirina said softly and ran to the tiny back room.

Through the shutter slats, pale moonlight illuminated a straw-stuffed cot where Amarta slept curled around the baby. Dirina had named him Pas, after a tasty fruit-filled pastry she had once eaten because every time she looked at him she felt as if she had bitten into something wonderful.

On her knees she reached over him, breathing a quick prayer that he would stay asleep. She squeezed her sister's shoulder.

Amarta muttered something into the layers of clothes and blankets, the muffled, flat tone telling Dirina just how exhausted she was. Then she opened her eyes.

"Diri?"

"A man," Dirina said. "He has seven falcons, Ama. Can you see for him?" She didn't pause for an answer. "You must." She brushed her sister's dark hair out of her face. "Seven falcons. He won't wait. My sweet, I'm sorry."

Her sister struggled to sit up, blinking, then pulled a tunic over the light clothes she slept in and stood. Dirina hastily tucked the blankets around Pas and then followed Amarta into the other room.

Amarta looked at the man, at the coins on the table, then back at the man.

His eyebrows furrowed. "You are the seer?"

Dirina recognized the tone. It was easy to understand, with Amarta's hair a dark, fluffy mess and her child's eyes lidded with sleep.

Amarta nodded and sat across the table from him on another stool. Dirina stepped back, leaning against the wall by the stove, a grab away from the oak stick on the floor.

The man put his hands on the table and leaned forward a little. In the light of the candle, Dirina could make out odd white lines crossing the backs of his hands and fingers. Scars, she realized suddenly. They were all scars.

Amarta put a finger on the pile of silver coins.

"We don't usually ask that much," she said.

"Then do good work, girl."

Her sister crossed her forearms on the table and lowered her chin atop them, squinting into the candle flame. Dirina gnawed a knuckle.

The silence lengthened. "Ama," she said, summoning her most encouraging tone, "what do you see?" She gave the man a quick smile. "Sometimes she needs a moment."

He tapped a fingernail on the table in a slow, annoying beat. "I don't have a lot of moments."

"Amarta?" She hadn't fallen asleep, had she?

Those who came to them for answers were desperate, their problems having pushed them to spend money they didn't have in the hope that someone else might know what was good for them better than they did. Usually she reminded her sister to say only good things to them. So often the future was not what people wanted it to be.

As the silence continued, her stomach went leaden, chest tightening. They needed this man happy with his answers.

The wind knocked a branch against the side of the house, and for a moment the candle flickered furiously, threatening to go out.

Then Amarta sat up, looking into the distance at something beyond flickering shadows and wood walls. Dirina knew the look, felt a flush of relief.

"There's a man," Amarta said easily. "He's looking for you. And you—you're looking for him, too. He's your brother, isn't he?"

The man nodded, very slowly, his attention now entirely on Amarta.

Dirina knew this look as well. No matter what people had heard about Amarta, no matter what they believed, this was the moment of shock, when she told them something she couldn't possibly know.

"Where is he?" the man asked.

"One of you will be dead before sunrise," Amarta said.

Dirina's stomach clenched agonizingly. That was not the right thing to say. What was Amarta doing?

That times might be difficult. That people would need to be strong. That things would get better. Yes, all that. Not this, never this.

Because people rarely changed their actions, no matter what she told them, because that was how people were. Small things, like where and when to plant, that they might do, but big things, like not going to market next month, or insisting that someone leave and never come back, that was much harder.

Some things couldn't be changed. Better not to speak of those things.

And yet the man did not look surprised.

"Where is he?" he asked.

"There's a woman," Amarta said. "She's going to be very upset with whoever lives tonight."

The man gave a humorless half-laugh. "He'll be spared that, at least. Will her father keep his word this time?"

Amarta tilted her head back and forth in a gesture that spoke of scales that had nearly come even.

"I think yes. The spring after next, or the summer following. Then . . ." She nodded. "He will—I don't know what it's called. Give her the crown?"

Dirina heard her sister's words but could not make sense of them.

"She will marry me," the man said. Not quite a question.

Amarta nodded again. "If you live."

"Where is he?" he demanded a third time, his voice strained.

Amarta glanced at the shuttered window.

"Not far. Four lanes to the north."

The man stood up, fast, and there was a knife in his hand. The flash of metal caught Dirina's gaze as surely as the coins had before. Her breath stopped in her throat.

"Tell me how to win against him."

At this Amarta shook her head.

"Tell me," he said in a tone so compelling Dirina ached to satisfy it herself with a reply.

"I don't know," Amarta answered.

"What do you mean, you don't know?" he growled. "Look wherever it is you look and tell me."

Amarta was breathing fast and shallow.

"It's not clear. I can't see it."

The man tightened his grip on the knife, the tip pointing toward Amarta. Then, laying the knife on the wood, he rotated it, hilt toward her.

"Does this knife draw blood tonight?" he asked.

He was clever. Most people never understood that Amarta could answer the small questions easier than the big ones, or that touching an object could help foresee its future.

Amarta brushed the bronze and leather-wrapped hilt, tracing her fingers along the flat of the blade. She pulled back and shook her head.

His eyes narrowed. "Try again."

"No," she answered, her child's voice unsteady but certain. "No blood on this blade tonight."

He scowled. "If I wanted to, I could change that." He took the knife again.

Amarta cringed away from the table. Dirina knelt down and picked up the oak stick.

"Tell me, girl," he said, his voice full of threat. "Is there blood on this knife yet?"

Amarta's shoulders shook. "No blood," Amarta whispered.

Dirina thought frantically. She would throw herself at him. Get between him and Amarta.

But if she sacrificed herself, who would protect them then? What should she do?

"Put it down," he said to Dirina, as if answering. "You don't want to challenge me. You wouldn't last two breaths." His knife vanished beneath his cloak, hands empty again. "I don't want your blood or hers. I said put it down."

Dirina's hands were trembling violently. The stick fell to the floor with a dull thud.

"Advise me," he told Amarta. "What must I do to live through tomorrow's sunrise?"

Once again Amarta was looking far away.

"Don't hesitate. Because he will."

The man followed Amarta's gaze to the wall and slowly nodded. He stood, turned, and walked to the door, seeming to have already stepped into the future Amarta had seen. He paused, glanced back at them both.

"You had better be right, girl."

He shut the door hard behind him, the walls shuddering with the force of it. Dirina hurried over and bolted it. Then she went to her sister.

"Ama?" After a moment her sister began to shake. Dirina held her until the ragged breaths turned calm, then pulled back, searching her sister's brown eyes.

"Why did you say that? About killing and dying?"

"He paid us. We need the money."

"But why him? Why not the brother?"

"He was here," Amarta said, her voice cracking. "Was I wrong? I tried to see further, but I couldn't."

"My sweet. You can't know everything."

"It was too far away. All I could see was tonight. I'm sorry, Diri," Amarta said, beginning to sob.

Dirina murmured reassurances, stroking her sister's hair, swallowing her own growing unease.

A mistake to let him in, perhaps.

She had made so many mistakes, their difficult lives the consequence. Like forcing them to leave the village of their birth with nothing in hand. Or selling Amarta's visions and needing to flee those who didn't like the answers.

Like getting pregnant.

He was so beautiful, Pas's father. She had known better but in the wanting had somehow ignored the knowing. He made her feel sweet and warm, put laughter into her bleak world, implying with every kiss that he would stay.

It had been a hard lesson to discover that he had gone. Harder still to discover that she was pregnant.

She loved the baby, fiercely, every finger and toe of him. But she should have known better. *Had* known better. Had been taught by her own mother to count the days of the moon, to mark time from blood. Her mother would be ashamed of her.

Except her mother was dead. And that, too, was Dirina's fault.

There had been solutions to the pregnancy, but they couldn't afford any of them. They couldn't afford the baby, either, but there was no choice about that. So they went hungry.

And sold Amarta's strange ability.

She hugged her sister close, the girl's body tight.

"It's over now, Ama. Let's go back to bed and get warm."

"No. He's coming back."

"What? Tonight?"

Amarta nodded.

Dirina bit back her next question. There were things it was better not to know.

Which was why she had not let Amarta see their parents' broken bodies in the canyon, four years ago. She'd seen enough for both of them. She remembered her uncle's hand tight on her arm. Yes, he would take them in, he said, words soft in her ear as his grip tightened, and all their parents had owned, but they had better be worth the trouble. He shook her for emphasis, holding her back from her parents' bodies. An obligation, he said, watching her closely. Hard work. Did she understand?

She had not. Not then.

When he had let her go, Dirina fell to the ground, her arms around the still-warm bodies of their mother and father as she wept. Her uncle collected the baskets of rare crevasse honey her parents had harvested from nests along the high rock wall, where overhead, so many lengths above, ropes and pulleys had somehow failed.

The next morning, Dirina had woken early with a suspicion of what her uncle meant to do with her and her sister and a sick certainty that he had set the ropes to unravel. There was no proof, but she could feel it in her bones. Before dawn she had gathered Amarta and had left on forest paths under a quarter moon to they knew not where.

Days later Dirina remembered how Amarta had woken her in the middle of the night before that terrible day to tell her of a vision of wall-nests and slipping rope, begging her for help.

Dirina had told her that it was only a dream and to go back to sleep.

To know what would happen and still not be able to

change it was worse than not knowing. Dirina no longer wanted to hear about the future.

Amarta stared into the light of the burning candle. Perhaps they should save what was left of it—they could not afford them as it was—but it comforted her sister, and—

He was coming back.

"Ama, is he—"

A sudden noise outside the thin walls of the cabin. An animal, perhaps, or—

She strained to hear, helpless to stop herself envisioning which of the many night sounds might be a man's last struggle for breath.

This was the last time, Dirina told herself. No more of Amarta's visions.

Then they would starve.

No, then she would—

There was a loud pounding at the door.

"What should I do?" Dirina asked, frightened enough to blurt out the question.

Amarta shook her head with a child's lost, fearful look. She didn't know. Or wouldn't say.

The pounding came again, rattling the door frame and walls. Dirina could too easily imagine him breaking the door in if she waited much longer. She dashed to unbolt it and let him in.

He pushed past her into the room, breathing hard, hood thrown back, hair and face smeared with mud. At his look, Dirina backed away.

From the other room came Pas's freshly woken howl. Before Dirina could move, Amarta darted to the back room, returning with Pas cradled in her arms, now quieted. Dirina felt a sick jolt at seeing her sister and son here, so near this dangerous man.

"You were right," he told Dirina, his voice low. "I broke his neck. Hold, twist, snap." His hands moved in the air, as if to demonstrate. "As we were taught. And yes—" He fixed a look on Amarta. "He hesitated, my brother did. As you said he would. He should have known better."

Dirina put a hand over her mouth.

For a long moment, the only sound in the room was the stranger's hard breathing.

His gaze wandered the room, as if seeing it for the first time. When his look came back to Dirina, he seemed to be weighing a decision.

It was slow, the motion of his hand moving out from under his cloak. He was shaking, she realized, despite that his face showed nothing. His hand went for the pile of coins.

For a horrible moment she was sure he would take all the coins and leave. It had happened before. Instead he put another coin on the table.

A gold souver. Dirina's mouth fell open.

"My life is worth this and more to me, so I'll give you some advice as well." He looked at Amarta and settled a weightier look on Dirina. "Charge more."

With that he left.

Heartbeats passed. When the cold night air finally broke her shock, Dirina went to the door, shut it, dropped the bolt. As if it would protect them from anything.

Her sister was sitting on the floor, curled around Pas, rocking, murmuring to him.

Dirina dropped down next to her, put her arms around them both.

"He's gone now, don't you worry," Amarta was telling Pas.

"We're safe," Dirina said, knowing the lie of the words as they left her mouth.

She helped her sister stand and drew them both back to the cot and under blankets. Dirina waited until she was asleep, then wrapped Pas in a blanket and took him back to the table. She gave him her breast to feed as she stared at the coins on the table.

All they had done was to answer the man's questions.

No, that was a lie, too; they had helped him kill his brother, a man who probably also had fine clothes, a horse, and a good deal of coin. Whoever he was.

It didn't matter who he was. Both men were gone, and the coins remained. Coins that would buy them food to keep them from starving through the winter. Perhaps some tar and straw to seal the roof and stop the drafts. Peat for the stove. Blankets. Food and shelter and warmth.

Or maybe a start somewhere else.

That's what they would do, she decided. At first light they would pack what little they had and leave. Begin again elsewhere, somewhere no one had heard about Amarta and what she could do.

When the coins ran out, Dirina would mend or clean or cook or whatever was needed to keep them alive. But no more answers for strangers. No more stumbling over long-held secrets or making enemies by telling people things they didn't really want to know.

For a moment she planned furiously, thinking of what they could take on their backs.

She stopped. It would not happen. Not this season, not the next. She could not take a child and an infant on a mountain trek to another village with ice on the ground and snow on the way.

Then, she decided fiercely, she would find another way. When the money was gone, she would rent herself to the village men for more. She would count carefully this time, and there would be no more mistakes.

That is, if the village men had any extra coin in the winter months at all. Well, she would find out, she decided.

Pas reached for her then, clutching the cloth of her shirt tightly in his little fist. She raised his hand to her mouth and kissed it, allowing herself this moment of sweetness. She tucked the fallen cloth back around his little body, and his head dropped onto her chest as he fell asleep.

She was his future. His only future. She would do what she must.

In his sleep, Pas made a small sound. She rocked him gently as the room lightened with the first hint of dawn.

Gold. They had a gold souver. Dirina took the coin in hand and looked it over closely.

Larger than the silver falcons and heavier, too. Nothing like the dirty, scratched copper quarter-nals chits she knew, that if you had the right four, you could piece together to make a picture of the Grandmother Queen with her moon-in-sky through the window and dog at her feet.

It was a wonder, this coin, heavy and smooth like a river rock. She brought it close, rubbing her finger over the shining detail.

A soldier on a horse, front legs high in the air, sword raised. Behind him were snow-capped mountains divided by a river. That would be the Sennant, the great river that ran through the empire, that they had crossed to come here to this village. Behind the horse, a palace. The Jewel of the Empire, which her mother had told her stories about when she'd been small. So many rooms. Food in every one of them.

What had Amarta said to the man who had given them this coin? Something about a woman who would be upset. Something about her father keeping his word.

Dirina turned the coin over. A bearded man stared back at her with an imposing expression on his face and a circlet on his head.

A crown. That was what Amarta had said. Something about a crown.

Dirina stared at the coin in her hand, her breath coming hard and fast. She dropped the coin to the table, where it rattled and went still.

What had they done?

In the dawning day, Dirina clutched Pas tight and watched gold and silver coins take on rich color as the prisms of her tears blurred them into wild, luminescent shapes.

Chapter Two

Bound in word and blood.

The monarchy's motto, and a part of Innel's long oath to the king. He looked at his brother's body in front of him, wrapped in burlap, laid across the shoulders of his mare, and wondered if he had now broken that oath.

He turned his horse from the road following along the thundering Sennant River to one that steeply ascended into the mountains. The horse snorted her incredulity at leaving the well-maintained, flat road but went where Innel directed. She was a splendidly well-trained creature with a glossy coal-black coat that he had taken in the middle of the night for the hard ride south to Botaros. Without permission. From the king's own travel set.

One more thing to answer for.

Her ears flattened again. She did not like the bundle she carried, wrapped in what Innel could find that dark, cold night. Did not like it at all.

Nor did he.

A confrontation, yes. Sharp words, even, given the circumstances. That he might have expected.

17

But this?

His mare slowed on the steep incline, stepping delicately over a fallen log. He pushed aside the desire to rush her. He wanted to be done with this, but there was no room for mistakes; she was not only carrying him and provisions, but a body.

Not a small body, either. Pohut had been a large man, powerful and fast. Had the fight been fair, Innel would have been a fool to bet on himself.

Yet he had won, the body before him testimony to that. His brother and he, resolved at last.

A cold autumn wind gusted across his face.

No, nothing like resolved.

Hours later the road leveled somewhat, weaving among the pines and patches of ice like a skein of silvered yarn, sometimes following along the roaring river far below, sometimes cutting inland, sometimes so overgrown it was scarcely more than a game trail. Once he and the horse disagreed on where the road was, and only after they had to backtrack from a dead end at an overhang that dropped to the white frothing water below did he defer to her when he wasn't sure.

The long way back to the capital, this detour from the main road, and that only to avoid the small risk of being stopped and asked what he was carrying. Growing up in the Cohort had taught him that sometimes there was a hair's width between triumph and disaster. As always, a balance of risks.

Like arriving at Botaros minutes before his brother did, finding there a child who could truly see into the future, and taking her advice.

A tenday ago, he would have dismissed the rumor of a seer as a children's fable, a ruse to some end. To find that his brother, supposedly aboard ship far south in the Mundaran Sea, had returned and was now en route to Botaros on a fast horse, had quickly decided him.

Deceit and treachery from anyone else, even Cohort siblings, he had come to expect. But Pohut?

So Innel had followed his brother. Hard riding, lack of sleep, and blinding fury at Pohut's most recent betrayal had put Innel there first. By a hair's width.

He went over the conversation in his mind, every word, how the girl had held herself. No deception that he could read, and she had known things she simply could not know. Now that he had time to reflect, he realized he should have gotten more answers, starting with what would have happened if his brother had arrived first.

No. He knew that answer.

He looked at the body in front of him again.

First he must return to the capital and find out how much trouble he was in. Then he would come back for the girl.

Innel stopped in the middle of a circle of alders and dismounted, tugging out the knots that kept the long bundle on his mount, easing his brother's body down onto frozen mud.

The mare's large brown eye met his in what might have been gratitude but was more likely a rebuke for putting her through this.

They had left the distant roar of the Sennant far behind. Other than muted birdsong and wind through high trees, the silence of the woods was thick and heavy. Such a contrast to Yarpin Palace, where every word, spoken or not, was loud with implication. Where the length of a shirt sleeve could spark backroom discussions and questions about one's loyalty.

Where he would need to arrive with a very compelling story about what he had done.

They were a royal investment, the girls and boys of the Cohort, the result of decades of tutelage and housing. Innel was going to need to explain why he was bringing one of them back dead.

Ironically, he wanted his brother's advice more than ever. What would Pohut have said now?

"You are the aggrieved party," he might have said. "With no opposing voice, the king will believe you. If *you* believe you."

"But what do I say?" Innel mouthed to the cold quiet around him.

"Sleep on it. You'll think more clearly tomorrow. You always do."

But tomorrow his brother would still be dead.

He stumbled away into the brush, hand against a tree, and leaned over to put onto the ground what little remained in his stomach. He heaved again and again.

His *brother*. He had killed his *brother*.

After a time he stood, wiped his mouth, and looked around at this too-quiet forest, dim and gray-green under frigid, flat white skies.

The past was done. Writ in blood and carved in stone. Unchangeable. No sense in dwelling on it.

He drank water and opened a bag of grain to hand-feed his mare, focusing on this simple act and nothing else; the feel of her lips on his palm, the sound of her grinding molars.

Just a package to deliver, he told himself, struggling the heavy thing off the ground and up and onto his shoulders and then across the horse, tying it securely. She snorted resentment, breath white like smoke in the chill air. As he swung up into the saddle, he resolved to have the stablehands overfeed her on their return.

A very, very compelling story.

The mutts, they had been called, from their first day in the Cohort. Together they had studied fiercely, the unspoken rules of palace life, the patterns of war, the moods of the princess. Together they had outthought, outfought, and outcourted the rest of the Cohort.

Together. Always together.

Perhaps it would be simpler for him to return to Yarpin without the body. Say he had not seen Pohut at all.

Or perhaps that his brother had cursed him and the king as well and headed for lands south, now both a traitor and a deserter.

"On a ship, Sire," Innel mouthed, to see how the words would sound. "Ashamed to face you after drawing his knife on me."

But no—uncertainty about Pohut's fate led to doubt about Innel's story, and there would be enough of that. The body had to come back with him, along with Pohut's knife. The knife he had indeed drawn on Innel but had never had a chance to use.

Because of the girl's prediction.

Or he, Innel, could go elsewhere. Leave the empire

entirely. Find some remote place to call home. A self-exile.

He could not stomach that either. They had worked too hard, too long. Year by year, spending what little influence they had being so close to the throne, grooming contacts, building loyalties. The two of them had been generous with favors but miserly in trust; raised in the Cohort among royals and scions of the Greater and Lesser Houses, he and Pohut had long ago realized they had only one true ally.

Since he could remember, the trust between them had seemed unshakable. But it was not; these last few years, it had eroded.

The king had told him, in words he could not mistake for anything else, that there was no longer room at the palace for the both of them.

And then his brother had betrayed him.

Now there was plenty of room.

"Damn you," he said to his brother.

There was a saying in the palace that blood speaks with one voice. It meant that what the aristo families shared was stronger than what divided them. This was why the king bred dogs and horses. It was why, when Innel's father had died a general and hero of the king's northern expansion, their mother and her three children were taken to the palace and inducted into the Cohort.

Breeding mattered. In dogs, in horses. In children.

As he stared at the bundle that was his brother's body, he could see Pohut's face and hear his voice.

Blood spoke, all right. He just didn't much like what it was saying.

✛ ✛ ✛

Innel arrived in Yarpin at the first hint of dawn's light, gray stone streets and tall brick buildings engulfed in pools of shadow under fast-fading stars. The mare picked up her pace, eager to get home.

Or perhaps she was trying to escape the stink. Even autumn-chilled, the stench of trash against the wall and the sewers was a foe no arms could subdue, a pungent insult to the nose that overshadowed even the nagging scent of his brother's body.

It didn't matter how many sewer pipes were installed down-city if the Houses on the hill consumed every drop of water for their baths and flower gardens. The palace was no better, with glassed-in gardens and soaking tubs.

The stench did not distinguish between common and noble noses; everyone gagged on entrance. Wealthy merchants, foreign dignitaries. The Houses and the king should have been embarrassed, but they simply ignored it. As soon as he and his brother gained some measure of authority, they would do something about it.

His brother.

He could still reverse direction, find a country far away, his actions this last tenday left unknown.

Along with everything else he had labored to accomplish. A ragged mutt with nothing. Common, in the truest sense.

No. He was not ready to give up.

Around him, tradesmen and clerks were rushing out into the dim light of the streets to start their day, stumbling out of his way, then staring. He had thought to attract less attention by seeming to be a trader going up-city to deliver a rolled tapestry, his soldier's uniform hidden under loose clothing and cloak, but it was now obvious to him that a body didn't hang over a horse's shoulders the way a tapestry would. A lesson that, oddly, none of his tutors had provided.

In doorways, rags moved, becoming scrawny children who scrambled to their feet and called out to him, promising everything from the impossible to the unlikely. One small boy pulled off his shirt, shivering in the morning chill, rubbing his tiny chest, describing in detail what he was offering. All, he assured in his high-pitched child's voice, for only three nals. Less, the boy cried out, as Innel passed him by.

A girl stood on the street reciting the names of tinctures at prices far too inexpensive to be sanctioned. There was something not quite right about her expression and distant stare that put him in mind of his sister, Cahlen. Would his sister and mother survive this day, if he did not? It seemed to Innel that he should care, one way or the other, but he was not sure he did.

The king's laws were supposed to prevent children from shielding black-market outlaws by setting the same penalties for the young as for those who hired them, yet it was still children calling from doorways, filling the prisons, and being sold to slavers when it was clear that no one was coming to pay their fine.

There was an upside, of sorts, he supposed; Innel had studied the empire's books and knew how much of the crown's income could be attributed to the sale of those barely old enough to count on their fingers, let alone make binding contracts. The king's accountants were fond of joking that children were one of Yarpin's most lucrative exports.

Except that it was true. Those backing these urchins could afford to bribe whomever they needed to. The city was soaked in such dealings, from the slums to the Great Houses. So many palms to which coin could stick.

And that was where the money went, on its way to clean the city, or to repair streets and water pipes. Another thing he and his brother would remedy when they—

Again he looked at the body in front of him.

A crow flew across the horse's path, squawking loudly, and Innel tensed, momentarily gripping the reins. The mare stopped, and he pressed her forward again.

The scent of baking bread caught his attention, making him realize how hungry he was. Absurdly he imagined stopping for rolls and herbed butter while the challenge before him simply waited until he felt like it.

Maybe someone would steal the body from his horse while he lingered, enjoying the bustle of the morning around him.

But it was just imagination, and he did not stop.

As his horse climbed the steep hill, the foul air cleared, replaced by briny ocean breezes. The Lesser Houses rose high and wide on either side of the street. Finch and Chandler, Glass and Bell, their familial sigils worked into patterns of trim, mosaic, groundstone, the dual-color flags of their patron houses flying high and bright in the rising sun.

In this prestigious neighborhood, House patrols kept beggars and other lurkers away. One patrol watched now, not recognizing Innel as one of the Cohort. The man looked him over; the fine black horse, anonymous cloak, body across the saddle. He appeared to weigh the evidence, then nodded a little and turned away.

From the palace, deep bells chimed the hour of dawn. Perhaps he should have arrived at midnight instead of at the start of the day, which he now realized would mean far more eyes on him.

No, there was no good time to arrive with this package.

At the summit, the street opened into a huge square at the center of which was a sizable fountain. Water poured from the mouths of a hundred carved marble flowers into the open beaks of a hundred carved birds standing on rocks in the pool below.

An apt model of the convoluted House Charters, he had always thought, the many streams of water—some parallel in effort, some at cross-purposes—that assigned contracts and Lesser Houses to the Great Houses. Few could make sense of all the relationships involved, even among the Cohort, even though most of them hailed from the Houses. He and his brother, though, they—

He veered from the thought.

The side streets were lavish with rows of trees and gardens fronting the gated compounds of the Eight Great Houses, each painted and jeweled in its two-tone colors, the roof lines sparkling brilliant in the sun's first rays.

And then the palace walls, beyond which was the Jewel of the Empire, dwarfing even the Great Houses with its size, stonework, and high towers, pink and alabaster stones sun-touched and glinting. The Cohort had sometimes been tutored in those towers, using the view of the ocean and surrounding forests to discuss the crown's history and economics, but most tower rooms were reserved as lodging for inconvenient royals, like the king's mother, whom no one ever saw. Housing for those the king didn't want to see but whose missteps weren't egregious enough for execution.

Not the worst outcome, he supposed.

No, he thought. He wasn't important enough. A mutt did not rot in the towers.

At the gate, his mare strained forward toward the promise of food, trotting to the front of the long line waiting for entrance, staring at him intently, as were the guards and bowmen two levels overhead on the parapet wall. He was recognized and waved through. One guard nodded sharply at another, who took off at speed.

Well, at least his welcome would not be overly delayed.

At the stables he dismounted. Stablehands took the reins, reached for the body.

"No," he said sharply. "Leave it."

With stiff fingers from the long ride and cold morning, untying the knots took frustratingly longer, but he would accept no help. He pulled the long bundle off the horse and onto his own shoulders, holding the legs and arms of the now-rigid body out to either side.

His mare was led away. Tired and hungry, but no worse for the journey.

Unlike his brother.

He met the widening eyes of stablehands. That he and his brother had left within hours of each other, very much without permission, was no secret from them. In their looks he saw them draw conclusions, step back.

Afraid. Of him. Of what he carried. Of what it meant.

A young woman rushed to the doors ahead of him. At a glance he took in the balance of her loyalty to the crown versus her allegiance to her House; dressed in the monarchy's red and black, only the yellow trim on her boots and cuffs marked her as a child of House Elupene. She yanked open both doors, dropped back and away.

Belatedly it occurred to him that it would have been prudent to have taken off his cloak to reveal his own red and black. To do so now would mean putting his brother down. He would not.

As he walked the path from stables to the palace's back entrance, he passed faces he knew. A green-and-cream-liveried servant. A pair of red-uniformed soldiers. A cook. A triad of scribes. All backed away, gazes flickering from his face to what he carried.

Srel, out of breath, dashed to his side.

"Ser, what. Ah—"

The smaller man fell suddenly quiet, his gaze solidly on Innel's burden.

Innel and his brother had rescued Srel from the streets many years ago, when he'd been a scrawny, starving teen, and Srel had given them his stubborn loyalty since.

"What—" Srel began again.

"Talk later," Innel managed. He wondered if Srel's loyalty would survive the day.

Irrelevant, though, if he himself did not.

The door of the palace back entrance opened inward. He climbed the steps. Scullery and laundry servants stared, gape-mouthed, hastily retreating back into doorways to make room.

Innel considered the various routes through the many-floored structure that would get him to the royal wing where the king might see him.

Or might not. Might have him arrested and thrown in the dungeon to await judgment. Might have him tossed into commoners' jail down-city.

Might have him questioned to find out what had really happened. Innel had witnessed a number of the king's interrogations over the years and had finally come to realize what should have been obvious all along: the king didn't torture people to get answers, but to make sure that those watching knew how willing he was to do so.

Palace life was all about who saw what, and certainly the fewer who saw him and his burden today, the better. With that thought, he took the servant's staircase up to the next floor. A tight fit in places, so he turned sideways.

As he walked another corridor, he realized it wasn't just his brother's body that stank, and wondered at the wisdom of seeing the king before cleaning up.

No. Worse to delay.

Again, his mind raced over what the king might do, the legalities involved. Innel had just killed a man directly sworn to the monarch, making Innel's actions closer to treason than mere murder. That he was similarly sworn might prove irrelevant.

Innel could end up at the northern end of the Dalgo Rift, counting the king's distant flocks of sheep and goats, lucky to still be in possession of all his limbs.

He shuffled forward over smooth marble flo

adjusting the balance of the heavy weight on his shoulders. This time of day, the palace ought to be bustling with servants and retainers, children of Houses and tutors rushing to make appointments. He might have a nod or a smile from a guard or aide. A moment's conversation about matters of the day. A Cohort sibling might have words for him, plans for a game of two-head later. Whispered politics. Favors offered, demanded, bargained for.

None of that now. Everyone was clearing the way before him, watching as if he were being paraded to Execution Square, another not-inconceivable consequence. With no House to back him, carrying a dead man on his shoulders whose identity anyone could make a reasonable guess about, despite—or possibly because of—his membership in the Cohort, he could think of no precedent.

He was contagious with implication, and no one would come near him until someone told them what they should think. That someone could only be the king.

Passing the eating hall by the kitchens where the Cohort had often taken informal meals with the king, he wondered if he would see the inside of it again. If he had eaten his last meal.

Once he and his brother, not much older than thirteen and fifteen, had arrived in just this spot, late for the meal, which would earn them a reprimand from the headmaster. They had needed the time to clean up. Even so, their faces were thick with purpled bruises from the beating that five of the Cohort had given them after luring them into a deserted basement hallway.

Pohut had taken Innel's already bruised arm in a hard grip, holding him back a moment from entering the room.

"You look like a whipped dog," he hissed.

"A good description of us both," Innel whispered back.

Pohut pulled him closer, speaking into his ear. "Act like it and you become it."

"Brother, we have nothing. No House, no bloodline, no patron—"

Another shake for his attention. Innel gritted his teeth at the pain, but Pohut's charming smile somehow gentled it, melting his anger. It was a trick that had opened many doors for his older brother.

"No House means we are freer, Innel. Lighter. A fast freighter. A pointed dirk. Beholden only to the king. We do what others cannot, say what aristos dare not. We'll win this."

This. Meaning Cern. The reason for the Cohort.

Innel had snorted in reply. "Your eye is purple and yellow, your toe broken. I think my forearm bone is cracked. We should tell the king."

"Say nothing."

"But—"

"Five on two. What does that tell you, about how they fear us? Think, brother. Think."

Innel tilted his head and considered. "That they do."

"How many of the Cohort has the king sent home, to the dishonor of their Houses, while we two remain? One of us will be consort; believe it. We will survive."

Survive they had, and more than that. Pohut was right: they could move and act more quickly than those with somewhere to retreat to if they failed.

Innel had never asked his brother which of the two of them he believed Cern would choose. Until last year it had been enough that it would be one of them.

The next time that those five Cohort brothers had found Innel and Pohut in that same deserted cellar hall, the brothers had been ready. They had put their attackers on the ground, leaving them there with broken bones, bloodied and bruised. One had a piercing headache that did not go away. A month later he was returned to his House.

No one tried it again.

Every year someone left or fell out of the Cohort. In one case, literally: a rooftop duel led to one boy tumbling to his death on the stone courtyard three stories below. The survivor of that duel had been sent back to his House, not because of the death, but because otherwise the two Houses would be at each other's throats, threatening to snuff lamp-oil deliveries to the entire city. Home the boy went.

By Innel's eighteenth spring, the Cohort had dwindled to eight boys and three girls. Then Innel and Pohut were separated, sent on campaign, assigned to serve various province governors, or kept close to serve in the palace.

But not together.

Innel sent Pohut letters by messenger bird, but his brother's replies were terse, demanding, critical. They saw less and less of each other, then not at all. Until Botaros.

A child's screaming laughter brought him back to the moment. A naked toddler had run in front of him and frozen, forcing him to a heavy stop to avoid plowing the boy over. The boy gaped up at him, then grinned widely, drooling with pleasure, as if nothing could delight him more than this large, grimy man, a dead body slung across his shoulders.

Out into the hall dashed a head-wrapped green-liveried servant who snatched the child up into her arms and stammered apologies, darting back into a doorway. The child's howl was muffled by a slammed door.

Innel struggled forward, keeping his expression as composed as he knew how. A colorful array of servants, clerks, and aristos in their House dual-tones stepped quickly out of doorways to line the walls to watch him go. Though it was usually a loud time of day, all he heard were his own footsteps.

Meat and bread and cheese, he thought, with sudden craving. A drink of something to clear the nasty taste from his mouth. A carafe of wine to clear the unpleasantness of his thoughts.

His brother's counsel.

A large, stocky figure stepped solidly in front of him, one foot and then the other, the high collar of the man's pressed red and black sharp against his doughy neck, gold trim on his neckline and down his arms catching the morning light from high windows.

"By the Eyes of the All, what have you done, boy?"

Innel felt a rush of anger at having to stop suddenly again. His shoulders ached.

More were gathering against the paneled walls to watch, quietly whispering to each other.

"Lord Commander," Innel said, choosing his next words with care. How to keep this conversation short? "I am on my way to see the king."

At that, surely the man would move aside. Anyone with sense would. But he did not. Lason, the king's brother, commander of the Host of Arunkel, did not much like Innel. Had not liked either of the mutts.

"What in the seven hells is that on your back?"

"The king, ser," Innel repeated.

Lason looked him up and down with a disgusted look. "You've gone far past the line this time, boy."

Innel bit back all the words that came to him and buried his all-too familiar desire to pummel the other man into senselessness. He could probably take him now—sixty-something, gone soft and slow since the days he had taught weapons in the Cohort by hitting them full force when they didn't get out of the way—but it would be the last thing he did. While Innel's friends in the military might hesitate, or even feel remorse, they would cut him down if Lason ordered them to.

Restraint, he reminded himself.

More importantly, the king.

"We will see," he said. Then with some effort he stepped to the side and around the Lord Commander, who turned in place to watch him go.

Lason spat and loudly. "You insolent, stupid, mongrel pup."

That would garnish the best dish of the day's news—possibly the year's, depending on how the rest of this day went for Innel—spreading as fast as feet could dash and tongues could twirl, from west gate to east wall. A half hour at most, he would wager, for the tale to reach everyone inside the palace walls, from royals to servants, aristocrats to soldiers, bathhouse to scullery. How Innel brought a body home and the Lord Commander had spat on him and insulted him.

Innel suspected that not much work would get done today.

For a bizarre moment, he imagined dropping the body and walking out the huge front doors of the palace and leaving. He wondered how far he'd get.

Probably not even to the doors. Far too late to change his mind.

Now his spectators were past pretending to be on some other task, but simply stood and watched. From the Cohort he saw the curly haired Mulack, entirely in the purple and white of his House. He stood by a smirking Sutarnan, who was claimed by two Houses and yet dressed entirely in palace colors. They were whispering to each other and would, Innel was sure, be more than happy to see his body laid out by his brother's by day's end.

A servant held a covered dish smelling like duck that made Innel's mouth water and stomach grumble. Just past him stood Tokerae, another Cohort sibling, slouching against the wall, his heavy chain of copper and charcoal iron his only nod to his House. The same age as Innel, Tok was finally thickening after years of being painfully thin and overly tall.

As Innel met his look, Tok gave him the smallest of nods.

Well, so, there was at least one person in the palace who even now supported Innel. He would not forget that.

Three years ago Tok had quietly told the two brothers he would no longer court Cern and would back the two of them instead. Still, Tok had said, it would be best if that didn't get back to his mother, Eparch of House Etallan, who was still harboring fond hopes of having a son married into the royal Anandynar line.

Ascending another long flight of stairs, shoulders burning, Innel walked another corridor. Word had preceded him, and this hallway too was lined with onlookers. He let his gaze slowly rake across their faces, seeing who looked back, who shifted away, who smiled in support, who grimaced with uncertainty. If he survived today, he would remember them all.

He headed toward the king's audience chamber. A likely wait of hours, given the monarch's usual schedule, but at least he could rest a moment, maybe even put his brother down.

To his surprise, one of the king's retainers waved him over, holding him with a gesture, then exchanged a few quick, urgent whispers with the king's seneschal, a gaunt man with graying hair who never smiled, who glared at Innel furiously over his papers. The seneschal then waved him through the just-opening doors of a lesser audience chamber.

He did as he was told and walked inside. Behind him the doors closed.

At the end of the room sat the king, white-haired, white-bearded, sitting in a heavy ebony and bronze chair atop a dais. He leaned on one arm, the other hand slowly straightening the collar of his morning robe, which was the color of red amaranth.

Restarn esse Arunkel. Restarn who is Arunkel. A thinning face betrayed his age, but the old man was still strong enough to give the impression the empire ran exactly as he wanted it to.

By him stood Cern, arms crossed, hands vanished inside the loose sleeves of her similarly colored robe, her face a mask of indifference, a mirror of her father's. That they both wore morning robes told Innel they had come from their rooms, recently woken. Possibly by reports of Innel coming back from his wandering, carrying a body.

Well, that was a kind of reassurance, that Restarn was willing to leave his bed to find out what Innel had brought home.

He could read nothing from them. The only emotion before him was at the king's feet, where a pair of his favorite royal dichu dogs sat on their haunches, faces brindled in black and tan, eyes bright, black-tipped ears up and forward, noses twitching eagerly.

One of the dangerous jokes that one never repeated came to him, the one about how the king's fondness for his bitches explained both the proliferation of dichu puppies and his single heir. Innel had heard it once, a long time ago, from a drunken scullery boy whom he had never seen again.

The king snapped his fingers and gestured. Both dogs dropped to their bellies, noses still quivering. Scenting his brother's body, Innel guessed, even from this distance.

Prudence would say follow them down, so he did. Innel let Pohut's body slide off his shoulders onto to the polished stone floor and went to his knees. He touched his head to the floor three times in the direction of his monarch and once to Cern.

Full formality. If ever there was a time for it, this was it.

"Your Most Excellent Majesty," he said, wondering what to say next.

"Show us," said the king.

Innel sat back on his heels, gestured to the knife on his belt. "With permission, Sire."

Restarn waved him on impatiently.

Innel cut the knots and rent the fabric covering the head. He pulled back the burlap to reveal his brother's face. Now no doubt remained.

In the silence that followed, Innel thought of many things. Of growing up in the Cohort, his brother at his side. Of their last, violent encounter. Of all his plans. With a small surprise, he realized he did care if his sister Cahlen lived beyond today.

He looked up. Cern's mouth was open, her expression stricken, no longer anything like impassive. It was one thing to suspect and another to know.

She had cared for Pohut. The devotion with which the brothers had courted the princess their entire lives had paid off a few years ago when Cern had finally allowed that she held some small affection for them both. Then her father had pressed her to choose one, so of course she would not, carefully apportioning her attention to them equally.

His brother would have been quite pleased at the grief on her face now.

"Well," the king said.

Innel got to his feet. What he said next could determine his prospects at the palace, his chances with Cern, and whether he would live to see sunset.

"He tried to kill me, Sire. Came at me with a knife. I had no choice."

Short. Direct. Perhaps it would carry the force of veracity.

And it was true, mostly, though Pohut hadn't actually used the knife, because Innel hadn't given him the chance.

Don't hesitate. Because he will.

Restarn's silence hung. Heavy with implication, weighted with consequence. The king looked him over; then his eyes flickered to the body.

Long silences were one of the king's tactics for getting people to talk. Innel had seen it many times in the monarch's adjudications. A terrified petitioner facing the king's expectant but wordless expression would babble. The mouth would open and damning words would pour forth.

Innel knew this, but even having watched innocent men talk their way to the hanging walls, he now felt an almost irresistible need to explain and defend. Clamping his jaw tight, he forced himself to think through what might be going on in the king's mind.

It was no secret that Restarn was impatient to have Cern produce issue, to continue the Anandynar line and the unbroken rule of centuries. But surely he must realize that if he took Innel out of the picture, Cern could become mule-stubborn, refusing anyone else. Tempted though he must be, the king could hardly shove her in a cage and wait for her to go into heat as he did with his dogs. She must say yes.

It was a standoff as old as Cern.

Innel and Pohut had become, he suspected, the only candidates that she and her father could agree on. Innel

was betting that the king could see that his life was worth
more than his death.

But the king did not like having his choices curtailed,
either, and might resent Innel removing one of the other
possibilities as much as Cern did.

The next moment was too easy to imagine: the king
would call an order, the doors would open, swords would
be drawn.

A few years ago, an overly witty ambassador was
beheaded exactly where Innel was now standing. By the
time Innel and the rest of the Cohort had come to gawk,
servants were mopping up the last of the blood and bits.
The head had been mounted on Execution Square's
hanging wall for a good tenday, a strangely thoughtful
expression on the ambassador's face.

At least it had been fast. Innel hoped he wasn't
important enough for the full treatment in Execution
Square. Those tended to take a very long time.

He swallowed, throat dry, wishing for water, and
looked down at his brother's face.

Always the calm one, Pohut, even now.

When at last Innel looked up, Restarn was watching
him, a terrifyingly thoughtful expression on his face.
Then the king made a clicking sound behind closed lips,
a sound Innel had come to know well: the monarch had
decided.

"He is to be despised," Restarn said flatly. "A
criminal's burial."

Relief flooded Innel, and he sucked in air. He would
keep his life today.

Cern stiffened, drew herself up, turned angrily,

stormed out. Innel might be her best remaining choice, but that was not the same thing as winning her.

But he had survived; he could manage Cern. A problem for later.

"I'll expect you at the meal," the king said, ignoring Cern's departure. "Get cleaned up."

"I should see my mother, Sire. Tell her. She should know."

"She already knows. The entire palace knows. Half the city knows."

Half the city?

Restarn said more with tone than he did with words, and woe to those who didn't hear. Like the witty ambassador. What did this mean?

It meant that Restarn thought Innel and his brother significant enough for the news to carry. And that meant Innel could push.

He met the king's look, forced himself to appear composed.

"I must see to my mother. To make funeral arrangements."

"No funeral. No gift ceremony. A criminal, Innel."

If Pohut had won, it would be Innel's body lying on this cold marble floor and Innel's dead spirit that would wander aimlessly, only the memory gift ceremony to help him find his way to the great Beyond. Without which, he would be ostracized by family and friends, lost forever, wandering the twilight of death.

Or so the story went.

More importantly, the most dangerous place to stand with the king was between compliance and challenge, where he would notice you but not respect you.

"Mother could not bear that, Sire," Innel said. "And so I cannot bear it." Not even close to true, and they both knew it, but the best he could do on short notice. "The gift ceremony. A full funeral. Please, Your Majesty."

The annoyed look Restarn gave him now made him wonder if he'd gone too far. But then the king shrugged, the shoulders of his robe barely moving.

"Be quick about it, then."

As Innel began to reach for his brother's body, the king said, "No. Leave it."

Leave his brother? For a moment he didn't know what to do. Days on end, aching to put him down, to have him gone, but now he did not want to walk away.

No. Pohut had betrayed him. He was rotting meat. Nothing more.

And it was the king's command.

With one last look at his brother's body, Innel bowed and backed out of the room. Around him the seneschal and various aides rushed in.

In the hallway the waiting crowd opened a path for him. He had walked out of his audience with the king. He met their eyes, looking for reactions. Many began to leave, perhaps coming to the conclusion that a free Innel was not wise entertainment. The crowd melted back.

He walked toward the residences, where his mother's room was. Srel fell into step with him. By now the smaller man would know.

"What would you have me do?" Srel asked.

So Srel was still loyal. He felt a flash of relief.

"Plan a funeral for tomorrow. Tell the Cohort to be there. Make sure they know I'm not asking."

Srel nodded and peeled off.

At the stairs up to the residences, Innel paused, alone for the first moment since he had entered the city. Really, since the night he had left the girl's shack.

Without his brother's body. Without a watching crowd.

He put a hand on the wall, his head hanging, breathing deeply for long minutes.

He had done it. He had said the right things. He had survived. This, the hardest trial of his life. His brother would have been proud.

His brother the traitor.

It didn't matter. Tomorrow Innel would lay his brother's body next to their father's in the tombs outside the city, paying close attention to who came to the funeral and who did not, whose eyes were correctly blacked and smeared in the nine directions to show their grief, and whose were not.

Now that he stood on Cern's path to the throne, anyone who did not attend the funeral was foolish beyond reckoning, and foolish beyond that if they did not seem to be glad that it was Innel who had returned intact.

He thought of his competition across these many years, Tok and Mulack and Sutarnan and others, of how they had stumbled in ways large and small, losing the king's backing or slipping in Cern's esteem. How finally only he and his brother had remained.

As he arrived at his mother's door, it came to him that

he truly was Cern's last, best choice. All he had to do now was win her back.

The king had been right: his mother knew. He could tell the moment he saw her.

She sat in a plush red chair, head turned away, face buried in a small handkerchief.

"The funeral is tomorrow," he said, pausing for a response. She snuffled quietly. "You and Cahlen will be there." A sound and a small movement with her head. Was it a nod or another sob? "Mother? Do you understand me?"

Both, it seemed. She curled forward, head down, shaking.

His mother had long seemed to him a fragile flower meant for other soil. Palace life had not suited her, not from the first.

"I had no choice," he said evenly, walking the small room, feeling the need to be moving. "He plotted against me. Had been arranging my downfall for three years. He came at me, Mother. He meant to kill me. Do you hear me?"

Again, the shaking, wordless sound.

He sighed his frustration, wondering why she was still here. The king did not make a habit of keeping in the residences those who were not useful to him. Like the women he'd bedded who produced no children. Cern's mother, the only woman to provide him a living heir, but unable to conceive a second one, had finally been sent to a small town in Epatel. Ostensibly for her health, though ironically she had died there of some high desert illness.

No, he knew why his mother was here. It was to

remind him and his brother of where they had come from and might be sent back to, if they did not perform. The simple power the king had over them. As if they might forget.

The door opened and in came his sister, Cahlen. She slammed the door shut behind her, eyes casting about, faced blotched with red.

Cahlen and his mother were both small, slender women, but there the similarity ended. His mother had survived palace life by being unnoticed. If she bore any ill-will toward the king for conscripting their father into the military for an expansion war that he quietly disapproved of, that had then killed him, and then giving her family business away, she never showed it. Silent, fragile, and well-behaved—she simply survived.

Cahlen was something else entirely. He remembered having to explain to his sister why she couldn't wear the green and cream of the servants, why she must wear the palace retainer red and black regalia instead.

"I like the green better," she had said stubbornly.

"That's not important," he'd said, already losing his patience with her but desperate to make her understand. He tried another approach. "Servants don't work with the birds."

That had been sufficient. The subject never came up again.

Today she wore appropriate colors, though her trousers were too long, her shirt overlarge, her shoulders spotted with bird droppings, and her hair uneven, as if someone had cut it in dim light using a dirty stew bowl as a guide.

Her gaze speared him and she charged, faster than he would have thought her capable. Once close, she began to batter him with tight, hard fists. He pushed back, trying to hold her at arm's length. With his greater reach it should have been easy, but his exhaustion and her wild thrashing made her nearly impossible to control.

While he was busy trying to keep her from hitting him she kicked him in the knee, quite a bit harder than he expected. He swore and stepped back.

Again she rushed him, lips pulled back, snapping her teeth. Instinctively he raised an arm, the way he would have with one of the fighting dogs, and cocked it back as if to hit her in the snout. He doubted it would even slow her down, though, not when she was like this.

Across the room his mother stood, holding her hands over her ears, and gave a piercing scream.

At this the door opened. In burst three palace guards, all of whom Innel knew. As he tried to make sense of this unlikely intrusion, Cahlen came at him again, and the three guards sprinted toward her.

This had gone far enough. He let Cahlen step in close and put his weight behind a full-force push to the middle of her chest, propelling her backward while the guards stumbled to the side to avoid her. Cahlen sprawled ass-first onto an open space on the carpeted floor. Now on her back, she stayed there, breathing hard, glaring up at him.

He turned his attention to the guards.

"What are you doing?"

He had never before seen palace guards break into a private residential room. Not for screaming, not for crashes of ceramic broken against walls. Not even for cries for help. Gossip would follow all that, certainly.

But guards? Never.

"Get out," he told them. They hesitated, the two looking to the one clearly in command. Nalas, a man he knew. Then, with more force, he repeated: "Out. Now." Nalas tilted his head toward the door, taking the other two outside.

Innel looked at his sister on the floor, still breathing hard, and wondered what was going on in her head. Cahlen could go from dead calm to bruising fury in an instant, then be over it in the next. A drenching rainstorm turned abruptly to blue skies. Once it had fully passed, the storm would be over. But had it?

Her expression shifted, mouth went slack, eyes unfocused. There it went, the storm. He waited a moment to be certain, then with a nod at his mother, who stood as if frozen, he left.

Outside the three guards waited.

"What in the seven hells was that about?" He stepped up close to Nalas, pushed him sharply with both hands, harder than he intended. Nalas stumbled back, tensed, and Innel found himself unreasonably hoping for a fight.

Nalas raised his hands in appeasement.

"His Majesty's orders."

At this Innel forced himself to calm. He wanted to hit something, but a fight here and now over this would be foolish.

"All right," he said, breathing deeply. "Why?"

"Protecting you?" Nalas replied, a tinge of wry apology in his tone.

"From *Cahlen*?" Innel said, incredulous. "But she's harmless."

Nalas gave a shrug that said he didn't disagree.

The king was guarding him? From what?

While he was formulating what he might sensibly ask Nalas, knowing that every word would get back to Restarn, Cahlen emerged. Behind her his mother's face flashed a moment in the doorway and then vanished, the door slamming shut. She wanted nothing to do with this.

Well, neither did he.

As two guards stepped to intercept Cahlen, Nalas stepped back, a hand on the hilt of his sword.

Innel could see this playing out very badly indeed. He stepped into the middle, a hand out to stop Nalas from drawing his blade.

Oblivious, Cahlen walked directly to Innel. To the other two guards, he held up a closed fist in an abrupt motion. Everyone stopped but his sister.

"Cahlen," he said sharply, to get her attention.

Innel could imagine the stories that would follow this: not only had Innel slain his brother, but the very day the king let him walk away from that, he had tried to kill his own sister in the hallway outside his mother's apartment.

It wouldn't matter that the king had ordered these guards, or that Innel had not drawn a blade; rumor had a way of following blood.

Untrained, unarmed, and half his weight, Cahlen was scarcely more dangerous to him than one of her messenger birds. But the guards were plenty dangerous; if she were seized by another tantrum now and came at him, they would take her down and hurt her, regardless of what Innel said or did.

He searched her face as she came close. Was she still angry?

Close enough to hit. Close enough to kiss. She did neither, standing scant inches from him, looking up at him, blinking rapidly.

"Cahlen?" he asked gently.

"Brother." She gulped for air. She seemed upset, almost about to weep. He had not seen her cry since she was a baby. But this was not a typical day.

"What is it?" he asked.

"I need to fix the east tower dovecote," she said, voice low. "The birds are too crowded. They don't fly well. Will you ask for me? The king, the ministers, whoever it is that you must ask."

When Innel and Pohut, five and seven, had been taken into the Cohort, the group had numbered nearly forty children, ten of them girls. Cahlen had been brought in two years later, but in weeks was sent back to live with their mother. Between the strange moods, insensible responses, and a tendency to become overly violent when confused, she was deemed unsuited.

Over the years Cahlen showed a strong talent with animals. Now she was an assistant bird-keeper, living in the tower-shaped dovecote, breeding doves, training them to carry messages back to the palace.

In this moment, her fury at their brother's death mysteriously dissipated, all she demanded from him was a favor.

"I will," he told her earnestly.

With that she turned wordlessly away, walking down the hall, only a small limp in her step to indicate anything had transpired besides conversation. As she went, she brushed her hand through her thick, short mass of hair. A bit of birdseed dropped onto the wooden flooring.

And now to Cern.

He waited a few days to let her fury ease, then visited her suites. Sachare came into the hallway to meet him.

Most of the girls of the Cohort had left early, somewhat less motivated by the often brutal competitions that so often comprised so much of Cohort life. Of those who had finished, Taba was now a navy ship's captain and Larmna had been put in charge of House Nital's amardide forests in the Kathorn province. Sachare had become Cern's chamberlain.

His Cohort sister was a tall woman, her hands tucked into the pockets of her red robes trimmed in dark pinks and gold, marking her as one of the princess's staff. A magenta sapphire glinted in her right ear. Cern's color.

"No," Sachare said, simply and clearly.

He hadn't expected Cern to let him in easily, and it was no surprise to have Sachare sent to stand in his way, but he had thought to get into the antechamber, at least. Not to have the conversation in the hallway, in front of a tencount of royal guards who had no reason to keep it to themselves.

"Her words or yours?" he asked.

"Mine are less polite."

"Oh?" He stepped toward her, too close, just short of what might have been considered threatening, a line his Cohort brothers and sisters knew well. "What would yours be?"

From her changing expression, he could see that she was weighing various answers. She shook her head.

"Again: no."

"He was a traitor, Sachare."

"So we've heard." A small, bitter smile. "In any case, it's not me you have to convince."

"Then let me in."

"She hasn't given a new answer since I told you a moment ago."

"I can change her mind. You know that."

"You may not enter, Innel."

That was clear enough. Cern would need more time.

Still he hesitated, wondering if he should give Sachare the gift he'd brought for Cern, a small book he'd been holding in reserve for such a need. Full-color drawings of birds of prey, their silhouettes, descriptions of their calls and hunting habits. The sort of thing that would appeal to the princess. Expensive.

"He was a good man," Sachare said softly.

This caught Innel off guard. He looked away, the words echoing in his head. When he had his feelings again in hand, he looked back, meeting her stare. "So am I."

"As you say." A hard tone.

He held out the book to Sachare. "Give her this for me."

Wordlessly she took it from him and returned to the princess's rooms, the sound of the door shutting behind her echoing in the corridor. Her guards watched him silently.

A gentle touch, his brother would have said of Cern now, so furious. *Close but not too close.*

Like the rope game they'd all played in the Cohort, each holding an end to try to pull each other off-stance with sudden yanks and misdirection.

Hold solid to the rope. Keep the line alive, not too slack, not too tight.

And never look away.

Weeks went by. Cern kept a stony silence. When he approached she looked away, rebuffing him openly, and he knew better than to come close enough that she might signal her guards to intercept.

Appearances mattered. When rejected, he made sure to seem pained and conflicted, like a hurt lover pretending not to care. He set his gaze to linger on her when she was carefully not looking in his direction. He passed by her suites daily, slowing as he did.

When he and his brother used to fish together, they would find the underwater creature's location from the eddies and ripples it caused across the surface. The palace was like a lake; even if Cern did not see his longing looks directly, the ripples would get back to her. He had to be patient.

But he did not feel patient. He lay awake past the midnight bells, mind circling around what he had done that day to draw her back to him, wondering if it was too much or too little.

Somehow he had to convince her that what he had done in Botaros made sense. The king would only wait so long before looking again at his second-best choices in the

Cohort. He had given Innel an opening. He wanted Innel to win.

Innel needed to get Cern to choose him. Nothing could be more important.

Almost nothing. One afternoon, a casual comment from Restarn made it clear that Innel was expected to attend the next day's trade council. Innel studied the trade ledgers deep into the night to arrive well-prepared, because the king did not make casual comments.

A few days later, he was woken at dawn by the unsmiling seneschal, who explained that Innel would oversee the rebuild of the burnt stable auxiliary. Yes, starting now. In his spare time, the seneschal added, Innel would provide the king an analysis of the ministerial council's resolution on a stack of tangled and conflicting House petitions.

Without delay.

Still being tested, then. He thought he'd proved himself worthy already to the king, again and again, but apparently not.

So be it; he applied himself to every task, working as hard as ever. Before he quite realized it, he was spending hours a day with the king. At meals, answering challenges like Cohort drills, then pulled in for fast minutes between appointments to suggest courses of action. Even attending the king at his bath, where he couldn't help but notice that the man was hale and healthy for near eighty.

And yet, near eighty he was. As the king aged, with only the one heir, who stubbornly refused to be wed— let alone impregnated—good wishes for the king's health took on new tension. Everyone wanted to know who followed Cern on the succession list. Restarn would not say.

Traditionally, this list lived in a strongbox under the monarch's bed and was thrice-sealed. A key, a press-trap, and one final means, unspecified, but quietly said to be mage-lock. If the monarch should die before Cern was queen and no mage came forward to liberate the succession list, there would be chaos among the king's siblings and their offspring, and pushback from the Great Houses and the Cohort children.

The other Cohort children. Not the mutts.

How well Innel was now passing the king's tests was not at all clear to him. The king showed neither approval nor disapproval, quite unlike the trials of Cohort childhood, when Innel's mistakes were made clear with beatings and missed meals.

Now that he considered that from the vantage of an adult perspective, he was not at all sure he liked this better. There was a lot to be said for clarity.

One day, without warning, Restarn tossed him a captaincy. That seemed an answer of sorts.

Best of all, it came with an increase in pay. Since the trip to Botaros, he had been chronically short of funds.

Botaros. The girl who had set him on this course. A frayed, dangling thread, one he needed to cut before it unraveled the entire garment.

At least the king hadn't charged him rent on the horse.

Again he went to see Cern. This time he was let into the antechamber.

"She liked the book," Sachare told him.

"Excellent. Let me see her."

"She still says no."

With a bit of a flourish, he held out his hand and opened his fingers, revealing a dark square. Sachare took it, sniffed it.

"She can get candy any time she likes, Innel."

"Not from me, she can't."

At that Sachare chuckled a little, put the piece in her pocket, and dismissed him.

Gentle persistence, he told himself as he walked away, knowing that his repeated rejection here was the subject of palace gossip.

So be it.

As winter froze the world outside the palace, Mulack, Dil, and, to his surprise, even Sutarnan came to see him, offering pleasantries that implied support, should things go well. As if the bloody, brutal Cohort fights across the years were merely playful roughhousing.

But Innel knew better than to reveal his grudges. If he succeeded with Cern, there would be time later to address those who had supported his cause only when the winds were in his favor. And if he failed, it wouldn't matter. He could be tossed onto the street with nothing.

Or worse yet, with his mother and sister.

One morning, these dark possibilities churning in the back of his mind while he struggled with an accounting error he'd been set to resolve, there was a pounding on the door to his small room. A set of servants streamed in, directed by the seneschal's second. Over Innel's objections, they picked up everything of his that they could carry. While he watched in wordless astonishment, they marched his belongings down the hallway.

He followed them, up a floor and toward the royal wing, to a double-room apartment. Stunned, he stood in the hallway, watching them array his belongings, the accounting book still under his arm.

Sutarnan stepped to his side. "Congratulations, Captain. Let's celebrate your new quarters tonight."

How did Sutarnan know about Innel's new rooms before he did?

He had been too busy; he had neglected his various contacts. Sutarnan knew because he had neglected no one.

The double room, it turned out, was not entirely for Innel; the second section had six cots laid out, and, as he watched, a set of guards were making themselves at home.

"What is this?" he demanded, struggling to regain some semblance of control.

"King's orders, sir," said Nalas, putting his things by the cot nearest the door.

Innel puzzled over this. Guards to protect him? From what? Jealous Cohort brothers? In case he might want to leave the palace again on some wild midnight ride?

That evening, Sutarnan came with a vintner's matrass of sweet red wine. Innel barked a loud laugh at the offering, watching as the grin fled the other man's face in rare uncertainty.

He clasped Sutarnan's shoulders enthusiastically.

"Friends, always," he told him with just enough mockery to keep Sutarnan on edge for the entirety of the two hours they spent drinking together. He pressed

Sutarnan to talk about old times, specifically to recount various events in which Sutarnan had been the agent of Innel and his brother's difficulties. Sutarnan had left uneasy, a result Innel found both petty and satisfying.

The wine, also, had been very good.

The next day he went to the king's seneschal and named Srel as his captain's clerk.

"I will have to confirm this with the king," the seneschal said.

"No, you won't. And Srel will need a raise in pay appropriate to his new position."

At this the seneschal's mouth worked tightly, as if he were sucking on a dirty rock. After a moment he nodded slowly and turned away. This told Innel more than all the rumors put together.

So what was he now? Consort-apparent? He'd never heard of such a thing in his studies of monarchical history, but it seemed so.

Except that Cern still wouldn't speak to him.

He continued his diligent attention to her, sitting near her at meals, coming to her suite daily, where he instead spoke with Sachare.

Cern would come around, he told himself. In time. Patience.

Innel ran the garrison every day, his guards following in his wake. It was important to make sure that those who carried weapons regularly in the palace grounds didn't forget he was still one of them.

Today at the fields, a game of two-head was just beginning, the teams marked by colored bands tied around foreheads. A small audience of off-duties had gathered to watch. The two teams tossed their respective balls to each other to warm up, one black, one red.

"Who do you favor, ser?" Nalas asked him.

At this, Innel considered what he knew about the players on the field. Overhearing, they paused, looked back at him, as did the off-duty soldiers gathered around. Those who had been talking stopped to look his way.

As some thirty people suddenly fell silent and waited on his next words, Innel felt odd. He did not know what to make of this.

And then he did. The guard suddenly made sense.

Not protection. Not to keep him at the palace. It was the king's way of setting him apart. Cern might not yet have chosen him, but the king had.

Other things now made sense as well. The apartment. The many new tasks.

The king was not testing him. Or at least not only testing. Rather he was putting Innel in the position of consort. If not by title and not by Cern's decision, by practical measure.

A tactical error where Cern was concerned, Innel knew. He wondered how Restarn could know his own daughter so poorly. No surprise that Cern's demeanor had chilled further. She now looked past him as if he didn't exist at all.

During meals he approached as near to her as Sachare would allow, letting himself look pained and frustrated as Cern turned away. He must seem just the right amount of concerned.

It was never far from his mind that Cern could still say no. The king could hardly keep him in this exalted yet nebulous position if she did. Innel would be no more than a mutt wandering the palace halls. Out of place, out of support. A frog in the open sea, amidst sharks.

He *must* get back into her good graces.

Deep winter hit the capital all at once in a heavy snowstorm with freezing rains that coated the entire hill in slick ice, delaying delivery of the massive amount of food the palace consumed daily, ending up ripping to shreds a delicately crafted deal between Helata, Nital, and Murice to build a new fleet. The three Great Houses refused to clasp hands over the deal, and hard looks followed between their scions in the palace.

Had they been able to predict this sudden storm, the contract could have been formalized earlier, rather than as it was now, taking months more to soothe the three sides and get them back to the table. Even a day's warning could have saved the contract, not to mention preserved the kitchens' larders and hence meals for thousands.

But who could have known?

His thoughts returned to a candlelit hovel in a snow-clad village where there was a girl who could indeed predict the future.

He must act to bring the girl close by, where he could get his own answers and keep a watch on her and what she said to who. Bring the sister and baby as well to ensure her cooperation.

He could not leave and collect her himself, keenly watched as he was now. He would need someone else to do it for him. Someone competent and exceedingly discreet. That would take resources he did not yet have.

But would, when Cern came around.

Chapter Three

"You're going out?" Amarta asked her sister. "Tonight? In this cold?"

Winter had come to the village of Botaros and settled in for what was now the fourth day of a hard freeze, with midwinter still more than a tenday away.

Dirina was changing her clothes. Putting on her good ones, Amarta saw in the dim light. Her best frock. Not so frayed, less stained, fewer mended rips.

"I won't be long."

Her sister went out more and more often.

As the nights grew colder, they had drawn the cot close to the stove. Amarta sat with Pas lying by her side, thickly bundled. His eyes opened and Amarta tucked the blanket around his neck to keep him warm.

How had it all gone so fast, the coins the large man in his fine cloak had left them? They'd gone to food and peat moss, of course. Repairs for the roof and cracks that were everywhere. They had one remaining falcon, saved against need, but Amarta didn't think it would last long.

And the gold souver, so beautiful and heavy, that she'd gotten to hold for a few moments before they'd spent it, that, too, was gone. The landlord had raised his eyebrows a long moment when he saw it, his mouth falling open, but then he had shut his mouth and taken the souver, giving them five months ahead on the rent without any haggling at all.

Since that night, no one had come to ask Amarta questions. Now Dirina went out at night.

"I could come with you," Amarta said, scrambling to her feet, looking around for her blue trimmed cloak. "I'll carry Pas. I'll bundle him good and—"

"No," her sister said. "Another time, maybe." She walked by Amarta, petting her head in passing. She moved around the room, readying herself.

"Where do you go?"

Her sister stopped and looked at Amarta. Amarta sat down again, her gaze dropping to a seashell she had been holding.

The village tavern, Amarta guessed as she turned the shell over in her hands. Whatever it was Dirina did there, she somehow managed to bring back food and fuel for them. Not much, but enough to keep them going.

A treasure, the shell was. When had her mother given her this? It seemed to Amarta the least she could do, to recall the last thing her mother had given her.

"I'll only be a little while," Dirina said softly.

Spring festival of her fifth year, Amarta was pretty sure. A festival gift. It made her want to cry, thinking of her mother.

No, she would wait until Dirina was gone to cry.

Dirina belted her dress with a cord, cinching it tight around her waist, then began to brush out her dark hair, gathering it in a length of blue cloth that matched the hem on Amarta's cloak. Dirina's bangs escaped the tie, falling across her face in slight curls. With the ends of the blue fabric she tied a bow behind her head.

Blue. Like the blue lines of the shell. Like the dress her mother used to wear, blue as a hot summer's sky. They had cut that dress up, over and over across the years, reused every piece of it, sewn strips of it onto the bottom of Amarta's cloak, taken more lengths yet to tie their hair with. They still had a few of those ties left. A bit of beauty against the undyed brown of everything else they wore.

The shell. The scraps of blue dress. But for memory, it was all they had left of her.

There had been a song, too, but it was gone. Sometimes, as Amarta was falling asleep, she almost remembered it. Her mother would sing about the ocean. Like a lake, her mother had said between verses. So big you couldn't see the other side. One day, she had promised, they would go and see it together.

But they never had. Because of Amarta.

With a thoughtful pout, Pas reached out a hand to try to take the shell from Amarta's hand. She gave him her other thumb instead, and he clutched it tightly.

"What do you do there?" Amarta asked.

"Not much. We talk." Her sister fastened her fraying cloak around her shoulders, tying it snug.

Amarta looked up eagerly. "Do you mean like telling stories? Like what I do, but for fun instead of—?" Instead of causing trouble with tales of futures that might be.

"Yes, like that." Dirina walked to the door.

"At winter festival," Amarta said, not wanting her to leave. "Will we join in?"

"Yes. Probably. You watch Pas. I'll be back soon."

"I'll wait up for you."

"No, you should sleep. You should—" Dirina exhaled, fell silent, then nodded once and opened the door. White flurries swirled in the night breeze. Then she left, yanking the door shut behind her.

In the silence that followed, Amarta found that her tears for her dead mother would not come after all. Pas had fallen asleep again, and she gently pulled her finger out of his slacking grip.

The pile of peat by the stove was small, too small. Amarta decided to wait until Dirina returned to burn any more. She was not so cold as all that, not yet.

Again she turned her attention to the shell. As she rubbed the blue and white ridges she wondered if some part of her mother's spirit lived on, in the shell. If she believed it to be true, might it become so?

She *would* believe it, then. She would keep the shell close to her, always. Perhaps if she slept with it in hand, she would dream of the song her mother used to sing to her. And then, when the weather warmed, she could tie the shell to hang in the window, letting it dangle in the sweet breezes, so that if her mother's spirit was in it, she would see the warm blue sky, hear the birds, smell the earth. Each solstice and equinox, Amarta resolved, she would take her mother's shell in hand, and think of her, remembering everything she could about her. Surely, she could do that much.

The flash of vision came and went so fast that she barely realized it had happened.

Thick fingers held her shell, turning it over and over. A man's voice. A thoughtful sound.

Her shell. Someone had taken it from her. A sick feeling came over her. She enveloped the shell in her hand, wrapping it tightly, as if to protect it.

For a moment she had a sense, almost a taste, of the man whose fingers she had barely seen, then it was gone. Someone she had once met? A long-ago memory or some possible future vision?

Or maybe it wasn't memory or vision at all, but only a snatch of dream.

It wasn't fair, she thought, pressing the shell to her cheek as if it were her mother's touch. The shell was all that she had left of her.

No, she decided, whatever it was that she had just seen, vision or memory—and whoever the man was—she would not let him take it.

Her throat tightened, and she gripped the shell tightly until the stove ran hungry and the room went dark.

Chapter Four

Pelting icy rain continued, slushy and cold. When it warmed even a little, the pouring rains washed the streets clean, flooding sewers and inland farms and lakes.

At least, Innel reflected, the palace's roof cisterns were full.

Midwinter festival arrived. Cern sat sullenly by her father, drinking herself into unconsciousness and needing to be carried to her rooms, to the scowling of her father. Sachare shook her head sharply at Innel's offer of help.

A tenday later, Cern's glares at him had softened, ever so slightly. Was that the smallest hesitation before she turned her back on him?

His patience was souring. Letting the king's assigned work languish, he watched for the right opportunity.

It was late afternoon when he followed Cern and her entourage to the glassed-in gardens of the southern court, warmed in the winter months with a ring of heated stones brought from the basement furnace. Inside the glassed-in room, fruit trees were in bud. Beds of green sprouts lined the windows.

Cern's guards stood arrayed inside and out, a double perimeter of protection. There had not been a successful attempt on the life of a royal since Nials esse Arunkel, the king's beloved grandmother, was a young queen, and her younger sister's attempted kidnapping turned particularly nasty, but some attempts had been sufficiently bloody—and politically messy—to inspire both diligence and a solidly capable royal guard.

Innel had trained with many of these guards and knew them well. He exchanged nods with the commander in the doorway, a stout woman with an instinctive and powerful close-in fighting style. She considered Innel for a long moment, then stepped aside to allow him entrance. She turned her back on the room, implying a privacy that was not, in fact, present.

Cern did not look up from the long-tailed red and blue Perripin bird. It stood on her leather-wrapped arm, clutching tightly with long talons. She was feeding it with tongs from a bowl of wiggling white slugs that sat atop a round red marble tabletop.

The bird turned its head sideways to give Innel a suspicious one-eyed look, then snapped up the offered slug, held it high, gulped it down. Innel watched a lump make its way down the bird's long neck.

Cern held out her arm, and the bird stepped onto the marble tabletop and then over to the bowl of slugs, helping himself as the princess turned an unwelcoming, loathing look on Innel.

"You are trash and a liar," she said.

He suppressed elation. After months of effort, she was speaking to him.

"Yes, my lady," he said, bowing his head, aiming for a contrite tone and expression.

"What kind of man kills his own brother? And a man as fine as Pohut was? You are a monstrosity."

Much warmer. This was the opening he'd been hoping for. And now to step into it.

The story he had given the king after his audience on return from Botaros had started with the truth: that he and his brother had gone to Botaros independently. From there it was invention: a woman, he told the king, claiming to be an unknown granddaughter of Nials esse Arunkel, now dead for decades, was said to look enough like the old queen to be her twin. The granddaughter was telling anyone who would listen that she should be on the throne instead of Restarn.

Treasonous talk, of course. Both he and his brother, Innel said, had gone to Botaros to find out the truth of the matter, intending to bring the granddaughter back to the king for justice.

But Pohut had changed his mind, barring Innel's way, claiming the granddaughter to be his discovery. Intending to use her against the king, Innel suspected. They had fought, and Pohut pulled a knife, forcing Innel to defend himself.

It was a relatively safe story. Even had the granddaughter existed, a short talk and a quiet relocation to the south border would have taken care of the matter. Not a threat that would much trouble the king.

Restarn listened impatiently, waving his hands for Innel to hurry it along. Clearly he didn't want details.

Or he knew it wasn't true.

In any case, he seemed to accept the explanation.

Innel had debated an alternate tale for the king, that it was the brothers' devotion to and lifelong competition for Cern that brought them to blows, but finally discarded that; if Cern found out—if she thought that Pohut had died for her—she would never forget him.

And that would not do; however long it took, he needed Cern to forget his brother and forgive Innel.

So for the princess he needed a more compelling tale.

He kept his tone soft and sorrowful. "There's more to the story than what I told your father."

A dangerous double game here, he knew, because with the guard listening, every word would likely get back to the king. Anything he said now had to both be convincing to Cern and transparently benign to Restarn.

A flicker of uncertainty in her eyes, a wary interest.

"You see, my lady, we wanted to find out if the rumors were true."

"The granddaughter," she said tightly.

"No."

"No? What, then?"

Innel shook his head ruefully. "I'm embarrassed to admit to it."

At that she gave him a look, still plenty hostile, but tinged with curiosity.

This was the reason the Cohort education had included the finest bards and minstrels of the empire.

"We were seduced by a story that could have been a children's tale. A cave outside a small village . . . a treasure trove: a cache of gold."

"Gold?"

By law, every flake of gold belonged to the crown. Every last bit, no matter its form nor how it had come into being. And no matter who now held it.

Innel looked around at the seedlings, the fruit trees optimistically preparing for spring in this last part of winter, and let the moment lengthen. He acted as if he were struggling with what to say next.

"We could not afford to be wrong. You know what they'd say. The mutts. The fools. We had to find the absolute truth. And we did. But my brother . . ." He paused. "He wanted it for himself."

"What, the gold?" She seemed incredulous at this.

"To sell it south, to wash it through Perripin traders."

"But that would be treason."

Sometimes it surprised him, how naive she could be.

"Yes, and I told him so. No, I said. He grew angry. Our loyalty to the crown, I said; nothing is more precious. He yelled at me, called me a fool, and when I would not budge, disowned me. And then . . ." A glance down, a ragged exhale. "You know the rest."

She considered his words skeptically. She was almost there.

He inhaled slowly, audibly. "We grew up poor, My Lady Princess. Two years older, he remembered it far more clearly than I did. No House, no family—then the king's generosity, to be sure, but nothing to call our own. Perhaps he sensed that his chances with you were waning and wanted something more substantial in hand."

"What? We would never have turned him away. A company command, at least."

Innel gave her a pained look. "You know how proud he was."

"No, it is not possible."

But it was not disbelief in her tone now. It was pain. Denial that someone she had known since childhood, someone she had cared for, could act this way.

And that meant she nearly believed him.

It was time for the final detail that weaves the parts of the story into a whole. He reached into his pocket, palmed a small, heavy item that Srel had bought for him from a south-end black market, a place it was barely safe to walk, let alone spend money. Srel, born to that side, had known what to do with the funds Innel had managed to scrape together. It had taken every quarter-nals Innel could lay hands on.

An investment, he told himself again. It would pay off. He only had to win her. This was the moment.

He walked slowly to the marble table.

"There was no cave, no cache. Just a hole under a rock, by the foot of a twisted hemlock pine, where we found this. Perhaps also the source of the granddaughter rumor. Now I give it to you, My Lady Princess, to put in the treasury. As is my duty to empire, king, and Your Royal Highness."

He placed the item on the table. At the sound and feel underfoot of the heavy metallic click on the stone, the bird quickly sidestepped away from him to the edge. He stepped back.

Cern reached forward and brushed the small, dully gleaming statuette with her fingers.

Four-fingers high head to shoulders, it was a passable rendition of Nials esse Arunkel, the Grandmother Queen, judging by the portraits that hung in the Great Hall. Cern picked it up, held it wonderingly.

"Pohut died for this?"

No, his brother died because he had crossed the line between competition and betrayal.

And because Innel had gotten to the girl first.

But he could say none of that.

"I'm sorry, My Lady," he said, knowing it was the only thing he could say, and resenting the part of him that meant it.

Innel found himself jolted awake from dreams of struggles in frozen mud, unable to get hold of his brother, grasping and slipping. Then suddenly, somehow, he had Pohut's head tight between his locked arms and twisted hard to the sound of a crack.

He was fully awake now, considering the split-second decision that saved his life, and the advice that had made it possible.

If he knew of her, others would. Of those who had heard the rumor, who else might care enough to go to Botaros to find out if it were true?

Innel now keenly regretted not having done something about the girl that night.

But what? He could hardly have dragged both his brother's body and a resisting child through the mountains and then into the palace, never mind the question of the sister and the baby.

It dawned on him then, the obvious, brutal solution: to slay her there and then, that very night. This problem would now be solved.

His thoughts flickered back to the candlelit shack. He considered the distance from the nearest neighbors and how far her screams might have carried in the gusting wind. The sister would likely have fought him, so he would have had to kill her, too. And then what? The baby as well?

He wondered if it was in him to do such a thing, to take sharp steel to the three of them, in order to keep the girl from whoever else might want her predictions.

Well, it didn't matter if it was in him or not. He hadn't. He would simply have to find a way to have her quietly brought to Yarpin, where he could control what she said and to whom.

Once she was here, he would have more options. For example, he could have her tongue cut out, solving the problem of her talking without any killing at all. He wondered if she knew how to write.

In any case, this could wait no longer.

Innel drummed his fingers on a table of dark wood into which was inlaid a scattering of paler woods showing the sigils of the oldest of the Lesser Houses. Bolah, warming spiced wine in the corner, filling the air with anise and cardamom, was adept at services quieter and less showy than the Great Houses might inspire.

Which was why he was here.

He realized he was drumming on House Finch's sigil. What was their motto again? *Loyalty through winter.* He considered that and paused in his drumming.

"Twunta, Captain?" The small white-haired woman offered him a long, silver pipe from a red mahogany stand.

With a head shake he declined. Wine only clung to his breath, while smoke clung to his clothes. He found it better not to have his indulgences so easily determined.

Getting away from the palace tonight had been no small feat. On this cold, overcast evening, Srel stood outside a soaking bath as if Innel were inside, where instead Nalas enjoyed hours of late-night soaking while a hooded Innel snuck out into the frigid city to meet with Bolah.

Now his eyes wandered the room, taking in the glinting, colorful, polished clutter. On one wall a thick tapestry hung on which people and animals feasted and fornicated, their bodies mingled and twisted together so that it was hard to tell where one limb began and another ended.

Bolah had a reputation for being able to offer the unusual.

On the table between them she set two tall circular porcelain tumblers, almost equidistant from him.

"Congratulations on your promotion, Captain."

Innel made a sound between acceptance and amusement. She would surely know that he expected to have another title as soon as he married Cern.

She slowly sat across from him at the small table. "It has been a long time, has it not?"

"Alas, I've been quite busy."

"I can easily imagine, ser."

Through the translucent sides of the tumblers he could see the dark, aromatic wine fill as she poured.

"The hope your pending marriage brings brightens this dismal night. I trust I may be allowed to say that the empire is most fortunate to have your hands so near what I am certain will be her most grateful reins."

"You may, but only once."

Her laugh seemed almost genuine. She waited for him to choose his cup. An old tradition, now mostly formality, but some believed that you could tell a great deal from which cup a person chose. He selected the closest. A gesture of simple trust.

"Surely there must be something this poor old woman can do for you in return for the honor and pleasure of your most excellent company."

Innel rubbed his thumbs over the geometric design on the cup and raised it high, examining the underside. "An impressive imitation of House Etallan's sigil, Grandmother."

"What keen eyesight you have, Captain, to notice the poor Maker's mark from House Keramos in this year's produce. I fear that as he ages, his hands shake, his eyesight dims, and his mark becomes—it pains me to say this, ser—rather sloppy."

The other word that came to Innel's mind, of course, was "forged."

"Perhaps I should have a word with Tokerae dele Etallan, to see if he can assist Keramos in finding a new Maker." Etallan was Keramos' patron House. He smiled wide to show he wasn't in the least serious.

She matched his smile. "No sense in bringing shame to House Keramos, Captain. We depend on them daily for our plates and cookware."

"As wise as your years, Bolah."

This was where Innel came when he needed

something uncommon. For his part, he saw to it that Bolah could do her business unencumbered by time-consuming questions from the crown's auditors about anything as insignificant as the veracity of the marks on her cups.

"And so, what can I do for you, Captain?"

"I need someone brought to me."

Bolah raised her eyebrows in question.

"With no mistakes."

She held out her hands, as if to say she was sad he asked for so little.

"Very quietly."

"What sort of someone?"

"A girl child."

"I know many who could do this for you."

Innel reached into his pocket and brought out two souver touches, placing the heavy, palm-sized coins on the table between them. It was the rest of everything he had, including the cache of simple souvers that he and Pohut had secreted away against some final, desperate need.

But he had no choice; he must get the girl in hand, and to do so meant the appearance of being able to spend this amount easily. If all went as planned, that would soon be true enough.

He placed them palace-side up, each stamped with a detailed likeness of the multistoried monarchical mansion. Not the side that showed the sigils of the Eight Great Houses. A clear message, one that she could hardly miss. "I want the best," he said. "And soon."

Bolah did a fair impression of barely considering the

coins, but Innel was not fooled; he had her keen attention. "The best, ser? In-city? In the province? Across the empire?"

"Yes."

"And soon as well? You ask a great deal, Captain." Her eyes flickered to the souver touches. "You will be spending more than that."

"I may need some credit extended to me."

"Ah," she said, drawing out the sound, a look of calculated sadness across her wrinkled features.

"I am going to marry the princess, Bolah. Who will one day soon be queen of the empire. What is that worth, do you think?"

For a moment she looked elsewhere, as if attempting to answer his question by calculating sums. Her eyes flickered back to him and she gave him a merchant's best smile. "I believe I can help you, Captain."

"You have someone in mind."

Bolah took a sip of her wine. "If he is available."

"Reliable? Discreet?"

"And talented and capable, with a solid reputation. My first choice, Captain, if I required such a service. And had I the resources of your princess."

He did not miss her point.

"It may take more than money to interest him. He chooses his patrons, not the other way around."

Innel swirled the wine in his cup, watching the red liquid slowly fall in tails down the insides. "What will it take, then?"

"I would not presume to suppose. You will need to negotiate directly with him. I will, of course, take my percentage of any coin, goods, or worth of services on which you agree."

"Of course."

"Shall I arrange a meeting?"

"Yes."

"With or without your name, Captain?"

He considered the benefits of anonymity. If the man was as capable as Bolah said, then Innel's own future status was part of the enticement. At the same time, knowing who he was would make him vulnerable.

A balance of risks, as always.

"Give him my name."

"Captain, in your interest I must say again that this man is expensive. There are ten or twenty in Yarpin alone who are strong, quick, and smart enough to assist you in this matter. Even a handful of them would cost less than this single man. Are you quite, quite sure—"

Innel lifted two fingers, and Bolah fell silent. The gesture was Cern's, and he was finding it an effective reminder to people of his changing position. He took a sip of the wine. Sweet and dusty, a hint of woodsmoke and pine behind the spices.

Bolah waited, giving every impression of being willing to wait forever with perfect delight. She had built a rich business on such impressions.

"I was ten," Innel said. "My brother had challenged me to a rabbit-hunting contest. The loser would present his clothes to the winner and spend the night in the woods. That year at spring festival my mother had given me an excellent hunting bow. To this day, I don't know how she afforded it." At Bolah's bemused look, he gave a bitter smile. "Don't mistake being raised in the palace for having money, Grandmother."

She inclined her head at this point, then raised her eyebrows for him to continue.

"I had planned to save the bow for when I truly needed it. A hunt with the king, perhaps, something I had not yet been invited to, unlike many others in the Cohort. The contest was only rabbits, I reasoned, so I took a smaller, lesser, and cheaper bow."

"No rabbits," Bolah guessed.

"A long, cold, autumn night I will never forget."

"There is no substitute for quality."

"Since then I have been fortunate enough to hunt with His Royal Majesty often. Though I fear his hunting days may well be in the past."

"Oh?" she asked carefully.

"He is not a young man any more," Innel said. Sometimes it was enough to breathe a little life into a rumor.

"I pray daily to the sea and sky for His Majesty's most excellent health."

"As do we all. But no one can stop the years. The moon is eaten and reborn. Seasons chase each other across the year." He paused. "Wedding horns sound. Knots are tied."

"Who can know what will come?"

She meant that he was not yet consort, Cern not yet queen. The coronation, even if the king's promises of abdication were to be relied upon, was still many steps away. There was a limit to how much he could borrow against a future that might not come to pass.

He recalled the girl's prediction. *I think yes.*

"The time is coming to place your wagers, Bolah."

"You have my full support, Captain."

He picked up the cup again, swirling the small pool of red at the bottom.

"More wine, Captain?"

"The price of metals is going up. Why are merchants hoarding, Bolah?"

"The markets are always in motion, Captain. Now it simply happens that metals are more in demand than yesterday."

"The rebellions in Gotar and Sinetel are minor affairs. They will not last long."

"Then I am sure the price of copper and tin will fall again."

"Tell your fellow merchants that even now Arunkel troops are putting down these rebellions."

"As you say, Captain."

He had debated with himself whether or not to say these next words. Even now he was undecided.

A balance of risks.

"Also," he said, "I need someone who can see into the future."

Her expression was uncertain, poised, as if ready to laugh at his joke, as soon as she was sure it was one. Seeing that he was serious, her tentative smile vanished. She shook her head.

"You have heard of no such?"

"Of course I have, Captain. Such rumors come and go with the sea winds. These days they blow with a young man's bluster. There are always such rumors. Always."

"Beyond rumor, though?"

"You wish someone without pretense, who can truly predict what will come?"

"I do."

"If I knew of such a person, Captain, I would have my robes made from House Sartor's silks, eat myself silly on Elupene's fermented Kukka berries, and only open my door to mages who would keep me young forever."

After a lifetime at the palace, Innel had faith in his ability to spot duplicity. He was almost certain Bolah was telling the truth. Almost.

"For such a person I would pay a great deal."

"Yes," she said with sober amusement, "you would. But I cannot find what does not exist. Even the most powerful mages cannot foretell the future better than a wealthy gambler."

So Bolah had not yet heard of the girl.

Or having heard, had not credited the rumor. Innel could almost allow himself to hope the knowledge was contained.

He stood. "Contact me when you find him."

"You will not be disappointed, Captain,"

He hoped she was right. He needed her to be.

Now Innel half wished he had not told Bolah to give the man his name. If the man were as clever as she had implied, how long until he figured out himself what the girl was?

A true seer. The possibilities were staggering.

But it was too late for regrets. He would simply have to be careful what he told him. And get the man under contract.

Bolah had arranged their meeting at the Frosted Rose, an expensive eatery near the palace where lamps were kept dim to cater to merchants and aristocrats who found it prudent to conduct business away from House and palace.

Innel had dressed in the simple, nondescript garb that a merchant might wear. Nalas was at another table in a similar outfit. After a sip of sunken ale, a fermented drink he didn't much like, involving roots and fungus that was currently popular, he went to the toilet at the back of the inn. Nalas followed and stood outside to discourage anyone else.

Inside, Innel opened a small vent above his head. He tapped the ceiling in a pattern of knocks based on a well-known ballad.

"Yes?" came a male voice.

"Identify yourself."

"I am called Tayre. Bolah sent me. In what way can I assist you, ser?"

The tone was not what he had expected. Mild, nearly deferring. Perhaps the tone of a servant.

"She speaks highly of you," Innel said with some doubt. "That you are without peer across the empire."

A thoughtful sound. "That seems likely." Was that disappointment in his tone?

Again, not the response Innel expected. "What you can do for me?"

"What do you need done?"

Innel hesitated. Every person who knew was a vulnerability. "There is a girl. I want her brought to me. Fast and quietly."

"In what condition?"

"Intact. Alive and well. She is traveling with a woman and a baby. I want them, too, but the girl is my first concern." He recalled how she had looked at her sister and cradled the baby. There were deep, isolated rooms in the palace dungeons that would house them all. He would clear one. "A bonus for the woman and baby."

"What do you want with the girl?"

"Does it matter?"

"It might," the man said. "I can't know until you tell me."

"I have questions for her that I don't want anyone else asking."

"Are others pursuing her?"

"No," he said firmly, willing it to be so.

"Will you describe her?"

Again he hesitated. But really, what choice did he have? He could not fetch her himself.

Once he married Cern, once she was crowned, his position would be secure.

If he had the girl, that was.

"Perhaps twelve springs old," Innel said. "Amarta al Botaros, or at least she was in Botaros last autumn." Had so much time really passed since then? "Brown hair, past her shoulders. A roundish face, light green eyes, short nose. Her sister is perhaps twenty, with an infant in arms. A boy, I think. Botaros is a mountain village, southeast, off the Sennant River."

"I know it."

"How long will it take you, do you think?"

"I don't know."

"What? No estimate?"

"Please understand," Tayre said, "that when you contract with me, you purchase my ability to deliver what is possible and no more."

Innel gave a soft laugh. "What does that mean?"

"It means that I deliver what you want, if it is in my capability."

"That's all you offer?"

"That is all I offer."

Innel waited for more, but he was silent. No explanations, no promises. For a moment anger sparked in Innel. Was he being toyed with?

No, he was not, he realized. Innel was overly accustomed to the arrogant, blustery talk that made up most of palace conversation. This man was not from the palace. Not from anywhere nearby, either, he guessed. This was simply confidence. "I see," he said slowly. "When can you begin?"

Spring weather had yet to arrive in force. Snow and ice still clung to the mountain peaks.

"As soon as we come to terms," Tayre answered. "I will go to Botaros and track her. One hundred souver touches now, against expenses, one hundred more when I deliver her. Another hundred for the sister and baby. All alive."

Expensive, but not nearly as dear as Innel had expected.

"And."

"And?"

"Unrestricted passage through Arun."

Arun, not Arunkel. Not quite an insult, but far from the patriotism Innel was accustomed to. "I can't even promise myself that."

"I will accept as sufficient a writ that neither you nor those under your command will detain me in any way."

"Not if you break laws."

Now there was open amusement in the other's voice. "Have you heard the saying that one can break the king's laws by sneezing, Captain?"

"Liberty *and* immunity? I can't give you that."

"I think in your future capacity as Royal Consort you can."

"Not indefinitely."

"Ten years."

"Five."

"I see Bolah has failed to explain me; I do not bargain. Those are my terms. Do you decline the contract?"

There was something about the soft tone of voice that blunted words that would otherwise have been insulting. It was just the sort of clever trick his brother might have used. He reminded himself what Bolah had said, that there were others far less expensive and nearly as good.

Nearly.

No. He did not have time for mistakes. "What would you do with such free passage if you had it?"

"I have no specific plans."

"I can't promise such liberty without knowing."

"Nothing to undermine your monarch's agenda. Whoever it happens to be."

"Or mine."

A short chuckle. "No, Captain. I can't afford to be caught between you and your sovereign. Choose one."

Innel started to answer, stopped. As long as the girl was free to give accurate predictions to anyone else, his plans could be severely and rapidly undermined. At the same time, those plans depended on his unquestioned loyalty to the king and, if things went well, to Cern.

One answer put Innel in danger. The other was treason. Bolah was right. The man was good.

"To protect the crown, then," Innel said, "you should first direct your loyalty to me."

Treason it was.

"As you say, Captain. Do we have a contract?"

"I want to see what I'm buying."

"Seeing me won't reassure you."

"You assume a lot about me for someone who doesn't know me."

"What makes you think I don't know you?"

That caught Innel offguard. After a moment's reflection, he decided the man was making a point rather than a threat.

"Also, consider this," Tayre said. "As I go about your business, if I should be caught and brought before you and your monarch, you may disavow me with veracity. There are those who can tell lie from truth, just by hearing it spoken."

"I have yet to meet such a person," Innel said. It was one of a long list of abilities that mages were reputed to have.

"They don't typically announce themselves."

"Are you a mage, Tayre?"

A single laugh. "If I were, I would charge more. Perhaps I would even bargain. Hire my reputation, Captain, not my appearance."

Innel preferred his contracts sealed with a formal

handclasp as well as words. It was said that one could judge how well a person would fulfill their commitment by the hands and eyes in the moment of binding. Innel fancied that he had that skill. Furthermore, he was curious about what Tayre looked like, curious if he would be disappointed. But the man was right in his points, and curiosity was not reason enough. It was, as always, a balance of risks.

"I accept your terms," Innel said, initiating the litany that sealed the bond.

"Our contract is made," Tayre replied, completing the verbal binding.

As Innel listened to the man's soft steps fade across the roof, he wondered which of the dungeon rooms would attract the least attention.

Chapter Five

"Must you go out again? Really?"

Amarta heard the whine in her own voice, but it was hardly fair that Dirina went out almost every night, while Amarta must stay and watch Pas. With snow deep on the ground, Amarta only went outside to the toilet, and the only people she ever saw were her sister and Pas.

Pas was trying to stand now, making a small, frustrated sound. He sat back heavily onto Amarta's lap, frowning, staring across the lamplit room at his mother. Amarta wrapped her arms around him, burying her nose in his neck instead of looking at her sister.

As the peat in the stove smoldered and spat, sending an acrid smell into the room, Dirina pulled a dress over her pale underclothes.

"We need more fuel for the fire," Dirina said flatly.

That was so; they did not even have enough to get through the night. By morning it would be wretchedly, bitingly cold.

"The tavern again," Amarta said, half-question, half-accusation.

87

"I'll be back soon."

It was nearly the same conversation every night. But when Dirina came back she brought food and fuel, sometimes a few nals. Though as winter held stubbornly to the land, the nals chits became worth less and less, and the peat ran out faster and faster.

Maybe it wasn't so bad, what her sister did at the tavern. Maybe it was one of those things that seemed worse than it was because Amarta was too young to understand. And just because Dirina's hair was tangled when she came back, and she stank of men until morning when they could heat water to clean themselves, that didn't mean that she didn't like it. Did it?

Amarta didn't really want to know.

"Why don't they bring me questions any more, Diri?"

Dirina's fingers were on the door handle. She paused. "I don't know."

Amarta didn't quite believe that. "Because it's so cold, maybe."

"That must be it."

The winter had been far colder than anyone expected. Even the king's red-and-black clad soldiers had gone, given up their search for the missing tax collector, a short man with a husky voice who had come during harvest, taken taxes, and left, apparently failing to return to the capital with his collectings. The soldiers seemed ready to stay until they had questioned everyone in the village over and over.

Then the snow had begun to fall in earnest. When it was four feet deep, the soldiers had left. The spring, now that it was here, did not seem that much different from the winter.

"When the weather warms . . ." Dirina said, hand still paused on the door.

"Please don't go."

Her sister's eyes widened in alarm. Amarta felt a sudden, sick guilt. "No," she said quickly. "I don't *see* anything. I just . . ."

Her sister's mouth twitched into a weak, fearful smile that settled the guilt deep in Amarta's stomach.

"Do they talk about me?"

"Who?"

"At the tavern. What do they say about me?"

"Nothing. They talk about the tax collector and how the king's soldiers drank all the best wine. How Grandmother Malwa laughs too loud in the night and returns to the wrong house when she comes back from the toilet."

But Amarta had seen the villagers scowl at her and had heard the whispers: "Magic, that's what."

The poor harvest. The wretched cold that would not break. They blamed it on her.

But it was no kind of magic, what she did. Only a way of looking at things and people.

Not magic. Magic brought destruction. Everyone knew that.

Dirina sighed, walked over, stroked Amarta's head. "When the cold breaks, and the ice melts, people will warm to us. You'll see, Ama."

Amarta nodded, though she didn't believe it.

Then Dirina left, pulling the door tight behind.

So cold. Amarta put one of the final pieces of peat into the stove.

The three of them had gone to winter festival, stood warming by the huge fire in the central square, listening to the music. While she looked around for a friendly face, Amarta recalled the saying that, in winter, no one could afford to be stingy, because who knew when you yourself might need something in the dead-cold times? But everyone kept distant from them; they had not been born here, so perhaps they did not matter.

It was hard to imagine that spring festival would be any different.

She remembered the last village, the forgiveness rite at spring festival, with the run up the cliff, flat stones in hand—as many as you needed—each one scratched or char-marked with the first letter of the name of those who had wronged you the previous year. Then, all at once, together, everyone would hurl their rocks as far as they would fly, so that they could go into the new year free of grudges and wrongs, all forgiven.

She had laughed with delight, looking around at the others, eager to see who might now be her friend again, but no one had returned a smile.

There had been no friends then. There would be none now. At this spring festival there would be no welcome, let alone forgiveness for the outsider who knew too much.

It was so very unjust—she had only answered the questions they had asked. How could they resent her for that? Surely, once they understood how little she really knew about them, they would forgive. At spring festival this year, she resolved, she would tell them everything. She imagined the moment, how she would stand up and speak up, and she would say—

The light of the fire went very bright.

There would be no spring festival this year, not for her.

A vivid image cut through her imaginings like a howl etched across the night's deep quiet.

The hunter stood in the shadows, face wrapped against the chill, eyes dark, watching her, waiting for her to come near.

Only once before had vision come on her this way, unbidden and overwhelming, and that was the morning her parents had died.

Tangled in a blanket, nearly smothered, unable to move, she fought and struggled to cry out. A thick wad of blanket went into her mouth, tight, impossible to push away, her cries no more than muffled grunts.

Amarta launched to her feet, heart pounding, and pulled on her cloak. She bundled the sleeping Pas. He whined about being woken, then about being wrapped too much, hands pushing at the blankets. She said something, forgotten the moment it left her mouth, and he stopped, perhaps sensing the urgency of her tone. She held him tight and was out the door.

A breezy, frozen night faced her, a three-quarter moon shining half around a cloud, making the drifts of snow glow white. The air bit her face with cold, snuck under her cloak, crawling around her neck.

A small sound in the dark. An animal in the brush. A mole, or a rabbit. Surely too small to be a man, but she froze anyway.

Suddenly she was unsure. Should she go back inside and wait for Dirina? Must she rush? Even if the vision was true, this could hardly happen so soon, not with the ground frozen and deep in snow. No one would travel in this.

But the last time she had waited to act, her parents had died. She had foreseen it clearly, and still her parents had died.

She pushed herself to a fast walk, trading silence for speed with every crunching footfall.

Someone was coming. She could feel it. Every shadow seemed a threat.

When she reached the tavern, she pushed open the heavy door and stepped inside, shudderingly grateful to be out of the bitter chill.

The small room was lit with lamps and smelled warmly of people, the yeasty smell of ale, the spice of woodsmoke. Every scent told her that all was well with the world.

For a moment she simply stood there, relishing the warmth, inhaling the scent of food, listening to the reassuring sounds of conversation.

"I'm not paying more," an old man was saying, "I'll tell you that. Not to make up for the collector's theft."

"Oh, you'll pay," a woman near him said, slapping the back of one hand with the palm of the other, a gesture that said hard currency, not trade or favors. "Get fixed with that. If they give you a choice between pay and your fingers, you'll find a way."

"Shit will sprout wings and fly."

"Brave words for a man with all his fingers."

The man loudly exhaled. "We don't earn more, they just take more. It's not right."

"If the king knew . . ." said a young man.

"Maybe you should go tell him, boy," the woman said.

"I could do. Would he listen, do you think, if I went—"

A laugh. "No. He wants your coin, boy, not your—"

The room fell silent as Amarta was finally noticed. In moments the only sound was the hissing of the central fire pit. Some who turned their heads to look at her she recognized from their shack, as those whose futures she had foreseen when the weather was better.

From their looks she could see that they remembered her, too.

"I don't—" she began. *Know anything about you,* she ached to say. So many people, so many possible futures, things that might never even come to pass—how could anyone expect her to remember it all?

Or maybe they thought she was foreseeing now, as she stood here with her feet and fingers aching from the cold, Pas whimpering in her arms.

"What do you want, girl?" asked the unsmiling innkeeper, walking to stand in front of her.

"Dirina."

"Upstairs," he said. "Busy. Go home."

"I need her."

"Not now, you don't. Go home."

Behind her someone opened the door and stepped inside, bringing in gusts of cold air. Sudden terror made Amarta pull away from the figure, clutching Pas tighter, but it was only the village healer, an old woman, not the monster from her vision.

The woman's lined face twisted downward. "What's she doing here?"

"Just leaving," the innkeeper said, a hand on Amarta's

shoulder. "Come on now, girl, people got to eat and you don't belong."

Then Amarta was outside in the chill again, the door shut tight behind her. Pas inhaled the frigid air, a deep, deep inhale, and then gave a shrill wail into the night.

Amarta wanted to cry, too. She rocked him instead, face near his, murmuring. He quieted, staring up at her with a petulant expression.

A mistake to come here. She would return to the shack, where, if her visions were to be believed, she would not live much longer. When Dirina came home, she would tell her what she had seen and they would figure out what to do together. Surely there would be at least that much time.

She thought of her mother.

There might not be.

Before she could reconsider, she pushed open the door again and stepped inside. Pas had stopped crying, but once inside he began again and everyone turned to glower at them both.

Amarta trembled.

"Hey, now," the innkeeper said sharply, moving forward, his hands out. "You can't—"

"Dirina," Amarta pleaded.

"Can't come in here, I said, girl. Now—"

"Dirina," Amarta cried out defiantly, raising her voice over Pas's howl.

"Out," he shouted, grabbing her by the shoulders, hard enough to hurt, turning her and propelling her toward the half-open door. She leaned back against him, resisting.

"Dirina!" she yelled as loud as she could.

And then she was again out in the night, the door shut, the bolt slamming down.

Pas was wailing in earnest now. She turned away from the inn, stumbling back down the path to the shack, tears of frustration and shame blurring her vision.

If the villagers hadn't liked her before, they would like her less now. A false hope in any case, that they might ever. But what if she had ruined Dirina's work as well? What would they do for food and heat?

Maybe there was no changing the future for yourself. She'd foreseen her parents' death but had not been able to prevent it. Maybe that was how it worked.

Or, she realized suddenly, she could leave by herself. Tonight. Go off into the mountain roads alone. Surely the villagers would accept Dirina and Pas if Amarta were gone.

She wondered at what would find her first. Cougars. Wolves. The cold.

The shadow hunter.

But then, if she died, perhaps she could see her mother in the Beyond. Tell her she was sorry. Maybe her mother would throw a stone for her over whatever cliffs the afterlife might have.

She wiped her nose as she walked, clutching Pas to her chest as he cried softly. So intent was she on the snow-crusted path in front of her, on swallowing her tears, that only when Dirina was right by her side did she hear her sister call her name.

Chapter Six

They took one last look around the shack.

"I'm sorry, Diri."

With a bleak expression, Dirina shook her head as if to reject the apology. "I only wish we could take the chair and table," she said softly. "We should have burned them for heat." Her sister adjusted the straps that kept Pas tied to her chest, nuzzled him briefly, picked up her heavy sack, slung it over her shoulder.

At least they didn't have much to carry.

Always leaving. Always because of her.

As they stepped outside into the frozen night, Dirina shut the door behind them. The heavy, dull sound of wood on wood echoed in Amarta's mind, and with a light brush of foresight, she knew they would never be here again.

At least she didn't have to worry about spring festival in this village.

Dirina was watching her, her expression a faint echo of the look the villagers sometimes gave her. Amarta felt a chill that had nothing to do with the night.

She followed Dirina past outlying houses and farms, now shut tight. Envy filled Amarta for their safe, cozy, warm houses.

As they left the village behind, snow crunching underfoot, the mountain road before them was free of footprints. No one traveled this road in winter. It was folly. She hoped her sister knew what she was doing.

But she was the one who had set them on this path.

High, thin clouds caught moonlight, casting barely enough light to show them the road as it led under tall trees and darker shadows. Pines and cedar and high maples cut black shapes against the night sky.

The thought of burning their chairs seemed so sensible now that she wondered why they hadn't done it before. They could die out here from the cold itself, never mind the eyes in the shadows that she might have only imagined. What if this were a terrible mistake?

"We go to the river, Diri?" she asked softly.

"Did you not say we must cross the Sennant?"

"That's what I saw," she said apologetically.

"Then we'll cross and go to a village a bit beyond. When the weather improves, we'll find a way downriver."

Somewhere new that no one had heard of them yet. Heard of her.

"Whatever is after us, maybe it only wants me."

"No."

"All I'm saying is that I could go to the river without you, cross and be safe, and you and Pas could go back to Botaros . . ."

"No."

"I just think that maybe—"

"Amarta." A sharp rebuke. "Whatever is coming, it isn't getting you. We won't let it."

Amarta sobbed a little then, but quietly so that Dirina would not hear. She wiped her face with her sleeve, leaving her even colder.

The last time they had crossed the Sennant, they walked a high bridge connecting two cliffs below which the river crashed and boomed, a terror of white foam that still gave her nightmares.

"How will we cross?"

"A raft on an overhead rope with a pulley. At the end of the road. Or so I'm told," Dirina added softly.

"I'm cold."

"I know."

Her mind numb, she marched behind Dirina, trying to step in her sister's footprints. "And tired."

"We should find a way-house between us and the river."

A place to be out of the cold. It sounded marvelous.

As they fled yet another home. How many had they left now? Three? Four? And how many more?

Whispers mumbled behind her heavy eyes, a swirling, muddy confusion trying to answer the question she had, in foolish exhaustion, begun to ask.

Taste and texture in her mouth, chewy and sweet, nuts and fruit and spices she had never tasted before.

Blue eyes above a wide smile. A warm hand squeezing her own.

Possibilities only. Nothing certain. She pushed it away angrily. A glimpse here or there, a tantalizing hint of warmth when she was so cold, of food when she was so hungry. No use. No use at all.

Distracted, she misstepped, caught herself. Dirina gave her a worried glance, then turned back to trudge forward, head bowed over Pas in her arms.

Amarta chastised herself. She must focus on the uneven ground in front of her. A poor step, a twisted ankle—she was already costing them so much.

"Ama," Dirina said after a time. "Do you think we could rest a bit?"

Amarta stopped, confused for a moment as to why her sister was asking her.

Because she was supposed to know. The one thing she could do to help them.

She let her sister's question sit in her mind like a lump of fat in a hot skillet. Atop some bread, perhaps, with a fried apple, or even some scraps of meat.

With effort she turned her thoughts back to the question. Was the shadow hunter close? Did they have time? A crawling sensation on her skin intensified. Warning or simply that she was freezing, she could not quite tell. "A few minutes, I think," she whispered.

So they sat, backs against a large, towering fir.

Moments later Amarta woke, heart pounding, dread propelling her to her feet and then forward along the path. Dirina silently gathered Pas and followed.

By the time the sky began at last to pale toward dawn, Amarta's legs felt leaden, and her eyes kept trying to close as she shuffled forward. With daylight, heavy clouds gathered across the sky and snow began to fall. At first it was a light sprinkling and then fat, wet flakes, the gray-green of snow-crusted pines the only color in a world gone white.

When Dirina stopped, Amarta plowed into her, and they caught each other, Pas objecting wordlessly between them. Dirina pulled her under a bough of thick cedar that provided a bit of shelter. They sat and ate a few bites of hard bread in oil, nearly frozen. Amarta looked back at the path.

Before them was a crossroads. To the south another road opened, leading temptingly downhill, unlike the ascending road that was their direction.

"The village south," Amarta said softly. "Isn't it closer?"

"The river, you said," Dirina answered. Was that reproach in her sister's voice?

"You and Pas could go south, and I'd go to the river. We could meet at the town of Sennant later, and—"

"No."

"What if there isn't really anyone after us? What if I'm wrong?"

"Ama?" Dirina's voice cracked. "Are you—"

"I don't know!" She swallowed the lump in her throat, looked into the woods. A winter finch fluttered to a fallen stick, pecked at it hopefully, fluttered away.

Dirina moved close and wrapped Amarta in her arms, the baby between them, and they huddled there a long moment. Then Dirina held Amarta at arm's length.

"We will go where your visions say," Dirina said, standing, helping Amarta up and hefting Pas in the sling at her chest. She caressed his cheek and, with a force that surprised Amarta, said: "We will not be among the fools who ignore your words."

At that Amarta blinked away tears, brushing snow from her lashes.

They struggled their way up the incline, heads down in the falling snow. After a time, the snow lightened to flurries.

"Diri, if it keeps snowing . . ."

"Will it?"

"I can't tell," Amarta said miserably, too tired to think, let alone ask questions her vision might answer. "What if the way-house isn't there? What if the raft is gone? What if the hunter—"

"What if, what if," her sister snapped. "I'm not leaving you for him to find. Say no more of that. You understand?"

"Yes."

A pause, the sounds of their footsteps crunching in snow.

"Ama. You must tell me when you foresee things. Even if it's about me. I know what I said, but it's different now. Yes?"

Suddenly Amarta felt cold inside as well as out. "Yes."

Exhaustion forced them to stop more and more often as the short day wore on.

At another rest, leaning against Dirina, again Amarta felt herself dragged into unconsciousness, waking minutes later, gasping for breath, lurching to her feet and stumbling forward on the path. Dirina followed wordlessly.

Daylight began to fade. Dirina picked up her pace, and Amarta struggled to keep up.

Something like pain hit her abruptly. An echo of pain to come, it was. A wrenching, sick moment of tearing.

"Diri," she hissed. "Stop."

"What?" Her sister looked around, face drawn, eyes wide.

"Something ahead. Something bad."

Dirina took a quick step backward, eyes on the path before them.

Amarta felt the pressure of the shadow hunter behind, urging her forward, an ominous warning. But before her on the road, something sharper and sooner.

"Pull the knife, Ama."

Reaching into the back pocket of Dirina's sack still on her shoulders, Amarta took out their only knife, gripping it in her hand, wondering when they had last sharpened it on anything.

They both went still and silent, listening to the deep quiet of the woods. Overhead a cloudy sky darkened.

Dirina watched her. At last she whispered: "What now?"

Hunter behind, a horror in front. Overhead, a gray sky darkening with night.

"I don't know."

Dirina rocked Pas gently to keep him from making any noise.

Again and again Amarta tried to summon a clear thought, a way to vision. Her thoughts felt stuffed with hay, sluggish with cold.

If they went forward, then—what?

The strange musky smell of wet animal. Pas's terrified wailing. Amarta tried to get to him but she could not seem to move. Pas's wail abruptly ceased.

Softly Dirina breathed out, "We have to go somewhere, Ama."

Amarta turned around slowly in the dimming light, looking for what, she didn't know. A tree, a rock—anything that might connect her confusing vision to direction. She took a small step off the road in one direction, then another, but nothing changed. Then forward again on the road. Was it still there?

The ground was hard and cold beneath her, Pas's broken, lifeless body just out of reach.

Amarta exhaled sharply, a soundless cry, and doubled over, fingers on the frozen ground.

"Ama?" Alarm in her sister's voice.

Struggling back aright, she stepped close, reached out to touch Pas's face where he curled in Dirina's arms. At this he opened his brown eyes, smiled. She put her lips to his forehead gratefully.

They must move. Where? Swallowing hard, she again took a step forward on the road.

It was suddenly free of disaster.

"We can go forward now," Amarta said.

"What? But why?"

"I don't know."

"But—are you sure?"

Another step. No warnings. "Yes." she said. Her visions were sure, anyway.

They went forward, hesitantly, Amarta in the lead, holding the no-doubt-useless knife in front of her.

They rounded a curve, the land sloping up on one side and down on the other, then rounded another curve. With every step Amarta listened for warning, heart pounding in her ears.

When at last they came to the place, there was barely enough light to see the broad, dark stains in the snow, the large animal pads where something had walked, the gouges where a body had been dragged away after a struggle.

Something had died here. Minutes ago. Instead of the three of them.

As they passed, they gave wide berth to the blood-soaked snow and bits of fur.

Darkness fell around them as the cold settled hard. Dirina took Amarta's hand and led her forward as if she knew where they were going, but of course she could not possibly.

Another flash of vision, and Amarta squeezed Dirina's hand, leading them by feel to the side of the road, then on a short path to a tiny cabin. The waystation, the dimmest of outlines. They felt their way inside blindly, finding the room empty and small enough that they could both barely stretch out on the wood floor.

But it kept out the wind, and the door bolted.

She woke her sister at dawn, feeling the pressure of pursuit.

By early afternoon they could see down the steep embankment to the river valley below. From this distance the Sennant was a thick gray and white rush, the sound a distant roar.

"You see," Dirina said, her tone one of relief as she pointed out a small square of brown at a wide, slow area on the other side of the river where the road continued from the rocky banks. "The raft. It's attached to a rope, strung between those two huge cedars. We'll be able to draw it back over to our side and take it across."

As they hiked down the switchbacked road to the river, the roaring was a welcome sound. Amarta felt her spirits rise. Underfoot, snow gave way to rockier land and patches of dirt.

Once they found the town, what then? They were out of food, had no more coin, knew no one there. A woman, a girl, a baby—how much generosity could they hope for in winter, when strangers were even less welcome?

It would not take long for the talk in Botaros to follow them. The first thaw's trade wagons would see to that.

"We won't be welcome in Sennant, will we."

A pause. "We'll see when we get there."

Beggars. That's what they were. As welcome as mice in a granary.

Mice who knew things they shouldn't.

They reached the riverbank, their feet crunching over rocks. On either side the tall rises were edged with snow-tipped firs and pines that rose to points against the flat, gray sky.

At last they reached the short wooden dock where a pole for the raft was waiting. Dirina handed Pas to Amarta while she set to pulling the dangling rope. On the other side, the raft jerked and began to move toward them.

Pas was restless, so she let him down to the dock, where he tried to stand, bouncing up and down, almost hopping. He looked up at her and smiled. Her fear eased. Dirina was right. She worried too much.

Then she looked back at the hills. At the high point of the road was a dark-clad horse and rider.

"Diri."

Her sister looked and inhaled sharply.

The rider was trotting toward them.

Amarta let Pas's hand go to help Dirina pull on the rope. Pas sat heavily on the dock and began to whine.

The two of them put everything they had into retrieving the raft. A glance back showed the rider halfway down the hills, now moving even faster.

No point in looking at him. She pulled harder, not thinking; grab and tug, grab and tug.

The raft bumped the dock on their side.

"Get on," Dirina said.

Amarta snatched up Pas and stepped onto the raft.

Now the horse was past the switchbacks and on the bank of the river.

"Diri?"

"Downstream," Dirina said curtly. She pulled the knife and began sawing at the ropes that held the raft to the pulley. "Not to Sennant town. He'll follow there. Understand?"

"Yes, but—"

"He'll track you along the shore," Dirina said, strands of the thick rope parting as she cut fiercely. "It's rocky, so you can go faster than he can ride, but stay to the other side."

"Diri. Get on."

The rocky bank slowed the horse, but not much. The sound of hooves grew louder.

The cut rope gave way. Dirina held tight to the end that held the raft. She turned on Amarta. "Take Pas. Hide. Pretend to be someone else. Find someone to take care of you. Use your visions, Ama. Use them!"

"Diri!"

"I'll stop him. You go."

With that, her sister released the rope. At the same moment, Amarta grabbed her arm with the hand not holding Pas. The raft struggled in the current, held only by Amarta's tight grasp on her sister.

"You have to come," she said, struggling to hold both Pas and Dirina at once. A seeing haze came over her, a warning. They had to leave, and now. If Dirina stayed . . .

The horse and rider were nearly on them.

"You won't slow him down," Amarta cried desperately. "Not enough."

Uncertainty flickered across her sister's face.

Amarta's visions were howling at her, one thing and one thing only: the shadow hunter was coming, and if he got her, she would not get away. Closer each heartbeat.

"I'm sure," she lied firmly. "Get on."

Dirina hesitated, a precious moment they didn't have. Amarta jerked her onto the raft, and she didn't resist, taking up the pole. With it she gave a hard push, propelling them away from the dock.

He was close enough now that she could make out details. He was well-wrapped against the cold, his chestnut-brown horse's hooves finding traction on the ground to come alongside them.

Amarta knelt down on the raft, holding Pas, keeping the two of them steady. As the raft wobbled, Dirina took a wide stance, poling into the water, pushing them farther away from shore.

Now the rider held reins in one hand and in the other a bow and arrow.

"Down," her sister shouted. Amarta went prone on the wooden raft, curling around Pas, who made frightened sounds. She whispered in his ear to comfort him, but he only cried louder. She went silent, letting him cry for the both of them.

Maybe there was no escaping the future. Maybe all you could do was trade one bad happenstance for another. She shut her eyes, not wanting to see what would happen next. But in the next moment she opened them, craning her head around to see him, this hunter.

Every part of the man was covered, gloves to high boots, a snug hood, only his eyes showing. He dropped the reins, but the horse continued forward as if nothing had changed. He took the bow in both hands.

"Diri!"

Amarta sat up, grabbed her sister by the arm, and tugged her down. Dirina dropped by her side, still managing to hold the pole. Around Pas they hugged each other.

A hard thunk on the raft. An arrow stuck upward, a scant foot from Dirina's back.

At that, fury overcame her. He was supposed to be coming after *her*, not Dirina. She was on her feet, struggling for balance. "Stop it!" she yelled at him. "Go away!"

The distance between the raft and the horse was widening slowly. Too slowly.

"Ama, get down!" Dirina shouted, grabbing at her

hand. She shook off Dirina's grasp and turned to face her pursuer.

He lifted his bow again, aimed at her.

She felt oddly calm, as though she had all the time in the world. She considered how he had almost hit Dirina with his last shot. From a moving horse. Aiming at a moving raft. He was very good at this.

Next time he probably wouldn't miss.

Especially if she were standing.

Or maybe it would be easier for everyone if he shot her now, killed her dead, and got it over with. Then, perhaps, Dirina and Pas would be safe.

"Ama!" Dirina screamed.

Still she watched him. She needed to see him, see this next moment. With every step his horse was losing ground as their raft was caught in the downstream current, but his bow was still pointed directly at her.

Now everything was moving: the raft, the horse, the banks on either side. It seemed to Amarta that the place where the bow in his hand crossed his arrow was the only thing in the world that did not move.

"What do you want?" she yelled at him. "What?"

"Ama," her sister hissed. "Don't."

As if in answer, he lowered the bow. His horse slowed, still following along the riverbank but falling farther behind.

Amarta sat heavily next to her sister. A half-hearted attempt to foresee only gained her a tangled, misty sense of fading danger as the man on the horse, still following along the shore, receded into the distance. At last they could no longer see him.

One thing she *had* seen clearly, though, was that she would meet him again.

Amarta began to tremble. Dirina held her, spoke soothing words, but she was shaking as well.

In time Pas calmed down enough to want to be fed and changed. Swapping one patch of moss for another, Dirina handed the pole to Amarta while she fed him. Amarta stood on the raft, keeping them at the center of the wide river. She glanced at the bank behind.

Would he follow?

Of course he would.

The skies cleared and the shadows lengthened. It was colder on the water than she thought it could possibly be without being frozen solid. They huddled together.

"We'll stop soon," Dirina said, bundling Pas in her arms. "When we find a road. We'll go—" She broke off, then started again. "We'll go—"

"Diri?"

Her sister was silent, inhaling raggedly, as tired and worn as Amarta. She had never seen her sister so shaken.

"We'll find a road on the other side," Amarta continued. "Go inland."

Dirina nodded as Pas reached for her hair. She kissed his forehead. "We will need to get off the river," Dirina said. "Find food and shelter."

But they would stand out wherever they went.

"Diri, if we cut my hair, could I seem a boy instead?"

Dirina gave her an assessing look. "Maybe. With a little change to how you move and what you say."

Amarta pulled out their knife, grabbed her shoulder-length hair around front in a fist, and began to saw through it as Dirina had with the rope.

"Here, let me," Dirina said, arranging Pas and herself closer. Then, after a time: "It will do for now."

Amarta held a handful of the cut hair, some of her tresses nearly a foot long. About to toss them into the river, she hesitated, recalling the eyes of the hunter. The strands might float downstream, tangling with fallen leaves and branches. He might find them.

She tried to foresee. The future was cold and swirling and uncertain like the water around them. She put the strands in her pocket.

"Look," Dirina was whispering to Pas, pointing to the moon in the deepening azure sky, "a shard of the first stone from which the world was born. And those lights? Those are stars, the children of the sun."

Dark banks passed to either side, thick forests, an occasional campfire.

Lamps from houses in small villages. Amarta envied them their warm houses, their families, their food. What would it be like to live in a place with the confidence you would still be there tomorrow and the next day? The next season? A year hence?

"There," Dirina said, pointing.

A road along the bank. Dirina stood, poked the pole into the water, maneuvered them to the shore. Amarta stepped off into the frigid water. Together they dragged the raft partly up onto the bank. Good enough. Or was it?

Dirina on the ground, blood oozing wetly from an

arrow in her leg. Amarta turning to see him atop his horse.

Dirina held Pas and the rest of their belongings.

"Diri, the raft. He's seen it."

For a moment her sister looked confused. Then she nodded. "We'll send it downriver."

They launched it with as much force as they could, and off it went downstream.

"Travel far, travel true," Dirina whispered.

Amarta didn't try to foresee the path of the raft. It would have to be good enough.

They stood by a tree at the edge of a fallow field, Pas deep in exhausted sleep against Dirina's chest, and stared at the lights of a farmhouse.

"This one, or do we go on?" Dirina asked, tone flat.

They had been careful, walking on rocks, considering every step. No broken branches. No stray hairs.

Tired, cold, hungry. Would whoever lived in this farmhouse take them in, at least until tomorrow?

Beggars in the night.

Amarta looked at the farmhouse again, trying to foresee. She felt empty. "Maybe," she said.

"Maybe?" Dirina said, her voice cracking. "Yes or no?"

They were both so tired that it was hard to say anything, let alone anything nice. Amarta squinted at the farmhouse. If they knocked on the door, could it lead to being warm?

The smell of hay. A place to lie down.

There was a way.

"Yes," she said, too tired to explain.

They walked the rutted path to the house. It stretched back and away from the road under a leafless oak, a barn nearby.

Dirina took a breath, and knocked.

A woman opened the door, gray at her temples, a frown on her face. "What do you want?"

"We are travelers," Dirina said, trying to sound hopeful and pitiful all at once. "Begging your mercy. With nowhere to go this wretched night. All we ask—"

"You're letting in cold." She scowled. "Get in."

They did so, pulling the door shut behind. A fire in a large wood stove breathed heat into the room. Two men, young enough to be the woman's adult sons, sat at a table and turned to look.

The smell of meat and spices hung in the air. They had food. They were eating. For a moment Amarta could think of nothing else.

"We were orphaned, ma'am," Dirina said, moving the blanket a bit so that they could all see Pas in her arms. "Our parents fell off a mountainside and died. Our uncle took everything we had. We're not beggars," she said. "We can clean and mend and care for children . . ." She glanced at the young men and faltered. There were no children here.

Dirina ducked her head, eyes wide. It was the look she got when they were most down on their luck. "We can cook and fetch water and collect wood and pick wildflowers and—"

Flowers? Dirina must be beyond tired. Her sister stuttered to a stop, only now seeming to realize what she had just said.

"Anything, really," Dirina finished softly.

The woman, clearly reluctant, shrugged. "The barn has hay. Be gone in the morning. The donkey is mean and will bite, so don't bother him."

But the last thing Amarta wanted was to leave this warm room to share space with an unpleasant animal in a cold barn. More than anything, she wanted to stay right here and eat whatever they were eating.

They would share what they had, if they wanted to. How to convince them?

The woman didn't trust them, Amarta could see that in her hard expression. What would it take to change her mind?

So tired. Too tired to look ahead.

Just a little ways ahead, then. Heartbeats in the future. A hint of what could be.

She caught it then, barely a whiff. A taste of stew from a future that might yet be.

"No," she said to the woman. "I mean—" She glanced at Dirina, who gave her a dismayed look. "That's not all of it."

"Not all of what, girl?" the woman asked, moving to the door to open it. "Loham, take them out to the barn." One of the young men stood and approached.

"It's true we're orphans," Amarta said, talking quickly, "but there's more. There's a man after us. I think he means to kill us." She spoke calmly. That was the thing, she realized, not to try to look ragged and pathetic. Dirina's approach had worked before, many times, but it wouldn't work now.

The woman gave them both a long look. "Why?"

"We don't know," Amarta continued. "But we have nowhere to go. We haven't eaten today because we have no food or money. But we're trustworthy, and we'll work hard for you as long as you'll have us."

"Not the king's men," the woman said. "We don't need that kind of trouble."

"No, not that," Dirina said.

The woman nodded slowly. Then, to Dirina: "Next time you let her speak."

Dirina looked down, face reddening.

"Cafir," the woman called to the other man, "put some blankets in the corner by the fire. Loham, ladle out two more bowls. You two, take off your packs, and—" she stepped toward Dirina. "Here, woman, give me that baby before you drop him."

Dirina hesitated a moment, then handed her Pas.

Amarta took off her pack and looked around the room, feeling dazed as the future she had glimpsed moments ago became the present.

Chapter Seven

Again Innel stood in the small toilet room at the back of the Frosted Rose. Against the patter of a light spring rain came a familiar series of knocks from the roof by the ceiling vent. Innel responded.

"Captain," came a familiar voice.

"Well?"

"I found them."

"Finally. Where are they?"

"Gone. When I arrived at Botaros, they had just left the village in some haste. I tracked them to the Sennant River, where they escaped me on a raft."

"They *escaped* you?"

"Yes. And here is the interesting part, Captain: they were warned that I was coming."

"Warned? What makes you think that?"

"They left a warm room and belongings to face a rough mountain road deep in snow with a babe in arms. At the riverbank they escaped me by mere heartbeats. What would you conclude, Captain?"

"That makes no sense. Who would even know to warn them?"

"An excellent question, Captain, since I told no one."

After a moment it occurred to Innel what the man was implying. He snorted. "I have no reason to send you after them and warn them as well. Not with what I'm paying you."

"No, you don't," the other responded mildly. "Perhaps it was coincidence that they left abruptly just before I arrived, and coincidence that they did not seem entirely surprised to see me at the river. What do you think, Captain?"

Innel thought that the girl had foreseen Tayre coming, as she had foreseen Innel's duel with his brother. But he would not say so.

He had underestimated the girl. She was more dangerous than he had thought.

Worse, anyone who found her would be similarly dangerous. He had to get to her first.

"I think we will know better when you have brought them to me. A woman, a child, and a baby. How hard can they be to apprehend? Did you follow them?"

"Yes. They are somewhere off the Sennant, which describes rather a lot of territory."

"They're poor. I don't think they will have gone far."

"Perhaps. But there are clearly forces here beyond the obvious, and thus many things become possible. Fortunes can change quickly."

Innel remembered placing bright coins atop a rough wooden table. Who else was overpaying the girl for her answers?

He exhaled. It came out a growl.

Before he could respond, Tayre spoke again. "What aren't you telling me, Captain?"

Innel hesitated. Careful, he warned himself. "I've told you what I know."

"My reason and your tone says otherwise. Keep your secrets, and I'll keep looking, but every day whatever it is that you won't tell me now might delay my finding her. My expenses rise. I will pass them on to you."

Innel exhaled, this time more softly. This was not going well.

"Captain, how badly do you want this girl?"

"Badly enough to hire you."

"That is my point. If this is that important to you, I suggest you tell me everything. Then I have a better chance of completing your business quickly."

Innel considered the man's words, aware that his silence was an admission. But perhaps the man was right. "You have a reputation for confidences."

"I do.".

Annoying as it was, he was starting to appreciate that Tayre did not use a lot of words to reassure him. But how far to trust?

A balance of risks.

"The girl is a seer," Innel said at last. "She predicts the future."

"She has done this for you?"

Should he admit that much?

"She has."

"I have been told by those who should know that there are no true Seers."

"So have I. Nonetheless, she is one."

A thoughtful noise from the vent, and a moment's pause. "I have had occasion to cross paths with many who can accurately predict outcomes, Captain, but what is cause, and what is consequence, can be cleverly reversed. I can arrange a demonstration if you wish."

A reply just short of condescending.

"No need. I know what a swindler can do."

"What has this girl told you, to make you believe this?"

That was more than he was prepared to reveal. "You'll have to take my word for it."

"As you say. Shall I resume the search?"

"Yes. And when you find her, I don't want her getting away again."

"I have no intention of letting her get away."

"My meaning is this: if you have to wound her to keep her from escaping, do so."

"I understand. How whole do you want her?"

"Alive. Able to speak, at least. Do whatever else you need to."

"And the woman and baby?"

"I no longer care about them. Do whatever you must, but get me the girl."

These last few days' drenching spring rains meant that Innel was more than a little damp when he came in from leading his ever-present guard at a hard sprint around the circumference of the garrison field, where he then beat on a rain-soaked straw-filled sack while his guard looked on, because no one would take up a practice weapon against him.

"This is absurd," he had said to Nalas.

"Captain," Nalas had said, with amused forbearance. "If I won't, they won't. And I won't."

"Why not? I assure you the king would not object to any of you hitting me. With force."

"No," Nalas said, nodding, "but His Royal Majesty might be less than perfectly pleased if we actually damaged you. We like our positions, ser."

So Innel beat on stuffed sacks that didn't hit back, while his guard and everyone else watched. A pretend opponent with all the wit and tactics he might expect.

When he was done, his guards trailing him into the palace, he stripped off his wet jacket and handed it to Nalas. Someone handed him a towel and he began to dry his head while he considered which of the many plans he was cultivating required his attention most.

Cern, of course. Nothing else would advance without her.

She had not so much as permitted him a touch since he returned from Botaros, now pushing a half year. From what his informants were telling him, she wasn't having any of the other boys to her room, either, and that was something, but he could hardly expect her to marry him until that door was open again.

The bitch makes the match.

No one would say that within Cern's hearing, of course, but the king had said it often enough to the Cohort that it stuck in all of their minds. From early on, the king would bring them to see his dogs and horses mate.

Bloodlines mattered, the king told them repeatedly, in any breeding match—he'd point out the preferred traits of his dichu dogs and coal-black horses—but if the female wasn't interested in the male, the offspring would always be flawed. So when the Cohort came of age, they were all sent to the *anknapa* for training, the boys especially.

The king liked his lessons vivid and bloody, so the point was driven home by his requiring every member of the Cohort to cull the weakest of those born to the kennels and stables. Slaughtering pups and foals that didn't meet the king's standards went a long way to inspiring the Cohort's focus on learning to make Cern happy.

Innel was certain that it had occurred to many to wonder just how pleased Cern's mother was with the king's attentions a quarter century back, but no one who valued their future would wonder that aloud.

From his lifelong study of the princess, Innel knew that his strategy back into her bed was simple: a gentle but relentless persistence. He had to seem confident, but not overly so. Just enough to be charming.

Well, he'd done it before; he could do it again.

He wiped the sweat from his face and neck as he walked the halls to her suites for what was turning into a daily rejection. Srel quick-stepped to catch up with him.

"Two of the Lesser Houses are meeting shortly," Srel said at a low volume. "Glass and Chandler. The lamp contracts. Elupene and Murice are sitting in to approve. They want amendments."

"Because the last ten amendments weren't enough?"

Srel made a sound that said he didn't disagree. "In any case, ser, the king's seneschal requires your presence."

"Of course he does. Well, I doubt this will take long."

Outside Cern's suite, Innel's guards arrayed themselves alongside her royal guards with now-familiar ease. This time he was allowed inside the antechamber, where his Cohort sister sat on a plush settee, a pleated, black long-jacket across her lap.

"What did you bring me?" Sachare asked, not looking up.

She was passing the long seams of the jacket through her extended fingers as if looking for something, which she probably was, and rolling and biting the buttons as if they might be poorly counterfeited coins.

"This," he said, tired of being polite, throwing the wadded-up sweat cloth at her face. Without looking up, she batted it aside. "What shall I bring you next time, Sacha?"

"Trillium wine, boy."

He snorted. Of course she would demand something impossibly rare and commensurately expensive.

"Something in season, girl. At least give me a chance—"

The inner door opened. Sachare stood quickly, jacket in hand. They both dipped their heads.

Cern gave them each a sharp glare, following it with a long, sour look at Innel.

The room was quiet for a long moment.

"Inside," she said to him.

He followed with alacrity. He did not waste the chance, navigating every caress she allowed him, steering by the set of her shoulders, the cords in her neck, the sound of her breath, the scent at her nape. He missed the hours-long House meeting entirely.

She was, of course, tight and angry for quite some time. Only partly at him, he knew, but it didn't matter—this was the opportunity he had been waiting for, and he applied himself entirely to it.

By the time they were done, she was a little more relaxed, and a touch less furious.

A good start.

The next morning, he came by again, and the following as well. She let him inside. He made a habit of showing up so she could get in the habit of saying yes, but left well before it might occur to her to wish him gone.

He was missing important meetings.

So be it.

The looks he was now getting across the palace told him that word was getting around that he was back in Cern's good graces.

The ladder goes up one rung at a time, Pohut would have said.

It was no time to get overconfident, though, so his every caress was planned, measured, carefully applied. Every look and laugh likewise, no matter how casual it might seem. He had to show Cern that he was strong in the ways she was secretly afraid she was weak, while at the same time avoiding any echo of her father's mannerisms. Unless they were the ones she even more secretly admired.

A delicate game. A meticulous seduction.

In another tenday, she nodded a welcome to him at dinner.

Another rung up.

When at last Innel judged he would be likely to

succeed, he politely asked if he might be allowed to sit next to her at dinner.

She shrugged.

Her father looked on.

Another rung.

One night, sitting by her side at the end of a particularly long and well-attended meal that saw nearly all the remaining Cohort in attendance, the king casually opined that autumn was a good time for a wedding.

The room went dead silent.

Cern gazed down at her plate, eyes narrowed, lips thin, and said nothing.

Which was, it seemed, good enough for the king. The next morning, some twenty royal retainers poured into Innel's apartment, took his measurements, made notes, and began planning what promised to be an astonishingly complicated and impressively expensive event.

But he would be wed.

To the princess.

A lifetime's goal.

In even better news, Innel was allotted an allowance to assemble a staff. As tempted as he was to instead put the funds toward finding the girl in Botaros, he now had far too many eyes watching him, so he did as instructed; he took Nalas as his second, and after he made him steward put Srel in charge of settling all the rest.

At least now, Nalas would do as he was told and hit back.

"Are you satisfied with the help I obtained for you, Captain?"

The days had lengthened and warmed, so now Bolah prepared the bitter Arunkel tea that the season's fashion demanded. She set a silver cylinder on the table between them along with two small matching goblets.

"Not yet, I'm not."

Bolah froze, the etched cylinder clutched in her spotted hands.

"What has happened?"

"Nothing has happened," Innel snapped, letting his annoyance show. "He searches but does not find. A glimpse; then the prey is loose again in the brush."

"Ah," she said, slowly completing her movement to fill his cup and then her own, setting the tea cylinder on the table. "Such things can take time."

"I am out of time." He took a sip, enjoying the tea, if not the conversation.

Bolah eased herself into the seat across from him and folded her hands together on the table. "Captain, if this man cannot obtain what you seek, it may be that the item cannot be acquired. Few, I assure you, are his equal."

"So you have said." Innel would venture a few inquires of his own, to see what others thought of Tayre's work.

Bolah seemed ill at ease.

Good. Innel was on the path to become royal consort. She should want him happy.

"Could it be that the item you seek is occluded by some . . . unknown aspect? Thus . . . distant and difficult to see?"

So many words to describe magic, all to avoid being direct. Even here in the privacy of her own home.

But she might be right.

"Perhaps."

"Then perhaps someone with exceptionally good vision could help speed the search."

Good vision. The euphemism for mages. Innel felt a little safer for sleeping in Cern's bed, but until he was wed to her, even that could be swept away in any number of unforeseeable ways. It paid to be careful.

"Are any of them in-city?" he asked.

"My sources say one, perhaps two."

"Are they . . ." He thought of how to put it. "Already on the gameboard?" Under contract to the king, he meant.

It was a dangerous conversation.

"One is, perhaps. But . . ." She considered her answer. "This is another level of expense entirely, Captain. Your credit will not stretch so far."

"I have funds."

Not long ago, his Cohort brother Tok had run with him during his morning's exercise and whispered to him that his mother, Etallan's eparch, wanted to be sure that the king was not the only one who had someone with good vision close at hand.

Some thought House Etallan, with its fingers on mines across the empire, had too much influence. Etallan had done well at the last Charter Court. But Innel knew Tok, and trusted him as much as anyone. If House Etallan was backing him, that was good for him and it was good for Cern.

As for the actual mage, Innel had mixed feelings. He'd met a few, quietly, and found them not much different than some of the touchy Anandynar royals, expecting to

be treated with great deference. *With mages, respect first.*
It paid to handle them like blown glass.

But if Etallan was paying, then—

"Tell me when you find one."

In spite of vivid tales intended to terrify Arunkel
children, negotiating with mages was mostly a matter of
tactful diplomacy. Offering them what they wanted,
whatever it was. Even mages must eat.

"My honor to serve," Bolah said, spreading her
hands.

"Your sister," Nalas said with a brief smile.

Innel made a face. "Yes, yes."

Srel slowed his work at Innel's elbow a moment, shot
him a warning look.

"I know. It should only take a moment."

Innel was almost late to attend the king in his bath.
Srel had been intently sewing an elbow rip in Innel's
amardide and leather jacket, and while the jacket would
come off immediately in the damp royal bath, Srel insisted
it was essential that he look correct as he walked in.

"Brother."

Cahlen's clothes, by contrast, were as far from
acceptable as was possible to be without her being tossed
out of the palace as a beggar. He sniffed a little. How
often did she change them?

"Sister."

"The east tower dovecote," she said.

"It's been addressed. The Minister of Palace says—"

"He says many words. I've heard them all. Nothing
changes. Nothing is fixed."

She reached under her loose jacket and brought out a bundle.

"I will look into it when I can, Cahlen. But right now I'm a bit busy—"

She put the item on his side table and unwrapped it. One of her messenger birds, gray and white, blood across its feathers and head, beak splayed, long neck limp. Dead.

"The males fight when they're too crowded," she said. "This was the best of my stud-cocks. Yesterday."

"I am late to attend the king," Innel said. "Do you know about my betrothal to the princess, Cahlen? Do you know what has been happening?"

"You killed my brother. Now you kill my birds."

He exhaled frustration. "Cahlen, you don't understand—"

But she had said what she came to say and turned away, walking to the door, brushing close by Nalas as she went. He quickly stepped back. She left.

Srel focused on the needle he held, tying off a knot, then motioning Nalas close to provide him a knife to cut the thread.

"We will need to do something about her, ser," Srel said, stepping back.

"Start by making sure she looks like she belongs in the palace. If you can figure out the dovecote problem, do that, too."

Innel pulled on his boots—again, despite the fact that they would come off as quickly as the jacket once he was in the royal bath.

Appearances.

And an honor, he reminded himself. A point of status,

anyway; not everyone had even seen the king's bath, let alone the king inside it.

Srel was kneeling at his feet, tying the straps of his boot around horn-cut buttons. He stood, reaching up to adjust Innel's collar and cuffs and run a comb through his hair and beard.

"Something in magenta?" Innel asked, thinking of Cern.

As well as Innel knew the palace language of clothes and color, Srel knew it even better. "Not yet, ser."

Innel nodded and left.

The royal bath was a large room, walls tiled in white stone, ceiling and sunken tub inlaid with black and red quartz. From the wide window, cut glass caught the light, casting shaped reflections on the walls that changed with the time of day. In the mornings, one could see birds and butterflies on the far wall and floor. Now, sunset, it was ships, moving slightly, as if on a sea.

Innel bowed as he entered, waiting for permission. Best to be careful; he'd found that when soaking in hot water, the Anandynar royals could be especially touchy.

"Yes, yes," Restarn said impatiently from the huge rectangular tub, waving him in. Steam rose to partially obscure the overhead mosaic, a circle of the sigils of the Eight Houses. Innel made sure that his glance up did not stop at any one sigil; it was the sort of thing he would have looked for, had he been the king.

A few servants were scattered about the room, bringing scented herbs and soaps, or sponging the king's royal back.

Innel's gaze stopped on the large male slave who suddenly stood before him, blue eyes downcast, blond hair falling in locks down his muscled shoulders. He felt his heart start to race. Only years of careful practice allowed him to keep his gaze moving past the man as if he barely saw him.

What was it about this particular slave that caught his eye?

The way he held himself, was what. So much like memory.

As the slave helped Innel off with his jacket, tension made Innel want to swallow, but the king's line of sight was direct. Instead he walked to the bench, forcing his movements to be calm and unhurried. Sitting slowly, he reached for the ties of his boot.

Another royal gesture, and a female slave knelt at Innel's feet, her golden hair cascading over her face as she bent over his boot. The man joined her. One on each foot, each unwrapping leather straps, removing boots and socks.

"She's new," Restarn said. "What do you think of her?"

Innel forced his gaze to the woman. She turned her face upward for inspection, looking beyond him.

Sky-colored eyes below long, golden lashes. A slender chin. Full lips. Beyond beautiful.

"Breathtaking, Sire," he said, hoping the king would mistake the oddness in his tone for awe.

The king chuckled.

Look at something else. Think of something else.

Through the far window the sun was setting in vibrant shades of orange and vermilion. From the Great Houses to the bay's shimmering sea, the city seemed gilded in gold. A marvel of glass-craft, this window, well beyond the present-day ability of House Glass. Mage-made, most likely.

Though again, not something to say aloud. Only the king could break both custom and laws with impunity.

Innel tried to remember which of the Anandynar royals had built this bath. The Grandmother Queen, he was pretty sure. A pragmatic ruler, Nials esse Arunkel, quietly rumored to have kept mages more openly than her descendants. Why Restarn, who revered her enough to have coins minted in her likeness, did not do likewise, he did not know.

When Cern came to power, well. Perhaps then.

"I'm thinking of breeding her, Innel. Her hair is soft as silk. Go on, feel it."

Willing his breath to slow, Innel put a hand on the woman's head.

Just like one of the king's puppies, he told himself.

"And the other. Go on, see how soft his hair is, too."

Gold inside as well.

Innel's stomach lurched.

It occurred to him that the king might be doing all this to unsettle him, but surely the incident had happened too long ago for him to think Innel would still be affected. He wanted to look at the king, judge his expression, but he didn't dare. Not until he had made a good show of doing as he was told.

He drew the woman's tresses through his hand. Then, affecting as much ease as he could, put a hand on the man's head as well.

How old had he been? No more than seven, surely.

Innel remembered standing in the hallway that day, head bowed as the king and his entourage strode past. Then he had made the mistake of looking up. At a gesture from the king, one of his guards grabbed him by the arm and pulled him along.

Later, Innel would come to recognize the expression on the king's face at that moment, an assessing scrutiny edged with amusement, and know that it presaged something unpleasant. Then, though, all he felt was pride that he had been selected while his Cohort siblings were left behind.

As he walked behind the king with guards and retainers, a man strode at his side, naked to the waist, blond hair falling to his mid-back. One of the king's fabled slaves, Innel knew, though he had only seen one at a distance before, at a musical performance in the Great Hall. A lithe woman, kneeling at the king's side, his hand on her shimmering head as the music began. Innel had stared wide-eyed at the exotic creature until Pohut, standing next to him, hit him sharply in the ribs to make him stop.

Walking alongside, the young Innel stole another glance at the blond man, trying to understand what about him was impressive. Clad only in simple black trousers, hands shackled in iron bands, he somehow looked anything but a slave. What was it?

The way he moved, Innel realized. How he held his head and shoulders. As if he were in command not only of this group of guards and retainers, but the king himself, even the entire palace. The king's royal guard did not

move as well as this man. Not even the king, he thought.
The slave put him in mind of the king's best stallions, who
strutted and galloped as if the world existed to serve them.

Innel found himself standing up straighter, changing
the roll of his shoulders, the tilt of his chin, even his stride,
as he tried to emulate the compelling blond man who
walked beside him.

The group descended one flight of stairs and then
another, then through a corridor Innel had never seen
before, to a room deep underground. They streamed in,
door thudding shut behind. At a heavy wooden table, the
slave was roughly shoved prone, held fast by a handful of
guards.

At a nod from the king, one of the servants drew a
knife. In a single, fast motion he sliced the man's throat
open. Gasping, thrashing, blood pulsed from the blond
man's neck, splattered across his pale chest.

The young Innel clenched his fists, mouth dropped
open, eyes wide. With a horrified shock, he realized the
king was watching him. He looked disappointed.

"You may go if you wish," the king had then said.

Only two years in the Cohort then, but the young
Innel knew perfectly well that these words were far from
true. He tightened his stomach, clenched his jaw, and
forced his gaze back to the man on the table, who was
twitching and taking a very long time to die.

"You think we'll find gold inside, Innel?" the king had
asked.

What was the right answer? He desperately wished
Pohut were here to give even so much as a glance for
guidance.

He knew the story, of course: how the pale-headed northerners had gold inside them, like pearls in oysters, which accounted for their pale hair. But was it true?

"I don't know, Sire."

Steady, he told himself. This would be over soon.

But it was not. The servants first cut the man's golden hair at the scalp. The long locks were closely inspected, offered to the king, then laid aside. Next they cut into the dead man's face and scalp, pulling skin away, digging out the eyeballs, handing each part to others who stood by to take it, making careful examination, often cutting it apart further on another table, before dropping the bits into buckets.

The slave's fingers were cut off, skin stripped away in small segments, ligaments pulled off bone, bones crushed with mallets against the stone floor. Each piece again meticulously reviewed, given to the king at a word to inspect. Blood dripped off the table, sluiced with water onto the sloped stone floor, oozing redly into a central drain beneath. They cut into the stomach and pulled out organs trailing intestines, dicing them into small bits on another side table. As one might prepare sausage for a stew. All the bits were then strained through a weave in a careful search, liquid dripping through.

Innel felt sick.

There was very little talk. The sounds of bones being ground. Bits of wet meat dropping into buckets. The room stank of blood, offal, and emptied bowels.

It took hours. Innel held himself as still as a statue, not daring to even look away from the table, terrified he might find the king watching him.

When at last the body had been completely taken apart, the table empty but for the tiniest bits, and soaked in blood, buckets of meat and pulverized bone lined the wall.

Nothing that remained was recognizable as the man who had walked beside him in the corridor.

Servants then hefted the buckets and left to take the remains to feed the royal pigs.

The young Innel found himself wondering if the blond man had known this was coming as he walked here so proudly. If he had, surely he would have fought it, even knowing that it would do no good.

Or perhaps he had indeed known, and knowing was what had given him the bearing that had so impressed Innel.

"Now," the king said. "we are finally and completely certain." And then he had laughed, a sound that haunted Innel for many nights after.

There was no gold inside. Not a single flake.

With a bow to the king, a servant offered him the long strands of gold-colored hair. Long, long locks of shimmering hair.

Much like the long, long locks that Innel now held in his hand as he sat in the royal bath room, under the king's close scrutiny from the tub.

Restarn snapped a finger, motioned, and both slaves stood quickly, the woman's long tresses flowing through Innel's hands as she pulled away. The two of them left through a side door.

Innel exhaled softly, finally daring a look at Restarn, finding his expression unfathomable.

"You seem distracted, Innel. Not getting enough sleep?" The king grinned widely. Of course he knew that Innel was sleeping with Cern.

"No, Sire, I am not." Innel gave a small smile in return to show he shared the king's amusement and met his gaze, but broke away first.

Just like with the dogs: show strength, but not dominance, not until you're absolutely sure you can win.

That would come.

"Innel, we must talk about the wedding."

"Yes, Your Majesty," Innel responded, relieved to be discussing the future rather than remembering the past.

"I need someone to go to Arteni."

"Arteni, Sire?" Innel frowned. A town along the Great Road, a central collection point for grain in the surrounding fertile lands. Contracted directly to the crown in the last Charter Court, as he recalled.

"They've made the poor decision to sell some of their harvest to traders at the Munasee Cut. Maybe they thought they could get a better price there. Maybe they thought we wouldn't notice." He gave Innel an unpleasant smile. "An insult to me, personally, and an affront to our hungry citizens. I need someone to go and sort it out. Someone I can trust not to be soft about it."

Innel could see where this was going. "It would be a great honor, Your Majesty. But with the wedding—"

"Exactly. I can't marry my daughter to a captain. It would be embarrassing." At this Innel felt a chill down his spine. "I could promote you, of course, but not without"—Restarn waved his hands as if searching for words, splashing a little water—"some demonstration of your capability to the generals. They think you're unproven."

"Unproven? They've been testing me for years. The Lord Commander in particular." He still had the scars.

"Yes, yes, I know. But they'll say pretend battles make for pretend soldiers."

It was one of the king's favorite maxims. Of course they would say it.

"I've been out on campaign repeatedly, Sire, and—"

"Not in command," he said sharply. "I have to give them something if I'm going to give you a higher rank."

There—he'd said it twice. The prize of advancement now dangled irresistibly in Innel's mind. Were it bestowed on him by the king, it would say a great deal about the monarch's faith in him. Given his lack of bloodline and House, *that* could matter, once he was wed to Cern. Could matter a great deal.

But Arteni was many days south. It would take him time to mobilize an armed force, even a small one. And how long would this sorting out take?

Innel could easily be gone months. That would delay the wedding. Take him from the palace. Away from all his plans, which might unravel quickly if he were not here to oversee them.

Away from Cern, whose interest might cool if he could not regularly remind her why she liked him.

No; there must be another way.

"You'll need to install a new town council," the king said. "Make sure they observe what you do to the old one—you understand. And the mayor, I don't have to tell you how to handle him, do I?"

"Sire, the wedding—".

"We'll put it off. Short delay, but for good cause. Midwinter, most likely."

Midwinter?

Innel thought furiously, quickly turning over what he might prudently say next. Not a time for missteps.

"Or," said the king, drawing the word out, "I could send Sutarnan. He's eager for the chance to prove himself. At times I think Cern might still hold some fondness for that boy, cheeky as he is. And Mulack—I still wonder if he might be a bit of a late-blooming rose."

Mulack was nothing like a late-blooming rose. He was eparch-heir to House Murice, and had no interest in getting his hands dirty.

But the point was now more than clear. He was being played on the king's board. To resist would mean being taken out of the game.

He had no choice.

"It will be my great honor to serve, Your Majesty."

"Yes, it will. Better get to it, then." He motioned, and servants came running to give Innel back his boots and jacket.

He'd been dismissed to what promised to be a sizable task. Standing, he bowed deeply, keeping his seething entirely on the inside.

Again his mind went to the Botaros girl. If he had her in hand, all this would have been avoided. Even now, she could advise him how to achieve a fast victory south.

Where in the many hells was Tayre?

Chapter Eight

As Tayre and his horse ascended the road to the mountain town of Sennant, he considered the many things worse than the freezing rain now finding its way around wraps and oilskin, under leather, to his skin, until only his toes deep in his boots were truly dry.

Many things worse. With a good fire and a little time, the chill he was now experiencing could be banished.

But doing his work in the open, for show—that could follow him for years. And that was worse.

They were proud of their name, the townspeople of Sennant. It gave them a sense of importance, of being part of the empire's mighty trade route up and down the river from which they took their name. That the village was not on the river and indeed could only be reached by twisting mountain roads did not seem to dampen anyone's enthusiasm; they were happy to visit the barge port once a week anyway, to trade furs, cider, jars of maple syrup, gossip.

Which was why it was here that Tayre would start

creating the rumors about himself that would circulate back to Innel, to quell his doubts as to Tayre's capability.

He'd considered ending the contract. Innel was sufficiently annoyed—and Tayre sufficiently expensive—that turning the conversation in a direction that would release him from the bond would have been easy.

However, he had no intention of allowing the contract to end. There was something about the girl that was still beyond his understanding. That she was a true seer he doubted, but something about her did not make sense. She was a puzzle that needed solving.

Find the unknown, his uncle had taught him. *And make it known to you.*

He rode past the town, circling First Hill, passing by Garlus Lake, the patter of frozen rain hard on the water's surface. Whatever fell from the sky, the lake would endure. Reputation was just one more tool, and his would endure this, too.

From the lake he entered the dripping canopy of forest and went to one of his hollowed-out cache trees. Suitably replenished, he found the Flute and Drum, where he knew they would take good care of his horse, who was certainly as tired of the chill rain as he was.

It would slow his work, planting stories intriguing enough to get back to Innel's informants. The best work left no trace.

But so be it. The job had simply become more expensive. Not entirely unexpected when dealing with the monarchy.

The next time he found the Botaros girl, he would watch her as long as it took him to arrange the best

circumstances for her acquisition, assure himself that she
was alone, with no transportation opportunities handy.
Learn her movements, isolate her, take her.

And if magic were involved, he would find a way
around it. He had done it before.

He entered the Flute and Drum, pulled the door tight
behind him.

A handful of people sat at tables around a central fire,
quietly eating. He limped a little as he made his way to a
wall-backed table and chair, taking in the room as he
went. Who faced whom, cut and fabric of clothing, how
they stood, skin tone variations, blemishes, hand positions.
He made quick assessments about history, wealth, and
agendas.

The limp was a small thing, like the way he held his
head a bit off-center and the mud ground into his worn
clothes. Enough to make him seem unlike the man who
had come through a nearby village a few days ago. People
watched strangers who came through, especially in these
cold months, and they talked about them. Now to make
sure they said what he wanted them to.

At the fire sat men and women eating bits of bread
from a greasy communal plate, drinking from mugs,
naked feet up on the stones clustered near the flames. On
the floor were short-boots and turnshoes propped up to
dry, socks draped between them like makeshift tents.

Glances came his way. As he sat, he lifted his hand in
a brusque, demanding motion to the innkeeper across the
room. The large man shuffled toward him on the unswept
wood floor.

"Time preserve the king's health," the innkeeper said

in an exhale. A traditional greeting, but also a warning that he was a law-abiding citizen and was not looking for black-market action. "What can I get you?"

Tayre knew that Binak was easily startled and would be obvious about it. Rolling his voice with a slight accent from the southeast, with a little Perripin thrown in and a tug toward the lilting tongues of the desert tribes, he spoke slowly, precisely. "Something with no dirt. Resembling food, if you have any."

The big man spat air through his teeth. "If you don't like it here, go somewhere else."

"Don't know yet. Bring it and I'll tell you if it's food. Hurry up." With that, Tayre spread a handful of nals across the table.

Shaking his head, annoyed, Binak turned away.

"Binak," Tayre said in another, quiet voice.

The man turned halfway back. Tayre let his expression change and turned his head a little.

"Seas and storms," Binak said softly, his shoulders hunching slightly, hands together in anxiety, mouth opening and shutting. "I didn't recognize you. What do I call you this time?"

"Call me Tayre."

"Sausage and fried bread, is that what you want? We have wine. Something from the north. Let me check, I—"

"Bring me whatever you would bring a stranger."

"Of course," the other man said, his eyebrows drawn together.

"I'll be here a few nights. Also messages up the coast and inland."

"I don't have—"

Tayre's hands met, back of one hand to the palm of the other. Hard currency. The big man's eyes flickered around the room.

"No one knows me here yet, Binak. Or our history. And won't unless you continue to fret, or mention other names by which you might know me. I trust that hasn't occurred to you."

"No, no," Binak said, seemingly horrified by the very idea. "The one man asking, I swear I told him nothing. Didn't even say I knew you."

"When was this?"

"Tenday and five ago."

"I will ask you about that later," Tayre said, gesturing to the other chair. "Join me."

The big man reluctantly folded himself into the chair across the table. He hunched over, head down.

"Your wife," Tayre said. "Tharna, isn't that her name?"

"Yes."

"Children. Four, if I recall. All healthy?"

"Yes."

"You had another, didn't you?"

"Died in childbirth."

"And the fishing?"

"Ah." Binak raised a hand, let it drop palm down on the table with a heavy sigh. "The river nets are empty two years now. The fish have found other places to swim, I think." A sudden glance at Tayre, worry laced with fear. "Please," he said softly. "I obey the king's laws now. I can't do what you had me do before."

"I don't remember any before."

Binak paled. "Of course not. I didn't mean, I—"

"Settle," Tayre said, his hands in a calming gesture. "I won't ask anything difficult. Nothing to offend the laws."

"I hear that in some lands, a debt dies with the owner."

"In some lands, the people have no honor."

"I don't need honor. I need fish in my nets. I need to be able to buy grain and wine for what it's worth, not five times that. Everything is too expensive all of a sudden. I can hardly feed my children."

"I could pay someone else in Arunkel silver instead of you. Shall I leave?"

"No, no. Forgive me. The times. The taxes. How can they expect us to pay more than we make? Whatever you need. I'll make up a room for you. A few nights, you say?"

"Maybe more."

Binak pressed lips together. He inhaled to speak.

"Be content, Binak. Don't ask for more. Or less."

Binak swallowed, nodded. "I'll bring you food."

"In my room."

"As you say."

Tayre stood and followed the large man upstairs, where he unlocked the first door, handing Tayre a long iron key.

"Next time someone asks you about me," Tayre said softly, "tell them I'm looking for a girl, a woman, and a baby. Usually I like you to keep silent, but now say that much. Understand?"

"Yes, of course."

"Also tell them I'm not a good man to cross. I think you can make people believe that."

Binak's mouth opened and closed soundlessly. Finally he swallowed and looked down.

"Food, Binak."

A month later, Tayre sat in a corner of a smaller, half-full public house of dock workers called the High Tide. Midday sun shone down through upper windows in columns, casting pale, smoky triangles across the floor and tables. The room smelled of cheap twunta, cut with pressweed and salted with cinnamon. Also heavy spice, the sort used to cover the taste of sour meat.

Sour meat. Impure twunta. Girls and boys wandering the streets in too few clothes for the weather, looking lost and hungry, cloaked figures lurking behind, prodding them forward. All signs of tightening times.

It was not only the rumors of the king's health weakening, not merely the uncertainty of the succession. Something was shifting oddly in the markets.

Arunkel metals had made the empire powerful for centuries, giving the Anandynar royals and their Houses enviable wealth and an uninterrupted monarchy, but it was a vulnerability, too; as the price of metals went up, the lines of influence across the aristos and Houses and royals shifted.

Tayre's morning's walk through this village's market had told him nothing about where the girl and her family might have gone, but much about the new taxations. Muttering and looks tracked him as he played the early season merchant, but the open talk about what unsanctioned goods could be bought without levy surprised him.

When the black market took over the gray, the king's rule was weakening. He wondered if the princess knew, or if Innel had any idea. If the king were smart, he'd hand the reins over to his daughter before she was left with a ship taking on seawater in the open ocean.

In any case, changing times meant opportunity. Even in his search.

As he sipped from a mug of tea, a tall man sat down across from him. The man held his arms and shoulders in a way that spoke of hard labor and fast reflexes. Dock work, perhaps. Tayre knew the type: he liked to fight, and his few scars indicated that he was used to winning.

Good; it was far easier to take down those who expected to win.

Tayre raised his eyebrows in question.

"Hear you're looking for someone."

"That's right."

"A girl."

"Right again."

"How much?"

"Depends on what you tell me."

"I'm muscle on a coast trade vessels. I get around. I like girls."

Tayre put a silver falcon on the table between them, falcon side up. On the coin, the raptor held a smaller, dead bird in its talons. Finch, if he recalled correctly. House Finch had been lobbying the crown to change the coin's design for some time.

"Southern Arunkel features," Tayre said. "Broad face, green eyes, clear skin. She travels with a woman and a yearling baby."

The other man reached for the coin, but Tayre's hand covered it.

"Sure, I've seen her," the man said, pulling back his hand.

Tayre searched the man's face a moment, then slid the coin into his pocket. "No, you haven't."

"I have," the man insisted, his chin jutting aggressively. "I can tell you where she went. And the woman, too."

"What sex is the baby?"

The man's pause gave him answer enough. Tayre pushed back from the table, standing while keeping the man in sight, then turned his back on him, walking to the door.

"Hey. You don't walk away from me when I'm talking to you."

Now they had the attention of everyone in the room. How to best use it?

He was unsurprised when the man darted between him and the door, facing him, arms spread wide to block his way. Sidestepping, Tayre slipped by, the man's fingers brushing him without gaining hold. He stepped through the open door just in front of the man's next grab.

In the middle of the cobbled street he turned to face him. Overhead the sky threatened rain.

"Around here," the tall man said, walking toward him, "you don't offer coin and then take it back. Rude, that. Guess you don't know, having been raised in a shit-pen. Give me the coin and we'll call it a pig's apology."

Behind the man, the tavern was emptying into the street to watch, hoping for good entertainment. Tayre would make sure that they got it.

"Why would I pay for your lies? Worthless, just like you."

At this, the man's face went red. He lunged forward, grabbing for Tayre's neck, a foolish move at best, telling Tayre how much this man depended on his size and strength. A quick but slight step to the side, a grab and a shift of weight sent the man forward in the direction he'd already been traveling, but faster. He stumbled forward, yelped once in surprise, caught his balance, and danced sideways, circling back, a grin on his face.

Turning his back on him, facing the audience, Tayre held his hands out in a gesture of mock confusion, giving the collected crowd a warm, humorous, and slightly self-deprecating smile.

These people would know the other man and not Tayre, but when this was over, they would remember Tayre and his modest, warm smile. Across cultures, people liked winners, but they always preferred the ones who didn't think too highly of themselves.

He watched their eyes track the man coming closer behind him. As his arm circled around Tayre's neck, Tayre dropped and stepped back, slamming his elbow into the other man's sternum, letting the motion carry his fist into his groin.

As the man grunted heavily and began to fold, Tayre spun in place, hands on the man's head, easily directing it into his rising knee. There was a gratifying crunch as his nose met Tayre's knee.

Then a gentle push with his foot on the man's less-weighted knee and the large fellow went sprawling onto the stony street.

Tayre followed him down, dropping atop him, straddling torso and arms. Taking his time, he wrapped a hand around the man's neck, a move that was more for the audience than the man under him, who seemed, for the moment, to have had the fight taken out of him.

The man squinted upwards at him and gurgled, a bubble of blood coming from his nose.

"You should take more care who you choose to annoy," Tayre said, making sure that his voice was loud enough to reach the gathered crowd.

The man struggled. Anger flickered across his features. Tayre's grip on his throat tightened, and the expression went back to confusion.

Clearly he didn't have much experience losing.

He tried to sit up, but Tayre held him pinned easily. Still, the effort implied a general lack of attention, so Tayre grabbed the top of the man's head by his curly dark hair, raised it slightly, and let it drop to the stone. The man gave a pained yelp.

"And it would be smart of you to show me some respect. You see how that might be wise?"

The man blinked a bit, then struggled again to try to get free, so Tayre repeated the motion with the man's head, raising and dropping it to the stone. The man's jaw went slack, eyes unfocused.

"Make more sense now?" Tayre asked.

The man attempted a nod, though Tayre was confident that he had no idea what he was agreeing to. Tayre nodded back.

"My name is Tayre," he said, careful to enunciate, loudly and clearly. He grabbed the man's hair again, but this time instead of resistance he was given a whimper of agonized anticipation. He lifted the head as high off the ground as it would go, holding the man's gaze with his own.

"No, no," the man whispered, eyes wide. "Please."

"Much better. What's my name?"

A croaking sound.

"Say it again."

"Tayre," the man whispered.

"Louder."

"Tayre."

"You won't forget, will you? I wouldn't like that."

"No, no, no."

"Good." With that, Tayre released the man's head a third time. It fell with a crack. The man exhaled once and was silent.

Nothing like the finesse and subtlety he preferred, this, but Innel's uncertainty meant that he needed to build a reputation quickly.

Tayre stood, brushed off his trousers, and gave the watching crowd a modest shrug and a friendly wave.

Their eyes were open very wide as they watched him. He'd made an impact, all right. They'd talk about him.

As he walked away, the tall man rolled over onto his side, moaning, seeming content to lie in the street awhile.

It began to rain.

In the sky a three-quarter moon broke the dark of night. Tayre greeted the stablewoman and handed her the reins of his horse. He knew her; she was the owner's adult daughter whom he had entrusted with his horse many times across many years, but she treated him like a stranger. It was not just his stance, expression, and clothes that caused her to fail to recognize him. Had he come with the same horse as last time, she would have looked at him twice. She cared about horses. People, less so.

After entering the eatery, he stood inside the door as if absorbed in thought, adjusting cuffs, collar, shirt folds. He would seem a wealthy trader, clothes new and light in color, with only a few splatters of mud.

By the time he looked up from this distracted fussing, all the eyes in this crowded room were on him.

The owner approached, a woman with gray streaks in the braid down her back. She wiped her hands on her apron.

"Season's blessing to you, ser," she said. "You can sit, let me see, right there." She pointed.

"Corner table, Kadla," he said, too softly for anyone else to hear.

She looked back, mouth opening to tell him what she thought of his correction. But she hesitated, gave him another look. This was one of the many things he liked about Kadla.

"You," she said, her tone as much amused as annoyed. "There." She indicated the table he'd asked for, as if it had been her decision.

He went where she pointed and sat. When she came back a few minutes later, he passed her two palmed falcons, which saw no light before they went into her pocket.

"Call me Enlon. Trading from Perripur."

Kadla smile a little. "I watch for you all year, then you stride in and I'm surprised. All over again. Fancy clothes this time, too. Didn't you have a beard before?"

"You look younger every year, Kadla. What rare herbs do you use?"

She snorted. "Mountain air, good water. That's what keeps me young."

He chuckled.

"Don't you laugh," she added. "I'm as strong as my best mare."

"And she's a looker, I admit. But you're far prettier. Smarter, too. Anyone tells you otherwise, I'll find them and explain their mistake to them. Then I'll come for you."

"You and your fancy tongue." She leaned down close to his face. "Still charming the young ones, are you? I've seen you work. They fall like cut grain, don't they? Rumor is you're worth washing the bedclothes for, but I don't think you're enough for me."

"What would be enough?"

Even though they had some version of this conversation every year, he could see her slight blush.

"You're a boy to me."

"Then teach me to be a man."

She stood back, made a tsking sound. "Go find yourself an anknapa. You won't get better food or drink this way. Your silver's good enough."

"Kadla," he said, mock-wounded, "you underestimate me. Come to my room tonight and I'll show you how much."

Her smile faded a bit. He could see her wondering how serious he was.

"A lot of food," she said. "And water. If I remember right."

"You do."

"And a room."

"Yes."

"Same room as last time," she said.

"Good. You'll have no trouble finding me tonight."

"Give it up."

He raised his eyebrows, met her eyes, held the look. "You sure?"

She inhaled as if to speak, thought better of whatever witty thing she had in mind, and said, with an expression uncharacteristically open, "You keep asking, one of these times I'll say yes. Then you'll have to deliver. Careful, boy."

"I'm always careful."

"Hmm."

"If anyone asks about me, under any name, I want to know about it."

"Call me shocked to the bone."

He chuckled at this teasing. He wondered if she would still feel this comfortable talking to him after the stories he was building for Innel made it back to her.

"I have messages I need delivered." He would ask his contacts if they had seen any unusual travelers.

"Can't imagine what you'll do," she said, making a show of confusion. "Oh, perhaps you'll give them to me and I'll have them sent for you."

"Perhaps I'll even pay you well to do it."

"That would be wise."

"Are your children well?"

"You want a story, wait for the harper. I have work."

As she walked back to the kitchens, he could see that she knew he was watching.

When she returned a few minutes later with thick stew

topped with a stack of hardbread dripping in fat, she was a little less smooth in her movements. She was thinking about it.

"Ah," she said in frustration as the fat dripped off the bread onto the table. She pulled out a rag and gave the table a cursory wipe.

"The best meals are messy," he said with a smile.

She smirked, put the rag back in her apron. No, he judged: she would not come to his room tonight. She wanted to, and he could have convinced her, but he wanted to see what she would be like when she came to him without influence. One of these years she would. He was in no rush.

At the side of the room, tables and chairs were cleared. A woman descended the steps from the rooms above, a large cloth case in her arms. As she scanned the room, Tayre recognized the expression. A horse master evaluating a new mare. A shepherd assessing a flock.

Or himself looking across a crowded room, deciding where to sit.

She perched on a table and unwrapped the harp. She set up a quick, playful tune. The room fell silent. She brushed a strand of hair out of her eyes that fell back immediately. Giving the audience a wolfish grin, she strummed a single, loud, attention-getting chord.

"Blessings of the season," she said into the sudden silence. "I'm Dalea. I'll give you my stories, and you leave me what you've got to spare. We could both go home happy." Her fingers did a quick dance across the strings, producing a sound like laughter.

There was a scattering of chuckles.

"Isn't this warm weather sweet?" Sounds of assent. "Don't get too used to it. How long is your summer up here? A tenday?" Chuckles.

Tayre studied her words, stance, and the small movements of her face. They were alike, the two of them, both making their way through the world by choosing what others saw.

Across the room Kadla leaned against the door to the kitchen, the bowl of stew in her hands forgotten.

Another stream of notes flowed from the harp and Dalea began to sing, smiling at the audience as if they were friends, as if they all shared a secret. It was an effective trick, her sincerity and vulnerability, irresistible to these people, who would be guarded with family and neighbors they knew too well. To a warm and attractive stranger, they would gladly give their hearts. Their coins would follow easily enough.

When she finished the last song, the crowd hit their thighs and made the trilling sounds that Tayre knew originally came from the tribes before the Arunkin took over. Quarter-nals and some half-nals landed at her feet and on her side table. A crowd surged to talk to her, the men ducking their heads like awkward boys.

Tayre ate another bowl of stew and waited until the room had emptied.

She was wrapping her harp, tying it into a pack.

"Beautiful," he said, giving her the uncertain smile he knew she would most expect.

"Thank you."

"I played a bit," he said, looking at the wrapped instrument, letting a conflicted expression flicker across his face for her to see. "Never any good at it. I studied with Melet al Kelerre."

"Melet?" she asked, surprised. Impressed.

"A little," he said, modestly. It was, entirely coincidentally, true, though he'd actually been better at it than he was implying. "My father was trying to figure out what to do with me. See what I might be good for."

"And?"

"And it wasn't music."

"Ah." Her curiosity was piqued. "What was it, then?"

"Oh, selling things. Jars and jewels, spices and extracts. A few books. Whatever's easy to carry on horseback. I do all right. And you?"

She gave a forced smile. "Tonight I'll eat. Sometimes I'm not so lucky."

Tayre dug into his pocket and put a falcon on the table.

"You're very kind, ser," she said in a tone clearly reserved for those who overpaid.

"Good fortune to you, Harper."

"And you."

He turned to go, then back to face her, as though something had only now occurred to him. "I don't suppose—did you come from downriver?"

"I did. Why?"

"Have you seen a young woman and a girl? A yearling baby, perhaps walking now?"

Dalea frowned thoughtfully.

"Cousins," he said, putting pain into his tone and eyes. "They had a falling out with my father. Took things that weren't theirs. Ran. They were scared."

"Hard times," the harper said sympathetically.

"Yes, but there's forgiveness for them if they want it. I have to find them to tell them so, but I don't know where to look. The woman is slender, the girl has sort of—" He held out a hand as if sketching in the air, "a roundish face. A cloak with blue trim." He smiled fondly. "She was always so clever with needle and thread. Sky blue. A distinctive touch. Hard to miss."

"Oh," she said slowly. "I think so. Downriver. A small village. I remember now. The girl is trying to seem a boy, but she's . . ." She shook her head to convey the extent of the failure of that attempt. The grin faded. "She seemed fragile, somehow. Afraid."

"That's her. Do you remember where?"

"A tenday downriver. On foot, that is," she added with a nod at his riding boots.

"May fortune bring you a horse," he said.

She laughed the rich, deep tone of a singer. "How would I afford to feed it?"

"A least a new pair of shoes, then."

"That is at least possible. I hope you find your people."

"Oh, I will."

In a corner of a nearly empty village greathouse that doubled as an eatery, Tayre fished the last bite of cold stew out of his bowl with a hunk of bread. The greathouse's windows were open to the evening's warm summer night. Moths flickered around the room's lamps.

The woman who had brought him the goods smoothed her dress as she brushed by his table. She stopped, turned, glanced around to see who might be watching, and sat down across from him, her elbows on the table and her chin on her fists.

"Want some dirt ale with that?" she asked.

"No."

"It's better than it sounds. We keep it in the cellar so it's cool. You'll like it."

"No again. What are you really offering?"

"I heard you asking around, about a girl and a woman and a baby. You're not the only one asking, you know."

"I do know that. And?"

"I'm wondering what I would get if I knew something about it."

"Depends on what you know." He tapped his bowl. "More of this."

She stood. "I'd want you to pay me first."

"I'm sure you would."

She pressed her lips together and left, returning with another bowl of the cold mix of meats, which she put in front of him. She sat again. "How do I know that you'll pay me if I tell you?"

"Because I said I would."

"Well, words don't mean much, now, do they—"

He leaned forward suddenly, took her hands gently in his. At his intense look, she fell silent.

"Mine do," he said mildly.

Her eyes widened slightly. She pulled her hands out of his light hold.

"Come now, pretty one; tell me what you know." He mixed a seductive smile with a commanding tone, a mix that usually worked on this sort.

"Some new folks. Arrived in spring. Don't see them

much. A woman and baby and a boy. Farm outside the village." She leaned forward again, lowered her voice. "Except it isn't a boy."

Tayre tore off a piece of bread. "Go on."

"I can tell what people are about, you know. Not like some who only see what you show them. I'm not so easy to fool."

Tayre made an encouraging sound and gestured for her to continue.

"So there he is," she said, "and I think, that's not a boy. Must be a reason he's pretending then and wouldn't that be interesting to know." She nodded decisively, looked to see if he was listening, then nodded again.

"Where?"

"Well, now," she said, tracing a greasy circle on the tabletop with a fingertip, "if I told you, it wouldn't be worth much for me to know it, would it?"

He chuckled. "It's not worth anything, otherwise."

"How much will you give me?"

"If it leads me to what I'm searching for, you'll see silver."

Her finger stopped. "Falcons?"

"If."

"I'm sure it's not a boy. Voice high. Too soft. Some people think they can fool anyone. Not me."

"Not you. Tell me where I can find them."

The finger resumed its circuit. "I don't want to be left with nothing," she said. "How about you give me something now, the rest after I tell you?"

Tayre leaned forward, grinning. "When I'm finished eating, your chance at silver ends as well."

She lifted her chin. "Maybe I should tell someone else."

"That wouldn't be wise," he said. "You can either tell me everything now, for the possibility of silver later, or tell me everything in an hour or so, for no money at all."

An uncertain look crossed her face.

He added, "I really do advise you to tell me now."

"Are you—Wait. Are you threatening me?"

"Silver," he said again. "I wouldn't want you to forget that part."

"Mmm." She exhaled. Then: "There's a small village. Nesmar." She shifted in her chair. "There's a farm east of there . . ."

Chapter Nine

"I like this, Diri. I want to stay," Amarta said softly to Dirina as they lay together on blankets by the fire, Pas between them.

Warm. Fed. The smell of woodsmoke. Spices in the air from the stew, surely the best stew she had ever eaten.

"We'll have to prove we're worth it," Dirina whispered back.

Amarta rolled onto her back and stared at the rafters overhead and wondered what made a person valuable enough to feed and shelter them.

Not her visions, certainly. As she looked at her sister and nephew, she realized that this morning on the raft, but for a few inches of luck, they would have had arrows through them. Because of her.

In memory she saw the hunter's eyes watching her, bow raised.

There was no reason for anyone to come after Dirina and Pas, except for her.

With that, she made a decision: she would do no more

foreseeing. Her visions were why they had been forced to leave every place they ever might have called home. It was what made people hate and fear them. Here they had a chance, with Enana and her sons, whom Amarta already liked enough that the thought of staying was a fullness of hope, filling her chest the way the stew filled her belly.

They would prove themselves. They would work hard. And Amarta would not speak of her visions. Not to anyone.

Another look at her sister, who had drifted off to sleep in exhaustion, and Pas, with his mouth open, his beautiful face sweet in the peace of sleep.

This was what she wanted for her family: food, warmth, and a safe place to sleep.

Better, she thought, would be to not have the visions at all, ever again.

So, she resolved, she would bury them. Deep in the ground, like some bit of rotten meat, where they would not be able to hurt anyone.

In the months that followed they threw themselves into the work, doing everything possible to help the family. Washing, mending, cooking. Planting seeds. Weeding.

Dirina made sure Pas was never a burden, always keeping him close by, warning him not to bother anyone, until it became clear that he had already charmed Enana and her sons, who were happy to supply him a lap or a hug and tell him stories at night.

When they left the farmhouse with Enana to go to the market, Amarta wore clothes as loose and baggy as possible, hair cut short and ragged the way the boys did here. She talked little, kept her head down, pitched her voice as deep as she could, and called herself by another name.

But mostly she kept to the farm. There was a lot of work, but it seemed easy, and she realized that it was the company that made it so; she had never before met people so willing to laugh, to make light of any difficulty, and to give each other a gentle brush or squeeze as they went through the day.

Spring became summer, longer days letting them do more in the fields, collect wild herbs, stack wood for winter. Harvest promised a good yield, if the rains came when they should.

But no—she pushed that thought firmly away. The rains would come when they did. She did not know any more about the rains than anyone else.

Bit by bit, Enana trusted them, giving them work to do without her, meals to prepare, even sending one or the other of them to market with a few coins for the grains and fruits and nuts they did not grow themselves.

Best of all, the whispers of the future grew fainter and fainter until Amarta could barely hear them at all. She had nearly forgotten how much a part of her life they had once been.

One dawn morning as the soft light of the sun promised another warm day that she felt eager to begin, it finally occurred to Amarta that she was happy.

She worked even harder.

Amarta adjusted the pack on her back as she hiked the

forest road. She'd found everything Enana wanted except pickled nut paste. Next week, the vendor promised, repeating how sorry he was, despite Amarta's assurances. By way of apology he had given her a bread roll shot through with thick berry jam.

She was speechless at this generosity. Perhaps this was what people did when they weren't busy hating you for knowing too much about them.

It wasn't that she was hungry—she ate better now than she could remember—but the roll was special. A sweet gift, something that was hers and only hers. She had forced herself to wait to eat it, wait until she was out of the village market, past the houses, over the brook, and near the halfway point back to the farmhouse, by a hollowed-out cedar. There she paused a moment, took it from her pocket, unwrapped the cloth, and took a bite.

The buttery bread and tart jam was delicious. Before she knew it, she'd eaten half. Save some for Dirina and Pas, she told herself sternly. She wrapped the rest, put it in a pocket.

Birdsong and squirrel complaints accompanied a distant hum of flies and bees contentedly going about their summer business. Her bare feet fell comfortably against the packed dirt of the road, calloused from months of barefoot walking made more attractive by her turnshoes having grown tight this last year as she got older.

A glance up to where pine and oak and maple met thickly overhead told her it was nearly noon, which meant plenty of day left to work the fields or help wherever Enana needed. And to share the rest of the bread roll.

Around her the underbrush was thick with ferns and

flowers. Having learned their names and what they were good for, she was tempted to stay awhile and pick red and white bleeding hearts or blue sour tangle. Even stinging nettles, now that she knew how to harvest them without getting stung. More likely, Enana would appreciate getting the bag of groceries sooner.

What a change, this life of such pleasurable choices. Living with Enana and her family, she nearly felt she had a home. Indeed, she was now willing to admit, in the privacy of her own heart, Enana reminded her a little of her own mother, so many years gone.

And all this gladness because she had silenced her visions. It had taken work, but in a way it was also easy: if she didn't ask herself any questions—not even half-questions or sort-of questions—the visions would not try to answer her.

Which meant her life was her own. Foreseeing a possible future seemed to draw her onto that path, making her a part of it, no matter what she wanted or intended.

Two squirrels furiously and noisily chased each other up a tree, over a branch, and leapt across to another trunk. There, she thought; just so: knowing which branch they would take would make no difference. It did not make her bag of groceries lighter. It did not make Enana's stew taste better.

The only thing her years of foreseeing had done was cause her and those she loved pain, put their lives in danger. That part of her life was over. Now she was like everyone else. Now she saw only what was in front of her.

For a brief moment, memory of a dark figure on a horse at the edge of a river.

No, that was the past. She pushed it away.

It brushed her, then, the barest chill of vision, like a sharp winter breeze stabbing through this thick, hot summer day. Images tried to form in her mind.

"No," she said fiercely, waving her hands as if to brush away flies.

A deep breath. She inhaled the smells of grass and earth around her, felt the light breeze that brushed her skin.

She thought of Pas. He would smile when she got back home, dash over to her, reach up to be lifted. She imagined his small fingers. Imagined, not foresaw.

No visions.

A nagging feeling came over her. The road before her curved around a blind rise.

Vision was trying to tell her something. She pushed it away.

After supper she would play games with Pas. She would teach him new words. Maybe Enana would tell them a story.

Her steps slowed.

He couldn't have tracked them here, not after so long. Could he?

She stopped, holding her breath. The future was struggling to unfold itself, like a map. She could not stop it from its motion any more than she could stop the moments from coming toward her. But she could decide not to look.

Resolutely she walked forward. Whatever it was, she would be surprised. Like anyone else.

Rounding the rise, heart speeding, she expected a dark

figure. He would jump out. He would have a bow. An arrow in her chest.

Instead, shafts of sunlight cut through tall trees, patches of light finding their way to fallen piles of leaves. Bird calls echoed through branches. A high breeze made the treetops sigh.

There was no one there.

In the distance she could make out the strand of trees past which was the road that would take her to the farmhouse. She exhaled relief, laughed a little to find that she was not anything more than a girl returning home from market. She shifted the bag to her other shoulder and hurried forward.

A squirrel poked its head around a tree trunk and stared at her, body and head frozen. Then it twisted, scampered up the tree, and was gone.

Behind her came the sounds of footsteps.

Vision came upon her like a huge stove fire: close, heavy, hot. Too strong to press away.

It shouted at her to drop, and she obeyed, bending her knees as instructed, barely missing the arm that swept over her head.

Again, vision barked direction and she thrust the bag that had come off her shoulders in the last motion behind, pushing hard. The bag pressed into leather-clad legs, slowed them only slightly. She struggled to her feet, turned.

For a moment she took him in: dark hair, hands open, empty, a pack and a bow slung across his shoulder.

He stepped lightly over the spilled bag at his feet and toward her. She turned and ran.

"Amarta," he called.

With part of her mind she realized that it was the first time she had heard his voice. She half remembered hearing it before. Vision or dream?

The tone was friendly, somewhere between a greeting and bemusement that she was running away. At this she herself might have been confused enough to pause, but vision was not. It told her to run, so she did, and his steps were hard on the dirt behind her.

The arm came across her face again, and she bit it, or tried to; it was covered in hard leather and pulled her tight against him, wrapping tightly around her head.

Strange, really, that she had time to think about the taste of leather, that it must be awfully hot to wear that much leather over your arms and legs, here in late summer. Serious, quite serious. About what he was doing. Which was—

She screamed, howled her rage and resistance. His wrap tightened, burying her face in the leather arm, muffling the cry. Not that it would matter—there was no one nearby to hear.

Then the arm was gone. Before she could blink, a wad of cloth was stuffed in her mouth, soaked in something sticky and bitter. She began to inhale; then realized vision was saying spit. She did, but even so the stink of it burned her lungs and made her eyes water. Her next cry came out as a croak. It hurt to breathe.

Now he had her arms and was pulling her off the path into the brush. She struggled, kicking fruitlessly. He twisted one arm behind her back, another around her neck. Pain shot up her shoulder as he yanked her backwards, stumbling across the uneven underbrush. She was slammed to the ground on her back, he on top, pinning her arms with his legs, a hand on her neck.

Above her, dark hair and face was framed by a thick green and golden canopy of leaves. In the air between them she could smell leather and the sticky stuff that still made her eyes water.

While she gasped for breath, they looked at each other.

Light brown eyes. Her hunter had light brown eyes.

She struggled, and he held her without any seeming effort, expression nearly blank. With his free hand he reached into his sleeve and pulled out a knife, put the tip at her face. A pinpoint of pain on the underside of her eye stopped her moving.

"You are Amarta al Botaros," he said. "The seer." There was no hint of question now, no pretense of friendliness.

How could he have found them, after all this time? They had hidden, changed their names, pretended to be other than they were. She hadn't foreseen for anyone, not since they had left Botaros. Not once.

"Answer," he said.

Vision had warned her, despite that she had pushed it away for so long; it had come when she needed it. If only she had listened sooner . . . But no, she had thought to be like everyone else.

Fear washed over her, pushed away reason.

"Please," she heard herself croak. "Please don't hurt me . . ." Once started, she could not seem to stop. "I'll do anything. Please don't hurt me."

"You've no cause to fear," he said gently, pulling the

knife back a bit. "I know who you are. I just want to hear you say it."

If she lied and gave him the false name she had been using—if she said it as though she meant it—would he believe it? Would he let her go?

An answer tried to form within. From determined practice these last months she pushed it away, then struggled to pull it back. Sluggishly, like an atrophied muscle, it began to unfold.

Slowly. Too slowly.

With a quick, fluid flip of the blade, his knife went blunt-side along his forearm and he leaned forward, the sharp edge now up under her chin. The move was so fast that it spoke of skill far beyond anything she had ever seen.

Vision gave her an answer: he would know a lie, but the truth would not serve better; the future promised capture, pain, blood, and darkness.

The blade would cut her throat. She would struggle. He would keep her pinned, gaze locked on hers as she lost consciousness.

It was near, that future, very near.

And would that be so bad? If she were gone, if he sent her to the Beyond, Dirina and Pas might finally be safe from the hunter and the ill-fortune that seemed to follow her.

Sounds and flashes, nothing certain. The future shifted like spray from a spun waterbag. She could not follow the drops, nor tell one from the next.

He tightened his grip on her throat, shook her a little. Her head swam.

"I only want to ask you some questions." His tone was soft, reluctant, as if to say that he hated to be this hard on her, that if she answered him he would certainly let her go. The grip on her neck loosened a little. The pounding in her head eased. "Who have you spoken to about your visions since you left Botaros?"

She thought the tone a lie. She searched her visions, frustrated at the fog-filled traces that led out of this moment. She should never have stopped practicing. A bit late for that understanding.

For all the half-seen flashes and muttering voices the future revealed now that she had opened the door again, as she peered along the dim paths that led forward, she saw only darkness.

There must be a way, a thread that led through the next handful of heartbeats, that would take her past the approaching wall.

She struggled harder. A cacophony of sounds grew, each crowing about what might yet be, a tumbling and turning, a thousand voices muttering, talking, screaming. Then a pinpoint of light. She hurled herself forward toward it, fear propelling her. She overshot her destination, went far distant.

A familiar scent of breath. A smile on a face that didn't smile.

She opened her eyes. He stared down at her.

"You are foreseeing," he said, watching her.

"Yes."

"Tell me what."

Relief flooded her, pouring over the many layers of vision, the myriad of noisy futures.

This—his curiosity—was the thread she had been searching for. She held tight to it while she opened herself to the dictates of foresight. Under his grip and weight she went limp, not fighting, letting herself sink into this moment and the very next.

The way he watched her, somehow he could tell her plans.

No plans. No thought.

On the ground beside her, fallen leaves brushed the skin of her pinned arms. The breeze filled the air with the scent of pine and bark, of grasses and rotting leaves.

It was quiet now. No wind, no bird calls. No squirrels.

"Amarta. Tell me what you foresaw."

Before the reason and terror made her reconsider, obedient to vision, she lifted and turned her head, pressing her neck into the edge of the knife he held at her throat. His eyes flickered, and he pulled the knife away, a little, shifting his balance. Not much, but enough.

Twist hard, vision said, and she did, all at once rolling to follow his slight movement, hard and fast.

The weight change took both of them into a half roll onto the dirt where he came off her. She kept twisting as vision demanded, hands now under her, pushing against the ground to keep herself rolling.

Now he was on his feet, knife in hand, stepping toward her where she sat on the ground looking up at him. She groped for the next move, pushing away panic, surrendering to the guiding whispers.

Move thus, they said, so she did. She tensed, twisted, and kicked from where she lay prone, at what was empty air, just as he stepped onto the spot. Not hard enough to hurt him, of course, but enough to force him to step to the side instead of forward, giving her another heartbeat of time. In that heartbeat she leapt to her feet and started to run.

He was right behind her. Vision gave her a particular feel as a hand reached for her hair. She shook her head sharply. The hand missed. When it came again she ducked and it grabbed empty air.

Deep in a flickering foresight, she saw him move, right before he did. She sidestepped. He lunged. She stopped suddenly, and turned in place. He stumbled past.

He froze where he stood, looking at her. He understood now, she could see from his expression. As he was considering what to do next, vision told her to go, and she did, turning to run, glancing back as she stumbled ahead on the road.

He took the bow off his back. A moment later she felt a pressure, a craving to stop, to step to the right, to brush a particular tree trunk as she passed, so she did. An arrow hissed by her ear, sinking into the ground beyond.

She launched away from the tree, a sprint forward, dodging bushes, running as fast as she could.

An arrow through the air, a finger width from her neck.

Suddenly she felt light-headed, giddy. The future knew where he would aim better than he did, and the future was hers. She sprinted past trees, bushes, mind jumping between now and a heartbeat ahead.

He was following, but he had to slow to put an arrow to his bow, take aim, and shoot, and he fell behind as she ran.

The pressure again. She stepped to the left, heard the arrow sink into a nearby tree.

Then something shifted. The next moment narrowed to a pinpoint, and the dark wall returned. Two options unfolded: an arrow through her ribs, or a fall to the ground.

She let herself fall, realizing as she went down that she had misstepped, ankle twisting painfully under her as she went down. Something bit through her shoulder, and she landed heavily on the dirt and leaves, pain shooting through her leg.

The pain broke her concentration. Fear came flooding back. Vision became blurry, indecipherable. She rolled over onto her back, reached for her aching shoulder, momentarily confused by the red wetness on her fingers. His last arrow had sliced through her shirt and skin like a knife.

Above her leaves flickered in the breeze like small blades. A crow called.

He stood over her now, bow in hand, arrow notched and pointed at her chest. She groped inwardly, searching for the map that had guided her thus far, but her mind was clear of anything but pain and terror. She gasped a sob, forced herself to stare up at him through her watering eyes.

"Where are your visions now, Amarta?"

Not a mocking tone. He was truly curious.

"Gone," she whispered, feeling all at once weak. "All gone. Before you kill me, tell me why. Please."

He was silent. Could he be undecided? He lowered the bow the smallest bit. "If I let you live, will you promise me you won't try to escape?"

Amarta tried to think, swallowed. Somehow he could discern a lie. But she would say anything to live. "Yes," she said.

He laid the bow on the ground behind him, knelt just out of her reach. "Don't give me reason to reconsider."

"I won't," she said, meaning the words as she said them.

He pulled away the loose cloth of her shirt, and she tensed against the pain, whimpered. He took out a strip of cloth from his pack and pressed where she'd been sliced.

"It will heal. This will stop the bleeding."

"Then you won't kill me?"

"I still have the option, Seer."

"Why are you chasing me?"

He reached into another sleeve, drew out a small leather case and from that a thin piece of metal. "There's tincture on this dart," he said. "Enough to make you sleep, not to harm you. I think this may stop your visions for a time. What do you think?"

What should she say? She nodded.

"We'll see," he said. "You understand me, girl? You'll cooperate?"

"Yes."

He put one hand on her leg to hold it steady. His other hand, the one with the dart, was already moving toward her leg when vision came upon her again, strong and urgent.

She moved suddenly, a sharp twitch. Instead of going into her leg, the dart went deep into his hand.

Then she twisted in the other direction, escaping his

hold, and scrabbled back and away on the ground. He pulled the dart out of his hand, tossed it away, and put his hand to his mouth, sucking and spitting onto the ground.

What had she done? She cringed, backing farther away.

From his sleeve he snapped out his knife and stood. A step toward her, and he swayed slightly. His hand opened, the knife fell to the dirt.

He dropped to his knees and hands, hands flat on the ground, still watching her.

"Your visions come back?" His voice was slow, slurred.

She nodded uncertainly. Was he really this drugged, this fast? Could it be a trick?

She sought guidance from her visions, but they were again silent.

"Why are you after me?" she asked.

He lowered himself to the ground, still watching her. "Why?"

He blinked twice, then his eyes closed.

Ignoring the agonizing pain in her ankle and the ache in her shoulder, she struggled to her feet. She looked back at him where he lay now motionless on the ground. Then she turned and limped home to the farmhouse.

She and Dirina stuffed what they could into their bags. Amarta looked around their small room, trying to keep the weight off her throbbing foot. What more could they carry?

"What do we tell Enana?" she asked.

"Nothing. Just go."

"Where we go?" Pas asked, grabbing a shirt at random and offering it to Amarta.

"Without even saying good-bye?"

Dirina hesitated in her packing, not looking up, tone edged. "Do you have another plan, Amarta?"

"No."

"The less she knows, the safer she is."

Dirina was right. But it felt wretched, after all the family had done for them.

"We can't take food from them, and we have no money. Where are we going? What will we do?"

"That's what I was wondering," came Enana's voice from the doorway.

At that, Pas ran to Enana, and she lifted him into her arms. The tall woman walked into their room, balancing the boy on her hip. Pas turned to look at his mother and Amarta, thumb in his mouth.

"Is this the same man after you?"

"Yes," Amarta said softly.

Enana had been so good to them, taking them in at midwinter, feeding them, letting them stay. What a wretched way to repay her, leaving now, before harvest, when they were needed most.

Amarta saw the hunter again in memory, lying there, his bow and knife a few feet away on the ground.

Why hadn't she taken them? She felt a fool now, thinking of it. It would have been so easy to just pick up his weapons and take them away.

Or, she realized with a chill, she could have taken an arrow from his pack, aimed for his heart, and let it loose. Standing right over him, surely she could not miss.

He could have been stopped, right then, for good.

"We're sorry," Dirina was saying. "So sorry. The wash is half done, and Amarta dropped all the groceries from market in the woods—"

"Down now," Pas said very soberly. Enana let him to the ground. He ran to his mother, hugged her leg.

Maybe the hunter would not wake at all. Maybe he lied to her about the dart not being deadly, and she had inadvertently killed him. She paused, wondering if this was likely. Reason said no.

And what would he do when he woke?

A dark figure in the night, a crescent moon at the treeline. He knocked on the farmhouse door. Enana's silhouette against the lamplight from inside. His tone was apologetic, gentle. Charming.

She felt suddenly ill.

"We'll go upriver," Amarta said quickly. "Back to Sennant. Or—"

Dirina looked a question at her.

"Home to Botaros," Amarta continued, making her tone as certain as she knew how, catching Dirina's gaze. When the shadow hunter came to ask Enana questions, Amarta wanted her to have answers.

"This man," Enana said. "Where did you say he was now?"

"He attacked Amarta in the forest," Dirina said, her hand on Pas's head. Amarta willed her sister not to say the rest, but she did. "Asleep on the ground, from poison on a dart. You said, Amarta."

"Yes," Amarta said reluctantly, "But—"

Enana's expression turned hard. "Tell us where he is.

I'll take the boys out there and we can take care of him where he lies."

Hope surged inside her. Was this possible? Enana and her two sons. Big men. Surely they could take one unconscious man.

Back at the house, the hunter in the cellar, a makeshift bolt across the door. Enana and her sons sitting at the table, discussing what to do with him, what would be right. What would be just. And then—

They would bring him back to the house, yes, and lock him in the cellar with the apples and the preserves. But sometime before dawn—

Enana in her bed, slumped over, arms twitching, blood trailing down her neck, the blankets soaked in red.

He would break free of the basement. The men would die first, quickly, but Enana slowly, after being asked questions.

And this because Enana and her family would not, could not, take the life of a man who had yet to do them wrong.

"He'll kill you," she said flatly.

"One man?" Enana snorted.

"No," Amarta lied. "He's not alone this time. He has a whole band of outlaws with him, hiding in the woods." She licked her lips, looking at Dirina. "Twenty or thirty. All armed with crossbows and swords. They're killers, Enana. Brutal killers."

"But they're only after us," Dirina added. "You and Cafir and Loham will be safe without us."

Enana frowned. "But I don't want you to go. We could hide you. The basement—"

Amarta shook her head. "He'll find us."

The tall woman looked between them both, anger sharp across her features. "No one tells me what to do—"

Amarta stepped close and took Enana's hands. "We must leave, and soon. So much safer for you."

Enana pressed her lips together. Then spoke, her tone low. She was still angry. "I have coins I can give you. I'll pack you some food."

Amarta hid her relief as she saw the future's tangle of threads twist a new way. Enana might live through the hunter's visit.

What could she do to make it more likely?

"Enana," Amarta said urgently. "He'll come here. He'll ask you questions. He can read a lie. Tell him everything you know about us. Let him in, feed him, give him drink."

Enana turned around slowly, her expression darkening further. "I won't feed a killer who forces you from my house. No one comes into my home I don't let in. Not even the king's soldiers with their manners of goats and brains of chickens. No one."

Amarta's ankle and shoulder were throbbing for attention now, distracting her. Dimly she thought she heard Enana cry out in pain, but it might be her imagination. Everything seemed to suck away her focus. "He's worse than the king's soldiers. Please, Enana, don't fight him."

"You want me to show him hospitality, this monster? To treat him well?"

"Yes."

"There is no sense in this."

"And," Amarta whispered, struggling with the last of her focus to seek a toehold in the future, not just for tonight, but farther, farther, "it will be dry until a tenday before the new moon. Then the rain will come all at once for three days, then stop." With that, Enana would know how to best harvest, when to cut the hay. If she believed it.

"What are you saying?"

Amarta and Dirina exchanged looks. Amarta licked her lips.

"The future sometimes . . ." How to explain? "It whispers to me."

Enana shook her head, disbelief on her face. "No one knows when the rains come."

"Amarta does," Dirina said simply.

Amarta spoke again, feeling a sudden urgency. "He will come tonight, Enana, as the moon comes over the rise." In her mind's eye she saw it clearly, the knock on the door, Enana backlit by stovelight. "If he comes when I say he will, will you remember my words? Don't fight. Treat him . . ." She swallowed, hating to say it, but knowing she must. "Treat him well. Tell him everything. It will go better for us if you do."

Enana stared at Amarta for a long, thoughtful moment.

"Get packed."

It was slow going along the forest road with Amarta limping. The walking stick Enana had given them was a help, but each step was full of pain that she resolved to hide. Dirina slowed so as not to outpace her.

The nals chits Enana had given them sat heavily in

Amarta's pocket, weighted with her guilt at the knowledge of how little the family had to spare. From the jabbing pain in her ankle to her shoulder, never mind the other places where her encounter in the forest had left her bruised and scraped, Amarta ached.

"Do you think we have until nightfall before he comes after us?" Dirina asked.

"I hope so."

"You hope? Ama, you said—"

A flash of hot resentment went through her, hand in hand with a sickening remorse. "I know what I said. Seeing is not the same thing as knowing. And now I don't see anything at all. Diri, everything"—*hurts*, she didn't finish—"is confusing."

Her sister said nothing.

"Up now," Pas said after they had let him walk a little way. Dirina hefted him and put him on her shoulders, holding his feet, wrapped with tiny turnshoes Cafir had made for him.

One more thing the family had given them, which they repaid so wretchedly. The gnawing ache inside threatened to eat through her. It was as if along with the seedlings she'd planted in the fields she had also put some of her self into the ground, and now she was being torn out by the roots. "Diri, where do we go?"

Dirina squinted at the sky and the sun. "The river. We'll get the barge. It comes five hands past noon, so we should . . ." She inhaled. "We should hurry."

"Down now," Pas said.

"You ride, sweet," Dirina said. "We have to go faster than you can go."

"I go fast."

"Then you'll have to carry me, too," Amarta said, giving him a smile. He looked at her, considered, and fell silent.

"He will come after us, Diri," Amarta said. "That's not"—she said, seeing her sister's wide-eyed look—"what I'm seeing. It's what I'm thinking."

She could have prevented it. Picked up the bow. Notched an arrow. Tried again if she missed. Or used his knife on him. It had been right there on the ground.

To have ended it right then, to be able to stay with Enana—but she had not. She prayed to the guardian of travelers and orphans that Enana would do as she had told her. As vision had told her.

"Ama?"

She realized that she had made a short, pained sound. "If he hurts them—"

"He doesn't want them. He wants us."

No, he wanted Amarta. "But how will we make money? How will we eat?"

"We'll clean, we'll mend, as we've done all along."

That wasn't what they had done. Dirina still thought Amarta might believe it, though, so she kept on saying it.

"I will do what you do to earn money," Amarta said.

"No," Dirina said, shocked. "You will not."

"Why not?"

"You're a child."

"Come spring, Diri, I'm of age."

"Years are not enough. Your first time should not be—like that. It should be someone you like. Someone who likes you."

"What do you mean, first time?"

An exhale. Then, softly, "You do not need to know."

"How long until I bleed with the moon, Diri? That, if not my springs, certainly means—"

"It doesn't. It means nothing."

"I'm not a child."

"You certainly are. This would not be safe for you."

"It's safe for you?" Amarta swallowed her frustration. "I'd know if it was safe. I'd be able to see before it happened."

"Would you, now? Really? Then why are we on the run again? You see danger when it's right on top of you, Ama. With a man, that's far too late."

Amarta wanted to say that it was more complicated than that, to explain that the hunter after them, whose eyes she had finally seen, was more dangerous than a single man ought to be. Then she looked at her sister's thin mask of confidence, saw worry and terror churning beneath, and decided not to. "All right," she agreed. "But I won't let us go hungry again."

"We won't," Dirina said. Another empty promise, but she would not gainsay it. Her sister was doing all she could to get them from one moment to the next.

Despite that vision had told her he would sleep for hours yet, she looked around furtively at the dark forest.

She would not, she resolved, push vision away again. Thinking of the forest and her hunter, she realized that she hadn't, really. The visions were inescapable. Like so many things in her life. Like having to leave places that might have been home.

A sudden scratching sound made her jerk around,

setting her heart to speeding, but it was only a squirrel, leaping from one tree to the next, now gone into the upper reaches of the thick canopy.

She hoped that the inescapable things in life did not include her hunter.

When they reached the Sennant River they turned along the road, walking past small houses and fenced pastures. Goats and sheep looked curiously at them as they passed.

Nesmar Port was little more than a sloping bank of stony shore and a wooden dock. People, horses, and wagons were clustered thickly, some leaning on barrels, voices loud and gestures wide over piles of sacks and stacked crates. Two well-dressed women stood together, consulting a board of parchment notes as a donkey laden with overstuffed saddle bags was futilely attempting to back up from between a stack of crates topped with cages of chickens. Someone began to laugh, someone else to call loudly to children who were staring and pointing at a pair of small, oddly striped brown, black, and tan-colored horses.

Amarta breathed relief. They had not missed the barge after all. At a large flat rock she sat gratefully, dropping her stick to the stones underfoot. She crossed her ankle over her other knee, rubbing it to try to ease the pain.

"Ama," Dirina hissed.

Her sister's gaze was intent, face tight. Amarta followed her look across the assembled crowd, not seeing the cause of her alarm. "What?"

A single carthorse was pulling a wagon of hay bundles slowly up and away from the water toward the road.

Elsewhere a man hefted a pack over his back. Two small, dusky-skinned men from some eastern tribe were securing a wagon cover.

Amarta felt her stomach drop. "Oh no," she breathed.

The man with the large bundle across his shoulders, his three children pulling a handcart behind him, gave her a sympathetic look as he passed. "Sad it is, but you just now missed it."

"No! Are you sure?" Dirina asked.

He pointed downriver. In the distance was a slowly receding barge, laden with wagons, boxes, animals, people.

The man's children looked at the two of them as they dragged the handcart behind him. Amarta saw how their gaze took them in. They would be remembered.

"Up now," Pas insisted, arms on his mother's leg, looking at her intently. She sighed heavily, pulled him into her lap.

The weight of the day, of this latest failure, settled heavily on Amarta.

Open and covered wagons were hitched to horses, packs slung over backs and into handcarts. The donkey escaped his temporary trap and was now making his way up to the road.

Leaving. They were all leaving.

"What do we do?" Dirina asked, her hopeless tone tearing at Amarta.

Would the hunter come here directly from the farm? Surely there was the rest of the countryside to search. He might go another way.

No, the barge was obvious. She could too clearly

imagine him walking through the riverside village, asking questions.

"A woman and child and a limping girl dressed as a boy? Oh, yes, I saw them. They missed the afternoon barge. They went that way."

"Do you think," Dirina asked, almost timidly, "we could—go back?"

To the farm, she meant. The only place Amarta was sure they could not go. "No," she said soberly.

"Then . . . ?"

She wanted to sleep it all away, like a bad dream. Wake to Enana calling her to the fields.

The final crates and barrels were loaded onto wagons, bolts of cloth and cages of rabbits rearranged on top. The sky was darkening. Everyone wanted to get where they were going before nightfall.

Nightfall. When he would wake.

Another moment she put off looking to vision, then another. That part of her was sore as well. At last she forced herself to look and listen to what could be.

Nothing but the chattering of people, the crunching of small stones under foot, hoof, and wheel. The smell and hush of river. High clouds caught the first hint of sunset.

Focus, she told herself sternly, closing her eyes.

When she found it, it was buried and crusted over, like some rusted-shut metal door that screamed to open even a crack. She fought back, pushed the question into this sorest part of herself.

Could they wait for the next day's barge? Find somewhere to hide for the night? Was it possible?

The smallest flash came to her. Barely a breath.

Darkness. Rough motion. The smell of horse strong under her, head pounding. Pas and Dirina gone.

"No," she breathed, pushing it away, not wanting to know more.

"Then where?" Dirina asked. Almost a plea. "Ama, we have to—"

"I don't know!" she said loudly.

An elderly woman gave her a reproachful look as she and her adult son, judging by his similar looks, slowly walked by. The man was breathing hard, carrying a pack as well as holding his mother's arm to steady her as they ascended the bank.

A slight depression in the ground, near a flowering plantain at the edge of a road. A leather-clad knee dropped down by it, fingers lightly brushing the dirt.

"Grandmother," Amarta said quickly, rewarded by another glare from the woman. Amarta struggled painfully to her feet, picked up the stick at her feet. "Please take this for your travels." She held it out. The two of them paused, the woman's expression softening.

The man nodded gratefully, took the stick and handed it to his mother.

"Thank you, child," the woman said.

"Blessings of the season to you," Amarta replied politely.

Dirina looked a question at her. Amarta looked toward the river.

Only a couple of large covered wagons remained. A dusky-skinned woman checked the harnesses of a team of four gray carthorses while the other of the tribespeople loaded up bags into the other wagon.

Standing apart from them were the striped horses, untethered, unhaltered, not even bridle or reins. Their markings were strange, with brown and orange stripes wrapping their wheat-colored hides, stretching from the tricolor fall of their tails up their backs through their manes to their heads, the fingers of stain reaching across their faces like some sort of midwinter festival mask. It was as if the chestnut-and-ginger-colored lines had been painted on their backs and sides by someone with more enthusiasm than skill.

"Mama, look: horses!" Pas cried loudly, pointing at them. At this outburst, one of the horses looked at them. Dirina kept a tight hold of Pas's hand as he tried to pull away to run to them.

"What are they?" Amarta asked.

Mutely, Dirina shook her head.

One of the striped horses turned in their direction and began walking toward the rock on which they sat.

"Diri . . ."

As it came near, Dirina and Amarta quickly stood and stepped back behind the rock. Dirina pushed the excited Pas back behind her as he struggled to break free of her grip. He reached out his other hand around his mother to the horse who had walked around the rock to reach him. Horse lips and small fingers met before Dirina managed to get between them, Amarta hobbling over to help.

"Stop that!" Amarta told the horse, who swung its head to stare back at her.

"Ho! What do you do here?" One of the tribesmen strode over. A smallish man, light brown hair nearly the same shade as his skin, glared at Dirina and Amarta as if they had somehow caused this problem. He turned on the animal, speaking softly to it with words Amarta did not understand. The horse snorted, tossed its head slightly and turned back to Pas again, snuffling. Pas held his hand out, again blocked by his mother. Pas giggled.

Now the man made a soft sound, a sort of warbling, interspersed with a clicking. When that didn't work, he put a hand on the side of the horse and pushed, with no obvious result.

At last the horse turned, slowly, but in the other direction, to take it closer to Amarta. She reached out a hand, fingers trailing across the neck and soft, warm hair, as it turned the rest of the way around. Somehow the animal conveyed an amused insolence even as it returned to the wagons to rejoin its similarly furred companions. With a snort of frustration, hands in the air, the man followed.

"'Bye horse," Pas said.

A tiny, wet animal colt trembling in the early dawn, dark brown with pale tan stripes, lips hungrily searching upwards.

"Oh," Amarta blurted. "She's pregnant."

Then, despite the pain and everything that had happened that day, she laughed in delight. A future flash of something not painful, threatening, or about to hurt her—she hadn't realized it was possible.

The tribesman stopped suddenly, looking between Amarta and the horse. He walked back to Amarta.

"Why do you say that?" he demanded.

"Take us with you and I'll tell you."

He shook his head, then went back to his wagons. The

larger gray horses were harnessed, and the tribespeople seemed ready to leave. The man and woman mounted their striped horses in a fast, fluid motion.

"It's a colt, the foal," Amarta called out to him in a final desperate attempt. The man glanced at her, then leaned toward the woman, speaking, head motioning back at Amarta and Dirina.

In truth, Amarta wasn't sure about that, but it would be almost a year before the mare birthed, whereas the hunter would track them here in—hours? A day?

Soon. Too soon.

The man turned in the saddle to look at her again for a moment. The wagons were leaving, the striped horses following. In minutes they were all gone.

Amarta turned her head to look at Dirina, wiping her eyes of tears.

"It was a good try, Ama," Dirina said, her arm around her shoulders.

The riverbank and dock, busy and full only a little bit ago, were now empty and quiet. The sun was dipping down behind the trees. Dirina pulled Pas onto her lap and held him tight.

"Ama." Her sister's voice was soft.

Where should they go, Dirina wanted to know. The sky was now awash in red and gold and deepening blue. In another hour, perhaps two, the hunter would wake. Go to the farmhouse.

The nightmare would begin again.

She sought vision, but it wasn't answering, the door shut and barred. She was too tired. Everywhere she looked she saw bitter failure.

"We'll be okay," she said with as much certainty as she could pretend, though she doubted Dirina was much convinced.

Perhaps vision would return after she'd rested. Or perhaps only when she was about to be captured, or her life threatened.

Pas wanted down again. Sighing as if defeated, Dirina let him go. He raced around the rock on which they sat.

"Here, give me your foot," Dirina said.

Amarta lay her foot in her sister's lap. Dirina turned it gently, and Amarta yelped with pain.

"Sprained," Dirina said wearily. "Then you walked another hour. No surprise it is swollen and red." She rubbed it gently for a time. Then: "We must go somewhere, Ama."

Amarta struggled to think of what to say, found nothing. She struggled to her feet, pain lancing through her leg as she put weight on it.

"Ama, where—"

"I don't know, but we can't stay here."

They made their way to the main road, Amarta's step slow and labored. Dirina insisted and Amarta let her take her pack, put it on top of her own. With Pas in one hand, she offered an arm to Amarta to steady her. Amarta refused, limping forward. Was she not already enough of a burden?

The main road was in shadow. Through shutters she could see flickers of lamps, stoves. Smoke rose from chimneys.

Not for her, a home and safety.

Pushing to walk faster, her foot collapsed under her.

She fell painfully to the dirt road, hitting an already bruised knee, curling around the pain.

For a moment she let herself weep, watched the drops fall into the fine dirt, making small puffs where they landed. If she could be so small, as small as an ant, she could sleep right there in the dirt, hidden from sight. Dirina knelt down next to her, squeezed her shoulder.

Every moment he was closer. Beyond her not to cry, perhaps, but not quite beyond her to stand. She struggled to her feet.

Her sister's encouraging smile was forced and fragile. Leaning on Dirina she limped forward. One step. Then another, putting as little weight on the bad foot as possible.

They would walk until she dropped again, she supposed. And then she would stay there until he found her.

The sound of a horse's hard gallop brought her head up. Dirina gently pulled her and Pas to the side of the road to get them out of the way.

The striped horse, the dusky-skinned woman atop, pulled up fast in front of them and stopped, as if showing off. The woman slipped down off the side, strode to Amarta, bringing her sharp nose right up to Amarta's face.

She smelled like horse, Amarta noticed, as she stumbled painfully back in surprise.

"You say pregnant," the woman said. "You say this. Why?" She glanced sidelong at her horse, who looked back. "Are you a healer?"

Amarta wondered if she could pretend to that. "No."

"You lie, then."

"No!"

"Say then, how you know."

"Take us with you," Amarta countered.

"You run from something. Someone," the woman guessed.

Dirina and Amarta said nothing. Their silence was answer enough.

"The king's Rusties?"

"The what?"

"Soldiers of the king. In red and black."

A knife at her eye. A blade at her throat. But her hunter had worn no red.

"Yes," Dirina said at the same moment Amarta was adamantly shaking her head no.

The woman hissed wordlessly in response, gave each of them a look. To Amarta she said, "She has been changed this last week. So it may be true, what you say. Did you guess this?"

"No."

"You say a colt. You can predict this for all animals?"

"Yes," Dirina answered determinedly. But the woman ignored her, looking the question at Amarta.

Amarta tried to remember the many times she had foreseen a baby. Goats. A few cows. Human children. She had not always been right about the baby's sex. People wanted to be sure, but babies themselves weren't always sure, not until later. Sometimes not even then.

"Sometimes," she answered honestly.

At this Dirina gave Amarta an incredulous look. "No. She sees things truly."

The woman gestured at Pas. "Can he be silent, the boy?"

At this both she and Dirina nodded together. But it was Pas, smiling up at the woman with his beautiful smile, who seemed to convince her. She looked down at him, considered for a long moment, petted his head, then nodded. "Come with, then."

Seeing Amarta limp forward, she added: "You ride." With that, she picked Amarta up, surprising her with how strong she was. Before Amarta quite realized what had happened, she had been set atop the small, striped horse. The woman swung up behind. The horse turned an eye to Amarta, then swung her head back and gave a soft neigh that almost sounded like a laugh.

"They wait for us," the woman said to Dirina, who now had Pas in her arms, packs on her back. "We must hurry."

Chapter Ten

This was hardly the first time that Tayre had been poisoned.

His apprenticeship with his uncle had included a close examination of many substances that took away a person's mind to varying degrees, including permanently. In particular, he had more than passing familiarity with the plant whose juice he had painted on the dart that he'd intended to use on the Botaros girl.

This was, however, the first time it had happened to him by accident.

Except that it wasn't really an accident, despite the girl's wide-eyed reaction when her own exceptionally well-timed twitch sent the dart into his hand instead of her leg.

He was now convinced; against all probability, Innel had been entirely correct: the girl was a true seer.

Tayre could feel the tincture working in his body. It was a fast, potent dose, intended to put the girl into something approximating slumber for a half day or more, which he had expected to be sufficient time to secure her in a way that even her foresight would not allow her to escape.

Then again, the dose was measured for her, not someone twice her size, so it should not affect him as much. If he could summon decisive movement, right now, he might still reach her, hold her, disable her. Stop her from getting away.

She was at this moment crouched on the ground, watching him fearfully, mistrustful of his slowing motions. He could turn that to his advantage, if he could act. Struggling against fading concentration and numbing limbs, he stepped toward her once, then again. His fingers loosened against his will, and the knife fell. He looked down at the foliage where it had landed and realized that the ground seemed too far away.

"Looks like you're going to fall, boy," his uncle had said from the rise above.

His ten-year-old self's hands were sweaty, gripping tight but slowly slipping from the branch from which he dangled, twenty feet over the ravine.

"What do I do?" he'd asked through gritted teeth.

"Sometimes you lose," his uncle had said conversationally. "Thing is, if you can wake the next morning, then you have another chance to win. If you die—well. You've lost entirely, then."

Another small slip, Tayre's grip weakening. He looked down at the steep slope below. At best, it would be a painful fall.

"I suggest, my boy, that you figure out how to land so that you can wake tomorrow."

Sometimes you lose.

With what fast-fading control Tayre still had, rather than let himself fall as his loosening limbs wanted to do, he lowered himself to the forest floor. On all fours, he considered what was most likely to happen next.

The road was not well-traveled, so despite hours of lying unconscious, there was a good chance he would wake. The girl herself was the greatest risk; she could kill him as he lay there defenseless. If she had the will. He didn't think she did.

Or she could bring back others who did.

As his thoughts slowed to an agonizing crawl, he laid himself on the ground, keeping his eyes on her as long as he could. She got up and limped away.

Escaping him a third time.

Tayre's final thought was that it was a shame he had been told to bring her back alive. He was almost certain that, had he been trying to kill rather than disable her, he would not now be lying here, falling unconscious, as she fled.

Tayre woke to wet darkness and sounds of night—crickets, high winds, and the light pattering of rain on leaves overhead. He sat up slowly and reached out to where he remembered dropping his knife. His fingers found it, curled around the handle, resheathed it. His bow, also, was where he dropped it.

Other than being damp from hours of lying in what was now partly mud, it was as good an outcome as he could have hoped for.

He stood, rolling out the ache in his limbs and breathing hard to clear the headache that the tincture had left.

It was very dark. He traced the mud and dirt road with his feet, following to the edge of the woods, in the direction she had fled. The rain slowed and stopped. Overhead he saw small patches of stars.

No rush now. She was hours ahead of him in any case.

With the advantage of being able to see things that had not yet happened.

He considered this for a moment.

Then he stashed his bow and knife under the leaves at the base of a large oak, drew a few lines on his face by feel with an oil pen from his pack in order to make himself look older and more tired than he already felt, and began his search again.

Tayre knocked lightly, stepped back, and threw off his wet hood to reveal his face in the lamplight that came from the house as the door opened.

The tall woman's eyes widened as she saw him. More than the surprise of a late-night visitor; she had been warned.

"Blessings of the season to you, good woman," he said softly.

She seemed undecided about how to answer this.

Warned and then some, it seemed.

He did not read in her face and body the look of a woman protecting children, which meant that the girl and her sister and the boy were no longer here.

That would have been his guess anyway; the girl was used to running, and people in fear for their lives tended to repeat what they knew best.

The woman stood aside to allow him entrance, the

invitation in obvious conflict with what she really wanted to do. He stepped inside hesitantly, hands together implying supplication, head forward, shoulders slumped.

At a table sat two men, likely her adult sons. On their faces Tayre read the simple suspicion of a stranger. So only the woman knew something more.

He turned an uncertain, grateful smile on her.

"Who are you? What do you want?" Her voice was hostile, charged with tension and challenge.

He glanced at the floor, let pain and regret settle on his features. "You must know that I'm following a girl, a woman, and a young boy." He glanced at her for confirmation, swallowed twice and went on, his voice cracking. "To whom I have brought so much wretchedness I am nightly tempted to end my life to escape my own shame."

On her face confusion warred with solid mistrust. For a long moment she said nothing.

"We have food and drink," she said grudgingly. It was an offer, but barely. An unwilling host. It would do.

He smiled bitterly and shook his head. "They must have told you about me." He saw the confirming flicker in her eyes. "Whatever they said, it was generous. Did she say I was hunting her? That I would hurt her if I found her again?"

The woman hesitated. Then: "Yes."

He nodded, put his hand on the still-open door, as if about to leave. "I don't deserve your kindness. Not a crumb of it."

Her expression had collapsed into confusion. "I don't understand."

"I don't claim to be a good man," he said earnestly. "But I could set all this right, if I could only talk to them for a few minutes."

"Why don't just you leave them be?"

He nodded. "I want to. As soon as I discharge my obligation and tell them about their inheritance. My cousin has left them everything. They are wealthy now and will never want for anything again. I need to tell them this, even if it's the last thing I do. It is the one thing I can do to make amends."

"I think," the woman said, her voice hard again, "you had better come in and sit down and explain yourself."

"You are kinder to me than I deserve. Let me tell you how it happened, and you can decide if you want to help me find them so I can repair some of what I have broken."

It hadn't taken long to convince Enana of the familial misunderstanding, of the better life in store for Amarta and Dirina and the boy if he could only find them. Of the possibility of them returning here—healthy, happy, and with money.

It was easy: they wanted to believe. Word by word he had used their expressions to guide his story. By the end of his tale, they had been interrupting each other to give him every detail from the months the girl and her family had stayed with them.

They even let him search the small back room where he had found a small blue seashell, a strip of blue cloth, and some hairs.

Apparently the girl had said they were going upriver to the town of Sennant, or that they might return to

Botaros. Tayre thought neither of these very likely, so he would follow their trail instead, take it as far as it led.

And the girl—how far into the future could she see? How clearly? If he decided to track them back to Botaros, then changed his mind and went to Sennant, would she foresee the one path, then the other, or only the final outcome?

Did she see potential paths, or only the one eventually taken?

It was clear that she was far from infallible. She might foresee well enough into the next few moments, when she thought her life depended on it, but perhaps that was all she could do. He had seen it before, people exhibiting exceptional abilities when faced with death.

But clearly she had limitations, or he would not have found her at all.

Still, he must rethink how to capture her. In the middle of his thwarted forest pursuit, it occurred to him that a sufficient number of capable men under his command might be able to surround her. Every arrow ready to fly could remove an avenue of escape.

But after watching her move and twist and drop to evade, he realized it would take a good many practitioners, nearly as skilled as he was, acting in concert, to accomplish this. An unlikely gathering at best.

With enough soldiers he might conceivably overwhelm her with sheer numbers, flanking and surrounding, but he suspected that would take hundreds.

Not out of the question if Innel rose to power as he clearly intended to, but for the moment, beyond any available resources.

And might she foresee such imminent, mortal danger far enough ahead to circumvent even hundreds of multipronged attacks? However carefully he set such a trap, might she simply avoid it by prediction?

Maybe. Maybe not. He did not yet understand the girl or her ability. He would need to study her.

First he would need to find her. Again.

Chapter Eleven

Amarta tentatively put weight on her injured ankle, suppressing a wince. Dirina helped her from the horse to one of the covered wagons.

"We take a chance with you," said Jolon, the small man they had spoken with at Nesmar Port. He lifted Pas from where he stood next to Dirina and set him inside the wagon.

"You won't be sorry," Dirina said with conviction as she helped Amarta limp forward.

"We hope this is so," replied the woman who had come back for them, Mara, with a sober glance at each of them.

Amarta did, too. Having left Enana and her family in the path of the shadow hunter, she wondered just how safe it was to help them.

With Mara's help she climbed up into the wagon, finding an open spot among casks and sacks of grain, bails of hay in the corners, and blankets wadded into the spaces between. Through a rip in the wagon's tarp, in the twilight, she saw another of the small, striped horses walking by. They settled in and then, from all around the wagon, voices began a trilling soot-soot-soot half-song. The wagon jerked forward and began to roll.

· "Where are we going?" Amarta asked Dirina as her sister took Pas into her lap.

"Away from here," Dirina said adamantly.

Away was a good direction. But he would follow, surely.

She could imagine him arriving at the riverside barge dock the next morning. But so many people had walked and ridden and wheeled up and away from the dock, across banks and riverrock. Surely he could not track them among all the others' footprints.

He could have lost their track anywhere between the farmhouse and Nesmar Port. In the forest. At crossroads. Surely it would be impossible for him to determine what direction they had gone, let alone that they had climbed into a wagon.

Just as it was impossible to know the gender of a foal whose mother did not yet even show her pregnancy?

With that troubling thought, Amarta lay back on the blankets.

The wagon stopped suddenly. Amarta sat up, waking, not remembering falling asleep. Outside, it was full dark.

Mara opened the tarp flap at the back, a lamp in her hand. "Come," she said.

They climbed out. Dirina took Pas off to a nearby tree. Around the wagons, the small tribespeople in their odd rag and leather clothes were making camp, feeding and watering their carthorses and the smaller ones with stripes. A fire was going, and someone was preparing food.

Mara looked at her. "We will feed you, too, lost girl. To sit here." She took Amarta's arm and helped her limp over to a fallen log.

Her mind was on their pursuer. He might even believe that they had gotten on the barge that they had just missed.

Somehow she didn't think so.

Around her, tribespeople were making camp with a practiced ease that she had never seen before. They had grown up together, she supposed, surprised at the intensity of the ache of envy she felt.

Jolon sat beside her on the log, a lamp in one hand, bread in the other. He handed her the bread, which she nibbled gratefully. "Do you still hurt?"

For a moment she was stunned—how could he know?

He meant the ankle.

"Much better, thank you," she lied. They could not afford to be thought of as a burden. Even if they were.

"Those you run from. You worry. It is not needful."

She shook her head, denying the worry, denying the assurance, not sure how much to admit. She looked for Dirina for guidance, but her sister was elsewhere with Pas, helping prepare the food.

And that was good: they must seem useful enough to be worth the risk, and hide the trouble they really were. Amarta saw another tribeswoman kneeling to talk to Pas, smiling, and she felt relief; if Pas was sweet, that might be one more reason not to leave them by the side of the road. Which they probably should.

She realized that Jolon was still watching her. She hoped she hadn't shown too much of what she'd been thinking. "Where are we going?" she asked.

He smiled. "Somewhere safe." He considered a moment, then crouched down in front of her, set his lamp on the ground, and motioned her close. Smoothing a bit of dirt flat, he drew an oval with a finger. On the lower side of the shape he made a long, thick, wavy line. "We follow the river road, here." On the near end of the oval he made a small mark. "This is where we camp now. This"—at the far end of the oval, he pointed—"is where we took you with us, at Nesmar Port. Where are the ones who follow you?"

Hesitantly she pointed to an area to the side of the oval. "He was here, I think."

"He? You mean he is one man?" At her nod, he gave a short laugh. "One is not enough. No more worry for you. We are Teva." At her look, he made a thoughtful noise. "You have not heard of us?"

She shook her head.

"We are Teva," he repeated, sitting back on his heels, a playful smile on his face. "We are so fierce that Arunkel kings and queens bribe us to be on their side. Some say it is our clever nature. Some say it is our laughter. Some say it is shaota."

"Shaota?"

"The horse you called pregnant. And her brothers." He gestured to the striped horses.

Amarta looked over at the small creatures, nibbling at grass. "You don't halter or tether them. Won't they wander away?"

"No, they . . ." He seemed to consider a moment, then stopped himself. "Yes, sometimes, it is true. But rarely. It is not like . . ." He moved a hand in the air, searching for words. "They are not slaves, like the carthorses. They belong to themselves."

"To themselves?" She had never before heard of such a thing. "Then why do they not leave?"

He frowned a little, his gaze on the horses. He made a guttural chuffing sound, and one of the horses turned her head to regard him for a moment before she turned back to her grazing. He suppressed a chuckle.

"They like us," he said with a shrug. "We are Teva. Who does not like Teva?"

The wagons continued south. Some days later, Dirina asked for and gained from the Teva thread and needle to repair the various tears in the seams on both sides of the wagon's tarp. Amarta watched her fiddle, thinking it more likely, given the rattling and swaying of the wagon, that she'd stab herself than mend anything.

But Dirina was right to try. The more useful they were, the better.

As she began to work on the tarp, Amarta curled around Pas on the blankets, awaking as the wagon suddenly jolted to a stop.

Dirina hissed, sucking on a finger.

Far distantly they could make out voices and shouts and something that might be screams. Dirina held her hands out for Pas. He crawled over to her. After a long moment, Jolon put his head in at the back of the wagon.

"We come now to a town. There is no way around it. You stay inside and be silent, yes? No matter what, yes?"

"Yes," Dirina said.

His eyes flickered quickly between them. "One last time I ask you. Tell me true. You do not run from Arunkel soldiers?"

"No," Dirina said firmly; and Amarta also shook her head, agreeing.

"Good," he said, but he seemed worried, and he looked at them a moment longer. To Pas: "You stay quiet, yes?"

Pas nodded.

Then Jolon left. The trilling soot-soot-soot song, and then the wagons jerked forward.

What were they going into? What was about to happen?

A pointing finger, followed by a shout. Hands grabbed for her, yanking her from the wagon. Sleeves of red and black. Dirina shouted. Pas screamed.

Amarta scrambled over the straw and crates to the largest of the rips in the tarp and clamped it shut with her hand, looking out the tiny opening that remained.

"Ama," Dirina whispered.

Amarta held a finger to her lips for silence.

As the wagon rolled forward, the voices and shouts grew louder. Amarta smelled smoke, heard distant wailing. She made a gesture to Dirina to get down. Her sister wrapped her arms around Pas and burrowed into the blankets.

A shout to halt. The wagons stopped. Horse snorts, footfalls. Amarta peeked through the pinhole opening.

Two large horses. Then three. Men atop them, wearing red and black.

"Identify yourselves," said a male voice.

"We are Jolon and Mara al Otevan," answered Jolon, who was mounted on his shaota.

"You have picked a poor time to visit Arteni, Jolon and Mara of the Teva. What is your business here?"

At the sound of the voice, Amarta felt a shock of familiarity. Where had she heard it before? Memory of the past, or glimpse of the future? She could not tell.

"No business here, ser. We only pass through."

Amarta tried to see the face of the large man atop the dark horse, but could not. His back was to her.

"Where are you going?"

"The markets of Munasee," answered Jolon. "To trade and sell. If there is anything remaining, perhaps on to Perripur."

"Captain," said a new voice, and Amarta managed to move a little to see a soldier on foot. "The town council and families have barricaded themselves in the basement of the mayor's mansion."

"Did you explain that it is the king's will that they put themselves in our custody?"

"Yes, Captain."

"Say it again. Slowly and loudly, so there is no confusion."

"Then break down the door and drag them out?" The soldier's voice had an eager edge to it.

A pause. "No. Burn it."

"Ser?"

"Give them a count of ten to come out and then burn the mansion."

"So that they come out, Captain?"

"No, so that they die. No one comes out."

"But . . ." Another voice. "They have children there, too, ser."

"Good. I want the townspeople watching to clearly understand what comes of disobeying the king's orders."

"Yes, ser."

Sounds of footsteps departing.

Another voice: "Shall we inspect the Teva wagons, Captain?"

"What do you say?" This from Mara, who was standing just outside Amarta's field of vision. "You cannot, we are—" She stopped suddenly. From a slight movement, Amarta guessed Jolon had put a hand on her shoulder. Jolon slipped off his horse to his feet and turned to the captain, hands wide and open.

"We offer no challenge, Captain. We only want the road. We are Teva, friends to your king and empire some three hundred years."

"I know this," the captain said. After a moment he tilted his head toward the wagon in which the three of them hid. "What exactly do you transport, Teva?"

"Shall we take a quick look, Captain?" Again, the eager tone.

Apparently the captain's hesitation was taken as approval; one of his men dismounted and left Amarta's sight, walking in the direction of their wagon. She pulled back, looking alarm at Dirina.

Jolon laughed—a loud, hearty laugh, full of such sincerity that it drew Amarta back to the pinhole to look. Through the opening she saw that she was not alone in this; everyone had stopped to look at him. She very much hoped that included the man who had been walking toward them.

"Let me show you, Captain," Jolon said, still sounding amused.

A long moment later the back flap pulled open. Dirina flattened and cringed, Pas tucked under her, while Amarta kept her hand clamped tight around the ripped opening.

Jolon looked around inside the wagon as if they were not there at all. He dug under the hay and blankets, bringing out a cloth-wrapped package. Then he dropped the flaps and left.

Back in front of the captain, all eyes were on Jolon as he unwrapped the item, then held it up.

It was a hand-high statuette of a shaota horse, painted in chestnut and clay colors, the tones and stripes matching the animals, who looked on curiously. After a moment, the captain reached down and took the offered item.

"Teva children," Jolon explained, "they paint these. The figures are well-loved in Munasee and Perripur among the high houses."

"And anyone can have one," the captain said. "Unlike the horses themselves."

Jolon ducked his head in agreement. "They sell so fast we cannot make enough. Also these flutes." With this he held up a small, round item that hung around his neck. "I will play. It makes the shaota laugh. Watch?"

Not far off, a shout turned into a shriek, then a keen howl, which stopped abruptly, sending chills through Amarta. She admired the way Jolon reacted not at all, simply waiting until the voice was done before he put the palm-sized oval to his lips and blew. It was a loud, high note, followed by a rapidly descending cascade of sounds. Behind him one of the shaota opened its mouth and made a similar throaty sound.

Jolon had been right: it almost sounded like laughter.

At this a few of the soldiers standing around also laughed.

"Captain?" came a new voice.

"What?"

"This man is the grain silo keeper. He says he can give you a list of names of the guilty."

"I can!" A strained voice. "I want immunity, ser Captain. A full list—everyone who spoke in favor of breaking with the crown's grain contract. Every name. I swear it on the harvest—all the harvests—for all of time, and—"

"Yes, yes," the captain said, waving the man to silence.

He looked at Jolon thoughtfully a moment. "Be on your way, Teva. Nalas, take a demi-squad and escort them through town. Make sure they get through without incident." He held the shaota casting down to Jolon from his horse.

"No, no," Jolon said, hands up to refuse. "A gift, Captain. For you. Or your king. As you see fit." With that, Jolon gave a small bow.

Only after the voices and smell of smoke were long gone did Amarta dare release the ripped seam she had been holding closed all this time, and only then did Dirina let Pas out from under her.

On they went, horses and wagons, continuing south.

A day later, forest gave way to wide lakes and bogs, then a day more and it was farms and fields again, quiet pastures of goats and geese. Then the land turned rocky and spare, with scrub and thick, squat trees that hung low, offering up furry red berries. As the days passed, Dirina and Amarta managed to repair all the rips in the wagon tarp.

Now the ground was a pale, milky-colored rock, dusted with sand, the grasses meager, the small plants few. At last they stopped.

Jolon pulled back the opening. "We are arrived. Gather your things and come."

They emerged to find the wagons in a small clearing surrounded by rocky rises of gray and ocher rock shot through with lines of orange and tan. A crow called loudly; another answered.

The shaota were gone, as were most of the Teva. Those remaining unhitched the wagon from the carthorses.

Seeing her confused expression, Mara said, "You will see."

Then, seemingly out of nowhere, came a handful of people. Amarta stared at them in shock.

Their hair was pale yellow, eyes the color of sky. Amarta had never seen such a thing before, had not even known it could exist. Dirina drew Pas close.

"Mama?" Pas pointed and looked up at her.

"Shh," she replied, taking his pointing hand in her own.

The pale-haired people and remaining Teva began to unload the barrels and sacks and hay that had been Amarta and Dirina's home these last handful of days, hefting them on shoulders and into handcarts, then taking them along a path that vanished around a small rise. No one spoke.

The carthorses were led away. Finally Jolon and Mara slung bags over their shoulders and motioned Amarta and Dirina and Pas to follow.

Around the rise the land sloped steeply down a dry creekbed, rocky banks rising on either side. The ravine snaked through one blind curve after another and ended at a large boulder. Only when they reached the boulder did she see the small opening beyond. They followed the Teva into a cave.

Mara took her hand as they walked in, indicating she should take Dirina's, and led them into the darkness. The way led forward and down. As her eyes adjusted, she saw the pale-haired people moving around and watching them from openings in the walkway.

Points of dim lamps. The flicker of candles. No voices.

Mara's hand stopped Amarta, and she in turn stopped Dirina. They were now in a large room with many low tables at which other of the pale-heads sat, now turning to look at them. Long shelves on the walls, filled with jars and cookpots and crates and barrels.

They stood beside Mara and Jolon, facing five of the pale-headed people, whose heads seemed the brightest thing in this dim, lamplit room. Pas clutched Amarta's hand tightly.

Of the five they faced, only a woman rocking an infant in her arms smiled back at them. Her blond hair fell in long, snakelike ropes down her shoulders. Her baby gripped one.

An elder man and woman spoke to Mara and Jolon in a language Amarta didn't know. The woman's pale hair was cut nearly to the scalp; the man's was blond to the ends, where it went abruptly dark.

Jolon answered back, and Amarta recognized their names. To them Jolon said: "These are the first and second of Kusan's ten elders, Vatti and Astru."

The elder woman, Vatti, spoke. "Welcome to Kusan, sometimes called the hidden city. Do you know these names?"

"No," Dirina admitted.

"Good," the elder man, Astru, replied. "That is as it should be."

"I am Ksava," said the woman with the long, ropelike gold hair, swaying slightly to rock the baby on her chest. She nodded at the other two, a boy and girl about Amarta's age. "My brother, Darad. Our cousin, Nidem."

The girl's cheekbones had three lines painted on one side and two on the other. She gazed back at Amarta with a pointed, unfriendly expression. She addressed Jolon and Mara. "You bring strangers here? Do our lives mean so little to you?"

"They seek a haven," Jolon said. "We thought you might understand this."

"That's a reassurance, then," Nidem said nastily. "What do they bring us? Supplies? News of our beloveds in the cities? Or do they only take, like Arunkin do?"

"Nidem," said Astru, in what might have been a quiet rebuke.

"We bring them," Jolon said to her. "As we bring you bags of grain and salt and nuts, bottles of spice and oil—

the many things you cannot get for yourselves, even in your out-trips."

"And in turn," Vatti said to him, her voice mild, a contrast to Nidem's venomous tone, "we supply you with water and hidden shelter for your people and your horses on your journeys north and south."

"Yes, and we are grateful to you—" Jolon began.

Vatti held up her hand to silence him, a firm gesture, and continued. "And you bring us coin when we need it. News of the world outside. Your counsel and knowledge."

Astru spoke. "Hear us clearly: the Teva are valued partners to the Emendi. You are welcome here." He looked at Nidem. "Nidem is a child and does not speak for us."

"We will help however we can," Dirina said quietly, respectfully.

"We will work hard," Amarta added quickly, looking between the elders and Nidem.

"You had better," Nidem said.

A sigh from Astru. "You gift us with your companionship as well as your trade, Teva," Astru said. "And now Nidem will gift us with her silence until she is told otherwise."

At that Nidem made a series of gestures with her hands and fingers. A clear signal, judging by the sharp reactions of those around her; Vatti pressed her lips together in what might have been annoyed forbearance, and Ksava suppressed a smile as she moved her baby to her shoulder. Astru looked long at Nidem, his eyes flickering back and forth.

Nidem scowled and stamped out of the room.

Astru made a gesture with both hands, a brushing of the air, somehow conveying a cleaning of the unpleasantness that had preceded. Vatti put her hands together at her chest, then reached out to Mara and Jolon in turn, fingers out. They met her fingers with their own.

"We honor your presence here. Your friends are welcome in Kusan," Vatti said.

"Our gratitude to you," Mara said.

"Come," Astru said, "show us what you have brought us." Then, to Amarta and Dirina: "Ksava will show you how to conduct yourselves here. We will see you at the meal."

As they left, Jolon paused, put his arms lightly around Dirina and Amarta's shoulders, head tipped downward, and said quietly: "Their forebears were enslaved by Arunkin. They can perhaps be forgiven for mistaking you for the enemy. Be patient with them."

"We have our meals here," Ksava said, motioning to the large room. From the low, round tables scattered around the room, pale-headed adults and children watched them with expressions from curiosity to looks rather similar to Nidem's. Amarta looked at Ksava rather than meet their eyes. "We eat two meals together each day. If you are hungry another time, go the kitchens back there. Someone is always present to help you find what you might like to eat."

What she might like to eat? This was wealth, to always have food, to be invited to have a preference. Her mouth watered, and she wondered if it was too soon to ask.

She would wait.

Ksava took a lamp from a nearby table. With Darad trailing behind, she led them down one of many bewildering cave tunnels. They passed numerous doorways, and she was soon lost, though she noticed letters carved into the stone at every juncture. As she stared at one of the signs, trying to sound it out, she noticed Nidem had joined Darad behind them.

A hand sign from Darad brought a smirk to Nidem's face that vanished when Amarta looked. Nidem gave her another hard glare.

"There are those among us," Ksava said, "who believe all Arunkin are slavers and not to be trusted. You are the first to visit Kusan in quite some time."

At this, Amarta moved a little closer to Dirina, wondering how long until they would be leaving.

Ksava gestured to a door much like the last handful they had passed. "I sleep here with my family. You are welcome to join us, or stay with the Teva." The room had six thick pallets across the floor, cabinets, and the soft sound of running water. Ksava motioned with her lamp toward the back of the room. "The water in the sleeping rooms is for drinking, not toilet or bath or clothes. I'll show you that next."

They descended wide stairs that Pas insisted on taking himself. Amarta was glad for this slowing; as they walked, her foot hurt more. She was resolved not to limp.

"The city descends many levels. Even we do not know the extent of the tunnels. Go nowhere on your own until you have learned all the ways. If ever you are lost, do this."

She sang out in a loud, clear, high tone that then dropped low, then climbed again. "Repeat that until you are found, yes?"

They nodded.

Motion at the floor of the corridor caught Amarta's attention. Darad knelt to the ground, and a long, thin creature with a ratlike face ran to him, then up his arm and onto his shoulder, nose twitching, sniffing his ear. Pas was reaching upward and making wordless sounds of longing. Darad dropped down and let Pas pet the creature on his shoulder.

"The ferrets are our companions," Ksava said. "They find misplaced objects in dark corners. They bring us home when we are lost. They know the tunnels better than we ever will. Be good to them."

Darad let the animal back to the ground. It ran to the wall and then paused, standing up on back legs. Ksava brought out a piece of something and tossed it to the ferret, who caught it between handlike paws and transferred it to its mouth. In a twitch it was gone again, back into the dark.

They descended another flight of stairs to a room with many holes, under which were the sounds of a rushing waterway.

"These are the toilets."

"Oh!" said Pas, tugging on his mother's hand.

"Don't drop anything in there," Darad said with a grin. "It goes all the way out to the ocean. You'll never see it again."

This was a toilet? Amarta looked around. Something was missing. "It doesn't smell," she said wonderingly.

"The shiny areas around the holes are mage-made. Nothing sticks. This helps."

"Mage-made?" Amarta said. "But that's . . ."

"Yes?"

"Isn't that . . . doesn't it bring death and bad fortune?"

Ksava chuckled, handed her baby to Dirina. She took Pas's hand, walking him to the edge of the hole, holding him while he peed into the hole. Pas laughed in delight.

When she returned, she said, "My people were brought into the worst of bad fortune when we were abducted from our homeland and taken in chains across the sea and made into slaves. Kusan has been a sanctuary for a thousand years and more, older than the Arun Empire. The gifts that mages have left for us here have been far more welcoming than anything the Arunkin have done. Who brings death and bad fortune, Amarta?"

To that Amarta had no answer.

"Are there other mage-makings in Kusan?" Dirina asked.

"Perhaps the waterways, but they may be simply cleverly made. It is hard to know." Ksava returned Pas to his mother and led them out of the toilet room. "We Emendi have been here only some hundred years."

"Do you ever leave?" Amarta asked.

"We visit the hidden gardens up top," Darad said. "To see the sun, when the keepers allow."

Nidem tapped Darad and signed at him.

"And," Darad added, "the out-trips."

Ksava spoke: "We travel to nearby towns to buy those things we cannot make, grow, or hunt. Darad might do so. Even Nidem, in a few months, if they study the ways of the outside well enough."

"I'll be in the trade wagon by year's end, sister. Watch and see."

She reached over to him and rubbed his head affectionately, laughing a little. "We'll see how your hair likes the walnut dye. Take Amarta to see if Nakaccha can look at why she's limping."

"I'm fine," Amarta said quickly. "It's nothing, really."

"Then it won't take long," Ksava answered. "I'll show Dirina and her young one the baths."

"She's good at seeing things that you don't want seen," Darad said to Amarta as they made their slow way up the stairs.

"But I'm fine." Amarta glanced back to see if Nidem was following, felt relief that she was not.

"Not me you need to convince. Oh, here," he said, pausing at the door of a room and bringing out from the darkness a flat, hand-sized rock, which he handed to her. "A pillow for you to sleep on tonight."

"This? A pillow? What?"

"Well, after it's been softened, of course."

"What?" Amarta said, bewildered, examining the rock more closely.

"Yes," he said, taking the rock back, knocking his fist lightly against it, then knocking his own head. "Our blond hair, you see. It's magic. It softens the rocks until they become so soft they're pillows. Tell you what: I'll give you my already-softened pillow for tonight and sleep on this one until it's ready."

Amarta's mouth hung open for a long moment.

He grinned wider.

"You're fooling me?" she asked, stunned.

He laughed. "Of course." At her expression, he sobered, adding, "I'm playing. Don't you play, sometimes?"

She wasn't sure how to answer that.

"Perhaps later," he said, giving her an odd expression. "Down this way to the hot springs. The soaking baths. Clothes washing. When was the last time you had a bath?"

"You mean to be submerged in water?"

"Warm water. You'll like it. Now here, see this huge opening?" He waved his lantern so she could see over the lip of the opening, which dropped down sharply some ten feet. "This is the lesser canyon, which opens way back there into the greater one. We hunt in there, but only in large groups. Don't go in here alone."

She peered into the darkness, for a moment thinking she saw distant movement, black on black.

"What is that, back there?"

"The ruins of old Kusan, now taken over by the night forest. It goes a long, long ways. There's a lake back there. Cavewillows and white trout. On the hills we harvest mushrooms and nightberries. That's where we hunt nightswine."

"Nightswine?"

"You must have heard. No? Ah. Pigs. They get fat on cave-truffles, white thistle, the fruit of spider trees. They taste better than any pig in the world."

"You're toying with me again."

"No, no. This is true. The Teva take our salted

nightswine to the great markets in Munasee and Garaya. Sell it for us."

In the lamplight she gave him a suspicious look. "Truly?"

"Ask the elders." At that, his face broke into a grin. "You can ask them about the pillows, too."

At the meal, Amarta realized she had never before seen so many people gathered together in one place. Hundreds, it must be, all sitting around the large, low, circular tables.

Ksava directed them to a table where the Teva and Darad and Nidem sat. The remaining open spaces were bounded on one side by Nidem, on the other by the Teva.

Well, Nidem already hated her; no sense in putting Dirina in her path as well. So she chose the seat nearest to the other girl, letting Dirina sit by the Teva.

They had come from visiting the woman named Nakaccha, who had taken Amarta's ankle in her lap. She'd pressed gently in places, turned it a little, and told her that it would be fine in a day or two. To Amarta's surprise, it felt better immediately.

When she had thanked her, Nakaccha had responded: "It is what I am called to do, girl. That is the best any of us can hope for, to be called to our work. What is it you are called to do?"

Amarta had mumbled that she didn't know. The encounter left her unsettled. Whatever it was that she did, she must make sure to do it very quietly here. She felt watched keenly.

Despite the hundreds gathered here in this cavernous room, there was no noise other than the soft sounds of wooden spoons against bowls, the brush of leather-clad or bare feet on stone floors. No one spoke.

Nidem pushed a large, full bowl of something that smelled wonderful in front of her, somehow making the gesture convey no warmth.

Mara crouched down behind her, hand on her shoulder. She said softly: "The Emendi are silent at meals, using only hands and eyes to speak."

"What should we do?" Dirina asked her in a whisper.

Now that Amarta looked, she saw the fluttering, flickering motion of hands and eyes across the room. Silent, perhaps, but there was plenty of talk.

"Speak if you wish," Mara whispered, "but they will not, here at the meal. As slaves they were forced to hide voice and thought, and this practice honors their ancestors who gave their lives in silence and obedience. After dinner there will be other rooms, where there will be plenty of voices and singing."

At her side, Nidem was laughing voicelessly at something Darad had signed to her. Amarta felt a twinge of envy.

After dinner, after the clearing and cleaning, the Emendi left in groups in various directions. Ksava invited the three of them into another, smaller room, while the Teva went with the elders.

The Emendi began to array themselves across the floor on blankets. With a laugh, Darad offered her a pillow, a real one. A kind laugh, as if they shared a joke between them, not as if he mocked her. She smiled back, feeling herself warm.

A woman with hair in loose curls around her face put a long, thin, stringed wooden box across her lap and began to pluck out a tune. A young man about Dirina's age brought out a small drum and began to lightly tap it with his fingers in time. Nidem sat in a corner, watching.

"Do you come from Yarpin?" asked another girl, not quite Amarta's age.

"No," Dirina answered, looking as ill at ease as Amarta felt, with the Emendi all watching them. Pas climbed off her lap, found a thick pile of blankets, and curled up there, asleep in minutes. At least one of the three of them was relaxed here.

"My uncle is still there. At House Helata," an older boy said. "Do you know it?"

Dirina and Amarta shook their heads.

Another spoke. "My mother escaped from transport when I was still in her belly." His voice dropped. "My cousins didn't. I hope they're still alive."

"We've never been to Yarpin," Amarta said again.

"How about Munasee?" asked another eagerly, a boy, perhaps nine. "We had to leave my sister there. At the governor's palace. She was young then, like your boy. She'd be eight now. If she—if she . . ." He fell silent.

"We have never been to Munasee, either," Amarta said, feeling oddly as if she should apologize.

The room was quiet a moment.

"Perripur, then? Sometimes they take us down there; some of the merchants there own us. They—"

"They say they don't," said a young man with a scraggly, pale beard. "It's a lie."

"They lie. They all lie. All Arunkin lie. What do you expect?" asked another.

"No," Amarta said. "We have never even been to Perripur—"

"Yes, yes," Nidem cut in from across the room. "We know now. You've never been anywhere. Why are you here?"

Amarta started to blush, saw Darad watching her curiously. It was his look that decided her. Guests they might be, but Nidem was treating them as if they had enslaved all her people singlehandedly.

Well, they were only here with the Emendi, whom she had never seen before, until they left with the Teva.

"Why do you have marks on your face?" she asked Nidem. "With all the water you have running through Kusan, don't you ever wash?"

"Ama," Dirina said, shocked, a hand on her arm, but it was Darad's amused smirk at her response that she sought, that gave her some satisfaction.

Nidem held up an index finger to the right side of her face. "Two generations free from my mother's side." She moved the finger to the other side. "Three from my father's. How many lines of freedom would you have, Arunkin?"

Anger flashed through Amarta as she struggled and failed to come up with a clever reply. She pulled her arm out of Dirina's tightening, warning grip.

"You have an odd way of welcoming strangers, Nidem," said a man standing in the doorway, one of his arms ending in a stump above the elbow.

"I don't welcome them at all. Who knows what they will say once they leave? To trust the Teva is one thing. To trust Arunkin is folly. We should know this by now."

"It's a little late to curse the door for letting in the wind," Ksava observed mildly from where she sat, her baby at her breast.

"Why would we say anything at all about you?" Amarta asked.

The room fell silent, looks exchanged.

The one-armed man sat down next to the young woman with the lap-harp. She handed it to him. Closer now, Amarta saw that his arm ended in a sort of crater, out of which poked a thumb's width of yellowed bone. She struggled not to stare.

He began to strum with his one hand, then stopped, meeting her look squarely. "Because we're worth a fortune, girl."

"Oh," Amarta responded, trying yet again not to stare at his arm. "But we would never do that."

"We know how to keep secrets," Dirina added earnestly.

"Go on, look at it." He held up his stump for her to see. "The king's law and justice, girl. Take a good long look."

Amarta was tired of being attacked, tired of being polite. "What did you do to earn it?" she found herself saying.

Dirina hissed. "Ama—"

He shook his head, negating Dirina's reprimand. "It's good she asks, woman. Some things should be said aloud." He fixed Amarta with his startling blue eyes. "I escaped my owner, is what I did. When I was recaptured, he brought out his axe. Smiled while he cut my arm."

"But . . ." Amarta trailed off, confused.

He waved his stump slowly in the air for her to continue.

Amarta felt herself warm again, wishing she'd stayed silent.

"Go on, girl. Ask your question."

Everyone was watching her. No one was smiling. She swallowed, hoping she wasn't blushing too redly. "Don't slaves need hands?" she asked.

He barked a loud laugh that seemed to echo off the cave walls, and then looked around the room, meeting the eyes of the others. When he looked back at Amarta, his eyes were dancing in dark amusement. "Some sorts of slaves need hands. Some don't. It all depends on what kind of slaves they are. Me, I was used for—"

"That's enough." Dirina said harshly.

Startled, Amarta looked at her sister. "Diri?"

"We don't want to hear about it."

The man's incredulous look matched Amarta's. "Woman, this is the truth of the matter. We are all old enough to hear such truths. Why do you object?"

"None of your business, man," Dirina said, standing and grabbing up Pas from where he lay. Pas frowned furiously at being woken, his arms now wrapped around his mother's neck, staring his displeasure at the room. Then Dirina grabbed Amarta's hand and drew her along to the opening of the cave.

"Diri," Amarta whispered, resisting.

"There are things it is better not to know. Yes?"

Amarta thought about her visions. "Yes, of course, but—"

"This is one of them."

Darad joined the three of them with a lantern.

"I'll take you to the sleeping room where the Teva are staying. You must be tired after your long journey."

Amarta abhorred his polite tone, ached for his teasing wit, and gave her sister a hard, resentful look.

"Yes, we are," Dirina answered Darad, ignoring the look. "Thank you."

That night and the next day, Dirina looked so tired and downcast that, as annoyed as she was, Amarta could not bring herself to say anything about the night before.

In truth, it was not her sister's fault that they had come here, that they had been forced to leave the farm, that they were on the run again. That was entirely Amarta's doing.

She would, she resolved, hold her tongue. Treat her sister kindly. It was the least she could do.

After the first silent meal of the day was done, Amarta happily fed with more wonderful food, she listened as the Teva discussed what goods they would leave here for the Emendi and what they would take forward with them to market. They mentioned cured nightswine jerky, which she found reassuring. Darad had been telling the truth about that, at least.

"Let me do something useful," she begged Jolon when he had a moment. He smiled and brought her to a well-lit room that had a loom and hand-mending tools. "I saw what you and Dirina did with the rips in our wagon covering. I think you can help them." The other Emendi sitting there knitting and working the loom made her quietly welcome.

For hours she sat there, absorbed by the work, relaxing for the first time since she had arrived. She repaired one shirt's torn seam, then another. She picked up a sock and darned it, then looked for more work.

"There you are," Darad said from the doorway. "Come on, I want to show you something."

She leapt up to follow him into the hall.

"How is your ankle?" he asked.

She had not even thought of it today. "I think it is all better," she said with surprise.

"Nakaccha is skillful." Then he took her hand, leading her along the stone tunnels. She was suddenly, keenly aware of the warmth of his fingers on hers. It felt very good.

"Have you lived here your whole life?" she asked to make conversation, to cover the awkward feeling suddenly coming over her.

"Kusan-born, yes. My grandmother came here after she was blinded by her owner. He wanted her eyes."

"Her eyes?"

"Gold flecks in the blue, you see. Some of us have them. Look." He stopped suddenly and held up the lantern. She looked into his eyes, which gave her an odd and not unpleasant feeling in her stomach.

Until she remembered why.

"That's awful."

"Yes," he agreed, simply, taking her hand again, resuming their walk. "She was lucky to find Kusan at all, blind as she was. Brave. So brave."

"Where are we going?"

"You talk too much," he said. But she could hear the smile in his voice that belied the words, and felt the squeeze of his hand.

More minutes passed. They went from one tunnel to the next, and she wondered, though not very seriously, if he was going to lead her around in circles and leave her here in the dark. She quietly hummed the distress signal, and he laughed, squeezing her hand again, a reassurance.

They entered a lamplit room lined with shelves of folded burlap where some ten children sat around at a table. Nidem was among them.

A silent conversation between Darad and Nidem commenced. Amarta was sure he could have more effectively used both hands, but he insisted on keeping hold of hers. At this she felt a sweet sense of something she had not felt before. He wanted her there. It was almost like belonging.

Then she met Nidem's look. She looked away at an open chair, then back to Amarta again. As Amarta watched this repeat, she realized that it was a direction, an invitation. Darad drew her with him to two open seats.

"It is a game," Darad said softly, his the only voice in the room. "A silent one. You'll learn. I'll help you."

With a combination of eye flickers and blinks and hand signs, they taught her the game, which turned out to be about moving each other from seat to seat with eyes and signs and rules that became clear to her as they played.

Before she knew it, she was smiling. And now she did feel as if she belonged.

Finally Darad let her hand go, but she was engrossed enough in the game that she hardly noticed.

The next day and the next the two of them helped in the kitchen, cleaning and preparing vegetables, and then set about to help mend clothes.

Every now and then she saw Dirina smile. So unusual, Amarta realized. Both of them were starting to relax, to breathe more easily. At meals Darad sat by her, teaching her more signs.

At the evening meal of the third day, the annoying and ever-present Nidem broke in between his instruction, interrupting with her hands. Resentment flashed through Amarta, so it took her a moment to realize that Nidem was telling the very joke that she'd made the day Amarta arrived, when they were first introduced. That she was telling it now for Amarta's benefit, repeating it slowly, making sure that Amarta understood.

Then the three of them laughed, soundlessly, together, and Amarta felt a joy she had never felt before.

She realized she hadn't thought about her hunter since she had arrived.

"Somewhere safe," Jolon had said. Maybe he was right.

On the fourth day at Kusan, Amarta was using the washroom for her own clothes, soaping at the lowest of the waterfall basins carved in the stone, rinsing upstream in successive basins. She had wrung out her shirt, then Dirina's as well, and hung them to dry on lines strung across an opening overhead that brought in dry air from the outside.

She sat on a low bench for a time and watched the Emendi across the room in their wash work.

Jolon sat next to her. At their feet was a small puddle of water that had gathered during her washing. Very softly, so that only she could hear, he motioned to it and said, "Is it in such water that you see the future, Amarta?"

Amarta kept her eyes on the puddle at her feet in which the lamps around the room reflected, points of light in dark water. "I don't know what you mean."

"We keep it to ourselves, Mara and I, but we guess it is so. Is it magery?"

"No," she said sharply, realizing her answer for the admission it was, then pressed her lips tightly together.

He brushed her shoulder. "I hear your words. That does not mean I believe them. No one else knows, and we keep secrets well."

She would say no more about it, she resolved. Not a word.

"I am also here to say good-bye," he said.

"What?" Amarta scrambled to her feet. He stood with her.

"We continue our journey south, to deliver the goods we have come to trade and sell."

"We can be ready in minutes. We—."

"No. We do not take you with us. Stay here. The Emendi have no more desire to be found than you do."

"They won't let us stay without you."

"They will. You work hard. They see this. We have spoken for you."

Spoken for them? Vouched for strangers they had known mere days? Jolon and Mara could not know what they had saved her from, but until this moment, it had not occurred to her how much they had risked in bringing them here.

But to be left here?

Her mind raced. She thought of Darad, of laughing with him. With Nidem. "Jolon, you have been so good to us. Why?"

He made a thoughtful sound, then drew a large circle in the air with a forefinger and jabbed at a point along the circumference. "Today you need something, so we give it to you." His finger continued along the circle, stopping at another point along the arc. "Another day you give something to someone who does not have what you do. That other, perhaps"—his finger traveled further and stopped.—"gives to another. And then"—his finger went back to the first spot—"who can say? It is a better place, the world, when we give what we can. But there is another reason."

"What?"

His face turned sad. "Long ago," he said, "a force came to Otevan, bearing weapons, claiming our lands. Before blood was shed, we showed them what we and the shaota do together. Not in challenge, but in display, you understand?"

She nodded.

"They saw the wisdom of having us by their side. So we fought with Arunkel and helped them take the lands, one hill after another." His eyes narrowed, the ends of his mouth turned down. "We sold ourselves for freedom. For some of us, it is a great sorrow and a sharp shame that our ancestors did this."

"But you had to, or—"

"Yes, it seemed so. But if we had all faced the invader as one? It cannot be known." He sighed. "Now we have a debt. To those who come to us in need, we give what we can."

"But it wasn't your decision. It was your ancestors'. How is it your debt?"

"What affects one Teva affects all. With you and your sister it is the same, yes?"

She hadn't thought about it that way, but now she could see it was so: Amarta's visions caused Dirina and Pas to suffer. "But if you leave us here—"

"We come back to Kusan next year. If you wish to leave then, perhaps we can take you. Yes?"

"We'll be here," Amarta said, but even as she said it, the words echoed hollowly. She pushed away the tickle of vision that wanted to deny her words. No; they would stay or go as they decided.

Jolon gestured to the puddle below them. "I have heard this is how the future is seen, in still water. It is not so?"

Amarta thought of those who had come to her across the years with dead rabbits and birds. "No. Nor thrown sticks, nor animal entrails."

"Then—since no blood or water is needed, will you tell me something of what is to come?"

She owed the Teva a debt, greater than they knew, but to foresee now felt like she was bringing her curse here into the tunnels, where she had the last few days felt safe and more.

Amarta glanced at the rest of the hall to be sure no one was listening. "I will," she said, a soft whisper.

"Those who we meet in Perripur, can we trust them?"

Amarta took a deep breath. As she let it out, she cast her mind into the open space that was the future.

Perripur, he said.

A world of green and brown. Air wet and warm, full of scent. Walking and more walking. A dark-skinned woman by her side.

No, no—not for herself. For Jolon and Mara. She reached out a hand to Jolon's arm, to help her focus. She saw the inked scars that circled his forearm and hesitated.

"Yes," Jolon said, offering his arm forward for her examination.

"What are those?" Amarta asked of the circles around his arm.

"We call them *limisatae*. Life-doors we pass through. Our first shaota. The first mate. The first child." He met Amarta's eyes, and she saw for a moment a flicker of something she could not name. "A life taken to keep our people whole. That is *limisatae* as well."

"What are yours for?" she asked.

He shook his head. "It is for me. Not about the telling, but the being."

Not about the telling.

That she could understand.

"Do you have a life-door to mark, Amarta?"

She thought of Enana. Of her parents. Of the attack she had thwarted in the forest. Had any of it changed her as his three marks must have changed him? "I don't think so."

"In time, perhaps." He took her hand and wrapped her fingers around his forearm. "Will you tell now? Those we meet in Perripur? How much caution? How much trust?"

With her fingers on his arm, she reached into his future.

Faint smells of flowers, spice, smoke, fish. A collection of people standing in a circle. Voices.

"This is your first meeting with them?"

"It is."

A knife separated links of heavy twine; a roughspun pouch opened. A deep-throated woman's voice, another language. Words, back and forth. Dark faces turning away, smirking. Secrets.

Amarta opened her eyes to the dark and drip of the cave, the images already fading, the meaning sorting itself out in her mind. Trust was too big a word for this meeting, too wide a river to cross. "I think you will offer them a lot. Too much?"

She closed her eyes again, tried to find the place in time where she had seen the dark faces, to see if another outcome might change their expression. It was hard to hold, hard to see.

The same faces, different expressions. Fewer bags.

"Keep back more of what you brought to trade. The bags of . . ." She tried to remember what she'd seen. "Rocks? See what they offer for a smaller set first."

"Then we will know what the rest is worth. I see. Thank you for that good counsel." He clasped her shoulder and gave her a gentle smile. "Amarta, if hundreds of Emendi are safe here, you might be, too.

Kusan has stood for centuries. You are safer here than anywhere in the world."

Could he be right? Here in the dark, underground, might she be safe from the hunter who pursued above?

"Now I must ask another thing of you," he said.

"What is it?"

"Nidem was not wrong to doubt us, bringing you here. The Emendi are safe only as long as Kusan is also secret. We have trusted you very much."

"We are grateful. We—"

"Yes, this I know. But Amarta, whatever it is you run from, do not bring it here."

"I won't. I promise."

Chapter Twelve

The first thing Innel did when he returned to the palace from Arteni was find a bath. Caked in dirt, blood, and the ever-present dust of Arteni's grain mills, he stripped off his clothes and kicked them away from the tub, lowered his aching body into the hot and salted soaking water.

"Burn them," he told Srel.

Srel made a sound intended to convey acquiescence but which Innel knew really wasn't. Coming from deep poverty, Srel was incapable of disposing of anything that could possibly be reclaimed or repaired. But Innel wouldn't see the clothes again, and that was enough.

As for Cern and her father, well, this time they could both wait. He would be clean and fed before he faced either of them.

"Is she still marrying me?" he asked Srel bluntly.

Another sound, this time thoughtful. "The wedding plans were put on hold when you left, ser."

Disappointing but not unexpected. The campaign had taken the three months he'd anticipated and then some, but if the slog of dirt and blood, the tedious meetings and hurried executions had earned him a promotion, it would be worth it.

Colonel, most likely, he thought. General would be far better, of course, but it would be a stretch. Still, if the king wanted it for him and pushed, it was possible. He wondered what the other generals, decades his senior, born to the Houses or royals, would think of the king promoting him that far, that fast.

"She has shown no favor toward anyone else, ser."

The other men of the Cohort were his only competition now. That she was seeing none of them was good news.

"And my reports to the king?" From the field, sent by Cahlen's birds.

"I am told he read them very closely."

Carefully written to achieve that very end. When the Cohort had been taught by minstrels and versifiers how best to fashion a story, Innel and his brother had paid keen attention. Thus Innel's reports were more than factual; each started with a triumph, however minor, and ended with an uncertainty, the pattern intended to make the king eager to read the next dispatch describing how Innel sev Restarn was taking Arteni in the king's name.

The people of Arteni had been astounded at the force that had been called down on them for attempting to sell grain outside their contract. They had at first presented some optimistic resistance that Innel crushed with heavily armored cavalry that crashed through the rusted iron gates. The line of millers and farmers, holding pitchforks and scythes, had broken fast. Those who had not run had died quickly.

Those who had run had also died, but more slowly.

After that it had been a matter of rounding up the troublemakers and giving them the choice between providing names and being hung with the next morning's executions.

Innel made sure bread was passed out to the watching crowds to help them understand that they now ate by the king's mercy.

What had taken the most time had been restructuring the town's governance. The old council had stood firm in their insistence that this should be a negotiation rather than a surrender, finally retreating with their families into the mayor's house, where Innel explained that they were wrong by burning it to the ground. The ashes didn't argue.

His nights had been spent crafting these missives to flatter and intrigue the king, working in repetition to cover for the one or two in ten messenger birds that weather or predation would prevent returning home to the palace.

Cahlen had assured him that all these birds would return. Every last one of them. She had come to his rooms early the morning he had left, a cowed-looking assistant in tow carrying cages of noisy and annoyed birds.

"My best," Cahlen had told Innel. "No hawks or bad weather will stop these." Her eyes were bright and too wide. "Don't put your hands on them. They bite." Innel glanced at the assistant handler's heavy leather gloves.

"They bite?" Before Cahlen, messenger birds were not known for their temper.

"Make sure you feed them," she had said, her tone cross, as though he had already forgotten.

He took the soap Srel offered him, and began to scrub.

"What was the bird count?" he asked, dunking his head, feeling months of tension and dirt come off in the hot water.

"Eleven."

He made a surprised sound. Cahlen had been right: every bird had returned. He must remember to tell her so. With luck, she would take it as a compliment.

When he toweled off, taking clean clothes from Srel, he asked: "Who should I see first?"

The smaller man dug into a pocket and held out something to Innel.

An earring. A magenta sapphire.

Cern it was, then.

"Took you long enough." Her first words were softened a little by her hand on his face. She gathered his fingers in her own and drew him into her room. He hid his relief that she was glad to see him.

When, much later, she called for a plate of food and drink, the food came arrayed like a miniature garden, cheese and olives cleverly cut into the shape of flowers, and surrounded by hedges of herbed breads.

This, he realized, was wealth. Great wealth. Not the mere substance of the food, which was by itself rare and extraordinary, as befitted a princess, but the presentation itself. For a moment he simply stared at the miniature landscape so painstakingly prepared, laid across a lace-cut red ceramic platter that sat atop a table polished to a deep mahogany sheen. Around the edge of the table, inlaid in ebony and cherrywood, was the star, moon, pickax, and sword of the Anandynar sigil.

"The earring is a nice touch," she said to him with a wry half-smile.

The irony of this struck him; the sapphire in his ear was worth a tiny fraction of what was arrayed before him, but it was his gesture that mattered to her.

I thought of you every moment I was away.

No, she wouldn't like that. Something more pragmatic. He smiled. "Let no one wonder where my loyalty lies."

To his surprise, rather than be pleased, as he had expected, her gaze swept away across the room, her half-smile gone. A spike of anxiety went through him.

"What excitement have I missed?" he asked lightly, pretending not to have noticed her ill ease.

Her lengthening silence did nothing to reassure him. She was, he realized, trying to figure out how to tell him something.

That by itself was impressive: the heir-apparent to the Arunkel throne was struggling with how to say something to him, the mutt. Flattering, to be sure, but it could not mean good news. He watched closely as she put on a grimace that meant she felt she had no choice.

And that meant it was about her father.

Dread slowly trickled down his spine. She could certainly take him to bed for entertainment and marry someone else if she chose. Had he been cast aside, after all? What had happened while he had been away?

She glanced at him, and he gave her yet another easy smile, the work of years of practice, hoping to calm her. Or himself.

At last she cleared her throat and gave a forced laugh. "How would you like to be the lord commander?"

Lord Commander? The highest rank in the military?

"Of the Host of Arunkel?" he asked, incredulous, his careful presentation of equanimity swept away.

"Yes," she said, tone suddenly dry, "that would be the one."

Could the king have decided to elevate him that far, that fast? Surely it was not possible.

But then, perhaps it was.

He could not suppress a smile of elation. "How would I like it?" He asked. "It . . ."

This was as far from bad news as possible, to be made the commander of the empire's armies. It made sense, now that he thought about it; coming as he did from outside the palace and far below the Houses, Innel could well imagine Restarn deciding such a rank would appropriately elevate him to marry his daughter.

Innel would need to get the generals on his side, and quickly. Lismar, the king's sister, first and foremost. Make a point of showing great humility. Have it known he was only complying with the king's direct command.

A tricky prospect, politically. It would take a not insignificant amount of effort to arrange. But it could be done.

Cern was watching him, waiting for an answer.

"It would be my great honor to serve the crown," he finished.

"Yes," she agreed, shortly, but she did not sound happy.

"What is it, my lady?" he asked, unable to contain his tension at this unexpected reaction. "Do you think it is a bad decision?"

It wasn't. The more he thought about it, the more convinced he was that it was a good outcome. A far better one than to promote him to colonel or even general. He was, after all, marrying the heir to the throne.

She stood, her hands waving about aimlessly, a motion that signified frustration. She turned away, took a bite of a smoked cheese flower and chewed slowly.

That she was not looking at him was not a good sign. With effort he said nothing, knowing better than to press.

"I'm to offer it to you," she said at last.

"You? Forgive me, my lady, but you are not—"

A sharp gesture cut him off. "I know, Innel. I'm quite aware I'm not queen. I'm not an idiot."

"Of course not, my lady."

"Of course not, my lady," she echoed, mockingly. "Because *he* told me to, is why," she spat.

The king.

"But—"

"Shut up, Innel. I know perfectly well what you're going to say. But here it is: you can have the lord commandership from my hand, or you can petition him for a colonelship."

Petition? That's what his hard, bloody work these last months had gained him? He would be allowed to *petition?*

Tempted as he was to reply, he had already opened his mouth once without thinking, and with Cern in this mood, that was a misstep. He clamped his mouth shut and considered.

He could not take the Lord Commandership from Cern. It would put him in a weak position and spark controversy, but to refuse it from her hand would be an insult to her, which he could afford even less.

A typical Restarn move, to force him into an impossible situation with no good choices.

He also could not push the decision back on her, tempting as that was; her faith in him was based in large part on his ability to navigate challenges like this one.

She watched him as he thought.

He desperately wanted to ask her to relate the conversation she had had with her father that had led to this outcome, to gain clues as to what was in the monarch's mind, but that would underscore her weak position with her father, doing little to reassure in this difficult time. Cern's confidence was already a thin thread.

It would be best to get through the wedding and coronation. Then any decisions she had made, like promoting Innel to the highest military position in the empire, would be far harder to question.

But here and now, what to do?

Well, he was wearing her colors. He had laid everything he had at her feet. Really, he could not refuse.

"It would be my great honor to serve you in this capacity, my lady."

After a time he convinced Cern to wait to name him as lord commander until at least after the wedding. It would seem a more obvious move then, he explained.

And she would be one step closer to the throne, all her pronouncements carrying considerably more weight.

"Whatever you think best, Innel," was all she had said. She was relying on him to make sense of the tangled political forces at play, a challenge she seemed to care little for. A challenge he had been studying his whole life.

She had been tinkering with one of her collapsible in-air creations, a set of wooden rods with twine and chain between them, some pulled tight, others balanced delicately on top of each other. In the years since she had shown him these works, he'd seen her use stiffened fabric, small lengths of metal and wood, and even straw.

This particular set was suspended from the ceiling, in an equilibrium of many parts. As she touched it on one end, the pieces of wood at the other clinked against each other, making an almost musical sound.

Collapsible so that they could be taken down and hidden quickly when her father came into her rooms without warning, as he used to do often.

From their conversations, Innel knew her father had not confided in her his embarrassment at her marrying a captain, as he had to Innel.

So be it. Innel would petition no one. Let Restarn decide how much embarrassment he could stomach.

Regardless, once they were wed, Innel would no longer be the mutt who had somehow survived the Cohort. He would be princess-consort.

The thought sent a chill through him. For a split second, he found himself thinking he must find his brother and tell him.

"I'm busy," Innel responded to Mulack, putting a snap into the words, even though it was a good idea; it had been too long since he'd felt out his support in the Cohort.

He was truly busy; the king had called him back into

service, and he now faced interminable council meetings
that required summary reports, ongoing House contract
negotiations with high-stakes outcomes, and again the
near-daily work of sitting in the steam-filled royal bath to
hear the king complain.

In a way it was reassuring that the king had not
forgotten him, but it rankled that he had not yet made
good on his promise to promote him, either.

Nor had he petitioned. Still a captain. But, as the
saying went, not all captains had the same rank.

"Taba is in port," Mulack insisted. "A good sign."

"It's no sign at all. She was scheduled to be here."

Mulack waved this away. "We must celebrate your
victorious return." He managed to keep his mocking tone
to a bare hint of derision. "You're a hero, after all." He
clapped him on the shoulder.

Innel looked down at the shorter, thicker man he had,
for excellent reasons, not liked since early childhood. "I
have a report to prepare for the king."

"Oh, come on, Innel. Give us a chance to spend too
much money on you."

Too much money? Was this Mulack's way of saying he
knew about Tok's investment and might be offering
similar backing? He couldn't tell, which was how Mulack
liked it.

"How can I refuse, when you phrase it so seductively?"
Innel said dryly, acting as if lack of coin meant nothing to
him, as he and his brother had always tried to do.

Mulack probably knew better; he had a nose for
money. Despite everything—the promotion to captain,
Innel's proximity to Cern, the assumption of wedlock to

come, and even Tok's support—with all the gifts Innel was giving to everyone from guards to maids to stablehands to keep rumors flowing toward himself instead of away, Innel continued barely short of poor.

A strange state in which to live, in-palace.

He hid it as well as possible, of course; only Srel knew how bad his finances really were.

Mulack, on the other hand, was House Murice's eparch-heir and swimming in the coin of the House of Dye. With Murice's multitudinous contracts for textiles and amardide, anyone who wore sanctioned clothes had paid to swell Murice's holdings.

Innel took a look at what his Cohort brother was wearing. Boots and gauntlets tastefully trimmed in red and black—a nod to the crown—but the rest entirely Murice's purple and white. A bit of a cacophony of color, but clear enough, as far as loyalties went. Mulack was clearly done looking for his future at the palace.

Mulack's father, as sardonic as his annoying son, was vibrant with health. Mulack would have a long wait to become eparch. In the meantime, though, he had plenty of money.

"Tonight we celebrate," Mulack said decisively. "I'll tell the others."

"So be it," Innel said, feeling it best to make a show of reluctance to impress on Mulack how busy he was with the king's business. "Where?"

"Pig's ass," Mulack said loudly, grinning. In another context this insult was one Mulack was likely to use, but now he referred to the back room at the Boar and Bull, an innocuous midcity tavern that the Cohort sometimes used when they wanted to be away from palace eyes and ears.

"I'll see if I can clear my evening plans," Innel said, turning away, already knowing he would. Srel would let Sachare know so that she could handle Cern should the subject of Innel's whereabouts arise.

Cern, the entire reason for the Cohort's existence.

Technically she was a member as well, but Innel was sure Mulack would not be inviting the princess to the pig's ass.

"Too many times," Taba was saying, laughing loudly. She was a broad-shouldered woman and had been so even in her teens. Her eyes were a light green, the color of the seas she had made her home, and matching the shirt she wore. A red and black surcoat marked her as belonging to the king's navy, but under that she wore Helata's colors, green and blue. A long tradition, that, the navy showing House colors so openly. No one in the army would dare.

Mulack was grinning as Sutarnan poured more of the strong black wine into his cup. Dil leaned back in his chair. Tok nodded slowly at Taba's story.

It had been some time since the Cohort had gathered, even this small a number.

The last time, all the other times, his brother had been there.

Keep a watch, Innel, Pohut might have said. *Stay sober*.

He intended to.

Around the table was a scattering of plates of food and mugs and glass goblets. A ceramic tumbler meant it was harder to track what had been drunk and what still remained. A clear goblet gave the appearance of not hiding anything.

Everyone was drinking. Everyone had multiple cups in front of them.

It was an old game, one they had played through the years to see who could be made to slip up while tempted by various intoxicants. Across the years they had tried every substance the wealthy boys and girls of the Cohort could get their hands on.

"Incompetence in a harbormaster is inexcusable," Mulack said from across the table, now on his third glass.

Sutarnan, who was still sipping from his first tumbler, made a disparaging sound. "Harbormasters are set for life, you know that. Supposed to keep them honest, that appointment."

"They're perfectly honest if you bribe them," said Tok with a straight face, at which Sutarnan snorted.

"Truss them and toss them off the pier! Problem solved!" Mulack said loudly, downing the rest of his glass and holding it out to Sutarnan for more. Mulack was slurring slightly, but that was one of his tricks, to pretend that he was drunker than he really was, to see what he could get away with. Sometimes he walked the line too closely.

A long, loud sigh from Taba. "If only."

"Taba, surely your eparch will listen to you." This from Dil, many steps removed from the eparchy of House Kincel but who made no secret of being perfectly happy behind the scenes, making sure his House of Stone had every connection to the palace it needed. Dressed mostly in reds and blacks, Dil was clearly planning to stay at the palace. Innel suspected he was lobbying to be Kincel's liaison.

"If only," Taba said again, laughing again.

"No one listens to us," Sutarnan complained. "You'd think they would, what with all the royal education our heads are fat with, but no."

"No one listens to *you*, you mean, and that's because you won't decide which house you belong to. Or have you finally made up your mind?" This from Tok.

Two Houses claimed Sutarnan. He was the son of a brief union between Sartor's and Elupene's eparchs, an unusual liaison, which—more unusually yet—the king approved. Restarn might have been distracted at the time by the second battle of Uled, some handful of years after Innel's father had died in the first, but whatever the reasons, Sutarnan's parents had stayed together long enough to produce him and then, after an impressive two-year-long fight during which time no armor was made in the city, managed to get a royal divorce.

"I have no plans to select one over the other. Two is better than one." He smiled widely, then his eyes settled on Innel and the smile vanished. Innel, who had no House at all.

Which would not matter, Innel reminded himself, as soon as he married Cern.

"You really should taste this, Innel," Dil said quickly, before the awkward moment had a chance to lengthen, pushing a small crystal bottle around the large table toward him. Taba passed it along to Tok, who, with a lopsided grin, handed it to Innel.

The room fell silent, everyone watching him expectantly.

A strange moment, this. It wasn't long ago that none of them would much care what he thought of the wine. Or anything else.

It was hard to forget years of Cohort hostilities, schemes, broken bones, and broken agreements. Harder yet to forgive. He had one friend in all those years, one person to trust at his back. That trust, too, had been foolishly placed.

But now, fed and wined, it was evident even these last holdouts of the Cohort realized how things had changed. No one at this table would benefit from bad will with the princess consort. They needed Innel.

Of course, he needed them, too.

It was time to rewrite history.

"We are all brothers and sisters here," he said, hands wide, smiling at them, putting as much joviality and warmth into his expression as he could stomach. He let his gaze come to rest on Mulack, arguably the most dangerous of the lot, and gave him the warmest smile of all, to which Mulack snorted in amusement.

With a nod of appreciation to Dil, Innel took a swig from the delicate bottle he'd been handed, not bothering with a cup. A deep, smokey concoction met his tongue and fairly danced down his throat. It was superb, and no doubt older than he was. Indeed, he would bet that every sip cost more than his boots.

He took another.

"You have the princess now," Dil said, stating the obvious, with what appeared to be a genuine smile. Dil was good with the charm. Almost as good as Pohut had been.

"To your pending marriage," Tok said, raising his tumbler to Innel.

Everyone did likewise, Taba making a thoughtful sound as she reached behind to the side table and selected another bottle, filling the cups of those who held theirs to her, putting some splashes in the rest, making the math more difficult. Not an accident.

"And how did he manage that?" Mulack asked no one in particular. "We all had the same damned anknapa. Why isn't Cern in my bed?"

"Because you're clumsy," Taba said, who no doubt had first-hand knowledge. The Cohort had done a lot of practicing.

"There was some actual study involved," Tok added. "Not something you really cared for, as I recall, Mulack."

"I studied plenty!" he said, sputtering drunkenly. "The anknapa, she had a—" He made a flopping gesture with one hand that caused everyone to laugh.

Study Cern, Innel thought, but didn't say.

"A toast," said Tok, motioning to Innel. "To the hero of Arteni. To whom we owe the very bread in our mouths."

"Huzzah!" said Taba. They all drank.

"I hear the king was pleased with your efforts in Arteni, Innel," said Tok.

Innel gave an affirming nod, despite that there had been no discussion with the king about the campaign at all. Which, he supposed, could well be taken as royal approval. The wedding was going ahead, and that was all the approval he really needed.

"To our beloved princess," said Tok, raising his glass.

Soon to be queen, Innel thought. But no one would say that. Not quite yet. It was too close to questioning the king's will.

"To the heir!" said Sutarnan with enough enthusiasm that he sloshed red wine across the table. A trick to help empty his glass? A distraction? An honest, drunken slip?

Did any of them make honest slips any more?

"Oh, we're not out of drink now, are we?" asked Mulack with a pout as he looked deep into his empty clear goblet.

"No, no," said Tok helpfully, pouring a liberal amount of ale into Mulack's goblet.

Glass number five. Ale, not wine.

"To our brother, Innel," said Taba, raising her glass to Innel with a sideways look at Mulack. "May he continue to bring honor to our beloved empire."

"And may the stench of his astonishingly good fortune permeate all our lives in like fashion," said Sutarnan with uncommon passion.

Innel remembered something Pohut used to say: *Poverty and power both require arrogance. Moving between them, though, often requires the appearance of humility.* He gave Sutarnan what he hoped was a modest smile.

"Good fortune!" cried Mulack with a large grin, the gesture overly wide, glass raised so quickly there was ale dribbling over his fingers. "To the heir's new and virile stud-to-be. May he succeed where all others have failed."

It was close enough to what should never be said

aloud, about the king's lack of heirs, that the laughter at the table died suddenly.

For some reason everyone looked at Innel.

"Do explain your meaning, Mulack," Innel said pleasantly.

"Why—marrying the princess, of course." He gestured around the table with his wet hand still clutched around his goblet. "A feat at which every one of us has marvelously failed." As if he were a lamp suddenly snuffed out, Mulack's drunken expression and smile vanished. "Where you, Innel, have succeeded so splendidly."

Looking over the rim of his goblet at Innel, Mulack emptied his glass.

The wedding, initially postponed because of Innel's campaign, was postponed again. First a tenday. Then two.

There was always a good reason, and of course it was always the king's decision.

Innel was sorely tempted to push, to point out that he'd done everything the king had commanded. Had butchered Arteni townspeople to prove his loyalty to the crown, to demonstrate his leadership ability.

Had gotten Cern to say yes.

He already knew what his brother would say; he had said it often: *Don't push until you must. Then go in with all you have.*

It was not time to push, so he must be patient. He had Cern's good will in his pocket now, and prudence dictated holding steady, seeming to be confident in the outcome. He put his focus on keeping both Cern and the king happy, as he gathered what support he could.

An odd position, this one in which he found himself: as long as he was on track to marry Cern, and she on track to become queen, his influence grew, but his coin did not.

With one notable, recent exception. "Make your hire," Tok had told him softly. "I have funds in hand." Meaning the mage.

He would have Srel send word to a down-city broker he knew, rather than go through Bolah. Best not to always use the same path to a destination.

No, on second thought, he would tell Bolah as well and see which pathway succeeded first.

Best to have them search outside the city. Any mage in Yarpin was likely already aligned with the old king. Innel needed someone new, someone who did not already know the Anandynars.

Then, one evening, alone with Srel, frustrated, he asked, "Is this damned thing going to happen or not?"

Outside, swirls of snow flew sideways past the window. In the gardens below, a dusting of white collected.

Srel followed his look, then poured hot spiced wine from a flagon with one hand while he dribbled cream from a small cylinder with the other.

"Coin has been committed to the feast, and a fair bit of it. That would seem a strong indicator of yes."

"Then why is the king still delaying?"

"Oh, that. Well, ser . . ." A small smile.

"He has mixed feelings?"

"Very much so, I think."

"The mutts," Innel said, using the title no one would now dare speak.

Srel made a sound indicating disagreement. "I think he likes being king, ser."

After all the times Restarn had pushed Cern to choose a mate and promised her the throne if she did, a wed Cern was one less excuse. He wanted his daughter to continue his bloodline, but was loath to give up the crown.

There was, Innel suspected, another reason. He thought Cern weak.

It was no secret he had long hoped Cern would blossom into a replica of the Grandmother Queen Nials esse Arunkel, a powerful ruler who kept the empire strong and expanding.

Innel had watched the king as he scrutinized his dogs in the fighting pits to determine which would be given the chance to sire the next bitch's litter. Innel had seen the intensity of his attention. Restarn cared about one thing: winning. As long as you managed that, some rules could be bent along the way.

Suddenly Innel understood that bringing back his brother's body had not made the king doubt Innel at all, but rather the opposite; it was what had convinced him that Innel was a suitable mate for Cern. The king thought he had sacrificed his brother to win her.

At this thought Innel felt sickened, closely followed by the fear that if he looked deep into himself, he would find it was true.

He pushed it all away. It didn't matter; it was the past. There was one direction open to him now, one path, and he'd staked everything he had on it. Unlike the rest of the Cohort with their Houses and wealth, he had no second-best option.

✤ ✤ ✤

"After that, the Lesser Houses will enter here and here, march around the columns here, stand staggered thus and so behind the Great Houses." The king's seneschal looked up sourly from his diagrams at Innel as if doubting he understood.

One wedding date had replaced another so many times that Innel had stopped paying them much attention, so he was more than a little surprised to be standing in the seneschal's office surrounded by a handful of assistants, the wedding still scheduled for the morning after next.

Might it actually happen?

Most of those who directly served the king, like the seneschal, had offices lining the side of the palace that looked over the walls of the palace grounds onto Execution Square. Innel was looking out just such a window, wondering when they were going to take down the two ice-covered torsos hanging on the square's display wall.

"And so the Great Houses are in front, represented by a count of—Innel, what is the count from each of the Houses?"

"Twenty-five per House," he answered, without looking away from the frozen bodies. "The Lessers each have ten." It was like being drilled, back in Cohort days; a part of his mind was always ready with a correct answer, trained by pain and hunger to never be without.

"Everything must be done exactly as specified. Any mistake will reflect poorly on the king."

How many times had he heard that admonition?

"Yes," he said.

"You must nod your head exactly the same amount for

each gift from each of the Greater Houses. And likewise, but in lesser measure, for each of the Lesser Houses. Did you practice with a mirror?"

In his peripheral vision, Innel could see the gaunt man look at Srel for an answer.

"Yes," Innel replied, trying not to sound as irritated as he felt.

"Now we will review the vows—"

"I know them."

"We will go over them again. There must be no deviation. Not a word. You see where this mark is between the words? That means you inhale at that time. Do you understand?"

"Yes."

Innel wondered if the Grandmother Queen had been as creative in her executions as was her grandson. He should ask his Cohort brother Putar, who had made a particularly detailed study of those histories.

"Srel, be sure he has them memorized." A rustling sound told him that the seneschal had handed Srel yet another set of papers. "Now—the roster of attendees."

A paper was being held up in front of Innel's face, blocking his view.

"I know them," Innel said.

"Be sure you do, ser. This list is as if chiseled in stone, and yet it may change at the last minute. So memorize also this secondary roster"—another piece of paper with hundreds of names on it—"of those who have requested to attend should something happen to those who have been directly invited."

That would make for some very interesting social

events the next two evenings. Innel could imagine fights breaking out among Houses at taverns and pre-wedding celebrations, reflecting quiet arrangements made in the shadows about who should infuriate whom and how much, and what they would get in return for such efforts. The Houses could be impressively cooperative when they wanted something badly enough.

Innel had been granted only two invitations, one each for his mother and sister. He would have been insulted if there had been anyone else to invite, not already on the list. There wasn't.

His mother had been profoundly relieved when he handed her the threefold envelope, expression as near pleasure as he had seen. For a moment it almost seemed she would look at him.

Cahlen, of course, didn't care. He must remember to have someone dress her, in case she decided at the last minute to come anyway.

"I was in the Cohort," he said to the seneschal. "You may have heard. I spent my life studying the damned Houses."

The seneschal handed more papers to Srel, who exuded his usual calm. Innel again made a mental note to buy something extravagant for Srel as soon as he had the means.

"Do not swear. Not about the Houses, not about anything. Not until your wedding night, and then only if it pleases Her Grace the Princess that you do so. Do you understand me?"

Innel clamped down on the many replies that leapt to mind.

Don't push until you must.

"Yes."

"Now—attend to this map. It shows the locations of all the Houses in the Great Hall—"

"Because I won't be able to tell who they are by their colors?" He could feel himself losing his patience. He looked at Srel, who was smiling faintly, as if everything were right with the world.

"Because, ser Royal Consort-to-be, I have worked very hard to achieve an equal count and arrangement among both Greater and Lesser Houses. Who stands next to whom is no accident. The ordering of the presentation of gifts was harder to arrange than the Charter Court's opening day feast—no trivial matter that, and I have arranged three of them in my life—and you *will* learn the locations of the Houses so that you know what to expect and when."

Innel clenched his teeth against what he wanted to say.

The seneschal seemed, for a moment, to be out of breath. He inhaled, then handed the last sheet to Srel with a pointed look, as if he would hold Srel personally responsible for any mistakes.

Then, to Innel: "The tailors will be in shortly to measure you."

"Again? Do you jest?"

"Never. Innel, do attend carefully to my next words: she can divorce you far more easily than she marries you. Watch where you put your feet."

He felt himself warm at this condescension and wondered what the man would think when Innel was made Lord Commander.

When Cern was queen there would, Innel resolved, be a new seneschal. And perhaps a new kitchen scullery boy as well.

For now, though, he would comply.

"I will step only where and when I am told to, seneschal."

On the day of his wedding, Srel woke him at the fourth bell, in full dark, a lamp in his hand, and presented Innel with a message sealed with the king's mark.

A shot of apprehension went through Innel. He ripped it open, his mind dancing across various possibilities, read it once, read it again, and handed it to Srel.

A strange, bitter feeling settled over him.

"Congratulations, ser Colonel." Srel looked at him. "You are disappointed?"

The smallest possible promotion. In time to prevent his daughter marrying a captain. Barely.

Having had the lord commandership dangled in front of him made this seem a meager achievement, where it should have felt a victory. Innel wondered if that had been the king's real intention, to keep Innel wanting more than he could have, with no plan of ever passing the throne to his daughter, or letting her make Innel lord commander.

But how long could the man keep ruling? His famous grandmother Nials esse Arunkel had stayed on the throne until she found someone she wanted to succeed her: her grandson Restarn. She had passed over her own children and their generation, dismissing them as unsuitable, then passed over Restarn's older siblings as well. She stayed tight by her grandson's side while he secured his throne, alive and active in palace politics until she was well over a hundred.

A long time.

And while it seemed unlikely, Restarn could still name someone other than Cern to succeed him.

Srel moved around the room with the ease of a silverfish, selecting underclothes for Innel, setting out various jewelry for the ceremony.

As he looked out the window at the late winter snow, he asked Srel: "Do you think it's too late for him to cancel it again?"

"Entirely too late, ser." Srel smiled, a rare expression on the small man.

It occurred to Innel only now that his steward had been waiting for this day nearly as long as he had.

In short order Innel's room began to fill with people. Houses Sartor and Murice had both sent so many people to dress him that they could not all reach him at once. The Houses clearly wanted to make their mark on his outfit and began sniping at each other about matters of buttons and tucks.

Finally Innel growled, "I can rip it all off and let you sew it back on."

After that they were more polite. Another hour went by with needles and other sharp objects moving around him, making Innel even more testy. All this in order to adjust an outfit that looked much the same to him as it had an hour ago.

When at last they left he was rushed to one of the Great Hall's antechambers to wait.

Like a working animal, he thought, not liking it much. He stepped out into the hallway and found a door that opened to the Great Hall, prying open a crack to look through. For a moment all other thought fled his mind.

In the hall stood a thousand murmuring aristos, packed tight in knots of House colors, each jacket and glove, cravat and earring bright in appropriate hues, long hair swept into elaborate towers draped with chains and sparkling gemstones. In stance and expression he could read the strains and linkages between the Houses.

In the galleries above, royals sat up front, the Lesser Houses standing behind. From the banisters draped chains of the various metals from which Arunkel derived wealth, red and black flowers woven through.

It came to him then that this whole event was going to cost the king a very great deal. It was an immensely satisfying thought.

The mutt was worth something.

Then the ceremony began. First a speech by the king about the necessary patriotism of every Arunkin, then a list of the accomplishments of the Anandynar line and a summary of the history of the empire. For a time it seemed he intended to discuss every one of the nine-hundred eighty-three years.

Next, loud, brassy music from the corners of the room, followed by a long and quite tedious gift ceremony for which Innel was ready with his practiced nods.

Next, the vows, which were impressively one-sided, with Innel promising his loyalty to the king, the royal line, the empire, the Houses, and finally to Cern, while the princess offered in return the vague possibility that Innel would be allowed to come near her from time to time.

The important part, though, was when the king said the final words.

"It is done."

And then, like that, Innel was married into the Anandynar line. Children, if Cern and he ever had any, would be legal heirs with a chance at the throne. He himself was now an almost-royal.

One more rung up the ladder.

For a moment, before he and Cern were swept out of the hall and into the now-crowded antechamber, he thought he saw his brother in the back shadows of the halls. The ache he felt within took a bite from the victory.

But no—had Pohut been here, he would have been fiercely proud. At least the man his brother had been before Botaros.

Innel had not forgotten the seer's predictions about the king's abdication to Cern.

The spring after next, or the summer following. Mere months from now.

In the anteroom, a swirl of aides separating them, Sachare hovering protectively, Innel caught Cern's eye and smiled. She returned a glare that he knew was not meant for him. The seneschal was too busy lecturing someone else to give them any last-minute instructions about the feast to follow, so Innel waded through the sea of people to reach her side. He took her hand, a gesture uninvited, one that he felt he could now risk.

"I hate this, Innel," she whispered to him.

"One step closer, my lady," he whispered back. To the throne.

At that she grimaced a bit, a brittle smile, but he saw through it to something like desire. He wondered what expression her face would take on when a crown was put on her head.

Within a month the king had changed his mind again. To wed was easy, he said, but best for Cern to make an heir first. Better yet, two or more. Don't make my mistake, he said. A few more years of seasoning. Make her better suited to rule the empire.

Innel was unsurprised, but as the days passed, Cern became more and more livid. She wandered the palace in a tight fury, clenching her fists and saying things that should not be said about one's monarch, certainly not an Anandynar, as fond as they were of elaborate executions. Innel did not think Cern was in real danger, given how much faith the king put in his own bloodline, but it would not be wise to test that certainty.

It was now, finally, the spring of the seer's prediction.

Innel mused on the plans that he had spent so many years assembling. Should he wait?

The spring after next, or the summer following.

He looked out his small office window to Execution Square to see how things were progressing. The twitching man was on day two of his dying efforts, suspended four feet off the ground, some thirty hooks embedded deeply in his flesh, from fingers to toes. Innel had found that a long look at one of the king's executions helped him order his priorities.

Act now, or wait? He considered the question for a day, and then another.

If he had the girl, he could simply ask her.

At last, while Cern's storming temper swayed him, it was the seer's words that decided him: it was time.

On the fifth day, when the man in Execution Square had stopped moving, Innel began. He sent Srel with herbs to calm Cern. She quieted, sitting for long hours in the glassed-in gardens, staring at her birds. Innel saw to it that she was carefully watched by his guards as well as her own.

As a result of meticulous planning and sand-clock timing, Innel was nowhere near Restarn when the old king stumbled, was caught by his guards, and carried to his bed, hot with fever.

The slave who was sent to tend to him knew to kiss him as he slept, but only after applying the lip rouge Innel had given her. She didn't know why, only that if she did as she was told, her sister would not be sent from the palace into House Helata's navy, to serve sailors at sea.

The apothecary knew a little more: to mix with the many ingredients for the tincture for the king's fever a new ingredient, by itself a perfectly benign herbal extract, in exchange for Innel making sure that no one would care about his drunken rant in the kitchens a few months ago in which he described the various compounds he had assembled for members of the royal family to treat various maladies, some of which were rather embarrassing.

The final ingredient was the doctor herself. He had chosen her with care; she was neither brilliant nor clumsy, and had few enemies. For her, Innel had brokered a quiet agreement with his Cohort sister Malrin of House Eschelatine to take the doctor's newborn grandson, a baby from a match not crown-approved, and have the boy tucked into the lesser House, to seem to have been born to an approved match that wanted a baby. In exchange, the doctor would put a bit of a certain powder on her fingertips before she inspected His Royal Majesty's mouth, to be sure his gums weren't bleeding.

They weren't.

The king's condition worsened over days, and then weeks. Bedridden and still feverish, Restarn was approached by his closest advisers, many of whom Innel had spoken to, to be sure they knew which way the wind was blowing. They asked the king, might it not be time to consider abdicating to Cern?

That is, unless he had another heir in mind?

Innel had been told that even as ill as he was, Restarn had been adamant in his reply. At his command the strongbox had been brought out from under the bed. He unlocked it, thrusting the succession letter at them.

Cern was at the top of the list. The rest of the names should have stayed quietly behind the eyes of those in that room, but of course that was not the way the palace worked. Now everyone knew the entire list.

Innel gave Cern no more herbs, needing her alert. But even sober she seemed uninterested in the process by which she might become queen, despite her anger at being denied it before. She only grudgingly participated in the council sessions that the king from his bed also grudgingly allowed. The planning sessions that might, if all went well, lead to her coronation.

With the affairs of state floating between an ailing Restarn and a sullen Cern, trade and House negotiations stumbled, contracts frayed and needed focused grooming to survive. As Innel struggled to keep Cern somewhere between too tense and too withdrawn, taking on as many administrative tasks as he could, he also made sure those who supported the king most closely knew there might be a place for them under the new queen. When she was crowned.

It was like juggling oiled knives in a dark room: any slip could cut. Or kill.

In front of Innel was a barely touched plate of food. He rubbed his head, trying to ease the ache and strain of a day already too full.

And now this.

"Be ready," read the simple message, written in the down-city broker's hand. He crumpled it and tossed it in the fire along with his sense of having been given an order.

This was how it worked; money was not enough to hire a mage. Even the appalling amount with which Tok had supplied him. They must be persuaded. Seduced.

He considered who he might send to do this. Sachare, Tok, Sutarnan, Dil, and even Mulack were all quite capable of convincing people to do things they didn't want to do. Pohut had been the best of the lot, of course. Had he been here, he would be the one to send.

No, there was no one else he could trust to do this. He would have to go himself.

Somehow. There did not seem to be an hour of the day in which he was not acting in some way essential to support Cern's cause or to undermine one of the others' on the succession list. Now that there was no secret who would take the throne if something happened to Cern, there were too many people eyeing the throne with interest and eyeing Cern speculatively.

He doubled her guards, taking the time to interview each one. Sachare and he had long talks about security.

He brought Cern more rods and flats and hooks for her various and delicately balanced in-air creations, hoping to keep her entertained in her own rooms.

The other royals on the succession list—two of the king's cousins, a great nephew now married into one of the Houses, and a toddler niece—were subject to more attention as well, which had the advantage of keeping them busy with new and fawning friends, but it also put the thought in people's heads that there might be options to Cern becoming queen.

Restarn had to name her, formalize the transition. Soon. How to get him there?

Innel could not, he now realized too clearly, let Cern name him lord commander. When the king was healthy and active it would have been clear that Cern had made the appointment with Restarn's tacit consent, but if she did so now, everyone would think she was trying to grab the throne out from under him while he lay ill, which would open the door to challenges they could not yet face.

She might be the heir-apparent, but he was still the mutt.

He must get Cern to the throne.

At Innel's direction, the doctor began to intercept the

king's advisers, explaining to them that he needed rest with no disturbances and hinting that there was a chance the disease was contagious. The king's visitors quickly dwindled down to none.

No advisers, no servants.

No beautiful blond slaves.

Only the doctor, who Innel continued to watch for signs of disloyal behavior. He made sure she knew how well cared-for was her grandson in House Eschelatine, and that there was a position for her with the new monarch, but only if the old one did not die unexpectedly.

Innel now stood outside the king's door, having decided it was time to see him. The doctor ran a hand through her hair, cut traditionally short, pink scalp showing through dark strands to demonstrate how healthy she was. For the sake of the listening guards, she explained to Innel that the disease might be contagious.

"My devotion to His Majesty will protect me," Innel answered, loud enough to be heard. Then more softly: "You have all the herbs you need, yes?"

"Yes, ser."

Inside, the room stank of illness.

"I'm sorry, ser," the doctor said at his expression. "Perhaps we should open some windows."

The windows were shut, heavy drapes across them, keeping it warm against the winter. But now it was spring.

"The princess would not want to further risk his health with the cold air."

Cern, he suspected, would be happier yet if her father were bricked up in a deep dungeon cell to rot. But they needed him alive, at least for now.

The shape under the covers stirred, eyes coming half open in a wrinkled face. He stared intently at Innel.

"You may go," Innel told the doctor. The doctor bowed to the king and left, closing the door behind her.

Restarn esse Arunkel. The man who across fifty-six years of rule had extended the empire from the Dalgo Rift to the ocean, united the warring provinces, and held the seas from Perripur to Chaemendi. Was it really possible he was now so frail?

Innel bowed. "Your Majesty."

The eyes blinked, seemed to struggled to focus, found him. Innel felt himself tense.

"How do you feel, Sire?"

"You fool. How do you think I feel? Where's Cern? She doesn't visit. No one visits. This your doing, Innel?"

"She is busy, Sire. Taking on the essential work of governing the empire while you recover. It is a trying time for us all."

"Yes, I'm sure it is," Restarn said sourly.

"I'm certain she will have more time after the coronation."

"Coronation?" Restarn frowned.

Anxiety sparked in Innel. Had the illness taken the king's memory? Had he changed his mind?

"You directed the council to begin the process of crowning her, Sire—"

"I know that," he snapped. "I'm sick, not stupid." A coughing fit took him. When he was done, his head fell back on the pillow, breathing hard from the exertion. He turned his head sideways to look at Innel.

"So you buried your brother and married my daughter."

He chuckled, then wheezed. "Not bad for the son of a down-city mapmaker and his wet-nurse wife. Aren't you fortunate that I took your family in all those years ago."

Dragged them from their home, their family business given away.

"A mapmaker whom you made a general, Sire," Innel said quietly. "A hero, you told me."

"But not so good for your brother, eh?" Restarn said, ignoring Innel's words. "I was betting on Pohut, you know. Not you."

Innel struggled to keep calm, forcing a smile to his face. "And yet, here I stand, Sire. Perhaps we could discuss some of your unwritten agreements with the Houses, so we could—"

"I can just see it," Restarn continued, starting to look pleased, "you and Pohut galloping across the empire to ask a snot-nosed commoner brat to tell your fortune. Did you ask her for the blessings of the wind and the mercy of sea as well, while you had the chance?"

With effort, Innel kept his breathing steady, letting only a shadow of confusion show on his face.

"Yes," Restarn said slowly, watching Innel closely and ignoring—or perhaps seeing through—his show of bemusement. "I know where you went. I knew the first time you fucked my daughter. I know every boy and girl she takes to her bed. What she likes, what she hates. You thought you could keep something from me?" He laughed, then coughed again, curled in on himself while his body was wracked with another fit. Then he wiped spittle from his lips, looked at Innel. "I know everything that happens in my palace."

"Knew," Innel said softly.

Restarn's smile faded.

"I have taxed you enough, Your Majesty. I will leave you to rest." He turned.

"Innel, no. Stay. What's happening on the borders? Tell me." Wheezing, the king struggled to sit up. "The Gotar rebellion. Sinetel. The Houses. This foul illness has kept me flat. No one tells me anything. I don't even have my slaves. Stay and talk to me."

Innel turned back. "There's a rumor, Majesty. About your mages."

"I never had mages."

"Rumor says otherwise."

"My enemies seek to dirty my good name."

"Then," Innel said, backing a step to the door, then another, giving a small bow, "you'll be pleased to know that there's nothing happening in Sinetel and the Houses are still standing. Rest easy, Sire."

The king's eyes narrowed as he inhaled sharply, no doubt to say something, but instead he started coughing again. The pain showed on his face. He turned a furious glare on Innel. "I will not have it said of me that I used mages."

"I have no desire to give voice to such filthy lies, Your Majesty."

"Horseshit," Restarn said. "Give me your oath, Innel. Not that it's much, coming from a man who would kill his own brother, but I'll take it anyway."

At this Innel's anger welled up hot from deep inside. He wrestled with it for a moment. Truly, the king deserved his admiration; even sick as he was, the man still knew the exact words that would infuriate Innel. "You have my oath," Innel said evenly.

"Gotar?"

"They are rebelling in Gotar."

Restarn hissed. "I know that."

"The mages. Names. Details. Sire."

Innel wanted to be sure that any mage he hired had not previously worked for Restarn.

The king glared at him a long moment. For decades this particular royal expression had often preceded extended executions. To see it thus was extraordinary. Like a rare view from a high, thin cliff ledge, sharp rocks and ocean churning below. Innel felt something like vertigo.

Then go in with all you have.

"Forgive my intrusion," he said with a bow, backing to the door where he turned on his heel, took the handle, and pressed it until, in the silence of the room, there was an audible click.

"Yes, yes, all right. I'll tell you what you want to know. You may want paper. I doubt your memory is as good as mine, even now."

Innel turned back, his own anger transformed into hard resolve. "Test me."

At this Restarn smiled wide. While his sunken eyes and pallid skin would not have looked out of place in any down-city street beggar, no beggar's eyes could hold such arrogance. "Sit down, Innel. I miss our talks. Tell me what's happening in my kingdom."

Innel felt a cold trickle of uncertainty. Restarn was not yet out of the picture. He could still shake their plans if he had a mind to. "I had understood it was to be Cern's kingdom, and soon, Your Majesty."

Restarn gestured, quite clearly, to the chair by his side. An order. The moment stretched. "It will be," the king said, sounding surprisingly hale. "Come on, boy. I knew you'd take Cern. I knew it all along. Pohut was too soft-hearted. It made him slow and stupid. Now come here, sit, and we'll talk."

"I don't have the time, Sire," Innel said, feeling stubborn.

"Oh, I think you do, Innel," he said with an unpleasant smile. "You never know when I might die."

Now that he had something of a yes from Restarn, Innel pushed as hard as he could. But moving the coronation forward was a choreography of coordination, conciliation, and inducement beyond anything Innel had ever experienced.

Too many people, from Houses to military, had an opinion, an agenda, or something else that Innel needed, that wouldn't be offered without reciprocation. Sorting out the pieces was confounding.

As events proceeded forward at an interminably slow rate, Innel discovered that the only thing worse than facing a seneschal who was annoying, opinionated, and stubbornly devoted to the crown was facing one who wasn't. He remembered the wedding, how it had come together, and reassessed the man's skill and necessity. Swallowing his pride, Innel went to talk with him, making clear that if he worked for the princess now, he would work for the queen later.

Also, Innel told him, this event, unlike the wedding, would not dip so deeply into the royal coffers.

"It's a coronation, ser Princess Royal Consort," the seneschal said, pronouncing each word with care, as if unsure of Innel's hearing. "It reflects the honor of the Anandynars. All near a thousand years of it. You cannot pretend it is a simple winter festival ball."

"What you propose is an obscene expenditure that—"

"That employs half the tradesmen of the Lesser Houses, and puts coin in the pockets of the Eight Greater Houses whose support the new queen might well need from the moment she takes the crown. Raised in the Cohort, you say?"

"Careful where you step, seneschal."

The gaunt man's lips pressed together, making his face look even longer than it already did. "Do you know, ser Royal Consort, what year it was I began to serve the king in my current capacity?"

Innel could not remember any other seneschal. He shook his head in answer.

"Just so. Before you were born. Many years before. You may find it beneficial to consider the empire's challenges during that time."

Innel took a deep breath, let it out slowly. It was a compelling argument. "As you say, then," he allowed. "But I want to approve all expenses."

"No, ser, you most certainly don't." Then, with a look that bordered on pity, he added, "You'll have to rely on me sooner or later. Why not start sooner, when I can do you the most good?"

"Midsummer, latest." Two months hence.

At this the seneschal laughed outright, annoyingly unconcerned about offending Innel. "Invitations alone will take that long. There are foreign dignitaries to be notified. House eparchs and aristos traveling far from home to be called back."

Innel made a sound that came out a growl. "Listen closely, seneschal: without a monarch on the throne, the empire and all her tangles of trade and production falter. Do you track the price of the metals that are key to Arunkel wealth?"

"No. That is not my—"

"No, it isn't. But I do. You are going to have to rely on me, too, seneschal. Spend what the council will approve, but the coronation happens by midsummer, even if no one shows for it. Send the notice. Now."

The seneschal exhaled, taking a very long time about it to make his displeasure unambiguous. His look told Innel that the man was wondering how sick the king really was and if he might be persuaded to come back to health and rule again.

He appeared to come to a decision. His head inclined very slightly. "As you say, Royal Consort."

Innel smiled thinly.

It was a good title, Innel reflected as he walked back to his small office, but there was another one that he wanted very much, and he meant to have it.

"What do they say about me today, Srel?" he asked as the slight man poured a dark stream of bitter tea.

"That the coronation is to be the grandest, most splendid affair since the Grandmother Queen was crowned one hundred and six years ago. That it will be a tiny affair sponsored by the Eight because the crown is bankrupt. That the king is not really sick, but only testing loyalties. That he is away on campaign, conquering the wild lands past the Rift. That the king is dead."

"That would seem to cover the range of possibilities," Innel responded. "Seed a few more: the king is delighted to see his daughter ascending the throne. The royal consort is about to be promoted."

Srel raised an eyebrow, but did not ask. "Yes, ser."

Best would be to have the king seen happily supporting his daughter's succession. Could the old man be persuaded to be at the coronation? To at least seem willing?

If Innel put it to him right, perhaps.

Time to ease the man's isolation. A little.

Innel's two guards stepped into his small office, escorting a small blonde slave. Her golden hair fell to her waist, her wide blue eyes flickered around the room.

"The slave Naulen."

She was a startling sight, small and slender, her white silk tunic hanging to her calves, a thin gold chain showing off her long neck. Dwarfed next to the tall guards, her slight build made her look even more delicate.

With a nod, Innel dismissed the guards, watching her while she looked around.

It was obvious why she was Restarn's favorite. Her face was something a master painter might have considered a life's work, from the pale, arched eyebrows to the wide, angled, sky-blue eyes. Even the way she rubbed her slender wrist, a simple move, was somehow exquisitely graceful. As she stepped forward slightly, Innel found himself distracted by how the heavy silk outlined her curves.

"The king trusted you," he said. "You slept in his room many nights."

"Yes, ser."

"Then I will trust you, too."

"Thank you, ser," she said, voice a delicate, breathy tone, like a wooden flute. She looked at him with a soft, grateful look that made his breath catch.

Yes, she would inspire the king to tell her things he would tell no one else. He could see why.

"He misses you," Innel said.

"Thank you, ser." Her look and tone were just the right mix of demure, uncertain, and eager to please.

"He may not be king for much longer. You understand that, don't you?"

"I do, ser."

He could not quite tell from her expression if she did or not. The Perripin liked to claim that dark hair and skin meant a capacity for sustained and complex thought. This was why, they said, the blond northerners had been so easily conquered and enslaved. The implication that Perripin were smarter than their lighter-skinned Arunkin neighbors was the foundation of a great number of Perripin jokes that were rarely told this far north.

"You work for me now. Do that work well and I will make sure you are not sent back to the slave's quarters. Perhaps kept privately by someone who will treat you gently."

"I will do all you say, ser." She stepped close to him, looking up with a flawless, eager smile. "Anything and everything."

He laughed lightly at the implied offer, sweeter for how unnecessary it was, and for a moment caressed her shoulder with his fingertips. He dragged his gaze from the large, mesmerizing blue eyes, with effort reclaiming his focus, and reluctantly drew his hand away.

"You'll visit him daily," he said. "You'll be brought to me afterwards to tell me what he has said. This conversation, though, you will not repeat to anyone."

She looked up at him, and her expression turned sober. "I understand you perfectly, ser."

This time he believed her.

"And Naulen, don't excite him too much."

Chapter Thirteen

In Maris's dream her parents were still alive. A breeze delivered scent of ginger vine and jasmine flower through the open windows, baking taro wafting in from the kitchen. Her father's resonant laugh, her mother's flute-like song. Home, where she had lived her earliest years in something very much like happiness.

A sweet dream. A rare, sweet dream.

In the dream he had knocked on the door, a rat-a-tat demanding response. She knew who it was, even before he stepped across the threshold, not waiting for an invitation.

Keyretura did not wait.

She cried out a warning, but her parents did not hear. They turned to him with gracious, deferring smiles, their Perripin hospitality unimpeachable.

Then his gaze found her, his dark eyes burning into hers.

She ran from door to door, searching for an escape, but he was always there. As the sweet dream turned ugly and rancid, Maris disgustedly took control away from her dreaming self and woke.

From under the warm blankets she spread her fingers and sent channels of thought out and past the walls of the small cabin into the overcast winter day, out to the perimeter of the property where her wards were woven through the land and the trees, tuned to warn her of any trespasses. Had he somehow found her?

No, he had not. Only a dream.

As she pulled her attention back into the cabin, she felt the new depth of snow on the ground. So much snow.

The first time she'd seen snow, it had been a marvel to her. White flakes falling endlessly from above, covering the world, making it seem clean. A canvas on which anything might be written. Even, somehow, her own freedom.

She remembered that moment vividly, sitting atop a bay mare, looking across the astonishing white fields. He was at her side, of course; there was no escaping him in those days. How she wished then that when she turned back to face him, he too would be covered in white, her life made clean of this black-robed man, releasing her from the nightmare of her apprenticeship.

Absurd, of course. Freedom did not come from bits of frozen water, praying to the nine elements, or wishing upon grains of sand. And when she turned back, he had still been there, eyes hard on her, assessing.

No escape. Year after year, lesson after lesson, that had become indisputable.

Then, at last, the test that did free her. An ordeal best forgotten, like Keyretura himself. In the years since, she had seen snow many times, had learned that it blanketed without discrimination, making all things white, from villages flattened by plague, to the dead of battle with pikes and flags sticking up like some odd winter flower.

But snow made nothing clean. It only covered for a time. When the seasons changed, it would melt away, revealing the debris beneath.

Now, in the waking world, the banging came again at her door. She sent a bit of herself outside, focus settling atop the boy, floating down over him. Youth came off Samnt in hot waves, the swirl of etheric flow around him bright and vibrant. She sank her attention in through his skin, feeling the press of blood in his veins, hearing his child's heart beat strong and fast in his chest.

Not a child, she reminded herself. Not for long.

She withdrew her focus back under warm covers. The door was unlocked, but unlike the monster of her dreams, Samnt would never enter without invitation. Not because she was a mage. Not because he was afraid to offend. Because it was not done.

"Come in," she called.

He threw open the front door, stamping inside, bringing in swirls of snow and wafts of cold air. This sent her burrowing deeper into the cocoon of blankets.

Grinning, he slammed the door behind. "My ma sends hello. And this," he said, holding up a burlap bundle, fist closed around the top of the bag.

He was breathing hard from the run up the hill to her cabin, exhaling a white fog into the air. He could have come more slowly, but no—passion drove him to speed.

So young.

With a thunk he landed the bag on the table. The sides slid down to reveal bread, a large hunk of white cheese, and a brown ceramic jar. His eyes flickered around the room, as if to assure himself that nothing had changed in the day since he had been here last, then he was at the window, pulling back heavy drapes to let in a gray light.

Next at the woodstove, prying off bits of wood for kindling, setting them in the stove under the logs he had chopped and stacked for her back in autumn.

What, she wondered again, was she doing in this wretched, frigid land? For a time she lay there, thinking of her home in Perripur, in the Shentarat Mountains, and how overgrown with green it would be now. How warm.

The stove fire was burning enthusiastically. She struggled into clothes and braved the air of the room.

"Didn't wake you, did I?" he asked, poking at the logs. Concern flickered briefly across his face, then his mind was elsewhere. "Snow later, I think."

"Such fortune we are heir to," Maris said wryly. "What's in the jar?"

"Applesauce," he said, "Our trees, our spices. Ma's quite proud of it. You'll like it, truly."

"Thoughtful of her. Thoughtful of you. You may stay."

He laughed and crouched down to put more wood into the fiercely burning stove and a kettle of water on top. She found herself smiling at him.

This, perhaps, was why she was still here.

"Let's get started," she said.

"Need more wood brought in."

"It will wait. It's not going anywhere."

At this he sighed and dropped into the chair by her

side. A moment later he was up again, tilting his head sideways to look at the books on her shelf. "Pa went to the village yesterday," he said, running his fingers across the leather spines. "Trading tools at market. Saw a book there. Cost so much." He turned back with a quick smile.

"What was it about, the book?"

A shrug. "He didn't know. Leather working, maybe."

"Next time you go with him. You read it for him, yes?"

Samnt nodded but without enthusiasm. That, she resolved, would change when he understood what books could be.

It had been so warm in autumn when she'd come here to wait out the winter in the mountains of Kathorn. Samnt had been eager to help stock the cabin, helping her lay in far more wood than she thought she would ever need. Now she found herself wondering if she would have enough to get through to spring thaw.

When the kettle boiled Samnt prepared tea from her dwindling supply that she had brought with her from Perripur. He sweetened it with local honey, just as she liked, without her even asking. A simple gesture, but one that touched her. He sipped his own mug, made a face, wiped his mouth with his sleeve.

The face of another boy came to mind, one who drank tea and wiped his face on his sleeve. Five years ago, was it? No, ten. The boy's parents were already dead, his feverish sister restless on the soaked, stained mattress. Maris did all she could for them, gave the last of her herbs, but the illness held strong, eating through them, their family, their village. Still she stayed and nursed them.

The boy had died last.

"Let's do some reading," she said to Samnt. "From the animal book."

"Teach me magic, Maris."

"What, that again?"

"Yes. Why not?"

"You don't need it."

"But I do. I'm a fast learner. You said so yourself."

To learn fast had little to do with it. Yes, he had the rare spark, but Maris would not wish the nightmare on anyone.

"Study something else."

"What?"

"Anything. You must learn to read. Then we'll go to numbers—"

Samnt cut in, exasperated. "Maris, I'm fifteen in spring. I'm going to plant grain, raise pigs, and dig crappers for my life's keep, just like my parents do. I don't need to read for that."

"Learn to read and who can say what you might do? You could work a trade in-city. As bright as you are with numbers, perhaps even become a scribe."

If he were lucky. If he didn't get his head bashed in a moment after stepping through the city gates. He would need skills and sense enough to keep his mouth closed to survive in a city. He would need friends.

Her mind was already on how she would manage it. For Samnt she would go to Yarpin. Make some introductions. There were those in the capital city who would be pleased to be in her debt, who would help her find a position for a bright farm boy. They would go in spring, she decided, when he was of age. Something to look forward to.

Samnt snorted. "If I were a mage, I could . . ." He snapped his fingers. "Well, I don't know, do I. Because you won't show me."

"You are correct in this."

"Save me from plowing and shovels and shit-holes, Maris. Teach me. I'll study hard. Please?"

He had no idea what he was asking.

Nor had she, at half his age, when her parents had put her small hand in the large hand of the black-robed stranger. Not until ten years later, when Keyretura had finally allowed her to visit home, where she sat by her father as he died, did she understand just how much her parents had paid to see their only child contracted in a mage's apprenticeship.

Her father had comforted her then, wiping away her tears with his shaking hand, eyes full of pride, saying her name with his final breaths. It had shamed her to the core of her spirit to realize that while she had been studying in Keyretura's mansion of glass and water, learning the impossible, her parents had been struggling to afford to eat.

She could tell Samnt that he had no spark, that this door would never open for him. But looking at him now, eyes sparkling, young face full of passion, she could not quite bring herself to give voice to that particular lie.

Pointing at the bookshelf, she took a tone she had learned from ships' captains, Perripin magistrates, and Keyretura. "That book there, the brown one. Get it now."

He watched her, expression defiant.

She remembered being so openly rebellious with Keyretura, recalled the agony that followed. Yet she had done it again and again.

Stubborn.

"Can you get the book with magic, Maris? Float it in the air?" He snapped his fingers again, up next to his ear. "Like that?"

"That one there," Maris repeated, still pointing with her one hand, the other dropping toward the floor, three fingers curled, the other two pointing a ground into the earth. She was annoyed at his resistance, felt her emotion rise to anger, let it build.

"Come on, Maris," he said, restlessly standing but not moving toward the shelves. "You don't wear black. Aren't mages supposed to wear black? Show me what mages can do."

Keyretura's voice was clear in memory. *Show me what you have learned to do, Marisel.*

Samnt wouldn't like to see what mages could do. What they had always done, from the Shentarat glass plains to the Battle of Nerainne to the melting plague, mages took what they wanted, destroyed what got in their way. Left the ruins for Iliban.

Iliban. The mage word for those who weren't.

Pushing aside such thoughts she stood and went to the bookshelf, pulling out the book she had indicated, hefted it in one hand. "Heavy. You were right to let me fetch it for you. Might have strained yourself."

Samnt rolled his eyes. "Maris, show me just one thing and I'll study. Whatever you say. On the harvest, I swear it."

Maris held up the book. "Behold the one thing. Valuable beyond any trick I could show you. Now we study."

He exhaled loudly, frustrated, just as Maris slammed the book flat on the table.

"Samnt, you must attend to my words—"

"—not the book," he said loudly at the same moment, standing, waving his arms. "I meant—"

"I know what you meant. I'm a midwife, too, Samnt. Why don't you ask me about birthing babies?"

"I've seen babies born. I don't need to see more of that. Lots of blood. Now I want to see—"

"In the Buravin Tel fire pits they bet on how many heartbeats the condemned will stand before they topple into the lava. Trust me in this: there are things better not seen."

But he was not listening. Too much curiosity, not enough sense. It tugged at her, his craving to understand, but it was a sharp blade and it would cut him if he were not careful.

"'Fear magic from a distance'," she said. "Have you not heard this wisdom?"

He waved it away. "I've heard it. I'm not afraid of you, Maris."

"Then you're a fool."

How had her simple desire to teach this young man to read and write turned so sour? It was her own fault; she had been kind.

Was this what came from being raised by loving parents? From being treated gently?

He shook his head, refusing to be cowed. She could

send him away, she supposed, but he would be back tomorrow, the same litany on his lips, the same hunger in his eyes. Reason would not convince him.

"So be it."

His face lit up. "I'll study after, I promise."

Maris nodded, feeling distant.

"Maris, you're not at all what I thought a mage would be. Friendly. Generous. I like you so much."

His words threatened to slice through the layer of numbness she now spun around herself, but she had learned her protections across the decades with Keyretura. Even Samnt's innocence could not cut through that.

"Sit down," Maris told him flatly.

He sat down in the chair, smile wide, face eager. She exhaled, went deep into his body. A touch here, a shift there.

"Now stand up."

He didn't move.

"Stand up," she said again, knowing he heard her.

He remained still.

"You wanted to see some magic, boy," she said roughly. "Now you have. What do you think of it?"

His only movement was shallow breathing. Maris turned away from him as something bitter and familiar settled inside her. She picked up her mug. She sipped at her tea.

Again she had failed. Pain and suffering following in her wake.

Again.

The mother and fetus had not been working well

together. She had given them all the healing herbs she could, and had delved deep into the woman's belly with her focus, trying to smooth the child's way out. One by one she tried to fix the many problems, but too much was wrong with the channels that connected them. Sunrise came, then midday, then evening. Another sunrise.

It came clear: she could save only one.

Somehow the mother had read this decision in her face and begged for her baby's life. But a glance at the father, a taste of his unsteady, weak spirit, told Maris that the baby would not live long without the mother. So she touched the small entity within, gave it what comfort she could, and brought it from womb into life and then to the door of death. She put the small body on his mother's breast.

The woman howled. Maris had been young enough then to think an explanation of how life and death were two sides of one thing, how neither could exist without the other, might help ease the agony, but it did not. The woman cursed Maris, the power behind her words fueled by the power of childbirth. The curse set deep into Maris's spirit with a penetrating venom that shocked her.

Maris had left, sick in body and spirit, taking herself deep into the wilderness, beneath the tall trees and into deep loam. There she burrowed into the ground, in search of solace and healing. It had taken months to recover.

It was a hard lesson, to discover that everything she had to give was not enough.

As it was not now.

The woman's words hadn't mattered—it was the intent behind them that had settled ill into Maris's body and spirit—but Maris would never forget them. *My grief to you, a hundred times, and a hundred times beyond that.*

Today, perhaps, Maris had made some payment on that curse.

Her eyes roamed over the room, stopping at the books of her small library, that had been comfort and friend, aid and insight. Now they seemed entirely senseless, an absurd weight, a foolish indulgence.

Much like her desire to teach this boy.

She reached a bit of herself into Samnt to check how his body waited. The pathways from his mind to his body were slowed, frozen. Brain and blood and breath still moved, but nothing else. If she wished, she could keep him there until he starved to death.

Keyretura would never have bothered with such a demonstration. He would simply have told Samnt how much the apprenticeship contract would cost, an amount that would ruin his parents as it had hers, and the conversation would have ended there. Samnt would have been disappointed, his curiosity about magic unfulfilled, but his body and spirit undefiled.

Kinder, perhaps, Maris realized bitterly.

Of course, if Keyretura had been master of the house, Samnt would not have been here at all. Keyretura did nothing for free.

Maris turned back to the book on the table about farm animals that she had been using to teach Samnt. It seemed they would not need it today after all.

"Stand up, Samnt," she said, hearing in her tone the hopelessness she felt.

Finally she forced herself to look at him, at his frozen, rictus grin, letting it make her feel wretched, taking penance for her mistakes. So many mistakes. Then she released him.

He fell forward, slumping over the table, gasping for air. He pushed himself to his feet, the chair's legs scraping against the floor, nearly toppling as he stumbled backwards toward the door.

"Magic," Maris said. "Now you've seen it."

From the look on his face, he would never want to again.

Well, she had given him that, at least.

His eyes darted around the room—the jar on the table, the book, back to her. A look of terror that she recognized.

There were other things that she could have shown him. A spark of light. Pictures drawn in the air as if with smoke. An ant following her finger. But these would only make him want more.

No demonstration was as powerful as the one that touched you deep inside, where, until that very moment, you had never questioned your own control. It was something Keyretura had taught her.

Samnt fumbled behind himself, feeling for the door handle, unwilling to take his eyes off her.

"You may go," Maris said unnecessarily.

He opened the door and turned, running, leaving the door wide open.

It was some time before Maris noticed the cold.

Another storm came and went, another foot of snow

atop the last, as if the sky felt an urgency to produce as much of winter's fruit as it could.

A tenday passed, then another. Absurd as it was, each day she prayed to the nine elements, the snow, and anything else she could think of, that Samnt would not return. As the days went by, that bitter wish seemed fulfilled.

But he was young, and she had given him a shock, so she waited a little longer to be sure.

The snow melted, the rains came, and the roads cleared.

Samnt was not coming back.

At last she collected her clothes, herbs, and most of the books, loaded up her pack, and wondered yet again how it was she kept accumulating things everywhere she went. More things than she could take with her.

She took one last look around the room. On the table sat the jar of applesauce, unopened and untouched since the day Samnt had brought it. She could hardly lift her heavy pack as it was, but she took the jar anyway.

Maris hiked to the coast, wondering if it were time to get a freighter home to Perripur, to her isolated home in the Shentarat Mountains, where she would not need a supply of wood to stay warm, or the help of a farmboy to get through the season.

At a harbor village she found a public house with the encouraging name of the Ill Wind, its facing gouged and dented from years of coastal storms and neglect. Exactly what she needed.

The Ill Wind was as gloomy inside as the name

promised, walls slimy and dark, floor poorly swept and into corners where it had been addressed at all.

Maris rapped the edge of one of her few remaining coins on the table to get the tavernmaster's attention. In moments she had a bowl of stew in front of her. She hadn't needed coin for a while, indeed hadn't worked for it in some time, so to discover she had only a few remaining, while disappointing, was hardly surprising. She'd spent the last of the previous collection on wood and foodstuffs in the mountains.

Even mages must eat.

Ship's passage, food—these things required money.

Mages could always find work in the cities. All she need do was go north to the capital. But the thought took away her appetite. She wanted to be no closer to the horror that was Yarpin than she already was.

Worse than the misery and stink of that city was the chance of running across her own kind. From high cuisine to imported twunta to ship's passage to lucrative contracts, mages went to Yarpin for the same reasons she was now considering doing so. She had no desire to cross paths with most of them.

The one in particular. All the world in which to roam, yet there he had been, at the very Yarpin bookseller where she stood amidst high shelves of books, so absorbed in a heavy tome that she did not even notice him there, watching her. He had spoken, she did not remember what. She dropped the book and fled the city.

He would not be in Yarpin now, not these decades later. He disdained Arunkin. He'd be back in south

Mundar, in his garish mansion of glass and water of which he was so revoltingly proud.

Perhaps she could find work here in this village, wherever here was. If someone had money and the work was not too offensive.

Or, of course, she could find a Perripin-bound vessel and trade on her robes, boarding with Perripin sailors who superstitiously believed that mages brought good weather.

No, she would not sink so low as to pretend to have value merely by wearing the right clothes and breathing, like the Arun aristos, or her own Perripin statesmen. That she could not stomach.

But she could sign on as crew without revealing what she was and work for her passage. The briny winds off the sea tempted her. A roundabout way to get back to Shentarat, to be sure, but there on the ocean, the chaos of undirected human passion was at least limited to the crew, giving her time to sort out the pulls and pushes among them, the wounds and past that each carried, slowly weaving it all together into a serene and settled braid.

She had even achieved a bit of a reputation this way, without anyone knowing she was a mage. When Maris was on board, some sailors said, the crew got along as smoothly as an anknapa's kiss, making for calm voyages that lacked unpleasantness.

She was not quite ready to be away from the land that long. The last time she'd been months with crew it had taken her time to recover, wandering mountains, deep forests, baking deserts. Then she had traveled to the high arid lands of Mirsda, toward the Rift, to see Gallelon.

The long lives of mages and the etherics they handled meant complex, tangled relationships, rarely based on anything as simple as affection. Gallelon was as close as she had to a friend among her kind. He was another sort of sanctuary, though necessarily a brief one; it did not take many months for the two of them to reach the limits of their tolerance for each other.

On their last morning as they lay together, her head nestled on his arm, she ran her dark fingers across his pale body, wondering at his body's ancestry and how he came to have the hint of ginger in the hair on his chest.

"Where do you go next, Marisel?" he had asked her.

"Home, perhaps."

"You should consider the capital. Yarpin would do you good."

"Do you jest? What a foul place."

He chuckled. "Excellent cuisine. Splendid wines. Passable ale. Some of the cleverest of the Iliban. Also some extraordinary collections."

Of books, he meant, knowing her weakness.

He was right about the food. The last time she had eaten in Yarpin, the chef had worked mightily to impress his Perripin guest. Fish from the ocean, goat from the high hills, spices from Perripur, rare ferns from Arapur. It was an artistry of subtle flavors, a symphony of scent and texture. A splendid meal.

Which the bowl in front of her now, here in the Ill Wind, was most certainly not. She couldn't even guess what the greasy lumps floating in a sluggish sea of brown might be, but she was hungry enough to eat anyway. A quick touch of her attention into the unattractive sludge assured her that consuming it would not harm her, so she reached for the spoon, but then hesitated, her hand hovering over the crumb-strewn table. From the cracks in the wood, antennae quested out, followed by the thin segments of a centipede. The creature took a large crumb from the surface in its pincers and slowly retreated to the undertable.

Maris pushed at the creature with her intention to make sure it went in the other direction, but it pleased her to share her table with the locals, as long as they weren't humans. She preferred places like this one for much the same reason she no longer wore black robes: sitting here, eating greasy soup, and sharing her table with insects, she could almost imagine belonging to the world.

Around her sat dour-looking dockhands, grubby in overalls padded against the ocean chill, slumped over cheap drinks, bowls much like her own. The glances they gave her were mere curiosity at a plainly dressed dark-skinned Perripin traveler and nothing more.

She'd worn the black for a time after she had been created, until the looks of hate and fear had become too heavy. It was a bad time for her, newly created and trying to find her way. She had gone to the Shentarat Plains and walked barefoot on the sharp ground until her feet bled. At the edge of the plains where the smooth rock gave way to barren ground and then hopeful grasses, she had stripped the robes off and buried them in the ground to rot.

Simpler clothes, she had discovered, made for a simpler life.

Now, catching the eye of the tavernmaster, she

indicated someone else's drink and that she would have the same. He nodded.

Best of all, though, the Ill Wind had cats. On a high shelf amidst jars and curled atop a pile of burlap bags was a black and white feline, ears twitching in sleep. From a corner, an orange tabby roused itself to stroll into the kitchen. And overhead, against the high windows through which a fog-filled sky shone like a lackluster pearl, was the silhouette of another cat, sitting still as a statue, looking down on the room.

With a finger of intention, Maris reached up to touch him.

Male, a few years old, his feline blood pulsing easily through his lithe, powerful body. He had the glow of recent sex about him, a contented relaxation through the groin, the warmth of hard use across his shoulders, the taste of female nape in his mouth. At her pull, he turned his head to look at her.

Softer than a whisper, she spoke a few words. Sounds more than anything sensible, the words being irrelevant. Her soft vocalizations were an invitation. Did he want to be stroked, she wondered. Perhaps some food, a bit of meat from her stew bowl?

The cat blinked slowly, eyes on her a long moment, then he looked away and began to groom a paw.

She laughed silently. She could not even summon a cat to her side. And people were afraid of mages.

With a thunk the tavernmaster put a ceramic mug in front of her. Glazed deep brown, inside and out—to make the liquid seem darker, she knew from discussions with brewers. As a matter of habit she dropped her focus into the cup to be sure it didn't hold anything she would have to fix once it was in her body. It didn't.

"Something else, ser?" he asked her. A large man, gone well to fat, brevity near surliness.

"A room for the night," she said, putting a falcon on the table. Overpaying, she guessed. He slipped it into a pouch beneath the apron, stained with enough colors to be a clumsy painter's spill.

Then, ambling from foot to foot, he drew himself upright. "We got a room, sure." He looked bemused, as if he couldn't figure out why she was here if she had that much to spend.

It calmed her, his lack of effort to please. Other than money, he wanted nothing from her. Like the cat's disregard, it comforted her.

After he left, a thin figure entered into the room, looked around, came to her table. Blood-shot eyes looked out from behind dark, stringy hair, a face slick with sweat, gender indeterminate.

A Sensitive.

Male, possibly, she thought as he swallowed nervously. She could touch into his body to find out, but it seemed an intrusion and so she refrained.

"Yes?" she asked.

"High One." A deferring dip of the head, breath shallow and short, tone flat. "I have been asked to contact you."

She sighed, lamenting the loss of anonymity this implied. A bit surprised as well: this far from the capital she had not expected to be so quickly recruited.

If mages were a sort of family, Sensitives like the one

in front of her were a distant, disfigured, and disowned relation. They were among the large portion of people who fell below the line to be considered for apprenticeship, yet were also not quite Iliban. Outcast among mages, deviant among Iliban, ostracized by all. She ached a little for him—with no choice about what he was, with no way to become more, his life could not be easy.

He might even be one of the extraordinarily rare Broken, those failed apprentices allowed to live. Unlikely; failure to finish the study was not well-tolerated. She remembered Keyretura dragging her, coughing and retching, from the deep water where she had tried to end her own. Not at all well-tolerated.

Certainly she could ask. *Did you fail the study? Is that why you live in this wretched land that abhors you?*

"How long have you been employed thus?" she asked instead.

He would not meet her eyes. "Since childhood, High One."

"Call me Marisel."

"Yes, High One."

Oh, well.

"I am to ask if you are receptive to a contract."

Of course. It would be some task that only magic could accomplish, that only the very wealthy could afford. A troubled conception to be smoothed. Treasures to be secured in strongboxes that would open only for one specific hand. An impossible decoration high atop some glittering, ostentatious spire.

But nothing as draining as the healing she had given across the countrysides, over and over, for no pay at all.

"A contract with . . . ?"

"It is not given to me to know, High One. May I tell them you are willing to discuss?"

Gallelon had said something about this when they were last together, as he had been repairing a saddle. "Do something other than tend to the endless ocean of suffering Iliban, Maris," he had said as his needle dipped through the hard leather. She suspected he was using magic to help make the holes, and, curious, she tasted the air around the needle, keeping her touch focused so he would not notice. He did anyway, grinning back at her. "Take an expensive contract. Get paid for your work for a change."

And she needed the coin.

"You may," she told the Sensitive. The waif slipped off the chair and sprinted out the door.

Maris drank down the rest of the ale in front of her, which was neither as bad as she had expected nor as good as she'd hoped, and wondered what the contract might be about.

A motion from the high window caught her eyes. A small gray kitten had found its way up onto the thin ledge and was walking toward the tomcat. He had stopped grooming himself as the kitten approached, coming rather closer than she thought prudent. The kitten then sat back on its haunches, intently watching the older male, who gazed out over the assembled humans as if he were alone.

Slowly, as if to test the idea, the kitten raised a paw, reaching toward the older cat.

Foolish creature, Maris thought, strangely absorbed by this drama. A sudden swipe from the big cat and the kitten would fly off the narrow ledge and fall some ten feet or so into the room of tables and chairs. It would probably survive. Perhaps with something broken. A painful lesson.

The elder cat turned a sudden, hard look on the kitten, and the tiny paw froze midair.

"Ser High One?" A whispered voice. A figure tentatively sat across from her.

Another Sensitive? Who had this much money—or desperation—to be so fervently seeking mages so far from the capital?

This one stank of poorly washed clothes, smoke, and cheap rotgut. Her face was thin, the cords in her neck raised. Maris was done being polite; a quick touch into her body told Maris that many substances swam in the woman's blood, that she ate little food, that her kidneys would not serve her much longer.

It tugged at her, this suffering. Sensitives had no choice but to use every means they had to quiet what they could not control. Lacking a mage's training, their lives would be cacophonous with the etherics of the world, that Iliban could not hear.

"Will you speak with my employers?" She spoke in a hoarse whisper. "They have a contract to offer you."

Well, she had already said yes once. "I will."

A quick duck of the head, and the woman slid off the chair and was gone.

Maris returned her attention to the high rafters, to the tomcat and impertinent kitten, to see where the drama stood. But they were both gone. With a disappointed exhale, she returned her attention to her stew, which tasted much better than it looked, and wondered who would show up next.

He arrived the next morning as she sat in the eating room, sipping at a dark and fermented bitter Arun tea, wishing for honey. His gaze swept the room, settled on her.

A tall man, broadshouldered and wearing clothes nearly as anonymous as her own. She dipped her attention into him to find that he was strong, with a large number of scars. A trained soldier, then, though she could have told this from the way he strode across the room to her.

In Perripur the wealthy and powerful did not send soldiers to talk to mages. But here in Arun, the monarchy and military were tightly entwined, explaining the empire's insatiable appetite for land.

What will Arunkin not eat? went the Perripin saying, expecting no answer.

He sat. "High One—" he began.

"Marisel," she said sharply, tired of the game.

"Marisel, then. I won't waste your time. The palace offers you a contract."

"Does it indeed? The red, beating heart of Arun*kel*? Where your king outlaws our very existence?"

At this he tilted his head. "Times change. I intend to see them change further."

Maris exhaled a short laugh, then sobered, considered this, and realized from his words and demeanor that she was talking to someone from the palace.

An intriguing notion, to see altered the near thousand-year tradition of loudly denouncing magic with one side of the mouth while hiring a mage with the other.

"What sort of contract?"

"To give the monarch the benefit of your excellent vision."

The monarch? She sat back, surprised. That the Arun king quietly employed mages when he could persuade them to come close, she knew. Gallelon himself had played that game years ago. He had told her about the king's library one warm night as they sat watching a storm of falling stars. His description had filled her with a kind of lust. She felt it now.

"The library is exquisite, but be careful of the Arunkel monarchy," Gallelon had added. "The snake bites."

Rumor held that the old king was ill. Maris had wondered whether his mages had abandoned him.

Was she being recruited to replace them?

"The old monarch or the new?" she asked.

A faint smile crossed his face. "The new."

In Perripur, state parliaments discussed every issue at length, often until it was far past relevant, producing treaties that covered inches-thick sheaves of papers. The Perripin government did not hesitate to hire elder mages to advise and remove deadlocks. Far less often for their magic, though to have a mage handy meant a show of power. A little like having a swordsman as a servant.

"You wish only my advice, Arunkin? I find that hard to believe."

He spread his hands. "I would be a fool to try to bind you beyond your will. Come to the palace. Let us show you Arunkel hospitality. When we need more than advice, we will ask, and you decide."

"You have a library."

He smiled. "Histories going back to Arunkel's founding and before. Poems from the masters. We have the most extensive collection in the empire. You would be most welcome there."

Hot baths. Good meals.

Books.

A memory of Keyretura's voice: *What are you missing, Marisel?*

"I will not wear the black for you," she said, suddenly annoyed at him, at herself. "I will not be used to put fear into your enemies or set your monarch on the throne. We do no king-making."

At least they weren't supposed to. The council of mages had uncompromising penalties for such actions.

She tasted the quickening of the man's heartbeat, though he hid it well.

"I don't need your help in that regard, Marisel. The princess will be crowned midsummer, or sooner."

Maris's mind, fickle thing, was already in the fabled library, imagining running her fingers across the leather-clad spines of books, velum scrolls, stacks of amardide sheaves. The treasures that must be there. Unique across the world. A sublime opportunity.

The snake bites.

"After your queen is crowned," she said, compromising with the warnings in her head.

He considered her for a moment. "Allow me to put you on retainer until then," he said. "Enough that you can stay wherever you like . . ." With this, his eyes flickered quickly around the room. "And then I will send someone for you, after the coronation."

Maris had already decided, she realized. To see the inside of the palace, the Jewel of the Empire, and browse its library . . . irresistible. The contract obligated her to little.

"So be it," she said.

He held his hand out, palm up. On it was a gold Arunkel souver, king-side showing.

She hesitated. What was she missing?

Hot baths, she reminded herself. Good food.

The library.

She put her hand on top of his, palm down, the gold coin between them.

"Our contract is made," she said. Their hands turned in place, the coin now hers.

After Samnt, she had despaired of caring about anything for some time to come. Now there was something she wanted, and she cherished the thought of it, pushing away the nagging sense that she was, indeed, missing something.

Chapter Fourteen

"He wants his dogs, too, ser," Naulen told Innel.

Easy enough, Innel thought, if that would get them the old king's cooperation in the coronation ceremony.

"And to see his daughter," she added.

That might be harder. Still, Restarn's cooperation was worth a lot to the strength of Cern's rule. It might be worth everything.

He gestured, inviting the small blond slave to sit at a table where a mug of hot wine and a plate of pastries waited. "Have all you like," he said.

She sat where he directed, seeming bewildered, each movement somehow a graceful submission. She touched the cream-filled confections with her fingertips, as if she had never seen such a wondrous thing before.

Enchanting, he thought, wondering how much was pretense. All of it, he suspected, though it was nonetheless compelling. Beyond her value as entertainment, Naulen was proving her worth by regularly relating to him bits of conversation from the old king, who talked a great deal now that he had no one else but his blond slave to listen to him.

Naming names. Innel was gathering a very useful list.

As for Cern, that had turned out to be the work of nearly a tenday, starting with gentle suggestions, outlining his reasoning, gingerly turning her objections into his own supporting arguments. In the end he convinced her to see her father, to even try to be pleasant to him. To take to him the dogs she hated so much.

The king had always held the beasts with voice and will, but Cern had wanted nothing to do with them. Innel knew the king's dichu dogs would fight harness and lead if Cern held the other end, so he had the kennelmaster give them something to make them more compliant.

The coronation, Innel had reminded Cern.

Outside the king's room Cern took the leads of the muzzled dogs from the kennelmaster and went in. Innel waited in the hallway.

When Cern emerged a bell later, she vibrated with pent-up fury. Innel took her to her rooms, signaling Srel to fetch for him the previously arranged-for wines and twunta and infused oils. He spent the next hours in attentive application of the collection.

Day by day, as the coronation date inched closer, Cern became, if possible, even more tightly strung.

The seneschal continued beyond annoying, insisting on extravagant expenditures that would dwarf those of the royal wedding. Again, Innel objected.

"You can have it when you want it, ser Royal Consort, or you can have it for less coin, but you cannot have both. Trust me, ser."

Innel bit down on his objections and again gave way.

If the ceremony happened—if Restarn did his part—if Cern was made queen—it would all be worth it.

It was high summer when the coronation finally began. It took the better part of five days, dawn to midnight, most of it loud and brightly colored, excessive and ostentatious. The spectacle would culminate with the single most important moment, the one in which the old king was to hand his daughter the Anandynar scepter, passed down through the generations, from monarch to monarch.

The object itself was a too-long, slightly dented stiletto encrusted with gems and worked through with various metals, so over-decorated and lightweight that Innel suspected it would break if one tried to use it for anything beyond ceremony.

At least it would not be too heavy for a sick old man. All Restarn would need to do would be to hand the scepter to his daughter. His heir and only progeny.

It seemed simple enough, so Innel worried.

During each day of ceremonies and all-night celebrations leading to the main event, Innel reviewed the seer's words to him that night in Botaros, and the extensive resources he had now put into finding her. It was starting to seem to him as if he were dumping coins into the depths of the ocean for all that his various hires, Tayre most expensively among them, were providing him.

When Cern was queen, he would have more funds. But once he started tapping the royal purse, he would need to be even more discreet. He might even need to tell her, in case this all came to light. Another problem entirely, and for another time.

The final day of the coronation—then the final hour—arrived. The king was carried in his chair to the Great Hall, wrapped in red and black and gold.

It was the first time Restarn had been out of his sickbed in over six months, and he looked startled, eyes too wide, gaze flickering here and there as if not quite certain where he was. Innel felt an edge of alarm. Had the doctor given him too much of the various herbs intended to keep him calm and compliant?

Surely the man would be able, at the very least, to hand Cern the scepter. It was all he needed to do. Such a simple thing. But even after a lifetime of studying the man, trying to read his thoughts through his eyes and turn of mouth, Innel could not tell what was in his mind or what he would do.

"Get his dogs," Innel hissed to Nalas and Srel. They hurried off, returning with the pair of brindled canines.

With one dog on each side of him, their heads in his lap, one licking his hand, the king seemed to calm, something like sense coming back into his eyes. Innel watched him intently.

When the moment finally came, the Great Hall packed with thousands of aristos and eparchs and royals, all falling utterly silent, the old king looked slowly around the room. His gaze settled on Innel. The moment lengthened. Innel looked back at the king, feeling sweat drip down his back.

Finally Restarn looked to his daughter, then handed the long, sharp scepter to her with a casual, almost disgusted look, as if it were an unwashed dinner knife that he was well rid of.

Innel could live with that. It didn't matter now. Cern was queen.

The next morning Cern announced Innel as her new Lord Commander.

Innel sat in his small office as the day went on, receiving visitors, noting those who came—some to ask questions, some to explain past decisions at length, and some to lecture, as in the case of the seneschal—and those who stayed away.

Conspicuously absent was the now-former Lord Commander, whom Innel could well imagine seething as he paced the much larger offices Innel was now entitled to. While Innel thought a military rebellion highly unlikely, he didn't want to inspire one by mishandling the king's older and now more powerful brother, either.

Don't push until you must.

Yes, but when must he?

Among his visitors were Cohort brothers and sisters, even those who had left years ago, all wanting to make sure he would not forget how passionate had been their support for him these many years.

"Put in a good word for me, when the time is right, hmm?" Taba had said, referring to the commander of the navy, whom Innel had yet to speak with.

"No, really, Innel—congratulations. Truly." This from Mulack, pushing toward him an excellent bottle of greened brandy, then eating the rest of the fruit plate Srel had brought, that Innel had barely touched.

"And the mage?" Tok had asked him.

"Under contract," Innel replied. "When things settle, I'll bring her."

Quietly. Tempting as it was, it would be some time yet before he could parade a mage down the hallways without upsetting a significant number of influential aristos with whom he was not yet ready to lock horns.

The Great Houses seemed content to let Innel's Cohort siblings represent their good wishes. Those Houses who had not been fortunate enough to have sons and daughters in the Cohort these last two decades instead sent notes. The pale red amardide envelopes were collecting in piles.

But a good many of the rest, generals and royals, eparchs and bloodlines, would be waiting to see how well Innel handled this powerful beast he had gotten on top of, over the next days. It was one thing to mount up, but another thing, entirely different, to *ride*.

They would be especially watching to see how he handled the former Lord Commander Lason.

He missed his brother's advice keenly now. Opening a drawer, he pulled out a metal arrowhead. It was the only thing he had kept of his brother's.

When he and his brother had been boys, during a particularly foolish game in the woods, Innel had grazed Pohut's leg with an arrow. While Pohut pressed his hand against his leg where blood seeped out around his fingers, he had explained to the younger Innel that injuring your allies is a poor practice. As an apology Innel had broken the arrow, then broken the bow as well. Pohut had called him a fool, mocking him for wasting a valuable weapon, so Innel was surprised to find the arrowhead from that broken arrow among Pohut's few possessions all these years later.

Holding the bit of metal now, he ran his finger lightly over the still-sharp edge and considered the former Lord Commander and what do with him. Innel had every right to pressure the man as hard as he wanted now—he could push Lason past his temper, if he chose. It was an extraordinarily tempting idea.

But it would be a short-term satisfaction. He did not need to push yet. He would give Lason a few days first to spend some rage and digest the meal of having been replaced.

Then go in with all you have.

At times it was difficult to believe Cern had been training to be queen her entire life. As Innel sat at the table of ministers, she was silent, tense, barely answering.

It was almost as if she expected her father to show up at any moment and tell her it had all been a mistake, or a poor joke. He supposed she, too, would need some time to absorb what had happened to her.

But if she appeared weak, then so did Innel.

When in the meeting, her answers proved truly inadequate, a few questioning looks came Innel's way. He returned them ambiguously. He would contact the ministers later, make sure they knew this was temporary.

Much later, when he was alone with Cern, she said, "It's too much, Innel. No one could keep track of all this."

"That's why you have ministers and advisers, Your Grace."

And me. Which he did not say. She had spent a lifetime being told what to think. He had distinguished himself, in part, by refraining from being one of the many who did so.

She wouldn't admit it, but he could see it in her body, and hear it in her tone, that she was scared.

"One step at a time," he told her, gently. "That's how we got here. That's how we will go forward."

"They expect me to be Nials," she said bitterly.

That was true. Many were looking at her for signs of her famous great-grandmother. Another thing he couldn't say to her.

"You will make your own mark. Together we will show them who you are." He put as much warmth and conviction into his voice as he dared, knowing she was used to being told all manner of flattering lies.

At this she laughed a little, but there was no pleasure in it. "Whatever that is," she whispered.

He looked into her dark green eyes. She turned away and went to the chest where she kept her rods and hooks, flats, and now the set of bells that Innel had given her as a wedding present. Eyeing the ceiling from which descended a small chain, she began to put rods between the links, starting another of her in-air creations.

Best to go now and let her comfort herself with this thing she did. But he could not bring himself to let the barely mouthed words go by without comment. Not after all he had done to get them to this moment.

"The *queen*, Cern," he said softly. "You are the queen."

Almost imperceptibly, she shrugged.

✤ ✤ ✤

"That was fast work," Innel said of his reflection in the mirror while Srel adjusted the buttons and collars, cuffs and seams of the red and black uniform. Especially remarkable given that it had come from both Houses Murice and Sartor, working together, in under a tenday.

Innel found his eyes locked on the reflection, especially the gold trim of neckline and arms that marked him as the queen's high command. He touched it wonderingly. "Did you give them my measurements?"

"No, ser," answered Srel.

Well, so, even more impressive: the two Houses had gone to some lengths to tailor a new uniform for Innel. They wanted him pleased and well aware of their support.

And he was. "What do you think?" he asked Nalas.

Nalas gave an approving nod. "You look very much the part, ser."

"The part?" He frowned at his second.

"I only meant, Lord Commander, that—"

Innel waved the explanation away. "Yes, yes. What do they say about me today, Srel?"

"That you are young and inexperienced. That you should give the position to someone else."

Innel snorted. "My age and credentials would never matter. It's my bloodline they object to. Would they rather keep Lason?"

"Some would," he said.

Innel suppressed annoyance at this undecorated answer. That Srel didn't dissemble, his loyalty manifesting in such directness, was one of the reasons Innel kept him close.

Nalas he kept close for his cleverness and speed, though his tongue did sometimes stumble. At least he knew when to keep his mouth shut. Mostly.

Lason had still not shown any indication of being aware that he had been replaced. What, Innel wondered, would the old king have done now, had Lason not been his brother?

There was no question in his mind, and Innel had seen it countless times. Restarn would say a few words, and Lason would vanish. Lason's wife and children would hastily relocate, far from the capital city. Lason would not return. If anyone went looking for him, they would not return either.

A lifetime of watching Restarn's ways had long ago resolved him to do things differently when Cern took the throne.

Nalas handed him his sword belt and sword. It was the first time in his life he'd carried a weapon openly in the palace, let alone a sword. To do otherwise was an implicit questioning of the king's power in his own house, an insult and offense. But now Cern was queen and Innel was Lord Commander. He buckled the weapon on.

They stepped outside his small office, where a tencount of Innel's new guard waited. Nalas and Srel had selected the set of them together. Innel was pleased with the men and women who looked back at him now.

Who looked back at him. Under Lason, direct eye contact was discouraged.

"Look at me," he had told them when he first met with them. "If you're going to protect me, you must know what I look like, where I am, and what I'm doing. Yes?"

Nods all around. A few grins.

Now he made a gesture, telling them to stay where they were, and only took Srel and Nalas with him.

"Is Lason still in my offices?" he asked as he walked.

"Yes, ser," Srel answered.

"Are you certain you don't want a few more than only the two of us, ser?" Nalas asked.

To go with force was to expect to need it. Something his brother used to say.

"I'm certain."

When Innel rounded the corner, Lason's guards, two on each side of the Lord Commander's office doors, shrank a little, looking away. That Innel had only Srel and Nalas with him made this even more remarkable. Innel would later have Srel and Nalas determine whether this cringing was driven by fear or prudence, to see if these four would keep their posts after today.

As he opened the door to the offices, none of them moved to intercept him. Once inside, Nalas and Srel left beyond, he shut the door and dropped the bolt behind him.

Maps covered the walls, hung between a scattering of swords, spears, and slings.

The gray-haired Lason looked up from his desk, his face twisting in fury. Under his hands was an old map Innel recognized. Pre-expansion. Lason was reliving an old victory.

"These are *my* offices," Innel said, cutting off whatever the man might have been about to say. "It's well past time for you to leave."

Lason slammed the flat of his hand hard on the desk.

"You are nowhere near ready to take over this office. You haven't any idea what it means. You are nothing like qualified."

"The queen disagrees."

Lason drew himself upright. "She's barely twenty-five. A child. When the king returns—"

"There was a coronation. Did no one tell you?"

A look of loathing. "The king will recover."

Innel plucked a dagger from the wall, hefted it to see how it balanced, waiting for Lason to object, which he did not. He put it down, walked the periphery of the room. "How old were you when you took this office?"

"Times were different then. She needs my expertise, now more than ever. No one trusts you, Innel."

Innel closed fast on Lason, stopping short of arm's reach. The other man took a startled step backward. "Lason," he said. "Your command is over. Step aside. Grow old in glory."

"I'm not done."

Innel glanced at the map on the desk. The northern expansion, some decades back. The one Innel's father had given his life for.

"You most certainly *are* done. I'll give you until this afternoon's fifth bell to leave my offices."

"The queen will see reason. I'll go to her."

"Don't challenge me. If you do, it will be the last time."

"It's all been so easy for you, hasn't it? Your rise to power. Just one long streak of good luck."

Innel was startled at these words. That anyone could see him as fortunate, in any way, as though he had somehow stumbled his way to where he now stood, was beyond his comprehension.

Lason snorted. "And all because your father managed to get himself killed in battle in some clever way that the king noticed. I assure you that being killed is not at all difficult, boy, and it doesn't matter how clever you are about it, because you're dead. Your father was clumsy."

Innel fought a craving to slam the man to the ground. He was simply not sure, once he started such a thing, that he'd be able to stop.

Bad for appearances, Innel beating the old king's brother. The queen's uncle. It would look as if Cern had married and promoted a man with an unstable temper, and that would do them no good.

But it was tempting. Agonizingly so. He struggled to keep his hands at his side.

"You mutt," Lason spat. "You'll ruin Arunkel, piss on this glorious empire, shit all over everything we've built."

One of the advantages of Restarn's ways, Innel realized, was that this confrontation would never have taken place.

Innel walked to the door, unbolted it. "The fifth bell," he repeated.

"I trained you, Innel. I know what you know. I've seen your mistakes, and I know every one of them. It's disgusting, what you did. We lost one of our best when you slaughtered your brother. Pohut had good sense, and patience. But you—"

Innel shut the door behind him and wondered if Restarn's methods might not have something to recommend them after all.

✢ ✢ ✢

"What else?" Innel asked, keeping his voice low, despite that the two of them were alone in this small cellar room, vegetables and bags stacked high on shelves.

Innel had made sure Rutif was part of the team that delivered fruits and vegetables to the palace. The man had one leg shorter than the other and always stood lopsided, now splaying a hand to lean against the wall as he spoke.

A dockworker from childhood, until a crushing accident had taken most of his foot and ruined his knee, Rutif had a knack for getting people talking, and remembering what they had said, so Innel paid him to sit in the taverns and drink, which the man liked very much.

"Ser. Well—" Rutif drawled, rubbing his head in thought. "They liked the coronation parades. Especially the part with the sweet bread thrown from the carriages, the ones with the royal sigil baked in? They liked that very much." He grinned, a gap-tooth smile.

That had been Innel's idea, which the seneschal had not much cared for, muttering about propriety and expense.

"Tell them it was the queen's idea. What else?"

"Yes, ser Commander. Let me think. Complaints from some of the captains." Rutif scratched the back of his head, examined his fingers as if to see if anything had come off under his nails. "Since His Grace the old king's been so sick, they haven't been getting their full take. Don't like it so much. Whining a lot."

Full take? Innel needed to have a conversation with

the Minister of Accounts. And a look at the ledgers.
Perhaps the ledgers first. "Names?"

"Ahead of you there, Lord Commander," Rutif said,
handing Innel a folded piece of paper that was stained
with what Innel hoped was only food.

"What else?" he asked.

"People saying how things are going to be better under
the new queen. They say she looks like the Grandmother."

She didn't, not a bit, and anyone with a whole nals
could see that, but it was a good rumor anyway. "I like that
one; keep it going. Meet again next week. Now, you can
get back to—" He waved at the stacks of vegetables.

"Oh, and there's a young sergeant, got her drunk the
other night, on about you and your brother. Something
about a hard ride south a couple of years ago."

At this, Innel froze. "Who?"

"Last name on the list, ser."

Innel stepped to the edge of the large sunken tub
where Cern bathed in steaming water. The royal bath was
now Cern's, and the old king was bathed in his own rooms
with a basin.

And yet here Innel was, almost as often as before. One
of the ways in which she was very like her father. Which
he would not say.

A slave boy knelt at the side of the tub, beginning to
work a scented paste into Cern's hair. When it was wet,
Innel could see the hint of mahogany that was
characteristic of the Anandynars. Like embers, he
thought.

"Good afternoon, Your Majesty."

Her mouth twitched at this coming from him, as though she could not quite decide how she felt about it. But Innel knew that his respect soothed her, and soothed she was more reasonable.

She stared out the window at the Houses and city spread below.

"Lason and I have spoken," he said after a moment. "It wasn't a friendly talk. He is refusing to leave my offices."

"Ah. That explains why he demanded to speak to me today."

"And?"

"I am busy."

Innel made a thoughtful sound, not sure if this was loyalty on her part, or avoidance. "Perhaps you should talk to him, my lady. You might persuade him that it is in his best interest to cooperate."

Her shoulders twitched in a shrug that sent ripples across the tub. The blond slave lathering her arm paused, sponge in hand. "You take care of it, Innel."

There was a fine line between her letting him make decisions, and appearing not to rule at all.

"I can hardly send him to survey the roads in the outer provinces, as your father would have done at this obstinacy, much as I might like to. He's your uncle."

Her mouth turned downward. "I will talk to him."

Innel rubbed his chin, fingers still surprised at the naked skin there. Cern didn't like beards, so now everyone shaved. Those who did not were watched closely, in the Yarpin style, by the many who did.

"I've been talking to some of the captains about the rails to the north," he said. It had been a challenge to find any who would confide in him about what was going on out there.

The slave poured water slowly and carefully over Cern's head. Innel could see the effort involved as the slave boy poured with great attention to avoid her eyes. It must have been especially challenging when she nodded, as she did now.

"Good," she said, distracted.

"There's widespread corruption. Transporting goods via rail, to and from the mining villages. Without House sanction or royal accommodation."

A second slave was tilting a bowl into the bathwater of dried flowers and scented herbs. Cern raised two fingers, and the slave froze in mid-tilt. Two more leaves escaped, fluttering down to the water.

"I suppose this has been going on for a while?"

That there were black-market arrangements up and down the Great Road and throughout the city, they both knew. How many, and how far it went, how much it was costing the crown, they had not. To grab hold of it, they would have to unravel the tangled knots that made up Restarn's web of unwritten arrangements.

"Yes. It will take a while to sort out." Some knots were better sliced across, but Cern's rule was yet too young to take such abrupt action.

"I have sufficient things to take my attention," she said. "Kelerre wants us to pay for repairs to their port, did you know that?"

"I had heard something about it, yes."

In truth, he had been up late the night before, studying years' worth of correspondence and trade agreements between the crown and the nominally Perripin city of Kelerre.

"The ministers demand I approve everything. Perripin trade agreements, currency exchange contracts, shipping schedules . . ." She trailed off, raising and lowering a foot, making small waves against the side of the tub. "Surely you can take care of this."

"Yes, of course, my lady."

The slave rinsed Cern's hair, and the other dried her head. It seemed a good time to leave, now that they had reached an accord of sorts. Perhaps the other subject could wait. He could do what he needed to do without telling her at all, but if it came to light and she did not know—

"However," he said, sitting by the edge of the tub, "to find the corruption and fix it, I must hire someone with . . . exceptionally good vision."

She knocked the boy's hands away from her head. "Out. All of you." Slaves, servants, guards—all but Innel left the room at a near run. She gave him a look. "You can't mean what I think you mean."

"I do."

"We do not do this."

Innel knew how far from the truth this was, and again wondered how she could know so little about how her father conducted business.

"That is not quite the case," he said mildly. "What we face is beyond simple graft and chit-bribes. Our soldiers are soliciting coin from towns to ignore taxation and Charter violations. The crown is losing revenue. And reputation."

"So root out the corrupt ones and send them to

Execution Square." She waved a hand. "You are now in charge of executions. Make it right, Innel."

"Cern, we need—"

"The laws exist for good reason."

He motioned to the wide expanse of window. "Do you really think House Glass made this? You promoted me to Lord Commander because you trust me to do the necessary work. This is necessary."

"You've seen the Shentarat plains, Innel. A wasteland. Nothing lives there now. Magic did that."

"A mage did that. Magic does not act by itself."

"They bring death."

"The same can be said of our army."

"They are like raccoons. Once they learn you will feed them, you can't get rid of them."

She had no idea how hard they truly were to come by, nor did he plan to tell her. "They sell their services like any merchant. Even mages need to eat."

"They bring ill-fortune. Stone that rots, babies born dead, the melting plague."

If he were to be more than Cern's consort, he must be able to hold his own with her. He took a deliberate, insulting tone. "Is that what your father told you?"

Her lips thinned, edges down. She looked away a moment, silent and angry. For a long moment her expression did not change, and Innel wondered if his rise to power might have found its ceiling.

"No mages, Innel."

Innel clenched his fist, tapped it lightly to the tile at his feet, and considered. He had worked hard for her throne, perhaps harder than she had. He knew he needed her; without her he was only a mutt, rising above his station. Perhaps she needed him, too, or perhaps she could do without him if she must.

Most important was what she believed. It was time to find out.

He shifted onto his knees then touched his head on the tile toward her, then did it twice more.

"Your Majesty," he said, "I will need you to scribe your commands for me, so that I miss none of them."

"What? Get up."

"A list of what I may and may not do," he said, head still down.

She snorted. "No mages, Innel. Do whatever else you like."

"Next week, my lady," he said, lifting his head and meeting her gaze, "it will be no mages and no elk-horn buttons. The week after perhaps no horses with spotted manes. Then—no yellow flowers. After that—"

"You mock my laws."

"Your father's laws. Perhaps you should put me in charge of the kitchens instead of the army."

"You are starting to annoy me."

If he annoyed her enough, she could divorce him. Quite easily, as her seneschal had pointed out. Or she could have him sent to the towers without fingers, as her grandmother had done with one of her consorts who had presumed too much.

If she were truly vexed, she could have him torn to pieces in Execution Square, relieving him of his oversight of that particular job. That would be an irony many would appreciate.

He was betting she was too smart for that. Betting rather a lot.

"Then, my lady," he said with a calmness he didn't feel, "give the job to someone else. Someone you trust to make such decisions."

"No mages," she said, slowly, forcefully.

"I'm sure Lason would take back his command if you offered it to him."

"Cold crack your balls." She slammed her hand against the side of the tub. "Do as I say."

Their gazes locked.

"I am your queen."

"Without question, ma'am."

"You will obey me."

"You've given me conflicting orders."

"No mages. Isn't that simple enough?"

She was not yielding. *Don't push until you must. And then go in with all you have.*

"Perhaps you should break the marriage, my queen."

A step too far, he judged from her sudden change of expression. She was furious now, eyes wide, fists tight.

Innel suppressed a wince; worse yet would be to retreat. So with effort, he stayed silent, letting his last words echo.

"I'll have you in charge of the kitchens first," she said at last.

"I am reassured," he said, dryly, to hide how reassured he really was. He sat back on the tiles, letting himself softly exhale. "The Houses use mages, Cern. We must have at least the advantages they do."

She gritted her teeth, splashed the water a little. "Be

sure your hire is a citizen of the empire. One who pays taxes."

Unlikely, given the laws about practicing magic.

But, he realized, she had just said yes.

"I thought it prudent to find one from outside Yarpin, outside Arunkel. Someone without obligations or ties here."

Her expression bordered on the incredulous. "You have already done this thing."

He hesitated, then wished he hadn't. "Yes."

"You broke the laws."

"Your father's laws, which he himself broke regularly. *Your* laws now, my queen."

"When did you—" She broke off, stared at him with hard, green eyes. "How long have you been planning this?"

He wondered what answer would pacify her most, decided to risk the truth. "A year and some, my lady."

To his surprise, she smiled. "When my father still ruled. You planned ahead, for me. I like that." Then the smile turned brittle. "But don't hide things from me. If there's a mage in my palace, I want to know about it. No secrets from me, Innel, the way you did with him."

"No secrets."

Cern moved through the water to come close to him at the edge of the tub, then reached up and grabbed the back of his head with her wet hand, slowly pulling him close. She kissed him for long moments.

This he had not expected. For a fair number of moments afterward she continued to surprise him.

When Innel returned at the fifth bell, Lason left,

finally and gracelessly, storming out of the office along with an entourage of his remaining loyal retainers. They left with the best of the old king's travel set. "Stole" might be the more accurate word, but it was unclear what the legal status of the king's royal horses was now that Cern was queen. From there the group had headed north, Innel was told, but to where no one knew.

It had better not be to cause trouble at the mines. He instructed Srel to send word to his people there to report back anything that sounded like Lason's work.

Finally the Lord Commander's office was Innel's.

He signalled Srel, who gestured to the many servants who were unpacking his things onto the mantles, making the final touches Innel wanted—new maps on the walls, weapons on racks so they were more accessible than ornamental—to stop. They streamed out the door, leaving only the young, uniformed woman who had just arrived. She stood arrow-straight, staring at nothing.

When the two of them were alone, he spoke. "Identify yourself," he said

"Vevan sev Arunkel, Lord Commander."

"Sit down."

Startled at this, she obeyed, taking the chair across from him. The manner in which people sat in chairs told Innel a great deal about them, soldiers especially. They were accustomed to being watched when they stood; sitting was what they did off-duty, drinking or eating, their defenses lowered.

"You have a lover," he said. "Bintal."

Her eyes widened. She stuttered in her reply. "Yes, Lord Commander."

"He spoke to you before you left Yarpin on campaign last year. About me and my brother, Pohut sev Restarn. Is that so?" He was guessing. Satisfyingly, the blood drained from her face and her stark expression made reply unnecessary. "What was said?"

"Some sort of plan," she said, her voice low. "Against you. By Lieutenant Pohut."

"Give me details, Sergeant."

"The lieutenant was asking someone questions."

"Who? Where?"

"In the mountains south? Some fortune-teller." She laughed a little, uneasily.

Innel's stomach clenched. "Who did you tell this to?"

"No one, ser."

"No one? Not one person in your company?"

"No, Lord Commander."

He leaned forward. "No talk about the lieutenant's funeral? No rumors about how he might have been killed? No late-night speculations about the new Lord Commander? I find this hard to believe. I can have you interviewed at length by someone who can tell the truth of your words if I have any doubt about your sincerity. You are far better off telling me. Now."

Her face went even paler, her voice barely a whisper. "I might have said something, Lord Commander. In jest. Once."

"How many might have heard you, had you said this something?"

Her mouth opened and closed and then again. "We were out. Drinking and smoking, Lord Commander. Truly, I don't recall."

She was too easy to read: she wanted anything but to recall.

"Guess," he urged.

"A tencount, perhaps, my lord."

"Just one?"

She swallowed. Her mouth fished open again. "Perhaps a few more than that."

There it was, then: a rumor based in fact, with plenty of time for it to have found life across the public houses of the cities and the fire pits of the camps. It would sound like typical aristo dalliance and excess, consulting a fortune-teller, but Pohut's death might give it more credence than he could afford.

Innel would start his own rumors to combat it, of course, far more outrageous. Pigs that snorted predictions, dogs that burped tomorrow's weather. This would help confuse anyone looking for a kernel of truth. He hoped.

The woman before him was slumped in her chair, face a mask of despair, gaze on the floor.

"You'll want to go back to your company," he said after a moment's consideration.

"Yes, ser," she said, her tone flat.

She did not expect to survive this interview. In Restarn and Lason's time, she might not have. Might have quietly disappeared, family and friends acting as if she had never existed at all. No funeral, no gift ceremony, no body. Innel had seen it countless times.

"I can't let you go back," he said, letting that sink in, watching her face collapse, giving her another moment to consider her mortality. "So I will post you here, on the palace grounds. Something modest, perhaps the cavalry inventory staff. Would you like that?"

She blinked a few times, doubt warring with hope, then nodded with fragile enthusiasm.

"You can keep seeing Bintal; indeed, I encourage it. But you will tell me anything that is said around you, about me or anyone in my family. My own people will be feeding you some of those rumors, just to keep you in practice. Understand?"

"Lord Commander, thank you, I—"

He waved it away. "You'll tell me you're loyal, that you owe me your life." He leaned forward, caught her gaze. "I advise you to make sure I never question having let you keep it. Yes?"

"Yes, Lord Commander."

Getting away from the palace was harder than it had ever been, taking hours to arrange. Again he made his way to the toilet room of the Frosted Rose.

"Where in the hells have you been?" Innel demanded of the vent overhead.

"Finding your girl, Lord Commander."

"And?"

"You were right: she sees the future."

"You have her?"

"No. And I will need more funds to continue my search."

Innel's fist trembled as he touched white knuckles to the wall of the small toilet room. Softly. "Hiring you, first and most expensively, was intended to resolve this matter quickly. Yet I see no resolution."

"Commander, this no simple girl. In each moment she knew what I was about to do next. A seer. Truly, this is extraordinary."

"It took you a year to come to the conclusion that I was right? And you are supposed to be the best?"

"Few escape me, even once. I doubt anyone will get closer to her than I have."

"We can celebrate that at least," Innel said, "because rumors of the girl are now everywhere. Let's hope your competition is even less competent than you are."

"Lord Commander, I urge you to allow me to kill her. She will be far easier to control when she is dead."

"Absolutely not. I need her alive." Cern's rule was yet weak, his own command under hers consequently tenuous. Innel needed the girl's answers far more than he needed her silence. "So you come to me with nothing?"

"Not quite. I have some items that once belonged to her. A small seashell, some blue cloth. You may wish to ask your mage about these."

His mage. Tayre was surely guessing. That Innel had every intention of doing just this as soon as he could bring Marisel dua Mage to the palace did not change the fact that it was still against both law and custom. He wondered if he should pretend to be offended for the sake of appearances. "Explain your meaning."

"You are an insightful man, not given to common superstitions during your uncommon rise." Mutt to Royal Consort to Lord Commander, he meant. Innel frowned a little at this, wondering if Tayre was flattering him. "You would have a mage."

Innel made a noncommittal sound.

"Though," Tayre continued, "I suspect the girl's ability to anticipate danger will work equally well against magical forces."

"Is that intended to reassure me?"

"If you want reassurance, ser, you'll find it for far less coin than what you've been paying me. But coin is the least of your costs if someone else finds her first."

The very thought that kept Innel awake at night. "This is neither news nor does it put her in my hands. If you cannot find her—"

"I know where she is."

"What? Why didn't you say that before?"

"Because finding her is not the problem."

Again his hand was clenched into a fist. "And yet it seems to have thwarted you repeatedly."

"Lord Commander, your other hires—have any of them reported finding her?" He paused. "Or reported finding me?"

"No," he admitted.

"I've threatened her life twice. If any of your other hounds had done that much, I doubt you would be here."

"Damn this. Can you apprehend her or not?"

"Her foresight has limitations or she wouldn't be fleeing from me in the first place. I will keep pursuing, but I can offer no promises."

Unlike the others Innel had hired, all of whom had been quite willing to give promises. That it would be easily accomplished. That they would have the girl to him shortly.

"She is still on the run," Tayre said. "No one else has her, either."

"Someone will."

A doubtful sound. "Perhaps."

So many ways to use the girl if he could only get his hands on her. He thought of the mountain regions, where towns thought taxes and House Charters didn't apply to them, or the Greater and Lesser Houses and their squabbles. Trade boats that had been lost in bad weather, costing the crown astonishing amounts. The shifting metals markets.

For whoever held her, the potential advantages were boundless. He exhaled in a long stream.

"If capture is not possible . . ." It would be a great shame to lose her. But far worse to let someone else have her. "Bring me her head."

"A prudent decision, Lord Commander. And the woman and the boy?"

For all Innel knew, the girl's exceptional ability ran in the family. It made no sense to remove the girl and leave alive two other potential and similar threats. It was time to finish this.

"Yes. If you cannot capture, kill them. All of them."

Chapter Fifteen

At the meal, Amarta looked for Darad, but he had slipped out some time ago, to where she did not know. Without even signing good-bye to her.

There had been a conversation the previous evening between the handful of them, the subject turning to the upcoming trip. Someone had pointed out that she and Dirina already looked like Arunkin, because they *were* Arunkin, and why, he wondered, couldn't *they* be sent on the out-trips instead of sending Emendi?

"That's a dumb idea," Darad had said. "They don't know what we need to get."

"So give them a list. They can read, can't they?"

"Not really," Amarta admitted.

"Why not?" asked a younger boy.

"I just never had to learn, I guess."

"I mean why can't you go on these trips instead of us?"

Another girl spoke up. "We risk our lives on the trips. It's no risk for you at all."

Amarta could not—would not—tell her how wrong

she was. But at this Nidem and Darad exchanged quick looks, making Amarta wonder how much they suspected about why she and Dirina and Pas were in Kusan in the first place.

"No," Nidem said adamantly. She gave Amarta a brief, unfriendly stare. "I've worked hard for my place in the out-trip. She hasn't done anything to earn it at all."

Amarta nodded her agreement at this, feeling both relief and gratitude to Nidem. Darad gave her a thoughtful, unreadable look.

Which was why, now, with him gone early from the meal, she worried that she had said or done something he didn't like.

The meal was finishing and Emendi were leaving. Some to the baths, some to the nursery, some to the music room, some to the coops.

Nidem caught her eye from the door. *Come with*, she signed.

Clean-up duty, Amarta signed back with one hand, holding a stack of bowls with the other, hoping she was properly conveying with the abruptness of her movements the frustration she felt at being stuck here. She desperately wanted to get Nidem alone so she could ask her where Darad had gone.

But no, it was beyond important that they be reliable here. To be worth the sanctuary and food the Emendi generously gave them.

Washroom Three, Nidem signed back. *Come soon.*

Maybe she could get Dirina to take her clean-up duty, she thought, looking for her sister. She was with Kosal, a young man she had been spending a lot of time with.

Judging by her happy look, her sister wouldn't be in a mood to wash dishes for Amarta.

Again Kosal was trying to teach Dirina hand signs by holding her hand and moving her fingers. It seemed to Amarta that her sister was taking a very long time to learn. But no real mystery there; Dirina grinned foolishly as he slowly manipulated her fingers.

It was good that they were making friends among the Emendi. Still, many Emendi would not even speak to them, despite how diligently she and Dirina had worked these last months to find a place here in Kusan, to make themselves valuable and trusted to the suspicious Emendi.

After the Teva left, Nidem had warmed to Amarta, joking that it was best to keep enemies as close as possible. At Amarta's hurt look, Nidem had rolled her eyes and cuffed her lightly. *Joking*, she signed.

Not long after, Nidem had taken Amarta on a night-rabbit hunt, the two of them standing well to the back of the group of adults who released the hunting ferrets to find and flush the rabbit warrens, where two of the hugest ferrets Amarta had seen waited. As the rabbits exited their holes, the ferrets clamped onto their necks, rolling hard to break them.

The rabbit stew had been delicious.

When conversation after that meal turned to Arun slavers, Nidem defended them, explaining adamantly that they had never owned slaves. Never even been to Munasee, let alone Yarpin.

Now Nidem flashed her a final sign: *Hurry!* and left the eating hall.

Amarta took dirty plates to the kitchen, passing by Dirina laughing with Kosal. She felt oddly uneasy. At the waterway where she soaped dishes beside others she wondered if it were premonition.

She had not looked for the visions these last months, nor had they come to her unbidden. She was not pushing them away—she had learned not to do that from her escape in the Nesmar forest—but also she did not ask for them.

No, she decided after a time, her unease did not have the feel of that other sort of knowing, the future scratching like tiny beetles in the back of her head, slipping in through the cracks. It was more that time was passing, and they were some kind of happy here. The happier they were, the more it hurt to leave.

And surely they would have to leave.

But if not vision, then perhaps it was not even true. Nothing bad had happened. The hunter had not found them. No one had suffered from her visions.

Yet.

As soon as she felt she could leave the kitchen, she grabbed a lantern and ran to the washroom two levels down. There a crowd had gathered at the far end of the room, by the waterway. Nidem saw her and motioned her over, leading her close in. On the floor lay a boy, his head tilted back in one of the basins, Astru and another man kneeling over him.

"What—" Amarta whispered, but Nidem hushed her with hand squeezes.

The boy grinned at her, and with a shock she realized it was Darad, his hair dyed black.

"He goes on the out-trip next month," Nidem said.

"This is the first time for the dye, to test his hair to see how it takes. So—a ceremony, you see. He is more an adult today than yesterday."

Was that pride in Nidem's voice? Amarta looked at the other girl, and decided it was.

That the Emendi studied for this, she knew, but she hadn't really understood how much it meant to them, this opportunity to leave Kusan for the world outside, even for a few days.

Darad sat up. The men surrounding him toweled his hair dry with a cloth already darkly stained.

"Enough," said Astru, waving at the various watchers standing around. "The rest is for Darad only."

Out in the corridor Nidem's eyes were wide and bright, her look at Amarta intense. "I will go in the next out-group. The month after."

"If you do well in the exams," the elder Vatti said, standing nearby, running her hands through Nidem's hair, inspecting it.

"Your tests are harder than Astru's," Nidem said. "That's not fair."

"Fair is what you take," Vatti said. "You'll be glad of the extra study if you ever get caught."

"Why?" Amarta asked.

"Because what Arunkin do to blond girls they do not do to blond boys," Vatti said.

"None of us have been caught out in years," Nidem said. "A decade and more. Maybe we need less preparation for a few days outside to the market than you think."

At this Vatti said nothing, but she signed, once, sharply, a sign that Amarta didn't know, and walked away.

Nidem lost her smile.

"What?" Amarta asked her when Vatti had gone. "What did that mean?"

Nidem shook her head.

"Come on, tell me."

Nidem looked subdued as her eyes traced around the empty hall and back to Amarta.

"It is the sign for 'slave.'"

"You didn't recognize me," Darad said to her.

"No, not at first."

"I'm going on the out-trip next month. I look like Arunkin now, don't I?"

"Not your blue eyes."

"We look down," he said. "Part of the training. No one will notice. You worry too much."

"Be careful," she said, now suddenly truly worried.

He laughed. "I'll be fine."

Would he? She tried to foresee the out-trip to the market and back. Would Darad be sound through all that, and return unharmed?

"When were you last up in the gardens?" he asked. Without waiting for an answer he took her hand, pulling her along to the stairs and up the levels. A black and white ferret followed them curiously. Amarta didn't much like going outside, despite being encouraged to see the sun regularly, despite how hidden the gardens were, nestled among high rocks. It reminded her that there was a world beyond Kusan. A world in which she was not safe.

"It's spring," he said. "You have to, now."

"What? No, I don't."

"Yes, you do. And now that I have dark hair, you can't argue with me."

At this she laughed. "Watch me argue with you."

"I will, and closely. Okay, you can argue, but I'll win." At that he stopped suddenly, putting the lantern behind himself while he pulled her close with the other hand. Before she quite realized it, he had kissed her on the lips. She felt herself warm all over.

"See? I'm winning the argument already," he said, pulling her along to the gardens as if nothing unusual had happened. "Up we go, to see the sun."

The kiss had left her wordless. At the end of the tunnel, the garden Keeper, a tall, slender man with a blond beard, nodded his permission to them to go out. The ferret following them jumped into his lap.

The two of them stepped outside, standing and blinking in the bright day. In the small, flat garden, tiny green seedlings poked up. They walked the small path under the blue sky and overhead sun.

Emendi caution told her she was safe here, that she would not be seen. But she felt exposed.

"Look at my hair, Amarta. Look closely. Can you tell?"

He looked as if he had always had dark hair. Even his eyebrows had been dyed.

"No, but—"

He brought himself very close to her. For a moment she thought he might kiss her again. His blue eyes were on hers, searching. She felt herself warm again.

"Where did you come from, Amarta?" he asked. "And will you go back there?"

"No, no. This is our home now."

He stroked her face with his fingertips, the touch sending chills down her spine. She wanted him to never stop. "But your eyes," she finished.

He laughed lightly and petted her head slowly. It was the most marvelous sensation she'd ever felt.

"You worry so much. Trust me, we know what we're doing. We've been doing this a very long time. Truly, I will be fine."

He was right, she decided at last. As the days and weeks leading up to him leaving on the out-trip went by, she looked into the future as often as she could. There was something odd coming, something to do with Darad, but it was after he got back. He would return safe and sound. She was reassured.

Amarta could give every one of their kisses a name. "First kiss" or "washroom kiss" or "the tossing-ferrets-joke kiss." Sometimes she named them for what he said before or after. A simple, "Hey, dark-hair" or "There, I think you won that argument after all," or "You taste sweet."

When she was not sneaking off somewhere alone with him, she replayed every word he said. She felt as if she were floating. While she ached to tell someone, she knew it would not be Dirina, who, she was somehow sure, would not quite approve, despite that Amarta was pretty certain she was doing something similar when she snuck off in the night with Kosal.

Nidem, though, she might tell. She wasn't sure she would approve, so for a time she stayed silent, but finally she could bear it no longer and whispered to the girl all that had happened, and how she felt. Nidem seemed uncertain for a moment, then nodded.

"It is good that you keep it secret, though," she said. "Some would not be so happy to see Emendi and Arunkin close. I am pleased for your joy, Ama."

Maybe, Amarta thought, this really was their home now.

The day of the out-trip arrived. Amarta went to see them off at the staging area, the same entranceway through which they had first come with the Teva, which she now knew had stables to one side and another huge room for wagons off to the other.

A tencount of Emendi loaded barrels and sacks onto the wagon, then water and food for the three days out and back. Astru and Vatti stood by, directing.

Darad came to her and took her hand, drawing her close. Then, despite all those standing near and watching, he kissed her again, longer than ever before, as if to make a point. As he drew back, Astru and Vatti looked on with unreadable expressions.

Well, it was no secret now.

Then, with one last look at her, he said, "I'll be back for more." He squeezed her hand one last time and smiled.

The huge stones were rolled back from the cave entrance and the wagons set out into the sunlight, carthorse hitched. From the front of the wagon, Darad waved at her as they went.

A handful of days. Practically no time at all. She was not worried; vision had told her he would come back whole. She waved back.

❖ ❖ ❖

Some seven days later, right on schedule, Darad came back. The group was well, returning with sacks of grain, dried fruits, seeds and nuts, bolts of burlap. Even some casks of wine. There were celebrations that night.

But something had changed. From the moment he returned, Darad acted as if the last kiss and all the kisses before had never occurred. She tried to catch him alone, to ask him what had happened, but somehow he was always busy, always walking away or talking to someone else. The next day and the next she tried again.

In despair she went to Nidem.

"He doesn't want to talk to you," Nidem told her.

Her stomach went leaden. "But why not?"

"I don't know," she said. "He won't tell me." Seeing Amarta's expression, she did not even make it into a joke.

"Did someone tell him not to? Because I'm not Emendi?"

"Maybe that," Nidem said, nodding slowly. "But just as likely it is that he is fickle."

"But . . ." He had said things to her, things that did not go away so fast. "I said or did something to upset him, perhaps?" Her throat hurt. Her chest was tight.

"He went out into the world, Ama. It is not easy for us to do that, to be in the day, all day. To see the freedom your kind has so easily, that we can never have. Sometimes it changes us. Perhaps it changed him."

"That much? I don't believe it."

Surprising Amarta, Nidem took her in a hug and held her a long moment, then pulled back to look into her eyes. "You are not the first to be bruised by Darad's changing affections. He is a fickle boy. Someday he will be a fickle man. Be glad you discovered so early, so easily."

It didn't feel easy at all. She shook her head wordlessly.

"It will get better in time, Ama. Your heart will heal. Trust me on this."

She did not believe it. She felt ripped apart.

Darad's inexplicable cold distance continued. Finally she gave up trying to reach him, throwing herself into all the work that was possible to do in Kusan, from sewing to cleaning to leatherwork. The harder the work, the more demanding, the more she preferred it. She even volunteered to go to the bat caves to collect guano, a job always in need of doing.

Be useful, she told herself. Busy enough to keep away the painful thoughts.

One night she woke crying, and realized that the ache she felt for her dead parents, for leaving Enana and her sons, and the tearing pain she now felt for Darad were all kin to each other.

It had not occurred to her before that she could lose someone and still have them be so close by.

At meals Darad sat with another group, no longer inviting her to his table, no longer coming to hers. His hands flew with humor, his silent laugh and smile tugging at her emotions even now, just watching him. It felt as she imagined a knife through her chest must feel.

She expected Nidem and the others she had befriended to sit with him, and they did, clustering tightly around him as they had before. Like moths to a lantern, how he drew people to him, making the world bright and full of warmth.

But only when the light was on you. Now that it was not, she felt a desolate chill.

A few days later at the meal, to her surprise, Nidem sat down next to her.

Fickle as a child, Nidem signed, gesturing toward Darad.

Amarta's spirits rose.

You are no child. she signed back enthusiastically. *Nor fickle.*

Friends last longer than pretty boys, Nidem quipped. They laughed silently together.

Across the room, Darad's gaze flickered to them, then away again when she looked back.

Good. Let him wonder what they were saying about him. Let him wonder where his favorite cousin had gone to.

To her continued surprise, Nidem sat with her again the next day, and the next, then began bringing her along to gatherings after meals.

When Amarta saw Darad, as she must now and then, it still hurt, but perhaps a little less today than yesterday. He spoke to her occasionally, when he had to, a word or two, but it was cool and told her nothing.

Whatever she had done to push him away remained a mystery.

Bit by bit she felt herself heal. Nidem was right, though it seemed to Amarta that the girl's companionship had helped make the prediction true.

Dirina, on the other hand, shone like a buttercup in the sun in the constant company of Kosal. Pas, too, was happily learning words and signs, charming the Emendi with his fast grin and sweet disposition.

Truly, they could not complain. They were warm. They had more than enough to eat. They slept on beds. One fickle boy did not change that.

Most of all, they were safe.

Or so she told herself, firmly and repeatedly, when she woke from snatches of dreams of fire and smoke, keening cries from the dark recesses of tunnels. Only dreams, she told herself, again and again, and nearly believed it. Until the day the flashes came to her when she was awake.

Arunkin soldiers, torches in hand, striding the corridors of Kusan.

No, that was impossible. Kusan had held fast and hidden for centuries. What could change that?

She knew the answer: she could change that. As she had changed the lives of others.

Hands grabbed the Emendi by hair and arms, dragged them up the levels, out into the sunlight.

No, no, no. It could not be.

She stood by the door to the gardens. The keeper nodded his permission for her to go out. There in the sunlight, blinking at the brightness, pushing away the memory of the last time she was here with Darad, she tried to think.

Around her small green plants were bright and tall, red and yellow buds starting to swell.

Amarta, do not bring it here.

She closed her eyes, the sun hot and red through her

eyelids, and pushed herself to follow the trail of the horrific images.

Outside Kusan, soldiers hauled weeping Emendi into wagons. One grabbed at Ksava's long, ropy hair. Another plucked strands from her baby's head. They laughed, holding Ksava, pulling her baby away. Ksava howled. The baby wailed.

Amarta bent over the seedlings, forehead to the ground, sobbing.

"No, no! Not to crush the seedlings!" The keeper knelt down next to her, lifting her hands and head gently off the young plants. He looked into her eyes. "Perhaps you've had enough sun for now."

Wordlessly she nodded and went back inside to the dark halls.

Certainty settled inside her: Kusan would be invaded. If she did not do something, the Emendi would all be made into slaves.

She took her lantern and descended the stairs, one level and then the next, down the full nine levels, to the opening of the caverns where Darad had so long ago warned her to never go alone, where Nidem had taken her to watch the rabbit hunt. For a time she sat at the edge of the opening to the cavern, listening to the sounds of the night forest, owls calling, rodents scrabbling, and distant sounds that might be brush trod by huge nightswine.

If she climbed down the rope ladder and walked into the deepest part of the forest, where the nightswine ran, if she gave herself over to them to rend and tear and eat, would Kusan then be safe? If she were the cause of the trouble, could she save Kusan with her life?

The truth was that she did not want to die to save Kusan, not even if it were the only way.

But if it were . . . ?

Perhaps they could leave, she and Dirina and Pas. Let the city fall, if fall it must. Knowing the threat existed, knowing this horror was coming, did that make her responsible for fixing it?

Do not bring it here.

I won't. I promise.

But maybe the invasion wasn't about her at all. Maybe the Arunkin soldiers had been coming all along, and she being here was only a coincidence.

She knew better. It was her doing. All her denial would not change that.

Brave. She must be brave.

She turned her thoughts to the night forest, imagining her own death. Would it save the city?

She put the question in her mind but held the answer firmly at bay while she filled out the image of what it would be like to go step by step into the vast caverns, down into the night forest with the tall, black trees and their spindly, pale leaves, the white lichen dripping down in thick strands. To call loudly in the dark for the nightswine to come.

To let them come. To stand as they ran at her. To die wretchedly. Painfully. Alone.

Because if she were not truly willing, there was no point to asking the future for an answer. That was what children did: ask questions they did not really want answers to, make grand gestures that were only for show.

Make promises they wouldn't keep.

When she was as sure as she could be that she would do this awful thing if the answer were yes—when her breath came hard, heart pounded, and she was as sickened by her imaginings of her own violent death as she could make herself be—she threw the question into that place inside her where the future breathed back.

The answer, when it came, sent a wave of relief through her, followed in equal measure by shame. She gulped air.

No. Her death would not prevent the invasion. It would happen anyway.

She would not have to die.

But—Kusan. She had brought disaster to the city. Could she somehow prevent it?

Putting the lamp on the ground beside her at the edge of the cavern she thought of Jolon, his map in the dirt. With her fingers began to draw. She would not, she promised herself, leave here, not until she had a plan to keep safe the many Emendi who had sheltered them when they needed it most. For hours she sat there, making sketches.

By the time she climbed back up the stairs, she was hungrier than she had been in some time, but it felt good. It felt right.

She went to the kitchens.

Then she went to Dirina.

"No," Dirina said.

"We must collect food, all this month and next. Hide it for the trip. Then, before the night of the following full moon—"

"No!"

"—when everyone is asleep—I think I will know the time when it comes. I hope so. Then we—"

"Be silent. Your words are wrong." Dirina said, and Amarta could hear the pain and fear twisted through her anger. "We are safe here. This is Kusan. Secure for a thousand years. It will not fall."

"He tracks us here, even now."

"You can't know that. Nothing can be seen from outside Kusan. There are more protections and precautions here than you know. This time you are wrong."

"Diri, he will find the city. He will come with an army."

"An army! What grand things you foresee," Dirina said harshly. "How is he to afford such a thing, this army?"

"The wealth of slaves," Amarta breathed, hating the words she was saying.

"What a child you are to imagine such things."

Amarta dropped her gaze to her feet. Her turnshoes were uneven where she had resewn them to make them a little larger for her growing feet.

Growing feet did not mean adulthood, did not mean understanding. If her own sister doubted her, the one person who understood her, who knew what she was, then maybe she really was wrong. "Diri, I—"

Dirina's eyes narrowed. "You are not privy to all the elders' plans, Amarta. Even if there is an attack, Kusan knows how to withstand such things. We go deep. We seal and lock the tunnels. In centuries past, Kusan has repelled armies. You are wrong."

Amarta could barely whisper her reply. "He will find where the water comes in to Kusan and do something to turn it dark. It will sicken us. Some Emendi will say it is better to live in bondage than die in thirst. They will fight the others to leave and surrender. When enough Emendi have died from fighting or drinking black water, the rest will open the doors above."

"How can you say such wretched things?"

She could not bear Dirina's look, so she stared at her shoes.

Some of the pieces of the future were clear, but many were not. Some had yet to form. Many were still moving. Her head ached, trying to fit them together. She had been drawing in the dirt a great deal. "I think we still have time, Diri, but we must do certain things. Soon, if we are to—"

"No more. You will not speak of this again."

Amarta considered leaving Dirina and Pas here while she took the hunter's attention away. That would be best for everyone. But in her visions, the only futures in which Emendi stayed in Kusan included the ones in which the three of them left together. Somehow that mattered.

"If you stay," she stuttered, "I think you and Pas— Diri, you might die with the others."

"Then I will die with the others!"

At last Amarta's resolve broke. She began to sob. If she could not even convince her sister, she was done with the attempt. She, too, would stay and die. At least now they wouldn't have to leave Kusan.

Maybe the Emendi really *did* have a plan that would save them. Maybe she really was wrong.

"No, no, no," Dirina said, taking Amarta in her arms,

hugging her so tightly she could barely breathe. Then softly in her ear: "Of course we must go, Ama. Forgive my selfishness and foolishness. There are too many here who have lives yet to live, who have given us so much. If we must go to save Kusan, then of course we must go. Tell me what to do."

It was not hard to smuggle food from meals, from the kitchen, and hide it in their blankets and packs.

More difficult by far was to pretend nothing was amiss.

With Nidem, who knew her better than anyone, she could pretend to still be sorrowing for Darad. Nidem, so elated to have been chosen for the next out-trip, was herself distracted.

When Amarta saw Dirina sitting with Kosal, laughing, touching the young man's face, she was furious. How dare her sister engage thus, knowing they were leaving? How dare she be happy while Amarta suffered?

Then she realized that Dirina, too, was pretending. Acting as if nothing had changed. Better than Amarta had. Convincingly enough to fool her. Dirina must hurt, as well.

Amarta's resentment melted.

At night she would go up to the gardens to see the summer stars and moon and track the days. She could not afford to make a mistake about when they were to leave, which she now knew must, for some reason, follow the next Emendi out-trip, yet come before the full moon. Somewhere in that handful of days they would leave.

She relied on vision to tell her when, but on her own eyes to know the day in which it might say so.

So many pieces. Often they made no sense. She might, if she were lucky, know the what, but rarely the why.

They must, for example, include in their packs scraps of yarn of certain colors, which she smuggled out of the mending room. She must give away her cloak, the one with scraps of her mother's blue dress sewn into the hem. They must leave at exactly the right hour, and take the right set of stairs.

Whatever they had to do, they would do. She and Dirina were agreed: more important than anything was to keep Kusan whole.

Nidem laughed at her reaction. "You didn't know me, did you?"

With the dark hair and tinted eyebrows, Amarta had walked right past Nidem before the girl had snickered and grabbed her shoulder, pulling her around.

"I look Arunkin, now, don't I?"

So very, Amarta signed. *No Emendi here.*

We hide in the walls.

Like the ferrets.

"I've never been out past the gardens before." Nidem was vibrating with eagerness.

A flash of vision: *Horse pulling wagon, a winding road on limestone turning to grassland.*

"We're going farther this time," Nidem said. "To a larger market. So many things there, they say. Tools, ink, spices—"

Amarta felt the present shift and the future follow; a puzzle piece was only now forming, just falling into place.

A body on the ground wore her cloak. By the blue trim was a dark, spreading stain.

Nidem saw her face change. "Listen to me, going on and on. I didn't mean to brag, Ama. Do you wish you could come, too? We could ask."

Amarta's stomach turned over. Her response stuck in her throat as if the words were spiked. She forced a smile anyway.

Nidem. It was Nidem.

She swallowed hard, pretending as fiercely as she could, pretending joy for her friend.

Kusan, she reminded herself.

"I'm only worried about you."

Nidem hugged her. "I want to go. Be happy for me instead."

At this Amarta managed a nod, her stomach going leaden as she forced herself to say the words that made her feel sick, the words she knew she had to say.

"I have something for you, for your trip. A gift."

The three of them made their way quietly from their sleeping room. This staircase, Amarta insisted, gesturing, not the other.

Even Pas was quiet. Young he might be, Amarta realized, but they had been leaving places for all his life, and he knew when to be silent.

They climbed stairs, walked corridors, and stepped into the chamber that led to the outside door.

"I knew you would do this. Sneak off in the night like cowards."

Darad stood in front of the door that was their exit.

How had she not foreseen this? She had seen what she had to, in order to save the city. She could not see everything.

"We must," she said. "It's . . ." Her explanation shriveled at the revulsion on Darad's face.

"For everyone's benefit," Dirina finished for her, holding Pas's hand tight. Pas wanted to run to Darad, as he always had. He pressed his small lips together in sorrow, somehow understanding.

"Without even saying good-bye," Darad spat. "After all my people have done for you."

"You didn't seem to care very much what I said," Amarta shot back, finding her own anger painfully aflame again.

"Why should I care? I knew you were only going to leave."

"How could you possibly know that?" Amarta felt a new idea cut through her anger. Could Darad share her ability to see into the future? For a dizzying moment she realized she should have confided in him long ago. They could have shared everything, and whatever it was that had torn them apart could have been overcome. If he saw the future, too—

"Because I heard. At the market. Who you are."

"What?" Amarta said, confused.

"What did you hear about us?" Dirina demanded.

"A man offered me coin for information about a girl, a woman, and a small boy. You three," he pointed, his finger trembling. "Runaways from one of the Great Houses, he said, on some grand adventure. They want you home, you know. Offering a reward for your return."

"No!" Amarta said, outraged. "That's not true. We've never even been to Yarpin. We have no House. We have nothing."

"So you've said, again and again," he responded with an ugly smile.

"It's true," Dirina insisted.

He sneered. "Don't worry. I've told no one your precious little secret, despite how tempted I was to make some good coin on you."

"It's easy to tell lies about people," Amarta said hotly.

"I agree with you there," he said. "So easy to lie. You ought to know."

"I never lied, never. I—"

"Hush," Dirina warned at the increasing volume between them.

In a way he was right: she had lied. To him, to everyone. About what she was. About why they had come to Kusan. About the danger she brought with her.

But not this accusation. This wretched story.

"You don't know," Amarta said. "There's so much you don't know."

"I know plenty."

"Ama," Dirina again, urgently. "The time."

He stood aside from the exit, gave a mocking, inviting gesture to the opening. "Have your fun little adventure, you wretched slavers."

"What an awful thing to say. We were friends to you. We—"

"We must go," Dirina said sharply.

"You were never one of us, Amarta al Arunkel. I am filled with joy to see you leave."

Amarta shook off Dirina's warning touch, facing him, wanting to say more, one last thing, something cutting and witty, or even sweet, something he would never forget, that one day he would think back on and somehow understand what had really happened here and how wrong he had been.

But no words came. Instead she simply stared, and he stared back, his smile carved as if from stone.

Dirina took Amarta's arm and squeezed until it hurt, finally breaking through her anguish and fury. "Ama," she said. "The moon. If we don't go now, none of this will matter."

Chapter Sixteen

Tayre was impressed with the residents of the hidden enclave and the lengths they went through to hide their existence here in the deadlands. But was the Botaros girl still there?

Judging by the many places he had been that she was not, he was fairly certain she had come this way, down the Great Road, into the deadland flats, and had not emerged. He had circled the area a good number of times, all sixty and some miles of it, watching riders and wagons come and go, noting tracks, keeping count. Almost all the wagons, riders, and those on foot who had entered the deadlands also exited the other side.

Almost.

One wagon had clearly originated in the deadland expanse itself without having come from elsewhere, and had headed east to the markets in the small towns, returning days later, and failing to emerge elsewhere.

He was becoming fairly certain he had stumbled onto the fabled hidden city of Kusan, an excellent place to hide.

If half the rumors about it were true, also uncommonly well-defended. He could not simply ride in and start asking questions.

So he scouted the area, looking for clues as to the people who lived in this, it turned out, not-mythical underground city. He made a methodical survey of the area, avoiding the deadlands themselves, staying well out of sight.

The Kusani, it turned out, were clever enough not to keep a schedule. Wagons left sometime during the waxing or full moon, when the skies were clear enough at night to light their way, so he expected another wagon to emerge from the deadlands soon, at which point he would have someone to question.

Such a community would be keenly aware of newcomers. If she were there, they would know. If he got his hands on any of them, he would also know.

Which he would shortly.

The wagons came eastward from the deadlands via a windswept rocky shelf of land, clearly intending to avoid the kind of tracking he was now doing. As careful as they were at hiding their location and travel, every human alive needed food and water. They could only do so much to hide from someone observant and patient.

So he waited.

When it came, the small covered wagon rolled slowly toward him, one cart horse, two people sitting at the front, he would guess another two inside. They would pass directly under where he now stood, on a hillside in brush and trees.

Then he would ride down from his vantage point and

have a conversation. With a bit of care, he could not only find out that the girl was there in the warrens below, but also induce them to bring her out to him. Willingly.

He could think of a number of compelling stories that might make the underground residents grateful to him for taking her off their hands, and he had enough coin to back any such story. This would be the tidiest of solutions: fast, direct, with least risk. He might even be able to take her alive.

But if he could not command Kusani cooperation, he would take them off the road into the woods where he could ask questions at length and see what other solutions presented themselves. Then, at least, he would know the girl was there.

As he watched the wagon roll closer he performed his usual checks: saddle, pack bindings secure, knives in place, close-in bow ready, arrows likewise.

Once he knew the girl was here, if his ideal solution of Kusani cooperation was not obtainable, he would go back to the capital and convince the Lord Commander to give him a small army. With enough soldiers he could surround and overwhelm the underground warrens, blocking every exit she might take, then thoroughly search every inch of tunnel. With sufficient eyes and hands and weapons, he felt sure her foresight could be overwhelmed.

Rumor said that Kusan was impregnable. That was not reason enough to take it, but it did make it intriguing.

And no one lived underground without reason. They were hiding something, or hiding from someone. Whatever that was would likely be valuable and further inducement to the Lord Commander to give Tayre the forces necessary. Another thing he would find out from the Kusani.

He swung himself up on his horse, eyes still on the approaching wagon, checking and double-checking that everything on himself and his horse was where he expected it to be.

He heard sounds from the hill west, another vantage point he had considered and dismissed as both too open and likely noisy, which it was now, as two horses came crashing down through the brush, half-sliding down the steep hillside on a fast approach to the wagon, which they now circled, the two riders shouting orders to those inside, to stop, to get out.

Tayre was already riding down the hill as fast as his horse would take him, watching as the two Kusani sitting up front dropped the reins to put their hands up in surrender, facing the first attacker as he let fly an arrow that sank into the chest of the first wagoner. The wagoner clutched at his chest, gasping and slipping off the wagon to the ground. Another shot and the second wagoner, a woman, screamed, and crumpled.

Tayre urged his horse to speed.

At the back of the wagon the second attacker was yelling at those inside to come out, to get onto their knees, which they did rather more quickly than Tayre had hoped. The attacker then pulled a short sword and clumsily but effectively ran it through the first of those. The figure went prone.

The other figure, a girl, lurched to her feet and began to run. The attacker's arrow caught her in the calf. She stumbled to the ground.

A girl about the age the seer would be now, wearing a cloak with blue trim.

Tayre's horse was on the road proper, forward at a full gallop, but in the seconds it took him to arrive, the other attacker had put a bolt into the girl's back. She went flat.

If it were indeed the seer, they had saved him a good deal of trouble. Somehow he doubted it would be that easy.

As he rode up, the two attackers turned to face him, the points of their notched arrows aimed at him. One seemed ready to speak, the one he had judged as the more competent of the two, when Tayre shot him through the stomach with his crossbow. He crumpled. The other man's attempt to shoot Tayre went far wide as he sacrificed accuracy for speed, which was what Tayre had expected him to do, providing plenty of time to put a bolt through his wrist to a loud grunt of pain and a dropped bow.

"Wait, wait—" the man said, stumbling back, his other arm raised to block the next shot.

"Turn her over," Tayre ordered, motioning to the girl, face down on the ground.

Clutching his wrist, giving an agonized look at his bow lying feet away in the dirt, the man lurched to the girl and pushed her onto her back with his foot.

She was not Amarta al Botaros. Disappointing, but not surprising. He doubted any of the other Kusani were still alive to tell him anything. Maybe the attackers knew something.

"Why kill them?" he asked. "Any of these could have led you to the girl."

Swallowing hard with pain, he said, "We only need the head."

"You do know it has to be the right head, don't you?"

"It *is* the right head."

"What makes you think so?"

"She has the cloak. The one we were told she wears."

Hunting the cloak. Not the girl.

Idiots. These two clearly knew nothing of the hidden city or the whereabouts of the seer.

"Who hired you?" he asked.

"No one. I—"

The next bolt went through his shoulder. The man screamed.

Tayre dismounted. "Who hired you?" he asked again.

"The Lord Commander. No, no, please don't, I—"

It was, alas, the answer he had expected, so he sent the third bolt through the man's throat to keep him quiet for a bit, but alive, in case Tayre wanted more answers. The man's mouth moved silently as he slipped to his knees, hands clawing at his throat.

Tayre bent down to touch the girl's neck. Dead. The cloak was definitely the seer's—he remembered the unusual strip of blue on the hem, now bloodied.

What did all this mean? That someone had taken the cloak from her was the simplest and thus most likely explanation. But she could see into the future, making this far from a typical situation. He had to assume what he was looking at now was no accident.

Did she know he would be standing here right now, watching this girl's blood seep out of her into the cloak, this garment that used to be hers? Had she predicted his intent here today and acted to thwart him? Or was this all instinct to her, as a horse knew to snap at a fly, or a cat to kill a mouse?

He confirmed that each of the Kusani was dead. As clumsy as the attackers were, they were competent enough against the Kusani; not a pulse remained to question.

Too bad all around, he thought, standing, gaze sweeping the land from the road leading west to the deadlands to the eastward hills that went to the market towns that were the wagon's original destination.

While the road was rarely traveled, it would be in time. The Kusani might even come to investigate when their people failed to return. Best to clean up and move on.

He put his knife blade up and through the heart of the attacker still gurgling and clutching his throat, and inspected the second attacker, a man so young he could barely grow a beard. He lay keening, curled around his stomach, the bolt having sliced through his kidney as Tayre had intended, accounting for the obvious discomfort. A few more questions of the young man gained Tayre no new insights, so he twisted the man's head sharply and let him die.

As he stripped the cloak off the dead girl for closer inspection, he came to the conclusion that the seer was no longer here. Not in the deadlands, not in Kusan. Her cloak on this girl, so close in age, could be no accident.

An intriguing mystery, Kusan, but for now one best left hidden. By the time he returned with force sufficient to take the underground city, he was confident she would be long gone, the trail again cold. He could not, with that level of expenditure and visibility, afford to be wrong again; it would exhaust what little credibility he still had with the Lord Commander.

So it seemed this event had changed his mind after all.

Had she foreseen all this? Was she clever enough to have engineered it? If he had decided to apprehend her alive, before he had the Lord Commander's permission to kill her, would she have acted otherwise?

How many moves ahead could she see?

He stopped himself from this line of supposition. Guessing at what she might foresee based on his intent would get him nowhere. Short of examining her up close and with sufficient time, this was no more than circles of speculation and excessive conjecture, a trap as surely as his previous underestimation of her had been.

He must reason from immediate evidence. He turned slowly, looking for any other clues in the scene of slaughter before him.

Another thought occurred to him, born of another set of rumors entirely. He knelt down and made a second, closer examination of the fallen Kusani, looking at their eyes, scalps, brows, and arms. They were all blond.

Even more interesting: Kusan, it seemed, was at least in part a slave refuge. It did not change his plans; while a city of Emendi was a prize of significant worth and something the Lord Commander might even be interested in, making slaves had nothing to do with this contract nor his determination to find the girl.

The seer had turned into a potent adversary. Acquiring her, breathing or not, was all that concerned him now.

He had to admit that it might not be possible. His uncle, the man who had raised him and taught him his craft, had also shown him how to find the edge of the possible and go beyond it. That meant finding the place where what you knew wasn't enough, where your very conception of the world kept you from understanding the next step.

Find the unknown. Make it known to you.

He would find her, study her, and complete his contract. However long it took.

With that thought he rode the dead bodies up into the high hills, putting them deep in the ground. The wagon and carthorse he would take to one of the small towns where those he knew would make it vanish for him.

Then he would search the deadland roads again for the girl, her sister, and the now-walking boy-child. Most likely she would continue southward, heading toward one of the coastal port towns or cities. Possibly even Munasee.

The trail was there. He would find it.

Chapter Seventeen

Maris wandered the coast and its many harbor towns, spending some of the money that Innel delivered monthly to her, listening to the news of the approaching coronation. When it arrived in midsummer, festivals unfolded across the land, turning into boisterous and inebriated revelries that Maris knew were mere echoes of the extravaganzas occurring in the capital.

It had been over half a century since a monarch had been crowned. Despite her cynicism Maris found herself caught up in the optimism embedded in the celebrations. She wondered if the queen might bring more than a new face to her coins.

But Maris did not enjoy the festivities for long, making camp in a deserted collection of lightly wooded hills at the edge of a beach, sleeping on the dunes. With the rise and fall of the surf, roar of the waves, scent of brine, and cry of gulls, she could feel the tug of the salt water and had very nearly decided to contract as crew and return to the ocean again.

Of course, she already had a contract. With the crown. For which she had taken coin.

She stayed.

She felt the man riding along the beach toward her before she saw him. Young, trim, clean-shaven, his rust-red and black surcoat hemmed with a messenger's white. Another horse followed along.

He rode up to her. "Marisel dua Mage?"

She nodded affirmation, wondering how long he had been searching the countryside and beaches for her. From the way his throat tightened and his heart sped at her nod, she guessed this was the first time he had met one of her kind. No surprise, his reaction, in this land where a loathing for magic was as common as poverty. Odd, she had always thought, when the Shentarat glass plains in her homeland should have served as a more terrifying reminder. Perhaps rumor was more compelling than evidence.

They were beautiful mounts, the horses. Large and brown, happy and healthy. It cheered Maris to draw herself up onto the saddle of this powerful animal that was well cared for and wanted no more from the day than the chance to run and to eat.

"Nalas," he answered as they rode north, when she asked his name.

"And you are . . . ?" she asked, prompting for more.

"Confused," he admitted with a rueful smile. At her look, he continued. "A half-year ago I was honor guard to the princess's intended. His second, I suppose. Now he's Lord Commander as well as Royal Consort, and all the other things he takes care of. So am I second? To which?

I rather doubt I'm second as consort to the princess—the queen," he quickly corrected, then shrugged. "Things have been a bit confused since the coronation. Forgive me for the lengthy explanation, High One—"

"Don't call me that."

He winced and fell silent. "My apologies," he said at last.

She nodded, the touch of regret at her sharp words tempered by the realization that this was probably why Innel had sent him, to be charming while escorting a potentially touchy mage to the capital. His manner was easy and kind, and she found herself relaxing somewhat. Credit to the Lord Commander for thinking ahead.

Her mood soured again when they reached the crowded outskirts of the capital, the crowds thick, a morass of struggles and impulses, of maladies and miseries. She felt them pressing in, their ills palpable.

She reached focus down through her horse's legs and into the earth, borrowing his animal ease, finding some measure of calm in each hoof step. Solidifying her ethereal shield muffled somewhat the increasing splashes of pain and hunger but did not block them out altogether.

Yarpin's city gates were twisted wrought iron, stretching upward, cumulating in high, sharp pikes, as if to claim even the sky.

What will Arunkel not eat?

When last she had been here, the Grandmother Queen was a handful of years dead and Restarn had finally produced his heir. These events seemed to spark a frenzy in Restarn, who had then set in motion another massive Anandynar expansion. As his armies spread across the land, stomping flat tribes and towns and city-states who had previously thought to rule themselves, Maris had gone deep into the countryside. Inspired by those with the temerity to resist Arun rule, she helped the many who needed her, applying skills she had herself only recently come to own.

She found herself at a village deep in disputed territory and advised them on how to resist the avaricious Arun army, only to watch helplessly as the village elders decided they would instead pay the tribute the new rulers demanded, even though it was obvious it would smash them into poverty and starvation. Her warnings fell on deaf ears; they simply refused to fight.

She moved on, giving what she could, but too many needed too much. She could not help them all.

The ocean of suffering Iliban.

When exhaustion finally drove her into retreat, she went back to Perripur, where unification fever had sparked to flame, the confederated states finally willing to put aside their differences to organize an army to fight against the encroaching Anandynars. A united Perripur would have been undefeatable.

But it never came to pass. Restarn proved too canny to tangle with his southern neighbor, keeping his forces well north of the border states.

She was bitterly disappointed. A conflict with Arun would have taken Perripin attention from domestic squabbles, put it north, where it belonged. But lacking a credible Anandynar threat, the states were content to stay independent and bickering. As long as Restarn did not cross the border, they would not bother to resist him.

While, above the borderline, the Anandynar king simply took what he wanted.

As their two horses passed through the gates, people surged out of their way, and they watched those who watched them. Here Maris's foreign looks brought curiosity; it was Nalas's uniform that attracted fearful, suspicious glares. The king's soldiers—now the queen's— had not been well-liked. That had not changed.

Was Yarpin, she wondered, truly worse than the other Arun cities, like Munasee or Garaya? Or was she letting the disturbing memory of Keyretura color her assessment?

It was worse, she decided: there was a keenness to Yarpin's heaviness, as if somehow the avarice of the empire burned hottest here, using the potency of human suffering as fuel, producing a dark smoke of agony that spread outward in all directions.

The actual stench was impressive as well, coming from the sewers and the corners of city walls that served as both trash heaps and scavenger piles.

As they passed, a ragged woman stood to watch, one side of her face intact, the other melted, the monarchy's sigil branded on her face where her other eye used to be.

The king's justice. The queen's now, Maris supposed. Before she quite realized it she had sent a bit of herself into the woman's body. Hunger, injury, pain. What had she expected? She withdrew quickly.

At the edge of an alleyway three men crouched in a circle. One threw dice across the stones, his other hand tight around the arm of a small boy. As the dice came to rest, he held up the boy's arm with a triumphant yell, drawing the terrified child deeper into the alleyway, leaving little doubt as to his fate. A sense of sick despair came to her.

She could make it otherwise. Dismount, follow them into the alley. Take the boy away from him. No one could stop her. But would she be anything more than his new captor? She could imagine the look of horror in his eyes as he realized what she was. To release him again only meant he would be back in someone else's grasp before long. There was no winning that game.

For a moment a man paced them, hopping along on one leg, hand trailing a brick wall for balance. Then he stopped, shook his cloak off to reveal a wrist stump, which he jerked up and toward them. Nalas looked straight ahead as if he had not seen it, though Maris suspected otherwise. The man wouldn't have dared the gesture, Maris knew, if not for the messenger's white that meant they were unlikely to stop. Maris had seen Arun soldiers dismount for milder offenses, and the offender had not even limped away.

What had the man done to lose two limbs? Touched an expensive item in the marketplace, perhaps. Or hopped too slowly out of the way of some aristo out for a ride.

Fingers extended, she reached her focus downward below the stones and dirt and basements under the buildings, deep beneath the layers of human remains and debris, farther past all touch of humankind, taking stability from the earth itself, bringing it back into her body and mind to keep the cacophony at bay.

The more of Yarpin she saw, the better she remembered why she didn't want to be here.

As their mounts ascended the steepening main road, eager to reach home, they passed merchant mansions. The lanes to either side widened. First the Lesser Houses, then the Greater Houses—estates of dual-color splendor, towers reaching high, sigils snapping in the ocean breeze.

But beyond, the glinting Yarpin palace dwarfed them all, rising above the palace walls. At the gates to the palace grounds they were waved through.

What, she wondered again, was she doing here, atop this fine horse, contracted to the very monarchy she abhorred?

It seemed that while Yarpin had not changed, she herself had. When she was done here, she promised herself, she would go home to Perripur.

Of course, memory waited there as well. Perripin faces swam in her mind's eye, those she had not been able to save, from her parents to friends to countless strangers. The few who had cursed her across the years were bad enough, but worse yet were the many who should have cursed her but who, instead, praised her with their last breath.

Even working for the Arun monarchy was better than that.

She was escorted through high-ceilinged halls lined with lavish tapestries depicting mining towns joyously celebrating beside Arun soldiers, or tribes expressing gratitude for Anandynar rule. History was written by those who owned the looms.

And now those she passed were well-fed and well-dressed. None missed limbs or were ill. She felt an ease come over her, and something like self-loathing followed close behind.

At a room with doors higher than anyone could need, with windows that looked out into the gardens of red tulips, stood the man she had met in the Ill Wind, whom she now knew to be the Royal Consort and Lord Commander.

"Marisel al Perripur," he said, dismissing the scribes and soldiers who filled the room. "On behalf of my queen, Cern esse Arunkel, welcome to Yarpin palace."

He was impressive in his uniform, the black collar glinting with royal gold, mixed-metal buttons down the front atop rust-colored amardide fabric. Maris realized that she had not truly met him before. These were his colors, not the nondescript clothes he'd worn at their meeting at the Ill Wind. Had he dressed thus in that meeting, would she have agreed to this contract?

"Please," he said, inviting her to sit at a table with him.

At the center of the table was a bowl of fruit. She picked out a green lilikoi, grown in southern Perripur, far distant. Such wealth.

"Our gratitude, Marisel, for coming to us here."

So very polite. *With a mage, respect first. Reason later.*

She had agreed to this obscene contract, she could say. She regretted it now and would return his money and go, she could say.

Instead she bit into the lilikoi, sucking out the pulp through the hole she'd made with her teeth, as she had when she'd been a child. Tart and sweet, it brought her memories of bright, hot summers full of ease and childhood delights. Before Keyretura. "And so I am here," she said, hearing the weight in her tone. "What do you want of me?"

"What can you do?"

"I have many skills," she answered, putting the lilikoi aside to pick out a ripe peach. "Among them arithmetics, high-elevation farming, circular harp, and birthing babies. Shall I give you a complete list?"

It smelled marvelous, the peach.

"We can discuss something else, then. News of Perripur, perhaps?"

This was how one caught an animal in a trap, with bait like the fruit she held in her hand. She frowned, put it back on the table. "Are you so badly in need of company that you must hire a mage to find it?"

His smile froze for a moment. "I meant no insult."

She waved the apology away. "We'll both be happier if you simply tell me what it is you want of me."

"I want to know who is loyal to the new queen."

"Ah. That is not on the list."

"No? You can't tell a lie from the truth?"

"No better than someone with good eyes. No better than someone who knows the person well, that's certain."

It often played out this way, explaining the limits of her abilities to those who had such high hopes. The impoverished and destitute, for all their misery, asked for simple things. To ease the pain. To live another day.

"It is said that magic can help find magic."

"Ah, you want something found?"

"Someone. Can you find a person?"

"In a house, perhaps," she answered.

"Across the empire?"

"That is another matter. It would be like touching each stone in the Sennant river to find the single one made of iron instead of rock."

"What if the person is a mage?"

Now she was on alert. To be hired to search for another of your kind was never a good sign.

"A Sensitive can find a mage in a small village if you give him time, but he must still know which village to search. Magic isn't like a blocked sewer that you can find by stink. More like the wind—you see its effects where it ripples the high grasses or bends back the trees. If a mage has done magic somewhere, I may be able to sense it, like a footprint in mud. The mage may be long gone but I could point at where they once stood."

"So if I were to tell you where someone was, could you"—he considered—"stop them from performing any magic?"

"You want me to fight another mage?" she asked, feeling her body and senses tighten.

"Perhaps."

Maris tried to hold her anger in check, then wondered why she bothered. She let it course through her and out her hand, slamming her palm against the peach, breaking it open, the hard pit all that remained between herself and the table. Juice oozed around the squashed fruit. "Don't you study history in that fine library of yours? When mages fight, everyone dies but the mages. How can you make the same mistakes, generation after generation, then—your cities flattened—bemoan your ill-fortune yet do it again? You are idiots, all of you."

At least there was this advantage to being a mage: she

could insult the powerful and merely be, ever so politely, asked to leave. She stood.

"Marisel—" Innel began, standing also. Apology or rebuke, she didn't care.

"If you want to set mages against each other, find someone else."

"Good," Innel said.

"Good?" She glared up at him. "What's good about it?"

"This is why I asked you to come. To help me understand. To advise. Stay, and I'll take what you offer."

Suddenly she saw that he hadn't been reluctant to push her at all. He'd been probing her to see what she could and would do. She had missed the obvious. She was rusty at these games.

On edge, being here, she admitted to herself. Too much wealth bought with blood.

She could leave. Give aid to those with real need. The injured, the ill, the pregnant. But no; she could not face it again, not so soon.

And she had taken his coin.

Anger drained into weariness. She wondered if he guessed how much she craved this respite. She exhaled, felt herself become subdued. "So be it."

He smiled at this, the smile of someone who had scored a point. "Join us for the evening meal, Marisel. The queen is"—a small pause—"wary of mages, but she'll change her mind once she's met you. Until then, perhaps a bath? A visit to the library? And . . ." He picked out another ripe peach, held it out to her.

Trap or no, she wanted the fruit. She took it.

The bath was hot, the scented soap lush with Perripin

spices—no accident, that. Even so, she made long and delighted use of the luxury.

The peach tasted marvelous.

To her vague disgust, Maris found she had quickly become accustomed to soft beds and splendid food.

And then there was the library.

"Tea, Marisel?"

Innel poured from a cylinder, a stream of pink liquid mingling with steam as it filled a clear glass mug. It was not the spiced, bitter tea Arunkin drank—out of embarrassment for their wealth, went the Perripin joke— but a smoked fruit and bark tea, imported from Perripur, no doubt at some expense. A gesture not lost on her.

"I have some items once owned by the person I am looking for." On the table between them he put a bundle wrapped in heavy black silk, tied with black cord. He slid it across to her.

She touched it. "You know something about magic, Lord Commander."

"Less than I might," he said with a twitch of a smile. "The old king was of the strong opinion that magic brings disaster to all it touches."

"He was right in that."

"That seems untrue to me, Marisel. You have prevented a number of disasters these last months."

At his direction, Maris had been keeping watch on him and the queen and a few others, one of whom was unimportant to palace politics but even so had been attacked five times in five different ways over the months she had been here. The poor man was only a servant, bringing stacks of bedding into the palace from the laundry. Slow attacks, all of them. Plenty of time for Maris to warn Innel and have him calmly send soldiers to take care of the matter.

Clearly Innel was arranging these. It was the next step after fear, testing, and only mildly insulting.

In truth she was barely annoyed. He was paying her astonishingly well to eat magnificently, bathe often, and keep track of a few people.

And there was the library. Truly as astonishing a collection as Gallelon had promised.

One day, as Maris had come into the book-filled rooms, she found an elderly woman there, dressed in the gray and brown of House Nital. Yliae was her name, and she was warm and well-spoken, engaging Maris in a fascinating discussion of the architecture of stone bridges and the challenges of harvesting amardide forests. Hours slipped pleasantly by.

The following week a man in Helata's green and blue proved eager to talk with her about the various ships on which she'd sailed. He was happy to tell her stories of the far side of Arapur, which he had been to and she had not yet. More hours slipped by.

Gallelon was right. *Some of the cleverest of the Iliban.*

Of course Innel was arranging these visits. But she could hardly complain when week after week, she was kept engaged, engrossed, delighted.

One day Yliae offered to take Maris into the city by carriage to hunt rare books from small, private collections. Now Maris had begun to amass another small set of tomes, one that would be hard to transport when she left.

It was a pleasant problem to have. Innel was working hard to keep her happy.

"Surely the old king had mages of his own," she said to Innel.

His eyes flickered, ever so slightly. "If he did, he has them no longer."

Maris had come across the old king as she had explored the palace. He lay in his bed, sick with something in his blood that should not be there. Something that, with some effort, she might be able to clean. "I could look in on him."

Innel shook his head. "The queen wouldn't allow it. And rightly so; if he gets better under your care, they'll say you had no part in it, but if he gets worse, they'll blame you." He smiled ruefully. "I'm afraid Arunkin have a ways to go to accept your kind."

"I don't need to be in the room," she said, suspecting he knew this. "Simply nearby. No one need ever know."

"No," he said firmly. "That is not where I want your attention."

It was obvious that Innel knew perfectly well what was causing the old king's illness. Whether it was Innel or the queen or someone else feeding Restarn something to keep him sick didn't matter; Innel did not want him to get better.

So be it. Not her concern.

But Innel was watching her keenly now.

Very well; he was paying her enough to have earned a bit of reassurance.

"The great halls are full of spiders, best left to do their work without interference," she said, borrowing a saying from Perripur. Innel's eyes narrowed slightly. He knew the saying, knew what it meant. Knew what she suspected.

"In Arunkel we honor spiders," he said. "They ensure appropriate behavior from lesser insects." By eating them, he meant. "You are wise, Marisel."

Wise enough to know who provided her with sumptuous meals, insightful conversation, and a library that rivaled any she had ever seen before.

Thus reassured, Innel unrolled the black silk, revealing a pale blue and white seashell, a strip of blue cloth, and a few strands of brown hair.

Maris put her fingertips on the shell, sorting out her impressions, separating out the taste of human presence from the vast backdrop that was the shell's many years prior in the ocean. She subtracted out the most recent and fleeting touches of whoever delivered these items to Innel. Few others had touched the shell since it had been parted from the great salt seas, so this did not take long. She let the impressions settle inside her, like tea leaves falling into patterns at the bottom of a cup. It was important not to rush, a lesson that Keyretura had drilled into her repeatedly.

One strong presence remained. An odd mix of terror and assurance and grief. "She is young," Maris said. "Still a child. There is the taste of knowing about her that most do not have so early in life. Is this the one you seek?"

"Yes." In his voice she heard the force of desire and a touch of surprise.

Well, that was unavoidable. Half her work to the wealthy was proving herself.

"Is there more?" he asked.

"Often tired. Hungry. Afraid. Cold."

"When?"

"I can't tell. Across many years."

"And the cloth and hairs?"

Maris shook her head. "They tell me nothing." Some parts of the body could say a great deal about the spirit who lived in them. A bone, even a bit of flesh. Maris saw no reason to tell him that.

"Can you find her?"

Maris focused on the man before her. "If she is where I happen to be looking, I will know her. But to find her in the world at large is another matter. You would do better to have your many informants search for her."

"I am already doing that. I want you to search for her as well."

"Perhaps you don't understand my meaning. I would need to search tile by tile through the palace. Each brick of each building. Every step along the Great Road."

"I understand. Start in Yarpin and expand outward. I don't believe she is in-city, but she might be. I need to be sure."

She looked at him in astonishment. "You cannot be serious. That could take a very long time."

"How long?"

"Years. Decades. Centuries. I don't know."

He nodded, stood. "Then best you begin soon."

"Finding her this way is impossible, Lord Commander. That's certain."

"It's only impossible until someone does it. All I ask is that you try, Marisel."

✢ ✢ ✢

Maris walked the halls, tasting those in every room she passed, searching for the girl. She suspected it would be faster to knock on doors and ask if she were there, but she doubted Innel would appreciate such a direct approach.

It occurred to Maris to wonder if this were another test. But no; there was an intensity and urgency about Innel's tone.

An absurd way to search, but so be it; as long as she took Innel's coin and enjoyed the palace's extravagances, she would uphold her end of the contract.

So she strolled along polished wood floors, trailed her fingers along painted walls, and sent bits of herself into each room, questing for the one taste that would match the owner of the shell. Despite not wearing the black robes, she gathered curious stares.

Not her problem. Innel could explain her as he wished. After enough hours, she would tire, and return to the library.

Weeks passed this way. She did not find the girl in the palace. But she found other interesting people.

Like the old king, whom she looked in on despite Innel's objection. She dipped into his body as he lay there in the bed, sweating and coughing, then into the body of the slave who slept in his room, and the doctor who came to treat him. A taste of what the doctor brought to him told Maris that this was the source of his illness.

That did not surprise her. What did surprise her was that every time the doctor rubbed the ointment into his gums, right before she did, the old king's body tightened and his heart sped.

He knew.

She thought of telling Innel but decided that it was best to stay out of the matter. He had made clear he didn't want her attention on the old king.

So be it.

Maris knew she would eventually need to take her search outside to the palace grounds, then into the city at large, but as the weather turned cold and wet, she found herself far more interested in staying warm and dry inside.

So instead she took the search deeper, into kitchen corners, back rooms, servant dormitories, underground storage areas, tunnels that led to garrison and dungeon. She touched on each person, passing quickly over the ones she already knew, telling herself that she was being thorough, that the girl might have somehow slipped into the palace while she wasn't looking. It was a weak justification.

The truth was that she had grown accustomed to being around those who were not suffering and in need. She delayed through autumn as the land slid into dark winter. With rains and then snows outside, she wandered the now-familiar palace halls, delving into basements, toilet rooms, deep closets. The deep, sealed tunnels. The spaces above and between floors.

Which was how she had come across a man and a woman sitting together in a small cellar room disguised as root storage on one side and a closet on the other. She knew them: the older woman was the Minister of Larder, the young man an administrator.

Both were afraid. Very afraid.

Usually she did not listen in on such things, wanting

to stay as far from Arun politics as Innel's coin would allow, but she was intrigued to find people where they should not be, where no room was supposed to be, and in such a state of agitation. She moved her consciousness fully into the room, curling bits of air on itself to give herself the equivalent of ears inside.

"We've waited long enough," the man said urgently. "Restarn promised us—"

"It doesn't matter what Restarn promised."

A frustrated sound. "Yes. All right. But look at how the price of metals rises, Oleane. We could make a profit now, one that would fund everything. If Restarn were on the throne, we'd have some liberty in our operations, and privacy, too, but now—"

"No, no, no," the woman called Oleane said, cutting him off. "Things are different now."

"Damn it, I want what I was promised."

"Keep your voice down, boy. My books are under audit. No more slop. We must be very careful. *You* must be very careful."

"I am, I am."

"You are not." Her voice dropped. "It's not Restarn any more. It's not even Cern. It's Innel you need to be concerned with. The sooner you get fixed with that, the better."

"It doesn't have to be Innel."

"I don't want to hear it. You stink of treason."

"He's sending the city into the sewer, Oleane. No one is following the old agreements. He has shaken the table, and game pieces are everywhere. The queen only watches. We must do something."

"When things are settled, perhaps—"

"Old woman, if we wait for things to settle, you will be cold in your grave and I will be too old to act. Cern turns whatever way the wind blows, and now the wind is called Innel. Let's change the wind's name."

"Hush!"

"There are others who think as I do, Oleane. Don't hide behind your hands like a child, or when the wind changes next you will be left behind."

"Don't threaten me. I'm old enough to be your grandmother."

"Maybe that's the problem. Best you leave these battles to those young enough to imagine what might yet be."

"Idiot. Leave war to the young and you repeat the same mistakes we made when we were young. That's why we have generals. Have you learned nothing in your short life?"

"Innel is not much older than I am. Look at what he has managed."

"He was in the Cohort, you fool."

"You are wise, Oleane. Will you be our general?"

"Ah." The woman's voice held a smile. "I see. You and your 'others.' Not a general among you."

"Truly, we need you. Will you stand with us?"

"Innel is clever. His people are everywhere."

"That could be a different name on your tongue soon, if you're with us. Maybe even yours."

"Don't flatter me, boy. I know who could take over from Innel, and it isn't me."

The man's whisper held sudden passion. "Then you

could be the one to choose. We've waited long enough. This is the time, Oleane."

"I'm not convinced. You can't just—"

"We are ready. Are you with us or not?"

A pause. "Do you know what you're suggesting, boy? How dangerous this is? Do you see who squirms in Execution Square this week?"

"I am not afraid. It is time to act. Yes or no."

A longer pause. At last: "Yes."

Maris chuckled at the drama, withdrew, wondering if she should relay this to Innel or not. As she walked the hallways, a window afforded her a view of the aforementioned square where two men hung by their feet, heads a hand's width above the ground, coated with some sticky substance that Maris guessed was honey. They had lasted two days thus far, despite the rats, but she did not give them much longer.

Yes, she decided, she must tell Innel. While her contract did not require it, it seemed to her that to take his money meant to tell him when his life was in danger.

The woman named Oleane and the young man with her were spiders. They had made their choices.

She went to find the Lord Commander.

The winter passed more comfortably than Maris would have thought possible so far north. Stoves and fireplaces were always warm.

And the library. She could live in it for a hundred years and still not exhaust her interest.

As for the search, as long as she continued to report

various corruptions and treasonous plots to Innel, he seemed happy for her to put off leaving the palace grounds. When the ice began to melt and spring came, though, he reminded her, ever so gently, that he still needed the girl.

So Maris took the search out of the palace with its warm halls onto the palace grounds, searching laundry and garrison, pig and goat pens. At the kennels and stables, she took her time with the dichu, the large Arunkel dogs, their black and tan brindled faces looking up at her eagerly, tails wagging, ears forward. Then the horses, strong and happy and eager to run. It was a pleasure to her.

The girl was not there, though.

When she could put it off no longer, she left the palace grounds. Above, a clear night sky showed the constellation of archer chasing the world-snake, a battle that surely would satisfy no one. She brushed herself with a touch of shadow and illusion, enough that anyone who looked at her would see someone paler, in poorer clothes, less interesting than a Perripin woman wandering alone at night in Yarpin.

As she walked past the Great Houses, she trailed her fingers across walls and iron gates, her attention raking through those within to see if they were the owner of the small seashell. When she had passed across every resident of the Eight Great Houses, she moved downhill and to the Lesser Houses.

None of this took as long as Maris had hoped. There were simply not that many girls, and none of them the one the Lord Commander sought. Reluctantly she expanded her search outward, lane by lane. Merchant houses. Inns. Public houses. Storefronts. Apartments.

And who *was* this girl on whom Innel was sufficiently intent to hire a mage at exorbitant cost to execute a fruitless search? She felt a twinge of sympathy for her, not wishing Innel's attention on anyone but spiders.

It seemed too much coincidence, the many rumors on the streets about fortune-tellers. Not only rumors, either— as the weather turned mild, girl children and young women flocked to street corners, shouting and calling, promising to reveal the future for a pittance and indeed a much lower price than the charlatan girl down the lane.

Some used stones or ointments or bits of metal to aid with the prophecy. One even insisted on first obtaining a drop of blood from the inquirer; a clever trick to get the quarry invested, to stretch credibility before a word of supposed prophecy had even been spoken.

Even so, Innel was too smart to believe such foolishness, and she could not imagine these tales at the heart of his motivation. More likely he had created the rumors himself to serve some intrigue or another. Perhaps the girl was some runaway aristo child, or the daughter of an enemy who could provide him some leverage once he had her in hand.

As she walked the streets and watched the displays, Maris found herself saddened at how credulous people could be. Accounts of prophecy swept villages and cities as would a catchy tune, belief cresting and crashing with rumor, only to rise again years later when people forgot. They were good at forgetting, Iliban were.

Or perhaps they remembered perfectly well, and these

girls with their small pigs and dogs and buckets of bloody entrails were merely entertainment now that the coronation was over and life had returned to a bleak misery.

In any case, if the new queen's Royal Consort and Lord Commander wanted the girl, one way or another, with or without Maris's help, he would have her.

At last the search took her into the poorest sections, down-city. Now when she slipped her awareness into the inhabitants of the apartment buildings, she found sluggish blood, chronic illness, searing pain. When she found such need, she might sometimes take a moment. Open a slow channel here, shift the balance of blood there. Smooth the working of an organ, remove a pinpoint tumor. Small things, things that surely she had the time to do as she went by.

Her search slowed. She tired more quickly. It left her aching, body and spirit, sparking images she thought buried, memories of those who had trusted her when they had nothing left. For them, she decided, she could give a little more, especially when so little was desperately needed.

One night she sat, her back to a dilapidated wall, working on twins, a boy and a girl, who had eaten some corrupted food. She eased the tightening of their throats, shifted the fire in their veins, and watched as they slept to be sure they kept breathing. Hours later, when she was confident they would live, she stood slowly, stretching her stiffness, walking back to the palace where she lay on top of her soft palace bed.

When at last she drifted off, the faces of the dead accompanied her into dream.

Chapter Eighteen

"Where is she now?" Innel asked Srel.

"In the library, ser."

Innel had given Marisel dua Mage some time to enjoy herself while his people kept watch and learned about her.

"Food and drink at regular intervals. Start with a large variety, then improve on the ones she chooses. I want to know every book she opens or touches."

"Yes, ser."

Innel took a sip of his heavily smoked, fermented tea. That it had also been the old king's favorite, and consequently everyone's for decades, had made Innel consider changing it when Cern was crowned. Even now, with fashion changing furiously, people copying—or those few refusing to copy—Cern's hairstyle, her three-quarter-length sleeves gathered with gold buttons—he could stand to have his tea in common with the old king. Still, he ordered it brewed stronger.

While Innel was finding ways to keep the mage happy and engaged, he sought a different sort of entertainment for the queen.

"Tonight's dinner?" he asked Srel.

"In your name I have invited House Elupene's Minister of Bird and Nital's Minister of Decoration."

"Make sure they know their job is to intrigue her, not lecture her."

Cern was still withdrawn, visibly tensing when called on to make decisions. Not acting much like the monarch she had been crowned to be.

Insecure she might be, but she was no fool and would easily see through a ruse. A fine line, Innel bringing aristos to dinner, hoping that they would make her feel competent without merely flattering her. It might be beyond most of them to walk that fine line, but it was worth a try.

"Yes, ser. The ministers of Coin, Mint, and Account have agreed to meet with you at the third bell." Srel took a tray of envelopes from a servant outside the door.

Agreed, Innel thought, knowing that Srel would have relayed that word accurately.

A balance; the queen could command them, but would not, at least not yet. Innel could only ask. The ministers would agree, not comply.

So be it. One rung at a time.

"Invitations to congratulatory dinners at the Houses, Lord Commander," Srel said, fanning out the stack of pale red envelopes.

"They can come to me," he muttered, his attention back on the treasury ledgers.

"Shall I say so, ser?" Srel asked, with a small indication of humor.

Innel sighed. It was hard to put aside a lifetime of

hearing about extravagant dinners at the Houses, dinners to which he and his brother were not considered important enough to invite. Now that he was that important, he found himself wanting to make sure they knew it.

But no; past grudges might be indulged in thought, but not in action. Not unless they served the present.

"Schedule them, but later."

"Even Etallan, ser?" Srel asked.

Etallan had backed him when no one else would. They would understandably expect something in return.

Besides, it was Etallan.

"No. Etallan soon."

Nalas knocked and entered. Innel glanced up, saw on his second's face an expression he knew: He had news he didn't want to deliver.

"What is it?"

"Your sister, ser."

"Yes?"

"Ah—" He exchanged looks with Srel, who shrugged with a look that Innel took to mean the smaller man was declining Nalas's request to rescue him.

"There's a corporal," Nalas said. "Been spending nights in her room."

"Doing what?"

At this Nala's and Srel exchanged another, very different look.

"No," Innel said in response to the unspoken, drawing out the word. "Not Cahlen." Then, at the continued silence, he frowned, musing on the implication. "Do you know him?"

"We do not, ser."

This was an oddity he didn't have time for. "Find out what you can."

"Shall we tell him to stop?"

Tempting as it was, Cahlen was, by the count of years at least, well above the age of consent. He could easily imagine her resenting his intrusion. A familial battle was not something he had time for, either. "No. I'll have a talk with him later. For now, find out everything about him. Watch him closely."

"Yes, ser. Also, a number of the generals want to talk with you."

"Is Lismar among them?" The king's younger sister was first among the generals. If he had her support, the rest might follow.

"She is, ser."

At last.

"I'll see her as soon as she's free."

For Lismar, he would interrupt whatever he was doing.

"The general, ser," Nalas said, standing smartly aside.

Lismar stepped inside, flanked by two guards standing at what was clearly a very precise distance behind her. Innel made a mental note to point this out to Nalas when he had a chance.

Her choice of seconds was a clear statement. Large men, both of them, tall and broad—Innel himself would not have cared to tangle with them. A demonstration of raw physical power, trailing her, this most senior of generals.

Lismar herself was average height or a bit less, with graying mahogany hair. But compact, as if she held within her the same power as these large men, concentrated to fit in her smaller body. An aged wine.

Without quite thinking, Innel stood at her entrance. Ten years ago he had been so far below her in the military hierarchy she would have known him only as one of the Cohort brats. Decades his senior, seasoned by countless battles and campaigns, she must surely wonder at the sense of reporting to him now.

It was not entirely uncommon for those of the Cohort to be promoted over others, just as the tower piece in some board games could jump other pieces. Given the animosity between Cern and her father, surely Lismar could not be surprised to have the new queen select a new Lord Commander.

Though he was still the mutt, and she was still the king's sister. She might have wanted a more worthy tower piece.

He wondered if succession was always this complicated. The written histories were not forthcoming. The results of battles, who wore the crown—all duly noted. But there were holes in times like these. Much left unrecorded.

"Welcome back, General," he said.

Her eyes flickered around the room, possibly comparing it to how it had been when her brother Lason commanded. She took in the maps, weapons, stopping a moment at the tan and striped shaota horse figurine in the corner. Her eyes narrowed slightly, briefly, followed by a small twitch of a smile.

Lason's forcible eviction from this office and position had potential costs. The good will of the generals, Lismar in particular, could be one of them.

Her look settled on him. "Congratulations to you, Lord Commander."

On his marriage? On his promotion?

On his survival?

"It seemed time to stop in," she added, "before I leave again tomorrow."

Telling him her plans, he noted, not asking him. Well, one step at a time. He decided to first address the obvious.

"I have every intention of bringing your royal brother back to the capital, General, as soon as we can find him."

"May he stay good and lost then," she said with a short laugh. At his look she continued. "You think I care about that waste of manflesh? The longer he's gone, the better." At this she made a sharp gesture with thumbs out to the sides. Her guards left the room.

Innel had not expected this dismissal of Lason. He reassessed what he thought he knew about Lismar.

Or perhaps he was too credulous; given how well-known Lason's dislike of the mutt brothers had been, this might be simple prudence, to take the side of the current winner.

She selected a chair and sat. No permission given, and none sought. Feeling a bit uncertain and hoping it didn't show, he sat as well. "If it's not your brother returned home that you want, General, what can I do for you?"

She studied him a long moment and it occurred to

Innel that maybe she was being careful. A power in the palace since he was first brought into the Cohort, now weighing her words to him.

He should, perhaps, try to put her at ease. His brother knew how to unlock people's tongues. What would he have said?

Innel leaned forward in his chair. "How can I hope to succeed without your counsel, Lismar? You have decades and experience beyond my own. What can I do to gain your good will?"

She gave a short laugh at this, as if amused by the show, but he held her gaze, willing her to believe his sincerity. At last she seemed persuaded. Or persuaded to seem so. "My siblings can see to themselves, Lord Commander. My children and their children, perhaps less so."

As he recalled, her children were scattered across the bureaucracy of the palace, the military, others married into the Houses, some with children of their own. A few had been on the old king's staff, and were now—where? He wasn't sure. "And?" he prompted.

"I want them protected."

"Protected from . . . ?"

"From the coming changes." She pursed her lips and drew in a breath through her nose. "From you, Innel."

From him?

It hit him then: it was one thing to be given the title and responsibility to take charge of the empire's armies, and another altogether to be treated as though he truly had. A feeling much like elation threatened to cut through his focus. He pushed it aside; there would be time for that later.

He drummed his fingers on the desk, considered his possible responses to her. "As long as your bloodkin support the queen, I see no cause for you to be concerned."

She smirked. "Come now, Innel. I was educated as thoroughly as my brothers were, under the thoughtful eye and harsh hand of our esteemed grandmother. I know that when the crown moves to another head, even loyal subjects can find themselves . . . reexamined."

Innel recalled how some names seemed to disappear out of the histories during the successions he'd studied. Lismar probably knew more about it than he did. "What do you want, exactly?"

"My progeny safe from the splashes of your impressive rise to command, ser."

"And in return . . . ?"

A small shrug. "My counsel. The loyalty of my command."

"Which should be mine anyway," he said, suppressing a sudden annoyance.

"Of course, ser, of course. Forgive my intrusion into your busy schedule." She gave him an overly warm smile and stood.

A misstep; he could not afford to alienate Lismar. He held his hands up, a gesture of conciliation. "Many call you grandmother, General. Surely you understand that I can't offer immunity to all your descendants."

"I expect no promises. You know what I want, and I know what you need. Do what you can for them, today and tomorrow. Beyond that?" She shrugged. "No one knows what will come."

Innel would not argue, though he was spending a good deal of money to find the someone who did.

Lismar was still standing. Feeling oddly like he was following her commands, and not the other way around, he stood with her. "I appreciate your candor, General."

She saluted. Precise, with a hint of a smile.

Was she mocking him? Surely not.

"I have every confidence we will do good work together, Lord Commander."

Having been raised in the palace, Innel thought himself immune to the extravagances of wealth, but this, Etallan's Great Room, where he sat at a table with Tok, Tok's mother the eparch, and various others of the House, strained his indifference.

From high ceiling to floor to table, nothing was fashioned of wood or stone or cloth or leather, but only those substances that the Etallan charters oversaw directly: metal, ceramic, and glass. The chairs were heavy, some mix of metals; the floor a black tile edged with bronze. The ceiling was a stained glass map of Arunkel, bright with glinting dots showing Etallan's mines. A starlike constellation.

The House's devotion to its charter produce was obsessive. And, should Etallan lose the charters of the Lesser Houses of Glass and Keramos at the next Charter Court, a rather expensive bit of remodeling.

Around the table sat Tok, his mother, her husband, and a number of Tok's siblings, cousins, aunts and uncles. Thus far the dinner had been full of flattering comments about the queen. Hot wine and succulent foods were offered first to him, so that he might have his choice of plates and glasses. He didn't expect anyone to actually attempt to poison him, certainly not in the open like this, but this tradition of caution had been established some centuries ago. Now it was simply polite.

The eparch was a small woman with loose, shoulder-length, graying hair and a plump face with an easy smile. At her nod, Tok continued his introductions.

"And this is my second cousin, Eoinae, who, with the crown's permission, would like to marry Nital's Thvarn. And here, this—"

Tok continued around the room, highlighting various hoped-for couplings. Innel had reviewed familial names and relationships before he'd come, so he knew who each of these were, but it had not occurred to him that he would be lobbied to approve matches. He must stop this before it went further.

"You must know that only the queen can approve marriages."

"Of course, of course," the eparch said brightly. "We only want you to meet them, to see how happy they are—smile, Eoinae!"—The young woman obediently gave Innel a beaming, if somewhat forced, smile. "And thus, what fine children she would bear to better serve the crown."

"Fine children," Tok said, nodding firmly. "Well-suited for the Cohort."

Innel looked his confusion at Tok. "The Cohort has been closed for years, Tokerae. What do you mean—" He fell suddenly silent, feeling foolish.

He meant the next Cohort, of course. The one that

would be formed for the next heir. The heir Cern had yet
to conceive.

With the myriad of issues he had been juggling, this
had not even come into his mind. It would be poor
form to say so, though. He could see why it would be
on the minds of the Houses, who were used to thinking
ahead. Having come into the Cohort from the outside,
at the king's command, it had not occurred to him that
there must be maneuvering ahead of time. Far ahead
of time.

"Ah," Innel said, feeling oddly self-conscious at finding
the outcome of his bedroom activities so openly discussed
in this room of near-strangers. "It has been a busy time."

"So many distractions for you both, I'm sure," the
eparch said, her smile constant. "But the Anandynar line
must stay"—pure, Innel was sure she was thinking, noting
the very brief pause in her words—"strong. It is good to
have choices. One can be so very surprised to find which
one ends up being the most robust."

Meaning him, of course. The mutt. Robust.

He examined her for signs of mockery, saw only the
wide smile. Still, for an unsettling moment Innel felt as
he had so early on in the Cohort: out of place, swimming
in a dark, open ocean.

This was a world away from that time. Now he was
Royal Consort. Lord Commander.

Or was it folly to assume that marriage to the queen
made him acceptable among the Houses?

*We do what others cannot, say what aristos dare not.
We'll win this.*

And win it they had. Or he had, in any case. He looked

around the room, forcing himself to focus on the politics before him.

"You'll like this, Innel," said Tok as a servant presented a small tray of thimble-sized glasses, like miniature goblets. "Adept-wine."

"Imported from the adept-hermits of Arapur-Selsane," said the Eparch's husband, Etallan's Minister of Chimes, a House-specific title that meant more than the words implied. A short man, matching his Eparch, with a deep, resonant voice. Innel had always wondered how two such short people had produced the overly tall Tokerae.

Adept-wine. Implying that the substance was somehow magic-infused. Ironic that this implication made the wine distinctive and sought after. A touch of magic made a thing exotic. As long as it had originated far, far away.

"I am told," the Minister of Chimes continued, "it is aged a century and a day, bottled at their yearly fertility festival."

Or perhaps the implication was that adept blood was shed to make it.

With that thought, Innel examined his glass. The liquid was a grayish shade of purple. He took a sip, attempting to refrain from emptying the tiny glass all at once, but there was so little of it that he failed.

It had an unexceptional, mild taste. He waited for any additional effect, noticed nothing.

"What extraordinary times we find ourselves in," the eparch said. "So much change. So many opportunities."

Innel's mind flashed across all the things aside from Cohort positions for the not-yet-conceived heir that she might mean. "If too many things change at once, Eparch," he said, "no one knows which way is up."

She laughed at this, and it seemed to him altogether too sincere. "Well put, Lord Commander, and exactly my thought as well. We had certain understandings with the old king, as I'm sure you know. We hope to have certain understandings with you and the queen as well."

To Innel's frustration, Restarn had never been specific about his arrangements to do with the Houses. Of course, the eparch could be wholly inventing this.

"The Charter Court comes barreling toward us, mere years away," she continued. "At every Court there is chaos, as warrants, charters, and contracts upon which we have depended for years are tossed into the air to perhaps fall in a new pattern, perhaps not. So much time and disarray. What a waste." She made a tsking sound, shaking her head sadly. Around the table other heads wagged slowly, echoing her.

"There is no getting around the Charter Court," Innel said, forcing a show of amusement at this dangerous idea.

"I do not dispute this," she said. "But perhaps some small change is possible? Rather than every sixteen years . . ." She paused, as if thinking the matter through. "Perhaps every twenty? Even every quarter of a century?"

Etallan had done quite well at the last Charter Court, taking on a number of new high-value Lesser Houses, including Bell and Eschelatine. No surprise they would like to put off the next one.

But a longer time between Courts was impossible. Innel could easily imagine the outcry should he even suggest the idea. Especially if he suggested it. The

Houses, Greater and Lesser, would howl in outrage. He doubted even the old king, with his influence among the Houses, could have altered the timing of the Charter Court.

While it was quite true that no one was ever happy with the Charter Court, it was just as true that they would fight to the death to keep it as it was.

"I rather doubt—" Innel began slowly.

"Of course not," she said, laughing, as if it had been a joke. "But perhaps, then, a rotating Court, with two of the Eight Houses every four years? To achieve some sort of—continuity of contracts? Less change and more stability—everyone would profit from that, surely."

An insanity of renegotiation every four years instead of every sixteen?

And who would go first into this rotating charter, like a fish tossed into the blades of a water wheel? He doubted Etallan intended to volunteer.

"He can't do that, Mother," Tok said in a tone of tolerant forbearance that seemed a bit showy to Innel. "The other Houses would mutiny."

"Surely it's worth consideration, though?" This from the Minister of Chimes.

Innel held up his hands in a gesture of half surrender. "I will mention it to Her Majesty." To amuse her, at least, he didn't say.

"So kind," smiled the Minister of Chimes, nodding pleasantly.

"What about the weapons contracts?" Tok asked with a guileless look Innel didn't believe for a moment.

Another impossibility, and Tok would know it. No

House had been given military weapons contracts in centuries; those contracts were spread around to the Trades, outside direct lines of Charters, because weapons in the hands of the Houses were not something the Anandynars ever wanted to see.

"No," the eparch said, giving a dismissive shake of her head. "We already have the great honor to supply the smithies with their ingots, and the great honor to take back the rejects for remelt. Conception and death—we can hardly ask for the honor of birth as well. So much honor would embarrass us."

A poorly suppressed smirk from Tok, who shared his amusement with Innel with a raised eyebrow.

Unless, of course, that too was for show, intended to give Innel the impression that he was in on the joke.

This was all testing, Innel was starting to realize, to see what he might say. To gauge his reactions. Thus far he had not actually been asked for anything that he could hope to provide. That, he was confident, would soon come.

In the silence that followed, everyone seemed to pause, as if to take a breath before coming back to the fight in earnest.

"Perhaps this, then," the Minister of Chimes said in a less flowery tone. "Our first forge, outside the city, along the Sennant."

"Oh, that." The eparch waved it away. "Hardly worth troubling the Lord Commander about."

"No, no. Please do tell me," Innel said, speaking the words he understood to be expected of him.

The eparch continued from her husband's start.

"Complaints from next door. About the noise. Odd, since we've been there—laboring to provide the empire's steel, as is our patriotic duty and considerable honor—almost three centuries now." She shrugged eloquently. "We understand that our great bellows and waterwheel hammers, all in service to the queen, might disturb their grand plays and elegant dances. Clearly something must be done." The eparch's smile dimmed a little. "Lord Commander, we beg your help on this matter. Perhaps you could move them somewhere else, sufficiently far enough away that we don't trouble them with our hard work?"

Next door, if Innel were not mistaken, was one of Helata's inn houses, for use of its rivermen and barge workers. A mansion in its own right.

Helata and Etallan had been at odds for some time, nursing a long-standing feud whose source seemed buried in history. But Helata, with its monopoly on ships and water trade, was also a House to avoid antagonizing.

"Naturally we would be happy to pay for the land," added Tok. "We could use a bit more room for the smithy anyway."

"Naturally," Innel responded dryly, knowing that the cost of the land was a trifle for Etallan.

Helata would be incensed at any such move, and when Helata was angry, ship-building contracts suffered. The monarchy had to stay out of this fight.

"I will mention it to Her Majesty," he said. Maybe he could put off a decision until Cern's rule was stronger.

"So grateful," said the Minister of Chimes. "Also we understand that the queen's forces have been spread a little thin in Gotar. We had thought, perhaps, that we might be allowed buy the warrant to collect taxes in that district on Her Majesty's behalf."

Now there was an interesting offer.

"Yes," the eparch continued. "When the mining towns misbehave it slows our production and makes us seem at fault. This is an affront to our pride in our work, and our honor as a House. You seem to have Sinetel well in hand, ser. Let us take our House forces and help you with Gotar."

The downside to this was that Etallan's in-house force could, and doubtless would, collect more than the given tax rate, and possibly some other things along the way. A hardship for whatever towns stood in their way. A hardship for the rebels of the mining town as well. It was, in some places, difficult to tell the difference.

But if Etallan had the warrant, that was an effort the crown would not have to finance or oversee.

Innel nodded slowly. Helata would have a hard time objecting to Etallan's smithy expansion when Etallan was showing such service to the new queen. The action might even inspire other Houses to be similarly useful.

"I will mention it to Her Majesty."

Indeed, he would advocate for it. Etallan would get their tax warrant.

"Excellent!" The eparch clapped her hands and gestured to the servant. "More of the adept-wine!"

If Helata and the other Houses offered similar support, perhaps these rebellions could be taken care of more quickly and with less cost to the crown than Innel had anticipated. Surely House Kincel would care as much about the rebellions along the quarry lands, Nital about the woodlands. Innel could customize tax warrants for all of them. A heartening thought.

He looked around the table at their smiling faces. He smiled back, then attempted to adjust his chair slightly closer to the table. It did not move at all easily, this chair made of metal.

Not obsession, he realized suddenly, of the sometimes-impractical metal, ceramic, and glass that composed every piece of furniture, walls, floors, and ceilings surrounding him. Rather, a demonstration of the range of their holdings. Of the extent of their power.

Good that he was finding ways to keep Etallan happy.

Another thimbleful of adept-wine was put in front of him, and, oddly, it tasted better than the first.

To Innel's surprise, the seneschal had immediately agreed with him that it was time to move the queen into the old king's suite. The old king, on the other hand, had complained bitterly. As had Cern.

Innel decided not to point out this similarity.

"Can't we simply brick the rooms up?" Cern asked, her tone almost a childlike whine.

"You are the monarch," he told her gently, taking her hand, not quite understanding the pain in her eyes. "You must occupy the monarch's residence. You understand, surely, my lady?"

She nodded reluctantly.

And so, during the move, Innel made sure the entire set of rooms was scrubbed thoroughly and repainted, the furniture all replaced either with Cern's existing set or with completely new items. Nothing would be as it had been before. Further, he had the large cages installed in one of the rooms for her birds.

He now stood in the completed suite, ignoring the two large gray and red birds making rude sounds at him from the cages, bobbing up and down to get his attention. Out the large windows were the rooftops of the Great Houses, their displays intended to be seen from exactly this vantage point.

Hence the combination of House and crown colors. Loyal subjects, the roofs seemed to say. Loyal, but keenly aware of their own power.

On Etallan's rooftop was a metal fountain, water sculpted in orange brass and black iron, the arcs falling and curling into a large pool of red and black glass, all cleverly arranged to seem fluid and in motion. Atop House Nital was a live, thick grove of amardide trees, bright green leaves sharp against the twisted red trunks, the surrounding brick walls a checked pattern of red and black—though perhaps a bit closer in tone to Nital's own brown and ash. Helata showed off a perfect replica of a sailing ship, complete with billowing blue sails, tilted sideways as if in a heavy wind, atop a red and black sea.

You had only to look at the roofs of the Houses to understand how each understood its place in the empire. If you knew what to look for, it was an excellent study.

When Innel was once again in his office, an aide knocked to announce a visitor.

"Colonel Tierda, Lord Commander. Reporting from Sinetel."

Tierda tracked in winter mud on her boots, the stink of horse clinging to her cloak and uniform. She had been a tenday in the saddle and smelled it.

Lason had once kicked out a messenger filthy from the road, insisting he be clean before reporting. That small delay had ended up costing the crown a lucrative trade opportunity with the Perripin state of Dulu. When Innel had taken over, he had made it clear that anyone with news should report to him immediately, and exactly as dirty as the road had made them. Tierda had taken note.

She bowed briefly. "Lord Commander."

Again, this strange shift in power, making it a curious meeting; she had been one of the Cohort's tutors years ago, particularly knowledgeable about the history of the mining villages to the north. Until recently she had outranked him. "Good to have you back. Your report, Colonel?"

"The governor of Sinetel has vanished," she said. "In his place is a trio of siblings who claim authority over Sinetel's mines and the rails to the river. We sent a scout to negotiate their overdue taxes. They sent back this."

She put an object on the table, something wrapped in white cloth stained brown with dried blood. The item was larger than a finger but smaller than a hand.

"The scout was male, I gather," he said.

"The rest of his body came back a few days later. Eyes burned out. Missing toes, fingers, ears."

Innel considered. Methods of torture were part of a land's culture, like food, shoes, and harvest festivals. Burning eyes was a practice of the high plains tribes, intended to convey that prying eyes were unwelcome.

Removing toes and fingers was a practice of the mountain people and had to do with the importance of being able to walk and climb.

So the tribes—conquered in the expansion wars, but never very compliant—were involved in the rebellion in Sinetel. Probably supplying them with support, possibly even weapons. Sinetel had gone a long way to find illegal trading partners.

"What did the scout know, that he might have told them?"

"Nothing, Lord Commander."

Innel wondered at her certainty. "You brought the body back?"

A puzzled frown. "No, Lord Commander. Should I have?"

There was information that could only be discovered by examining the remains. Lason would have criticized her for this, though he was himself always missing such details. But Lason was gone now, and no one knew where. He would turn up; it was not like an Anandynar to be silent for long.

As for the mining town, perhaps they thought that this was a good time to attempt some form of independence.

They were wrong.

"Take another four companies back with you, Colonel." More than enough to quiet the notion of rebellion. "When you have order reestablished, hang those who resisted. From the rest I want death-oaths of loyalty. Anyone who lacks appropriate enthusiasm for their words should have their toes broken."

"Toes?"

"Yes. And not with hammers or swords. Rocks between the toes, cinched with rope. You know the method?"

She nodded slowly.

"You don't understand."

"No, Lord Commander."

"They can work with broken toes. Eventually and with pain, but they can work. It is the long-term reminders that work best, Colonel. Go and take back our lands."

Once Cern had been crowned, Innel had found even Restarn's most loyal retainers surprisingly easy to buy off and quite willing to accept new assignments. Innel had been most concerned about the loyalty of Restarn's mages, but he need not have been; they had long since left the city.

So, according to Innel's network, Restarn was now completely cut off. All he had was what Innel allowed him to keep. And what was still in his head, much of which was nowhere else.

"Be careful," he told the doctor in what was barely a whisper. "Keep him alive."

"Yes, ser."

"No mistakes."

"No, ser."

One of the things Innel had allowed the old king to keep was curled up like a cat on a palette on the floor, her blond hair a tangled, pale waterfall, her beauty still breathtaking.

Restarn looked up at Innel from the bed through half-closed eyes, his small form so withered and sunken that he was nearly lost in the sea of blankets. The room stank of herbs and sickness.

"Blessings of the season to you, Sire," Innel said, aware that it was winter.

From the bed it seemed a very different man who stared at him, not much like the man whose gaze Innel had grown up under. He cautioned himself to be wary; fifty-six years of rule did not happen by lucky accident.

Naulen looked up at Innel, her perfect mouth and blue eyes wide, face like a frightened faun, no doubt intended to evoke in him a desire to protect.

"Leave," he said, suddenly disgusted with her. She stood gracefully, quick and lithe, clutching the edges of her tunic, and fled the room. Restarn's eyes opened. He watched her go.

How ill was he? He was tempted to ask Marisel.

But no, not only did he want her focus on the search for the seer, he didn't want her tempted to improve the man's condition. Despite the very expensive contract, Marisel dua Mage was answerable only to herself. He would trust the doctor, whose loyalty he could control.

"Innel," Restarn said in a raspy voice, drawing the name out. "At last. What is it this time? Did you drop the signet down the shithole? Want to know how much to pay a down-city whore?"

Every time Innel came here, he had more sympathy for Cern's moods.

"I came to see you," Innel said. "And now that I have, I will go."

"The girl," Restarn said. "That was thoughtful of you."

It brought him up short, this rare appreciation. "Yes, it was."

"So?" Restarn asked. "What is it? What do you want?"

"I had questions." About the tribes and towns now resisting Arunkel protection, which they had previously been happy to accept. About the one tribe that had sovereign status within Arunkel borders. About arrangements that had never been written, agreements with Houses. Things Restarn knew that he needed to know. That Cern needed to know but would never ask her father.

But suddenly he did not want to be here, playing this game. "I see how sick you are, Sire. I will not trouble you." A lifetime's worth of anger seemed to come over him at once, tightening his throat. He went to the door.

"Don't be a fool, Innel. Stay and talk to me."

He turned back. "You will tell me what you know." A half-question.

"That may take a while. A little today, perhaps a little tomorrow. I tire easily, as you keep pointing out."

Innel gritted his teeth. What choice did he have? He took a step back toward the bed. "The Houses claim you made them various promises. Some of them are clearly invented. Treasury ledgers aren't balancing. The Teva—I saw some in Arteni, riding those strange laughing horses. Could they be supporting the rebelling mining villages? Garaya's taxes are short again. Start by telling me about the Houses."

An annoyed grunt as the old king slowly sat up and then drank from a nearby cup. Innel did not offer to help.

"I want to see my daughter."

"She's busy."

"You can make her come to me, Innel. I know you can."

Innel gave a humorless laugh. "I rather doubt that."

The king looked at him, silent a moment. "You took my dogs away. Bring them back."

"I will look into it. But first—"

"Don't trust the Houses."

"Yes, I know that, but did you promise—"

"Of course I did."

"What exactly—"

He waved a hand, as if it were of no consequence. "Make them new promises. As long as nothing's written or witnessed, you can play them like two-head."

Innel frowned. "But—"

"Remember the Karmarn Range battle? No, of course not—you were an infant. False understanding of the enemy, boy. Kill you every time. We had ten companies. No, fifteen. All those villages with their adorable little farms and trout streams? Should have been easy. Wasn't. The Teva made that win for us. Those laughing horses. I'd trade every hoof in my stables for a breeding pair." He snorted. "Don't make enemies of the Teva. Forget Garaya. Get me my dogs." He coughed a little and lay back.

"Sire. I need to know exactly what you said to the Houses."

"Bring the dogs tomorrow. I'll tell you about the Battle of Uled and exactly how your father died. He was a hero, boy. You know that? Seems a good place to start, don't you think?"

✤ ✤ ✤

At a long table sat the queen, Innel, and the ministers of Accounts, Coin, and Treasury. At the other end were many tens of large books, most open, a number of clerks standing beyond.

"Your Majesty," said the Minister of Accounts, a man with a roundish face. "It is not possible to make the numbers come out equivalent. There are simply too many variables to be tallied thus. For example, accounting for our changing currency and metals markets—"

"Yes, that," the Minister of Coin broke in, her voice throaty and soft. "Now that we are modifying the coinage to reflect Your Majesty's new and may I say exceptionally handsome visage, invariably there will be some shifting in value of the old coinage being returned, and we must—"

"Allow me," said the Minister of Treasury. "To account for that difference, these minor inconsistencies, our agencies make adjustments. Do you see . . ." He motioned to three clerks who hurried over with books, opening each of them in front of Cern in sequence. "Do you see here, and here, and here, and how those numbers are the same?"

"Yes," Cern said, uncertainly.

Innel rubbed a hand across his eyes, spared a glance for Nalas and Srel at the side of the room.

"Just a moment," Innel said. "Do I correctly understand that we are losing fifteen parts in a thousand of our tax and levy revenue to—what do you call it—inconsistencies?"

The Minister of Accounts was already shaking his head. "Not at all, ser. The adjustments account for these differences, which I have already explained, so that the ledgers tally, here"—another clerk, another book of numbers opened, and a finger pointing to a particular line—"and in the master ledger, equal to the amount here, in the coinage and collections books. Do you see?"

"Are we losing money or not?" Innel asked.

"It is hardly that simple, ser," the Minister of Accounts replied with poorly veiled condescension before turning back to the queen, his expression tidy again. "Your Majesty, these practices are entirely consistent with those that His Royal Majesty Restarn esse Arunkel approved for the entirety of his 56-year rule. Nothing here is in error. Furthermore, the treasury is robust."

"Inconsistencies, you called them," Innel said. "Does that mean the clerks can't read each other's numbers? Do they need handwriting lessons? Or do you mean something else?"

"Perhaps the Lord Commander's attention might be better spent overseeing the security of the empire, Your Majesty?" the Minister of Treasury asked the queen.

"I assure you that I—" Innel began.

"You must be so very busy in this difficult time," said the Minister of Coin to Innel, her face a sudden mask of sympathy.

"Yes, of course, but that isn't the point."

The Minister of Accounts looked at Innel. "Ser, no monarch in near a thousand years has been able to remove all of the minor record-keeping inconsistencies that naturally arise in the course of accounting. Do you think we ought to be more capable than our esteemed ancestors?"

"You call them inconsistencies—" Innel tried again.

The Minister of Treasury stroked his bare chin as he spoke in a flat tone. "We are happy to call it anything you like, Lord Commander, though what this has to do with the administration of the armed forces is really quite unclear to me."

"The military accounts for a large portion of the crown's expenditures. If there's corruption, and I suggest we call it that, because I think that's the word you're looking for, then those missing funds are not going to horses and wagons, ships and soldiers. The crown does not keep its influence across the empire merely by fattening the purses and midlines of aristos and bureaucrats."

"Of course not, ser," replied the Minister of Coin without so much as a hint of a smile. "That's why we have the Charter Court."

For a moment Innel suspected the minister of humor.

"Innel," Cern said. "Perhaps they're right. They have been doing their jobs for some time."

"Thank you, Your Majesty," replied the Minister of Accounts with obvious relief. "We are grateful to you for your confidence in us. We do know our trade; we have devoted our lives to it."

It was too rich not to respond to, but Cern's hand was on Innel's, keeping him from replying. With effort he stayed silent.

"We are done for now," she said. "You may all go."

The ministers stood, bowed deeply and stayed bowed for the time it took their clerks to bow to Cern, gather the books, and somehow bow again with the books in hand. The crowd backed out of the door.

"You, too," Cern said to Nalas and Srel, who left much more quickly.

"Your Majesty—" Innel began as soon as they were alone.

"Innel, we can't fight on every front. You yourself told me that I needed to trust my ministers. Do you intend to restructure the treasury? Audit all the ledgers? Count all the coins in the mint?"

"The numbers—"

"It's paper and ink, Innel. Not the thing it represents, which comes from the empire's lands and her subjects. The treasury is, as they say, healthy, and you, I think, do indeed have other things wanting your attention. Is this not so?"

It was. He nodded uneasily.

The books were wrong. Given how much he himself was tapping the very healthy treasury, hiding some expenses in the complications of accounting, he knew perfectly well they were missing something. And if they were missing one thing, they were certainly missing more than that.

So it nagged at him. But she was right, and it was, perhaps, best to let it sit quiet for a time.

Innel glanced at Nalas standing at the window, watching Execution Square's single resident this cold spring morning.

Colonel Tierda stood at attention in front of him, her eyes flickering to the same view before returning to look straight ahead. She would be keenly aware that he would not have called her back from Sinetel if he had been pleased.

Outside, now at day four, the man was still and impressively alive. Around his neck was a leather thong, tight enough to have sunken into the red and swollen skin of his neck. His hands were tied behind him, only the noose keeping him from falling over. The other end of the leather thong traveled over a scaffold, where it was counter-balanced by a series of lead weights attached to a water bag just in reach of the man's mouth.

As Innel watched, the man turned to the nipple of the water bag, legs trembling. Then, instead of drinking, he turned his head away, expression a mix of agony and resolve. Thus the balance of water did not shift, the weights remained the same, and the noose did not tighten.

The man's self-control was admirable, but eventually he would be thirsty enough to drink, and the noose would tighten sufficiently to slowly strangle him. The tricky part of the contraption was making sure the water nipple was always close to the man's mouth. Putar was to be congratulated for the design.

Had Innel cared to bet, he would give the man until sunrise tomorrow to succumb. A handful of men and women who did care to bet stood at the edge of the square, hunched over, wagering on the man's future: days he would live, times he would cry out, sips it would take before he died.

In their youth, Innel and his brother had slipped in among those wagering to hone their understanding of the process. They had gotten good return for a time, and then Mulack had reported them to the king, and they had been instructed to stop.

For a time after the coronation, executions had fallen

off and the in-city holding dungeons had swollen to capacity. Innel had given Putar a position in the complicated hierarchy of the execution team and told them to clear it out. Now Yarpin's criminal population was cautious again.

Innel considered Tierda, still standing silently in front of them. When her reports by messenger bird were not encouraging, then were not detailed, he had sent for her. Disruptive, he knew, to take her away from the conflict. "I would have thought three months and four companies enough to quell the trouble at Sinetel. What is the problem, Colonel?"

A tense exhale. "Ser, the townspeople hide in the woods, picking us off as we approach. They know the mountains better than we do."

He wanted to tell her this was a weak excuse, that other mining villages along the northern range were watching, slowing the ore they owed the capital city. That every month this continued, the crown looked increasingly impotent. "You must end this treasonous resistance, Colonel."

"Yes, ser." From her tone and expression, he could tell there was something else she didn't want to say.

"Speak."

"Not all those hiding in the woods are townspeople," she said reluctantly. "Some are ours."

"Ours? What do you mean?"

"Deserters, ser."

Innel scowled. "How many?"

"Perhaps—five in a hundred, ser."

At this Innel stood. "That many?"

"Yes, Lord Commander. I—ah. I think they may be aiding the insurgents, from some of the"—she hesitated. "Arrows we are now facing. Our arrows."

Tierda, he reminded himself, had a fine grasp of tactics and a fast eye. Her troops respected her. She was far from incompetent.

"Bring them back for me, Colonel. I want the deserters there." He pointed out the window.

She followed his look. "I assure you, ser, I've done everything I can. I—"

"I know. Enough."

There must be a way to encourage the soldiers to continue to fight, beyond the threat of death.

"Settler's rights to the soldiers if this is won," he said. "Provisional land grants, certified only after they produce at least two heirs who have come of age in their homes." Land and children tended to effectively turn soldiers into loyal citizens, keeping them where they were put. Better to lose soldiers to the countryside than to the rebels.

"Yes, ser."

"Land and children," he muttered. "Your child. He now lives with your sister's family."

She paled, swallowed. He knew the trouble she had gotten into under Lason, having the boy at her high rank.

"He belongs to my sister's family now," she said, keeping her look distant.

"A mistake anyone could have made," he said, watching her face. "Was it? A mistake?"

She focused on him, clearly considering what might be the prudent answer. She exhaled. "No, ser, it was not."

Good; she had spoken directly, even under this duress.

She didn't know, and he wouldn't tell her, but this had been his test of keeping her rank, that she would speak truthfully to him.

"I'm not Lason," he said. "I don't care if you drink or smoke or make babies. I care that you win. If your command suffers for any reason, I'll take it from you. If it's a child, I'll feed it to the royal pigs. Do you understand?"

"Yes," she said, her lips twitching in a near-smile, then sobering, as if she had suddenly decided he was not joking at all.

Good. Now for the reassurance.

"Some people think women make better commanders. What do you think, Colonel?"

"Some do, ser."

"Well said. If it were up to me, every soldier, man or woman, would bear at least one brat before taking a command position. The pain you go through makes you better equipped to understand the necessities of battle."

"I'd have to agree with that, ser."

"And less hesitant to share pain. On your way back to Sinetel, go through the other mining villages. Make sure they know the price for disobeying the queen's orders. Examples should be clear and easy to understand, and, like the broken toes, should not prevent them from working the mines. We must keep the ore flowing."

"Yes, ser."

"I will expect to hear of your successes soon."

She bowed her head and left, looking in equal measures relieved and troubled.

Innel sat back in his chair, taking a long look at the

young man who stood at attention on the other side of his desk. He thought of his mother, then of Cahlen, and found himself oddly at a loss as to what he might say.

The man was twitching, struggling to hold still. Nervous. More nervous than surprised.

"Selamu, is it? Selamu al Garaya, yes?"

"Yes, ser."

Innel was fiddling with Pohut's arrowhead. If his brother had still been alive, if they had come to power together as they should have, as they had planned to, he had no doubt Pohut would be the one to handle this now. What would his brother have said?

"How long have you been sleeping with my sister?" he demanded.

Not that, he was sure, as soon as the words left his mouth.

"Ser." The man's mouth moved silently for a moment, and he gulped as if he did not have enough air. "Some three months, ser." It came out a croaking sound.

"And what advantages do you think this gains you?"

"Ser Lord Commander?"

"Don't fence with me. I'll win. No delay, either. Speak."

Selamu's eyes went as wide as they could go, and he swallowed over and over.

Innel sighed with frustration. Now he had terrified the man into silence. He looked at the arrowhead, put it on the table, clicked it against the wood while he considered. "Answer," he said, trying for a gentler tone, suspecting he was not succeeding.

"She's beautiful, ser."

"Cahlen," Innel said, not quite a question. "My sister? What are you attempting here? What do you hope to acquire in this?"

"Acquire, ser?"

Innel had already looked into this man's records. Reliable. Obedient. No mention of being simple-minded or addled. "Tell me what it is you want. Say it slowly. Breathe."

The man stuttered, began to tremble violently. "Ser. I—nothing. She is. I only. Just to—"

"*What?*"

"Continue."

Continue?

The man blushed deeply, which Innel found curious and yet somewhat reassuring; it was far harder to pretend to blush than it was to lie.

"You are saying that you *like* her?" he asked, finally coming to the only remaining conclusion.

At this the man nodded eagerly.

Innel stood, came out from behind his desk. Selamu visibly tensed as Innel slowly circled him. Average height, without visible scars, his shoulders square. He seemed healthy enough and to all appearances unexceptionally average.

Cahlen?

When Innel had finished his inspection, he sat on the edge of his desk. Sweat was now beading on Selamu's brow, trickling down his face. The vein in his neck was pulsing fast. "Did you think to keep this secret?"

In a whisper, Selamu replied: "We tried, Lord Commander."

"You're a fool."

"Yes, ser."

Another long silence as Innel tried to imagine his sister having sex, with anyone, let alone this man, and failed. He pushed the image away. "Don't for a moment think this gives you any advantage in your unit, in your barracks, or even so much as an extra crumb of bread with your meal."

"No, ser."

"And don't be clumsy."

"No, ser. Yes, ser."

Innel drummed his fingers on his desk. "Did you have an anknapa when you came of age?"

"No, ser. We were too poor."

"I will send one to you."

"Yes, ser."

"You will study. With devotion."

"Yes, ser."

Innel had no idea what else to say. "Go."

The man saluted and then fled, his relief obvious.

Innel stood in the toilet room of the Frosted Rose, which smelled far worse than he recalled. "You do not have her."

"Lord Commander, it might be best if I resign this commission."

Innel had been thinking something similar. But now, hearing the words, he found himself not much liking the idea. The fact remained that Tayre was the only one of his many hires who had even reported back to him. "Why do you suggest this?"

"I have been seeking your quarry for over two years

now. Perhaps someone else might do better. I will return your souvers to you and go on my way. All you need do is say you wish the contract over."

"No." That Innel would not say. Not yet. "How is it that you have lost them now—how many times?"

"Oh, I know where they are. They are in Munasee."

"What? Then why are you here? Why does she still breathe?"

"Munasee is a crowded city, Lord Commander, with an abundance of places to hide, and she has gained some new sophistication in her evasions."

"So you can't catch her and you can't kill her? Perhaps you need help."

A laugh. "I've seen your help, ser. They make more rumors than they follow, create more trails than they uncover. I've had to kill some of them to clear my way. I assure you, ser, when I need help, I'll hire it myself."

Innel wondered how much coin he'd wasted on searchers who were now dead by this man's hand. "The cost you'll pass onto me, of course."

A single syllable that might have been tamped-down amusement. "You have a mage. All the help I could possibly hire would cost less than that one bit of trouble."

It was hard to argue with that. Tayre's expenses were small beside what Maris was costing him, who in these last three seasons had found nothing.

Maybe she was the one who needed help. Now that he had his hands in the treasury, that was an option. He put the thought aside for later.

"Lord Commander, if you really want this girl, we must change our tactics."

"Oh, we must, must we?" Innel's could hear the strain in his own voice.

"Yes. I believe that we can approach her directly, if we give her nothing to be wary of."

"Explain your meaning."

"Allow me to offer her a contract with the crown. To give her the monarchy's protection. This will assure that there is no threat for her to foresee."

Innel made a doubtful sound. "A contract to . . . ?"

"To advise you, ser. Is that not what you want her for? But for it to work, there must truly be no danger to her or her family."

"By which you mean . . . ?"

"You must genuinely forgo your goal of killing her or harming her in any way. You must change your intention."

Innel imagined the girl and her sister and nephew in the guest wing of the palace. He could explain that they were cousins of his, targets for kidnapping, and he had brought them close to protect them. It wasn't even that far from the truth.

"To secure her under contract . . . that would be acceptable."

"I might be able to improve her impression of such an offer by making sure that what she and her sister are doing to make money isn't enough. See to it that her rent is raised. Arrange to keep her wages low. To live in Munasee is already expensive; this could make her more desperate."

"Won't she foresee this as well?"

"I doubt it. She foresees danger when it is imminent, a skill that is improving daily as the attempts on her life by various hounds give her ample practice."

Innel wondered how many of the hounds after her were working for someone else. Or, having started in Innel's employ, had figured out what she was and were now pursuing her for their own ends with no intention of bringing her to him. Tayre, at least, kept coming back.

As if reading his mind, Tayre continued: "They won't catch her by force any better than I have, Commander. Their efforts might even work in our favor—frequent threats will make her more willing to come under your protection. Indeed, a few additional attempts on her life prior to presenting your offer might be useful. I can arrange those."

Innel considered the proposal for a long moment. "All right. Go ahead and bait the trap. If you can get her under contract I will put aside my passion for having her head in favor of having her well in hand."

Chapter Nineteen

Amarta woke with the sun's first light, crawling out from under the blankets on the floor of their one-room apartment, shivering in the morning chill. She put on one layer, then wrapped a wide strap across her waist, crossing it around her breasts, then back again, tying it tight.

Dirina struggled to sit up on her side of the cot, where Pas was still sleeping. For a moment her sister simply sat there unmoving in the dawn light through the small, high, shuttered window, like one of the sea-sprite statues on the white terraces of Munasee's governor's mansion that spanned the great canal.

Amarta paused a moment. Dirina was beautiful, she realized. Beautiful and so sad.

No surprise, there, though. If Amarta let herself, she had plenty to be sorrowful about, too. At least Dirina didn't have to entertain men anymore to keep them fed. She should be happy enough about that, but she was not.

Grieving Kusan. Grieving Kosal.

Amarta had no sympathy for either. They had both lost

Kusan, had both lost another place they might in time have called home and people who had made the mistake of caring for them.

Like Nidem.

As for Kosal—at least her sister had had such sweetness for a time. What had Amarta had? A few kisses, painful when she forgot to keep them from memory.

Amarta turned away to finish dressing. Dirina pulled on her clothes and set about to mix hot water with the fats and oats and farrow that made up most of their meals.

"You out all day, again?" Dirina asked.

Amarta pulled on another layer against the spring chill, then another on top of that to bulk out her stomach. She'd cut her hair short again, and while it was harder to seem a boy as she grew—even her face was changing now—with a hood and downcast look and the right movements she could fool people for a few moments. In this city thick with people like grass in a meadow, a moment was often all it took.

"Yes."

In truth it was only maybe, but she'd discovered that uncertainty meant Dirina was more likely to argue, and she didn't have time for it, not with Magrit looking to give someone the messages to deliver and others who would take them if Amarta were not first. She now made more coin as a courier than Dirina had ever from going with men. She felt rich when she was paid, so rich. But that feeling ended at the market. How could everything here cost so much?

"Ama," her sister said quietly, as if reading her thoughts, "I can make money for us, too."

Amarta pushed aside her sudden flush of anger, instead looked down into the warm mash that her sister had handed her. She had as little desire for it as she did for this conversation. She mixed the mash with her fingers, as if that might help, scooped it out, pasted it on her tongue, swallowed before she could taste.

It eased hunger, she told herself sternly. They had eaten far worse and far less.

But they had also eaten better and enough, and it was too easy to remember those times.

No. Life was about leaving the warm places with food and people you liked so much, so that you could protect them from what was following you. There was no sense in lamenting what could not be avoided. She put more of the mash into her mouth.

"Ama, I can—"

"I heard you the first time," she snapped.

Her sister gave her an angry look. "Then—"

"You are not going with the men. Never again. It's not safe."

She remembered, from their first night in Munasee, Dirina's swollen face, purple eye, how she hunched over. Dirina had left Amarta and Pas in a field outside the city to make coin the fastest way she knew how. Instead she'd come back badly beaten, told she couldn't do that sort of thing, not here, not without permission, and she wasn't getting that without paying for it. They'd hit her hard and repeatedly to make sure she wouldn't forget.

Dirina refused to cry that night, so Amarta cried for her.

It would not happen again, Amarta had decided,

furious with herself for letting this occur. Late that night while Dirina slept fitfully, curled around Pas, Amarta crept into the streets of Munasee, found a lamplit circle of women and dice, and put down the last of the nals they owned, using foresight to predict, narrowing her focus to that one thing, that turning cube and its symbols. They must eat, she told vision fiercely, willing it to listen, to behave, to deliver.

And it did; she correctly named each roll. On the third roll the women were surprised. By the tenth, they were outraged. They grabbed for her. Vision warned her, barely in time. She'd had to drop all the coins to get away.

From this she learned it was not enough to know how the dice would roll or even to know the game rules. She also had to know the people rules.

As dawn lightened the sky that agonizing morning, thin red clouds banding the sky like bloodied blades, Amarta walked the streets of this strange and terrifying city crammed with people, despair and hunger heavy on her, demanding that vision find a way to feed her.

The city was overwhelming. She had not realized how big Munasee would be, how many streets and tall buildings that blotted out the sky, more people than she had ever seen at one time, every direction a crush, the noise even at dawn near deafening. Future flashes were many and contradictory, so jumbled she had to push them away just to think.

She walked the streets, looking for answers, propelled by the anger at what had happened to her sister and the gnawing hunger in her stomach.

Between guesswork and flashes not much clearer than

the dirt-caked stones beneath her feet, she stepped into a tiny storefront. There a trader named Magrit eyed her suspiciously but with hope; she needed a message delivered uptown to something called the third district and her messenger had not shown yet. It had not been easy to convince the trader to let a girl she didn't know take a message for her, and even harder to accomplish it in this huge city of buildings and canals and bridges.

It had taken all day, but she had done it, and when she returned to Dirina, furious and wretched with worry for her, she had brought both food and money.

It had been months since then and Dirina was still not happy about it. "What you do, Ama, it's not safe, either."

Again, this discussion?

"I can see the future, Dirina. I am protected."

An overstatement, to be sure. Since they had come to Munasee, Amarta had reached a sort of truce with her foresight, one that kept her free and alive, though sometimes not by much.

It seemed she had to wait until nearly the last possible moment to slip between the confusing chaos of too many futures and the clarity of immediate action. Vision had kept its side of the bargain, though: she was still alive.

So many people, so many possibilities. That was why they had come to Munasee in the first place, to lose themselves among great crowds. To hide from the hunter. Like a drop of water in the ocean.

"Yes, Ama, but—"

"I'm safer on the streets in the middle of the night than you are in broad daylight," she said. "Get fixed with it, Diri: I go out and work. You and Pas stay here."

Pas was awake now, sitting up, looking from one of them to the other, displeased. Dirina handed him a bowl of mash, which he regarded with the same expression.

"Since when do you decide what I do?"

"Since I started bringing back coin."

Dirina was silent for a moment. Then, looking away, with an almost apologetic whisper, as if she were somehow to blame: "It's not enough, though, is it?"

It was not. Some days Amarta returned to their rented room with only nals in hand, having spent the rest on some tantalizing bit of food after going hungry all day running the city. Each time she resolved to save some for Dirina and Pas, but hunger somehow kept putting it all into her own mouth.

"I'll bring back more." She sat on the floor, pulled on her turnshoes, now tight again.

A pause. "When?"

She'd put it off, asking Magrit for a larger portion of the delivery fee. Watching the trader bargain with merchants, she had learned that no price was ever fixed, that the first offer was never the best, but even so, every time she decided to ask, she changed her mind.

Magrit might say no. Might decide Amarta was too much trouble. Then what would they do for rent and food?

"Today," she said, willing it to be true.

"Those are tight on you."

"Leave off, Diri—I'm fine."

They were a long way from being able to afford new shoes. Everything cost so much, from rent to food. Rumors of shortages from the farms, freighters coming in light—everywhere she looked, what would have seemed a fortune in Botaros was a pittance.

At least it hadn't snowed their first winter here. The ocean, a day west, kept the air warm, people said. Then they said it was the canals, or the stones in the ground. But when the winds blew from the eastern, white-topped mountains, and snaked through Amarta's layers, she wondered if that was the sort of thing people said to make themselves believe they were warm when they really weren't. Like pretending the mash in her mouth tasted good.

She put the half-full bowl onto the floor and went to the door. Dirina followed her with a worried look. Did her sister's face know any other expression?

"When will you be back?"

"Later."

"Amarta."

The courier work required confidence beyond sense. She must seem sure in every word and step, or she had no hope of traversing this dangerous city or escaping the near-daily attempts of the hunter to catch her.

"You want to eat more than mash, Diri? Let me work. Stop nagging. I'm safe."

And she would be. She and vision had an understanding.

Amarta touched the coins tucked tightly in the wrap under her chest, the ones Magrit had given her, to reassure herself they were still there. They replaced the small folded message she'd delivered earlier. Magrit had given her the larger portion without argument. If Amarta had known how easy it would have been, she would have asked months ago.

She frowned at this thought. Why hadn't she?

It was the many layers that vision gave here in Munasee, fuzzy and befuddling. Too many threads to follow. An unsolvable maze, right up until whatever danger tried to grab her was nearly upon her.

But there was another reason. Magrit's future was as wretched as the rest she passed on the street. Magrit would not keep her business. She would be lucky to keep her life. Amarta had seen enough.

She wove through the crowds of the Ocher Market, so named for the pale bricks that ringed the square. She ducked under shaded booths, listening as she went to the sounds of laughter, shouts, and insults, for anything out of the ordinary.

Something tantalizing was being fried in a brazier at the center, distracting her. She pushed away thoughts of food. Not today; today she would go home directly, decide with Dirina what to spend the money on.

Heading toward the Great Canal she stepped into the lines of people slowly moving onto a green bridge. It occurred to her as she shuffled forward up steps onto the bridge that all the people around her were like the sand in a sand-clock, slowing and narrowing at the neck to trickle out the other end in both directions. At the apex of the bridge, where the crowd sluggishly came to a standstill, she craned her neck to see what blocked the exit. A fallen cart, perhaps, or some other altercation—she couldn't see. While she waited, she gripped the railing and looked out at the water in which various bits of who-knew-what floated.

Up canal, short of the huge governor's mansion, was another green-blue bridge. Beyond that the ruins of a yellow one.

The War of the Bridges, it was called. House Helata built most of the bridges, the one she stood on being the first, and built them high enough to allow their oceangoing ships to sail to the governor's port. Then the other Houses had built bridges, not high enough to allow Helata's tall ships to pass. These new bridges mysteriously fell in, in one case taking some forty people into the canal as it collapsed. Helata took them over. As more and more of the bridges had become green or blue, House Helata's ships, large and small, took over the canals.

In front of her the flow of people began again, the tight crowd carrying her forward.

A hand on her arm yanking her off the green stone steps into a carriage, a hood over her head.

Vision took over. She followed instructions, dropping to a crouch, and half-crawled her way through the forest of legs to the far side of the bridge, where the flow of feet took her in the opposite direction, expelling her again into the Ocher Market. A dash left to the Fishermen's Inn, a pause, then it was over, the danger past.

She exhaled a laugh, walked easily through the crowds and over another bridge, passing the Key Market, named for its shape: long and thin, booths on both sides ending in a circular area with a public well at the center. Frying bread and vegetables and meat made her mouth water. She slowed, wondering how much of today's coins she could spare.

None, she told herself again sternly.

A man stumbled across her path, smelling of smoke and drink. *He would lurch left, then right, then drop drunkenly into the shadows of the alleyway beyond.*

Instead he stopped in front of her, stared at her curiously, his future shifting as she watched.

He had stopped, she realized, because she had stopped. She herself had changed the moment, and that had changed his attention, thus his future. This was why she must adopt a plan, any plan, and stay with it until vision's alarm. Otherwise it was like trying to catch a spilled bag of beans before they all touched the pavement. Too much, too many, too fast.

Like the night a handful of men had surrounded her, each one a glimpsed spray of possibilities, too many to sort through. In a near panic she ran, vision a confusing and mumbling advisor. Only when she had begun to run in earnest, dashing down into a basement stairwell, hiding in a tight corner, did vision give her a clear sense of direction: stay and wait. A mouse in the dark. They had gone right by her, inches from where she hid.

There was no reason to tell Dirina about that escape. Nor the many others.

She backed away from the drunk man, turned down another alley.

"Coin's good," came a woman's thick, slurred voice, heavy with a Munasee accent. Amarta realized she was the target of the comment. "You have the face for it." The woman's long features were deeply lined, eyes wide and unfocused. Amarta felt no alarm, so she did not try to see more. Nor did she want to; the woman's desolation clung to her like a stink. "I give half. Not many do anymore, you know."

This was what Dirina would turn into, if she whored here in Munasee. Amarta did not slow, as if she had not heard.

A boy, perhaps five, cut across her path, turning as he ran to look behind, then dashing away. He'd stolen something, something small from the sound of the half-hearted cursing that preceded a man wielding a large wooden spoon like a club. He looked around, then, having lost the boy, retreated the way he'd come.

The boy looked a bit like Pas might in a couple of years. If he didn't get better at stealing, someone was going to take him to a magistrate and chop a finger off. More, if he took something expensive.

No, she saw suddenly, the boy would not lose any fingers. He would not live long enough. By autumn he would be dead, beaten to death. She saw his body, twisted, head half-pulped like rotten fruit.

She had stopped again, hunched over. She felt as if she had eaten dirt.

To stop suddenly in the city, to seem unsure for even a second, was to attract attention. Eyes were on her now, suspicious and calculating. An old woman hobbling across the alley. A man carrying a sack. A young man giving her a thoughtful look. She turned abruptly, summoning the certainty of step and posture that she'd lost in that moment.

As vision came over her, the world went bright. Forward momentum changed to a turn. Her inhale seemed to take a very long time. Plenty of time to continue the turn, to look at what vision wanted her to see.

Her destination was a brick wall. The turn complete, she fell into a sprint toward the inviting wall, wondering what she would do when she got there. As her palms hit the sooty, gritty red brick, she glanced up the street. A tarp-covered carriage was barreling toward her.

The old woman threw herself backwards out of the path of the oncoming wheels. She landed on the ground with a cry. The boy flattened himself against the wall.

From the carriage a crossbow poked out, then another below it, pointed at her.

Deep in vision now, she felt the nudge to move to the side, but only slightly, and she did. A bolt hissed by her ear, hit hard brick, fell to the ground.

A small step to the side and forward, just so. Little more than a twitch. Another bolt went by.

She counted steps as she ran—one and two and three and—freeze. Another bolt and then another. It seemed too many, surely, which meant—what? That the hunter had help?

It didn't matter; she didn't need to understand. Vision knew. She only needed to follow where it led.

Rounding the brick corner she pounded down steps, then saw a small window, hidden from the street, open. She wriggled into it, dropping a couple of feet into a basement. Hooves and wagon wheels slammed loudly past, horses chuffing. Someone yelled to stop. Footfalls on the street behind her.

Run. Down a dark hallway, toward daylight at the other end.

Out, vision urged. She dashed out into the day, again in the Key Market. At vision's direction she slowed, snaked her way through the thick crowd, came out the other side. An alleyway invited, so she took it, finding herself now by a stone fountain. A fast dash, then a cross-step to change her direction. She was under the awning of a cloth shop closing their doors for the day.

All at once the pressure faded. The world sped up. She was breathing hard, pulse pounding.

She had escaped. Even though she trembled with the exertion, she felt elated, a giddy joy. She almost enjoyed these threats that she could now slip through.

Two years since she had faced him in the woods of Nesmar. A lifetime ago. She no longer had to flee the hunter—she was safe, right here in Munasee. He could not, would not, lay hands on her, not when she could move through the city like a snake in the grass, a fish in the canal.

This was a game she knew how to play and could win.

The evening sun dipped down behind tall gray stone and red brick buildings. She touched the pouch at her chest to make sure the coins were still there.

They were.

"You're going out again?" Dirina had her arms crossed in the light of the tallow lamp. Her tone said so much more than her words.

How late it was. How dangerous to be on the streets at night.

Amarta sighed. Through the spring and long summer, despite the raise in pay from Magrit, it had not gotten easier to afford food. She was working all hours of the day. Then the rent had been raised.

That they had tallow at all was due to Amarta, so if she decided to stay up late, or to work all night—or really, whatever she wanted to do—Dirina had no business giving her trouble about it.

"For a little," she said, as evenly as she could, tugging her feet into her turnshoes, lacing them loosely. At least it wasn't raining this spring night. She hated having her feet wet for hours, the shoes no longer watertight.

"What kind of work is this?"

"I'll know when I get there."

At this Dirina looked even more upset. All the more reason to leave.

"Magrit didn't tell you?"

The trader had asked her to meet with someone to talk about a new job. Who or what the job might be, Magrit didn't seem to know. More unusual yet were the falcons Magrit had given Amarta in advance, just to show up.

"There's coin in this," Magrit had said. "For both of us. Don't be late."

And coin meant food. Tallow. Maybe meat. If it was enough, she could even dream of a new pair of shoes.

"Where?" Dirina demanded. "Where are you going? What kind of work is it, this late?"

Of all the times for Dirina to insist on details.

"I'll tell you when I get back."

"You'll tell me now."

Amarta reached into her pocket, brought out the handful of silver falcons, put them into her sister's hands, wrapping her fingers around them, enjoying her shocked expression.

"Ama, how did you get these? You had better not be—"

"Going with the men? Taking my clothes off?" she asked mockingly. At this her sister looked even more aghast. "Diri, no, it's not that. It's—" She didn't know. "Courier work." Sound confident, she reminded herself.

"He could still be out there," her sister said softly.

"Who?" If she pretended not to know, maybe Dirina would think the hunter gone.

"*Who*?" her sister echoed in outrage. "Why did we leave Kusan? Because *he* was after us, you said. We never saw him, but you said, and I believed you. Now you ask me *who*?"

Her sister was breathing heavily, furious, and Amarta felt her face go hot.

"Mama," Pas said, wrapping his arms around her leg. "Not so loud."

Dirina was visibly controlling her temper now, a hand on Pas's head. "Did we leave Kusan for nothing, Amarta?"

Tell her sister of the narrow escapes she'd had these last months? Or let her resent Amarta for taking them away from Kusan, from Kosal? There was no good answer.

"I'll be late, Diri. But there's coin in this. A lot." Magrit had said so.

Dirina took Amarta by the shoulders and searched her eyes. "Ama," she said, "if anything happened to you—"

"I'll be careful, Diri. I promise. I'll be fine."

Dirina wanted to say more. Maybe a lot more.

"I must leave now, Diri."

Her sister pressed her lips together and nodded reluctantly.

Amarta's visions would keep her safe, and she would keep her sister and nephew safe.

The meeting was up-city, at the Ox-bow Inn, near the twist in the canal where the governor's mansion squatted across the huge waterway. The houses here were huge, bright in House colors and wrought iron.

She stood across the street in this warm night of late summer. The inn was gray stone with pale trim and many windows. A high and heavy wooden door, ornately carved. A place of money. Not the sort of place she usually went to, not to deliver messages for Magrit, not for any reason.

For a time she simply stared. She told herself she was giving vision a chance to warn, but in truth she felt awkward, unsure how to act, to speak, certain that anything she did would be out of place.

Now she truly was late. She went to the door, took the metal knocker—an iron wolf head, she realized, once it was in her hand—and let it fall. The sound resonated, not entirely unlike a bell.

The door opened. An expensively dressed woman opened it, saw her, and stood aside to invite her inside. "You are expected. Will you follow me?"

The woman led her down a long hallway. Amarta tried not to gape at the inlaid floors, deep brown velvet-cushioned chairs, walls painted with images of forests in such detail she could see birds and the buds of spring among the green leaves.

The woman opened a door, then stood aside, gesturing

Amarta inside. Lamps flickered from the walls. A man sat at the far end of a wooden table. There was an empty chair close to the door.

"Please come in," he said, smiling warmly. The door shut behind her. "There is tea for you, if you like."

"Thank you," Amarta said, sitting down. She wrapped her hands around the mug and inhaled. Fruits and spices. It smelled expensive. She took a small sip, astonished at how rich and sweet it was.

She was sure she did not know this man, yet there was something familiar about him. His voice, perhaps. Maybe she had spoken to him in the market. Or delivered a message to him once.

Vision was not warning of any danger. Still, the voice—she peered at him again in the lamplight. She felt certain she should remember where she had met him.

Something about him. Something—

Memory fell into place, like large stones falling from a great height, hitting the earth with such force they shook the ground.

Flickering maple leaves. The scent of rotting leaves. A knife at her throat.

She was standing now, though she could not remember having left her seat, the back of the chair clutched tight in her sweating hand. A step backward to the door, and another, her eyes glued to him.

"No premonitions?" he asked.

Had she passed him on the street she would not have looked twice, bearded as he was now, dressed so finely. Now that she looked again, though, she knew his eyes.

Her hunter had light brown eyes.

But vision had not warned her. All the times she'd escaped him and here he stood, mere feet away. Where was vision? Her heart pounded in her ears.

"The door is unlocked," he said. "You can leave if you like. I won't stop you."

"What do you want?" she whispered.

"I am here on behalf of the Lord Commander of the Arunkel Empire to offer you a contract with the crown."

He was speaking words, but she could not seem to make sense of them. "The what?"

"Do you know the name Cern esse Arunkel?"

Of course. Who did not?

"The queen's Royal Consort, Innel sev Cern esse Arunkel, has sent me here to offer you employment. A position on his staff."

She should leave, she thought. Now, while she still could. Her fingers groped for the door handle behind her. "Doesn't he already have messengers?"

"Not as a messenger. As an advisor."

She felt foolish. Of course. He would want her for her visions.

And where were those visions now to warn her? Was there truly no risk here?

She could dimly sense future danger coming out of this moment, but it was distant, complicated, the sort that was more direction and shadow than flash, that would take hours or days to unravel, if she could manage it at all. She only had a sense that whatever she did here tonight would be of consequence.

"You're shaking, Amarta. Please, sit a while. Your foresight should tell you no harm will come to you from having tea with me. Surely you trust your vision that far, at least?"

Of course she did. Was he was trying to make her doubt herself? That would not work. Not on her. Not anymore.

With that thought, she came around the chair and sat resolutely, swallowing, facing him. She was not afraid of him. She could leave anytime she wanted. Vision would protect her. "I don't think I should believe anything you say."

His mouth twitched as if considering a smile. "You can believe the message I deliver. Tonight I am a courier, like you. I would never work again if I gave a false offer from the crown. You don't have to trust me to trust the offer I convey."

She didn't move, barely breathed, hands clenched into fists. "Who are you?" she asked.

"You want a name?"

"Yes."

He made a thoughtful sound. "If you have a name for me, it will change the way you think of me. Are you sure you want that?"

"Yes," she said firmly, not at all sure.

"Tayre," he said. "And yours?"

"You know my name," she snapped.

"I know what others call you. What do you choose to be called?"

"Nothing by you. You are no friend."

"No, I am not, Seer."

The title sent a shock through her, from head to toes and back, an echo backward and forward in time. She sat back in her chair as if hit.

"On this night, I am here in peace, and bring you no threat. The crown wants your attention, and asks you to consider this offer."

With that, he put on the table a coin. A huge coin. It was gold and palm-wide. Amarta's mouth fell open. She had never seen a souver touch before, though she had heard of them. Ten times the worth of a gold souver.

"The offer is genuine and generous, Seer." He slowly pushed the coin toward her on the table until it was close enough to take. "There's more than this, if you agree."

More? She put her fingertips on the wide disk of gold, tracing the outline of the overlaid moon, star, pickaxe, and sword at the center of the coin.

"You've been running from me a long while, Seer. Are you not tired of this chase?"

Resentment stirred inside her. "No. Are you?"

"When I'm tired, I sleep. No one comes for me in the night."

The anger stayed, along with a fear she refused to feel. "I could have killed you," she said. "Right there in the forest. With your own bow. With your own knife."

He clasped his hands in front of him. "But you didn't. It didn't even occur to you until you were far, far away. Am I right?"

How could he know that?

"Amarta, end this hunt, right now. Take the crown's protection."

"I'm fine where I am. I escape you every time you come for me. Day or night."

"Ah. You think it's been me after you, all these months here in Munasee." He grinned a little, shook his head.

"I've only been watching. Has it not occurred to you to wonder why your pursuers all seem so inept?"

At that, doubt crept into her mind. She shook her head, tried to push it away.

"Sooner or later someone will find a way around your magic," he said.

"It's not magic."

"As you say. What about Dirina and Pas?"

He knew their names. She suppressed a shiver. "Who?"

A small tilt of his head. "You courier for the trader Magrit. Your sister and nephew eat by your work, when they eat at all. I know the room in which the three of you sleep."

"I'm not going to tell you anything."

"You just did. And while you're out delivering messages and evading clumsy attempts on your life, who is protecting your family from those who pursue you? Indeed, Seer, who is protecting them right now?"

He was only trying to scare her. But it was working. She wanted to run home right now to make sure they were okay. Did he really know where they lived?

"The Lord Commander offers you and your family the sanctuary of the crown. He is more than the queen's consort; he is the commander of the army. You could not be safer anywhere in the empire. Anywhere in the world."

"So you say. You who have been hunting me for years."

He spread his hands. "The crown extends the offer. My task is to present it. To bring you safely to the capital, after you accept."

"So," she said, putting as much insult in her voice as she could, "you're no more than a hired hound."

"I am exactly that, but no longer the only one in pursuit."

"I'm not afraid of you."

But she was gasping as if she could not get enough air. What if he were telling the truth? What if all these months in Munasee it had not even been him coming after her?

"Consider, Seer: safety for your family. Plenty of food. Shoes that fit."

She looked at him, aghast. How could he know about the shoes? "If I say yes, then what?"

"From that moment forward you will be under contract to the Lord Commander. You and your family, under his protection and secure. A life of ease and luxury in the queen's palace. This is a rare opportunity."

And a stunningly good offer. Yet she hesitated. Why?

"How do you answer, Seer?"

She looked back at him, forced herself to meet his eyes. It seemed she had been facing him her whole life.

To stop running. To eat regularly. A new life for the three of them. One of unimaginable riches.

A far better life than she could ever hope to earn for them in Munasee.

"I have to think.".

"Think fast. This offer will not be open long, and when it closes, Amarta, the life you have found here may no longer be so easy."

Easy? What was easy about it? But if the attacks she was escaping weren't even his—

She had felt so clever, avoiding the hunters, day after

day, confident in her vision's guidance. But what if, rather than the result of her ability to navigate the city, and her foresight to guide her, the attacks had been merely inadequate and poorly done? Weak, compared to what he was capable of?

If she said no to this, he would come after her again.

"I will give you a day to consider, Seer. Come here, by this time tomorrow. Bring your sister and nephew, or not—we can fetch them easily enough. All you need do is agree." He leaned forward. "All three of you: safe, secure, never hungry again. Surely this is everything you have wanted?"

It did seem so. What would happen if she said yes?

The future seemed to exhale upon her like a great beast, teeth sharp, breath of smoke and burning flesh. In the roar were human screams. In the air a salt brine from an ocean she had never seen. Around her shoulders, a cold and bleak freedom.

Then it was gone, leaving her in the stark silence of a small room, sitting across from the man who hunted her across the years. She opened her mouth to say something, but all that came out was a small, wordless cry.

No safety here. Not now. Not ever. She leapt to her feet.

"Be very careful, Seer," he said as she went to the door, his tone edging to warning. "The Lord Commander wants to hire you. Others only want your head."

The flash of gold from the table caught her eye.

All hers, if she said yes and agreed to something she did not quite understand, that seemed too good to be possible, and for some reason scared her to her very bones.

She fled.

"We would live in the palace?" asked Dirina.

"The palace?" Pas asked eagerly.

Their few things were scattered across the floor. What to take? What to leave behind? No matter how little they had, it seemed they always left things behind. Things that mattered.

The seashell. Bits of their mother's dress. People and places. Enana. Darad.

Nidem.

Was it the right decision, to flee now?

"The palace," Dirina said softly, wistfully.

After all their running, he had tracked them here to Munasee. Her visions had only rescued her from the lesser hounds. Where could they go that he could not follow?

Perhaps better to say yes.

"And more coin, too, you said?"

It always came back to money. To cold mornings in the mountains, without firewood. To long hungry nights. To tight shoes that did not keep out the wet and dirt of the world.

Amarta nodded mutely, watching her sister. Dirina inhaled and looked at Pas, who was looking between them both.

"What should we do?" her sister asked her.

"Diri, we could eat, plenty, every single day. Be warm at night. Sleep on soft beds."

Together they silently considered this seductive vision. What did a palace look like? What might they eat? How soft were the beds?

What would life be like if they were no longer on the run?

"Maybe we should say yes," Amarta said, voice low. "How bad could it be?"

Her sister laughed once. "Ama. You see the future. Look and tell us."

She had tried. It was like swimming through a bottomless lake of blood in which swam disembodied faces.

"It's too big. I can't."

In truth, it was too awful.

"You can," Dirina said, a sudden fierceness in her voice. "Again and again you have kept us safe. Amarta—"

"No! I made us leave, over and over, is what I did. What if I was wrong those times? What if I'm wrong now?" Amarta exhaled a sob. Dirina drew her down to sit on the cot. Pas was at their feet, his arms wrapped wide around both their legs. His eyes were wide, the trust in his face so clear.

Every time they had needed to flee, Dirina had stayed with her. Had refused to be separated. This, her only family, was at risk because of her. How could she give them less than everything she had?

She glanced around at the mess of the room, willing herself to look beyond it, to what might come.

A flicker here, a short flash there, then it was all tangled again—hundreds of threads in all directions, choices yet to be made by those who didn't even know they would make them, all coming together in thousands of different ways, a tapestry with threads of smoke. As she looked, it moved and changed. None of it, not one piece, was certain.

She exhaled frustration.

Dirina and Pas watched silently, patiently, their faith in her as solid as her visions seemed smoke. She wanted to cry.

None of that, she told herself sternly.

She would start over. Begin with this moment. Find the thread, the next moment, then the next, until she found the one where she might decide to put herself into the hands of her hunter and his owner.

Time passed, Pas and Dirina's long, quiet breaths the only sound in the room. She found a tangle of decisions and held it tight, feeling its shape as it squirmed to take many forms.

Not merely tomorrow. Not next month. But farther. Not only for herself. For Dirina and Pas, for Enana and her family. For Kusan and all who lived there. Mara, Jolon.

Kusan invaded by brutal mercenaries, this time, not soldiers. Emendi in cities, on platforms, sold in chains. At the farm, Enana's sons overwhelmed by gangs with sticks, beaten to death for the bags of grain they had in the barn.

No, no, no. It was too much, to care for everyone.

Her cheeks were wet with tears, lips trembling.

Only Dirina and Pas, then. Only them.

He would let her see them, he said, when she gave him the answers he wanted. They would be hurt, he warned, tall in his red and black, if she did not comply. But no matter what she said, there were no right words to keep them safe, and she did not see her sister and nephew anymore.

When at last she opened her eyes and spoke, her voice

was a hoarse whisper. "If we go to the palace, we will never leave."

And they would be hurt, Dirina and Pas. She could not bear it.

Her sister sighed heavily. "Then we will not go."

"Then we must leave Munasee."

"Then we must leave."

Again. Amarta shook her head as more tears of frustration came. She hated knowing enough to run away but never enough to stay.

Chapter Twenty

By nightfall Maris had reached the poorest of the neighborhoods. It was late summer, the air still and reeking of burning tallow and human waste and rot. She walked among the half-tents and broken buildings of the Arun slums, picking her way over a cobbled road missing so many stones that wagons did not come here at all. Nor did the sewers flow. The stench was pervasive.

This was her last neighborhood to search, then she could tell the Lord Commander with fair confidence that the girl was not in Yarpin.

She would be done. Not done with the library, no, that magnificent collection of books that she was now certain was the finest accomplishment of the Anandynars. But even that lure was weakening when set against this place she walked through.

No more healing today, she told herself again.

The children were hardest to pass by. The elderly, the ill—even the infants—she could ignore. Life and death—two sides of the same thing—but those who had struggled to their sixth or seventh year, who had survived what calamities and woes Yarpin could hurl at them—who might yet come to vitality, and possibly even adulthood— these she could not seem to pass by.

Only one more, she would find herself thinking. Only this one.

Overhead a clear night showed a haze around the moon, promising early morning fog. The stars of the compass again tempted her to the ocean and escape.

No. She would complete the city first.

As she walked past tents and open-air camps, she kept the work fast and quick, her palm out to taste each person's etherics only long enough to rule them out.

From a crumbling stone archway a man emerged, stinking of rotgut and smoke and unwashed years. He stumbled a little, catching himself, then lurched toward her. He stopped, peering closely, somehow seeing her through the dusting of illusion and disguise in which she had wrapped herself.

Shock went through her. He was far too light-skinned, missing an ear, but otherwise he looked like her own father, dead these many decades.

A wide grin was on his face, and he stepped close to her, stumbling again. She caught his arm to hold him aright. His tension seemed to melt then, as if he had finally found what he'd been looking for, and he went half limp, a hand down, seeking the ground. She helped him lower himself, following him to sit at his side, one hand going to his chest, the other to his forehead.

He was muttering something. She was, she realized suddenly, leaking tears as she delved deep into his body, where, organ by organ, the tumors and damage were more places than they were not. She could not fix it. Oh, she could make a start on cleaning his blood, but to what end? To sober his mind so he could more keenly realize how diseased he was? Return to him the pain he had worked so hard to silence?

He coughed and sputtered, spittle and drool on his lips and chin. "Hush," he slurred up at her with a gap-toothed smile, somehow reading her thoughts. "It is good enough. Just help me go."

"What is that you say, ser?" she asked, blinking her tears away.

"Help me go," he said more slowly. "Help me die."

She looked at him once more and realized he looked nothing like her own father. He was only one more dying drunk on the streets of Arun.

But as she tried to rise, to leave him to his fate, he held her wrist and pulled her close, begging her with his eyes, and she found she did not quite have the will to push him away. Finally, with a shuddering exhale, she put her hands on him, and she led his spirit to the edge of life where she opened the door for him.

His grip on her arm relaxed.

Maris got to her feet, refusing to let herself think or feel as she walked back to the city's main street and then climbed the long, steep road to the palace.

Once again in her palace room, she fell onto the bed, staring at the ceiling.

The old man's spirit clung to her the long night, and she could not sleep. Again, she could not quite bring herself to push him away.

✢ ✢ ✢

In the early morning, Maris cleaned herself in every way she knew how, scouring body and mind and spirit until she felt raw.

Raw but not much cleaner.

How had it come to this folly again? How had she let herself become so weakened? *The ocean of suffering Iliban.* She must rest, replenish, recover.

She would do no more searching today. Instead she would go to the library, let herself wander aimlessly among the books and scrolls and boxes of scrawled treasures stacked up to the high ceilings. There she would find something to ease her battered spirit.

And so she did. Once among the books she was so absorbed she did not notice the servant who brought her tea along with a plate of small, cream-filled pastries so delicate and moist they might have been spiced butter in her mouth.

Not restored, not so fast as that, but her stomach at least was content.

Again the seductive trap of the palace. Knowing she could leave at any time made it that much easier to stay.

She took another pastry.

"Good morning, ser." Srel inclined his head to her.

Respect first. Reason later.

But did she truly object? This same respect gave her access to this library.

"The Lord Commander asks your company and attention, if you will permit," he said.

At this she felt a flicker of hope. Perhaps the girl had been found, or something else had occurred that might honorably allow her to stop her searching.

Putting one last pastry in her mouth, she followed him to Innel's offices.

"The queen is most grateful," Innel said. "The conspirators you most recently identified have been spoken to, their efforts appropriately redirected."

Maris had wondered at the new residents of Execution Square she had seen through the windows, their limbs spread in what seemed such uncomfortable positions. Redirection indeed.

"How is the search, Marisel?"

There was something new in Innel's tone. Had his interest in finding the girl waned?

No, that wasn't it. It was something else. What?

A faint and familiar scent clung to the Lord Commander. Actual smell or etheric impression, she could not quite tell. She sat across from him at the small table.

"I am very nearly done searching the city," she said, distracted by the barest hint of something on Innel that she knew but could not place. She took the mug of tea he offered her—Arun tea, not Perripin—and took a tentative sip. Bitter. She made a face.

"It is time to make a change," he said. "To speed this work."

"I warned you it would take too long, this search. But you—"

"Yes, you have done all that I have asked and more, Marisel. I am grateful. But I can wait no longer, so I have acquired some assistance for you."

Maris froze, the cup in her hand. "What is this you say?"

"Two mages, it is said, are better than one. I have hired another."

She slammed her cup onto the table, splashing hot tea over the sides onto her hand. "Our contract does not include this."

"Nor does it exclude it. Two mages in cooperation could surely accomplish far more than one. Find my missing girl, perhaps."

She looked at him, gaping incredulously. "You cannot throw two mages together without warning, as if they were ingredients in a stew. You should have consulted me first. Mages are generally unpleasant. I'm a rare exception."

His hands were up in a placating gesture. "Most certainly, Marisel. But cooperation under a contract is simply a practical matter. Even mages must eat, yes?"

At this Maris stood, mouth open in astonishment. "Eat? This has nothing to do with food."

He stood, too, hands still up. "I ask you to meet him first, Marisel. Then you can decide."

"What? You've brought him here? You fool—"

As the words left her mouth, Maris hurled her focus out in all directions, questing as fast as she knew how, searching for the etheric spoor that a mage left behind as he walked the world.

"Who?" she demanded, finding none of her kind nearby.

Could Innel be lying? No, that would make no sense.

She strained harder, swirling through the passages and rooms of the palace that she now knew so well. Up and down floors. Out to the edges of the building and back. Down into the tunnels and up to the roof. She felt herself stretched thin.

Foolish, foolish: she had pushed herself too hard these last months, let herself become wearied. Lulled to distraction by these soft beds, good food, an unending supply of books, she had forgotten the first and most important lesson of magery: self-protection.

Still she pushed, casting her attention wider. The stables. The laundry. The garrison.

Nothing.

Could Innel be mistaken? Could he have found a Sensitive or Adept incautious enough to claim to be a mage? Or perhaps a mage recently created, so young and inexperienced that they trailed only a tiny wake that she had yet to find?

Or one so powerful they could choose to leave no trail at all?

"I am sorry, Marisel," Innel said, his tone sounding uncertain, as if he had not quite anticipated this reaction. "I did not realize—"

She snorted her disbelief. Surely Innel could not have been so ignorant.

But she could not reason about this matter and search at the same time, so she put analysis aside.

"In any case," Innel went on, "he's assured me that you two will work well together."

She absorbed these words slowly. As the meaning came clear, she yanked her attention back from the kennels. "What is this you say? How can he know that? *Who is it?*"

Watching her, Innel opened his mouth as if to answer, then grimaced, backing away from her toward the door, his expression betraying something close to fear.

About time.

"Let me send for him, Marisel. That will, I think, save a lot of explanation."

"Tell me, damn you, before I—" She bit off the words.

Before she what? She could think of nothing she could do that would help this situation.

Who was it?

To Nalas, standing outside the door, Innel spoke a few fast words. "Get him," Maris thought she heard.

All right, then: she would begin again. Maris slammed her attention through the walls and doors of the palace, touching and dismissing people as fast as she could. If he was here, she would find him. She must.

What are you missing, Marisel?

Catching her breath, she brought herself back into the room and forced herself to think in an ordered fashion.

Perhaps panic was unnecessary and her exhaustion was making her assume the worst. The other mage, she now realized, could well be Gallelon, having taken his own advice and come to Yarpin for the good food, books, and conversation whose qualities he had extolled to her. It was just the sort of thing he might do.

Indeed, he could have been recruited by Innel as she had. She could easily imagine him telling Innel that they two would work well together.

She exhaled her tension, throwing etheric taps down through her fingers and feet and into the earth, seeking ground to settle her agitation. Yes, it all fit; likely it was Gallelon.

Then, all at once, she found him. As he was stepping into the room. No longer hidden, no longer cloaked.

Not Gallelon.

She yanked her awareness fully back into her body.

Innel moved back quickly out of the invisible line that stretched between her and Keyretura, that etheric connection from him to the deepest parts of herself, that now felt as if it were made of fire.

Innel's expression was guarded. She read no surprise, but she would not spare thought for his culpability, not now; all her attention was on the dark-skinned man in black robes who faced her from the door.

Her creator. Her *aetur*. The man whose side she had left the very first moment she could. She had not even said good-bye.

The dark, wide-set eyes sent a familiar, stomach-dropping sensation through her. She felt herself begin to tremble, struggled to control it. Which he would notice, of course, along with her racing pulse and the fatigue in her body. He never overlooked such things.

His gaze slowly took her in, a familiar, faint smile on his face.

Innel said, "Marisel al Perripur, this is—"

"We've met," Maris said shortly.

"Marisel," Keyretura said, drawing out her name. "It has been a long time."

She switched to the ancient language of mages. Formality, Keyretura himself had long ago taught her, was the best refuge when conflict was possible. And with mages, it was always possible. "Teacher." The words felt clumsy on her tongue. "In this place, at this time, on this flow, I greet you. My respect."

In a way, it didn't matter that she was so exhausted; even fully rested she would be no match for him. If this came to conflict, she could not hope to survive. So it must not come to that.

"Uslata," Keyretura answered in the same tongue. "I have faith that you are well."

In a language rich with indirection and ambiguity, his reply could mean any number of things, among them, that by asking, the asker considered the answer in doubt. In the right context, it was an insult. So how did he mean it?

Why could he not have simply said he was pleased to see her?

Because he was Keyretura.

Anger and embarrassment made shards of her focus. He would know that, too.

"Well enough," she answered in Perripin, where nothing was so subtle. She turned to Innel, her back partly to Keyretura, conscious of the slight, reprimanding herself for being foolishly petty. "You told him I was here. But you gave me no warning. What is this?"

"I need you both."

Breath escaped her in a humorless laugh. At least now she knew where she stood.

"Lord Commander," she said tightly, summoning all her focus for what she must say so carefully in Arunkin, "what splendid good fortune for you, to have Keyretura dua Mage with you in contract. There is no labor or sagacity I could provide you with that he could not offer you in greater measure. To even attempt it would be to risk disrespect to my aetur, for which I could never forgive myself. With deference to you both, I absent myself."

"Marisel. Surely you can make the effort together?" He looked a question at the black-clad mage.

"We labored together for twenty years," Keyretura said.

Her apprenticeship, he meant. That was something else entirely.

She walked to the door, keenly aware of each step, expecting the familiar touch that was the etheric equivalent of being grabbed, the tug that would mean Keyretura meant to do more than talk. She took the door handle in a tight grip to stop her hand from shaking.

Surely Keyretura would not throw away twenty years of apprenticeship over a moment's unexpected encounter, however unpleasant. Surely.

What are you missing, Marisel?

How very dangerous this moment was.

No, she could not stay. It was all she could do to hold herself where she stood. To slow the pounding of her heart.

Turning halfway back to meet Innel's look, she said, "Two mages are not better than one. The original saying, Lord Commander, is this: 'Distract one mage with another and escape while you still can.' It does not mean what you think it means, and you, ser, are a half-wit."

It was a small satisfaction to insult Innel. Keyretura would not care; Innel was beneath him. But it did her no good; it was childish.

"I intended no offense," Innel said. Respect? Regret? Whatever he had intended, it was done now.

"No," she said, realizing the truth of it as she spoke. "You paid me well for work I did poorly. I should have left long ago."

"Marisel," Innel said. "Surely—"

"She has decided," Keyretura said. "She can at times be mule-stubborn and impressively free of the influences of reason. No one could change her mind now, least of all me."

A look back at him. Teacher, creator.

Aetur.

Mouth downturned, eyes narrowed, a tightness across the brow: he was disappointed in her. Of course he was.

So much time passed, but nothing changed.

For a moment she thought to give voice to her thoughts. He lifted his eyebrows in question, daring her to speak, but she knew better. Without the apprenticeship contract in place she had no protection from him at all, and she must at all costs avoid infuriating him, something she had never been very good at.

Say nothing, she told herself. In the decades since Keyretura, surely she had learned to do that much.

Swallowing words of anger and rage, she left.

Chapter Twenty-one

Tayre stood in the center of the tiny and abandoned apartment. Food and clothes and blankets had been taken. Little remained but trash. There were no clues as to where the seer and her family might have gone.

In his discussion with her the previous night, he had read her as suspicious and afraid, yet strongly inclined to taking the contract. Had there been a wager, he would have put gold on her saying yes today.

Even so, he had made sure he had hires across the city to catch her if he were wrong. By dawn the reports told him that the three of them had left together at first light, packs on their backs, and slipped into the crowds of Munasee.

Competent and experienced city trackers, his hires. They knew how to follow people. It should have been simple enough to keep the three of them in sight.

They had lost them.

Whether by skill or instinct, to escape the net he had arranged was no simple matter. He himself would have been hard-pressed to do so. For two women and a small boy, it should have been impossible.

The trackers reported seeing them come out of the building, slip into the streets, and then into the crowds. Tayre had anticipated this as a worst-case possibility and had set watchers at all the roads leading out of the city, as well as ports and docks. Anywhere the exceptionally lucky trio could find an exit from Munasee.

None had seen them. There was not even a rumor. They might as well have vanished.

West to the Great Road then southward again would again be his first guess, continuing her momentum away from where she started. But she had been learning, as evidenced by her ability to not only avoid capture but thwart the multiple attempts on her life he had seen play out these last months.

Despite what he had told her, not all the attacks were incompetent. Some should have worked. She should have been dead many times over.

The other possibility was that the three had not left at all, but had gone to ground right here in Munasee. A thorough search of the city would take some time, but he had to be sure he was not being tricked into thinking she was not where she actually was, one of the very best ways to hide and just the sort of tactic he would use in her position to put a persistent hunter off the trail. If he left the city now and she were still here, he would be searching fruitlessly for a very, very long time.

He did not think her quite that clever, but he had been wrong about her before.

He would need to take a close look at the Munasee

underground: the basement warrens, the labyrinths of storage, the coils of wine cellars. After Kusan it might well be on her mind to go into an underground for refuge.

She had a knack for getting people to take her in. Perhaps he should also look into the aristos of Munasee, even the Houses themselves. Who knew what she might manage?

An expensive search. He would need more coin. He had come to the point where he could no longer get funds from the Lord Commander without more in hand than an explanation of how he had lost her again, so he would need to do a bit of unrelated work. Something that paid especially well, which meant it would most likely be quiet, bloody, and illegal. That would take time as well.

As he searched the apartment once more, again finding nothing, he considered the pursuit in large scale, and wondered if he should continue.

It was easy to be deceived into thinking that coming close to a quarry was nearly the same as having it in hand, but this was the very thing that kept people gambling away all they owned when a sensible and dispassionate evaluation would tell them to stop.

There was his reputation to consider, certainly; failing to satisfy what was, at least to all appearances, a simple, straightforward contract would make it difficult for him to get the more lucrative and interesting contracts in the future. It would be best to tie off the loose ends and finish what he had begun.

But this now went beyond loose threads, reputation, and contracts.

Find the unknown. Make it known to you.

He had to understand her.

His offer to Innel to resign had been purely for show, to keep the man from making the suggestion himself. He would continue this search, even if the Lord Commander ended the contract.

What had gone wrong with the plan this time? He had seen the way she looked at the souver touch. Even her fear of him had been overcome by the promise of relief from his deadly pursuit, and the temptation of a life of comfort made strong by years of deprivation.

She must have foreseen something. The weak link in the plan had always been the Lord Commander himself. If, once he had her in hand, he would threaten her or her family, she might foresee this. Tayre thought he'd made clear to the Lord Commander how thoroughly his intention must change for this approach to work, but perhaps the man could not so easily change his intention.

In any case, the cause was unknowable. Tayre would simply have to go and find her again.

Now, at least, Tayre had the range of options available to him. He did not have to take her alive, which would make this much simpler.

There was no point in reporting back to the Lord Commander; that would only frustrate him to no good purpose. Tayre would return when he had her in hand. Or her head.

Chapter Twenty-two

A cold freedom, just as she had foreseen.

Amarta pulled the blanket tighter around her, wishing for another atop it, and gripped the rail as the ship rose and fell, watching the darkening blue line where the astonishing expanse of ocean met the sky, as a bright orange-red sun burned down into the sea. Above, the sky was brushed with strands of high, pink clouds, a few stars.

Some said the Beyond was up there, among the stars. Was it like this railing, she wondered, her parents looking down on her as she looked on the water below? Did they blame her for their deaths? They should; but for her lack of courage, they would be alive.

She missed her mother tonight, a pressure in her chest, a pain behind her eyes. What was that song her mother had sung to her about the ocean? Now would be the time for it, at least to hum it, a bit of remembrance for her mother. One last thing to hold, now that the seashell was gone, along with the strips of blue.

Even the blue trim on her cloak, with which Amarta had marked Nidem to die.

No, her mother's ocean song was gone from memory.

Gone, gone. All gone.

It was bitingly cold. As the sky darkened it chilled further, but Amarta refused to go back down, below deck. Too many people. She was sick of people, even her sister and nephew. She ached everywhere, most painfully in her stomach.

To bleed for the first time should have meant something. A gathering of friends. A feast to celebrate the moment of becoming a woman. Her mother by her side. Now all it meant was one less shirt, torn up for rags. She wondered what women in the palace did when they bled, and what they ate, and if they were warm right now.

Getting from Munasee to the ocean port at the Munasee Cut, then onto this ship had not been easy. Amarta struggled to stay in a haze of foreseeing, indicating in each moment where to go next. First it was the markets, this many steps this way, and then that way. Down to Button Port and under Trout Bridge, around the russet stone fountain but not too close, then double back and down two levels underneath the huge First Bridge to the stables where large wagons waited for the day's loading.

There, at a particular moment, they climbed inside a large box already atop a cart, nestling down into rolls of cloth to wait. An hour later the cart jerked to motion, taking them they knew not where.

They emerged at the ocean port, where a huge ship stood ready to leave. A fast departure seemed wise.

Somehow their few remaining nals got them waved on board; they'd bought themselves a small stretch of floor in steerage near some sealed barrels, below other passengers who had claimed the ledges. It was wet, it stank, but they had escaped.

Now, overhead in the twilight sky, a gull paced the boat, high among the sails. It must be flying, she realized, even though it seemed only to hover. Like the ocean's edge against the sky, which seemed a flat line but must be full of the same watery ravines and hillocks she saw looking overboard. Sharp waves, changing valleys, and the occasional spray in her face as the water spat upwards. Far distant, things could seem so much simpler than they were up close.

With the wind in her ears and her eyes on gull and horizon, it took her some time to notice the figure standing only a few feet away at the railing, watching her. For a moment fear seized her—somehow he had found them. How could he be everywhere, even here?

But no; another look told her it was not him.

"Blessings of the season to you," came a woman's voice, mildly accented, her feet set apart on the rocking deck, hand lightly on the railing.

Amarta clumsily sought through the next few moments for danger, but nothing signaled her. Perhaps the woman was no more than a fellow passenger. "And you," she answered cautiously.

"Cold out here," the woman said, voice loud enough to carry over the wind. She turned to look out at the ocean. "I'll be glad to get home."

Now Amarta saw the woman's dark skin in the

deepening gloom. A Perripin. She had seen them in Munasee, taken messages to them from time to time.

"Not very long ago," the woman continued, still facing the blackening ocean, "I held a small seashell in my hand, striped with blue and white. Yours, I believe."

Amarta gripped the railing tightly. Everyone seemed to know things about her, from the shadow man to this stranger. Where was vision to warn her?

The woman turned to look at her. "Come to my cabin where it's warm," she said. "We can exchange names and stories. I'm sure you have some interesting ones, like why the Lord Commander of the Arun Empire is looking for you."

Amarta's heart began to pound. Where to run to now, on a ship surrounded by ocean? Mutely she shook her head.

The woman's voice held a smile. "We do not stop until Kelerre. Will you hide in steerage all that time to avoid me? I have food and drink and warmth to share."

Amarta was so cold she thought she might freeze and shatter. Again she tried to foresee danger, but found nothing. It did not much reassure her, not after the talk with the hunter, in which vision was also less than forthcoming.

"I'm going to my cabin," the Perripin woman said at last. "Follow or not, as you please." With that she turned away.

It was too cold to stay on deck, but she did not want to go back to the crowded hold to see what bits of food they might still have left. She followed the woman along the inner walkway. Out of the wind, she felt better, a surge of guilt coming over her as they passed the ladders going down to steerage, where she belonged.

Near the front of the ship, the woman opened a door into a cabin with two bunks. A table. Lamps.

Warmth.

Amarta sat uncertainly as the woman opened a cupboard, taking out mugs, pouring red liquid from a wineskin, handing one to Amarta. A taste of the fermented, spiced liquid sent warmth into her belly.

"I am Marisel al Perripur," she said. "Maris will do. Who are you?"

"You know my name," Amarta snapped. Poor grace in return for this warm cabin and good drink, but she could not seem to summon more polite words.

"But I don't," the woman said, seeming more entertained than upset. "I never thought to ask." Seeing it was empty, she refilled Amarta's cup. "A year in Yarpin searching for you and I find you on board, going south." She chuckled. "Innel would be livid."

Despite the calming effect of the drink, Amarta felt sudden alarm. "Searching for me? Why were you . . ." She trailed off.

The seashell. The Lord Commander. *Searching.*

A weight settled on her.

Someone will find a way around your magic.

"I think," she said softly, "you are a mage."

The woman considered her for a moment. "Yes."

Now Amarta understood why her visions had been silent. He had been right, her hunter who now had a name: someone would find a way around her visions. Someone had. This someone.

Oddly, Amarta felt relief more than anything else. All of this was finally over. Nowhere else to run to. No more hard choices to make.

But Dirina and Pas.

"I travel alone," Amarta said quickly. "So, now, stop the ship"—could a mage could do such a thing? She had no idea—"and take me to Yarpin. I won't resist. But—we must go right now, right this moment. Or something bad will happen. My foresight tells me so." She licked her lips, wondering if she were at all convincing.

At this Maris sat back, mouth slightly open, looking surprised. "Your foresight. I see. I think you misunderstand. I am not searching for you anymore."

It took Amarta a moment to make sense of the words, and then she was not at all sure she believed them. It must have shown on her face, because Maris added, "I have no further obligation to that contract, and no interest at all in delivering you to the Lord Commander. Certainly I don't care for him very much. Perhaps you are reassured?"

If that was true, then she was not caught after all. Still running from the hunter.

She hunched over the drink, looking down into the red that sloshed with every rock of the ship. A bone-weary exhaustion came over her.

"Here," the woman said, holding out a square of nut chew, dark and gooey.

Amarta took it, bit a little off. It was sweet, nuts and seeds and dates and spices all wound together in a delicious whole. She ate the rest hungrily, all other thought gone. So used to ignoring hunger, she had not realized how empty she was.

"I—" she began, struggling to find an apology for her earlier unpleasantness. Maris handed her a second square. She took another bite, then thought of Dirina and Pas, guiltily tucking the rest in her pocket. Seeing Maris's look, she felt a shot of uncertainty go through her. Had she given something away?

"Saving it for later," she muttered. Could she do anything right tonight? "My name is Amarta."

"Amarta al . . . ?"

Munasee? Kusan? Botaros? The town of her birth, whose name she no longer remembered?

"I come from too many places," she said softly. "And none of them home."

"Where are you going to, then?"

Amarta started to answer, thought that perhaps that was unwise, then realized that she was too tired to reason. "Away. Far away. From . . ." She shook her head. "From the hound on my trail. From the man who sent him. Anywhere. Somewhere safe."

Maris tilted her head. "That will be hard to find, this safe place, given who pursues you."

She thought of the years she had been running. A tightness came to her throat, a pressure behind her eyes. "There must be somewhere."

"Some think safety is found in knowing what will happen tomorrow."

Amarta snorted derisively, shook her head, took another sip. "They are ignorant fools. The future is . . ." She waved a hand. "Always changing. Like the ocean. It might seem a flat place if you look far away, but up close it is so much more complicated, with waves and gullies and splashes. You might as well ask what the sea will be tomorrow as to ask what the future will be."

"Tomorrow," Maris said, "the sea will be wet."

Despite everything, Amarta laughed.

"And other people," Maris said, now smiling, too, "think safety is had at the front of an empire's army."

Amarta felt all the weight return. "He is surely safe," she said.

"You might be surprised at the threats he faces."

She was tired of being surprised, tired of everything. "I hurt," she confessed.

"That is to be expected with your first blood. The pain, the short temper, the ill-ease."

Amarta's mouth fell open. "How did you know?"

"Here. This one is for you and only you." She handed Amarta another square of nut chew, which Amarta put in her mouth, feeling sheepish as she chewed, but also feeling comforted.

"And . . ." Maris opened a small bag, rummaged through and brought out a small, cylindrical metal container from which she took a pinch of powder, which she sprinkled into Amarta's drink. "This will help ease your ills."

Amarta gave the powdered drink a look.

"You think I might try to poison you? Truly?" She seemed amused.

Half-ashamed and half-angry, Amarta scowled. "Some have tried."

"You say you can see the future. Can you not simply look and know that it is safe to drink?"

"There is nothing simple about it," Amarta said, not

much liking the resentment in her voice. She was tired of foreseeing. She wanted nothing more than to rest.

Vision, she decided, if it really cared, would tell her. She put the cup to her lips and drained it.

A storm came in the night, tossing the ship, soaking the decks, sending streams of saltwater down the walls of steerage where the three of them huddled, trying to stay dry.

The next morning, when Maris found them and suggested they move into her cabin with her, none of them had raised a word in objection.

Despite the food and drink—the powder that, as promised, made her menses far more bearable—Amarta did not quite trust this woman. She had, after all, admitted to being hired to find Amarta. Perhaps Maris had claimed to be quit of the contract only to gain their trust, intending to return them to the Lord Commander when they made landfall.

Words, after all, were easy.

Pas, naturally, befriended the Perripin woman instantly, climbing into her lap as if he owned it. Maris seemed happy with the arrangement.

Perhaps too happy, if Amarta let her suspicions guide her. Trying to gain their trust through Pas, to make them do something they otherwise might not.

And yet, day after day of the journey, when Maris offered them food and shelter in her warm, dry cabin, gave her drink and powders that eased the pain, Amarta did not object.

No surprise that Dirina and Pas were both so trusting

with strangers; they had always had Amarta to be suspicious for them.

When the storm was over and the sun out again, the four of them stood at the railing, watching the land go by. Villages and towns, small harbors and great cliffs.

"What is that?" Pas asked of a long, high stone wall that followed the shoreline, rooftops showing beyond.

"Garaya," Maris answered. "One of the last walled cities to fall to the Grandmother's fourth expansion, some eighty years ago."

"Were they Perripin before that?" Dirina asked.

"No. They ruled themselves, answerable to no one, proud, independent, and more than a bit arrogant. When Nials brought her armies south, no one stood by them. After a very long and brutal siege, they fell."

"Fell?" Amarta asked.

"Half the people dead, the city broken, most of it burned to ash. They have been building back ever since. A risky business, self-sovereignty. Now they answer to Arun, like everyone north of Kelerre."

Kelerre. Where they were headed.

The hunter had found them in Kusan and Munasee. Would he find them in Kelerre, another country altogether?

Pas tugged on Maris's clothes, held up his arms. She picked him up, propped him on her hip.

"What is Perripur like?" Dirina asked.

"Warm. The air rich with life. Fruit everywhere. North of the Mundaran Sea is green and lush. Inland are sugar flats, the Shentarat Plains. Beyond that the mountains—

tangles of thick forests, bright with birds. That's my destination."

"I want to see the birds," said Pas.

Amarta would need to find another Magrit in Kelerre, another trader she could convince to give her work.

"You'll stand out like falcons in bright sun," Maris said, as if tracking her reasoning.

"We will find a way," Amarta said, not wanting to confide in this woman, who might yet send her back to her pursuers.

But Maris was right; even vision could not make her invisible.

As they approached Kelerre, Amarta waited for vision to warn her. Nothing came. She watched Maris to see if she could tell if the mage were doing something to block her visions. But what might that look like? She had no idea.

As Kelerre came into view, Pas dashed from side to side, poking between the legs of those standing at the crowded railing, somehow making them laugh rather than be annoyed. The next time he ran by, Dirina grabbed for him, but he slipped from her grasp. Maris reached out a hand, took hold of his shirt, and swung him up into her arms, where he wrapped his arms around her, bouncing with energy.

Pas was not the only one excited. Perripin passengers also bounced where they stood, waving and yelling toward the shore, where answering calls came from those on the nearing dock. Seagulls cried overhead. Amarta followed one with her eyes, envying it its freedom.

She looked at Maris, holding Pas. It made her uneasy, how close the two of them had become.

"Mama, look!" Pas pointed to the shore, where tall silver towers stretched to the sky.

"What color, sweet one?" Dirina asked him.

"Metal," he said, rubbing his head against his mother's face as she tried to kiss his forehead.

Dirina did not seem worried. Counting on Amarta to make everything right, she thought sourly. She would not confide her uncertainties in her sister, either.

"It looks less crowded than Munasee," Amarta said, thinking of what they would do after they disembarked.

"Kelerre and Free Port are two ends of a stretched city. Though you're right: not as many people as your packed Arun cities. We would say this is because we are more clever than Arunkin and live better, not so tight together. A Perripin saying holds that the farther south you go, the smarter people are. Think of how far north Yarpin is, yes?" She chuckled.

Amarta remembered the Emendi and their pale hair and skin and eyes.

Darad. An ache went through her, too fast to prevent.

"Is it true?" she asked.

"No," Maris said. "People everywhere, in every possible color of skin and hair, are fools."

"Then you are not so smart?" Pas asked with a grin.

"Smart enough, little one," she said, bouncing him, smiling.

Sailors called back and forth to dock hands, ropes were thrown, pulled, knotted on shore. Passengers loaded up knapsacks and lifted belongings.

"We are grateful for all you've given us, Maris," Dirina said politely.

Amarta held out her arms for Pas, but both the boy and Maris frowned at this, if anything clutching each other more tightly. Amarta did not lower her arms, silently insisting. Finally Maris let him down, and Amarta took his hand firmly.

"Come with me," Maris said suddenly.

Amarta shook her head. "We have business in Kelerre."

"Can't we do it in Shenter—the name?" Pas asked her. "With Maris?"

Maris made a low sound in her throat. "While I'm tempted to stay in Kelerre to see how it is you make coin, Amarta, I think you will attract far more attention than you realize. Let me help you get farther away. I'll buy your passage to Shentarat."

A good offer. Surely too good. Her sister gave her a familiar questioning look. But could she trust vision, with this mage so close? She closed her eyes and sought the future beyond this docking.

Nothing and more nothing. She glared at Maris, who returned a confused, not-quite annoyed look.

Again, she tried.

Pas's small hand tugging on Maris's larger, darker one, demanding she come. A many-colored frog, he said. It would not wait.

She opened her eyes, shaken by this sweet moment, this flash without threat. Dropping her head in a silent, furious sob, she shook her head. No. They would not again be drawn to people and places that seemed so welcoming, only to be forced to leave again. They had each other. They would rely on no one else.

Seeing her expression, her sister said, "Thank you, but no."

"Yes." Amarta found herself saying.

Maris looked between them.

"Ah—" Dirina said uncertainly. "Then—yes?"

If Maris intended to take them captive and send them back to Yarpin as soon as they left the ship, surely she could do so, whatever they said now. This might all be pretense with betrayal soon to come, but there was no reason not to agree.

"Yes," she said again.

"So be it," Maris said, taking Pas's hand again.

As the ramp to shore was lowered with a bang, she considered that with all Maris had done for them, she might be sincere.

As if that mattered; Amarta had sincerely cared for Nidem, yet put her own cloak on the girl. Betrayal had many mothers.

"We'll walk to Free Port," Maris said, gesturing at the city. "From there get a boat to Dasae Port."

"Is there no way from the ocean to the Mundaran Sea?" Dirina asked.

"Oh, there is. Around the reef, right there." She pointed with her free hand. "But it's littered with the corpses of boats that have tried, no thanks to your selfish, short-sighted, half-witted Arun monarchs."

Amarta drew in breath sharply, glancing to see if anyone had heard this dangerous talk.

"We need a canal, you see. Right there." Maris

gestured sharply, as if she could almost make one with her hand. "Kelerre and all the Perripin states want it. They've been ready to start on it for forty years."

"Then—why?" Dirina asked.

"Your king demanded an obscene share of the tolls, claiming a transport tax so high that no one could afford to build the damned thing. So the canal remains undug and we must walk to Free Port. Perfectly senseless. Perfectly Arun*kel*."

Again Amarta looked around to see who might be listening. If anyone was, they didn't show it.

As they walked down the ramp onto solid ground, Amarta watched those around them, wondering who might be in the Lord Commander's employ, half expecting them to be somehow captured at this very moment. She watched Maris, wondering what the mage would do with her magic.

But all that happened next was that they walked for a couple of hours to get to the other side of the reef and Free Port, which did not seem much different than Kelerre.

This was a strange land, from the bright green trees that dripped with thick vines to the birds trilling and squawking and flapping across the road. Buildings were bright in bewildering splashes that clearly had nothing to do with the Great Houses' dual tones. Flowing clothes, wide-brimmed hats, foreign words, and curious tones.

Long stares at the four of them.

When they arrived at the docks, Maris had them wait as she walked the piers, stopping people who seemed to know her to clasp hands, to laugh, gesture, and talk. Arranging their passage, supposedly. Or perhaps instead arranging to send them back north to the Lord Commander.

Surely if Maris meant to betray them, she would have done it by now? Still Amarta moved close to Dirina, took Pas's hand tightly in her own.

They were beyond poor now: they had nothing. No money, no food. No words in this strange place. They were good and truly lost.

If they were so lost, might they also be hard to find?

Maris motioned them over to a boat far smaller than the ship before. Not large enough to travel back all the way to the capital, surely.

Or maybe she was taking them elsewhere for the Lord Commander.

Then again, maybe she only meant them well. Still vision refused to even hint at danger.

But that meant nothing, only that someone had indeed found a way around her visions.

Despite her suspicion of Maris, a day on the boat began to relax Amarta. The Perripin sailors were friendly and warm, eager to answer Pas's questions, happy to tell him the Perripin words for anything at which he pointed.

She could almost forget that they were running, that Maris might yet betray them. Here on the warm Mundaran Sea, with water all around them and the hunter so far away, she could almost imagine that they were free in the world, going where winds and whimsy might take them. She felt her spirits lift, played with Pas, listened to the Perripin sailors tell tales at night, understanding little of the words but somehow gleaning the stories themselves.

When, on the fourth day, they came to the Shentarat coast and Dasae Port, she sobered. In the distance a line of blue-gray mountains overlapped a paler range. Distant clouds seemed made of the same blue-gray stuff as the mountains, as if they had been formed from sky itself.

Dasae was a small town with flat-roofed buildings and a harbor full of fishing boats. Thick bushes and vines threatened to engulf everything from walkways to piers.

So much green everywhere. Perhaps they could simply hide in the underbrush. Flee into rabbit warrens.

"Surely he will not come this far to find me," she said to Maris as they watched at the railing, looking sidelong at the other woman for any hint of duplicity.

"Why not? I think you can assume Innel sev Cern esse Arunkel will continue to commit his queen's extensive resources to finding you."

Of course he would.

"Did he pay you a lot, to find me? Does he still?"

At this, Maris's expression went oddly flat. Despite the warm breezes, Amarta felt a chill.

For a time there was silence between them. Amarta felt herself flush, regretted her words. What was she thinking, to risk angering the one person they knew here, who had thus far treated them so well? And a mage, whatever ill-fortune that might also bring.

"When we disembark," Maris said at last, as if Amarta's questions had not been asked, "what will you do?"

"We'll find something."

Perhaps when she was far enough away from Maris's magic, vision would return more fully to guide them.

"He will send people here to search for you. The deeper into Perripur you go, the more you'll stand out. My countrymen are no fools; they'll know you're on the run. Some of them will gladly turn you in for the money he'll be offering."

Or already had.

"What do you suggest, then?"

"My house in the Shentarat Mountains is remote. It should be as safe as anywhere, even when I'm not there."

Dirina and Pas had just joined them.

"We go to the mountains with Maris!" Pas said happily.

Amarta turned her back on the town, fully facing the mage. "Why?"

"Why?" Maris laughed a little, expression turning sober. "You've no money, you speak no Perripin, and the most powerful man in Arun is after you."

"That's why for us. Why for you? You are strangely generous for someone so recently employed to hunt me down."

"Amarta," Dirina said with shocked reproach.

"And you're awfully suspicious for someone who can supposedly see into the future. Why don't you tell me what I'm going to do?"

"It doesn't work that way." Not exactly, anyway. People changed their minds, and the future altered.

But she had looked, and vision would not name Maris as a threat. Or could not. *A way around your magic.*

"I see," Maris said with an odd tone. "Perhaps I want

help cleaning a house I haven't seen in years. Perhaps . . ." Her gaze went to Pas, hung there a moment. "Perhaps it seems to me that Innel has too many advantages in this, and I want the contest closer to fair."

"Fair is what you take," Amarta said sharply.

At this Maris's eyebrows raised. "Then take my strangely generous offer, Amarta."

Could it be that Maris was offering only what she seemed to be offering? If so, it was even more important that they refuse.

"No."

"No?" Maris's laugh seemed more astonished than amused.

"Ama," Dirina said. "Do you see something?"

So many had paid dearly to take them in. If Maris only meant them well, then—

They were the last ones on the boat now, a few of the crew remaining to coil ropes and take down sails. One Perripin sailor approached, looking as if he were about to speak, perhaps to shoo them off the boat. Maris held up a hand and he nodded, backing away.

"Those who help me come to harm. Or worse," Amarta said softly.

"You are concerned for my welfare?"

Amarta nodded.

Maris looked at her a moment. "That's quite . . ." She seemed to search for the right word. "Unnecessary. I don't need your protection."

"Everyone tells me that. Everyone. And then they—"

"You know little of mages and the work we do, do you?"

"Yes, but—"

"I'm a little harder to hurt than those who've helped you before. I will take my own risks. Come with me."

Amarta looked at Dirina and Pas, and nodded. "We will come."

"We will help you clean," Dirina said.

"Me, too," Pas said, nodding enthusiastically.

"It will be good, to have help," Maris said, smiling down at him.

"Maris," Amarta said, again regretting her hard words earlier, "you've been so kind and generous and I—."

"No." Maris said, cutting her off curtly. "Don't say that."

They walked through the town of Dasae, a small city of wide houses with low roofs—some, Amarta noticed, with only roofs, no walls at all. Here they attracted long stares and even lengthy whispered discussions. Maris was right; there would have been no hiding here.

They walked the road out of town, through farms of thick green bushes, orchards of bright fruit, pastures of goat and spindly creatures who made trilling sounds as they passed.

If all this walking were indeed a ruse to convince them they were safe, only to turn them over to someone who would take them back to Arunkel, well, it seemed too elaborate. Maybe vision showed her no threat from the mage because there truly was none.

As the mountains grew closer, they passed tall fields of canes. They walked over rises of thickly tangled trees. When the land went flat again, they began to approach what distantly seemed an enormous dark gray seashore.

At the edge of the gray-green flat that might have been a frozen sea, they stopped, the three of them staring in silence.

Maris took out a water bag, shared it around.

"What is that?" asked Pas at last.

"A monument to the ruin that my kind brings to the world."

"The Glass Plains," Dirina breathed.

"How was it made?" Pas asked, eyes wide.

"Some mages got into an argument," Maris answered. "When it was over, the cities of Shentarat, Mundara, and Tutura had been flattened into molten earth. Tens of thousands dead. Farms, towns—every tree and rock flattened. This is what remains." She gestured.

"Was it very exciting?" Pas asked.

"I was not yet born, little one."

"The mages, did they die, too?" Amarta asked.

Maris laughed, bitterly, shook her head. "I am told they reconciled. Not much comfort to the dead, that."

Along the edge where the glass ended and earth began, grasses and small shrubs grew. Amarta knelt to examine the surface. Like dirty, frozen water, but solid and hot to the touch. Up close it was riddled with sand-filled cracks and bits of hard shards.

"It's sharp, Amarta. Watch yourself."

Amarta touched an edge, pressing her thumb onto it, drawing it along, feeling it cut into her skin. She pulled back, put her thumb to her mouth.

"You see? It cuts. I walked barefoot here once."

"Why?" Amarta asked.

"To give something back to the dead. To pay on a debt my kind is rarely called to account for." A small shake of her head. "A debt beyond measure. What we bring the world, it neither wants nor needs."

Amarta put her foot onto the surface of the glass. Under her the plate of gray-brown gravel shifted a little. She looked out at the expanse stretching away into the distance.

"Did your blood bring back the dead?"

A snort. "Nothing can bring back the dead. Or make up for the plains. Or for Nerainne. Or the Rift . . ." Maris paused. Her voice fell to a whisper. "I would see my kind melted flat here as well, though it is no reparation to those we so casually ruin with our petty, destructive whims. All we've done. All we've failed to do."

Amarta followed Maris's eyes to the horizon, past the plains, where the distant mountains faded into murky, heat-warped gray.

Strange words, but they also felt right in some way she could not name. Blood to pay for blood.

Behind her eyes, vision stirred. She sat down on the warm, hard surface and pulled off a shoe so worn it was no more than a tattered leather sock.

"What do you do there?" Maris asked.

"I take off my shoes."

"I can see that," the mage said sharply. "Refrain."

"I have a debt to pay, too."

"You? With your few years? Do you mock me?"

Amarta looked up at the mage in surprise. Maris's expression had a furious intensity about it.

"The world would be better off without me, too," she whispered.

"You presume. This debt has nothing to do with you. You are no mage."

"What am I?" Amarta yanked off the other shoe.

"A woman-child who understands little of the world. Who had best do as she is told lest her actions and words lead her shortly to lament."

"Amarta." From Dirina a warning that she already heard clearly in Maris's tone. Pas looked from her to Maris and back again in dismay.

She took a breath and paused, her shoes in hand, staring out across the plains, wondering what she was doing. A sort of double vision came to her: the world as it seemed, in which she was angering the only person they knew in this strange, hot land; and the dim flashes that something was giving her. Not foresight. Not quite.

"You will put your shoes back on. Now."

It was a tone she had heard before. In the shadow man's voice telling her to comply. From the tall stranger in Botaros years ago, demanding from her the visions that had made him powerful enough to try to kill her. Now in her body and blood she felt all the times she had done as she was told, hoping it would lead to safety, or at least out of danger. The times she had fled, wanting only to survive.

To whom did she truly owe this demanded compliance? Where was her duty?

Dirina and Pas. That was her duty. For them she saw no danger here and now and in the moments ahead. All that was at risk was herself.

She struggled to her bare feet. The sun-warmed glass

was nearly too hot to stand on so she shifted between her feet, facing Maris, forcing herself to meet the growing storm in the mage's dark eyes.

"Maris, how can you be responsible for this? You weren't even alive then."

"Do you intend this as challenge, child?" Maris asked with a sudden and frightening softness. "Or is it merely a foolish lapse of judgment?"

In her chest she felt the fast heartbeat of the prey. So many years of running, of being the rabbit. She wanted to be something else.

"I am not a child," she replied, voice quavering. "And you will not hurt me today."

At this Maris raised a hand, her fingers spreading slowly, pointing at the sky, her other hand a fist at her chest.

Not the right thing to say, Amarta realized quickly, sensing the future shift away from the one in which her last words had been true. As she watched Maris and tried to figure out what to do next, she dimly recalled having seen Maris and this moment before in vision, years ago.

No more running, she decided suddenly. The mage began to hum, very low. Vision began to warn that something was coming that might hurt.

"Maris," she said. "My parents are dead because of me. All those who took us in came to harm or death. Dirina and Pas have nothing, no home, because of me. Let me walk the plains as I must. Help me understand. I beg you."

At this the Perripin woman inhaled sharply, and turned away, dropping her hands.

For long moments there was no sound. Distantly, away from the plains, a hawk cried. Amarta dared not move, despite the heat of the glass under her soles.

When Maris turned back, Amarta could feel the mage's look though she did not understand it.

"There is an old saying," Maris said. "'With mages, respect first, reason later.' I wonder, should reason be mentioned at all?" A thoughtful sound. "He was so quick to anger, my teacher. I loathed him. More than you can know. And look at me, threatening you. I sound almost exactly like him."

"Not to me," Pas said quickly, shaking loose his mother's grasp and going to Maris, taking her hand, looking up. "You sound like you."

Maris seemed more shocked by this than anything that had come before. She picked Pas up in her arms and held him, burying her face in his hair and neck while he hooked his legs around her waist.

Finally she lifted her head and looked back.

"What is it you want, Amarta?"

"To walk."

"The shoes."

"They're too tight. If I'm going to hurt anyway, let me choose how."

Maris was silent a moment.

"So be it."

"Amarta," said Dirina softly as she walked behind with Pas, Maris leading, "this is foolishness. If you cut your feet, how will you walk the rest of the way? What if your cuts go bad?"

"They will not go bad," Maris said.

Amarta's focus was on the dark glass underfoot, soaking up the blazing sun, returning the heat to her with each step. Some spots were smooth, others rough and sharp. Maris was right: in places it was edged like a sharpened blade. In some places tiny plants grew in crevasses, small and prickly, tenaciously grabbing what life they could from the sand and dirt that had collected there.

She would not slow for the ground. Not for thorns, not for heat, not for cuts. Nor would she let vision guide her. She would follow where Maris led.

Her debt could never be paid back. Her parents—she could tell herself that she had been too young to understand and thus save them, even though the vision had been clear. But Enana and her family? She had known danger followed them to that house.

And then there was Nidem.

A friend. Perhaps the only one she'd ever had. Someone who had laughed with her, hugged her, and whom she had killed as surely as if she had herself sent the arrow into her heart.

To save Kusan, a small voice seemed to cry inside her.

No. She could have tried harder. Used her foresight more deftly. If she and Dirina and Pas had never gone to Kusan in the first place, Nidem would still be alive.

A cut to her right foot, deep and sudden. She bit back a cry of pain.

Because of her, Nidem was gone from the world. Because of her, their parents were dead. Enana and her sons, urged to let a deadly hunter in their door who might have done them grievous harm. How many more would die because of her?

She let herself cry, very softly, for all who had suffered for her coming into their lives, and for those she had put on the road to the Beyond.

Now she was leaving blood on the glass underfoot with each step. It did not absolve her of Nidem's death. Nor her parents'. Not even a little. Not a hair's weight on a merchant's scale. Nothing could make right what she had done.

Yet it seemed right and necessary, each pained step a kind of balm to her spirit. They walked in silence for a while.

"Enough," Maris said at last. She had Amarta sit, and examined her feet, dabbing at them with a cloth. "It's not as bad as it looks," she told Dirina. "She'll heal fast." Then, to Amarta: "Did you find what you were looking for?"

"Some measure of it, perhaps."

"At times that is all that is possible." Maris touched her face a moment, looking into her eyes, and Amarta felt some long-held pain seep out of her. For a time she trembled with sobs, then brushed the wet from her face and stood, ready to continue.

"Amarta," Maris asked, "do you truly see the future?"

"I—" She looked at the woman curiously. "It seems so, yes."

"Then tell me something: these plains—a hundred years hence—what do they look like?"

There were some things in the world that, as they changed across many years, left little room for deviation. The land before her was like that, and when she looked, all the futures seemed to lead to similar places, making them easier to see. Like the ocean at a distance.

"Small trees," she said. "Over there, a large town. That way, farms. Green, everywhere, breaking through the glass. Taking back the land."

Maris exhaled a long sigh and handed her back her shoes. She could barely pull them on now with her skin raw and cut as it was, but she did anyway. As the land rose into hills and they hiked, climbing away from the plains, the pain seemed to fade, turning to itch, and then to calm.

"Thank you," she said to Maris, who nodded.

As they hiked into the mountains, she thought of the unforgivable things she had done, the unpayable debts, and realized Maris was right: it was necessary to pay against the debts anyway.

They hiked the next day and another after that, passing infrequent houses, an occasional fox, and some oddly shaped four-legged animals with long snouts who bobbed their heads as they went by. At last they came to Maris's high mountain desert cabin.

The house was made of orange brick and a flat roof surrounded by a long-overgrown garden. Once inside, they put down their packs on a floor covered with a thick layer of dust. One wall was entirely covered with shelves of dust-gray books. Pas struggled in Dirina's grip, wanting to explore. Dirina held his hand tightly, keeping him close.

"It is a shambles, but the well works. With a little effort, the garden will return full force."

"Even this late in the year?" Amarta asked.

Maris smiled. "You are in Perripur, where everything

grows with great passion. I will go to the nearest town for supplies tomorrow. The two rooms in the back are yours."

Amarta turned a startled look on Dirina. Sleep without Dirina and Pas by her side?

"Or take the same room," Maris said. "This is your home, as long as you wish."

"Let go, let go," Pas complained up at his mother. Once released he took Maris's hand, staring up at her with what Amarta had come to think of as his charm-spell. Maris petted his head with her other hand and trailed the small boy while together they made an inspection of the house, opening doors and cabinets.

Amarta's suspicion had faded, and she felt instead something like gratitude, almost relief. Here in Maris's remote mountain home, Dirina and Pas might truly be safe. And that meant Amarta might be able to—what?

Be something besides afraid for them.

"Home," Dirina said softly, walking around the room, looking wonderingly at Amarta, giving her a tentative smile.

She looked around. Furniture. Food. A fortune in books. A warm, dusty smell.

Home. She mouthed the word to herself to see how it sounded. Could this really be home?

Snow crunched underfoot. A winter sun shone weakly through tall fir and pine.

Angrily, she pushed the vision away. It wasn't fair, the way the future so often ruined the present. She realized Dirina had gone somewhere else in the house.

"Ama?" came her sister's voice from out of sight. "Come see our room!"

"Coming."

Chapter Twenty-three

"What do they say today, Srel?" Innel asked.

A knock at the door of Innel's office delayed his steward's reply. Srel opened the door, took a large platter from a servant with one hand, and closed the door with the other. As he walked to Innel's desk, he passed by Nalas, who reached for a slice of mutton. Moving the platter just out of his reach, Srel arrived at Innel's desk. Finding no available space among the books and ledgers and maps, he sighed, setting the platter of food on a side table.

Innel glanced over at the array of food. Olives cut open like tiny flowers, pâté arranged in swirls on small toasts, slices of mutton precisely fanned out as spokes on a wheel, sausage and onion and who-knew-what-else bits of vegetables on silver skewers, neatly piled in stacks.

So much fuss.

Then there were the bowls of dipping sauces.

He and Srel had had a number of conversations about how dipping sauces and important documents did not get along well together, but still his steward could not be persuaded to obtain simpler and less messy food. "Appearances, ser," is all he would say.

"Well, ser," Srel said, considering Innel's question as he adjusted the plates on the tray. "Many are concerned about the insurgencies at Erakat, Lukata, Rott. The consequent import shortages. Speculation that rebellions are spreading. Some say Sinetel is holding back on shipments again, making our extended military efforts there seem ineffective."

"Continue," Innel said, suddenly in a bad mood.

Srel poured a mug of wine for Innel.

"Then there's Garaya's many years of tax shortfall. A large city, much like our own, and so there is concern the problem could spread to Munasee or even Yarpin, like a disease."

"Pah," Nalas said, stepping toward the platter of food. "Garaya is nothing like Munasee or Yarpin. Barely touched by the Houses. Barely a port, for that matter, and a far smaller garrison, whereas—"

"Agreed, ser," Srel said, interrupting as he arranged a plate of food while managing to position himself between Nalas and the table. Srel handed the plate he'd prepared to Innel; then moved aside to finally allow Nalas access to the food. "But what is said is less about veracity and more about coin and who thinks what about whom."

Innel looked for somewhere to put the plate Srel had given him that did not endanger some important document. "Go on," he said.

"Then there is your mage, ser."

Palace denizens might have suspected Marisel of

magery, given the strange way she wandered the halls and looked as if she were not entirely present, but Keyretura's traditional black garb left no room for doubt. In truth, Innel had expected more than whispers. The lack of outright objection told him that he had made the right decision in bringing Keyretura to the palace in the open.

"What do they say about him?"

"That he guards the queen. That he is making the king whole and hale. That he selects children for the upcoming Cohort. That he's been turning iron into gold—or the other way around, depending on who is speaking. Is seeking certain of the queen's relations for execution. Or commendation. Again, depending on who you ask. Is enchanting the army. Is helping the queen conceive a child. The list goes on."

The last caught Innel by surprise. He considered the old king and his single child and wondered if there was some historical basis for that particular rumor.

"Oh, and the Minister of Accounts wants his books back, ser. No rumor, that—he addressed me directly in the hallway a few minutes ago."

"Tell him he can ask *me*."

"Yes, ser."

"Do you think I'm hiding something, Lord Commander?"

The Minister of Accounts stood before him, nearly vibrating with emotion.

Innel had cleared the office of all but Srel in case the minister was inclined to confess to anything, though his current demeanor rather discouraged that hope.

Putting aside the temptation to answer as bluntly as the question allowed, Innel replied: "I am trying to understand the extent of the"—what was the best phrase?—"involved and subtle work you do for the crown, ser."

"How is this your purview?"

"I sleep in the queen's bed, Minister."

"Not every night, Commander," he said, words clipped.

Nowhere near confession, it seemed. Innel was sure the minister would never had said such a thing to his predecessor, Lason.

He put on what he hoped was a polite smile. "You are quite right, Minister. Our time apart whets our appetites nicely, and those nights I do spend with Her Majesty we talk very little. But some. We could, if you wish, talk about you."

The man pressed his lips together, jaw working as if he were sucking on something sour. "I want my books back. I do actually use them."

"You have copies."

"Creating the originals is my work and my life, Commander."

"I'm sure it is, Minister. Bring me copies and you can have these back. I'll have my retainers verify both sets to be certain."

The Minister of Accounts' jaw worked again, faster, harder, for rather longer than Innel had expected.

Finally: "Yes. All right, Lord Commander." Then he bowed, an exaggerated motion that Innel chose to take as entirely sincere.

✢ ✢ ✢

In a corner of Innel's office, Srel spoke softly with the queen's seneschal about scheduling and the trade council, while in another room the many ledgers of accounts were being compared to the copies that the Minister of Accounts had delivered.

Nalas looked out the window at the newest execution Innel's oddest Cohort brother, Putar, had designed. Large screws drove belts that went to various sharp objects that moved slowly into the hands and feet of some five traitors, each turn of each screw based on a nonstop game of cards and dice the guards were overseeing a stone's throw away, where a long line of Yarpin citizens waited to join in.

Wagers on the results of executions were a long-standing Yarpin tradition, but Putar had cleverly reversed cause and effect, making Execution Square's activities even better attended than before. Innel wondered if Putar would make a good Minister of Justice, finding himself a bit queasy at the thought. But then, so would others, so it was worth considering. Perhaps when Cern's rule was stronger.

Innel turned his attention to the bird-sent report from Garaya's governor and re-read it to see if he was missing anything in the man's words. At least these days he could be confident that he missed no letters; Cahlen's new birds were achieving an impressive reliability record, topping nine in ten returns.

The cost for this performance seemed to be that only Cahlen would work with them. Her arms, hands, and fingers were always covered with bandages, doing little to inspire others to come near the birds. Innel briefly considered the wisdom of one day making her Minister of Bird.

Putar and Cahlen as ministers. Should those things come to pass, the palace would be an odd place indeed. He winced and put the thoughts aside.

Nalas poured himself some spiced wine, putting Innel in mind of his own cup, which he raised to his lips, finding it empty. He held it out silently until Nalas noticed and hastily refilled it.

"What does he say, ser?" Nalas gestured at the report with his cup.

"He uses a great many words to reiterate their continuing inability to make up the shortfall." An entire city. A significant amount of revenue for the crown. "He's blaming the merchants for creating unrest among the citizens. He wants our support, urges action."

"Action? He wants us to send force?" Nalas frowned. "To Garaya?"

"Strongly hinting, yes."

Innel did not imagine that any of the Houses would find the warrant for this particular tax region at all appealing. It was one thing to march across the countryside collecting taxes and who knew what else, and another entirely to march into a walled city and demand an accounting.

"Find someone who knows Garaya. As I recall, Sutarnan has business investments down there and is there often. Probably knows all the merchants personally. See if he'll go along as an envoy. Tell him I'll give him a rank if he helps us solve this."

Nalas's eyebrow rose at this. Sutarnan was one of the

Cohort with little military service who wanted a rank anyway.

At the door, Innel heard Srel say: "Yes, of course—go in."

Innel looked up. This particular queen's guard was one of a number that Innel had handpicked. She knew to report to him directly when she needed to.

A quick dip of the head, a fast salute.

"Ser," she said. "The queen was visiting the old king. When she emerged, she ordered the dogs taken away, which the handlers did. Then she went to the kennels. She says she wants them killed."

Srel made a wordless, distressed sound. "That would not be good."

A bit of an understatement.

With Nalas and Srel trailing, Innel left at a near run. Down the stairs, onto the palace grounds.

Arriving at the kennels, he exchanged a fast look with Sachare. From her expression and almost imperceptible shake of her head, he knew Cern was not likely to be reasonable.

"Where are they?" Cern demanded, striding back and forth past the cages of iron and oak. "Where?"

Seeing Innel, the kennelmaster almost swooned in relief, stumbling a few steps in his direction. "Lord Commander!"

Innel ignored him. "Your Majesty," he said softly to Cern, coming close but careful not to touch her. "I am here now. Let me take care of this for you."

"If by 'take care of it,' Innel, you mean run them through with your sword, as I watch, yes. Do so."

He inhaled, considering what to do about this rather unambiguous command. While the dichu were generally looked on with more fear than affection, slaughtering the king's favorite two dogs would, at best, be seen as lack of respect for the old king and all he represented—including a half century of imperial expansion and prosperity—and at worst seem a kind of treason.

Cern's popular regard in the palace might not yet be able to digest such a meal.

"Perhaps we should reflect on this somewhat first, my lady," he said.

"They growled at me, Innel. They snapped at me." She turned around, looking through into the cages of brindled black and tan dogs, all of whom sat up eagerly, heavy tails thumping, as if she might have snacks. "Which ones are they? Tell me!"

The kennelmaster's mouth was opening and closing as, wide-eyed, he looked to Innel for guidance.

The two dichu she wanted sat in one of the corner cages, in plain view. With surprise Innel realized that though the two dogs had sat at the king's side for years, Cern could not tell them from the others. Willful disregard on Cern's part; she did not want to know anything about them.

That she hated the dogs was not a secret. Understandable, even, given how her father had used them and their forebears as object lessons, bringing them to Cohort meals and studies, extolling their virtues of wit and ferocity, using them to demonstrate how mating was properly done, his gaze pointedly on Cern all the while, while Cern pretended not to care.

Here and now, with guards standing ready but confused, hands on hilts, and the dog keepers fluttering about in near-panic, news would spread like a flash fire across the palace if the dogs were slain at Cern's command. He had to stop this.

"Your Majesty," he said, "let me—find them. I'll bring them to you in your rooms"—no, she wouldn't like that—"better yet, my offices. Surely this"—he waved a hand vaguely, as if to include possible slaughter, "is better done in private?"

She turned around, seeming to only now notice the many eyes on her. She gave an abrupt, angry nod and walked off, trailing her guards and Sachare, who paused long enough to mouth at Innel: "You had better fix this." He gave her a small nod.

With Cern gone, he gestured at the two dichu in the corner cage, the ones she had been looking for.

"Leads and muzzles. Bring them."

"Lord Commander, I beg you," the kennelmaster said. "Her Majesty startled them, I'm certain of it. They're good dogs, sweet and smart, they would never—"

"I know what they are. I'll save them if I can. Do as I say."

Innel gave the dogs' leads to Nalas to take elsewhere and went back to his office without them.

Cern was already there. Innel tipped his head to get rid of her guards so they could talk alone. They looked to her for confirmation, then left.

Sachare, of course, ignored this command, leaning back against a wall to watch. She was, Innel realized, nearly as good as Srel at fading into the background when she decided to. For a moment he wondered what the children of that particular union would be like, and whether Sachare found Srel at all appealing. He was arranging matches, he realized to his annoyance, and pushed the thought aside.

"You're going to tell me I can't, Innel," Cern said in a brittle tone. "Somehow you'll convince me it's a poor plan and that I should look past this to some larger picture."

"Yes, exactly, my lady. They are . . ." How to explain? "People see them and think of the king. I know how you feel, but we're not yet ready to have them see butchered animals where he once stood."

She was silent a moment. "You are right. But he may no longer have them with him. If I want to see my father—I, the queen—no animal will stand in my way."

He bowed his head. "It will be as you say, Your Majesty." This would mean finding another bargaining chip for the old king, but there was always the slave.

"Even now they obey him and only him. Anyone else, they growl and snap."

"I can address this poor behavior, my lady."

"You can?"

"Of course." He was nowhere near as confident as he pretended, but when compared to everything else he was addressing, it seemed a small thing.

"Then they may live."

Bowing to Cern, he caught Sachare's smirk. He knew what she was thinking, that he had just agreed to train the old king's dogs. He gave her a flat, humorless look, and she smiled even wider.

❖ ❖ ❖

"Keyretura dua Mage al Perripur, ser," Srel said, standing aside for Keyretura and dropping his head slightly. At Innel's gesture, Srel left, along with the rest of the crowd Innel's many-roomed office seemed to collect, staring at Keyretura as they went.

Innel pushed away the ledger he'd been working on and the long lists and diagrams representing troop movements and supply lines. He set it atop the pile, watching the mage walk into the room.

The Cohort had been a rich study of those who intended to hold power. From early on, he and his brother had watched everyone keenly to understand the roles they intended to take, studying how to act in all ways like the aristos they could never become and the military leaders that they someday might.

Late into the night they would whisper, comparing the stance and mien of foreign dignitaries to Anandynars royals. Watching at dinners as House eparchs and governors ate and laughed with the king, noticing all the little ways that power played out—the grip of a goblet, the twitch of a mouth, the incline of a head, the changing measure of a gait. Face and posture, word and tone, the entirety of one's physical presentation was a language that revealed thoughts and intentions, that showed how each person swam through the political surf of palace life.

Now he watched Keyretura, who briefly looked around the room for a chair. Innel had already moved the only other chair to the far side of the room. He wanted to see what the mage would do.

The way Keyretura moved was unlike anything

Innel had ever seen. Smooth. Spare. Confidence in each step.

No, it was more than confidence; it was beyond that. Some would call it arrogance, but Innel recognized it as competence.

Keyretura took the chair Innel had placed so far away and turned it to face Innel. Then he stood, watching Innel, seeming content to stand there and wait until his point had been made.

Innel gave it a long moment to see if he would do anything else.

"Let me get that for you, High One," he said at last, going to the chair and bringing it close to his desk. When Keytretura and he were both seated, he considered what he wanted of the mage.

He knew what Keyretura would see when he looked at him: bloodshot eyes, haggard expression, days' worth of beard. Cern had not yet said anything about the shaving, but he must make time to do that.

Keyretura spoke. "You need rest."

"I need a lot of things," Innel said. "I need Sinetel to start producing ore instead of bodies. I need Lukata and Rott to stop sabotaging the rails and resume shipments to Houses Etallan and Nital. I need Garaya to stop whining about tax contracts they agreed to seven decades ago. And I need the girl's head, since no one seems able to bring me her mouth."

Innel had hesitated to tell Keyretura about the Seer and his now years-long search for her, but at this point there seemed little point to silence.

"Affairs of state will go better if it is not generally

known that a mage is involved, especially a Perripin mage. The obvious politics I leave to you. As for the Botaros girl . . ." Keyretura paused.

"Yes?"

"The man you have pursuing her. The expensive one. I know him. If anyone can find her, it will be him."

Tayre, he meant, who was overdue to report back on his plan to hire the girl, making Innel suspect it had not gone well.

"In three years he has yet to deliver any part of her but for some hairs. The others I've hired have done even less."

"Have your searchers look south, to Perripur."

Innel leaned forward in his chair, suddenly feeling more alert. "You know where she is?"

"If I knew where she was, she would be here. It only makes sense that she would go to Perripur, fleeing you."

"Don't you think she'll reason similarly and then go somewhere else?"

"I don't think she reasons at all. I think she simply has an unusual instinct for speculation."

Speculation, not prediction. Well, Innel understood that; he had doubted her ability as well, once. Then he had become Royal Consort, Lord Commander, and Cern had been crowned.

"My expensive hound believes he can persuade her to come to me."

"Perhaps he can. But if he can't, you want her dead. Do I correctly understand your intent?"

"You do, but finding her—"

"Finding her is the harder part. If you can find her, I can take care of the rest."

His confidence was heartening. A far cry from Maris's objections and explanations.

"What about her ability?"

"No one is invincible. From what you've told me, she needs at least a little time to speculate, then act. I will not give her that time."

"You would fight one of your own?"

A small smile. "She is not one of mine, Lord Commander. I have no reason to believe there is any magic in what she does at all. At best it is untrained potential." He steepled his fingertips together. "But it does not matter; I have no intention of fighting. I will take her consciousness, then I will take her life. There is no struggle. It is quite simple."

Keyretura's words were like holding a well-made sword of good steel, straight and clean and ready. For the first time in the years since Botaros, Innel had the sense that this matter might truly be resolvable.

"I will find her," Innel said. "Then, perhaps, I will have you do this thing." He glanced back at the stack of books on his desk. Another thought occurred to him. "Do you know anything about accounts and ledgers?"

"Of course."

"There is something not quite right with these," He said, indicating the stack. "Would you consider taking a look?"

"Audits are far more effective when all involved know a mage is conducting them. I suggest you obtain for me a list of the names of everyone who has helped assemble and most particularly those who have signed the books you want examined, making sure everyone knows who is examining them."

It was an excellent suggestion. Now Innel understood why the Perripin hired mages as advisers. "I shall do so."

"In the meantime," said Keyretura, "have them sent to my rooms."

"Your slave misses you, Sire," Innel said, bringing a chair close to the bedside.

Between being busy and not really wanting to see him, Innel had been coming less often to visit the old king. Today he had finally summoned both time and resolve.

"What now?" the king asked with a wheeze. "Your pizzle too small? Have your mage thicken it for you while you sleep, which I'm assuming is alone, since I hear nothing about my daughter's growing belly."

How could a man ill and bedridden for nearly two years continue to be so offensive? Should he not be made meek by this extended illness?

No. This was Restarn esse Arunkel, chosen by the Grandmother Queen to rule instead of her own children, whom she had found wanting. He was made in the same mold as his formidable grandmother, and mere illness would not make him compliant.

Perhaps it had even made him less so, having nothing left to lose.

"I have questions, Sire," Innel said, finding it impossible to keep his resolution to stop using the honorific.

"Bring me my dogs."

"Naulen, perhaps. Your dogs are ill-mannered and upset the queen."

"She's easily upset. I should have had her beaten more often. Go on, boy, amuse me with your questions."

Well, then; no sense in being polite. Or drawing this out.

"I had Sinetel in hand. Months of the expected ore shipments. Now the numbers are short again and they claim not to know why. Also Erakat, Lukata, Rott. I can't send force everywhere to keep order. What should we do?"

"Ah, Erakat. Grandmother's eighth consort came from there, did you know? His family still owns a large estate. Breeds dichus, very fine ones indeed. A little delicate, but fast and mean. Maybe they could send me a couple to replace the ones you stole."

Innel ignored this. "Garaya is short on taxes. The governor wants us to send force."

"They have you dancing to the tune of their farts, boy. Stop letting them drag you about by your balls."

It would be so easy to hit this thin, weak old man.

Just once, in repayment for the countless times he and his brother had been hit. Just once.

No, tempting as it was.

"I sent soldiers to the mining towns, Sire. They resumed shipments, then—"

"Then it all turned to shit or you wouldn't be here whining about it. Halfwit! It's not about your soldiers. It's about you."

Innel found he was breathing heavily. "What do you mean?"

"If it were me sending the army, ore would be flowing into the city like water, and Garaya wouldn't be showing you their puckered asses instead of the coin they owe. They don't respect you, Innel."

Innel reminded himself that testing and needling was what Restarn was best at. Finding weaknesses. Eroding confidence.

But it put him keenly in mind of his outsider origins.

No. He was the Royal Consort. Lord Commander. His lack of bloodline no longer mattered.

"What do you suggest I do, exactly?"

"Show them you'll stop at nothing. I thought you knew this. Why do you think I selected you from the Cohort?"

"You didn't select me. Cern—"

"My daughter is a poorly trained dog. You think you'd stand where you do now without my hand directing the matter? Are you really such a fool?"

Innel left his chair, kicked it to the floor.

"Next time, Innel, bring Naulen," Restarn said.

Innel swallowed hard, struggling to contain his temper. "What about Garaya?"

"Pah. Garaya is a pragmatic old whore. She opens her legs to the strongest. She spread for my grandmother and if you make a brave show with drums and fanfare over the backs of a few thousand men, she'll bend over and spread for you, too."

"Shall I send him in?" Srel asked.

It was increasingly difficult for Innel to go anywhere unnoticed. He had given up meeting his informant Rutif in the basement root cellar. Now the man came to see him at his offices, in the open.

"First take them somewhere else."

The two dichu dogs to which he referred were sprawled in front of the fire, taking up, it seemed, as much floor space as they possibly could. Innel had not yet had time to do anything with them besides keep them away from Cern.

Srel gave the large creatures an uncertain look. One of the dogs slowly thumped her tail a few times then returned to a gentle snoring.

"Yes, ser. Where did you have in mind?"

The two dichu made people almost as nervous as Keyretura did, but interviews went better without the dogs present. "Her Majesty didn't recognize them before," he said. "She probably won't now. Take them back to the kennels. Then send in Rutif."

It took a few minutes to rouse the sleeping beasts and put them on leads, but then the dogs were gone and Rutif stood before him instead. The man listed slightly to the side of his shorter leg, a gap-tooth smile on his face. He gave a short bow.

"Lord Commander. I have something for you." From outside the room, Rutif drew a small figure inside. A boy, perhaps nine, dressed in overlarge clothes with sleeves and cuffs rolled back, and matted, greasy hair. Someone had tried, though not very hard, to make him presentable.

The boy looked around the room, gaping, eyes wide, then dropped to all fours, his forehead on the wood. A full, formal bow.

Innel snorted, gestured to the man to get him up. The boy fearfully resisted, seeming to prefer the floor. Finally Rutif grabbed a fistful of the boy's oversized shirt and yanked him to his feet, shaking him.

"What is this?" Innel asked Rutif, feeling the press of the books and maps and ledgers that demanded his attention.

"You'll want to hear this, ser. He walked here from Varo. Tell him what you saw, boy." Another shake of the child. He released him to stumble forward toward Innel.

"Your Majesty—" began the boy, grinning a wide, uncomprehending smile.

"No," Innel said sharply. "That is what you call your monarch, your queen, which I clearly am not. Your queen: Cern esse Arunkel. Surely you know this?"

The boy gave a sheepish look followed by a shrug.

"That he doesn't know," Rutif admitted, "Tell him what you do know, boy."

"If he's not the king, who is he?" the boy asked Rutif, whose hand flicked out to slap the boy's head. The boy yelped.

"Where you came from in Varo. What you told me."

"What should I call him, then, if not 'Your Majesty'?"

"Lord Commander, you call him," said Rutif. "Tell him about the goats."

Innel lifted a finger, about to signal Nalas to remove both of them.

"The goats!" the boy said, turning back to Innel. "The wagon stank, Lord Mander. Like a shithouse, you know, because it was. A goat shithouse!" he laughed.

Again Rutif flicked.

"Ow!"

"Just tell him, boy."

"I was hiding behind a tree, watching. One of the goats

escaped out of the wagon when they weren't looking. He ate some nettles. Then he pooped gold."

Innel lowered his finger. "Gold? From a goat's ass?"

The boy nodded vigorously.

Across the room, Nalas was visibly suppressing laughter. Innel gave him a hard look, then turned the look on Rutif. "You waste my time with this."

Rutif held up his hands, as if to beg a moment. "So I thought as well, Lord Commander, but no—the boy is a loyal citizen. Allow me to give you proof." He held out his hand and in a showy gesture slowly fanned opened his fingers to reveal a lump of pale ore perhaps a finger's width thick.

Rutif and the boy watched Innel as he walked around his desk and took the item from Rutif's palm, examining it closely.

"It's clean," the boy said unnecessarily.

It was also, without question, gold.

Someone in Varo had goats who were eating gold ore. Or perhaps being fed it in an effort to quietly take it somewhere else.

"You did well to bring me this," he said. "Where in Varo, boy?"

"Outside Seele," the child said, the smile suddenly gone from his face.

"You walked all the way from Seele to Yarpin?"

"Yes, Lord Mander."

"Alone?"

The boy's mouth twisted downward along with his gaze. He nodded.

"Where are your parents?"

A shrug. "I don't know. My village was burning, so I left."

"Who burned it?"

"Didn't see. Too busy running away."

The answer was too quick. An obvious lie. The boy was scared. He might not know who ruled his empire, but he knew the colors of the Arunkel military.

"Were they wearing red and black, like what I'm wearing?"

The boy looked right, left. A hard swallow, then another. He gave a single, small nod.

Most interesting; Innel had directed no military action in the province of Varo.

Of course, there should be no gold ore in Varo, either.

Innel nodded his dismissal at Rutif, who grabbed the boy and drew him out the door, a triumphant smile on his face at the credit with Innel this would have earned him.

When he was gone, Nalas made a sober, thoughtful sound. "Deserters, you think? Looting and burning the town?"

"Likely," Innel said, not wanting to think of the alternative, that it was his troops doing a little unauthorized tax collection. To Srel he said, "Rutif knows to keep his mouth shut. Get him extra coin to make him even happier about it. The boy . . ." He exhaled. He had no choice; a child that age could only be forced to keep secrets. "Get him to the slave market, somewhere far from the city where no one will care what he says."

"Yes, ser," Srel said softly.

"Nalas, send some reliable and trustworthy scouts to Varo. Have them look for signs of gold."

Chapter Twenty-Four

While the rest of the household slept, Amarta stood in the garden listening to the sounds of birds beginning their loud discussions as the morning brightened. She examined the vegetables and spices they had planted, and knelt to pull weeds, tossing them into the wild tangle of jungle beyond, where vines and grasses were ever eager to take over their garden.

Perripur was a marvel to her. Gentle rains and fragrant flowers, succulent fruits that grew wild in the encroaching forest, all just steps from the house. Warm nights and bright days. This was winter?

In only three months they were eating from the garden they had planted. The land was rich, Maris explained, the sun powerful.

A beautiful land, a comfortable home. Plenty to eat. And no winter. It was hard to imagine anywhere she would rather be.

If only she could stay.

✢ ✢ ✢

Maris left on her own every tenday or so, returning days later with food and supplies, clothes to replace the ragged ones they had been wearing. They offered to go with her but she declined.

"Best keep you out of sight. You are safe here, and I need the time to myself."

Dirina seemed to come into full color these months, like the flowers thick across the high mass of green that shaded the house. She looked happier each day. Perhaps it was that they were no longer hungry and tired and running.

Amarta felt her spirits lift as her sister hummed as she prepared food, as Maris showed Pas how to weed the garden. When the three of them helped Maris reassemble the pipes leading from the well to the house that gave them running water inside as well as out, Amarta could not remember being so happy.

One day Pas burst in from playing outside. He ran to Maris, grabbed her hand, began to pull. "A frog, Maris. Orange eyes. Come see. It has orange stripes!"

She remembered this moment in vision, felt a pang of sorrow amidst the sweetness. She smiled at him and asked: "Can it wait?"

"No!" he said loudly, with a face of such delight that it seemed her heart would burst from joy.

It was time.

Maris smiled and shrugged, to show how helpless she was, and rose from her chair at the table where she had been laying out strands of plants to dry, letting him tug her to the door.

"You should go see it, too," Amarta gently urged

Dirina. A look of confusion passed her face, but she, too, went to see the frog.

Alone in the room they shared, Amarta pulled out her pack and began to gather her belongings.

By the time they returned, she was packed to go. Pas's face and hair had somehow accumulated a great deal of dirt. He was happily breathing hard from some exertion.

"Pas," Amarta said. "Remember about wiping your feet on the mat at the door?"

"Yes. But helping in the garden. More important than feet." He sat on the bed, saw the pack, frowned. "I don't want to leave."

"Good, because you are not going to," Amarta said. "You stay here with Maris and your mother."

"What do you think you're doing?" Dirina demanded.

There was no way out of this moment that did not end in tears. She took her stunned sister's hands in her own. "He will come here. Not tomorrow, not next month, but soon. He will come. We all know it."

"Maris will protect us."

"And when the Lord Commander hires another mage? Will she fight against him for us?"

"Yes!"

"Then shall I be the cause of another Shentarat Plains? No, I will not." Amarta saw another shirt she should take. She stuffed it into her pack.

"But in Munasee you always knew the hunter was coming and you got away from him. You kept us safe every day."

Her sister had known, then. All along. She sighed. Why couldn't they tell each other the truth? "He will find a way," she said. "And how many are looking for me now? In time, someone will silence my foresight." Perhaps another mage, one who didn't have the affection Maris had for them. "And then what?"

Then Dirina and Pas would be in danger again. She had to leave them while they had this chance.

"We're safe here," Dirina said stubbornly. "Maris will protect us."

"Shall we risk her, too, as we have so many others? No." Pas was determinedly untying a knot on her pack. She drew her sister to sit next to her on the bed, pulling Pas's hand away from the pack, holding him tight. "Diri, you and Pas have a home here. I have wanted this for you, a place you could both be safe. Here it is. But only if I am somewhere else."

"You can't, you—"

"There's going to be a war. I have pushed the visions away, but they haunt me every night. All across the empire. Fight and terror. Illness and hunger."

"There have always been wars and illness."

"Not like this."

"You can't prevent it."

That might well be true. But staying here was the same as letting it happen, the same as letting her parents die.

Enana. Nidem.

Now that Dirina and Pas were safe, comfortable and happy, she would draw the hunter's attention back where it belonged. To her.

She stood, looking around to see if there was anything else to take.

"Where do you mean to go?" Dirina asked.

Her sister surely knew this answer, at least some part of her knew, but she did not want to. Amarta understood that, all too well.

She could answer that she was going farther south to lead the hunters away from them. That she planned to cross the sea to the lands beyond, and there she would be safe from all of this.

Had it always been this way between them, pretending, telling each other half-truths to keep each other going through all the achingly wretched times? Here and now, in these last minutes together, should she say something comforting and untrue?

Amarta met her sister's eyes, trying to be brave enough for both of them. "To the Lord Commander. To answer his questions. To stop running away."

"No!" Dirina took the pack off the bed, hurled it to the floor, as if that might somehow stop Amarta from leaving. "We have spent years running from that monster. Enana and Kusan and Munasee—so much struggle to get this far away. You would throw all that overboard, all those who helped us? All who sacrificed?"

Her sister did not know about Nidem's death, perhaps did not know how clearly Amarta had seen their own parents' death. But what Dirina did not know about how many had paid so dearly to see them escape, Amarta did not intend to tell her.

Dirina's voice rose in pitch. "You said that if we went there we'd never be able to leave again."

We. Dirina was not listening. Did not want to hear. Despite the warm air, Amarta felt a chill. "You and Pas will stay here."

Pas's arms were around Amarta's legs, his head resting on her hip.

"But we always go together."

"Not this time."

"You can't go."

"I can."

At this Maris walked in, took in the scene. Dirina went to her. "She's saying she'll leave. Go back to Yarpin. Maris, tell her no."

"I just left that stinking sewer of misery. Why would you even consider such a thing?"

Farther north than she had ever been; it seemed a very long way indeed. It was, she suddenly realized, still winter there. Real winter.

She sat down on the bed. Could this wait until spring? Even summer? Another year?

No. The longer she waited, the more likely someone would find them and hurt those she would sacrifice everything to protect. She had to get away from them.

"Maris," she said, "when we stood on the glass plains, you told us about the many who had died there."

"And?"

"That blood—that debt you paid against—it is in the past. I see that suffering and more in the future. If I can make the Lord Commander understand, I have a chance of changing it."

"I know him, Amarta. He won't change course at your words."

"He did once."

"He did?"

"Yes," Amarta said, remembering the dark night in

Botaros, when her words helped changed Arunkel's history. "He might again."

"That seems—optimistic, Ama. Even foolish."

"If you had foreseen what made the glass plains, Maris, would you have stood by and done nothing? Even knowing that any action you took to try to prevent it might have been both optimistic and foolish?"

Maris did not reply.

Dirina's voice cracked. "Maris, he'll hurt her. He might kill her. Tell her no."

Who were they talking about now? The hunter? The Lord Commander?

Was there a difference?

"Shall I guard her day and night?" Maris asked softly. "Shall I take her mind away so that she no longer has will or remembers her intent?" As Dirina seemed to consider her words seriously, Maris shook her head. "No, I will not."

"But what will happen?"

"Why don't you ask her?"

Dirina was silent a moment. Then: "Ama? What do you see?"

So familiar, the question, along with her sister's faith in her answer. She swallowed a painful lump.

"And this time," Dirina said, "you must tell me the truth."

The truth? Could her sister bear such a thing?

She looked at Dirina, for the first time trying to imagine what it must have been like for her to leave home after their parents had died, to take a girl so young she might have been her own daughter from the only home she had ever known, in the deep dark of night, out to an unknown world, with only sense and reason to guide her. Then to flee Botaros, a baby in her arms, on the say-so of a child.

Amarta had been young enough then that Dirina's actions had seemed—not easy, no, but surely what anyone would do.

But now she understood it was not so. She could not imagine herself having done the same.

Her sister, she realized, had courage beyond her understanding. Yes, she could bear the truth. She was stronger than Amarta had thought.

She sat on the bed, clearing her mind as the three watched. The question seemed to take a long time to arrange in her head. Perhaps because it was about herself, or perhaps because the very act of seeing made her part of much that might happen, making the threads blurry and sticky, slippery and shifting.

It was like a merchant's scale. Herself, whole and sound on one side; on the other, the lives of uncountable peoples across the lands. One side might come out right, or the other, but both? She did not think so. Or, if it were possible, it was remote, too distant and intertwined to see. Pieces in motion that had yet to begin. Decisions by those who had no clue they would ever need to make them.

She could see this much: if she did not go, if she did not try, there would be bodies in piles, blood in the gutters.

But here in Perripur and inland to these mountains? Surely this far . . .

She looked again.

The violence would be only rumor for years: the crumbling, northern Anandynar empire, safely distant. Perripin would hear of the broken alliances, betrayals ending in burnings and slaughter. But it would be very far away. For a time.

Then it would come. She saw Kelerre's tall silver towers torn down, their ruins a mocking tribute to the long friendship and trade ties between the two countries. Arunkin, hungry and destitute, would flee to Perripur, where the air was sweet and warm and food grew wild, fanning out along the Mundaran seashore, bringing desperation and destruction with them.

Pas would be a young man by then. Grown tall and strong, fighting for his Perripin home. A fast flash, barely there and it was gone: a Perripin force overrun by Arunkin, Pas facing death in some useless battle.

She opened her eyes, unable to keep the horror from her face. She looked at Pas, who watched her intently, his child's eyes and mouth open wide.

"Amarta?" Dirina asked.

"There is no simple answer," she said, looking at the three of them, Pas last of all, where her gaze seemed to stick. "This is bigger than me. I will make him listen. I must."

Dirina's face crumpled in agony. "I'll never see you again."

"You don't know that. Even I don't know that. Maris, will you look after them until I . . ." Until she what? Did she really expect to come back? "Will you look after them?"

"You can't go," Dirina said, choking back tears. "I forbid it."

Amarta swallowed a laugh, took her sister in her arms and held her while Dirina sobbed into her neck.

For so long Dirina had been strong, keeping them fed and free. To leave her here, where she could have a sweet, warm life, was the best gift Amarta could think of. This painful day would pass.

Dirina wiped her eyes with her hands. "Maris, will you take her where she wants to go? There are so many on her trail."

"I will be okay."

"Maris, please?" Dirina was crying openly now. It tore at Amarta, and tears gathered in her own eyes.

Then Pas was in front of her. "Up," he said firmly.

"Oh, sweet one—"

"Up," he insisted.

"You're getting so big," she said, hefting him into her arms, where he hugged her tightly.

"I'll take you to Kelerre," Maris said to Amarta. "Get you some kind of passage north to the capital. If you're decided."

"I am." Amarta looked around the house. "Will they be safe in the weeks you're not here?"

"Upon my house and my land is every protection in my power to make. A fair bit. They are as safe here as anywhere."

"But what if someone comes and—" Amarta said. "If you are not here and—"

"What, now—you, too? Nothing is certain. You of all people should know this."

"Yes, but—"

"You're the seer. Look. Decide for yourself."

It was hazy, like mountains through a distant rain storm, but she could feel it: a chance for her family. A chance they would not have if Amarta stayed. That they would not have while Innel sev Cern al Arunkel sought her.

"Then," she said, looking at Dirina and Pas, wanting to drink them in with her eyes and never forget them, "let us go. Now."

Pas ran to his mother, who picked him up, sobbing. His expression was stark as he watched Amarta over her shoulder, then he, too, began to wail.

A winter storm, mild in temperature but very wet, delayed the boat's departure from Dasae to Free Port. En route another storm soaked the decks, keeping the two women in the cabin.

"Maris, is what I do magic?"

A thoughtful sound. "I don't know. I have yet to see you predict something that might not have been a lucky guess."

"I understand. Have you a coin?"

Maris dug into a pouch, brought out a full nals.

Amarta nodded. Maris flipped the nals in the air. Before it landed on the cot, Amarta spoke. "The Grandmother."

The Grandmother Queen, dogs at her feet, moon-in-window above, the cross that went through the coin where it might yet be broken, dirty with age.

"Again," Amarta said and as Maris tossed it into the air: "The river."

The coin landed, river side up. A switchbacked river, trees on each side.

Maris flipped the coin in the air again.

"River. Grandmother. River. River. River. Grandmother."

They kept going for a time. Finally Maris took the coin and put it back into the pouch. She took a deep breath and exhaled slowly, a thoughtful look on her face. "You ask if it is magic. Yes. Also no. Among my kind, your ability is rare enough to be mere rumor; it is said that an elder mage with restored fertility might, in the last moments of her labor, when the child moves from womb to air, open a portal to prophecy." A small shake of her head. "Otherwise, no; it does not happen."

"So, not magic, then?"

"But when you call the coin, I feel it in you: a small, pinpoint spark of magic. The rest of the time, not even as much motion as an adept might have."

"So, then, what am I?"

"Unique beyond reckoning. Little surprise you are sought with such passion and fervency."

As this sank in, Amarta found herself taking deep breaths, her pulse speeding. "I think I am afraid."

"You would be a fool not to be."

The boat came to Free Port in early evening. The two of them stood at the rail to watch the city spires and buildings against a deepening sky. Gulls circled above, diving into the water for food, taking easy flight whenever they chose. Again Amarta watched them with envy.

She had had second thoughts and third ones as well. But they were simple, sensible fear. The decision stood.

Maris said, "A carriage to Kelerre. Then a room for

the night. Tomorrow I will ask around, see how things lie, and then we will decide how best to get you north."

"Not a ship?"

Maris shook her head. "It is storm season on the coast, and not the small, warm swirls we faced on the Mundaran. We would have trouble finding a ship northward from Kelerre and more trouble yet if we took it."

"So I must walk?" Yarpin seemed a very, very long way away.

A laugh from Maris. "Such a walk in winter would take you a very long time indeed, if you made it at all. The crew has heard there are bandits along the Great Road when it passes into Arun. Even the high mountain route—no easy trail the rest of the year—is said to be blockaded at many points north." She shook her head. "Your people are finally fighting back, but instead of turning on their rulers they turn on each other. Your country is wounding itself. What fools."

"Then how am I to go north?"

"I will ask around. I do not desire to go into Arun, Amarta, but someone will. We will find them."

"The Teva," Amarta said. "If they were here, I could travel with them."

A curious look from Maris. "That tribe's home is a very long way from here. How do you know of the Teva?"

She thought of Jolon and the inked scars around his forearms. Life doors, he had said. *Limisatae*. Had she, she wondered, yet earned such a mark?

No, she decided. She had not.

"They rescued us, some years ago." So long ago now, it seemed.

"Well, if there are Teva in Kelerre, I will find them. If not, perhaps some fortified trader caravan determined to make Yarpin by spring and well enough armed to make it so." She shrugged. "In any case, we will start by buying a good horse for you."

Buying a horse? "Aren't horses expensive?" she asked.

The other woman chuckled. "Compared to what?"

Horses, Amarta decided, were expensive.

"Have you ridden before?" Maris asked.

Amarta considered the short time she had sat on the shaota with Mara at Nesmar Port. "No. Maris, I can never repay you for all this."

A wave of her hand. "Not of consequence."

"But if the Lord Commander pays me, maybe I can, at least—"

"If you take his money, you will become obligated beyond reason."

"But—"

"Ama, I have coin aplenty. Mages always have work when we want it. It may be unpleasant work, like searching for a girl on the run, but it pays obscenely well."

"I could foresee for you," she said.

"Refrain. I have no interest in knowing what is to come. The past is hard enough. I'll face the future as it arrives. Does that seem odd to you?"

"No."

"Are you ever surprised?"

"All the time. The future is not one thing. It spreads and tangles and fades. Like game trails in fog. There one moment and gone the next."

The ship gently bumped the dock. On shore in the

fading light Perripin strode past the port carrying bundles, pulling carts, pressing horses and wagons forward. On dock people yelled, waving at the sailors, pulling ropes tight and tying them to the pier. Above were the first stars of evening, pinpoints through a darkening curtain.

Maris picked up her bag.

Then, all at once, the deep blue sky seemed to go hard like a rock wall. The boat beneath Amarta's feet felt slippery. Her grip on the rail tightened. "Maris, he's here."

"Who is here?"

"The hunter."

"The one Innel sent to find you? Here in Free Port? Kelerre? Are you sure?"

"Yes," she breathed shallowly. "Any way I go. The Great Road, the mountains. Even by ship. He's always there."

Maris laughed. "That's quite a trick. I wonder how he manages to be everywhere at once. Even mages can't do that." The other woman's voice seemed far away. "It's all right. We'll get you to Yarpin safely. After that, I cannot say."

All the other passengers had left the boat.

"Ama?"

He had always been there. He would always be there. She could not get past him. How had she thought otherwise?

"Amarta. You are afraid. There is no need."

It took a long moment for her to realize that Maris had spoken, and more time yet to make sense of the words.

She blinked a few times and realized Maris was right. Things were not as they had been. The cause for such fear was in the past. It had changed.

Slowly she unclenched her hands from the railing.

"Are you sure you want this, Ama?"

"Yes," she breathed.

She was done running. If he was here, so be it.

Amarta watched the city go by from the open carriage, tensing each moment they passed an alleyway or a wagon's shadow. She expected the hunter to jump out, to climb the carriage from the back, to drag her into the street. But he did not.

They left the carriage at a public house and went inside. Maris ordered them food. Amarta looked around the crowded room, wondering which of the many people he might be.

"Eat, Ama," Maris urged, but Amarta was not hungry. "We will take a room," the other woman said after a while. "Busy time here, but they have one open, and tomorrow—"

"No. I must find him tonight." She needed this to be over.

"Find him? Tonight? You must?"

"Yes."

"Why?"

"I don't want him to surprise me again."

"Unless he is one of my kind, Ama, he cannot surprise you with me by your side. Tonight, at least, I can protect you from that."

"Please."

"What does he look like?" Maris asked.

Amarta considered all he ways he had seemed to her

across the years. "He is clever with disguise. He can seem any number of ways. Light brown eyes."

A laugh. "I'll look for the eyes, then."

By the light of moon and stars they walked the streets of Kelerre, the cool winds of the ocean in their faces despite the high wall that kept the worst of the sands and storms seaside. In the dim light Amarta trailed her fingers along the seawall with its embedded shells and starfish, looking ahead to every gap and opening.

Where was he?

The wall was in ruins, the rocks and seashells broken along the crumbled stones.

She pulled her hand back from stone wall.

"Not here, then," Maris said. "Let's go uptown."

They walked an hour and more. In a small, empty square surrounded by buildings Maris stopped.

"He must be here somewhere," Amarta said.

Doorway after doorway, her heart would speed and she would hold her breath, thinking that now, surely, he would jump out at them.

"Let's bed down for the night and try again tomorrow," Maris said, breaking into a yawn.

The din of another pub came from a nearby building. She had lost count of the public houses they had entered, the many who had turned to look, marking the curiosity of a Perripin woman and a young Arunkel woman together.

He must be in one of them. Surely.

Maris pointed upwards. "We call that one the flying

fish, those six stars there," she said. "Your people call it the scales, though. I think it tips a bit to that side. What do you think?"

Amarta turned around, noting every darkened doorway.

Maris put a hand on Amarta's shoulder. "You panic at every door. Your blood is filled with exhaustion and fear. If he is everywhere as you say, Ama, then he will be everywhere in the morning, too. Rest tonight."

She was at a loss; he had never before been so hard to find.

Of course, she had never been looking, either.

Amarta went to the door from which muffled laughter came. She put a hand on the wooden wall, half seeing it burnt to ash in many possible futures.

Could she relax, knowing how close he might be?

"Two lanes down is the Sleeping Cat Inn," Maris said. "A comfortable place. We will go there."

"I want to look inside."

A tired sigh. "All right. I'll wait here."

Amarta pushed open the door and stepped inside, blinking in the room's lamplight.

She could feel it at once, a pressure and thrumming behind her eyes; by entering, she had put something into motion, something to do with the hunter. Which of these people was he? Most were Perripin. But he was so good at disguise, perhaps he could even darken his skin at will.

On the floor in a cleared area a small dog stood on hind legs, cloth around its middle and shoulders. The animal made little barking sounds, like bird chirps. Some fifteen men sat around the edges, clapping and laughing and tossing bits of food to the dog.

"Jump, Cern!" one man yelled, tossed a bit of bread. The dog leapt, caught the bread in midair, continuing to make small yelps.

"My harvest taxes," another man called in broken Arunkin. The dog launched upward to snap at the morsel he had thrown, staying perched on two legs.

"Levy for the hairs on my head," another shouted, tossing another bit. The dog snapped it out of the air. "And the hairs on my toes. And this one is for—"

She had been noticed. The men fell silent and turned to look at her. The dog dropped to all fours.

None of those was him, she was nearly certain. Odd, because she could feel him somewhere in her next few minutes. Close. So close. Where was he?

"What do you want, light-skin?" one Perripin asked.

"I'm looking for a man," Amarta said, surprised at how confident having Maris just outside made her feel.

"We are men," said one, spreading his hands with a grin.

Another said: "You have money, Arunkin? I rent by the hour."

A third man laughed. "You're too ugly for her. You'd be the one paying." Then, to Amarta: "There's a man looking for someone described like you. He was light-skinned and bearded. That maybe who you're after?"

Mutely she nodded.

"In here a bit ago. We see him again, want us to tell him you were here?"

Her answer, she knew, wouldn't matter. "Yes, thank you."

She turned her back on their stares, pushed open the door, and went outside.

The dark street was empty.

"Maris?" Amarta called, then bit her lip.

If Maris had been pulled away, something was truly amiss. For Amarta to call aloud was to give herself away to danger. She had come to rely too much on vision. Perhaps she should also learn to not make mistakes in the first place.

But there had been no warning. Did that mean she was safe?

Or did it mean something else?

Think, she told herself. Lack of vision did not mean lack of reason. She forced herself to stillness, to silence. To listen.

Voices came from around the side of a building. The laughter was Maris's. Relief flooded her. She walked toward the voices, rounding the corner where Maris stood, speaking Perripin. As she neared, Maris turned.

"Did you find him?" Maris asked.

"He was there, but he's gone now."

"Ah, too bad. This is my friend Enlon. We studied together at Vilaros university. I crewed with him for a year, too. How long ago, Enlon?"

"Oh," the man said, his voice a heavy mix of accents, "I say seven, maybe. Not a long time for you, mage."

"Long enough," Maris said, chuckling. "I shouldn't be surprised to see you in Kelerre in these times. You always had a sense for where opportunity lay. Good to see you, my friend." She clasped his forearm, and he clasped back.

"It is good," the man echoed. Then his voice changed, so subtly that Amarta barely noticed the change until after the words were said. "Warmth and health to you, Seer."

Amarta stumbled backwards, her heart pounding.

Maris frowned. "Enlon, you know—?"

"Maris," Amarta whispered, still only half certain. "That's him."

He wasn't anything like she remembered, not in how he looked—now with a headwrap as Perripin captains did, his beard braided—nor in the way he stood—a little stooped, head to the side. Not in his accented voice. Nothing about him looked right.

But as he returned her stare, she saw his eyes.

Maris had said she would protect her, but if she was friends with her hunter, then what? She stood as if frozen.

"No," Maris said, drawing the word out. "This cannot be your hunter. I know this man." As the moments slipped by and he did not speak, not to deny, not to explain, her expression slowly changed.

He said something to her in Perripin, something quiet.

"Indeed," she said in response. "How—unexpected. You, of all people. Well. This woman is under my protection. You understand me?"

"I understand," he said. Then, to Amarta, in a tone and accent that she now clearly recognized: "I am told by those in various establishments in Kelerre that you are looking for me tonight."

Amarta swallowed. For a moment she couldn't speak. "Yes."

"Why?"

At his look, she felt sick, her stomach turning. She

sucked in breath, one deep inhale after another, as if she were drowning.

"I am done running. I want to contract with the Lord Commander."

"Ah. This is good. We are now aligned in purpose."

"It has nothing to do with you," she said, hoping she sounded more confident than she felt.

"I understand that, Seer. But these are dangerous times. I can offer you my protection en route to the palace and the Lord Commander."

Amarta exhaled a laugh of disbelief. "You?"

"Yes, me."

"Why should we trust you?" Maris asked.

"What cause have you to mistrust?" His voice took on the strange mix of accents again. "I'm no less Enlon than I am the one the Seer has been fleeing. Remember the sudden storm off the islands when we fought waves fifteen feet high? You trusted me then. With your life. Why trust me less now?"

Maris shook her head, clearly annoyed. "You are contracted with Innel. You take on disguises to deceive."

He laughed a little. "Did you not also serve the Lord Commander, Maris? Where is your mage's black?"

"It is not the same thing."

"As you say."

Others only want your head.

"Yes," Amarta said to him, breaking in. "I will take your protection."

They both looked at her, Maris surprised. "Amarta, are you certain?"

If she did not run from him, he could not chase her.

Was it not better to have him close, where she could see him, than following behind?

Best to keep enemies as close as possible.

She forced herself to meet his gaze.

The price of not being hunted, it seemed, was facing these eyes.

"I am," she said.

Chapter Twenty-five

"I have found what you've been looking for, Lord Commander," Keyretura said as he stepped into the office.

For a short-lived moment, Innel thought that the mage had somehow found the seer. But no—three green-and-cream-clad servants trailed him into the office, carrying the stacks of ledgers Innel had given him to look over. He motioned them to his desk, where they set the stacks, then he dismissed them. They left quickly.

The mage looked at Srel and Nalas and gestured to the door. More disturbing than seeing Keyretura dismiss Nalas and Srel was how quickly they obeyed him.

The mage sat and tapped one of the heavy tomes in front of Innel with a long nail. "Page seventy-two. Note the name of the clerk signing. His accountings are accurate to the quarter-nals and without error. The problem begins here."

"Perhaps he is simply good at his work?"

"No. The only clerks who make no mistakes are those with something to hide. Search his quarters."

"I shall," Innel said, noticing how much like an order that had sounded.

"Next is this: adjustments in accounts—the inconsistencies your ministers are so fond of excusing—are nearly always used to account for too little in places where there should be more. However, across all these books you have the opposite set of corrections."

"The opposite set of—"

"You have too much coin to account for. This is a recent change, perhaps the last handful of years, and not at all a common problem in your empire. It certainly wasn't the case when I audited these same accounts some thirty years ago."

"Too *much*?"

"Yes. A number of clerks have been taking extra—some ministers as well—but more importantly, someone is putting unaccounted-for funds into your treasury. This is why, with all the extra being taken out, your clerks are both befuddled and yet able to make the numbers come out even."

Innel sat back, stunned. "Who would do that, and why?"

"A good question. Perhaps it is time for another talk with your ministers."

Innel considered this and the mage sitting in front of him. "Would you, High One, be able to help me assess the veracity of their words?"

"I assume Marisel told you that mages don't read thoughts."

"She did, indeed."

"That is so. However, I do read bodies, and your kind

lies both poorly and predictably. More importantly, those who believe I can detect deception are likely to reveal it without my needing to do much at all."

At this Innel found he was smiling. "You seem to know a good deal about how people work. Mine in particular."

"Yes, I do."

It occurred to him that the mage might well have had a similar conversation with someone else the last time he audited these books, long ago. Just how old was Keyretura? He stared at the mage a moment and wondered why he had taken this contract. "What does my body tell you, High One?"

"That you are tired and need sleep. That you eat too little. That you sit too much."

Innel snorted. "True enough." He kept meaning to find time to take Nalas into the garrison and practice with him until they were both dripping with sweat, but there never seemed to be time. He looked at the ledgers and then at the mage. "I am fortunate to have you advising me, High One."

"Yes, you are."

"But it's midwinter and very cold outside," Nalas said. Then, catching Innel's look, added slowly, "Which is a fine thing, because there's little I enjoy more than fencing when there's frost on the ground, ser."

"That's what I like to hear," Innel said. These days he seemed to always find a good reason not to. That stopped today.

Trailing a handful of guards, the two of them went to the practice yards outside the garrison and selected red-oak practice swords. By the time they were both good and sweaty, with a handful of bruises each, Innel ended the workout, handing his sword to one of the many guards watching and accepting a towel in return. As they walked back to the palace, they came upon a game of two-head between Kincel and Helata, with Tok watching from the sideline.

"I commend you for staying in good condition, Lord Commander," called Tok.

"You should join us."

"Na. Smarter than I am fast, as you may recall," Tok said with a grin.

"Not saying much."

As the Helata team slammed their blue and green ball into the goal, Kincel threaded theirs between the legs of Helata's defenders, trailing a wake of curses and blows. The arbiter blasted a horn to indicate a goal on one side while Kincel's gray and tawny ball went flying out of bounds.

"Good thing my mother finds me so charming, then."

"I understand congratulations are in order—I hear she has named you Eparch-heir."

Tok smiled wide.

"Speaking of which," Innel said, "please tell her how very much the crown appreciates the good work Etallan has done with the tax collection warrants in Gotar."

"I shall, ser. She will be quite interested to know if I have inside information into the timeline for the next Cohort. Do I?"

"You do not."

"I thought I might not. And the other matter?"

Helata's riverhouse mansion. Helata had been somewhat less than enthusiastic about the notion of selling their land and house to Etallan, at any price; their counteroffer to buy Etallan's smithy included an extensively detailed accounting of the last ten years' ocean-going freighter trade, with the portion that went to the crown underlined a number of times. Innel had put the discussion aside in the hopes that tempers might cool.

All because Etallan seemed to need to run their screaming grindstones and waterwheel-powered hammers all through the night.

"Out of my hands, Tok. Bring it to the queen," Innel said, knowing the seneschal would never find time in the queen's schedule for that particular matter.

Tok gave him a brief, assessing look, then turned back to the field, eyes flickering across the shouting, rushing players in House colors. "Who do you favor today?"

"I can hardly choose one House over another, Eparch-heir."

A laugh. "It's only a game, Lord Commander. Hardly anything at stake but reputation."

"Then I suppose I can say both teams seem enthusiastic."

"Truly? I think Helata looks worn."

No reason not to give him something to gnaw on. "I admit I'm surprised to see them sticking with the diamond formation on defense."

"But look—the woman on the left, doubled over and heaving? Their foremost. I don't think she'll make it to the end of the game."

"Perhaps not."

"Neither team a match for Etallan in any case. We lack for challenge among the Houses."

Innel noticed Nalas talking to a just-arrived messenger. Nalas gave Innel a look and a nod. "Perhaps your house should try its skill against the down-city teams." Aligned with the Houses, but only barely, wearing House colors and taking on matches that were more slum brawls than anything else. Still, better to have them in House colors, nominally answerable to someone, than wearing rags and answerable to no one.

"Pah. Anyone can win a game if they ignore the rules."

"A good point."

"Ser," Nalas said, stepping close.

"Good day to you, Eparch-heir," Innel said, leaving.

"Always a pleasure, Lord Commander."

As they walked back to his office, Nalas said, softly: "The trade council. Another scout report from Varo. A bird from Sutarnan in Garaya. Another from Colonel Tierda in Sinetel. Also, the queen."

"All this while we were hitting each other with sticks? Will I be happy with either of the letters?"

"You won't like the one from Sinetel."

"Ah."

He thought of Tierda's child and the implicit threat he'd made, wondering if she were worried about what he would do. In truth, he was too busy to do anything, let alone feed a child to pigs. Which would probably not, in any case, give him quite the reputation he was looking for.

Once in the office, Srel delivered a platter along with a flagon of something hot and steaming that smelled of fermented apple. The plate held herbed marrow bones, and small toasts with brie. And, of course, the ever-present bowls of dipping sauce. He ignored them all for the cider, taking a mug and downing it.

"The queen?" he asked, sitting.

"She's in the kennels, ser."

He stood. "What? Why didn't you alert me?"

"She's only watching, ser," Nalas said. "Watching the dogs. We would tell you if it were a problem."

"Watching? But why?"

The two of them exchanged a look.

"Perhaps," Srel said, "you might ask her. You see a bit more of her than we do." The smaller man winced at his words.

Innel waved it away. It was no secret that they spent as many nights apart as they did together. He had vetted the others who entertained her for their skill and sense, making sure she was solidly well-guarded. The most important thing was that she was pleased, and pleased to see him when she did.

Innel had studied the histories of royal consorts and similar pairings and marriages. He knew the prevailing wisdom of making such unions last.

"The trade council?" he asked.

"They want you at this afternoon's meeting," Srel said. "Kelerre."

The council was not happy with Kelerre's reluctance to renegotiate contracts or the explanations that they hesitated because of violence along the Great Road. The recently levied import and export taxes on Yarpin goods were an additional insult. Cern's rule was weak enough that Kelerre was pushing back.

It was Cern they should be asking to attend that meeting, not him.

"Sinetel," he said heavily, holding his hand out for the letter, which Nalas put into his hand.

Nalas had been right: he was not happy.

Innel looked at the Minister of Accounts, Coin, and Treasury, who stood on the other side of his desk. He had not offered them chairs and indeed had made sure there were none in the room besides the one in which he sat and the one in which Keyretura sat.

The ministers' eyes kept sliding sideways to the black-robed mage, seemingly hard-pressed to decide which of the two men they should be more concerned about.

"Minister?" Innel asked, looking at the Minister of Accounts.

"The clerk Dyrik, whom you named, ser. We searched his room and found souvers below the floorboards. You were quite right to be suspicious. But the man himself— alas. He is dead." The minister's mouth worked furiously, as if whatever he were sucking on were fighting back.

"How?"

"A flash flood in the mountains, where he was visiting his ailing mother."

"Where is the body?"

At this the man looked startled, then confused. "Swept away, ser. In the flood."

"Ah, I see." To Nalas: "Send someone to question the ailing mother. Be sure she has enough wood to get her through this cold winter. Find out what else she has."

"Yes, ser," Nalas said.

"And the rest of this?" Innel asked, gesturing at the books Keyretura had audited, looking at each of the three of them in turn. "The extra funds that have been, it seems, coming *into* the treasury?"

"I do not know how that came to be." The Minister of Accounts said quietly.

"Truth," Keyretura said.

Eyes fluttering as if fighting a fainting spell, the Minister of Accounts spoke again. "Lord Commander, I have no need to lie; I have done nothing wrong." He glanced quickly at Keyretura, who shrugged, almost imperceptibly.

Innel turned his attention to the Minister of Coin. "Minister?"

She dipped her chin in a bow. "We are taking in a great many souvers these days, Lord Commander, as we re-mint for the queen's visage. We do count them all, every one of them"—she paused, looking at Keyretura, who nodded—"but some inconsistencies are unavoidable"—another hesitation, another nod from the mage—"as I have said before. I will look into it, ser, and audit our process." Her eyes were wide, and she seemed to be breathing heavily.

Innel made a thoughtful noise. Finally he looked a question at the Minister of Treasury.

"The treasury is healthy, my Lord Commander," said the Ministry of Treasury, looking at Keyretura, who nodded for him to continue. "If there is an issue, well, I have no choice but to conclude it must stand with Accounts." With that he looked back at the Minister of Accounts and was joined in this by the Minister of Coin.

Well, at least it was clear who was being thrown to the pigs now.

"I have no authority over any of you," Innel said when it was clear they were hanging on his every word, "but I suggest that you look more closely at your agencies. If you need help, Keyretura dua Mage has told me he would welcome any opportunity to assist."

None of them looked happy at this suggestion.

"It is not ours, Lord Commander. We did not mint this."

The Minister of Coin held the gold souver up at arm's length, lips pursed, her eyes refocusing past it, on Innel, then back to the souver. She offered it to Innel, who took it, turning it over and over in his fingers.

It looked like a souver.

"Are you sure, Minister?"

"Quite sure. And now that we are looking for them, we are finding rather a lot of them."

He rubbed the metal of one side, then the other. "Is it not gold?"

"Oh, it's gold. Most assuredly. Weight, displacement, and slot tests bear that out. Which is why we didn't notice before now."

"Then how do you know it's not one of ours?"

She brought out another gold souver and held it out for Innel to see. Glancing between the two coins, one in her hand, one in his, Innel said, "I still don't see a difference, Minister."

"Look at the horse's teeth, ser. You can almost count them."

"No, I can't. I am holding the forgery?"

"You are." She brought out another, held them up, side by side. "I see attempted forgeries all the time, ser, but none this good. Never. This side—the king's face. Do you see His Royal Majesty's eyes? Such detail. You can almost see him blink."

Still Innel could not see a difference. "Improved engraving on the dies, perhaps?"

"No, Lord Commander."

"Then how can you—?"

She held both coins edge for Innel to see. "Just a bit too thin. Do you see?"

He made a doubtful sound, and she touched them together. Now he saw that one was very slightly thinner. Hardly perceptible. "Ah. Yes."

"There is more gold in this forgery than there is in a standard souver."

"More? What? But why—"

"Exactly, Lord Commander. And this is what puzzles me most: this coin would cost more to produce than a souver is worth. It makes no sense at all."

"Not a problem."

Sutarnan del Sartor del Elupene, recently returned from Garaya, sat in front of Innel eating boiled eggs dipped in oily saffron sauce and crab-filled pastries baked into the shapes of starfish.

"An entire city, remiss on taxes for nearly two years, and you say it's not a problem? Care to elaborate?"

"My pleasure." Sutarnan licked red oil from his fingers and took a sip of the black wine he'd had brought from his own collection. Then he leaned back, smug and smiling. "It's not the merchants. Well, it is, but not the way the governor has whined to us. Oh, they're full of spark and fury, all right, but the real problem? The governor. He's been eating his seed corn, the bastard. Not a little, either; the entire royal garrison has been gutted, turned into an army of beggars."

"What?"

"He hasn't paid them in over a year. The barracks are falling down. Some of them have sold off their weapons and armor just to afford to live. Others have gone off into the countryside."

More deserters. And close enough to the Perripur border that the word would spread.

Innel exhaled sharply. "This is why the merchants are troubled and taxes are in arrears. No one to collect and keep order. Where's the city council?"

"Well-fed wethers. They speak his words, simper and equivocate and defer, then go back to their houses to eat and fuck. Useless, all of them. Not that I object to eating and fucking, you understand."

"I'll have his head," Innel said darkly.

"A change in leadership might be just what the city needs. Even wants. Fortunately for you, Lord Commander, I can arrange this for you."

"Explain your meaning."

"The private militias aren't going to want to get involved, and the governor's guard has lovely uniforms and shiny weapons that they don't want to dent or dirty. Still, the walls and gates are sound and solid and very sturdy. I could defend them with a hundred good men.

Yes, even me." He laughed. "Imagine. I'm starting to like the idea."

Sutarnan had always been annoying. "Don't let me rush you," Innel said sweetly.

Sutarnan leaned forward, holding up a pastry then biting off one of the legs. "But the walls won't matter. A number of merchants are good friends of mine, and it turns out quite loyal to the crown. They've agreed to open the poorly guarded eastern gates when the queen's army shows its colors. You'd be surprised how many are eager for that moment to arrive."

"You arranged this?"

"Don't sound so surprised. It's not only you bone-crushers who can take cities. Sometimes it requires a bit of"—he waved a hand at the food and wine—"friendly conversation."

"I am—impressed. Well done, Sutarnan."

The other man smiled. "And this," he said, "is why you're going to send me back at the head of an army to take Garaya. I've always wanted to be a general."

"Ah." A bit more of a title than Innel had intended to give him, but perhaps reasonable under the circumstances. In any case, it was unlikely Sutarnan would want to repeat this experience. "I might send someone with you. Keep you from getting into too much trouble."

"Certainly. A little advice might be useful."

Innel thought of who he'd send with Sutarnan and the companies most familiar with Garaya. Then he thought of Cahlen.

"One of the companies I'll be sending with you has a corporal, named Selamu. I'd be very unhappy if something happened to him. Keep him safe. Back with the birds." Cahlen would like that. "Understood?"

"You have a boy companion? How charming, Innel. I would not have suspected you of such—sentimentality."

"He's my sister's. Just keep him alive."

"So noted, ser," he said, with a lopsided smile and a sloppy salute that Innel did not think was unintentional. "I'll send my clerk around tomorrow for the writs of command. I'll have to have a uniform made, too, I suppose, and select a new horse. My parents will be delighted. Let me know when I'm nearly ready to go, will you?"

"Of course," Innel said wryly.

Innel went to his suite at sundown, bone-weary and aching for his bed. He was starting to make little mistakes, letting important items slip by, getting angry with people over small things.

He could not allow little slips to turn into big ones, small annoyances to ripple out into the fabric of palace politics.

As he shut the door of his suite behind him, he saw her standing by the windows, dressed in soft, flowing magenta silks. She faced away from him, looking out the window at a city bathed in a golden sunset and the dark band of ocean beyond.

"Your Majesty," he said. She was in his room. Why?

She did not turn around. "What are you doing, Innel?"

He gritted his teeth. It was a sufficiently vague question that he could not guess at what she might mean. There was no good answer. He recognized the tactic from her father. Intended to put him off-balance. And working.

Restarn's daughter, after all.

He started unbuttoning his vest. "Getting undressed."

Now she did turn around. "I don't want all the details of how you keep order, but there are some disturbing rumors."

"Which particular rumors are you thinking of?"

"The one where you are spending a very great deal of money trying to find a young woman. A fortune-teller. Normally I ignore such idiocy, but this rumor has been surprisingly persistent."

"Rumors are always persistent. That's what makes them rumors. The more outrageous, the longer-lived." Innel pulled off his shirt.

"What is the new mage doing, Innel?"

He was beyond tired. "Helping me with a number of matters," he managed, tossing the shirt on the floor.

"Is one of them this fortune-teller?"

It was tempting to tell her no and have this done with, but if such a deception came to light, nothing would infuriate her more.

Besides, she liked to be right once in a while.

"It is."

She growled softly. "Is this a jest?"

"It is not. Do you now want the details?" His tone was too rough, he realized, struggling for calm.

She turned away in the darkening room, standing for a moment in profile against the fast-dimming sun. She touched a low-burning lamp and it brightened the room, underlighting her sharp features, giving her a formidable appearance. She looked a lot like her father now. "I do."

"My lady, I'm desperately tired. Can't this wait until morning?"

"Of course it can wait," she said, voice chillingly soft. "If you think it prudent to deny your sovereign answers when she asks for them. I wouldn't, in your shoes, but perhaps you know better than I do."

"Forgive me," he said quickly, feeling his blood rush at her words, grateful for the momentary clarity it lent him. "Whatever you want to know, you have only to ask."

"Why are you searching for this young woman?"

"Because she can see into the future."

Cern snorted in disgust. "Must I find a new Lord Commander? What a stunningly witless thing to spend on. You're as bad as my father."

"I would agree with you," Innel said cautiously, "had I not heard her speak. That she has evaded my best trackers is not coincidence."

"Anyone can get lucky."

"Not this lucky. Not for three years."

"Three *years*? Fates, Innel. How much is this costing?"

One of Restarn's faults was that he rarely asked for a close accounting. For a moment, he missed the old king. "Shall I walk you through the ledgers, Your Majesty?"

"Oh, it's going to be like that, is it?" Her words did not invite answer, so he did not offer. Instead he sat heavily on his bed and pulled off his boots.

She sat down across from him in one of the thickly padded chairs. "You realize how witless this sounds, Innel?"

"Yes. But it is worth the cost to find her, even if all she

does is sit and mumble, if our enemies believe she might be able to predict tomorrow's weather. And they do."

"I hear my uncle is on the Labari coast. Perhaps a royal pardon would bring him back to resume the Lord Commandership."

Innel laughed at this weak threat, even knowing it was a mistake. He was just too tired.

"You laugh at me? You dare?"

"I'm sorry, Cern," he said, belatedly realizing he wasn't making things better by addressing her informally. "But the thought of Lason trying to manage the military conflicts we are juggling—he'd change every allocation, just to show he could. He'd plunge us into outrageous, costly battles that could never be won. Besides, you don't even like him."

"I don't like you, either."

"But you trust me. Because I tell you the truth. As I am doing now."

She snorted as if in disgust and disagreement, but he saw her shoulders relax. He knew how she had been raised. When he thought about it, it was surprising that she could relax at all.

A vivid memory came to him of her as a small child, perhaps four or five, her expression one of utter, agonized frustration following some harsh and confusing conversation with her father. She had stood still and silent, small hands clenched into furious shaking fists, but eyes dry.

Now she stretched her arms up over her head, hands tightening into fists, betraying her tension. After a moment she gave him an odd look. "I went to see him today," she said.

Despite Innel's exhaustion, there was no question who she meant. He blinked hard, trying to clear his mind. Then, to buy a moment: "Who, my queen?"

"My father."

She crossed a foot over her other leg, pulled off her thick slippers and began touching her toes on their tips, one by one, bending them back and forth, as if testing each one to make sure it still worked properly. Innel was one of the few who had ever seen this odd habit. She only did this in private when she was sorting out details.

He must make sure he didn't end up as one of her details.

"That was good of you, to go see him."

"He likes you, Innel. As much as he likes anyone. Did you know that?"

"I admit it strains my credulity."

"You want to keep Arunkel whole, our borders strong. So alike, you two, he says." Her smile lacked warmth.

"Similar goals do not make similar men."

"I am glad to hear you say so."

There was something coming. Innel could feel it, like the pressure before a storm. He inhaled and braced himself, again willing himself to focus.

"He also says you are poisoning him."

There it was.

Someone had let something slip. The doctor? He thought of the doctor's grandson, now two years old, walking and talking at House Eschelatine, and what might happen to the boy if Innel discovered that the doctor had betrayed him.

Or could it be the slave? No, she could not possibly know, not unless someone told her.

Perhaps, after all this time, Restarn had simply guessed. Foolish of him to voice such suspicion, but he had now been sick two years. Perhaps his judgment was fraying.

And perhaps the king had outlived his usefulness.

"Does he," Innel said.

He met Cern's gaze. He would not offer more. She would have to ask.

After a moment, she went back to her toes. "He wanted to talk, as if all we were was father and daughter." Her tone was flat. "I went to leave and he—" She looked up from her toes, looking beyond Innel. "He begged me to stay. Begged me, Innel. He seemed on the edge of tears." Now she focused on Innel again. "He said you were going to kill him. That I was the only one who could save him. That if I left, I would not see him alive again."

Innel could well imagine Restarn enacting that particular drama. He knew how to control his daughter. "And then?"

She took a deep breath. "Then I left."

Or maybe he didn't.

"He isn't at all well," Innel said slowly. "Not thinking clearly. He could say anything. Might even believe it to be true."

"Yes," she said. "A very sick old man."

And still she had not asked.

Innel had worked his entire life to win Cern's trust. With her the coin of honesty was the hardest currency he held. Even so, now that she was a hair's breadth away

from asking, he wasn't sure how he would answer. Some
things were better left unsaid.

Standing, she put her feet back into her slippers. "Get
some rest, Innel." She walked to the door, paused. "If you
were not so tired, I would ask you to entertain me
tonight."

"So very kind of you, Your Majesty," he said quite
sincerely. "Would tomorrow morning please you?"

"Yes. Come see me then."

As the guard outside closed the door behind her, Innel
realized that she was not going to ask him. She did not
want to know.

He let himself fall back on the bed. Exhaustion came
over him like a fog.

Chapter Twenty-six

"Ama, there is no need for this."

Between market day and the loud masked comedy show in the courtyard of the inn, only one room remained available. An expensive one. It was huge, with a large bed in one corner.

Really, thought Amarta, there was no sensible reason not to share it with him.

He stood at the other end of the room, watching. Waiting.

"And what about later, on the way north?" Amarta asked Maris.

He had taken off the headwrap, brushing fingers through his dark hair and unbraided beard. "She makes a good point," he said to Maris. "I can hardly protect her all the way to Yarpin from a separate room."

But this was not merely a practical matter; Amarta had worked so hard to bring the dog inside where she could see him. She didn't want him back on the street where he might vanish into the shadows again, watching her. Hunting her.

Maris looked at each of them and shrugged. "As you say." At the bed, Maris pulled out the cot tucked underneath, moving it to the other end of the room where he stood. Then she took a chair at the table, unlacing her boots, pausing as she realized Amarta had not yet moved. "If we are to share a room, then you must also rest. He will not trouble you tonight, that's certain."

Amarta watched him as he walked the room, working the locking mechanism of the door, checking behind the pictures on the walls, dropping down to examine the carved base of the circular table that sat near the bed. At the window he opened and closed the slats, looking outside where swells of laughter and applause came from the watching crowds in the courtyard and on the walkway outside the room.

Finally he sat in the chair on the other side of the table from Maris.

Amarta sat as well, dragging her gaze from him, taking off her own boots, the ones Maris had bought for her. Elkhide, heavy, and so comfortable, with horn buttons to wrap at the sides. Without question the most marvelous and expensive things she had ever owned.

One more debt she could not pay.

He spoke to Maris in Perripin and she answered shortly, clearly still annoyed. But he kept on talking, his face animated, and after a while Maris laughed, a sound that shocked Amarta. She watched as they talked, gesturing, switching between Arunkin and Perripin and back.

"The ship was sold," Tayre was saying, having dropped the other accent entirely. Or maybe he had simply adopted a new one.

"A terrible shame," Maris said.

"An excellent price," he replied. "Most of it to the owner, some to me."

"And then?"

They spoke like old friends, Maris and her hunter. The way Maris acted, as if he were an ordinary person, made Amarta feel very strange indeed.

"Spice tariffs are a symptom," Maris was now saying.

"Then why does it cost more to transport spice legally through a few Perripin states than from Kelerre to Yarpin? That's the Perripin confederacy in action, I'd say."

"The states are lazy, is why. Distracted by their own political dances," she said, then switched to Perripin again.

Amarta's eyes wanted to close. Surely if Maris said she was safe tonight, she was.

"Have you heard," he was saying, "Kelerre's council levied a tax on goods in and out of Yarpin?"

Maris made a surprised sound. "That's a change that ought to get the capital's attention and inspire a healthy black market. Just your specialty, Enlon. Pah," she exhaled in frustration. "I keep calling you that. How many names do you have?"

"A sufficiency."

Maris snorted. "I don't like it."

Unless—the thought came to Amarta—he had no intention of returning her to the capital at all, but meant to kill her the moment Maris left. Her eyes snapped open again.

The look he was giving Maris now was full of mocking concern. "Forgive me my unintentional deception, High One."

"Watch your tongue," she said, but she was smiling as she said it.

"What does that mean," Amarta asked. "'High One'?"

Maris raised her eyebrows at Tayre, inviting him to answer. As he turned his look on Amarta, she felt a chill.

"It is the formal address for mages," he said. "No one else uses it, not even the most arrogant of monarchs, not even the Anandynars, for fear of offending mages who might overhear. The large ears of mages."

Maris snorted. "Yet you make it sound an insult." To Amarta, amused: "He enjoys taking such risks."

"As he enjoys killing," Amarta said. In the silence that followed, she wished she'd stayed silent.

"Is that what you think? I kill for amusement?"

She gave a shrug, not knowing how to respond. He stood and slowly walked toward her, stopping a few feet away from where she sat on the bed, crouching down to bring his head level with hers.

"I take contracts," he said. "If the work I have agreed to requires killing, I kill."

Anger flared inside her. "You take the lives of strangers for money."

"Would you prefer I kill only those I know?"

"You should leave the innocent alone."

"Ah, now you want me to decide who is innocent and who is not?"

"You twist my words. You hunt those who have done nothing to hurt you, merely for coin."

"No one suffers from your visions, Seer? You never take coin to tell people what tomorrow will bring them? All those who pay you are innocent?"

She shook her head. "I did not choose to be what I am."

"What makes you think I did? We both use our abilities for our benefit, even when there is a cost to others."

"No. I am nothing like you. I would never do to anyone what you've done to me these many years."

"Never? Truly?"

"You're a killer. A dog. A monster." Years of fear and anger drove her to spit insults, but the satisfaction faded quickly.

He spoke softly. "I watched a girl wearing your cloak die near what I suspect is the hidden city of Kusan." He paused. "Ah, you are not surprised to hear this. So I ask you: Did that moment have your touch upon it?" He watched her a moment, then nodded. "We are not so different, you and I." He shrugged a little. Suddenly, smoothly, there was a knife in his hand.

Amarta jerked backwards on the bed.

"Enlon," Maris said in warning.

The knife rotated in his hand like flowing water, black hilt pointing toward Amarta. He lay it on the floor by her boots and stood. "Now that we walk the same path, to the same destination, you have nothing to fear from me. You should have a knife. This is a good one. Take it. A gift."

He withdrew to sit again in the chair across from Maris. They resumed their conversation.

Amarta reached to take the knife, turning it over in her hands, examining the sharp blade, the black hilt carved with designs of waves. This knife, she was somehow sure, was the very knife with which he had threatened her in the Nesmar forest.

She looked at him again, and he looked back, offering

a small, friendly smile that from anyone else would have set her at ease.

Touching the flat of the knife blade, she failed to foresee her own blood, but she no longer found that particularly reassuring.

At last she drifted off to sleep, the two of them still talking. When she woke hours later, her back to Maris, moonlight through the slats showed her his sleeping form on the cot at the other end of the room.

He slept. Like an ordinary man.

She did not. In the morning they packed and went to buy horses.

"I will see you a ways north, I think," Maris said, looking between the two of them.

Amarta recognized Tayre's horse as the same one that had run along the rock banks of the Sennant River while they escaped on a raft. He was big and beautiful and dark chestnut colored, with white forelock and feet. He nuzzled her hand.

"Not your fault, to have such a monster ride you," she whispered, petting his nose.

Maris helped her up on the spotted mare chosen for her, larger than the Teva's shaota Amarta had once ridden before. As Amarta sat there, clutching the tawny mane in terror, she wondered how it could seem so much farther to the ground from atop the animal than it had from the ground.

They left the city, taking a smaller road north past farms and orchards. He rode in front, which suited Amarta. Better to watch him than have him watch her.

After a time, Maris came even with him, and they began to talk again in that confusing mix of languages they had, telling each other stories, told so compellingly that they caught her imagination right until they continued in some other language.

At her frustrated sound, they both looked back at her.

"I can't understand that. Would you go on, but in Arunkin?"

They did.

Light showers came and went, cooling the heat of the day, wetting the dusty roads into mud. When the sky darkened toward night, they stopped at an inn where Maris arranged for them two adjoining rooms. "One night for you to sleep without fear of him," she explained softly to Amarta.

When trays of stew and bread came, Tayre took his into the other room. Amarta watched him go, feeling slightly less reassured than she might.

"He is no danger to you, not with me here."

"And after you're gone?"

Maris dipped bread in her stew, took a bite. "You're looking in the wrong place for your problems. You should be considering the Lord Commander and what he will want from you."

"You don't know what Tayre is capable of."

That earned her a sharp look. "You don't know what I'm capable of, either. But know this: his word is reliable. If he says you are safe with him, you are."

Amarta did not believe that. They ate in silence. When they were done, Maris said, "We have another long day's ride tomorrow. Do you think you can rest now?"

"Yes."

But while Maris breathed deeply in sleep, Amarta watched the door, remembering the ways and times she had fled this man, how close he had come each time. How close he was now.

This was absurd. She of all people should be able to know what he might and would do.

But his future was strange; it seemed to shift each time she looked. A fog of possibilities.

Vision warned of no particular threat from him, at least not tonight. Somehow that was not enough.

She must have fallen asleep, because she started awake from a nightmare in which he chased her across mountain paths, barely missing with each grab. In dream she scrambled up and down drifts of snow, climbing and falling, sounds of pursuit close behind. When the knife he had just given her in the waking world was in dream again at her throat, she had woken, gasping.

A bit of moonlight came through the shutters, a shining line across the wooden floor.

"Ama?" Maris asked. "What is it?"

"He is in my dreams."

"Are my assurances so worthless? He will not touch you."

"He has tried to kill me so many times."

"More in your dreams than in truth, I think. Will you take some herbs to help you sleep?"

"No."

"You must sleep."

"No."

Maris sighed, pulled back the covers, rose and lit a lamp. "Go talk to him."

"What? Now?"

"We have days of riding ahead, and it will only get more difficult as we pass into Arun and onto the Great Road. I don't want to have to tie you to your horse to keep you from falling off in exhaustion. I'm here, Ama. Even with the door closed, you could not be safer."

"You can protect me from him, even through the door?"

"I can."

Amarta wondered how that worked. But then, people probably wondered how her ability worked, too.

So she stood, pulled shirt and trousers over her underclothes, and walked to his door and stopped. What was she going to say? Feeling foolish as she stood there, knowing Maris's eyes were on her, she pushed the door open, stepping into the dark of his room, and shut the door behind.

She heard nothing. Surely he would have heard her come in?

"Hello?" she whispered.

"I'm here," he said, from closer than she expected.

She pressed back against the door, hearing him move in the darkness, his feet brushing the floor. Surely he could move more quietly than that; why would he want her to know where he was?

A flame sparked to light, the lamp in his hand, showing him standing there, dressed, eyes on her. He put the lamp on a table, still watching her. "What is it?" he asked.

There was no safety anywhere. Not in questions, not in answers.

"I have nightmares about you."

"I know."

"You know? How can you know that?"

"I see it in your eyes. I hear it in your tone. The way you hold yourself. I have been feared before, Amarta. I know what it looks like."

"I want you to stop chasing me. My visions tell me you won't hurt me tonight. That to travel with you is probably safe. But—" Her voice caught. She took a step forward, as if daring herself. "But I don't believe it. And my dreams don't believe it."

"What can I do to reassure you?"

She took another step toward him. Close enough to touch. She raised a hand, then stopped, not sure what she intended.

"Go ahead," he said.

Holding her breath, she touched his arm. Through the shirt she felt muscle, warmth. She pulled her hand back. Was he really made of the same stuff she was? Not a shadow at all? "Are you truly done hunting me?"

"You say you want to deliver yourself to the Lord Commander. As long as this is so, I have no cause to pursue you."

She bit her lip, quick, hard. "What could I give you to make you stop coming after me and my family, forever? To give me your word you won't ever hunt me again?"

"I only take one contract at a time. Nothing you can offer me will change that. While your intention and my contract are aligned, you and your family have nothing to fear from me."

"But after that? You could come after me again."

"I could, I suppose. I hope not to."

"Why not? Because the dog can never catch this rabbit?" Her taunt felt childish. Maris, she reminded herself, would not always be so near by.

He chuckled. "In time, Seer, I would find a way."

"Then why not?"

"As long you're running, you're weak. I'd rather see you strong."

She shook her head, angry at this pretense. "You're a liar. I don't believe anything you say."

"Sensible, especially with me. But don't listen only to your fears, Amarta. Listen to your reason. Why would I lie about that?"

"I don't know. I'm sure you have reasons. Why would you want me strong?"

"If you don't believe anything I say, why should I answer you?"

"Tell me," she said. "I want to hear it."

He put one foot in front of the other and, with a startling, simple grace, let himself down to the floor, arriving cross-legged, looking up at her.

What was this? Was he trying to reassure her somehow by making himself seem smaller? That was absurd; she knew better. To show him so, she sat down on the floor in front of him, though not as smoothly.

"I'm curious," he said. "About what you'll do when you're not running away."

"I don't believe you."

He held out both hands, palms up, toward her. A clear invitation. She shook her head. Refusing what, she wasn't sure.

He waited, hands held out, unmoving.

"What do you want?" she asked at last.

"Take my hands."

"Why?"

"Please."

His voice, so often light and even, now held some entreaty. But that, too, meant nothing—he lied as easily as he took in air. He could pretend anything.

Still he held out his hands. Would he wait all night?

Maris, she reminded herself. Near by. With a deep breath, she put her hands on his. As her fingers touched his palms, she felt a brief flash. An echo of the past, a whisper of the future.

"Are these the hands that terrify you, Amarta, that give you bad dreams?"

She nodded.

"Feel them. Are they warm? Are they alive?" He gently pressed her hands with his fingers and thumb.

Again she nodded.

"Where are these hands?"

She frowned in confusion and looked at his fingers curled up around the sides of hers.

"Here," he answered for her. "Not in your dreams. Here. On the ends of my arms."

She giggled and tried to stifle it, which only made it worse. He smiled in response. She felt a subtle shift inside herself, as if he were, for the first time, truly on her side. He didn't seem the killer who chased her down forest paths, or the shadow that stalked her through the mountains.

She quickly pulled her hands back. "This is another game. You toy with me."

"Go back to your bed and sleep, Amarta. Dream of something else. And in the morning," he added, standing, again fluid in his motion, his hand downward in an offer to help her stand, "you'll still be safe from this hunter."

"You could be lying."

"Of course. But since you can't be sure, is it not sensible, at least for this journey, to assume I mean what I say?"

For this she had no answer. After a moment she took his hand, let him help her stand.

They rode across the border, into Arunkel, and then north through Gotar Province. At the Munasee Cut, they paused before the floating bridge, and Maris looked a question at Amarta. She looked into the near future, the one that included them crossing the bridge safely, and nodded. They walked the horses onto the wide wooden floating bridge and across without incident.

Munasee, a day's ride east. Where she and Dirina and Pas had last fled, from the man at her side. Who was no longer, however temporarily, her enemy. Such an odd change.

From there they rode north through Olapan Province. Mountains rose to the east, snow heavy and white on distant, jagged peaks.

Day after day Amarta steeled herself for Maris to leave, but she stayed. She would leave, she kept saying, just not yet.

Waiting until Amarta was at ease with him? That would not happen, she resolved.

But Tayre was friendlier each day. A little warmer.

Smiling at her. It was easy to forget the many things he had done. Too easy.

A knife at her eye. A blade at her throat.

He was right: she had no way of knowing if he meant what he said. Perhaps it was better, as he suggested, to trust that he did.

Or was he only saying that to distract her from sensible suspicion? Surely if they were aligned in purpose—at least until she was in the Lord Commander's hands—she could trust him. Unless, of course, he was only saying that to confuse her in some way. She shook her head, unable to follow the convoluted motives she could ascribe to him if she gave herself the chance.

She found herself trusting him in small ways, to let him load her pack, to carry her things, to bring her food.

When he told Maris where he'd been since they'd seen each other last, she could almost forget where she was and where she was going, the sound of their horses' hooves on the road lost in the howl of raging seas or storms, or the drums and pipes of distant lands that he made come alive with words. She felt a hunger to go to those places, to go somewhere out of choice, to see what was there. Not to run from—

This man. Who rode beside her.

Maris told tales of merchants and musicians and governors. "And, of course," Maris was saying now, "the problem with providing witness for that snarled contract was that then I had to enforce the damned thing. It's usually not worth the trouble and time."

"And yet, it pays."

"That it does."

Amarta shook her head in wonder. All her life lack of money had meant hunger and cold and rank, ragged clothes. For these two, it was like drawing water from a well that never went dry. When they wanted more, they worked and were paid more than they needed. It was a mystery to her, how some could have so much while the many had so very little.

Maris was in the lead when Amarta began to recognize the hut-shaped rises of rock and scrub plants and yellow grasses.

At Tayre's look over his shoulder she kept her face as blank as she knew how. His horse slowed to ride alongside her. Much as she wanted to look around at the deadlands that held Kusan secret, she kept her eyes fixedly on the road ahead.

At last he spoke. "The hidden city. A slave city," he said. "Am I right?"

If only she had made the three of them leave Kusan as soon as she had foreseen the threat, he might not now know this.

"I thought so," he said to her silence, as if she had answered.

Ksava and her baby. The elders. Darad.

As he watched her, she struggled to keep her breathing even. She had to blink to clear her eyes, lest the tears show.

"I only suspected," he said, "until now."

"Damn you," she said, exhaling a soft sob.

"I have no need to tell the Lord Commander or

anyone else. Provided you do not change your mind about where we are headed."

Could he be relied upon that far? She looked at him.

"My word is good, Seer."

"I don't trust you."

"You don't have to. Stay on the course you have begun, and I will keep my silence."

They had stopped. A distant, gray column of smoke rose into a pale winter sky.

"Chimash, I would say," Tayre said. "A rather large town. That much smoke would mean most of it is on fire or already ash."

So they left the Great Road for the High Traveler's Road, a detour that twisted its way up into the mountains, taking them up steep switchbacks through forests of evergreen and bare, twisted orange and gray limbs. As they rose in the mountains, the snow deepened, and the cold began to bite.

Tall pines painted dim, cool bands of shadow across the snow-covered road, fading then coming bright as high clouds moved across the sky. Wet, cold sprinkles fell, becoming white points of snow as they rode under the intermittent light of a fading, weak winter sun.

Maris and Tayre turned their talk to the inn where they planned to stay that night.

On either side of the road, snow-crusted banks rose. All at once Amarta felt the sharp pressure of immediate warning. She cried out wordlessly, yanking her horse's reins. Tayre snapped out his bow, notched an arrow, and turned in his saddle.

Stepping out from behind the high bank was a horse and rider, blocking their way. On both sides of the banks above them were a handful of riders and horses with bows pointed down at them. Behind them another group. Sharp whispered commands, shouted cautions. Where had they all come from?

Motion exploded everywhere, suddenly. Amarta lowered her head to hug her horse's neck, heard the twang of arrows, of shouts and screams. Looking sideways across the tawny mane she saw a man on the rise crumple, then another.

The pressure of warning vanished even while frantic movement continued. She looked around curiously, lifting her head. The man on the horse who had blocked their way slumped over in his saddle, then slipped down onto the snow-patched dirt below.

Then Tayre was facing her, bow up. Before she could move, he let fly an arrow. She yelped and again contracted tight against her horse's neck. Behind her someone howled in pain.

Suddenly there was silence.

Mere heartbeats had passed. Only now did it occur to Amarta to pull the black-handled knife that Tayre had helped her strap to her boot. Her hand was shaking as she reached to draw it. She sat up, feeling foolish, the blade useless in her hand.

Maris spoke. "Ama, are you all right?"

"Yes," she croaked, trying to keep her hand steady enough to put the knife back into its holster instead of into her leg.

"You foresaw this," Maris said.

"Only at the last moment."

"Sufficient for our needs." Maris said. "Don't underestimate the value of an eyeblink's warning."

Why had the sense of threat vanished so suddenly, even before the motion was done?

Because of Maris and Tayre, she realized: the attackers might have put an arrow through her during that first moment, but with Maris and Tayre there, that first instant had been the only one in which she was likely to be harmed. Past that instant the danger was gone, so the warnings had ceased, even though the action had not.

Maris turned her horse around and surveyed the bodies on the ground. "Who are these idiots, Enlon?"

"You two did nothing to disguise yourselves in Kelerre. Word spreads, and Innel isn't the only one who wants her. Mountain tribe, by the look of them."

"Are they dead?" Amarta asked timidly.

"Asleep," Maris said. "They'll wake in a few hours."

"And come after us again," Tayre said.

"Four are dead from your bow, Enlon. If the rest don't take that as a clear message, next time I'll see to it that none of them wake."

"It would be better to leave them unable to say anything about us."

"I see no reason to take more life here."

"We have a ways to go yet," he said. "Let's not make this trip more difficult than it already is. Shall I take care of it?"

Maris was silent a long moment. "No. It is done. These will tell no tales of our passing here."

Amarta looked at Maris, realizing what these words

meant. That it was easy for Tayre to kill, that she knew, but Maris as well?

She looked at each body as they passed, wondering who they were, if they had families and people at home who would miss them—surely they must—and what they had hoped to gain here by her death. Or her life.

As they rode in silence through the tall corridor of trees that darkened with nightfall, Amarta's thoughts returned again and again to the men lying on the ground. Death seemed to come so easily. Like a sharp gust of wind taking a candle flame. How many more would die because of her?

Slush squirted out from every step of her horse's hooves, splattering Tayre's horse's back legs ahead of her. Above, beyond the trees, blue sky mingled with white, hinting that somewhere there might be sunlight. How long had it been since she had looked up and seen anything but white?

From a distant hush the sound of river steadily grew into a roar. When the hillside dropped away on one side, Amarta saw the wide, broad Sennant through the trees.

"Wait," she said, pulling to a stop. "I know this land."

"What do you mean, Ama?" Maris asked from behind her.

Tayre looked back at them.

"Enana," Amarta replied, looking at him. "Her family. What did you do to them?"

"Would you believe any reply I gave you?"

"Answer me anyway," Amarta said.

He turned his horse around on the path to face her.

"I told her that I had wronged you, that I sought now to make amends, to bring you an inheritance. She believed me. I left them unharmed."

"Is it true?" she asked Maris.

"How would I know? His body has always been a cipher to my reading. I believe him, if that is sufficient."

She stared at him, trying to see truth or lie with her own eyes, even knowing she could not. "I want to see them."

"Where are they?" Maris asked.

"East of the Sennant," Tayre said. "Near a village called Nesmar. I can lead you there if you wish."

That was part answer, then; if he knew where the farm was, he had been there.

"Yes," she said.

They continued on. The High Traveler's Road met and followed the Sennant River for a time, veered off, snaked back.

Images of Enana and her family flickered through Amarta's mind. The tall woman lighting the lamp at night, her wide smile, the games they would play after eating their fill of a stew that was never the same twice but was always astonishingly good.

Then: the feel of hard ground under her, a knife at her throat.

She inhaled the brisk air, put a hand on the warm neck of her horse, and brought herself back to this moment. He glanced at her.

"Why should I believe you at all?" she demanded angrily.

"You shouldn't."

"Then why answer me?"

"Because you asked."

Curse him for giving her reason to hope and to doubt at the very same time. Why did he do that?

She began to recognize landmarks. There, by the bend in the road, was where he had first surprised her that warm summer day in the forest, where vision had crashed over her, impossible to ignore. There she had lain on her back under the high green canopy, then rolled him off of her long enough to rise and run.

A twisted tree, there, grown but recognizable, one that she had spun around in her dash to escape.

And there, where she had dropped to the ground, ankle in searing pain, staring up at him, his arrow aimed at her heart.

That man there, who rode before her. She could have killed him that day.

No, she could not have. It had not been in her to do so.

Would it be now?

He led them off the main road where he had once chased her, a side road, up onto a hill. There they stopped in a wide ring of alders, small buds dusty mauve and green with early spring, and dismounted.

Through the trees and down the hillside, through pine and bare branch, she could see bits of Enana's farmland and house.

"Is that it?" Maris asked.

Amarta nodded.

"Know this, Seer," he said, "before you go to them:

you risk them, doing so."

"What do you mean?"

"It is likely we are being tracked. Any who follow us will ask them questions. Less skillfully than I did."

"Or maybe you don't want me to see what you did to them."

"They are your friends; risk them if you wish."

"Why should you care?"

"I care about getting you safely to the capital, and I prefer not to leave behind a trail of signposts. If your friends have not seen you, they can't tell anyone you were here."

"I want to know if they are well."

"And you won't believe whatever I tell you, so—" He stopped, made a thoughtful sound. "Perhaps you can find your answer without risking them."

"What do you mean?"

"Decide to see them. Then look into the future and see what would occur when you go to the house. If they are well, change your mind and decide not to go. If you can do such a thing."

"Maris?" she asked.

"He's likely correct," the mage said, "that we are being tracked and your friends would be endangered if you went closer."

She felt a vast longing to see them, but that was not reason enough to put them at risk. Surely she had already cost enough people so much.

Leaning against a tree, she stared at the distant farmhouse and tried to ease her mind into placidity. She closed her eyes, pushed herself into the future.

She would, she resolved, go to the farmhouse. In a few minutes. She would do this.

And then . . . ?

A walk down the hill, leaving the others behind. A scrape of the back of her hand on a thorned brush she had not seen, wrapped around a trunk. She would wipe the bit of blood on her trousers. A knock on the door. There was Cafir, Enana's youngest, now with a full beard, filled out solid across the shoulders. It would take him a very long moment to recognize her, and she would be smiling so wide, and then he would call out excitedly to his mother. Enana would run, and she, too, would smile, and Amarta's heart would swell with joy as she swept her into a hug, and—

She pushed further, days hence.

Would someone else come, asking questions?

A boot on the ground, one she did not recognize. A hand on a tree trunk, examining a broken thorn. A heavy knock on a door. The look on Enana's face as she opened it to see the men who stood there.

Amarta opened her eyes, blinking away vision, struggling to come back to this moment. The one in which she would not go to the farmhouse.

Tayre had been telling the truth. And that meant what?

It meant nothing.

"Amarta?" Maris asked softly.

Taking the reins of her mare, she put a foot into the stirrup, pulled herself up into the saddle. "I don't need to see them," she said.

✢ ✢ ✢

More days of travel took them back to the Great Road, having circumvented Chimash and the trouble there. More nights in inns, more days of riding.

In the evenings, Maris often left them for a time to go walking by herself. Tonight Tayre was performing his usual movements, his stretches and twists, turns and jumps, drops and rolls. He would start slow then speed up, the fast, flexible motions sometimes hard to follow. A lethal dance with an invisible attacker.

It was stunning to her, what he could do with his body. Until she had seen him do all this it had not even occurred to her that he would need to practice. Nightmare creatures did not need to practice to be what they were.

When he finished tonight, his face damp with sweat, he sat and drank water, turning his chair slightly to face the door.

Guarding her.

"You have been south of Kelerre? To Dulu? To Timurung?" she asked.

"I have."

"What are people like in other places?"

"Strip away language and dress and they are much the same. They eat, sleep, make babies, and die. Some talk, some dance, some do fancy tricks with rows of beetles, some sit burning thin scented sticks, waiting for the day when their luck will change."

"I would like to see all that."

"Perhaps you will."

At this her smile vanished.

"Look what I found," Maris said cheerfully when she

returned. She set a carafe of wine and some small ceramic cups on the table and poured, handing the cups around.

"Do we celebrate tonight, Maris?" Tayre asked.

Maris downed her cup and poured another. "I have come rather farther north than I intended to, my friends. But now that I am satisfied that you"—she gestured at Tayre with her cup—"will see Amarta safely to that wretch Innel, it may be time for me to go. I thought we could all use a little help brightening the prospect. That is, unless you've changed your mind, Amarta, and will return home with me?"

Amarta felt her stomach go leaden. She had come to like this, she realized, being in company with Maris. And, yes, even Tayre. It had become easy to forget what this was about, where she was going. And why.

For a moment she let herself imagine returning to warm lands. To Dirina and Pas.

"No," she said softly. They would not be safe with her there. She took a sip. "Oh," she said, her mind suddenly and entirely on the rich, smoky wine. "How marvelous."

"It had better be, for what I paid for it."

"So like a Perripin to pay too much for wine," Tayre said.

"Certainly not," Maris said. "Just enough."

It warmed her throat and stomach, easing the ache of sorrow she felt deep inside. She held out her hand for more. Maris refilled.

"Aren't you having any?" she asked Tayre.

A shake of the head. "It would slow me."

"You don't have to be fast, at least not tonight."

"It'll slow me tomorrow some as well, and who knows what I'll have to be tomorrow?" He smiled.

Maris chuckled at this, and for some reason it struck Amarta as funny, too. "He's fast," she said. "Have you seen him move? So fast. Like that time with the dart."

"Not fast enough, though, was I?"

"That wasn't you. That was me. I saw it coming. So I"—He had come so close that day. So close. Now she was willingly going to the man who had sent him. She had reasons, she reminded herself. Good ones. "What will happen to me at the palace?" she asked.

Maris snorted softly. "Why ask us? Don't you see the future?"

"I don't, always. It's"—she exhaled frustration, trying to clear the haze of her thinking enough to explain—"too much. So many images I can't make sense of them. Or understand how one thing that only might happen could lead to another that only might happen, if that and tens of other things happen in just the right way."

The future was always shifting. Trying to hold it was like trying to hold a live fish with greased hands.

"But sometimes you know," he said.

She looked back. "Sometimes most paths lead to the same place."

"What do you see now?"

She took another sip and another and put the cup on the table. The truth was that her dreams had been full of horrors. She picked one.

"We ride through a smoking town. On the ground someone's been cut open from neck to groin, skin pulled back, still alive. Making a horrible sound. Then we pass a barn with smoke coming out of the windows. Soldiers in red and black stab anyone who tries to get out the door or windows, throwing them back inside. At the edge of town are heads on the point of the gate. So much screaming."

She inhaled raggedly, looking down at the red liquid in her cup.

"A hard future you see, Ama," Maris said softly.

Swallowing the rest of what was in her cup, she held it out for more.

"The wine does not interfere with your foresight?" he asked, pouring.

"Not enough." She shook her head, which made her feel a little dizzy, but was also sort of pleasant, so she did it again.

"Empty," Maris said dourly. "I'll be back." She took the carafe and left.

Amarta stared at him. He looked back. Her and the hunter. Together. Again.

"You're not so frightening anymore," she said, feeling oddly accustomed to this shadow man. Comfortable, even.

"A pleasant change, I would think."

"Yes," she said adamantly. "I know what you are, but now, just now anyway, you seem almost like . . . I don't know. Not a nightmare creature. A person."

"I am glad to hear it," he said.

"Or am I saying that because of the wine?"

He was watching her, but his only answer was an easy shrug, as if to say that it didn't matter. He was right; it didn't. Not anymore. Her path was set.

It would be nice to lie down and forget all that for a

while. But the bed was all the way across the room. It seemed very far.

Surely not so far. She stood and was suddenly dizzy. Grabbing for the edge of the table to steady herself, she missed, knocking her cup into his full and untouched one. As one cup began to topple into the other, both heading for the edge of the table, he reached out both hands and took one in each, setting them back aright.

Not a drop had spilled.

"Oh," she said. "That was clumsy of me. I—"

She stared at the cups he had set upright, imagined the red wine splashed across table and floor. He had caught them barely in time. She could never have done such a thing, not feeling as she did.

Or, really, ever. She was simply not that fast. Not that alert.

"Oh," she said again, more slowly.

Why he hadn't had any wine. What he really was.

The chill cut through the warmth of the wine, the warmth of the room, the comfort she had been feeling a moment ago. She remembered a frozen day on the banks of the Sennant on a raft. A hot afternoon in a thick, green canopy of forest.

He was no friend. He was not an ordinary person. She had let herself forget.

Slowly and with great care she walked over to the bed and sat. He was no longer watching her, but she was sure he knew exactly where she was and exactly what she was doing.

When Maris came back, Amarta did not drink any more wine.

✦ ✦ ✦

"I leave tonight," Maris said as she stepped into the inn room, setting her pack by the door. With a long look to Amarta, she said, "It is time."

Amarta sat heavily on the bed, watching as Maris took Tayre by the shoulder and spoke softly and earnestly to him in Perripin.

The capital was less than a day away. Tomorrow Tayre would bring her to the man she had truly been fleeing all these years.

She hugged her legs, put her head down on her knees. And then?

She saw things, certainly: high ceilings, endless questions, a room that locked from the outside. Flashes of color: red and white walls, the pink of slices of meat. The green of a shirt, the feel of fine linen.

Beyond that little was clear; there were too many crossroads and too many people who must yet decide to walk them.

This room in which she would sleep tonight—the last night she would be free, she realized—was as lavish as anything she had ever seen. Windows of clear glass showed a colorful, busy street below. A stone fireplace kept the room warm. Tapestries lined the walls with images of flowers and swords. The furniture was carved in similar patterns, the table decorated in red and black woods.

It was astonishing. Yet she would have traded it all for a packed dirt floor, a hungry belly, and windows and doors that leaked cold air, if it put Dirina and Pas by her side.

Until the moment Maris left—fast approaching—she could still change her mind.

Maris walked to her and drew her to her feet, taking her by the shoulders, looking into her eyes. "I ask you one last time, Amarta dua Seer: Are you set on this course? Innel will not treat you gently. You can still return with me to Perripur."

It was so very, very tempting. She thought of Dirina and Pas.

No, nothing had changed. War was coming, a war so wretched and sweeping that it would threaten even her family, far away as they were. And even if she could do nothing to change it, they were safe only as long as she was not with them.

She looked at Tayre and wondered, without any real intention of finding out, what he would do if she left with Maris right now.

Follow, no doubt.

It didn't matter; she knew her course.

"I must do this."

"So be it." Maris closed her eyes a moment then touched Amarta's forehead with two fingers. Amarta felt something, then: a calming, a soothing. "Courage to you, Amarta, to go where your path takes you."

Amarta nodded, blinking back tears.

Maris nodded at Tayre. "He has given me his word he'll see you safely to the palace. It's as much as I can ask of him, and as much as I could do for you myself."

Amarta wondered what Tayre's word was worth to someone who did not hold his contract, but saw no reason to ask.

Then, wrapping her in one last embrace, Maris spoke softly in her ear. "Innel is formidable and clever. But you, also, can be these things, Amarta."

She nodded slowly, soberly. "Will you take care of them for me?" Dirina. Pas.

"I will." Then Maris picked up her bags, spoke sharply to Tayre in Perripin one last time, and left.

Amarta exhaled slowly, softly, as she listened to the footsteps fade in the hall outside, letting fade the final imaginings of opening the door and calling after Maris that she had changed her mind and would go with her.

When it was silent at last, she turned to look at him. She should be afraid, perhaps. Or even just wary. But he'd done his work so very well. She cursed herself for letting his pretense fool her so completely that even though she knew what it was, what he was, she still felt at ease now with him.

He smiled a little.

"What did she say before she left?" Amarta asked.

"That my word was binding. She made a threat on my life, should I fail to deliver you whole."

"To the Lord Commander, who may well kill me the moment I arrive?"

"You are of more use to him alive."

"But you would say that, would you not, to keep me on course?"

He nodded to accept the point. "Nonetheless, it is so."

"I can trust you one more day, then."

"Yes."

Once in the Lord Commander's hands, she would no longer have any choices. But now, at least for tonight, she still did.

She wondered about the future. Not the far future, not even tomorrow, but now, these next few minutes. Wondered about it, but didn't attempt to foresee. For this moment she needed her senses more than her vision. And courage.

Tayre watched her approach. Relaxed. Ready. Always ready.

Heart pounding, she stepped close to him. Close enough to smell him, to hear him breathe. Deliberately, slowly, she put her hand flat on his chest, looked up into his eyes, tried to smile, faltered.

He blinked. Other than that, he might have been made from stone.

"What is this, Amarta?"

"I ask that you be my first time."

He covered her hand on his chest with his own.

"*Do* you?"

"Yes."

"Your first time could mean a baby if you lack sufficient understanding."

She felt her face go hot, pulled away. "I know that."

"You didn't," he said, his voice betraying surprise.

Now she understood Dirina's moon counts, why her sister would arrange pebbles in a row so carefully when she went with the village men. It was so obvious. How could she not have known?

"No one told you? Not your mother?"

"I was five when my mother died." Who she had let die. She pushed the thought away.

"Dirina?"

Amarta shook her head. "She thought if I didn't know, I wouldn't make her mistake."

"Many children are born to that particular misunderstanding."

"Then teach me."

"You should be taught by an anknapa. An older woman. Not me."

"Don't give me that," she said, tension making her testy. "You know all this and more. You must."

His brief smile faded to unreadability. "What has changed so that you would invite this hunting dog so very, very close, Amarta?"

Her face was still warm. "Tomorrow I give myself up to the Lord Commander, which I may not survive."

"That is not reason enough to choose me."

"I say it is." Her voice sounded uncertain in her own ears. "I say it is," she repeated more firmly.

For a long moment he watched her. She waited uneasily. He might say no. He couldn't say no. She didn't want him to say no.

"I could die tomorrow, Tayre."

"This would change how you think of me, Seer."

"I don't care."

"You might well care in the future."

"So be it. I still ask. Please."

He was silent again for a long moment. It was all she could do to keep her gaze steady on his.

Brown eyes. Hunter's eyes. She swallowed, refusing to look away.

At last he nodded, stepped back, stripped off his shirt to bare skin.

"Men," he said, "are different, in ways both obvious and subtle." Standing on one foot he untied and removed a boot, making it look easy, then switched feet and took off the other. He pulled off his pants and the silk underneath and stood there without clothes, silently inviting her to look.

After a few moments he chuckled. "The woman who can look into the future has never before seen a naked man."

"I've seen Pas."

"Pas is a child."

He gestured to her to come closer, held his hands out, and turned slowly, inviting her touch. She put her fingers on his stomach, his chest, feeling the skin and hair as he turned, giving her time to explore. When she stood back and nodded, he took her hand and wrapped it around his penis.

"Most of the visible difference is here. Like with animals, yes? Notice how this feels? Firm, but the skin smooth?"

"Yes."

"Like a water skin," he said. "It gets tight with blood, then shrinks when it empties. Firm to soft, throughout the day and night. Most men can't control this, but some can. Sometimes it is a result of desire, but not always. You understand?"

She nodded again.

He guided her hand down to the looser part underneath. "These are like sacks, where the seed is kept, the seed that makes a woman pregnant. A man always has seed, so that doesn't matter as much. More important is when the woman is fertile. If you bleed with the moon, you are unlikely to be fertile now, but it is still a costly gamble. I want you to look into the future and be certain: Is there a possibility that you are pregnant in these next months?"

Amarta looked along the line that was her own body's future. A glimpse of darkness and agony and terror, but unrelated to this; she pushed it aside. Nowhere in the near future did a life grow inside her. "No."

She bent a little to get a better look at the seed sacks. She took one of them between her fingers and pressed to see if she could feel any of the seeds inside. He grabbed her wrist, tightly, precisely, and her fingers loosened of their own accord.

"Don't press like that unless you're trying to hurt me, in which case you'll need to know quite a bit more than you do. That's an entirely different lesson."

"Oh."

He moved her hand up to his mouth, where he brushed her fingertips with his lips.

Her heart begin to speed. She tried to remind herself to be wary, but it was only words in her head. If she was afraid of anything, it was that he might stop.

Something occurred to her. Feeling her tense, he stopped, waited.

"Do you like me?" she asked.

"Does that matter?"

"Dirina said a first time should be with someone who likes me." In the Nesmar forest, as Amarta limped along in pain, her sister had said this. As the three of them fled this very man. For a moment she felt dizzy.

"I think that quite sensible advice."

"And do you?"

He stared at her a moment. "Yes." Then he came close, bent down, and touched her lips with his own.

So much more gentle, this, and startlingly so, than Darad's quick, brusque kisses in Kusan. Like the difference between the weak wine she'd had before and the rich, smoky drink Maris had brought them.

He slowly moved his lips down her face and to the side of her neck. Somehow it relaxed her. Half relaxed and half something else.

Suddenly she began to shake all over, unable to stop. He drew her down onto the bed and sat beside her. As she sobbed soundlessly, he pulled a blanket over her. When she could again breathe easily, she rolled over to face him, grabbed his hand, pulled him down next to her.

"Continue," she said.

"Are you sure, Amarta?"

"Yes." Eyes closed, she brought her face close to his, finding his lips again.

So this was a first time. It filled her with a kind of longing, a deliciousness. A hunger. She opened her eyes, looking into his.

The feel of forest floor under her back. Smells of rotting leaves. A knife pressed to her throat. Oblivion a moment away.

Again she curled away from him, trembling. He put a hand on her shoulder. A comforting touch.

How could she be taking reassurance from this creature, this monster?

And yet she did.

"This was bound to be difficult, Amarta," he said. "There is no need to continue."

She turned back to face him. "Yes, there is. I ask you to teach me."

"A strange courage you have, Seer."

"Practice for tomorrow," she said with a half laugh, half sob, and pulled him close, their noses touching. This time she would keep her eyes open.

His slow and even breathing calmed her. Then he moved his lips on hers in a slow circle that made all other thought cease.

It was so unlike anything she had ever felt that images of the past and future finally quieted. He was, she realized, bringing her into the present, a place that she very much wanted to be.

When she awoke, a gray early morning cast a watery light through the panes. Outside, the wind gusted with the start of a spring storm. He lay on his side, watching her.

She reached out a hand to him. Something had changed between them, but something else had not. He reached back and wove his fingers through hers.

To look at him now was an intensity of fear and longing. He smiled a warm smile.

A smile on a face that didn't smile.

Pretense or no, it worked. Her spirits lifted.

"Why did you say yes?" she asked him.

"It is in my contract's best interest to have you compliant."

"What does that mean?"

"Your trust in me has grown, has it not? You want my touch. You care for me. You are less likely today to change your mind."

"That was why? Not because you like me?"

"Can it not be both?"

"But, then—why would you tell me this? Wouldn't that make me suspicious of you?"

"More than you already were?"

Were. In the past. But she could not deny it.

"Then—why tell me this at all?"

"Why indeed? Think on it. Are you in any pain?"

"Should I be?"

"I was careful. Still, tell me if you hurt."

Did she? Only in spirit, at the thought of leaving this room. "I want to stay here forever and—"

"And?"

"And have a second time."

He nodded, not agreeing or disagreeing. "We have time for that, if you wish, though not much. Best we arrive at the palace in daylight."

His words swept away the sweetness of the night, replacing it with the hard clarity of what she was about to do.

And what she had just done. She had shared a bed and sex with her hunter. Had wanted to, had asked to. Wanted to again.

He was right: she trusted him in a way she had not before. But there was something more, something he did not know yet. She shut her eyes a moment, recalling the reasons she was here, that had forced her on this path to seek out the very man who had sent the hunter after her.

She sat up. "How many people have you killed?" she asked.

"I don't keep a count," he answered, sitting up next to her.

"Really?"

A tilt of his head. "I used to. When I was a child."

A *child*? He had killed as a child?

But then, hadn't she as well?

"Twenty? Thirty?"

"More than that."

More than thirty lives ended, because that was his work. More by far, she would guess, from the tone of his answer.

"If . . ." She considered how best to say it. "If your contract said to kill me, right now, would you do so?"

"Yes."

"Even after last night?"

"Yes."

"Even if . . ." Her voice dropped. "Even if, I don't know, even if you liked me a very great deal? Even if we had made a baby together? Even then?"

"I only accept contracts I intend to fulfill. Yes, even then. Why?"

"How much did he give you, to find me?"

He shook his head. He wouldn't tell her.

"I only want to know how much such contracts cost."

"That depends on many things. The contract. The various terms. Who holds it. You, perhaps?" She started to answer, but nothing came out. "As I have said, I can't take another contract now. I still have this one to fulfill."

This one. To deliver her.

"But when this contract is done . . ." Done with her.

One way or another. "When this is over, you could then be free then to take another?"

"Tell me what is in your mind."

She glanced at the window. Clouds rushed past against a blue-gray sky. "I don't have the kind of money the Lord Commander does."

"Few do. Tell me, Ama."

"I need someone to . . ." She took a breath. "To help me understand what I am. To teach me to use vision in a way that does not cause more suffering."

"You think I can do this?"

She looked down at her hand, still in his. "You aren't like anyone whose future I've seen. Most struggle toward something or run from what terrifies them. As I've been running for so long." From him. She looked away, at the sharp sword in the tapestry on the wall. "I can see what might happen tomorrow, yes. But you . . ." She could feel him there, listening intently. "You see what happens today and now. I think that might be just as rare. I must learn to see better so I can avoid making futures I have no business making, and hurting people I want to protect. If I can't do that . . ." She looked at him. He met her gaze evenly. Watching, always watching, with his hunter's eyes. "Then I will need someone to help me stop. To help me die. I don't know who else I could ask that of, who I could trust."

He leaned toward her a little, the intensity of his look startling.

"Don't trust me, Amarta. I am not in your employ." Nor was he her friend. She knew this.

"But if you were—if I could somehow get the

money—I could trust you to do what I had hired you to do. Yes?"

"Yes. If."

"If I ever get free, I want to see things. Learn things. About myself. About the world. I need someone to guide me. Just—if." She lay down next to him. "Will you think on it?"

"Yes."

"Now, will you show me what a second time is like?"

He laughed a little and smiled. For a moment it seemed to her that she could believe this reaction. True or not, she smiled in response.

"Yes," he answered.

Chapter Twenty-seven

Triangles of bright sun cut dust-filled shafts from the ceiling and high walls of the long-house, casting bright shapes on the dirt underfoot. At a table sat an old man, his skin nearly as tanned as the deer hide he worked, his straight, white hair braided into three tails, a shock of black through the one that swept back from his face. "I think you are mistaken," he said.

On either side of him sat two white-haired women. They might have been mirror images of each other but for the pale blue jacket one wore where the other's was orange. One woman was slowly feeding two lines of thin dried stems through her fingers from a nearby basket, passing them across a heavy double spool that sat on the table in front of the man. From there the lines went to the other woman, who wound them together onto a spindle, feeding the resulting twine back to the man between them. With a large needle he pulled the twine through holes in a skin on his lap.

"Do you want to trade places, then, and you can do my work instead?" the woman in orange asked mildly.

An amused snort from the other woman. The elder man smiled.

From the end of the long-house a large door came slightly open. A small, striped horse, nose first, pushed its way inside, walking slowly along the length of the house toward the woman in orange. He stopped there, nosed at her shoulder. She halted her work, forcing the other two to stop as well, turning in her seat to face the shaota, a chuffing sound coming from her throat. She bore the animal's affectionate nuzzling and then the slightly wet snort that followed, patting the horse's side as it turned away, flicked its tail, and wandered back outside.

The woman in orange turned back to the table. The three resumed their work.

"Perhaps you are not wrong," the man said after a time.

At this the woman in blue laughed a little.

Another door opened, a smaller one nearer the table. In came a man and woman breathing hard. The woman brushed her dark hair back out of her eyes. The man clasped his hands together.

"Forgive our intrusion, Elders. We have urgent news."

"We listen, Mara and Jolon," said the man, not looking up from his work.

"Our unpleasant associates come riding on their large, clumsy horses. A ten count."

"Ah."

The three elders' hands stopped their motion. The old man put his work on the table.

"Were they followed into our lands?"

"They were not," said Jolon.

"What do you wish us to do, Elders?" asked Mara.

The three elders found each other's gazes, small expressions flickering across their faces.

After a moment the woman in the coat said, "What choice is there? None. Bid them welcome."

The Arunkin, who they knew better than they wanted to, stepped inside the long-house. Two of his kind followed, each standing on either side of the door as if they owned it.

He was tall, the Arunkin, feet set wide on the dirt floor as if to claim the land on which he stood, perhaps by virtue of his size. There was little in this Arunkin's wordless message that the elders had not seen before.

He adjusted the cuffs of his long riding coat, cuffs and lapels woven through with silver thread, extravagant to the point of impracticality. The rest of the outfit was brown. Not the deep, rich soil brown of one of their gaudy Houses, but the brown of trees in winter, the brown of their dull horses.

"Elders," he said, dipping his head.

The woman in blue spoke. "You make a path to us, like a painted arrow. Do you mean to show someone the way?"

"This problem is urgent and can't wait for a circuitous approach."

"We listen," said the old man.

"People are asking questions in Varo and Sio Provinces. About gold. Nuggets. Coins. All the ways you ship across your borders. Someone has started to talk."

The old man said, "In the years we have been about this, it had to happen that someone would ask such questions."

"Yes, but the problem now is that someone is answering the questions. One of yours, I suspect. Your townspeople. Or the strays you take in."

"No," said the old man. "It is not any of ours."

The tall Arunkin snorted. "You are so confident of their loyalty?"

The old man replied, "The Hanathans are our own. We protect and care for them. They would no more tell our secrets than would the shaota."

"And the deserters you keep taking in?"

"Why would they betray us when we give them sanctuary?" asked the woman in orange.

"You shock me with your naivete. Have you never met those who want more than they are given through largesse? You think these who deserted their sworn obligations are so full of honor?"

"Do you think them so full of ingratitude?" the old man asked.

The woman in orange put a hand over his on the table. To the Arunkin, she said: "We make you welcome in Otevan, and then we argue. Let us save time and say you are in the right. What do you want us to do?"

"My people will do what we can to quiet the rumors and obscure the arrow that leads to you. But you—you must send no more shipments. Delay your next caravan. No figurines, nuggets, coins or any of the other myriad of ways you have been transporting gold out of Otevan, not until things are quiet again."

"This we can do," the woman in orange replied. "What is ready to go now, though, you take."

"No. Too many are watching the roads from Otevan through Sio and Varo. When it is again safe, we will tell you, and you can resume your deliveries."

"Again," said the old man, "we take the risks while you take the benefit."

The woman in blue spoke up. "We relied on your promise to empty the mine."

"It is not our fault the vein turned out to be so unusually difficult to exhaust."

"This was to be finished years ago," the woman in orange said.

"Plans must change as circumstances change. You will pause your mining operations until we tell you otherwise."

A grunt from the old man. He looked to the woman on one side, and then to the other. Then to the Arunkin he said, "Do not mistake our hearing you for compliance. We ask you to take all that is above ground, and we forgo claim to our part. The mine we can bury, as we originally intended."

"No, you can't. There is no burying a thing that can be dug up again. Too many know. Your people. Ours. The only way forward is to empty it."

"And yet this seems as impossible now as it did when you first thrust this bargain upon us."

"Dig faster. Use more of your grateful Hanathans and those deserters you are so fond of."

"There is only room in a hole for so many before they are mining body parts instead of metal. Take what is ready to leave Otevan and go, or we will dispose of it ourselves."

"Dispose of it?" the man asked, confused.

"We have an even larger hole to the east of us."

"The Rift? You will not. Half of that is ours."

"All of it is yours if you take it now."

"I say again, that is not possible. You will wait until we tell you to resume shipments. Then you will do so."

"Arunkin, we have spilled a great deal of blood these last three centuries to insure we are beholden to no one."

"I wonder how the crown would react if they knew what you've been doing here these past six years."

"Yes. The threat. Again."

The Arunkin shrugged. "You've broken the queen's law. Not merely mining gold, but selling it, and forging coins."

"At your insistence."

"Harboring deserters. Now listen to me: be patient, be quiet, and we will soon be back to our previous and beneficial partnership."

"We hear your words," said the old man.

"Do more than hear them, Elders, unless you want to test the strength of the Anandynars' respect for your borders."

Silence fell on the room for a long moment.

"Don't make enemies of Arunkel, Teva."

The Arunkin waited a time for the Elders or Mara and Jolon to answer, but they were silent. Finally he nodded slowly and left, taking his men and brown horses with him.

"Bury the mine?" asked the woman in blue of the other two.

"He is right," said the old man. "If you can bury it with a shovel, you can uncover it with one."

"Do we change direction and veer away from these associates, despite their threats?" asked the woman in blue.

The woman in orange nodded her head. "Because of their threats. I say yes."

"Let us circle this question again," said the man, who then addressed Jolon and Mara. "You have traveled among the Arunkin. What do you advise?"

A humorless snort. "Do not trust them."

"That we see." His eyes searched those of Mara and Jolon. "If you stood where we stand, what would you do now?"

"Can we not simply wait," Mara asked, "As he advises? Are we so weak we cannot take advice from someone who insults us even when it may be the best path? Can we not let him quiet the arrows that point to us, and, at least for now, do nothing?"

Jolon said, "But how long do we ride in their shadow?"

"A time, perhaps," said the elder in blue.

"Is there wisdom in this?" the old man asked each of the women.

"I say we have had enough," answered the woman in orange. "It is time to come out from the shadow."

"I say we can wait a time longer," replied the one in blue. "Mara's words have sense in them."

The man tilted his head at them both.

"We will wait, then," answered the woman in orange. "But we must consider and prepare for the worst possible outcomes."

A long moment's silence. Jolon and Mara watched the elders, all of whom seemed deep in thought.

"Is Gallelon still living in Mirsda?" asked the old man.

"You speak of the mage, Elder?" asked Jolon.

"If this goes very badly," said the woman in orange, "we may need to ask his help."

"We will go and see if he is still there," answered Mara.

Chapter Twenty-eight

"I think you are delaying, Seer."

"No," she said as she packed her things, but her hands and her mouth seemed to belong to different minds. Fingers trembling, she could not seem to tie the knots on her pack. He watched a moment, then took over for her.

All too soon they were ready to leave, atop their horses, and riding north on the Great Road.

The wide road was now crowded. Donkey-pulled wagons, hand-held carts, hundreds of people, all urgent to get somewhere, shouting and shoving, but getting out of the way of their horses. Tayre's occasional glances and smiles at her seemed distracted. She finally realized he was watching the many people around them, looking for threats. She could have reassured him that vision told her she was not in danger of bodily harm, not until the palace itself, but she would not expect him to rely on her word any more than she would rely on his.

The gates of the city were huge and heavy, many times the height of a tall man. She watched them in wonder as they passed, picking out the many symbols twisted into the iron and spikes.

So many people. Even in Munasee there had not been this many people, swarming in all directions, children slipping behind gawkers around a puppet show, being pushed away, vendors calling their wares, people shouting. As they rode, thunder cracked across the sky, sending a brief fall of frigid rain that cleared the street not at all. Such a chaos and array of colors, sights, and sounds, that Amarta found herself looking back at the man who had been her hunter just to see something familiar.

He gave her a smile whose sincerity she no longer bothered to consider. She smiled back, but it felt weak, fragile, and insincere.

As the horses climbed the steepening road, vision tightened, a near ache in her head and neck and shoulders, confused half-warnings, tantalizing snatches of what it would be like to drop from the horse and lose herself in the people and buildings of this strange city. To avoid this day's conclusion. She pushed it all away.

At last they reached the summit of the hill where a huge square opened, huge sprawling houses on each side in dual colors, their gates and walls so ornate and beautiful that she could not quite take her eyes off them. The Houses, she realized with a shock. The capital city was where the Houses had all begun. Where the empire itself had begun.

At the center of the square rose a pale pink marble fountain, carved into sprays as if it had been transformed from a geyser of water, birds and flowers frozen in the water.

Then she turned her attention forward again. Ahead another large gate. Walls atop which men walked. And beyond that—

The palace was huge. Silvered windows reflected the sky. Flags of red and black and white rippled in the high breezes. She could not take it all in at once. Her mouth dropped open.

"Amarta," Tayre said softly from the ground. She tore her gaze away to look down at him. He had dismounted, and signaled her to follow. Then he was talking to someone, handing them something that looked like coins, and the horses were led away. She patted the side of her mare affectionately, sensing the unlikelihood of seeing her again.

From there they walked forward toward the palace gates. Terror slowed her step. She found she had stopped.

Tayre took her arm, gently pressing her forward. "No hesitating now, Seer."

Red-and-black clad soldiers stood at the entrance. Traffic in and out of the palace gates was thick. A crowd clustered before them, waiting to be let in. They were being checked, one by one.

"Thank you," she said softly to him. "For saying yes."

He still held her arm, and she let herself believe he meant to impart some measure of reassurance, not merely to convey his readiness should she at this last minute change her mind.

He spoke softly. "Once inside, for your benefit as well as mine, I am not Tayre. You understand?"

She looked ahead at the gate and not at him. "Yes."

He came closer yet, put an arm around her shoulder,

his mouth by her ear. "Do not depend on me, Amarta, not even in thought. My loyalties are to the Lord Commander and not at all to you. Expect nothing from me."

"I know."

"You know it in thought only. Listen carefully: when we walk through those gates I will leave you. There will be no good-bye, no more time. So, now: is there anything else you want to say to me or ask me before then?"

Was there?

How do I survive this?

No. She had given away hopes of her own survival or she would not be here now. "Your advice. Anything at all."

He made a low, thoughtful sound. "Your instincts have served you well these years you've run from me, escaping every time. Trust them, but go further yet: ask questions. Think on the answers. Consider the intentions behind spoken words."

"Thank you."

He pressed her forward again. She took a breath, then another. Then a step. Then another.

Close enough to the gate to look through, Amarta had not until now realized the palace was a single, enormous structure, larger than any she had ever imagined. The walls stretched up four and five stories tall, glittering pink and white stone interlaced among sparkling glass windows, towers and etched spires climbing higher yet.

The Jewel of the Empire. No one who saw this immense palace could wonder why it was so named.

Foresight was whispering urgently, warning that in moments she would walk into a dire darkness without escape. She pressed the whispers away, instead studying the palace windows, wondering who was inside and might be looking down on her now.

When they reached the front of the line Tayre spoke quietly to one of the guards. They were motioned inside, beyond the gate. The guard left at a jog, another stepping up to replace him, looking them over curiously.

Too late to run, though vision kept pushing, suggesting quickly closing options.

Tayre watched her attentively. Ready. Always ready.

Hunter's eyes. Still. Always.

Minutes later the guard returned, a tencount or more of soldiers trotting alongside, large men in red and black. The two of them were instantly surrounded, her arms were pinned, and she was nearly lifted off the ground as she was rushed forward to a destination she could no longer see. Fighting panic and trying not to struggle, she could see little through the black and red uniforms. She and Tayre were swept forward, toward and through huge palace doors to the inside of the Jewel of the Arunkel Empire.

Glimpses of long hallways, colorful throngs of people stepping quickly back from the mass of guards rushing forward. Stairs and more stairs. Another long hallway. They stopped a moment. She tried to catch her breath. Then movement again, and they were inside a high-ceilinged room. The guards released her. Unsteady and shaking, she looked around.

Walls a pale pink with delicate red swirls. A floor of gray wood and milk tile. High windows letting in light but showing nothing but flat sky.

No one moved. The guards stood silent and large, making even Tayre look small. No—he was making himself look small. The way he held himself. One shoulder dropped. Head tilted. Eyes wide, mouth slack, as if he were as stunned to be here as she was.

When we walk through those gates, I will leave you.

He had already left. The man standing beside her was not the man who had held her in his arms only that morning.

The door to the room opened. In walked another large man, his red and black uniform glinting with gold. His gaze went to her and stayed there a long moment, then went to Tayre, then back to her.

Looking as he did now, she would not have recognized him from her memory of that dark night, years ago in Botaros.

"Lord Commander," Tayre said, bowing deeply, bobbing slightly at the deepest part of the bow, as if nervous and uncertain, which Amarta was certain he was not. His voice was accented with a lilt Amarta had not heard him use before. "I am servant and messenger. This girl, I deliver her to you. I am to tell you she has come of her own will. That she gives herself to you without influence."

Should she bow as Tayre had done? She watched the Lord Commander as keenly as he now watched her, hoping for a clue, finding none. Why hadn't she thought to ask Maris or Tayre enough to prepare for this moment?

All her vision and resolve had not prepared her for this. Not even to ask the right questions.

"Yes," the man said. "This is the one. You may go. Tell your master I will contact him. Tell him he has done well."

Tayre bowed again and again and backed to the door.

She had known he would leave, yet he had been right: it was only in thought. She felt a rising panic, a curious transfer of her fear from Tayre from these many years of running to the man in front of her.

Who was, after all, the man who had sent him. The holder of the hunting dog's leash. The man in whose hands her life rested. Who had killed his brother, because she had told him how.

If she had been able to look further into the future, then, back in Botaros—if she had seen more clearly— would she have chosen his brother instead? And then, might she now not be standing here? Perhaps his brother would have been worse.

It didn't matter: there was no asking about what might have happened in events already passed. That was not vision; that was regret.

The Lord Commander gestured, and the rest of the men followed Tayre out. Suddenly the room was empty but for the two of them, the echo of the door closing the only sound in this quiet room.

The Lord Commander seemed to look everywhere but at her. "Amarta al . . . ?" he prompted.

She swallowed. Tension was a pressure in her head and throat, fear a tightness in her chest. She sensed every word she spoke would matter. "Nowhere," she answered. Her voice sounding small in her own ears. "There is no home."

"Amarta al Arunkel, then," he said roughly. "And that's far from nowhere."

It took her a moment to understand his words, to comprehend their meaning, to realize she had already earned his annoyance.

"Yes, ser."

"When last we spoke, I was short on time, and you were short on sleep. Now I have plenty of time. Is it true that you come here of your own free will?"

"Yes, ser." He had a way of asking questions that made her want to answer. Her hands were clenched into tight, damp fists. With effort she uncurled her fingers.

"You have no need to fear me, Amarta al Arunkel. All those years running—all a misunderstanding now addressed. You are safe here. Safer than you've ever been."

She didn't believe him. But it didn't matter; she had not come here to be safe. For him to say this, though, what did that mean? Was he trying to reassure her? Or make her more afraid?

He motioned to one of the chairs. "Sit. I'll have food sent for. Later, a room for you. A clean bed in which to sleep. Perhaps even a bath. Yes?"

She sat, clutching the loose fabric of her travel-stained trousers to keep her hands busy. She felt out of place in this room of high ceilings and heavy doors, of chairs of polished wood. It made her wonder how much Tayre had been paid to deliver her here, and decided that she would rather not know. She thought of Dirina and Pas and, bizarrely, what they would think of this room, of this moment, of this man.

He had, she realized, asked her a question, but she did not understand it. As he walked the room, watching her, vision played dimly at the edge of her awareness, shifting like flame-cast shadow.

He was the largest thing in front of her. From him came warm blood, and cold stillness, and the echoing screams and cries of thousands.

He stood at the door now, speaking to someone about food. She was too afraid to feel hungry. What she felt, she suspected, was no longer of much consequence.

The sound of his boots on the wood and tile reminded her of a moment in half-dream, some years ago. Vision or memory? Or both?

"Amarta, where are your sister and her child?"

Her gaze snapped to his, then down at the floor's tile of gray and milk.

He pulled a chair around to face her. He took his time as he sat, his every movement unhurried. "Will you not answer?" His tone seemed to hint at consequence, at displeasure, at the unacceptability of silence. It cut through her thoughts, making it even harder to think of a reply. "I assumed you would cooperate with me now, since you came here willingly. Perhaps I assumed in error."

She looked at him, afraid to see his face, afraid not to. His expression threatened some kind of heat, like dry tinder waved near a fire.

"My first question, and you refuse. This does not give me much confidence in you, Seer." To her continued muteness, he made a dismissive gesture. "Never mind. I'll find them if I want them. Why are you here?"

She must answer. Pushing away the dread she felt at these words, she stuttered. "To—to answer your questions, Lord Commander."

"You rejected my offer only last year. Has the future changed so much since then?"

"The future is always changing."

"Don't play word games with me, Amarta," he said, his tone forceful. "What has changed?"

She cringed, swallowed. "I have, Lord Commander."

"In what way?"

Children screaming, burning in basements. Heads sitting atop walls on spikes. Bodies swinging from trees.

What would he understand? What would he believe?

"I want Arunkel to be a good place for my nephew to grow up."

"In what way is it not?" He sounded annoyed.

This was completely the wrong beginning. If she were to have a chance to make him change his mind about anything, she would have to gain his confidence, and she was already failing. It was not enough to convince him that she was sincere; she had to show him that she could help him in ways he cared about. She had to win his faith. But how?

The way Tayre had with her. Building trust, one careful detail at a time. Without pretending the past had not happened. That was why Tayre had told her his various reasons for doing what he did: he was building her trust.

She must be useful to the Lord Commander. Predict something both soon and likely. That had, perhaps, already happened, but that he had not yet heard about.

In his future she saw him slam a fist against a desk, furious with someone. With many someones. With a town. Many towns. People would die under this fury, but still he would not get what he wanted. And what did he want?

Smithies stand idle, he spat, *waiting for ore.*

"There is a mine, ser," she said, struggling for elusive detail, forcing herself to sound more confident than she was. "More than one. But one in particular."

"Go on."

His voice revealed nothing. She hesitated, then pressed ahead.

The rails.

"The rails." She had never seen a rail-wagon or the rails it rode on, had barely heard of them until one of Maris's long stories in one of the many inns.

"What about them?"

Rocks. Large rocks.

"They will break the rails. With rocks."

"That would be astonishingly reckless of them. The mines and the rails are all that stand between them and my troops razing the town to the ground."

"They want control of their land and future. They want it badly enough that they will sacrifice the mines, their homes, everything they have."

"No, they won't. No one goes that far."

Amarta thought of her journey here.

"Tell me how to put this rebellion to rest, for good and for all, Seer."

An impossible question; nothing could be that certain. She licked her lips, trying to see his future and those around him. What they might say. What they might do.

Too much detail.

What path took him to an ended rebellion?

"Give them ownership of the mines, ser." Part guess, and it wasn't quite right, but she could not see more.

"Impossible. The mines were opened by the crown at great cost. Find me another solution."

Another solution? And this one already so hard to obtain? She must have looked as lost as she felt, because he said, "But later. First we come to an understanding. Who convinced you to come here? The man who found you, perhaps?"

He meant Tayre. "No."

His eyebrows drew together. Clearly he did not believe her. "Despite your lack of contract, the crown will pay you for your service."

"No," she managed.

"No?" He sat back, seeming startled. "You refuse the queen's gold?"

"Yes, ser."

"No pay and no contract puts you entirely at the crown's mercy. Is that really what you want?"

Surely she was already at his mercy? What was this game?

And what to say now?

He made a thoughtful sound. "You are tired after your journey. We will discuss it tomorrow. If you are, as you say, here to help the crown, the crown will take care of you. That is why you're here, isn't it, Amarta al Arunkel? To serve the queen?"

To change the future. To change this man's intention.

"Yes, ser."

"Then we are, at long last, aligned in our purpose."

Amarta looked at him. At his wide smile she felt a chill.

Chapter Twenty-nine

Innel looked out the large windows onto the gardens below from the huge and high map room, his thoughts darting from one issue to the next, fitting together like pieces into puzzles.

Failing to fit.

Sinetel. Troop movements. Supply lines. Ore production.

The seer.

Outside, the gardens were bright with spring greens, dotted with rich blooms of red and white roses. Orderly and neat, a quiet contrast to the pictures in his head sketched from reports of bloody skirmishes on the borders and along the Great Road.

Innel was acutely aware of Keyretura sitting by the windows, a striking figure in his dark skin and black robe. Innel found it oddly reassuring that the mage seemed willing to sit for hours, listening and watching, his expression seeming to say that little could surprise him.

Good. He had not hired him to be surprised.

A knock at the door. Amarta was brought into the room. The simple green and white servants' dress made her seem almost as if she belonged at the palace. He had thought it best to clothe her as if she were unimportant, though the guards surrounding her rather belied that implication.

Years of searching, handfuls of hires, and exorbitant expense, all to get her in hand. It was time to see what he had bought.

She looked around the room, at the walls of maps and ornamented swords and daggers, her wide-eyed expression one of bemusement. He waited while she walked the room, staring at the various gifts he'd been given by the Houses, from Helata's extraordinarily detailed miniature sailing ship to the ornately carved rosewood and ebony box from Nital. At the painted shaota figurine with its lines of chestnut and amber, she stopped, reached out her fingers to touch the horse's head.

The figurine put him in mind of the Arteni campaign two years back. That town, at least, had continued to behave well—very well, indeed—since he had replaced their leadership and explained to them in detail how Arunkel justice was applied.

Sufficient force. A willingness to make swift examples.

She turned to the huge table that dominated the center of the large room, covered with sculpted mountains and valleys, green and brown and white-tipped, small red markers where the troops were located.

"The empire," she breathed, eyes lighting with understanding. He watched her gaze travel down the coast to Kelerre, inland, and back.

Catching on quickly. Interesting. When at last her gaze found Keyretura, it stayed there.

"Keyretura dua Mage al Perripur," Innel said. "Amarta al Arunkel."

"Blessings of the season, High One," she said.

Innel was a little surprised at this. Where did she learn the formal address for mages?

Keyretura smiled. "Good manners for one so young, in a country so full of loathing for my kind. Warmth of spring to you, Amarta."

She looked at him intently. Foreseeing for him? Keyretura looked back, expression flat.

"Amarta," Innel said, gesturing to the table, "do you see these markers? These are troops. Do you understand what I want?"

"You want predictions."

"Yes. You are safe here," he added, hoping to reassure her.

She stared back at him. "You have wanted me dead for a long time."

"All in the past, Amarta. Tell me your visions and I guarantee your continued safety here."

She put a clenched fist to her mouth, doubt across her face. Understandable, he supposed.

"I have a suite of apartments set aside for you and your family. Quite a nice one. All you need do is cooperate with me."

"I want my family safe."

"Yes. As I said, I have a suite and—"

"From you."

She had interrupted him. With a demand, challenge,

and an implication. He suppressed his desire to explain to her how to speak to him respectfully. There was no time to teach her proper manners.

"Simply tell me your visions without evasion and—"

"My sister and my nephew remain safe, even if you don't like my answers." She held her arms across her stomach, as if she were in pain.

He wasn't liking her answers much now. But he was understanding her, better and better. "I will agree to that."

"Then I will have a contract with you, ser."

"You will, will you?" he asked, finally letting his annoyance show. "Do you have a list of terms for this contract you now require?"

Her shoulders hunched at the force of his words. Perhaps he had spoken too sharply.

"I will answer your questions about my visions, ser," she said. "As long as my sister and nephew are safe."

"It is hardly in my power to look after the welfare of a woman and child at some mysterious location," he said evenly. "But tell me where they are and—"

"Safe," she repeated, again interrupting him. "From you. From the queen. From anyone you command."

Clever, he thought, reassessing her, but she had left out key details. No mention of compensation. Or, glaringly, her own safety. Oversight? Or foresight? "Is that the entirety of the contract you require?"

Convenient if it were; under such a contract he could go so far as to have her killed and not even have to break the agreement.

Uncertainty flickered across her face. She looked at

Keyretura, who was watching with more interest than he had yet shown. "Safe," she said softly.

"So you said. But it is beyond my power to account for the actions of every person, horse, dog, or bird who marches under the banners of the empire, Amarta. Surely you can see this."

Her eyes flickered between Innel and Keyretura as if looking for answers.

"What should I say to that?" she asked the mage.

Keyretura's brows drew together. Was he actually surprised?

Innel certainly was. He was not used to a negotiation that involved asking the opposing side for guidance.

"I have no bond with you, Seer," Keyretura answered. "Why would you give credence to anything I might say? Would you not expect me to lead you astray?"

"Yes," she said. "But whatever you say, and however you say it, I will know something more than I know now."

The mage made a sound, half thoughtful, half amused. "In some lands they say the advice of an enemy is gold. Perhaps you should ask the Lord Commander himself. I am merely his advisor."

She glanced at Innel, then back at Keyretura. "But I ask you, High One. Please."

The mage looked a question at Innel, who nodded slowly, not quite sure he liked where this was going.

"Then I will advise, Amarta al Arunkel." He considered a moment. "It is clear the Lord Commander's will stretches far beyond his words and touch. Perhaps you wish the contract to say that whether by action or stillness, through his hand or another's, his power permitting, he has an obligation to keep your sister and nephew whole of body and to refrain from putting them at risk or harm."

"Yes." She looked at Innel. "That is what I want."

"Good," Innel said, "then—"

"But also you must give them food and water and shelter, if they ask you or those you command."

"Ah. Anything else?"

"For their entire lives."

"You ask a lot, Amarta al Arunkel, in return for something whose worth has yet to be proved."

She lifted her chin, met his gaze. "You said I should charge more."

And so he had. He remembered that night in Botaros keenly, when she had given him the advice that had brought him to this position, and this moment.

"Very well; I agree to all you have said, and I agree on behalf of my queen. Are there other terms?"

"No matter what I say, no matter how I answer your questions."

"You repeat yourself," he said, fighting irritation. This much challenge he had not expected.

She turned to Keyretura. "Will you witness, High One?"

Innel's mouth opened in surprise. Where in the seven hells had she learned about mage-witnessing of contracts? It was a rarefied enough practice that he himself had yet to see it done.

Keyretura looked a him, eyebrows raised in question.

"Go ahead," Innel said.

"I will witness, Seer," the mage responded.

Now she looked entirely lost. Capable of negotiating a contract, of this complexity, with someone of his standing—even to ask for witnessing—but she had no idea what to do next? She was a fascinating mix.

"Are you ready to make this contract with me and the monarchy of Arunkel, Amarta al Arunkel?" he prompted.

Her eyes flickered around the room. "Yes." She looked terrified.

Innel walked to the door, spoke with a guard, and returned.

"A contract of this importance is typically sealed with gold, gems, or other such valuables. Since you refuse payment, the queen will not insult you with those things. Instead I offer this simple nals as a token of value to seal our contract. Will you accept it as such?"

She nodded, still looking like a misplaced lamb.

He held out his hand, the shiny copper nals on his palm. She did not move.

"Now," he said, "you put your hand on mine and say: 'Our contract is made.'"

Hesitantly she stepped close to him and put her hand palm down on top of his. At the touch, her eyes opened wider. What, he wondered, was she seeing now?

"Our contract is made," she whispered.

"Our hands turn, together, thus, so that the coin is left with you." His hand now facing down, he drew it back.

She looked at the coin as if she didn't know what it was, then looked back at him.

"And now, Seer, you will answer every question I have, for as long as it takes, and with no more objections. Do you understand?"

Mutely, she nodded.

"What do they say, Srel?" Innel asked.

His stomach was grumbling. Again he had forgotten to eat. Srel held out a platter from which Innel took a bite of something fried and crunchy, salted and peppered, that tasted mildly of fish. He took another.

"That she is the king's bastard daughter. Your bastard girl. The queen's . . ." He paused, clearly not wanting to finish that sentence. Innel gestured for him go on. "The mage's bastard daughter—though looking at them both, I don't know how anyone could think that. That she is the seer of rumor, or that she is not, but you are pretending she is. That she is next on the succession list. That she is going onto the hanging wall next week. That you are using her to test loyalties—though I can't quite sort that one out either. Shall I go on?"

"Enough."

Notably missing was the rumor he had deliberately seeded, about her being a distant cousin of his, orphaned in the recent unrest south. Not salacious enough, clearly.

Nalas entered. "Colonel Tierda has arrived," he said. "On her way to report, ser."

Innel sighed and looked out the window to Execution Square, considering what Tierda would see this time.

"How long have they been dead?" he asked of the odd arrangement of limbs suspended on various ropes above the cobblestones of the square.

"Ah . . ." Srel said. "Six days, I think, ser."

"Enough. Clean it up. Close the curtains." No sense

in making the colonel fear for her life on top of her child's life.

"Yes, ser," Nalas said. "Oh, also—the queen. She's stopped watching. She's in with them now."

"In with the king's dogs? Again?" Innel stood. "Do I need to—"

Nalas shook his head. "No. Sachare knows to send word if Her Majesty gets any sort of murderous look in her eye. The keeper's in there with her and has a new litter of pups she seems to have taken an interest in. No blood has been spilled yet."

He had warned Cern that the king's dogs were unpredictable, that they could be violent. "I know, Innel," she had said, "but it's time I understand what my father sees in them."

"Eat more," Srel urged him. Innel accepted a tiny roll with a curl of green-herbed cheese atop, washing it down with warm, spiced wine.

A knock. Tierda. He pushed the food away.

Her expression as she saluted was dour and resolved. She knew what was coming.

"This," he told her, "is turning into a very expensive problem."

"Yes, ser."

"And still the smithies stand idle, waiting for ore. Sinetel was supposed to be in hand. Last year."

"It was in hand, ser. Truly it was. Then word came about Erakat's mining towns demanding a bigger share. Then Rott and Lukata started to complain, and—" She fell silent. She had the miserable look of someone who had run out of ideas as well as words.

"And?"

"Masked riders, carrying torches, spooking the horses. Riding off before we could catch them. Attacks on the rails. Large rocks rolled onto the tracks in the night. But we put out the fires," she added, as if hoping that might pass for good news.

"Rocks on the rails," he muttered, recalling the seer's prediction of this problem. Now, if he could only get her to deliver a solution. The foundation of the empire's wealth was being chewed away, mine by mine. Town by town. "What do you need—a soldier at every cross-brace of track to keep it secure? What does it take?"

Correctly sensing from his tone that he didn't want a response, she stayed silent.

Sufficient force. Swift examples. He rubbed his head.

"I'll get you more troops and cavalry, but then I expect you to see to it that the wagons go through on schedule. Make it known to all the towns that anyone who approaches the rail without authorization will be executed. Then do it. Publicly and with a lot of noise and blood."

"Yes, Lord Commander."

He gave her an assessing look. It was one thing to attack an opposing force well-equipped with weapons, but another to take the lives of townspeople who carried nothing more dangerous than rocks.

And another thing entirely to make people howl for mercy and continue to cause them to suffer and die. This was why the old king had so often forced the Cohort to long observation of interrogations and executions. To make sure they understood the difference.

Tierda, he judged, was exhausted, not only in mind but also in spirit. This problem needed someone with resolve. Casting his mind over the members of the Cohort who had seemed most keenly interested in those particular lessons and who might currently be free of House obligations, he said to Nalas, "Find Putar. See if he wants a captaincy and the chance to cause some pain."

"Yes, ser."

"My Cohort brother Putar will help you with the least pleasant parts of this matter," Innel said to the colonel. "You will restore order. I will look in on your child." Part reassurance, part reminder. "Do you understand?"

"Yes, Lord Commander," she said, voice low and quavering.

He was tempted to replace her, but she still knew the area and issues better than anyone. Would another commander do better? Would it matter?

More questions for the seer.

Innel watched Amarta stare into space and drew on his reserves of patience. Enough hours had gone by for Srel to have sent for multiple meals. Even Keyretura had come to look less impassive than bored.

Keyretura could afford to lose interest. He was not responsible for the welfare of an empire.

Amarta put the tips of her first two fingers on the tops of the northern mountain range that stretched north to the ocean through the Labari Province.

"In the warm months ore shipments resume," she said. "In autumn they slow. By winter they cease."

It was the same answer she had given the last ten times

he had asked this and similar questions. He had tried every variation he could conceive of.

"How can it not matter who leads the troops?" he asked.

Again, the far-away, slack-jawed look. How much of her expression was pretense, intended to convince him that she was actually seeing the future?

"Within the year, yes, ser, it changes. But three years hence, it is the same result."

"Then—ten companies here—" he said, moving the small, painted red wooden markers. "Four to Lukata, four to Rott, the rest to Sinetel." He looked at Amarta. "Well?"

She moved her fingers to the coast of Labari, drawing them across the paint and fabric of hundreds of miles.

"One year," she said softly. "Two. Then three. The same result, Lord Commander."

He swept five more red blocks north. "Here. Enough to destroy Sinetel entirely. Labari, Lukata, Rott—they'll come into line if Sinetel goes down hard. Three years hence. Answer." He could hear the harshness in his tone.

She had developed the habit of sucking on the knuckles of her right hand, which she did now. He was beginning to find it annoying.

"There are still troops here." She pulled her hand from her mouth to point at the northern mining towns. "The miners refuse to work. The ore shipments stop."

"You know nothing of this situation," he snapped. "Look south. The mines of the Karmarn Range. Erakat. Garaya." He walked down the side of the table, set troops beyond Munasee in Gotar's mountain range.

"The cities, they—" She stopped, looked at him.

"Go on."

"They claim independence."

"No," he said. "They do not."

Garaya at least was in hand. He had sent Sutarnan south with twenty companies, well more than enough to stiffen the spine of the counter-rebellion his Cohort brother had cleverly arranged. Sutarnan had a general with him, an experienced veteran in the south, who had assured Innel the plan was sound. Innel had made it clear to them both that he wanted the corrupt governor brought back alive and whole to stand before the queen. The man had earned that at least: a spectacular and lengthy execution, one impressive and bloody enough to be told and retold across the empire.

Sweeping markers down the thin line of the Great Road, then east to the raised areas, he said, "Twenty more companies to Erakat and the Gotar Mountains."

She was silent long enough that he looked from the table to her face. She again had that startled look of fear. So much emotion. It had to be pretense.

"Answer."

With an inhale she walked around the table to the south end. Her hand trembled as she lifted the black and gold chain that separated Arunkel from Perripur and slowly dragged it north and west over small rises and dips, with a single movement taking cities, mining towns, and hundreds of miles of Arunkel Empire and turning it into Perripin lands.

"The cities, they claim—" she began.

"This, then—all these to the Munasee Cut, by ship." He moved small blocks onto the blue of ocean and then south to below the borderline, moving the chain back where it belonged. "They march north from there to hold the trade routes, here and here. Favorable contracts to Erakat and the Gotar mines if they provide immediate support with no lapse in production. A new governor in Garaya. Lowered tax rates for merchants trading with Kelerre."

She put a finger on the chain.

"Take your hand off that," he said. She quickly pulled her fingers back. "Answer."

"The mountain regions will declare independence because Perripur will offer them . . ." She faltered, glanced at Keyretura. "What the empire does not."

"Which is what?"

"The chance to rule themselves."

"No troops, then," Innel said. "Half the tax rate. Protections for all trade. What now?"

"The mountain towns will seem to cooperate, but within five years they will claim independence and—"

"Enough," Innel said. "There are other answers. You don't know enough yet. But you will."

"Yes, ser. Maybe—" she began.

"Maybe what?"

"Maybe it's like a fishing net with too many fish. If you try to hold them all, the net breaks."

It astounded him, the things that she thought it sensible to say. He walked toward her. She took a step backward.

"Have you ever held such a net, Amarta?" She shook her head, retreating as he advanced. "You would stand with it at the edge of the water and you would starve.

You are here to tell me what I want to know, not to blather about nets and governance revealing the astonishing depth of your ignorance. If you want to keep your tongue, you will use it to answer my questions. Is this clear?"

She swallowed repeatedly, nodding. "Yes, ser."

Maybe Keyretura was right: maybe she only had an instinct for speculation. Flawed and unreliable. He exhaled frustration and turned from the table, still seeing red blocks against green lands from his hours of focusing. "Land grants to leaders in the mining towns and to the new governors of the cities. What changes?"

"These areas." She pointed to the southern provinces. "They have Perripin names now."

"What?" he shouted, outraged, aware that his temper was fraying. He turned his back on her and walked to the window. From here he could see the Houses of Nital, Sartor, and Kincel. But even these Houses, working in wood and stone and textiles, needed metal for their tools. Metal was the spine of the empire.

And Perripur—he could almost feel the country to the south watching, biding its time, wondering if Arunkel was still strong enough to defend itself, or ripe enough to bite. The chain must not slide north.

He turned back to the table and moved all his red wooden markers to the chain.

"Look again, Seer," he said. "With care." He looked at Keyretura. "Every troop to the Perripur border. All of them. Now what?"

Keyretura did not even blink.

For some time she stared, the blank look again on her

face. The minutes stretched until he could stand it no longer.

"Well?"

"There is no more red and black here," she whispered. "So much death."

He ignored this. "Where is the border? In five years? In ten? In twenty?"

She looked around the room, at the high walls, the weapons, then back at him, wide-eyed, silent.

This was what all the years of searching and expense had bought him? A blank stare and useless answers? He felt a craving to hit her until she spoke sense. "Answer," he said.

"In twenty years only this city will call itself Arunkel."

His entire empire reduced to one city? It was beyond possible. What was she attempting here?

At his look, she cringed.

"You are tired," he said flatly. "Not seeing clearly. We will try again tomorrow."

He went to the door, instructed the guards to take her back to her room. Then he carefully moved all the troops back to where they belonged, adjusted the chain minutely.

"Well?" he asked Keyretura at last. "Is she lying?"

"Many people believe their visions. That does not make them true."

"Her answers are unacceptable."

"Perhaps you're asking too gently."

"Perhaps."

"And perhaps you give her too much credit for a few clever guesses, and some of them not all that clever."

"She can predict the toss of a coin, High One."

"So? A coin is a small thing. The answers you want are a bit wider in scope than that. If her answers are not sound, ignore them, and keep her as a token to frighten your enemies. Or kill her and be done with it."

"I think she is keeping something from me."

"The location of the sister and nephew, at least."

This thing that she seemed to care most about. A loose end he would prefer not to have dangling.

"If I want her dead?"

"Easily done. Do you want this now?"

"No." Not yet.

He gave the mage a thoughtful look. Mage, yes, but also a Perripin, from a land where many stood to profit from the confusion and strife the empire was already facing.

"Should I be concerned about your loyalty to your homeland, High One?"

The mage barked a rare laugh. "You trust an ignorant commoner girl to advise you on troop movements, yet you doubt my word? A Perripur-Arunkel war would merely entertain me, and my home is remote enough that I could watch it in comfort. Our contract is sound, Commander."

"Forgive me, High One, I had to ask." Something else occurred to Innel. "The sister and nephew. Without knowing where they are, even what country they might be in, does it not seem to you I am constrained in how I can keep them safe from all those over whom I have command or influence?"

The mage gave Innel a look. "You propose to circumvent the contract?"

No chasing the subject around, then. But that was one

of the advantages of Keyretura: he existed outside the usual web of delicately spoken truths and layers of veiled lies.

"I question how much safer they might be, guarded by the forces at my command and your excellent attention. Many of those who act at my direction will not know of their protected status. These are dangerous times. Anything could happen."

Was that a flicker of amusement across Keyretura's face?

"Let me be sure I understand your intention, Commander. After assenting to my witnessing this contract with the seer, are you now asking me to make sound a pursuit of the sister and nephew within the scope of that contract? Or are you asking me, under the terms of my contract with *you*, to compromise my witnessing obligations?"

And this, Innel was quickly coming to understand, was the problem with dealing with mages: they were often already standing where you were only looking to go.

"Let us say the first of those options, the one that keeps the seer's contract whole."

"The terms of the contract are that you and the crown of Arunkel do not harm the sister and her child, and further that you give them food and shelter if they should want it. Nothing was said of their liberty."

"Though—abducting them . . . ?"

"I am confident that I can preserve the safety and full bellies of a woman and child while I move them somewhere safer."

"You?" Innel blinked in surprise.

"Yes."

The mage's overwhelming confidence was a heady drink.

Innel made a thoughtful noise, then a dismissive one, and turned back to the table. "Irrelevant, though; they could be anywhere in your country or mine. I have no time to start another long search. Yes, if we happen across them, but otherwise—"

"When the seer came from Kelerre with your hire, there was someone else with them."

Innel turned back. "What?"

"On your seer is the faint but unmistakable scent of my *uslata*, Commander. Marisel has touched her."

"Are you sure?"

"Of course. I know my own."

Marisel dua Mage, also traveling with the seer? He wondered what that meant. "And so?"

"And so I now have a very good idea of where the sister and nephew are."

This was entirely unexpected. "Where?"

"I might obtain them in a matter of weeks, perhaps a month, in a manner consistent with and within the bounds of the contract that I witnessed, provided you have a safe and comfortable location to which I can deliver them. I suggest something well away from the city. Isolated. Quiet. Fortified."

Innel could find such a thing. The crown had a number of distant residences.

"Truly? You can do this?"

"Do you need me to repeat myself? Shall I speak more slowly?"

"No, High One. I—" He what? It seemed too good to be possible. "Yes. I understand you."

Innel's contract with Keyretura was costing a very great deal of money, and perhaps this was why: because the mage could do what he said he could. He stared at the mage and wondered briefly what was between them, Keyretura and his former apprentice Marisel, and what the mage intended.

"If you wish, I can leave immediately," Keyretura said. "This is, however, a greater level of effort on my part, and does not fall under our current contract."

"Ah, of course." *With mages, there is always more to pay.* "What more do you need, High One?"

"Not coin. Marisel dua Mage."

"I can hardly deliver her to you. I could not even keep her here."

"You need do nothing. If she comes here, when she does, you agree not to interfere."

Interfere? How would he interfere?

Unbidden, the image of the glass plains came to him, from the one time he had glimpsed them from a distance, desolate and vast.

He inhaled, let it out. "I am told that when mages fight, everyone dies except the mages. Perhaps this is not a wise plan, High One."

A small smile. "That risk only exists when the mages are of similar power. This is not that circumstance. Do not presume you know my intent. I assure you, not a stone on your precious walls will be so much as scratched."

"Then—it seems a price easily paid." Perhaps he should ask more, find out what this might be about. Or perhaps the business of mages was best left to mages. "I accept your amendment."

Keyretura stood. "I will need a set of your fastest horses."

Maybe you are asking too gently.

The next morning as Innel dressed, he thought of the seer, her answers, her motivations. That she had not negotiated for her own safety, only that of her family, meant what? That she was confident of her safety? Sure he would not hurt her?

Perhaps you give her too much credit.

She had known about the rails and the rocks. Years ago she had known about his brother. He was not yet ready to give up on her answers.

A long night's sleep had done much to restore his good humor, but he had slept far later than he meant to, reading histories of the southern provinces and cities into the early morning, so he was surprised to see Srel and Nalas waiting outside the door for him.

"Don't you two have other things to do than wait on me?" he asked, half serious.

"No, ser," said Srel, at the same time Nalas began with, "Well, now that you—" Then, hearing Srel's answer, added: "No, ser."

"Arrange a meeting with the hire," he told Srel. It was time to pay Tayre and ask him a few questions.

A messenger dashed up to them, coming to a fast stop, dipping her head in a bow. "Lord Commander, the queen wishes your presence at the aviary viewing walkway."

The bird yards?

It did not sound urgent, but it was Cern, and possibly the unpredictable Cahlen as well, so they walked quickly.

The queen stood at a balcony, various attendants and guards arranged about her in a set of interlocking circles that Innel reviewed weekly for security, despite that this required a certain amount of struggle with the existing hierarchy. A quick glance at the expressions on the faces of Sachare and the queen's seneschal told him that this particular stop in the queen's schedule was not exactly expected.

A path opened to allow him access to Cern.

"Your Majesty," he said, coming close, giving her an exacting and proper bow, since they were observed.

"What is she doing, Innel?"

Three stories below, in the courtyard of the aviary, Cahlen stood, a bow and arrow in hand, instantly alarming him. At his sharp look, Sachare shrugged.

Fortunately, the bow and arrow in Cahlen's grip was not pointed upward but held loosely as she watched the flying birds above, seemingly oblivious to her royal audience. On the verdant grass that grew happily under the droppings of so many messenger birds lay ten dead gray and white carcasses, an arrow through each.

Other bird-keepers scattered around the yard watched Cahlen nervously. Whatever Cahlen was doing, they were deferring to her. Even the Minister of Bird, it seemed, standing at the back with a tablet, making notes, was content to let her do whatever it was she was doing.

Which was what?

"I'll find out, Your Majesty," he said, motioning to Nalas, who drew the correct understanding and headed down the stairs at a quick trot. A few moments later, Cahlen looked to the side at her called name and left the courtyard.

"Another thing," Cern said softly, and he came close so that they had a measure of verbal privacy. "The ministers, House liaisons and trade council are concerned about the various troubles north and south. I told them you had it in hand."

He thought of the map room and the seer and the answers he thought he'd have by now.

"I do, Your Majesty."

"Good," she said. Below in the courtyard the other keepers picked up the bird carcasses and followed Cahlen off the field. The drama seemingly over, Cern looked thoughtfully at Innel then left.

He headed to the dovecote. Anyone but Cahlen he would have had sent for, but she might not come, and his reputation did not need another failure of obedience from his own sister. He found her in the high, wide dovecote tower, atop a ladder, checking nests, handing down a handful of eggs to an assistant below.

Raising his voice to be heard over the calls of the birds, he spoke. "Cahlen."

"Brother."

"What was that about, in the yard?"

She turned on the ladder, grinning widely, another handful of eggs in her hand. "Culling the weak."

"The weak? Do you mean the birds foolish enough to be killed by your arrow shot?"

"Yes." She turned back around, poking into the nests.

"Explain this to me."

She climbed down, handed the eggs to the keeper, who put them in a basket and with a fearful look at Innel fled the dovecote, leaving the two of them alone.

"They're going to die when I send them into battle anyway, so best to kill them now, so that they don't drop any messages as their final failure."

"You are saying, then, that—"

"Don't you have other things to do, brother?"

He ignored this. "—that your birds know how to avoid arrows?"

She scowled. "Not all of them, obviously. But the ones that go out with your troops, yes. Nineteen in twenty now come home." Her smile went very wide.

"That's very—" *Impressive*. He was pretty sure that between bad weather and predatory hawks, no one had ever achieved that rate of return before now and certainly not at the distances at which action was happening across the empire. "Very good, Cahlen."

"Not good enough," she said, angry again. "They will get smarter. The ones that don't will die."

At some point he might, he reflected, need to make Cahlen Minister of Birds, despite her strangeness.

Subsequent sessions with the seer produced no answers he liked better. Either she was holding back what she knew or her visions were indeed little more than speculation, as Keyretura had suggested.

Disappointing, perhaps, but Innel had done well enough without her these years since Botaros, making troop deployment assessments using the same tools Arunkel commanders had used throughout the years:

military theory, a study of history, and the advice of veterans.

He sat now with General Lismar, who looked at the paper maps he had given her, glancing back and forth to the notes he had made.

"Yes," she said at last, leaning back, though her expression indicated she was still considering. "There is room for argument, of course, as there is in any plan, but I see no place I would make substantial changes." She looked at him. "Transitions are always difficult times, Innel."

"Even when your brother took the throne?"

She smiled, a hard smile, eyes crinkling. "I sat by his side for a similar discussion. After Lason made a mess of things."

This Innel had not known. "Why did you keep Lason as Lord Commander so long, if he was incompetent?"

A shrug. "He wasn't, not quite. More importantly, he made friends easily, and a lot of them were the previous generation's generals and aristos. We needed the support. As you do now."

"I am grateful, General, for your backing, and—"

The door to his office slammed open. Two of the queen's guards stomped in, dragging between them the slave Naulen, her long blond hair falling over her eyes. Innel and Lismar stood.

Cern followed tight on the heels of the guards. One look at her face silenced any objection Innel might have been forming. Cern looked around the room, her eyes wide and furious.

Lismar must have known the familial expression; she went to one knee, dropping her head low. Innel quickly debated following her down. A lifetime of studying Cern, but he had never before seen this expression on her face. Trusting his intuition, Innel only dipped his head, then met her furious glare.

"Is this your doing, Innel?"

The slave looked up, her mouth opening and closing silently.

"Your Majesty," Innel said. "What has happened?"

"Leave," Cern said to Lismar, who lurched to her feet and left quickly.

"This—trash," Cern said, waving her hand at the slave, "was with him. Your idea, Innel?"

Her hand was shaking. Innel looked at the guards and gave Cern a questioning look.

"They stay," she said.

Innel felt his stomach clench. This should be a private conversation. Something had happened. But what?

"Yes, Your Majesty: the slave was my idea. To ease the king's discomfort, perhaps calm him in these difficult times."

"I know that, you bastard. You put her there to spy on him."

"Of course."

"And?"

Naulen suddenly went limp. Pretending a faint, Innel suspected. The two guards lowered her to the floor in a small heap.

"And she has been reporting to me, as I instructed," he said.

"But not today, I'm fairly certain. Today when she was done with him she came to me."

"To you?"

He wondered if Cern was deliberately drawing this out to induce fear in him; it was the sort of thing Restarn would have done.

No, he decided, she was upset, and profoundly so, even having trouble talking.

His pulse began to speed. If her anger found him the best target, his world could change very quickly.

Her face twisted into something stark. She put her a hand on either side of her own head. "He's dead, Innel. She killed him. This worthless piece of shit killed him."

Naulen cried out from the floor, a sound of anguish. "He ordered me to collect his spit, Gracious Majesty. Please, I only followed his direction. I would never hurt him, never, but he insisted. Mercy, Your Majesty, I beg you."

Cern's face went hard. "Get her up," she said to the guards. They yanked Naulen to her feet and Cern put a hard fist into the small woman's stomach. Naulen grunted, doubled over, gasping for air as the guards held her taut, and began to retch.

"Get her out of here," Cern said.

"You are both bound to silence," Innel said to the guards as they drew the slave to the door. "Any word of this is treason." He hoped that would keep them quiet long enough to talk to them both later.

When the door was shut, they were alone. Hitting the slave had helped her mood, Innel judged, though she was rubbing her hand and a bitter expression was on her mouth. An improvement over rage.

"He saved his spit, Innel. For days or weeks. I don't

know. Held it in his mouth until the doctor was gone, spat it back out into a skin she smuggled in and out for him, wrapped flat between her breasts. Today he swallowed it all at once."

Clever, Innel thought.

She was pacing the room, holding herself with her arms. "I thought I'd be glad to see him dead. But damn her, that blond rat—she had no right. Give her to the streets. Make her run. I want to see what they do to her."

He knew exactly what they would do to her. Better, he strongly suspected, than Cern did. "She'll last minutes."

"Good."

Keeping his tone calm, he said, "If that's what you want, my lady, I will see it done."

"I do."

Better to have her vent her fury on the slave than on him, but with the king dead a number of decisions needed to be made quickly. Killing the slave this way, this soon, would imply things. The wrong things.

"Cern," he said, risking the familiarity, "she didn't kill him. He killed himself."

He was careful not to use the other term for suicide: the coward's way.

She looked up at him, suddenly suspicious. "Did you set this up? Tell her to do this? Did you kill my father, Innel?"

"No and no and no," he said with precision, meeting her wild-eyed look with every bit of certainty he could summon.

"The medicines the doctor has been giving him. The truth, damn you."

"Yes, the doctor is mine and acts at my direction. Enough herbs to keep him abed these years, yes to that. But not to kill him. You know me, Cern; if I wanted him dead—" A small shrug. "He killed himself."

Restarn had even warned them. They had simply ignored it.

Well, it was done.

"Damn him," she said. "No gift ceremony. I don't want him remembered. Let his spirit wander the Beyond in silence alone. That's what he deserves."

That would make Cern look bad, worse even than Restarn's suicide. The Houses would be furious without the chance to show how wretched was their grief, and losing an opportunity to own something of the king's. Cern's unsteady rule would grow more precarious. But he could not say any of that, not now.

"Would that satisfy you?" he asked. "Would it be enough? To bury him as an unknown? A criminal?"

Her face fell and she exhaled, seeming to deflate. He decided to risk touching her, putting his hands on her shoulders with every bit of confidence he could.

"I hate him," she said.

"With cause," Innel responded, letting his face and tone mirror her own. "Even so. Let's make no plans now. Wait until tomorrow to decide."

Cern looked up at him, her face tight. "He always made me wait, Innel. Always tomorrow, never today. Then it would never happen, what I was waiting for."

But never had finally arrived: the king was dead.

Rumor would spread like wildfire. Even threats would not stop the meaningful looks of those who knew what had occurred, nor guesses by those who watched and listened. Everyone would speculate. How to control that inevitability?

"That's all over now. Whatever you want, it shall be so."

Slowly her expression softened. "Tomorrow, you say."

"That would be most wise, Your Majesty. A little time to consider, to clear our minds." In those words he heard his brother, and for a moment the ache threatened to take his attention.

"Yes," she said. "You are right. Very sensible." A deep breath.

He gave her what he hoped was a reassuring smile.

"The wretched slave said he gave her a last message to give to us. If the rat is to be believed."

"What was it?"

"'Keep my empire whole.'"

Plausible; it sounded like something he would say and not much like something a slave would invent.

"I intend to."

Cern smiled. A hard, brittle smile. "It's not his empire any more, Innel. It's mine."

"Of course," he said quickly.

All she had to do was hold it. She would need him for that.

"I want to talk to your seer, Innel."

That took him by surprise, but he hid it. "Of course. If there's no rush, my lady, I'll deliver her to you as soon as I can spare her."

"All right."

Now it was even more important to find out what the seer was hiding, if Cern was going to talk to her.

Cern's voice went quiet. "I'm going to my rooms."

"Yes, my lady."

"Come with me."

So much to do. A story to invent and quickly, one to get them through the night until Cern's decision could be solidified.

They could not allow it to be said that Restarn had killed himself. A common man might do so, but the empire's king was another matter entirely. What would the people think of Restarn's rule, and consequently Cern's, if they found out that, at the last, he had possessed not even the courage to live?

Innel needed to find out who had seen the slave dragged through the halls. Cern's fury had to have been noticed. By whom? What were they saying? Where were the guards he'd sworn to silence? And the doctor? He must speak with a number of people, and quickly.

But there were priorities.

"Of course, my lady," he said, following her.

After Cern was asleep, Innel confirmed the king's body was being well-guarded, and told the stunned-looking seneschal to start planning the funeral.

"Yes, ser," the seneschal said quietly.

Not long after, Innel stood in his office, Nalas and Srel before him. "What do they say?"

Soberly Srel replied: "That the king is dead of his long illness. Killed by his guards. By his dogs. By the doctor, who has fled. By the slave. By you. By himself. Is healthy and well and in hiding, to test loyalties. The queen is pretending his death. Again, to test loyalties. That the queen's birds killed him, and his eyeballs dangle from their beaks. That's most of it, ser."

"Nalas?"

"I've isolated the doctor, the slave, and the guards, each individually. They're all eager to comply with your desire, ser."

"Good. What else?"

"New talk about the insurrections in the north. Rising costs of imports. People comparing the old king to . . ." Srel trailed off.

"The queen?"

"To you, ser."

"*Me?*"

"Some say the queen is only doing what you tell her," Nalas added.

"Pah. If only that were true," he muttered. An interesting balance. He needed the aristos and Houses to respect him, but only so far; it was Cern who had the right to rule. If people thought that Innel was the real power, respect for them both would plummet. "What else?"

"That if Restarn were still on the throne, the insurgencies would be done with. There wouldn't be shortages. Garaya would be compliant."

"How quickly they forget. There were shortages then as well. Restarn nearly exhausted the treasury with his expansions."

"Yes, ser."

"Any word from Sutarnan?"

"A status letter from Abinar Province," Nalas said. "Mostly he complains about the slowness with which an army moves. And the food. He has suggestions as to improving the latter."

"I'm sure he does."

"Instructions, ser?"

He and Cern had come to an accord that morning in bed. A good place for it.

"Yes. The doctor and guards—send them away for a time, far from the city, until all this has had time to quiet. Make arrangements for an execution for the slave Naulen. Something simple but visually compelling. Beheading, perhaps. I want everyone to know about it except her."

"Yes, ser."

A shame to waste such beauty. "I want her heavily sedated. The best of what you've got and plenty of it. Be sure she does not know where she is or what is happening to her."

They could not make the execution seem too quick or too painless, but they could make sure she didn't feel it.

Nalas and Srel gave him uncertain looks. They didn't understand. Srel shook his head, as if to say his own understanding was irrelevant.

But it wasn't. He needed them to be able to make decisions without him.

"How do you think the old king died?"

Srel gave him a surprisingly formidable look. "Until you tell me, ser, I don't know."

At this show of loyalty, Innel smiled. "Nalas?"

"He's been sick more than two years. Surely that's answer enough."

"Indeed. But what will they say if the queen orders his favorite slave to execution the day before his funeral?"

"They will wonder what the slave did to gain such royal attention and so formal a death," Srel answered.

"And they'll want to see it. The execution," added Nalas.

"What will they say next, do you think?"

Srel considered. "They will speculate that the slave killed him, while he was ill. Or—" Srel hesitated.

"Or?"

"Oh," said Nalas.

They exchanged looks.

"Yes?"

Srel exhaled in a long stream. "They will wonder if the king killed himself, with the slave as the only witness. Then the queen would be protecting her father's reputation by maintaining he died of his illness rather than by his own hand."

Nalas continued. "The honorable thing to do, executing the slave, thereby implying more than is ever actually said. Protecting the king's name."

"The most immoderate of the stories that might go around, I think."

Also, ironically, the true one.

"Agreed," Nalas said.

"Do what you can to quietly give this story a good launch. While the palace is talking about a slave's execution, perhaps they will talk less about border skirmishes and shortages. That, perhaps, will give us a few moments of quiet."

"I very much doubt it, ser," said Srel.

Innel sighed. "Probably not."

✛ ✛ ✛

Innel stood in the toilet room at the back of the Frosted Rose, feeling stiffness in his shoulders from the tension of these last days. Much to do and little time. But this, too, was important.

"I have your final payment," Innel said into the overhead vent. "With a bonus for delivering the girl alive."

"No," Tayre answered. "It is not my doing that she is here."

"So your messenger said. But surely you convinced her?"

"She came on her own, for her own reasons."

"What reasons?"

"I think she hoped her answers could achieve some measure of peace across the empire."

"Those who want peace had better first be ready for war," Innel said. "Thus far she is not helping much. Would you be interested in another contract?"

"Perhaps. To do what?"

"Bolah tells me that when you ask questions, nothing is held back. I want to be sure there isn't anything she knows that she's not saying."

"You don't like her answers."

"I think she's not telling me everything she could. Whatever her true agenda is, mine must prevail."

"Surely you have others who can interrogate her."

"Of course. But I don't want to have to explain this to anyone else if I can help it. You've studied her, traveled with her. You know her and what she is, or pretends to be. She may even trust you somewhat."

"She may. What if her answers to me reveal nothing more?"

"Then I will know better what she is."

"In what condition do you want her after? Scarred? Blind? Missing limbs? Dead? How far do you want me to test her answers?"

If she had no new answers, would she still be useful to him? Again, best to keep his options open. "Leave her as whole as you can, but do what you must to be certain."

"I understand."

"How long will you need?"

"A few days, perhaps."

"That fast?" Innel was surprised. He had watched lengthy questioning before. One such famous interrogation had lasted nine years. It was considered an accomplishment as much for keeping the man alive as for any answers it had provided.

"With complete control and no interference, yes."

"I would like to see this."

"It will take longer if you are there."

For a moment he considered insisting. Then: "So be it. Can you begin immediately?"

"Payment in advance."

"Yes," Innel said, realizing he could now easily afford this man's services. What he couldn't afford was the seer keeping answers from him.

Chapter Thirty

Something was coming.

Amarta wrenched awake, heart pounding, the red and white room around her a momentary mystery.

She took gulps of air, trying to exhale the shadows that still clung to her from another long night of dark dreams in which she fled from the monster, squeezing through tunnels of knives to escape, looking over the edge of an impossibly high cliff, the shadow right behind. She had been trying to work her courage up to jump to her death rather than be caught when she instead awakened.

The soft, cream-colored sheets and blankets were soaked in sweat. She kicked them off, got to her feet, realizing as she took deep breaths that each one brought her closer to whatever was coming.

She paced, trying not to think, looking around the room in which she was locked when she was not answering endless questions. So many marvels, from its sheer size to the delicately painted designs on the walls—white on rust, rust on white—interlocking circles and spirals.

And the corner fireplace, now quietly banked with coals, lined with alternating red and white bricks, each inlaid with copper and silver. The royal mark of moon, star, pickax, sword. Not enough to keep the room warm, it seemed; it must have the crown's sigil as well. Each brick must be worth more than anything she had ever owned.

At the wooden cabinet that held her folded, clean clothes—more than she could ever need—she opened and closed drawers, wondering at the craft required to make them move so easily, stroking the smooth wood with her hand. If only she could show this to Pas. So easy to imagine him delightedly opening and closing them again and again.

Almost, she asked the question of whether she would see them again. Almost.

Pushing away, she went to the windows that also did not open from the inside and touched the smooth glass. Dirina would love this, this window so clear one could see four stories down to the tantalizing gardens below, where red and yellow flowers were blooming. She could pick a flower, hand it to her sister. The craving she felt, thinking of them, was a welcome distraction from her dread.

She took another breath. As if spending another coin.

Despite the height of the room she had no view of the city, like the glimpses she could catch as she was led from her room to the Lord Commander's offices and back again. Instead the view was a nearby wall of pink and white stone, the side of another section of this massive palace. Looking up between the buildings she could just see a patch of sunlight, a bit of blue.

Locked from the outside. Guarded. The Lord Commander did not trust her.

But where would she go?

Not that it mattered. She had made a contract. Given her word. She was not going to even try to leave.

Never had she used foresight so much across so many days as she had these last ten. She had learned that while her vision could be made weary by days of questions, she herself could be brought to exhaustion and tears by relentless examination of her every answer, each word and detail, always ending with the Lord Commander's frustrated dismissal.

Yet the next morning she would stand before him again, waiting while he reviewed the previous day's reports, comparing each to her predictions, asking about every deviation until her head swam.

Then the questioning would begin anew, her every word studied like a piece of bread on which someone at the palace had found a speck of dirt.

And still she couldn't give him the answers he wanted.

She stripped out of the sleeping gown and pulled on a green and white dress. She had an outfit for sleeping and one for being awake, both finer than any clothes she'd ever worn. When she had said so, Srel had brought her more clothes yet—a day outfit: dark green with white trim, belted, with matching trousers. A servant's outfit, he'd explained.

The door clicked and opened, and she started at the sound. But it was only Srel, bringing in a tray of food, a cylinder of tea. Behind him the door locked again.

Srel was a slender man, with light green eyes, a quick,

sympathetic smile. He seemed to enjoy doing things for her. There was something about him that made it seem, for a few minutes each day, as if someone here liked her.

"I've brought the bread sticks you like, with"—he gestured—"a peppered cheese béchamel, hazelnut paste, duck pate. Also mutton sausage and rice pudding. Try to eat some, won't you?"

Again he had brought nearly as much food as she used to eat in a single day, if she were lucky.

She took a bite of the roll and made an appreciative sound. Srel smiled brightly, as if he had been waiting for this. He poured her tea, mixed in honey and set it on the table, then stood as if to leave.

"Srel, you could stay and eat with me. You always bring so much."

He shook his head. "Not today."

Of course not. Today something was happening. Something was coming. She put down the roll.

"One small bite?" he chided gently. "I know you can do that much."

"I think I am not going to the Lord Commander today."

He gave her a wary look. "Surely you can see such things?"

She looked down at the platter, with the delicate bowls and small silver spoons. So much. Too much.

"Sometimes it is better not to know."

"I understand," he said.

"Srel, will I have long to wait?"

"A little while," he said softly.

"Thank you."

"Try to eat, won't you?"

A cold fear came over her. Vision warning again, like a keening animal. "Srel," she said urgently.

"Yes?"

She took a breath, looked into his future. Two years, three, then five. For a time, at least, his life would be surprisingly constant, somehow withstanding the storms of violence that crashed around him at the palace and in this city. "You've been very kind to me. Thank you."

"You are very welcome," he said with a smile that seemed tinged with sadness. "Very welcome indeed." For a moment more he stared at her. Then he left, the door locked behind him.

The food was so beautiful, she could stare at it a while, but dread ruined her appetite. As she paced the room, the morning bells rang, marking an hour, then another. The time she would usually have been taken to the map room came and went.

Vision warned again. The light was too bright, the quiet too loud, and she saw flickering hints of unlikely escapes that she could still attempt.

"No," she said aloud.

The lock clicked. The door opened. A shock went through her.

Tayre entered the room, shut the door behind him. Gone was any disguise.

He was clean-shaven, simply dressed. So very different, but she knew him.

He walked to her, put his hands lightly on her arms, his touch at once comforting and unnerving. Inside her, dread and hope mixed so tightly that there was no room for reason.

"I'm here to question you," he said mildly, without preamble. "To find out what answers you may be keeping from the Lord Commander. Solutions you have not yet offered him."

"I have told him everything. He doesn't like my answers."

"I am paid to disbelieve you."

She twisted away from his touch and stepped away. "I thought your contract with the Lord Commander was over when you brought me here."

"It was. I made a new contract."

Her heart sank. "Why would you do such a thing?"

"If I were not here, someone else would be. Someone less careful. I know the Anandynar interrogation style. It lacks precision."

She shook her head. "I've answered his every question, a hundred times and more."

"And if you were anyone else, that might be enough. But you have an ability you do not entirely understand, and the Lord Commander has an important puzzle that needs solving. There may be pieces you can give him that you will not see until you've looked harder for them."

"You are the dark cloud, come here to hurt me."

"Am I? What do your visions show you now?"

All at once the weight she had felt since yesterday was gone. The room seemed bathed in a calm, gentle light, as if going from night to day in an instant. Her mouth fell open in surprise.

He smiled a little. "The future of this moment does not hold pain for you, so your fear vanishes. Yes?"

"Yes," she said wonderingly, searching his face for understanding.

He exhaled slowly. He stared at her, then past her.

Dread tore through her like the teeth of a ravenous animal. She was foreseeing—suddenly, vividly, inescapably. She inhaled, hungry for air, the pain of the future so vivid she could almost feel it all through her limbs.

The smell of burning lamp oil. Wetness on her face. Agony twisting through her, washing over her like waves.

Panicked, she backed away from him. The bed caught her legs and she lost her balance, falling back onto the soft surface. Before she could blink he was there, cradling her head in his lap. She curled around herself.

"The future has changed, hasn't it, Amarta?"

"How—"

"I changed my intent." He touched her head, stroking gently.

"I'll tell you everything, anything—"

"There's nothing you can say to stop this, Amarta." Again the touch. She wanted to push him away, but she did not.

"I thought I was done being afraid of you."

"I know." Not sympathetic, not reassuring, just understanding.

Again vision warned her, then fell silent. And again.

Pain, darkness. A keening and sobbing.

For a moment she wasn't sure if it might be memory. She hoped it was memory. Blinking, she came back into the present.

No, it was still before her.

"I use your foresight to build your fear. You will tell me everything I want to know, as many times and in as many ways as I want."

She sobbed a denial, pushed against him, stumbled to her feet, went to the window.

"I'm good at this, Amarta."

She looked out at the gardens below, a world away, hearing his slow steps come close behind.

Could she break this glass and throw herself to the gardens below?

Shards of glass fell away from the opening, but she herself could not get through because he held her.

"Remember the forest, Amarta? How you slipped by me, over and over? I think you could do that now, perhaps better than ever before. You might even get out of this room. If you need to prove to yourself that you've done everything you can to resist this, I understand. Go ahead and fight me, if you wish."

What would it gain her?

Guards, so many the room was packed, each one cutting off a possible escape. She was held, tied, carried out of the room.

Tayre knew what she was.

"It is the same," she said, looking down onto the garden below, wanting to drink in every bit of color she could before the world turned dark. She stared at the pink and white stone wall across the way. "I'm afraid."

He put a hand on her arm and from behind her spoke. "I know you, Seer—you can do this."

The words startled her, like a shot that went deeper

than it should. She turned her back to the window to look at him. His face held a hint of a smile. She felt—what? A touch of hope.

Was this another way to draw her in, to make her fall harder and farther later?

"So," he said. "Will you fight, or shall we walk there together?"

"Tayre, I'm not ready."

He took her hands in his. It was, she foresaw, one of the few gentle touches she would feel for some time.

"There are things you can't be ready for. This is one of them."

They descended into the palace's basements, through dim corridors, down steps carved from dark stone. The windowless, lamplit room into which they were led was suddenly quiet as the many guards escorting them streamed out.

He dropped the bolt on the inside of the door and set a large pack on one of three large, wooden tables. On one was a paper map of the empire, on another a white cloth, and on the third, nothing.

Her gaze stayed on this last table as vision gave hint of the grain of the wood, up close.

"I will tell you how I will do this," he said as he opened his pack. It was the same tone he might have used when they had been traveling north from Kelerre, perhaps discussing a possible route or the care and feeding of the horses.

He took a folded bundle out of his pack and unrolled it across the white linen, revealing a set of knives. He set them on the white linen one by one as he spoke. "First I make you afraid. I make sure you believe that I will hurt you past your ability to bear. I think we have achieved that." He looked at her. "Yes?"

She struggled to slow her breathing. "Yes."

He took out from the pack a coiled rope, then another, setting them atop each other. "With you," he said, "this is somewhat easier; I set my intent to hurt you, and you believe me because you can see it happening in your future. It's almost as though you read my mind."

Next he brought out three sets of pliers, each one smaller than the last, setting them beside each other on the table.

The pain would not stop, no matter what she said. She could not breathe.

She gulped air.

"You, in your terror," he continued, "hide very little. It is almost as if I can read *your* mind. You see?" He paused in arranging the tools and looked at her thoughtfully, a look she could almost mistake for concern.

She was shaking now and could not seem to stop.

"Next, I ask you questions—some I know the answers to, some I don't—to better judge your responses for veracity. As it happens, I know you pretty well already, though"—he gestured to the room—"a different place and time means I will need to fine-tune my perceptions. Do you understand all this?"

"Why can't I just tell you what you want to know and you don't hurt me at all?"

"Why indeed?" he replied, taking out from the pack an iron-headed mallet, then three more, of varying different sizes, setting them next to each other. "Because of your ability, I can only deceive you so far with my pure intent—the things I conceive must actually occur in order to convince your foresight. Equally important, the Lord Commander will find it challenging to believe my work was effective if there isn't convincing physical evidence. He must see the signs of it on you, and his guards must hear something through the heavy door to report back."

"Are you saying this is all for show?"

"There is no such thing. Presentation is not distinct from substance." More items from the pack. A chisel. Large needles. He looked at her. "Do you trust me?"

"No."

He held large shears now, opening and closing them, putting a touch of oil on them from a small jar. He set them at the end of the set of tools.

Somehow she could not seem to look away from his hands arranging the tools.

"That is a lie," he said mildly. "Try again."

It was hard to force the words out. "I don't want to trust you."

"Now *that* I believe. Good. Where are your sister and nephew?"

"What?" For a moment anger overcame the terror that had frozen her where she stood. "My contract protects them. I don't have to tell you that."

"I know what your contract says. You will tell me."

"I won't."

Or would she?

No; she would not look to find out. If he were right, she couldn't bear to know.

Air. She needed air.

She had been holding her breath. She gulped an inhale.

In his hand was a flat stone. He picked up one of the knives, began to draw it across the stone. Sharpening the knife.

Again her breath caught.

"Lie to me," he urged.

She swallowed hard. "They are in Munasee."

"Good." For a moment the only sound was metal against stone. "Now tell me the truth."

"He'll find them. He'll kill them. No. I can't. I would rather die."

He made a thoughtful sound as he placed the sharpened knife on the linen. "I believe you, but I won't let you. I will, however, break parts of you. Let me show you how." He picked up one of the metal mallets with one hand and with the other hand patted the edge of the empty table. "I will tie you here, with your hands over this edge—see these metal rings? Very snug. Finger across here, then a sharp hit and they break. Where are your sister and nephew?"

"You'll do it anyway," she managed, suddenly sure, nauseated at the pain that accompanied the flash of vision.

"Yes. But how many fingers? Which hand? Can you tell?"

She shook her head wordlessly.

"Because I haven't decided yet. What is the most important thing the Lord Commander needs to know?"

"That the future he asks for—*no* path will lead there. The empire *must* become smaller. Or . . ." She looked around furtively. After all these days with the Lord Commander, it felt like treason to say aloud. "Or end. Entirely."

He nodded, walked to the map, studied it a moment. "He thinks you have answers you are keeping hidden. I think he is right."

"What? No! I've told him everything. Everything he's asked. I've—"

"What do you want, Amarta?" He gestured at the map. "Show me."

She looked at the map table. "Peace in the empire."

He laughed a little. "There has never been peace in the empire. I don't believe you. Answer again. Dirina and Pas, perhaps?"

"Yes, I want them to—" She looked south on the map, toward Perripur, with a shock realizing that he was watching her. She looked back at him, hoping she had not already given too much away. "I want them safe. From you. From him." From the man who had come in the night so many years ago, asking questions.

He nodded. "What else?"

"I want to stop the Lord Commander from causing so much suffering."

"What do you care if strangers suffer?"

"I care," she said, suddenly angry.

He shook his head. "I don't believe you. Try again."

"I pray you to the deepest hell." She pushed away from the table, walking away from him and the map, as far as the room would allow, coming to the table with the tools.

She picked up the mallet. "This? You threaten me with

this?" Without thought she hurled it at him. It sailed end over end. For a moment her aim seemed impossibly good; it flew toward his face.

Then he raised his hand and somehow caught it by the handle, held it a moment for her to see, then tossed it on the empty table, where it landed with a heavy thud. "I'm going to let you choose which hand, Amarta. Since your right hand is your strong hand, I recommend the left."

"You're a monster." She grabbed the linen of the table in her hands and yanked it as hard as she could. The tools scattered across the floor. She was trembling all over. Gasping.

He walked toward her, stepping over the tools on the ground, seeming unconcerned.

"Do you trust me?" he asked.

"I hate you."

"Yes, but do you trust me?"

"You told me not to."

"So I did. And?"

She shouldn't. She knew better. "Yes," she admitted.

He stepped close enough that she could smell him, tangling her feelings. He took her shoulders, looked into her eyes. "Then tell me everything, without hesitation, and I'll take you through this as well and as quickly as I can."

"You'll hurt me."

"Less than anyone else who would be standing in front of you right now."

"No."

He released her and went back to the table with the map. "You say the empire becomes smaller. Tomorrow? Two days hence?"

"Not so soon. He asks for outcomes in years. Decades. There are no answers that satisfy him."

"It is the nature of people to ask poor questions. Ignore his words. Consider his needs. What gets him a step closer to his intention? Not years hence, but tomorrow?"

"Tomorrow?" She shook her head. "What he does tomorrow will not give him what he wants in ten years."

"Perhaps not." He put both hands on the map table. "But every step he takes changes him, and that, I think, will change what's possible. What understanding can you give him, Seer, however small, to achieve his hopes, however distant and unlikely?"

She walked to the other side of the table and put a finger on the western edge of Arunkel, where it met the sea, and considered the question.

Not what would happen, and not what someone might do to achieve some end. Rather, how a person might need to change, so that they could go in a particular direction.

The sun rose. Where sky met earth a dark, uninterrupted band of near-black stretched wide across the land.

She looked at the map, following the great road with her eyes, so familiar from days of standing in the map room. "He so often looks north and south," she said. "I think he should look east."

"How far east?"

"I don't know."

"What do you see?"

"A thick, dark line on the horizon."

"Ah. The Dalgo Rift." He touched one side of the map

where there was a heavy, straight line, north and south. "The edge of the Empire. Back to you, Seer: tell me what you want most of all."

Not to be facing this man, who had somehow had gotten inside her mind, gaining her trust. "To be somewhere else."

"And if you were there, this somewhere else, what then?"

The dark room flickered in the light of wall-mounted lamps. Why was he asking this? She did not understand.

But he was right, she trusted him.

What did she want, if she could have anything? It was not something she had considered before.

"I say a thing and people die," she found herself saying. "I stay silent and people die. I want to be free."

"And what do you need to know? What is your next step toward this freedom?"

For some reason she had stopped trembling.

"Go on," he urged. "Look. Just as you would for another."

It was harder to foresee for herself. Painful. Her eyes went to the table where the linen and tools had been, then to the floor where they now lay.

She held up a hand. He nodded slowly.

"No," she breathed.

Watching her face he said, "I think yes. A good beginning, in any case. What else? Look again."

She didn't want to, but there was something in his expression now—a warm smile—that somehow compelled her. Almost as if this, what they did here together, would not be so bad.

How did he do such things with a few words and a look?

"Freedom," she mouthed, looking around the room. At the map, the tools on the floor, the empty table, back at him. What was a step forward in that impossible direction?

Dead bodies lay strewn in every direction, as if someone had scattered loads of firewood across the field. She stood in the middle, turning and turning, looking at the sky and the thick column of smoke over the rise. Someone, somewhere, called her name. She had been the cause of their deaths, as surely as if she had cut each one down herself, yet all she felt was a fierce joy.

"No," she breathed in horror.

"Again, the ring of truth," he said. "Now the same question, but for the Lord Commander. Not in a year or five or even twenty, Amarta, but in a matter of days. What does he most need, to come closest to his intention?"

The sound of a gold coin being set decisively on a wood table. Someone spoke, an urgent tone. A warning.

"A souver, on his desk. Someone says something. I think it's an accusation. He will wonder if it is true."

"And is it?"

"Yes. Though the speaker is . . ." She shook her head. "Not telling him everything. Still it is true. That's all I see."

"Well done, Amarta." The gentle clink of metal brought her gaze back to him. He picked up a tool and the linen from the floor, arranged them on the table. Dread trickled back into her.

"Your sister and nephew," he said. "Where are they?"

It would be her final failure to tell him this, the last

thing that gave her life its worth. But as she looked at him, she knew he would take it from her. She could not allow herself to tell him, but she sensed she would anyway. What to do? What to say?

Suddenly she knew.

She breathed out, not quite a laugh, then walked to the map, put her finger on Munasee, met his look evenly. "They are with Marisel dua Mage, under her protection. If I tell you where that is, I think you will be answerable to her for any outcome. Shall I move my finger from Munasee to where I left them, or no?"

For a moment he stood unmoving. Then, with a slow smile, he said, "That is sufficient answer, Seer."

She exhaled her relief.

He picked up the remaining tools from the floor and laid them out again on the white linen. Then she remembered what this was. Why they were here.

"Fear is like a wolf," he said as he aligned the knives. "It howls at the door. It distracts and unnerves. But fear is a shadow, not the wolf at all."

A shadow. As he had been her shadow for so long.

"Are you saying that I should not be afraid now, that the wolf has no substance?"

He glanced at her, then back at his tools. "No. The wolf is quite real. But they are two different things, the wolf and the fear. Only the wolf can bite. Fear makes you bite yourself. Do you understand?"

She hugged herself, considering. "I think so."

"Good."

So many shadows. She took a step in his direction, paused, then took another and stopped.

He looked at her. For a moment the only sound she heard was her own breath.

"This one," she whispered, holding up her left hand.

Amarta woke slowly, reluctantly, at first not understanding why she would be holding herself so still. At a slight movement memory rushed back, helped along by a series of sharp pains and aches across her body. Her throat was sore. Her ribs ached. Her feet burned.

Again she went still.

The room around her was quiet and bright with daylight. In vision, there were no dark clouds of pain. In the past, finally.

Her left hand was heavily bandaged. Despite the shooting pain, curiosity drove her to move each finger. The middle three, it seemed. He had broken three.

There had been more questions, many of them the same. She had started with the truth and ended with it as well, having no more reason to lie, but in between, when the pain did not cease, she had said things that she had not expected to, little of it to do with the course of the Empire. She confessed to him how she had let her parents die on the side of a mountain one day because she was afraid to believe what she had foreseen the night before. She cried her terror of Dirina and Pas dying, caught in the horror of war and death that would sweep south.

In a strange state brought on by pain and exhaustion, not awake and not asleep, she became lost in images and memories and visions, unsure what was in the past or the future. Horses and fire. The Lord Commander angry again. Someone laughing. Someone screaming.

Or perhaps she was the one screaming and laughing. She was no longer sure.

She could not quite remember when it ended, though it seemed to her there were more people in the room, the Lord Commander among them, that she was inspected, spoken of, and wrapped in blankets, carried to her room, laid down in the soft bed.

She hugged the bed and wept. Nothing, it seemed, in the brief moments before she lost awareness, had ever felt so good.

How long she had slept, she did not know. But now, in the light of day, her body a mass of aches and bruises, ointments and bandages, she recalled the various things she had foreseen under Tayre's questioning and wondered what, if anything, had changed.

When she next started awake it was from a dream. His hands were in front of her face, holding sharp metal tools with glinting points and edges that flickered in the lamplight. Then they were his empty hands, which somehow could also make so much of her hurt so astonishingly.

The red and white room settled around her, quiet, bright. She was still so very tired. A heat burned across her body and through her head, each heartbeat bringing a dull ache, joined by many other points of pain. For a time she simply lay there, dozing.

She woke again when the lock clicked and the door opened. In walked the Lord Commander with a tray of food and a cylinder of tea. He put it on the table by her bed, brought a chair close and sat at her side.

She struggled to sit up. Silently he helped her, then offered a bite of bread. She shook her head.

"This, then," he said, offering a cup of tea. She took it, but her hand shook enough that he took it back, holding it to her lips while she drank. He set the cup down and took her chin in his hand, turning her head each way, examining her face.

He nodded. "You'll heal."

She looked up at him, this man who had hired so many people to capture her, to threaten her life, to question her. He had, she suddenly realized, spent a lot of coin on her across many years. She had not, until this very moment, quite understood that, and what it might mean.

"Your questioner has relayed to me the visions you revealed to him. He assures me you now know how to give me better answers, answers I need, and it won't be necessary for us to do this again. Is this so?"

Do this again? She swallowed, wincing at the pain that followed.

So many days of struggling to give him the answers he demanded. But that was wrong, she now understood.

Fear is a shadow. Only the wolf bites.

"Well?"

She searched his eyes. Then, as sore as she was, inside and out, she searched his future.

A fist clenching around something sharp. A hand coming away from a shoulder, bloody, shaking. A bone die, turning over and over, coming to rest sun-side up.

"I think so, Lord Commander."

"I am pleased to hear it." He stood, gave an abrupt

nod. "You will rest. Tomorrow and the next day. Then we resume."

What was he, wolf or shadow, this man who had hunted her and bought her as one might buy an animal or a slave?

"I don't think so, ser," she said.

He turned back, eyes narrowed, expression hardening, but she could see behind his quick temper a touch of uncertainty. Had that been there before? Had her own fear blinded her?

Tayre was right: fear made you bite yourself.

"Explain," he said brusquely.

She struggled to sit up straighter, inhaling as pain shot through her. "I think you will be busy, ser."

"What do you see?"

A swirl of colors, of brown and beige, blue and green, orange and gray. A spark of gold. A puddle of blood.

But what did he need to know? To do?

"Horses. Wagons. Soldiers. I think you are assembling an army."

"In three days?" He did not believe her. Again. She chuckled a little.

Now he was annoyed. "What amuses you, Seer?"

She shook her head, sinking back into the bed and blankets, exhaustion coming over her again.

Something was coming for Innel sev Cern esse Arunkel, some set of forces that had been in motion for some time. But what, exactly, she could not tell, not yet.

As she began to drift off to sleep, she heard the door close and the lock click.

Chapter Thirty-one

After a few hours, the shrieking and howling had put Innel into a rather testy mood.

Standing these many hours beside and a bit behind the queen, he had time to reflect on the vast difference between the howl of pain of a freshly orphaned child and the lamentations of a House ingénue determined to be remembered for a display of grief.

Around him was a small crowd of those royals who happened to be in-city at the king's sudden demise. Together they watched the trail of aristos slowly feed into the Great Hall, winding around like a sluggish sewer.

Their first stop was the queen, each one to offer obeisance and demonstration of fealty with a full formal bow. It seemed a good time for it, with the king finally and truly dead. Some, once on hands and knees, needed help to rise before they continued in the slow line toward the king's body.

The king was laid out grandly amidst plush reds and deep blacks on a platform carefully constructed in appropriate proportions of metal, wood, stone, amardide and so on—every substance created and overseen by Houses, Greater and Lesser, so that no one might be insulted at the lack of their product being part of the king's last foundation.

There the displays of anguish reached greatest intensity as clumps of aristos, with a look at the king's face, keened cries of shock as though they had not, until this very moment, realized the truth of what they had been told. Rending of clothes seemed to be the current practice at this point, but it had been added onto with a stumble off the single-step platform, then a crumpling to the marble floor beyond, as if so overcome with sorrow that they could not stay standing another moment. There they lay, wailing until one of the properly solemn retainers attempted to help them rise. Some refused, still howling inconsolably into the marble.

This did nothing to speed the line.

The queen sat on a great high-backed chair, a neutral look on her face that Innel knew she was working hard to maintain. He stood among those who were, by virtue of birth, at least his equal in influence. Small, polite smiles told him that they did not think of him similarly.

But the most interesting displays were at the Table of Memory, the final stop of the shuffling, twisting line. Here the empire's most powerful families fussed among the king's belongings as if haggling at market, their artfully composed expressions of bereavement and studiously scratched faces giving way to avarice, even building toward outrage, making for something resembling an unguarded moment. Soft but urgent discussions had surrounded the Table of Memory since the very first person—Eparch of House Etallan—had stepped up to choose her memory gift.

During the rushed planning of this event, the queen's seneschal had pointed out to Innel that oversight at this table was regrettably needed, or every glove, candlestick, chalice, and comb would quickly be taken. "I will do it, ser," the seneschal had said sourly. "I did it the last time."

Memory gifts were said to focus the prayers and thoughts of the living to help guide the departed's spirit to the Beyond. And, of course, to be kept after, when the dead spirit had presumably found its way toward wherever it was going.

Another loud screech cut through Innel's contemplations. It seemed a number of people were determined to find out if volume could be a substitute for the appearance of sincerity.

While many had come in with faces already artfully scratched to show the depth of their sorrow, now, having little else to do, some had taken to such self-mutilation while standing in line. Most of the line was currently House Sartor, a strange and severe bunch even at the cheeriest of times. The youngers of the House were using something sharp to mark their bare arms, most likely a needle, given the produce of the House. Their red marks were bright enough to constitute a noticeable color tribute to the crown, and quite visually striking when combined with the austere gray and black House colors. A not-very-subtle show of loyalty. Clever, Innel thought.

Was one of them actually dripping blood? She was. Innel was curious to see if the House following would make a point of stepping around the drops of blood or into them.

At last the Great Houses had finally wound past the Table of Memory and out the other end of the large chamber to the next hall, where small delicacies were being served until everyone was through the procession and the formal speeches could begin. Then the feast.

The Great Houses would bow and give homage, wail and rend, wait their turn to own something of the old king's, and listen to long talks about the might of the Empire, but afterwards they would expect to be fed.

The Great Hall's balconies were draped with dark flowers woven through mesh and chain, the many tapestries depicting Restarn's great exploits lining the walls, the decorations as lavish as they had been for the coronation.

"You will want it so," the seneschal had told him with a humorless smile, "because they will compare the two, and further compare this funeral to the Grandmother Queen's—those who were there. Best they find this compares favorably to the extravagances of memory."

The extravagances of memory. In death the old king's reputation had been polished to a brilliant, impossible sheen. The dead could not be held to account.

As the Lesser Houses now bowed to the queen, then made their slow way to the king's body, Innel noticed that the red lines of scratched faces were accompanied by welts on arms and necks, allowing yet more fabric to be rent and torn to reveal this additional grief-induced suffering.

At the king's body, the gray-haired Eparch of

Chandler raised the stakes of how much clothing one could tear off in grief, his welted torso showing bare as he took off his tunic and threw it on the ground, then tore his shirt to shreds, howling in grief, his deep, loud cry cutting across the huge room, catching the eye of the queen—no doubt his intention—who Innel could see was nothing like pleased.

But there was no mistaking any of these screams for true pain. Nothing like what he'd heard yesterday outside the dungeon room door, at the end of the first day of the seer's questioning. He found it reassuring that despite the long stretches of silence coming from the room, something was going on in there besides talk.

He judged that enough time had passed that he could now briefly step away from his place by the queen's side. He spoke softly in her ear for permission and she nodded slightly. He retreated off the dais, Sachare and Srel both converging on him as he tried for the back exit.

Sachare arrived first.

"When this is all over," she whispered to him, "she will not be in a good mood."

"Wine, twunta, sweets. Me," Innel replied. Srel joined their small huddle.

Sachare turned to Srel. "Can we get her aside, before the feast, for a few minutes?"

"Certainly," Srel said.

"Good. I'll get one of the pups for her to hold in the antechamber." To Innel she gave a half smile and apologetic shrug. "It'll help. Trust me. Then—you and the rest."

Innel swallowed the start of indignation. "I defer to you, Cohort sister."

A quick touch on his shoulder to come closer, and he did. "You must talk to Mulack," she said.

"Must I," he said, letting some of his tension show. Then Srel drew him away and out into the corridor, where the Minister of Coin waited, looking dour.

"Minister. What is it?"

She waited for a bevy of servants with platters of food to press by.

"That matter we discussed some months ago," she said softly.

The souver forgeries.

"Yes?"

She cleared her throat, looked again around to be sure they were not overheard. Srel stepped back a few feet into the hallway, subtly describing an area around the two of them that no one would intrude upon.

"They are coming in greater measure, from many directions."

"What?"

"Taxes, merchants. We re-mint them all, of course, but the fact remains: they are in circulation. Prices are rising in the markets. Contracts are being broken, held up for renegotiation."

"But the treasury is—"

"Healthy, yes." She pressed her lips together, and the edges curled down. "So the minister keeps telling us. But that is not enough. To be on the safe side, ser, we might want to buy up some Perripin *aldas*—"

"What?" he hissed at her, outraged. "Never. Arunkel coin is steady—"

"Value, Lord Commander," she whispered back, "is

not the same as numbers. If this keeps up, we are going to have a problem. Or rather, the queen is going to have a problem."

Separating herself from the monarchy. Openly.

"You cross the line, Minister," Innel said sharply.

From beyond the door to the Great Hall came the barely muffled sound of another piercing shriek, accompanied by a deep-throated howl. Yet he could hear the Minister of Coin breathing hard.

"My apologies, Lord Commander," she said, looking down.

"You might by such comments affect the very coin you are sworn to protect. Your words have power. Keep them to yourself."

"Yes, ser. Of course, ser. You can rely on me, ser."

"That had best be the case."

"It is done."

Keyretura sat down across the desk from Innel, looking at ease and as rested as if he had spent the last twenty-four days at the palace rather than riding the monarch's fastest horses across the span of the empire.

"Done? So very quickly? The woman and boy in hand?"

"Yes, that is what 'done' means. Shall I repeat myself?"

Innel decided it was best to ignore the reprimand. "And are they well? Are they safe?"

"They are both. The woman was not reluctant to give earnest and frequent voice to her objections, but that is not particularly surprising. The boy was more capable of finding pleasure in the journey. They are now at the residence you provided, where I made it clear to the chamberlain that they are to be shown every possible comfort within the walls of the manor. You look shocked, Commander."

"No, High One." But it was true, he was. "I am simply not used to such efficiency." To put it mildly.

"You have little exposure to my kind, Commander. Marisel is young. Inexperienced."

At least by comparison, Innel thought, a little dazed by the realization that he actually had the seer's sister and nephew in his possession.

Keyretura spoke again. "You will keep the seer's family safe and secure in your custody, under the terms of the contract I witnessed. An inconvenience for me, if I must enforce that contract; I promise you would find that quite unpleasant. What have I missed here during my little detour?"

Innel digested this threat and nodded his understanding. "I had the seer questioned."

"And?"

Innel had met with Tayre after and found that the man had been entirely correct at their first meeting to say that seeing him would not convince Innel of his ability. Visually the man was entirely unremarkable. But he had gotten useful answers out of her.

"She suggests I look to the Rift."

"All five hundred miles of it?" Keyretura asked, openly amused.

He knew the mage's opinion of her ability and had idly wondered if traveling with her family might change it. Apparently not. "She didn't say."

"Of course she didn't. Vague answers are far harder to test. Planning a trip, then, are you, Commander?"

He ignored the mocking tone. "No."

Not yet, in any case. If she were right, that he would be planning a campaign in a mere matter of days, with no hint of it now, much would need to happen and soon. It was as good a test of her predictions as any.

The Dalgo Rift stretched in a straight line from the northern ocean to the southern Mundaran Sea. The continent continued eastward past the line, but there was no crossing the Rift.

Innel had seen the Rift when he'd been younger, along with the rest of the Cohort, on one of the extended forced marches they'd made under Lason's sadistic education. They were instantly stunned into silence by the mile-wide chasm that descended so far the bottom faded into black, sheer obsidian walls on both sides as slick as ice. Stories of those who had tried to cross were grist to frighten children.

Now he looked around the room, searching the walls for a map that showed that straight, dark line. His gaze caught on the painted shaota figurine and he remembered that day in Arteni, the noise and smoke and screams. The Teva and their strange laughing horses. The man handing him up this very figurine, which he had decided to keep rather than give to the old king.

Following his gaze, Keyretura spoke. "Ah yes, the shaota toys. I've seen them in Kelerre. Popular among the governors' households and the patrician's brats."

Innel stood and walked to the painted metal horse with its brown, black, and tan lines, from eyes to tail. He hefted it in one hand, carrying it to the map. With a finger he traced Otevan's roughly oblong shape, flat side against the edge of the Rift. A bite out of the empire of Arunkel. He looked southward on the map, nearly to the floor, and thought about roads and distances.

"Does it not strike you as odd," Innel said, staring at the map, "to transport such merchandise so very far?"

A small shrug. "Shaota are popular in children's stories. Some parents have an excess of coin and a paucity of sense. Even so . . ." Keyretura gestured for Innel to hand him the figure, and he did.

The mage was silent for a time, holding the small horse between his hands. Innel resumed his seat. Keyretura gave a soft, thoughtful exhale.

"What is it?" asked Innel.

"Wherever these were cast, someone has also been handling gold, in sufficient quantity to leave small amounts of it mixed into the lead."

"*What*? Gold? Are you sure?"

Keyretura set the lead horse on a nearby table and gave him a look. "Is my accent flawed? Did I use a word you didn't understand?"

Innel found himself flushing. "No, High One. I am merely—surprised."

"With some cause. Lead mines do not, as a rule, contain any gold. The contamination implies this foundry is pouring both lead and gold. Which, if I understand your laws correctly, should mean it was done here, in Yarpin, at a particular and well-guarded foundry called the mint. Is that correct?"

"Yes," Innel said slowly. "It is."

Keyretura laughed a little, now seeming even more

amused. "Maybe your fortune-teller is right after all," he said.

That night Innel awoke in the darkness of a moonless night to the sound of the door to his suite opening, a bit of light coming from the hallway lamps, then dark again as the outer door softly closed. No cause for worry; there was only one person his guards would allow inside.

Unless, of course, some treachery had occurred. Now that the king's funeral was gloriously and expensively completed, some across the palace were acting incautiously and unpredictably. Had they really thought Restarn would come back from his illness and take control again?

Innel kept track of them all through his spies as best he could, letting a few plans continue unhindered as long as they did not come to completion. The current turmoil seemed to be pushing people to action, to increasingly blatant attempts to shake Cern's position.

And consequently his own. He could not be too careful.

He rolled out of bed, dropped softly to his hands and knees, pulling the long knife he kept between the floor and his bed. He stood to a crouch, fast, blade ready.

"Innel." Cern's voice.

He sighed, set the knife down again, watching her shadowy form. She kicked off her slippers, stripped off her shirt, let it fall to the floor. Usually she at least toed it to the side. That said something. What?

He lit a lamp. "Your Majesty."

"I've been walking, Innel. Outside, in the gardens. Thinking."

Where she could be picked off like a low-flying duck, from any window, even with guards all around her. "I would so very much prefer that you think indoors, my lady," he said.

She looked out to the gardens below. "I know."

Cern had no succession list, despite his urging. If anything happened to her, the Ministers' Council would very likely consult the old king's list, and Innel was under no illusion that anyone on that list would keep him in his current position of Lord Commander.

He had been focusing so hard to shore up her reign, to keep the empire's borders strong, to bring the mining towns back into line, that he had not given enough consideration to his own situation should Cern's reign truly stumble.

Concerned for her safety, he had told her repeatedly, not mentioning his own. But she was no fool.

"You won't be on the list, Innel," she said, following his unspoken thoughts. "You couldn't hold the Houses."

"I understand that, my lady."

It rankled, but he knew it to be so. He had worked harder to achieve his position than any of his Cohort brothers, and his father had been one of the king's generals, but it was not enough. Never enough.

She turned to face him. "I've wanted to be free of him my whole life. Now I am. Why doesn't it feel like it?" Something about her expression reminded him of her when she had been so much younger, a child. When he'd finally understood that he would devote his life to being the mate she needed.

And he had.

"The ladder is climbed one rung at a time," he said, quoting his brother. He wondered a moment too late if she would remember this as well, and if that were a good plan. If she did, she didn't show it.

"My father wanted to push the border south into Perripur. He always thought Kelerre should be ours. Did you know that?"

"I heard him say so, once." A rare, late night chat with a handful of the near-adult Cohort, drinking and smoking with the king until first light.

"The mountain mines," she said. "The tribes. The borders. So much defiance." She shook her head. "We are in very deep now, Innel."

"Transitions are difficult times," he said, echoing Lismar. "We will take them all in hand. It will be settled. Soon."

"These battles are costing us, Innel. It will cost us more yet to win them. If we even can. Perhaps we should stop spending so much to war against our own people. Let them withdraw if they want to."

From anyone else, words of treason. Innel suddenly felt very tired. "My lady—"

"We could at least talk to the mining towns," she said. "Find out what they would do with their independence if they had it."

"Cern, that would be—you have no idea what kind of rebellion that would encourage."

"No idea?" She turned on him. "Don't you think I might have some idea, Innel? Some small glimmer of conception, after the many years I also spent in the Cohort, studying beside you and forty of the most cunning and unpleasant of the empire's aristo whelps?"

"I only meant—"

"I know what you meant, but I will not be insulted. Yes, I know there is a cost to asking those questions. But what is the cost of continuing as we are now?"

"We cannot know."

"No? She named the die roll, Innel. Every time. A hundred times."

He had known it was a mistake to let Cern go off with the seer, but there was little he could do besides point out that the young woman was still recovering from questioning, that it might be best to let her heal. Cern had not been dissuaded in the least, simply directing her guards to carry the girl, blankets and all.

"Dice are simple," he said. "An empire is not."

She laughed humorlessly. "That much is clear. You don't believe her, that if we fight to keep the empire whole, it will crumble into pieces. You spent so much time and coin to get her in hand, Innel, to bruise and break her, and now you ignore her advice?"

"What does she truly know? It is easy to make predictions," he said, realizing he was echoing Keyretura.

Cern exhaled. "I don't want to believe her, either. But it is not going well on the borders. Or in the mountains. What of Erakat? Garaya?"

"Garaya and Erakat will comply. I will make sure of it."

A victory at Garaya would turn all this around. He thought of Sutarnan leading a force to take back the walled city, mere weeks from arriving. He wondered if he should have sent more troops.

"Are you sure? Innel, are you sure?"

Was he? He had better be. "Yes. I can quiet this unrest. I only need a bit more time."

"I don't know how much of that we have left," she said softly. "I've been on the throne nearly two years. People are starting to wonder if things will ever be better than when I took it."

He could not argue with that. Restarn's passing had made people think fondly of past glories. That the old king had borrowed against the future to fund his expansions, that these debts were now coming due—no one wanted to hear about that.

"Innel," she said, "maybe . . ."

He held his breath. His mind, unbidden, found many ways to finish that sentence.

Maybe she had promoted him too far, too fast. Maybe he should resign. Maybe . . .

He waited, keeping his musings from his face.

"Maybe now that he's dead, things will be better."

"I'm sure of it," he said with relief.

After a long moment, Cern took his hand and drew him under the covers, silently pulling his arms around her as she curled into a half-ball. As she began to breathe evenly, he lay there, unmoving, feeling her warmth against the front of his body and wondering what he would do if it all came crashing down.

"I like what you've done there." Mulack motioned with his wine goblet out the window of Innel's office. Innel and the Eparch-heir of Murice had run through the polite conversation available to them. It hadn't taken very long.

"Putar has returned from Sinetel," Innel said, explaining.

Through the window, Execution Square looked like a huge cat's cradle with the three traitors as hands. Returned from Sinetel as rebels, they had been allowed to keep their clothes on for the execution, a rare allowance, but now that Innel saw what Putar had in mind, he saw why. The hooks were embedded deep into the fleshiest parts of the three of them, simply going right through the cloth, as if to say that there was no hiding from the retribution of the empire.

Each hook was pulled taut by cables that moved freely around grooved tracks in vertical posts thoughtfully arranged around the square. Each was further hooked into another of the three traitors, such that each one who moved affected the barb in another's flesh. Such movement could not really be avoided, not when the geared spikes mounted on the very same posts clicked forward into the skin of each sufferer, advancing with the bells of the hours.

From the looks of it, the three had stopped discussing the strategy of lessening their suffering by working together and were now screaming at each other.

Pain and impending penetration could do that to people.

"Ah, of course. I should have recognized his touch," Mulack said.

"He has a knack," Innel agreed. "As much as I enjoy your company, Mulack, I do have rather a lot to do. So—"

Mulack held out his cup for more wine.

Eparch-heir, Innel reminded himself, refilling the cup

with as much courtesy as he could. Mulack drained it noisily, leaving his lips wet with the dark red wine, wiping his mouth on the sleeve of his purple and cloud-white jacket, leaving tracks on the cuffs.

The message was neither subtle nor new: Mulack could easily afford to replace his expensive jacket every day of the year if he so chose. The only stains on Mulack's clothes would be the ones he enjoyed.

Innel sat back, hoping his stare might inspire the man to come to the point.

Mulack's gaze roamed languidly around the room. At last, adjusting his now-wine-stained jacket, he placed his dripping cup on Innel's desk, rather closer than Innel liked to the detailed map of the Rift he'd been studying. Innel moved the map away.

"Last night," Mulack said, with the air of someone about to say something of consequence, "I was sitting on the crapper, thinking about you. Thinking, indeed, about the many conversations I've been hearing in which you are mentioned. It occurred to me that I must do something about it."

"You needed to see me alone to tell me how well you wipe your ass? Congratulations, Eparch-heir. I'll see if I can arrange a parade."

A small laugh. "Listen to me or not, but I'll be eparch in a few years, Innel, no matter what happens to you, *Lord Commander*."

Innel very much wanted to wipe the smirk off Mulack's face. Instead he forced himself to slowly exhale. "More wine?" he asked politely.

"Yes, I think so."

Innel poured, focusing on this action to both clear his mind and his temper.

Mulack took his cup, his smallest finger uncurled and pointed at Innel. "I know we've had our differences across the years. But here it is, straight as an arrow: people are talking about you."

"They always talk about me."

"Yes, but it's no longer about your uncommon rise to position or your pretty face. Now they are asking who else could be Lord Commander. People are losing faith in you, Innel."

"*People* are, are they?" Innel said, hearing the edge in his voice. He could not count the times Mulack had said such things to him and Pohut as they came up in the Cohort. Mulack was very good at sowing doubt. "Why should I credit this, coming from you? Given our, as you say, differences?"

Mulack's expression turned serious. "Surprising myself as much as anyone, Innel, I want to keep you here. I know the others who could take this position from you, and much as it makes me want to empty my stomach onto the floor right here and now to say it, good wine and all, you're the better choice."

"I suppose your reluctant support is better than the alternative."

"Far better, I assure you."

"Is there advice coming, Eparch-heir?"

A wide gesture. "Pah. Why bother? You're not going to listen to me."

"The advice of an enemy is gold. We've had our differences, Mulack, but gold is always welcome."

At this Mulack laughed. "So it is. Smart move, the mage. No one knows for sure if he's the real thing, so you've got everyone on edge. Amazing what a quality black robe will do, isn't it?. I think Murice should start making them. Tell me, is this woman you're having interrogated in the dungeons really the fortune-teller of rumor?"

Innel's stomach clenched at this fast change of topic and how Amarta's story had traveled. He forced himself to chuckle. "Good," he said. "I was worried the story would seem too far-fetched. She's a cousin of mine who has been saying some unflattering things about my dead father. We are—reconciling our differences."

"Ah, that makes more sense."

"So. Your advice, Mulack, Eparch-heir?"

Mulack leaned forward, his gaze steady. "Win something, Innel."

Toward the evening of the second day since Innel had finished having the seer questioned, Srel opened the door to his office to let in Tokerae dele Etallan.

"Eparch-heir. What a pleasure. What can I—"

"There's something you should know. I think it's rather important."

"Go on."

Still standing, Tok set a gold souver firmly on the desk in front of Innel. Innel picked it up and examined it closely. He knew what to look for now. The horse's teeth. The king's eyes. But first to be sure Tok and he were talking about the same thing. "And . . . ?" he prompted.

Tok's grimace gave Innel the distinct impression that

Tok knew perfectly well what the problem was. The other man settled himself into the chair across from Innel and gave a long sigh. "You should have told me, Innel. We've been working on the same problem."

"We have?"

"It's not as if Etallan wouldn't be the first House to be suspected, brother. We do know our metals."

So Tok knew, and that meant Etallan knew. Who else knew?

"You do indeed. And so—" He gestured to the coin, raised his eyebrows.

"An excellent forgery. Good enough that we had no idea, until . . ." Another look. "I really shouldn't tell you this. My eparch mother would be quite unhappy if she found out."

"I wouldn't want to get between you and your eparch, Tok."

Tok waved this away. "Ah, well, there comes a time to take control away from them, doesn't there? Something I think you already know." He gave Innel a conspiratorial smile, which Innel found unsettling for its implications about the king. He kept his expression tidy. "You will keep my secret?" Tok asked.

"You can rely on me."

"Good. So, here it is: we test souvers regularly, to see what the Minister of Coin is cooking up in each batch. Dimensions, mix, and so on. I dare say that our records of changes to the silver and copper in the gold are quite possibly even more detailed than the Minister of Coin's."

"I'm hardly shocked."

"One thing to know it, another to admit it, yes? In the course of doing our, hmm, informal audits, we discovered that this particular coin stood out. Far purer. It's clear this and its like didn't come from the crown. Tell me I'm wrong."

"I can't," Innel admitted.

"We suspect Helata of this treason."

"Of course you do."

"Hear me out." He leaned forward, his tone earnest. "We don't even make their boat anchors any more. You know this, Innel."

"Even Sartor has smithies, Tok."

"By that logic, it could be Nital, or Elupene, or even Kincel."

"I think you've made my point for me. What makes you think it's a House at all?"

"That is another, perhaps more disturbing possibility yet: it could be a foreign power. Which I thought might concern you rather directly, Lord Commander."

This Innel had not considered. If Perripur were forging the coins—

No, they could not take on Perripur. Even Restarn, wanting Kelerre as badly as he did, had not tried. If their neighbor to the south were forging souvers, that could be a real problem. Still—

"That makes no sense. Perripur has a solid currency. They have no need to forge our currency."

"I don't mean Perripur. We traced the circulation origin of these coins to Sio."

Sio. The province east of Varo. The one right before Otevan.

Innel leaned back in his chair and exhaled in a long stream, making a hissing sound between his teeth.

Tok watched closely. "You don't look nearly as surprised as I thought you'd be."

"No."

On the morning of the third day since the seer had finished being questioned, Innel was up well before dawn. He nodded to the guards outside Amarta's room, who opened the door for him, and he went in.

By her bed he sat, watching her sleep. Thinking.

He saw no reason to mention her sister and nephew, not yet, not while she was being cooperative. Something to hold in reserve against need.

She must have heard him move, because she made a noise in her sleep, a startled, soft cry. Her eyes came open and she sat up quickly, using her unbandaged hand to push herself back to the headboard. Away from him.

Her eyes were wide, face yellowed and purpled, noticeably swollen on one side, lip split. But her gaze tracked him without issue. Her mind was sound.

What was she thinking now? That he might question her again? What went through her mind?

Or was she looking into the future?

"This morning," he said, "I go to the queen and tell her I must arrange a force to send to Otevan. To find out what they are doing there. You were right. You foresaw this."

She nodded.

"Here is my question, Seer." He paused a moment, considering how to phrase it. "In order to keep the empire whole—as whole as is possible—whom do I send to command this force? Handled correctly, it is possible it need not come to conflict at all. Who best to command?"

She looked at him and then looked distantly. "I think you, ser."

"I thought the same." He considered who else to take. Who knew the Teva best?

"General Lismar," he said. "A short woman. Cropped gray hair. Is she there?"

She blinked, seeming to consider. "I think so, ser."

"Good." He stood. "It will take some time to arrange." Cavalry, infantry, supply wagons. There was work to do. "You," he said, "will also come."

It was not a question. That would be too close to asking her permission. Still, he waited, in case she had a reply.

"Yes, ser," she said at last, but he could not tell if she were agreeing with him or speaking from foresight.

It didn't matter; she would come, and she would help him, and they would win this.

After a moment, he nodded and left to get started.

Chapter Thirty-two

Maris slept poorly, and the closer the three of them came to Yarpin, the worse it got. This morning, now only a day away, she felt the tension all through. A tightness in her shoulders, a pressure in her head. Too close to him. Far too close.

So she'd finally said good-bye to them both, leaving Amarta and Enlon with suitable encouragement and warnings. She checked her horse's packs one last time and glanced up at the many-storied inn to the window of the room in which they had stayed the night.

Someone had decided to use every House color possible and a few others besides. She still couldn't quite decide if the varied paint betokened extreme courage or shocking obsequiousness. Perhaps an effective show of loyalty to the Houses, Maris could not say, but it was certainly a cacophony that suited no aesthetic.

Her horse snorted.

"It is truth," she said softly to him in Perripin, and mounted up, turning south, eager to put distance between herself and the capital city.

She had meant to do so some time back. At the start her goal was to help Amarta past the worst of the strife that was tugging loose the threads of the empire's cohesion. Then she had come to enjoy the journey itself. Enlon was one of the few Ilibans she could stand for long. Nearly a friend, she supposed.

The terror he invoked in Amarta had given Maris another reason to travel with them, to stay another night, then another. Each morning she would tell herself that Amarta was well on her way, that it was time to turn around, but she would find new reasons to continue.

Dirina and Pas would be well enough without her, with the garden and fruited trees thick around the house, jars filled with preserved meats and grains. They had enough food to see them through a whole season if they needed it. There was no need to rush back.

Yet there was no good reason to have come this far, either.

She was almost sure that Yarpin was too far from here for Keyretura to sense her, but it was as if she could feel him anyway: a weighty, ominous presence.

Or maybe she could; she did not entirely understand the bond between *aetur* and *uslata*. That the connection endured, she knew, but how far away he could feel her, she was less sure of.

In any case, she was leaving now. She had decided to take the Traveler's Road through the mountains. Fewer people and more trees. A welcome distance from the draining presses and pulls of too many Iliban.

At least that had been her intention, but as she let her wandering inclination work through her horse's hooves, taking one detour after another, she found herself climbing a familiar path up a mountainside.

So be it.

She tethered the horse where he could nibble the tall summer grass and walked the road upwards to Samnt's parents' farm, dusting herself in shadow with a hint of leaves and mottled sunlight. At the base of a large oak at the edge of the farm she sat and waited.

When Samnt at last emerged from the farmhouse, she found herself smiling. Two years had grown him tall and lanky, shoulders broader, face longer. And was that was a hint of downy fuzz on his upper lip?

For a time she simply watched as he inspected the knee-high amaranth seedlings. He seemed melancholy and somber, but when a younger sibling came out, he laughed and put an arm around her. Perhaps Maris had not, after all, with that last, hard lesson between them— so much like what Keyretura might have done—done more than bruised his spirit.

As she watched him, she wondered: would she, had she known then what she knew now, have fought the unsmiling, black-robed man who had taken her in his iron grip, plucking her away from the only home she had ever known?

Perhaps Samnt had been right that he was too ambitious and clever to be content as a farmer, digging ditches, planting, harvesting. Or maybe he was lucky beyond reckoning to have no one to take him from this warm, sweet home.

Grimacing, she stood, brushed off her trousers, and walked down the hill.

✣ ✣ ✣

Each day she rode south through the mountains she felt herself ease a bit further. Days would pass where she saw no one at all, only trees of substance and age, branches towering over thick ferns and saplings, all atop a living loam of underbrush and roots, lush with life going deep into the earth.

The Traveler's Road saw her through these thick forests that then gave way to high grasslands and hills. At summits she could see the lands stretch away in all directions, clouds rushing by overhead.

At a deserted crossroads where madrone and salal and hemlock grew, three men on horses surrounded her, pulling out long, notched knives and heavy sticks. They ordered her off her horse and made threats and demands.

She put fingers of thought into all three at once, so none of them would be distracted by the suffering of their companions as they doubled over in pain, unable to breathe, struggling to stay in their saddles, which Maris made sure they could not. They slid off their horses, finding their way to the ground with heavy thuds, writhing in silent agony with their various breaks and bruises.

When she was sure she had their attention, she spoke for a time, sympathizing with the difficulty of identifying a mage who didn't wear the black, commenting on the inadvisability of being rude to travelers, and conveying her annoyance at being thus inconvenienced. She urged them to share this cautionary story with others.

The land and trees had put her in a generally good mood, so she let them live. They'd heal in time, but it would be a long and challenging walk back to wherever they came from, because she gave their horses a small spark of encouragement so that they would be happy to be quickly gone from the area.

Then she continued south.

It was a delicious time of year, the scents of the land rich and full, flowers and trees intent on the business of life. Her nights were abundant with stars, mornings glorious with birds.

Another week south and then another, and she was passing brown and green patches of newly planted fields in the highlands, goats reaching their heads through fences, bleating hopefully, chickens chattering and calling.

On a warm day she stripped off her overshirt, stuffed it into one of the side packs, then stopped her horse at a bend in the road to watch an old man standing there. He held a large stone and stared at a pile of rocks by the crumbling remains of a wall that had once held the hillside back from the road.

He was speaking something that sounded like a long, thoughtful curse. Seeing Maris, he stopped in mid-word.

"Perripin," he muttered. "Don't get many of your kind here."

"Blessings of the season to you, grandfather," she said.

He grinned, showing more gaps than teeth. "Yes, yes. Blessings and so forth. You get old, you forget to say polite things. You look at one thing and another pops into your head, and then a third thing comes out your mouth. Ah—" He waved a hand. "You'll see. My woman tells me I'm just a forgetful old man. Then she tells me something else, but I can't remember what." His grin widened.

Maris smiled at the ancient joke.

"Not this one," he said tossing the stone he held to the outer edge of the pile. He bent to pick up another one, standing slowly, wincing, a hand on his lower back. "Pah," he said, and dropped the second stone as well, grunting as he pushed rocks out of the way with his foot, walking around the pile. "Where did the long, flat one go?"

"How many times have you rebuilt this wall, old man?"

He snorted. "What makes you think it's mine? Maybe I just happened by. Could be my neighbor's and I'm being helpful." He bent his knees, crouched down over yet another rock.

"Could be. But I think you've rebuilt it before."

"Nothing wrong with rebuilding."

"If you use mortar, it might stay up next time."

"The stones fit fine without any of that fuss."

"Except that they seem to have fallen down."

He stood, frowned, looked at her. "Yes, woman, they fall down. Then I put them back. You just going to sit on your horse and watch? Or you going to help?"

Maris chuckled, swung down onto her feet, and picked up the stone he had been looking for, handing it to him. He placed it on a gap in the wall where it fit snugly.

"There," he said, proudly. "You see?"

"I see. But it will fall again."

"Then I'll put it back up. As long as the wall needs me. Until my last sleep."

Maris touched into the man's body. He had a strong heart. He could easily live another ten years, maybe twenty. "And when that last sleep comes, man, what about the wall?"

"Every wall falls," he said. "Pah. Too much talk. There,

that one." He pointed. Maris lifted it up, handed it to him. "Can't worry about tomorrow. Got my hands full of today. And today . . ." He stood again, holding his back, looking up at the sky. "Today is not so bad."

Maris laughed a little at this bit of wisdom.

"Where are you bound?" he asked her.

"Perripur."

"Long way. Help me fix this wall and you can have some stew off our pot tonight. A soft place to sleep."

It was tempting. She picked up a rock that she saw would fit. "Just to set right a few stones?"

"Well," he glanced sideways at her. "When your stomach's full, you might tell us about Perripur. My woman, she's always saying we should go south where it's warm. Maybe if you tell her how awful it is there, how the sand storms will take your skin off, she'll stop nagging."

"For a place to sleep and a bowl of good stew, I could talk a bit. It is good stew, is it?"

"Oh, yes. She's had decades to get it wrong, and I'd say she's got the knack now." He grinned.

A bed. Warm food. Even some company might be welcome. But something stopped her.

She was, she realized, weary of the charade of pretending to be other than she was.

"Only a fool invites magic inside, old man," she said gently. "Best fear it from a distance."

He snorted. "Magic is a foreigner's problem. We don't have any of that here."

Holding the rock in her palm, she touched below the surface, felt there the compression of eons, the dust of life long passed, the tightness of heat and cold wrapped up so small. Along the surface she made changes, shifting one thing into another, and the stone in her hand began to spark and sputter, sizzling and popping, tiny bits flying off in a spray like stars, its surface suddenly the color of the sun.

Then she let the stone's shifting fires quiet.

The man's mouth fell open, his eyes wide. He took a step back. "I meant no disrespect," he whispered.

"I'm as old as you are," she said tiredly. "But I hide. Why should I struggle so, only to make the likes of you less afraid of the likes of me?"

The stone was cool and gray again. She held it out to him. She could feel his heart pounding, his mouth drying.

Terrorized.

And that, she reflected, was what mages were good for. What she was good for. A sorrow settled on her shoulders as she saw that he would not move, would not take the stone.

She walked to the wall and placed it. "A snug fit."

"Well," he said. "Well," he repeated. "Well."

She turned, put a hand on her horse's neck, and swung back up into the saddle, taking the reins in hand, pressing forward down the road.

"What is this?" he called from behind her. "I offer you my hospitality and you walk away without a word?"

She stopped, bewildered, turned her horse around to face him. "What? You still offer?"

"My back still hurts, doesn't it?" He glanced at her furtively, then down at the pile of stones. "My wall still needs building, doesn't it? Come on, woman. Mage. However it is you are called. Help me set this wall aright."

He stood there, wobbling, arms crossed over his sunken chest.

"What is this you say?" she asked softly. "Are you not afraid?"

"Of course I'm afraid," he snapped, eyes flickering to her. "But you want food and a bed. I want this wall built. Can't live my life by the dictates of fear. Old as me, you say? You ought to know that, then. That one there." He pointed at another rock, his hand shaking.

Moved by this odd courage, Maris dismounted again. She picked up the rock he still pointed to and put it in his shaking, outstretched hand. He set the rock into the wall and turned back, breathing hard, looking around at the pile and not at her.

She was surprised, and surprised to be surprised. Taken off guard by a gruff old man and a pile of stones.

It made her smile.

The stew, it turned out, was better than the old man had promised, and the company more nourishing yet. When she left the next day, she felt oddly content.

It was full summer by the time Maris reached Dasae Port, and Perripur was hot and bright and green. She stopped at the market, finding herself idly considering a toy, wondering if Pas might like a limestone spinning-top, painted black and white, and spun to make color. But no—she could only carry so much. Instead she loaded up on spices, cheeses, dried meats and nuts, her packs filled tight.

A few more days of riding the plains and she was nearly there, eager to see Dirina and Pas.

So many things to do, once she had unpacked. First they would feast on olives and cheeses, on the thick, sweet paste of cacao, and celebrate her homecoming.

She knew they were gone the moment her horse's feet stepped past the outermost of her watchstones, the heavy lodestones that marked the boundaries of her land, where her wards were set.

Heart speeding, she pressed the horse to a trot and then a run up the hillside path that snaked over brush and through falls of red-flowering vines trailing across the road like blood. As the path curled around the sun-oak, she pulled him to a stop, slid down, and ran the rest of the way herself, up the tightly switchback hillside, past puff-flowers drifting on a too-quiet breeze.

At the house, breath coming hard, she yanked open the door and ran through the rooms, calling for them in each room, even though she knew they were not there.

Empty. It was all empty.

A fine layer of dust covered the main room's table. They had been gone days at least. Weeks, more likely.

Fury built inside her. She let it come, damming the flow so that it would not escape, not a drop of it, saving it for the someone who had earned it. She walked the rooms, touching every surface, looking to confirm what she had already knew, had known from her first touch onto the watchstone.

Keyretura. He had come to her home, broken her wards, violated her protections, and taken Dirina and Pas.

Despite how tired she'd been a moment before, how keen to end her journey, rest was nowhere in her plans. She would not stay a moment longer than she needed to.

How dare he?
He had taken Dirina and Pas.
She would find him.
She would make him sorry.

Chapter Thirty-three

Amarta was tired of being hot. In the heat of this tiny, enclosed wagon it was as warm as Perripur in summer's midday sun. When a guard came to bring food and water and take the chamberpot, ducking as she stepped into the small space, Amarta begged her for an opening in the sides of the tarp.

"I'll ask," she said with a sympathetic look, wincing at the heat under heavy leathers, then she was gone.

Smaller and more secure than the Teva wagon in which she'd ridden to Kusan, there were no torn seams to peek out of as she was jostled on the road, not a thread out of place in the heavy covering to allow a small hole. She knew; she'd examined every inch of it.

She was still sore from Tayre's questioning, and her fingers ached painfully under the splint and bandage. Even one-handed, she would have far preferred to ride than to be in here, day after day. She wasn't being kept here to rest and heal, but to be isolated as around her army marched. A captive.

And wretchedly hot in her stinking prison.

As she struggled to sit up, the wagon lurched to a stop, sending her flat again on the mattress, sharp pain shooting through so many parts of her.

Are you ever surprised?

All the time.

It didn't matter that she could see the future if she didn't happen to be looking.

Voices around her wagon indicated they had stopped to make camp. She wanted to be out of here, even if her every move was watched by a tencount of armed guards.

A gold coin on the hard straw mattress.

First, it seemed, she would have a visitor. As she watched, the tarp's knots were untied and the flap opened, bringing with it the barest hint of evening breeze.

The Lord Commander ducked low, climbed inside, and sat on the tiny bench nailed to the side of this tiny wagon over her tiny straw-filled mattress. At his feet, in front of where she sat, he dropped a gold coin.

"Tell me about this."

No words wasted to ask how she was, if she were still in pain, if she needed anything.

She picked up the coin, remembering a time when she would have been shocked to hold such a thing, with its image of the king's face on one side and a horse and rider on the other. Then it would have meant something: food, warmth, and safety for her and her family.

Now all it meant to her was that someone wanted to own something and could afford to.

That's what she was, she realized: an owned thing. No more than a slave. It put her in mind of Nidem and Ksava and Darad and the hundreds who lived underground in Kusan, rarely glimpsing the sun. But free.

"Well?" he demanded.

"It looks to me to be a gold souver, Lord Commander," she said, tossing it back in front of him on the mattress.

He was silent a moment, looking around the small space, the water skin, the collection of clothes, and then back at her. "I understand you might be tempted to be impertinent with me, Seer, and I also understand why. But if you speak to me that way again, I will make sure you regret it."

Amarta felt her face go hot. She swallowed an angry fear, looked away.

No, she told herself, focus on his words. His future.

She spoke. His returned look bordered on panic.

She blinked in surprise, trying to imagine what it would take to change the face in front of her to the one she'd just seen in vision.

"The coin," he said forcefully. "What happens to it?"

She took it in hand again. "It travels a time, ser, then it is heated to liquid. I can't follow it forward from there."

He took the coin back from her with a dissatisfied sigh. Then: "You told me to look east. We have been days on the road in that direction." That Amarta knew, she thought sourly, from the few moments she was allowed to go outside. "Tell me what I will find there."

The smell of smoke. A man on his knees, one hand on a tree trunk, vomiting onto the ground. The scream of a horse, thrashing wildly, a spear through its neck.

Despite herself, she made a small sound, a soft cry.

"What?"

"A man is sick," she said. "A striped horse screams. Something burns."

"What does that mean?"

"I don't know."

"You'll have to do better than that, Seer."

"I see the *what*, Lord Commander. The why"—she shook her head—"is not always so obvious."

"We have a contract. You have given me an oath, Seer."

"I remember, ser."

"See to it that you do."

The three Teva elders sat across the table from another three youngers, a woman and two men. Between them was a large skin on which was drawn a map.

"Bury it all there, Elders? Are you sure?"

"Yes." This from the elder woman in orange. "Every last bit."

The door to the longhouse burst open. Two Teva entered, breathing hard.

"Jolon. Mara," said the elder man. "What?"

"Arunkel comes in force. Their scouts crossed our border. The rest are only days away."

"Ah," said the woman in blue, drawing out the sound.

"They have sent an army, Elders," said Mara.

The young man across from them stood, strode angrily to the end of the longhouse. "We knew this would come."

"We knew this *might* come," the elder woman in blue corrected.

"I said that we should not give refuge to so many. Our welcome should not be stretched so far."

"You have said many things, Makan," the elder man affirmed. "We heard you then. We do not need to hear you now."

"Will they talk or attack?" asked the elder in orange of Jolon and Mara.

"If we go to them first," said Jolon, "show respect—"

"Not too much," Mara interjected.

Jolon nodded. "Not too much. Then, by their own laws, they must talk first."

"You go. Take others"—a glance at Makan standing to the side—"those who will behave as you direct. Find out what the Arunkin have come for."

From Makan a hot exhale. "We all know what they have come for. It was a mistake to treat with those greedy, filthy aristos. Every word they speak is an illness."

"What choice did we have?" asked the young woman who had sat next to him. "The earth cracked open like an egg with a hard, bright yolk."

Makan turned to face her. "Worth so much. What silence might we have bought with it, if we had not agreed to share it?"

"Silence is not bought with gold," said the elder man. "And we waste time and breath here."

"We knew not to trust them. Look how it turns us against each other," Makan said.

The other young man was now standing, glaring at Makan across the room. "We are not turned against each other. You find argument where there is none—"

The sitting elder woman in orange clapped her hands

sharply. "We grow old as you bicker like foals wishing to be stallions. The horse is running; there is no time for regret at having mounted."

"We should have—" the young man began.

The woman in orange stood, staring at the young man. He fell silent. "You interrupt me, Nahma?"

The young man dropped his gaze to the floor. "Forgive me, Elder."

"Make yourself useful, Makan," said the elder man. "Have the farms take food and everything else of value to Hanatha." Then, to Jolon and Mara: "You know the Arunkin best. Go and treat with them. Do what you must to make them leave."

Jolon took a deep breath. "If they already know, Elder, what then?"

"Then our associates at the capital have made of us a sacrifice," answered the elder in orange.

"Is this likely?" asked the woman in blue of her.

"The Arunkin change loyalties as often as they change their encrusted clothes. It is possible."

"We have not fought the Arunkin for centuries," Jolon said.

"Not openly," added the woman in orange softly.

"Not openly," the elder man agreed. "That path leads steeply uphill, to a treacherous cliff. We must turn away from it, if we can."

"Find out what they know," said the elder in blue. "Find out what they want. Find a way to make them leave. Nahma," she said to the young man, "send a message to our associates at the capital. They hold the other end of the dangerous rope we have helped weave. That we both hold our ends tight, they must know. Perhaps they need reminding."

"And the mage," said the elder man. "It is time."

A humorless laugh from Makan. "He's going to want something, Elder."

"We will find a willing foal."

"That is not what he wants, Elders, and you know this."

"He cannot have that," said the elder woman in blue.

"First get him here," said the elder man. "Then we will talk."

Innel swung up onto his horse. He, Lismar, and Nalas rode forward from the camp. The scouts had reported back, so they now had a reasonable map of the area. He had sent more scout teams north and south to look around.

Mines. Foundries. They knew what to look for.

At a steep rise the view opened up to a valley sloping down and away into the distance. Smoke rose in thin streams from the walled town to the south. From here they could make out, though barely, the figures going in and out of the town.

Innel looked at the northern town, a collection of squared and circular dark wooden buildings, stacked like a scattering of children's toys, around which were people and horses that seemed to watch them in return.

Beyond them both, to the east, was the Rift, distance graying the line of black obsidian to a dark streak that stretched across the horizon.

Lismar pointed. "That is the Teva town, Ote. That"—a

gesture to the rectangular walled town to the south—"Hanatha. Teva serfs, from what I gather, though their arrangement has never been entirely clear."

"This?" Innel asked, bemused, looking over the valley, the town, the buildings. "This is the capital of Otevan?"

He had expected more. A great walled city, perhaps. A city-state of massive roads to support their famed shaota horses. Not two small towns with a few handfuls of buildings.

"Don't be misled," Lismar said. "The Teva have acquitted themselves well in battle many times."

"Against other tribes."

"Not only."

"Even so"—he waved a hand at the whole area—"we have more soldiers than every man, woman, and child who could possibly reside here. If it comes to force, it will be a slaughter."

"Have you examined the battle reports of the Southern Expansion in which my esteemed grandmother Nials esse Arunkel hired the Teva to repel the tribes encroaching on lands she'd granted to the Houses?"

"I was in the Cohort when you taught us about it, General. You may recall."

"I do recall. You were an attentive student. Before the treaty was signed, the Teva fought against us with the cave tribes. Did you know this?"

"Against us? I have seen no such account."

"It wasn't recorded. My ancestor, Evintine Three, would not allow it. He thought it insulting to the crown."

What idiocy. You could not learn about an enemy if

you ignored the records of their victories. How many of the problems the empire faced today could be accounted for by suppressed accounts due to the sensitive pride of monarchs?

It would not happen under his watch, he resolved. No losses would be hidden from the war scribes, not one. Every account would be faithfully made and placed in the libraries, where it could be used to strengthen the empire's military might.

"How do you know this, then?" he asked.

"Proscribed accounts did survive. My grandmother bought them on the black market."

"She didn't find the insult intolerable?"

"She knew the wisdom of examining defeat. Even so, she kept the accounts hidden, under mage-lock. I know she passed them to my brother. I'm surprised he never showed them to you. Perhaps he thought it best not to burden you with such things."

A thinly veiled insult. He supposed he should not be surprised, given who she was.

Given who he was.

"There has not been time to sort through all his belongings."

"Of course not, ser."

"Hundreds of years ago, that. When was the last time the Teva fought a real battle?"

"When was the last time you did, Lord Commander?"

At that he turned in his saddle, facing her smirk and green eyes squarely. Arteni, he almost said, but stopped himself; she would respond that keeping order against a milling town was hardly a battle.

The old king's sister, he reminded himself. First among generals.

"That's why I have you, Lismar. To help find whoever is committing treason against the crown. To counsel me on resolving this matter. Do so."

She looked past him to the towns. Her smirk faded. "Have you studied the battles in which the Teva lost?"

"Apparently I was not to be burdened by those accounts, either."

"There are none," she said, giving him a moment to consider. "There is a reason we brought sufficient force, Commander."

The thousands of soldiers and cavalry behind them, now making camp. It had seemed too much, by far, an excessive expedition, outrageously expensive, but Lismar had insisted. Looking across the small towns before him, he found himself wondering what she could possibly be thinking. What was her true agenda?

Or maybe, being an Anandynar, she did not think much about cost.

Well, satisfying Lismar was worth something, both practically and politically. Maybe even this much.

In any case, they would end the affront to the crown, Teva or no, wherever it had originated.

Mined gold. Forged currency. Theft on an empire-wide scale. He would not allow it.

To Nalas he said: "Bring her."

Lismar snorted.

"She can be useful, General."

Lismar raised her hands in mock surrender. "Evintine Three," she said, "would eat a fistful of raw garlic before every battle, calling it his etheric shield. The Grandmother Queen slept with the severed paws of a mountain lion in her hands the night before a fight. Ramtor the Fearless kept the skulls of his enemies on long mahogany shelves and would kiss each forehead before dressing in uniform and armor. Whatever gives you confidence, Lord Commander."

Well, he reflected, at least there was no longer any need to keep the seer's existence a secret; Lismar would make sure everyone knew.

When Nalas came back, he had Amarta in front of him. Her bruises, Innel saw, were fading to yellow and brown. She was doubtless still uncomfortable. Good; he did not want her to forget.

"Well?" he asked, gesturing to the grasslands below.

She looked across the valley, from the walled town to the rounds of thatched Teva buildings. "I think there will be a battle," she said.

Lismar laughed, and Innel glared at her.

"What else?" he asked.

"Many dead across the valley."

"Who dead, exactly?"

A pause. "Arunkel soldiers, ser."

"You are mistaken," he said. "We outnumber them, many times over." He looked back over his shoulder at pavilion and tents being assembled at the army's camp, then back to the towns of Otevan. "Look again."

She hesitated, as if she were considering her words. Good; he wanted her careful.

"There may be other possibilities, ser. If you don't retaliate. If you comply with their instructions."

The general sneered. "Perhaps treason starts here with this one, Lord Commander."

Amarta looked quickly between them. "Do you think I lie to you, ser General? Lord Commander? That I betray my oath? I do not, I assure you. I stand by my word, ser, I—"

"Yes, yes," Innel said, waving a hand to silence her. "Is there a hidden force somewhere here, then?"

"I do not know."

"How can she know the one thing and not the other?" Lismar asked him.

"You cannot win this, ser," Amarta said to him urgently. "Not if you fight."

Yet again her words made no sense. He scanned the towns of Otevan, round tiered houses, circles within circles, tiny shaota beige and brown in the distance. He thought through the numbers. Unless there was an impossibly large force hidden somewhere nearby, the Teva and the town together simply could not challenge the size of army behind him.

He motioned to Nalas. "Take her back to her wagon." The horse turned and left.

Lismar was smiling widely. "I am sure the cooks have brought garlic, Lord Commander. Perhaps you'll find it tasty."

After a moment's consideration he decided to ignore this. "We are here to find and fix treason. The Teva are allies, and we will honor the treaty, as far as we are able."

"A shame to bring an army all this way to do nothing. Soldiers with weapons want to swing at something. At least get an eyeful of the famous horses and see what the Teva can do."

For a long moment Innel looked at the distant towns of Ote and Hanatha, musing on the deep blue of the lands on the other side of the Rift.

Whatever Lismar's agenda, the consequences of what happened here would fall entirely on Innel.

"Best to resolve this without conflict, if we can," he said.

She nodded. "If we can."

As Innel stood on the rise with Nalas he thought of the supplies, troops, and horses that spread out behind them. He missed Srel.

"What do they say, Nalas?"

"Ah," said Nalas, scratching the back of his head thoughtfully. "They complain, of course, ser. The food. They miss wives or husbands or lovers. Not enough wine, henbane, twunta, whores. Competitions between factions. Some fights." A shrug. "Nothing unusual."

"Factions? The Houses?"

"Some claim allegiance, connection or ancestry, of course, but no one is wearing House colors. At least not openly."

"They'd better not be."

From the distant town, a handful of Teva riders set out in their direction, carrying a white flag. Nalas motioned guards to fetch Lismar.

As Lismar arrived, the five Teva rode to a point roughly halfway to the rise then stopped.

"That seems clear enough," Lismar said.

"Let's go meet them."

Innel counted seven Teva. In addition to Nalas and Lismar he took enough of their own to match that count. They rode down the rise to meet them. As they came close, Innel took in their appearance: the rough clothes made of undyed weave and leather, sewn without trim or decoration. Long knives at their sides, bows on their backs.

And small. He had not remembered from Arteni quite how small the Teva and their shaota horses were. Well, perhaps their fighting horses and warriors were larger.

At the front of the group were two horses and riders, a man and a woman. Did he know these two?

"Greetings, Arunkin," the Teva man said.

"Greetings, Teva," Nalas replied on behalf of Innel and Lismar. "You here address the Lord Commander of the Host of Arunkel, Protector of the Realm, Royal Consort to Cern esse Arunkel; also Her Grace, Lismar Anandynar, Duchess of Kastin and Her Majesty's First General."

The Teva man exchanged a quick look with the woman by his side, then looked back. "I am Jolon al Otevan. This my sister, Mara."

Now he remembered where he had seen these two before. At Arteni. Years ago.

Jolon's eyes flickered past Innel, to the sound from the camp of stakes being pounded, loud enough to carry. "You come with many troops, Arunkin. Do you come to challenge us?"

"We come to ask questions," Innel replied.

"You bring a mighty force to ask questions."

"We are seeking to cut away the diseased skin of treason. We bring the necessary tools to do so, no matter where on the body we might find it."

"Treason? Against whom? You are"—he gestured—"making camp on Teva lands."

"Against the queen whose lands you live within, Teva," answered Lismar.

Jolon looked confused. "It is the Teva you wish to ask these questions of?"

"It is."

"Ah. Then we will require a writ of truce."

Innel gave Lismar a querying look. She nodded. "So be it," he said to the Teva. "I offer you a ten-day truce for discussion, in force immediately. Send your leaders to my pavilion and we will sign the decree."

A few words were spoken between them in the fast, atonal language of the Teva, which Innel did not know. Two of their riders left. "They go to notify our people of this truce. You will do the same?"

Innel motioned to Nalas, who gave an order to two others, who similarly rode off.

"We accept your word," the Teva man said, "And we two will sign the treaty, then hear your questions."

Innel frowned. "You? We expect to meet with your leaders."

"My sister and I hold authority to speak for our Elders and people. As you hold the authority to speak for your queen."

"I see."

Barely short of insulting, to compare their elders to the monarch of the empire.

Jolon pointed. "Do you see that rock outcropping there, at the top of that mesa?"

"I do."

"We will come to sign when the morning sun touches there. We wish you to rest well this night so that when our discussion is complete, you and your many soldiers may return to your homes."

With this Jolon of the Teva gave Innel a wide, guileless smile.

Innel nodded slowly. "Tomorrow, then."

As sun touched the rock on the mesa, seven Teva dismounted outside the newly erected pavilion.

Everyone in camp who could arguably have had reason to be close to the command pavilion was there, watching as the Teva slipped down from their small, strangely striped horses. The camp's horsemaster stepped toward the shaota, looking lost as she realized the horses had no reins to take.

Mara spoke to her. "They do not need your help."

"But," the horsemaster began, looking to Innel for direction.

"As they say," he told her.

Jolon spoke to one of his companions, saying something fast and low. "He will stay here, with the shaota," he said to Innel.

"So be it."

Innel led the remaining six into the pavilion, to a long table. Silver cups marked with the Anandynar sigil had been set out in a row. When all were seated, Innel and Lismar on one side, the Teva on the other, an aide poured wine into every cup, moving them into a semicircle equidistant from Jolon and Mara.

Jolon considered the cups, exchanging a quick glance with his sister. He then slid the cups from the ends of the semicircle in sufficient number to pass to his companions, leaving the center two.

Interesting.

Innel and Lismar took the remaining cups.

After they had all sipped, Innel nodded to a clerk, who brought a paper forward, along with a quill, ink, and seal. Innel made his mark and pressed his seal into a pool of red wax the aide dripped onto the document. Another pool of wax was dripped, and Jolon took from around his neck a long, thin seal that appeared to be woven from horsehair, pressing the Teva mark. As it came away, Innel saw a set of stripes much like the pattern on the backs of the shaota.

"Thus is the truce confirmed," Innel said after the necessary marks were made.

"Then"—From Jolon, an open hand, a gesture—"ask your questions, Lord Commander and First General."

Innel took another sip of the dark wine, considering the group before him. "Where is the gold coming from?"

"Gold?"

"In any form. Nuggets. Bars. Counterfeit coin. Statuettes. Those who make these items commit high treason."

Jolon appeared to consider this as he sat back. Then: "We regret we cannot help you with this."

Innel studied the Teva, thinking of Keyretura's words about the figurine and its casting and traces of gold. This man, this Teva before him, had handed that figurine to Innel as he sat on his horse at Arteni. Behind the Teva had been trade wagons.

Wagons Innel had decided not to search. Wagons that might have been full of these figurines, some of which might have been made of less lead and more gold. It was all starting to make a kind of sense. Innel suspected that Jolon and Mara, like the Teva itself, were not quite what they seemed.

But all that showed on their faces were looks of innocence.

"We want to check your foundries," Innel said. "Search your lands."

"We do not permit this," Jolon said easily. "Whatever you seek on Teva lands, it is not yours. We are sovereign—"

"Within Arunkel borders," Lismar said.

"—sovereign under the treaty of Nipatas Two," Jolon continued, his gaze still on Innel, "a treaty signed in blood, renewed by Hesindae One, Evintine Three, and Restarn the first of his name, your queen's own father. All esse Arunkel."

"We know the treaty, its ratifications, and what it means, Jolon al Otevan," Innel said.

"And we have been your neighbors in peace for over three hundred years."

Lismar leaned forward, jabbed a finger at the two of them. "Listen, Teva: no treaty gives you the right to violate Arunkel law. Your sovereignty does not swathe you like a babe. If it is not you doing these things, then you surely know who it is, and you will reveal this to us."

Jolon spread his hands. "We deny violating any law. We have nothing to tell you."

"Then you will not protest if we look around," Innel said.

"We do protest. It is our land. If you go farther, it is trespass."

At this tense moment, an aide stepped inside the pavilion. At this interruption, Innel shot Nalas a sharp look. Nalas quickly conferred with the aide, gave Innel a look that said the matter was urgent. Innel motioned him to speak.

"A scout from the southern team, Lord Commander," Nalas said. "She reports the other nine on the team are dead, slaughtered in a gully at a watering hole. She is wounded. Barely escaped."

Innel was on his feet. "Who did this?" he demanded.

Nalas's eyes flickered to the Teva. "Dressed in simple clothes, from the scout's description. Much as they are, ser."

No one was sitting now. The Teva spread out slightly from each other, fingers spread wide. Not yet on weapons.

Innel gave his full attention to Jolon. "Hours into our truce and you murder my men?"

"Not us, Lord Commander," Jolon said, hands up in a gesture of placation.

Innel glanced at Lismar. She trusted them no more than he did. "You deny much, Teva," he said. "Our credulity stretches thin. Someone has killed our scouts. Someone commits treason against our queen." He gave Nalas a sign. Nalas dipped his head, little more than a twitch, and was gone.

"What we wear," Jolon said, "it is simply practical. Many wear such clothes. On our lands and yours."

"Very well," Innel said. "You claim this is not your work. For the moment we will consider the truce whole and refrain from retaliation. But we will have answers. One of your people may leave to tell your Elders what has happened. The rest, and you in particular, Jolon of the Teva, will stay here until we get what we came for."

"What?" Jolon seemed shocked. "You cannot hold us against our will."

"I think you will find I can."

A twenty count of guards were streaming into the tent, weapons ready.

Jolon spoke softly to his sister. They exchanged urgent whispers. With a loathing look at Innel, Mara turned to leave. At Innel's signal, the guards parted to let her through.

"Disarm the others," he commanded, noting Lismar's expression. She approved.

The remaining five Teva did not resist as they were stripped of their blades and bows and arrows. Outside were the sounds of two Teva and their horses—Mara and the one already there—riding off.

And now, finally, satisfyingly, Jolon showed an expression beyond wide-eyed innocence. An intensity that Innel could not quite read. Fear, perhaps.

Good. It was time the Teva took them seriously.

"Food and water for their horses," Innel told an aide.

"Leave them be," Jolon said. "They come and go as they wish."

"We will pen them. For their own protection. Until this matter is resolved."

"Lord Commander," Jolon said. "This is unwise."

"So is your silence. You will give us the answers we need."

He gestured to Lismar to step outside with him.

He and Lismar watched as the camp's horse handlers surrounded the shaota and attempted to usher them into a fenced enclosure. The small horses seemed undecided about this, but after a few minutes went where they were directed. The horsemaster had water troughs and feed brought while she yelled at the collected crowd to get back.

"If I had brought the mage," he told Lismar softly as they watched, "instead of leaving him at the palace to protect the queen, I would bring him into this questioning, because his very presence loosens tongues. This is the reason for having the rumored fortune-teller in hand."

"Is that so? Are you telling me you don't credit her prophesy?"

"Predictions are easy to make," he said with a wry smile. "But I must seem to believe her if I am to convince others that her predictions carry truth. Once they believe that, her presence in questioning can be of great use."

Lismar studied him a long moment. "That is clever. You and my brother were well-matched." At his look, she added: "My brother the king."

"Then I am flattered," he said. "How so?"

"You are determined to win. Even when it came to

Pohut. My brother the king thought he was playing you against each other, but you saw right through it. Your willingness to sacrifice your own brother—" A soft snort and a nod. "That is the character and attitude it takes to hold an empire." A tilt of her chin in the direction of the Teva towns. "Or conquer treason."

Playing you against each other? What was she saying?

"Yes, General, it is," he said with a certainty he didn't feel. He would consider her words later when there was time. "And what do you advise now to ferret out this treason?"

"I say the truce is broken. We should take the towns. Someone there will talk and tell us what we want to know."

A simple, clean victory. Very tempting. But as their captives had pointed out, the Teva treaties were ratified across both centuries and monarchs. To take the towns in blood would not only bend that covenant but shake the confidence of any potential future allies.

You cannot win this, ser, not if you fight.

"Best we keep conflict as a last resort," he said. "Give the Teva Elders a chance to consider the wisdom of cooperating with the empire that surrounds and upholds them. They'd be fools to do otherwise."

"Fools or a people hiding something. Not too much time, Commander."

"No, not too much," he agreed.

Tayre crouched down in the scrub and brush, a look of bored contemplation on his face, just one of the many uniformed soldiers hovering around Food Square, waiting for the meal, as out of the corner of his eye he kept track of the master cook and her various assistants.

Something was wrong.

Nothing unusual about the cook wanting a measure of privacy in a camp this crowded. He'd watched her direct the drovers with a fair bit of grumbling to surround her cook-camp with a square of wagons, restricting access to her territory.

Again, not particularly uncommon.

She looked around, eyes moving constantly, as if she were afraid she were being watched, her movements hunched, abrupt. She tucked a good deal of henbane leaf into her cheek, and drank a fair bit of wine, easily accounting for her lurching, stumbling movements.

She was hiding something. He had a good idea what.

With no actual part in the command structure, Tayre was able to make his way around the various camps and tents. As long as he moved confidently, said the right things, made the right jokes, and occasionally passed along a wrap of twunta, a slug of henbane, or a flask of rotgut, he was only noticed when he chose to be. If that didn't work, a bit of good jerky went a long way. All of which he had in abundance, having prepared for this campaign with quite a bit more coin than was available to the ordinary soldier.

When, on the second day, the cook's furtive looks reached a peak, Tayre was sure she was about to act on whatever it was she had been nerving herself to do.

And then, as he watched, she did.

He roused himself from his hiding place and injected himself once again into the pattern of camp movement, taking a roundabout way to the wagon where the seer was being kept. While he had no particular desire to save the entire camp from the cook's ministrations, and thought it likely Amarta could protect herself, he wanted to be sure.

"Hey," one of the guards around the wagon said to him with a nod and a grin.

"Hey."

They knew him now; he'd been here every day, having managed to replace the regular aide assigned to this task.

"Got more of your special mix? I want an aunt like yours."

A potent in-cheek powder that was both stimulating and calming, which had been credited to a nonexistent aunt.

"I might," Tayre said. "Play again tonight and I'll let you try to win some."

Another guard spoke up. "Count me in."

"Me, too," another said.

"So be it, then," Tayre said with a wider smile, then let it vanish suddenly. "For now, though, I am still the clod who does the chamber pot and brings slop to the—" He thumbed at the wagon. "Lord Commander's cousin. Or whatever we're calling her today."

The group had already used some rather unflattering titles for Amarta.

"She's got hardtack and water," said the first, "but Lord Commander said to treat her well, so—" A shrug.

"I'll go find whatever's being dished out and bring some back."

"Bring us something, too."

"I will."

❖ ❖ ❖

At least, Amarta reflected, her small wagon prison was no longer rattling along rutted roads. She could rest, even contemplate. She was, currently, musing on how her vision worked.

That it was sometimes wrong, she already knew. Whether this was because events were constantly in motion and what she saw one moment would simply be impossible the next, because the present had changed to make it so, or if the fault were hers because she imagined a thing rather than actually foreseeing it, like a snatch of memory that turned out to be a dream rather than a true memory, she wasn't sure.

Or perhaps vision was not wrong, but was revealing an event so unlikely that it might as well be imagined or dreamed. Highly improbable but not entirely impossible.

Perhaps the problem was that she didn't think about how one thing might lead to another. So much of what she knew came to her without her needing to understand anything at all. She had come to realize that if all she did was live by her visions, she would never understand such things. She must learn to reason, not simply believe anything that came through her head.

For example, right now reason told her that the brief flash she'd had of Tayre bringing her food and talking quietly to her here in the wagon was in the category of imagination. It was clearly far beyond possible. That he was on her mind was not surprising, given her broken fingers and bruises and cuts, but that was not reason enough to envision him here.

Tell me what you want most of all.

Still she had no good answer. It was almost as if wanting was the opposite of foreseeing; vision didn't care about desire, only about action.

Not that her wants factored into things much now, captive as she was.

But she'd had a thought about that, too. In the dark of the previous night, listening to the laughing and chatting of guards outside, it had occurred to her that she might find a moment, a tiny opportunity between moments, when the guards were rolling dice and not paying close attention, the tarp perhaps not secured quite perfectly, when vision might help her find a way to open it and slip out of the wagon.

And do what? She was bound to the Lord Commander by her contract and oath, and the reasons she had come to him: to prevent death and suffering.

What do you care if strangers suffer?

All right, then: to prevent his actions from harming her family. Dirina. Pas.

It soothed her, as the heat began to ease somewhat with the coming night, to imagine them in Perripur with Maris, out in the garden, weeding or planting, eating peas and cabbage leaf, endive and luff, Pas's smiling face and fingers smeared with avocado.

He could be there right this moment, laughing and pointing at a brilliantly colored bird or lizard, demanding Maris tell him what it was called. She smiled at this, lay back, let her eyes close.

"Sure, go on in," said one of the guards.

She sat up, watching the tent flap open. As Tayre stepped up and into the wagon, she gaped in astonishment.

He put a finger to his lips, set the tray down, and closed the flap behind, coming to sit right next to her.

She was too startled to even be scared.

Not imagination.

"Do not eat the stew," he whispered in her ear. "I believe it is corrupted and will make you ill."

"I—"

Before she knew it, he had taken her bandaged hand, unwrapped it, examined her fingers, then replaced the splints and re-wrapped.

"You are healing well."

Certainly he seemed real enough, she thought, still staring. Smelled real enough, setting her feelings into a tangle.

A dark room. Metal against a grindstone.

Could the Lord Commander mean to have him question her again?

"Another contract?" she managed.

"No. I am beholden only to myself now."

"Then why—"

"I can't stay long or the guards will wonder. How does it go with the Lord Commander?"

"He demands answers, doesn't like them, then threatens me and sends me back here."

He examined her face, and she felt his look like a touch. "There will come a time when you must show him what you are capable of, Seer."

"My words do nothing."

"Innel is a wolf, Amarta."

That was so; every time the Lord Commander talked to her, she felt a rush of fear, closely followed by anger.

Fear is a shadow.

"Yes," she said, recalling his words in that dark room. "The wolf is real. The wolf bites. But the shadow—"

"Amarta," he said, putting his fingers to her lips to silence her, the touch a shock. "Listen: he is a wolf. But so are you. That is what I came here to tell you, and what I could not tell you before."

The sun began to dip to the west. Innel and Lismar watched the single Teva making his way toward them, carrying a white flag high on a pole. As he arrived he said nothing, only handed to an aide a rolled message, then turned and galloped away.

The aide handed Innel the message. He read the broken Arunkin written there, and snorted, handing it to Lismar.

Release our horses and people immediately.

"Now what do you advise, General?"

"There is a time to do what is clear and obvious. No more delay. Attack."

Surrounded by guards in the dimming light of evening, Amarta was taken from the wagon through the camp. She inhaled the cooling breeze greedily, happy to be smelling something other than herself.

They passed through a city of tents, horses, and red and black uniformed soldiers. Someone, somewhere, was sharpening a blade. She shuddered.

Vision tickled, and she pushed away the flickers. She did not want to see any of these people's futures.

At a large pavilion she was pushed inside. Candles

burned in an overhead chandelier of silver and copper. Heavy red and black silk lined the walls, embroidered with the monarchy's sigil. Two intricately carved center poles held up the heavy canvas and glinted with inlaid gemstones.

So much wealth. It was, truly, astonishing.

Then she saw the long table, at which sat the Lord Commander and the general. Across from them sat five small men and women.

"This"—The Lord Commander waved a hand at her—"this is the seer. She predicts what will happen. To see the future is to see beyond deception. Tell me again, Teva, that you know of no gold mine."

"Again, Lord Commander, we deny—"

Amarta met Jolon's gaze. He paused briefly then looked back across the table.

"—violating any law, and furthermore—"

"Your girl knows this man," the general said.

Could she hide nothing at all? The Lord Commander stood and walked to her.

"How is it that you know this Teva?"

He had saved them from the shadow hunter—from this very man before her—even at the risk of Emendi lives. He had given them the hidden city, safety, and—for a time—something like a home. He and Mara had been generous when she and her family were most desperate. He was one of the few people who had helped her who had not suffered for it.

Yet.

She remembered how they had met, as she told him his shaota was pregnant, that the baby would be a colt. It would be born and grown by now. For an absurd moment she thought to ask him whether she'd been right.

"Seer," the Lord Commander said sharply. "I asked you a question."

She tore her gaze from Jolon.

"Need I remind you of your obligation?" he asked, voice low.

Lifting her bandaged left hand, she said: "I think you have reminded me enough, ser."

"Then answer."

Fair is what you take.

"Our contract says I answer your questions about the future, ser. Nothing was said about the past."

His eyes narrowed.

"Lord Commander," Jolon said. "Release us. We can still calm the rippling waters, but as time passes, it will be too late."

He turned to the Teva. "I know gold is coming from Otevan, Teva. I have enough evidence to convict you before the queen. I give you one more chance to tell me what I need to know."

"We deny breaking any laws—"

"Seer, where is the gold mine?"

The wrong question, not the sort that she could really answer, which he ought to know by now. She thought to say all this.

"You fight the wrong battle here, Lord Commander," she found herself saying. "It will end in death for so many—"

He turned, very fast, grabbed her shoulders, fingers gripping painfully, and shook her hard, taking her breath away. Then he released her. She stumbled backwards.

"My patience runs dry, girl. You keep your sister and nephew safe by virtue of this contract whose edges you keep testing. Very well, I will rephrase: What must I do to find the gold these Teva hide?"

He is a wolf.

Breathing hard, she sifted through the rushing roar of futures, discarding image after image of the screams of soldiers.

The feel of her fingers, rubbing together, something gritty and wet between them. It was red. It glinted.

But so are you.

Blinking in the candle-and-lamplit pavilion, she moved her fingers over each other as she had in vision, staring at her empty hand. Was there any future in which the Lord Commander got what he wanted without blood?

"There is gold here," she said. "A lot of it."

The general snorted. "I am shocked to hear this."

No, not what he wanted. What he needed. What was that?

Lines of Teva atop shaota, streaming out of sight, A battle horn sounding. A child's howl, a woman's cry of anger, horses' hooves pounding dirt.

"Release the Teva," she said, sorting through fogs of images. "Offer them the crown's apology."

An outraged, wordless howl from the general. "This is sedition you tolerate. Now hear my prediction, Innel: we have come to correct a treasonous wrong against our queen. This is no moment to bleat like a lost lamb." She looked at the five Teva, now standing. "I tell you why they win, Commander, and you might do well to pay heed: they do not give in."

To Amarta, Innel said, darkly. "Try again, Seer."

"Pah!" The general exhaled loudly. "You take this one's advice over mine? You mock my decades of experience, Commander. Perhaps you two really are relations." She stormed out of the pavilion.

Amarta realized it wasn't enough to tell him what would come. She must tell him what to do. But first he had to believe her.

One step closer. But to what?

To a future where the wars of the empire didn't spread like a killing flood, ever closer to her family.

Something must change. But what?

Under a starlit night a striped horse jumped a fence. Men howled. A horse screamed.

It wouldn't work, she knew, but she had to say it: "Let the shaota go."

Finally she looked up at the Lord Commander. He was beyond anger, hands flexing and releasing as if looking for a target.

And indeed, in one of the next moment's many futures, he hit her hard enough to knock her across the room, sending her into a table at the edge of the large, tented room. In another future she ducked the blow, but his anger only escalated. He called guards. She was overcome. Sent back to the wagon. Captive, again.

No: she was done being sent back to that wretched, stinking prison.

She drew herself upright, and met his furious look, feeling the next moment's options narrow. "A horse dies in the next few minutes, ser. Then there will be more blood."

At this, Jolon began a sound, a warbling trill, deep in his throat. The rest of the Teva joined him, their voices combining into a loud eerie call. From outside the pavilion came echoing calls, the shaota's not-quite whinnies, the sound that was almost like laughing, but wasn't.

"Don't let them out," Innel said to the guards as he left.

Standing at the edge of the corral, Tayre was one among the thick crowd gathering to gape at the five oddly colored horses. The sun was going down, its last rays touching the animals, turning their chestnut-and-ocher striped bodies into lines that nearly glowed.

The horses were restless, testy. The crowd pressing in was not helping.

Suddenly there came a loud sound of song, a warbling, from the commander's pavilion. The ears of every shaota pricked up. Together they turned to the east.

East. Where the town of Ote was.

Tayre could immediately see where this was going, as he could clearly see what the horsemaster and the large crowd around the corral did not.

Better to be elsewhere. He ducked down, wormed his way backward through the press of people, the space he vacated quickly filled. He backed away until he was well clear, then climbed atop an open wagon, joining a handful of others watching the action.

One of the shaota backed up, clearly—to Tayre,

anyway—to get a running start at the fence, which was high enough to keep the much larger Arunkel warhorses confined for a short time when the horsemaster needed to. The first shaota lunged into motion rather faster than he expected, heading for the fenceline.

A sudden, eerie silence took hold as the crowd and handlers realized what was about to happen, then struggled to clear the space where the five horses were now clearly headed.

As the first shaota cleared the fenceline, the crowd scrambled to get out of the way, but they were too thick, packed in too tightly. As the rest of the horses jumped the fence, landing atop the human carpet, there were sounds of breaking bones, roars, and screams.

In the midst of this panic, one white-haired soldier calmly took his spear and launched it in a smooth arc at the next-to-last shaota to land. The spear took the shaota through the neck. As the animal began to twist and buck, flattening even more people as it fell, flailing, the shaota just behind it landed in a small clear area. It made a fast motion, a sort of stutter step almost too quick for Tayre's eye to follow, an odd sideways motion. As it launched again, jumping to clear the rest of the crowd and follow the other shaota, it gave a final kick. The white-haired soldier who had launched the spear flew backwards. It looked like he would not get up again.

"Oh, shit," someone next to him breathed.

Now the crowd turned loud, shouting, calling. Screaming. Tayre guessed a tencount or two Arunkin had been killed, another tencount broken in various ways that they might or might not survive.

"Demon horses!" someone called and the cry was taken up. Most were fleeing, some tending to the howling injured.

As he jumped off the wagon, retreating farther from the fray, Tayre wondered if it were time to leave the army. The night would be chaos.

Well, he thought, as he left the action, at least everyone who had been so eager for a good look at the nearly mythical horses now had it.

Amarta heard the sounds of men shouting, breaking, screaming. Then a sharp, inhuman cry.

At this one of the Teva howled and launched himself at the guards. The other Teva exploded into motion as well. A struggle followed, but the greater count of guards overcame the unarmed Teva and tied them, hand and foot, setting them on the ground.

The one Teva man was sobbing, his grief obvious.

His shaota, Amarta realized suddenly. The dead horse she had foreseen. It had been his.

Jolon caught her gaze. He looked to one side, then the other, then back at her, blinking oddly. It took her a moment to realize he was giving her an Emendi signal. She did not at first recognize it; it had been too long.

He repeated it.

Help us, he was signing.

A glance around the room. She could not imagine a way to free the Teva, not with so many guards.

But she didn't need to imagine; she could ask vision. Was there a way?

Distant screams. The flicker of fire. Guards distracted.

In an improbable moment guided by vision, she strolled past the Teva, dropped a knife on the ground out of view of the guards.

They would cut their bonds. One by one, passing the knife along behind them. And then—

No and no: she had a contract. To free the Lord Commander's prisoners was far from any reasonable interpretation of her oath.

Sorry, she signed to Jolon. *So sorry.*

His look of disappointment tore at her, as did the continued weeping of the man by his side.

The Lord Commander returned. He looked around the room. At the Teva. At her.

Stepping close, he dropped his voice. "The Teva heard your prediction, Seer. Now there is a dead horse. Are you foreseeing the future or creating it?"

"I did not kill that creature," she answered angrily.

"Predict something useful for me, then." His tone matched hers.

Many columns of fire. Sparks against a starry sky.

"You can still rescue this, ser. But it must be soon. Go to the Teva leaders with a white flag. You must—"

"Your visions are not serving me well, girl."

"—apologize to them. Otherwise, ser, there will be so much blood and death and you—"

"Can you predict nothing else?" he asked loudly.

"Can you do anything but slaughter?" she demanded.

She could see she'd gone too far. Faster than she expected, the back of his hand snapped to her face. She turned a little, just enough, changing the distance a tiny bit. His hand barely brushed across her cheek.

He reached for her shoulders. She twitched her upper body. His hands fumbled, failing to find grip. Next he lunged for her neck. A fast rock-step back and forward. His fingertips barely missed the front of her neck.

She was in the same position from which she had started. Making a point that she hoped he understood.

His eyes widened briefly and his hands dropped to his sides. His expression turned hard. "I have your sister and nephew, Seer."

"What?" she breathed. "No, you don't. You can't."

"But I do."

"Our contract. You said—"

"Safe, I said. And they are. Very safe. Indeed, it was the only way I could be sure they *would* be safe, to use my power to keep them so."

Amarta gulped for breath, dread and pain lancing through her. A tightness gripped her throat; fury threatened to overcome her. She sank into a haze of seeing, pawing through the futures that fanned out from this moment.

She craved this man's destruction. Not merely his death, but to somehow tear him apart, to take everything for which he cared and rend it to shreds.

In many futures she next launched herself at him with a howl, ready to tear, hit, bite. But the struggle was short-lived; she had never before used vision to attack someone and did not know how. Vision agreed and told her this would fail. He and his guards would knock her to the ground, tie her. Her options ended.

In other futures, she yelled at him, revealed to him the worst things the future might bring him.

But telling him changed the very outcomes she predicted, and her threats became empty, his faith in her eroded even further.

And nothing changed.

She stood still, vibrating with frustration, mute with anger.

"They are well," he told her. "Do you understand?"

"That was all I ever wanted. Them to be safe. From you."

"And they are. Our contract is intact. Do you hear me? I simply needed to be sure of your cooperation."

Where was the future in which she was no longer captive to this man? The one that made of her a wolf?

"Take her back to her wagon," he said to his guards.

You can do this, Seer.

"No," she shouted. "I won't go back."

He put up a hand. The guards stopped.

Flashes of metal. Howls of anger.

Moments were passing. The future was shifting. Options were closing. In truth, the battle had just now begun.

He reached for her, then hesitated, fingers hovering. "Come," he said instead, walking to the edge of the partitioned area at the rear of the pavilion.

What else to do? She followed him to the back, behind the heavy drapes, where there was a large bed. A world away from a straw mattress in a stinking wagon.

"Don't challenge me, Amarta," he said, voice low. "You will obey me, or your family—"

"You won't hurt them, ser. Not before you leave Otevan, and by then you—"

By then he might not be able to. Flickers of how Innel sev Cern esse Arunkel might finish this battle were still foggy, unclear, and changing.

He might survive. He might not.

She had no idea if her family were safe from him or not; she had simply lied. In a way. Foresight had told her that to say this would give her a moment more to act, a moment more of his attention before he called his guards.

And there it was, the answer to his earlier question: Did she make the future or predict it?

Sometimes both.

In the next moment, guards would drag her back to her hot, smelly captivity. She could not slip through a net of twenty strong men.

Yet.

"I *what*, Seer?" he prompted, and she knew from vision that this was her last chance to change the path forward.

"You will wish you had listened to me."

"I am listening to you now," he growled.

But he was not.

"It has already begun," she said.

"What has? Tell me, damn you."

She turned her gaze away from him, staring at the hanging tapestry. A deep red silk with the monarchy's sigil in black brocade, like a field of blood over which was laid an iron blade and pickax.

And what was she in this tapestry?

Unique and beyond reckoning.

She was a short length of dyed thread, and that was all

she would ever be, until and unless she was as willing to be the wolf as the man in front of her.

"Amarta, your oath. Do you break it now?"

"No, ser. I do not. But you ask the wrong question. Until you ask the right one, my answers will not serve you."

"What is the right question?"

She looked at the Teva across the room. "What do *I* want, Lord Commander."

"You?" he asked incredulously, hands again clenching into fists. "*You*?"

He waited for her to speak, but vision told her that any word she spoke now would only infuriate him further, so she stayed silent. He looked around the pavilion, at the tapestries, the bed, and finally back at her. "Very well; what do you want, Seer?"

"Untie the Teva," she answered. "I already know you won't release them, but you can treat them better than this." She met his gaze. "An attack is coming, Lord Commander. I see no future in which it does not occur, but there are things you can do to make it better. If you do them soon. And I know what they are."

His eyes narrowed at her, his expression darkening. Then he went to the guards. "Untie them. Send for cots, food, wine. And you—" He rounded on her, close and breathing hard. She struggled not to flinch, not to step back.

After a moment, with an exhale, he stepped back. "Tell me."

"The stream from which the camp gets water," she said. "Get more."

Chapter Thirty-four

Always a delicate balance, thought Cern, looking out her window to the tranquility below, a garden of flowers and herbs and sparkling gems, while on the other side of the palace someone was dying in Execution Square. Behind her Sachare checked the bedclothes, the mattress, and the pillows.

A delicate balance, a bit like the creation of rods and tubes, hooks and chains in the next room. Her most recent creation attached to the ceiling and two walls, pressing and pulling upon itself. A wooden rod in a large ruby's concave hollow, the rock pulled in two directions by delicate jeweled chains. The whole of the work would collapse if each piece did not depend on at least two others, and better yet three. Otherwise it was a weak arrangement, fragile and ready to fall to the floor. Forces from multiple directions were necessary to complete the puzzle, to draw it together into a single entity.

Now Sachare was grumbling. Someone had made the mistake of changing Cern's bedding without Sachare's oversight. Chambermaid and bodyguard both, Sachare was attentive and cautious.

As Cern must be. In action. In appearance.

Such a delicate balance.

The courtyard below was said to be the finest of the palace's many gardens, looked upon, as it was, by the reigning monarch. At the center red and black chrysanthemums formed her family's sigil, walkways radiating out in eight directions past walls of gemstone, iron trellises, and wooden sculptures, each of which had its own cascade of fragrant herbs, thick with flowers. Benches of stone, wood, metal, and coral were set about the circumference, kept exactingly clean in anticipation of the possibility that she might actually use them.

That was one of the many delicate balances, right there. No matter how carefully her guards were chosen, no matter how restricted the view onto this garden, when Cern sat on a bench, the House who had gifted it to the crown would soon be notified and then everyone would speculate on what the action implied.

The Great Houses who did not deal in substances that might reasonably be fashioned into benches must be satisfied in other ways, so tapestries and wall-hangings hung in a nearby room carefully adjudged a similar status to the garden below. That room, then, she also must be sure to visit on a regular basis while somehow making it seem as natural as a visit to the garden. One of her aides' primary task was to keep track of what Cern had done to honor or neglect which House and to arrange ways to even the score.

Cern could never simply sit.

"What are you thinking about?" Sachare asked her softly.

"That time I sat on House Etallan's bench, watching an ant try to drag a worm back to the nest."

"I remember that. He wasn't very happy."

"No."

Her father had called her to him and explained her error at fair length. She was to sit with good posture, at the center of the bench. Not slumped over, staring at the ground. It was insulting to the House. Did she understand?

She did.

The Houses. Ever-attentive, easily offended, and mercilessly unavoidable. Yet again she wondered if she could possibly move her suite to the other side of the palace, where she would instead have a good view of Execution Square. Let the Houses figure out what that meant.

But of course she could not; it would send all the wrong signals, among them that she mistrusted Innel's oversight of executions.

No such message could be allowed. The aristos loved their executions. The more cunning and elaborate the better, and they relied on the Anandynar royals to make a good show of them.

That her family had a reputation for exacting brutal retribution against those who opposed them, she knew. That she had to live up to that if she were to keep the crown she also knew.

But while she might condemn a criminal to be bound and pierced, crushed and broken—all the various ways to achieve a meticulous and agonizing death that were the trademarks of her family—Innel handled the truly messy part. Trained for it. Raised in the Cohort.

Particularly well-suited. This was part of why Innel had been her first choice. Pohut, for all that he was handsome and charming and full of wit, simply did not have Innel's keen edge of single-minded ruthlessness. Innel could do what needed doing.

But that wasn't quite all of it. It had also become clear to her those last few years that despite how close the brothers were, whichever of them she did not marry would need to swallow a sort of humiliation. Pohut, she had reluctantly concluded, would take this with somewhat more grace than Innel. This had factored into her choice.

What would have been her choice, if Innel had not taken it from her.

Single-minded ruthlessness, she reminded herself. She needed a man like him at her side if she were going to hold the throne through these first and most difficult years.

"And now what are you thinking about, my lady?" Cern could hear the smile in Sachare's voice.

A short sigh. "The Consort."

"Ah." Sachare returned a pillow to its casing, fluffing and setting it on the bed.

Cern's training had been a little different. When Cohort lessons became too full of blood and parts, she had been pulled away. She was to rule and judge, she was told, not slice and stab.

Rule and judge she now did. Finally free of her father, she would sink or swim entirely on her own. Innel was right that she must somehow make her own mark, become distinct, if she were to avoid being thought of as Restarn's own mother—her grandmother—a monarch in name only, a stumble between the formidable Grandmother Queen and Restarn One, who had taken in hand the last holdouts between Perripur and the ocean, uniting the empire.

But to take it was not the same as to hold it. If she could not hold the areas her father had taken, no one would care what benches she sat on or for how long or what murmured appreciations she made while staring at some amardide tapestry.

The mining towns. The border cities. Smuggled gold. Counterfeit coins.

If this continued she was well on her way to being another interim ruler, a stepping stone for someone else in the family, enthroned only until someone with more fortitude could be found.

The way the other royals looked at her was disturbing. Bemusedly, as if wondering why she had been on her father's list at all. From a handful of cousins her own age to Lismar and her Cohort, there was no shortage of those eager to try their hand at her position.

She knew she must make a succession list. The problem was that her father's list already contained the obvious successors, and all of them knew it. To make a list the same as his felt like the worst kind of defeat, and stiffened her resolve not to die anytime soon.

Innel was entirely out of the question. Naming him, should anyone find out—or worse yet, the list be needed—would incite a war among the royals, something they'd managed to avoid for some time. Or even a coup from the Houses, by whose collective patronage and loyalty the Anandynars kept their throne.

"Do you worry, Your Grace?"

Always. But Sachare meant Innel. A safer subject than her thoughts, certainly.

"Not with the numbers of troops he's taken," Cern said.

He had also insisted on taking the seer, leaving the mage with Cern. She would have preferred it the other way around, finding the black-robed man a disturbing presence in her palace, but she had accepted Innel's reasoning.

"No one ever lost a battle by taking too much force," Sachare said.

"Well, he'd better not lose this one."

Sachare made a thoughtful, noncommittal sound, something she did well.

If Innel lost this, she was going to need to seriously consider the not-very-subtle advice of her ministers about replacing him as Lord Commander.

He would not take such a step backwards gracefully.

Now Sachare was sorting through Cern's just-delivered clothes. She took a red-as-blood silk jacket, creases pressed to knife-sharp edges, shook it, turned it inside out, and did it again.

"You really think the laundry a threat?"

"Not everyone is as delighted to have you enthroned as I am, Your Grace," she said, tracing the hems and collar by running the seams through her fingertips.

So many ways to be afraid for your life. As she was growing up, her father had told her that ruling was never as splendid or amusing as those watching seemed to think, but he himself had managed to make it seem otherwise with his feasts and hunts and campaigns. She had not believed anything he said anyway, because it was clear he did not care much about the inconveniences of the truth, and that he would give himself every advantage no matter who might pay the price.

Like her mother. She pushed the thought away.

Now that Cern held the throne—for however long that lasted—she discovered her father had been telling the truth about how unpleasant it was, at least. Ruling was far from glorious.

Really, it wasn't even much fun.

She was beginning to understand his various indulgences. Why not suck the marrow from every moment you could? Otherwise life reduced itself to a constant calculation of risk and reward and struggle and little else.

Could she take a stroll outside? Not if fog clung to stone walkways where shadowy corners could hide threats, or if the sun shone too brightly and her guards might be momentarily blinded. Should the Ulawesan envoy be allowed to petition her in person, accomplishing a more favorable agreement with that wealthy Perripin state by flattering the envoy? Not if he had never been in the royal presence before, and certainly not with that many retainers by his side.

Sachare gave a small cry.

"What?" Cern asked.

"A pin," Sachare said, sucking at her index finger. "An accident. Most likely." She examined the offending bit of metal. "But this"—and here Sachare jabbed the air in Cern's direction with the pin—"could as easily have been a spring-snap coated in a tincture designed to take your mind and rot it from the inside like a bad fruit."

"Thank you for giving me more nightmares, Sacha."

"My pleasure, Your Grace."

"You seem healthy enough."

"These things take time," Sachare said dryly and resumed her inspection. She glanced up a moment, as if checking to see that Cern was still there.

Because she might escape? Climb out the window? Somehow wander off alone?

Stop that, she told herself sternly. If she could not trust Sachare, then she was truly lost, and her best hope was for a quick and painless death.

With a snap Sachare shook out a magenta tunic trimmed in lace overstitch and a repeating brocade of the monarchy's sigil.

"Yes, my lady?"

Cern had been staring. "I envy you your long hair, Sacha." A small thing. A tiny freedom.

Sachare's face showed mild confusion. "Surely now you can wear your hair any way you choose."

Cern's hair had been cut too short to gather since she was old enough to walk; a practical cut, bangs at an angle that became more pronounced as she got older, allowing one short, token lock at the right side that might be tied or braided in decoration.

"Think of the many images of the Grandmother Queen. I can no more change my haircut than I can change my family's colors."

Sachare held up the magenta tunic. "So—a little?"

"A little," Cern allowed.

A small chuckle from her chamberlain. Her friend, in truth, and possibly her only one. Certainly her closest companion of the most years. The boys of the Cohort, grown to men and heirs, were not friends, but something else.

Innel was a necessity first and foremost, though he would be more than the Grandmother Queen's consorts, and more than her own father's string of women.

Which put her in mind of her mother again.

As a child she had once secretly hoped to find that Restarn was not her father after all, but as she aged the facial resemblance became undeniable. Good thing, really; he might otherwise have disowned her as easily as he had discarded the many women he had bedded who were no more to him than dams to breed his hoped-for litters.

And all he had to show for it was a litter of one. Herself.

A knock at the door of the inner chambers. Sachare went to consult with the guards in the antechamber, the also-guarded space between the already-guarded hallway and her inner chambers.

So many chambers. So many protections.

As always Cern noted the voices, the sounds, the patterns, listening for aberrations.

Srel followed Sachare inside. This was rare, for Sachare to let anyone in her chambers. Something had happened. She fervently hoped it wasn't bad news about Innel.

"Your Majesty," Srel said with a bow.

"Speak."

He took a breath and paused. Cern was used to this, but not from Srel, who usually knew better than to waste her time. It did nothing to reassure her.

"The Royal Consort's sister," he said. "Cahlen."

"I know her name," Cern snapped, tension overcoming her. "What happened?"

"She has taken a horse from the stables and left Yarpin at speed."

"*What?*"

"As you may know, Your Grace, she is subject to—instabilities of temperament and inconsistencies of mind, so—"

Cern waved a hand. "Yes, yes. Where has she gone, and why?"

"We don't know that. Yet. Quite. Though there seems to have been a message, arrived by bird."

"What message?"

"Again, your majesty, I am so very sorry, but we don't know. That the message arrived was confirmed by her assistants, but only the Consort's sister read it. Cahlen took the message and apparently some of the feathers of the bird that brought it."

"That's"—Cern glanced at Sachare—"strange, isn't it?"

"Yes, Your Grace," Sachare confirmed.

"Send someone after her. Find out what happened."

"Yes, Your Majesty."

"What direction did she go?"

"East, Your Majesty."

✧ ✧ ✧

Cern felt her mind wander again, and drew it back. The eparch of House Brewen was still speaking—how long had it been now?—a new posture with each point, holding his arm up, or a hand to his forehead, then a deep, ragged breath before resuming. Then the eparch of Finch would stand, interrupting, her high voice shrill as she became increasingly agitated. House Flore's eparch shook his head at all this, making impressively loud clicking sounds to show his disapproval. With what, she wasn't sure and didn't really want to know.

She doubted she could bear another minute.

Much as she hated to admit it, her father was right: there was nothing grand about being queen. It seemed to be largely about reassuring everyone around her, most particularly the Houses by whose lands, holdings, and efforts Arunkel produced food and iron and ships. She was to make sure they were secure in the monarchy's attention so that they might continue to do what they did best.

Her real job, she was coming to understand, was to seem certain. In the Houses. In the monarchy. To infuse all meetings and conclaves and negotiations and adjudications with an appropriate sense of gravity, history, and credibility.

How had her father always made that part seem so easy? He had about him a sort of size and weight that no one would even think to argue with. *Restarn esse Arunkel.* Who was Arunkel.

For a moment she found herself wishing she could ask his advice on how to be more like him.

She stood. The arguments and clicks trailed into silence.

"Eparchs and representatives," she said as politely as she could manage, "you will have to excuse me."

Guards preceded and followed, encircling her instantly, mixing with the seneschal, courtiers, aides, secretaries, and the ever-present Sachare.

So many people. Always so many people.

As she strode down the corridor, her seneschal walked backwards to face her as he spoke.

"Your Majesty," he began.

She flicked her hands, a gesture both of rejection and acceptance of the carefully worded point he was about to make. "No one will be served if I lose my temper."

Cern was beginning to understand why her father sometimes interrupted meetings to veer off into irrelevant stories about his travels and campaigns. Or fell into sudden, scowling silences. Beginning to understand it all too well.

"Without you there, Your Majesty—"

"I know," she said with more force than she'd intended. He was retreating before her as smoothly as if he had been walking backwards his entire life. Well, maybe he had; she could not remember another seneschal. "Send wine and whatever happens to be good from the kitchen. They will wait."

The seneschal gestured at an aide, who ducked his head and slipped away between the moving rings of people around her.

It wouldn't be so intolerable if this weren't a discussion about something that should have been settled already, at the last Charter Court. What was the point of having the Court's chaos every fifteen years if the Houses then refused to honor those damned charters, seeking every possible means to undercut the contracts and demand new terms?

As tempting as it was to throw them all out and force them to come to terms without her, these were Elupene's Lesser Houses, and Elupene had fingers on every side of mutton, basket of vegetables, and bag of grain. The empire had many mouths, and of all the things the monarchy could be said to be responsible for, keeping people fed was high on the list.

Elupene, like the other great Houses, could not be ignored. It followed that even their Lesser Houses must be attended to.

"May I at least suggest to them how long it might be until your gracious return, Your Majesty?"

"Give me a bell." Not quite an hour to walk off her foul mood.

The seneschal bowed and peeled off, worming his way through the orbits surrounding her as the entire constellation moved down the hallway.

She had intended to stop at the garden and simply sit at whatever bench was most in need of her attention, inhaling the scent of lilac and honey flute, thinking of nothing for a short while, but her feet took her past that exit and out the doors. Sachare gave the smallest of amused exhales, and Cern glanced sidelong at her, but by then her chamberlain had set her face back to neutral.

Ah well; Sachare could think what she wished. The dogs would help replenish the cistern of Cern's temper, and that was good for everyone.

As she arrived at the kennels, she found herself

comparing the dogs and the eparchs and finding the eparchs wanting. Once you had established an understanding with the dogs, they didn't change their minds and try to renegotiate. Yes, they tested you, but they tested in the open, without subterfuge and endless posturing, and when they were sure of you, they stopped challenging.

It had taken her time to understand all this, weeks of talking to the handlers, watching her father's dogs in an attempt to make some sense of what he'd seen in the beasts.

Then, to her astonishment, she had begun to. It was as if, as she sat outside the cages watching Chula and Tashu observe her, she had begun to take their measure in return. To understand their scent as they understood hers.

At the kennels' door everything slowed as some urgent discussion ensued about who in her retinue would go, and in what order, and who would remain outside. They all did something important, she was sure, though it was sometimes hard to keep track of what. They sorted it out fairly quickly, leaving half her guards and most of the rest arrayed outside, allowing her to take a lesser crowd inside with her. Sachare and the inner circle of guards joined her.

Not alone, never alone.

Kennelmaster and assistants dropped whatever they had been doing and bowed, standing ready. From their cage, Chula and Tashu huffed, a sort of throaty sound that they'd been bred to make in lieu of a full bark, which they could also produce, but did rather less often. Something about being able to stay silent in battle, she'd been told.

She was, she realized, smiling. The kennelmaster opened the cage door, and Chula and Tashu came bounding out. Cern dropped to her knees and hugged them as they snuffled at her head and ears and neck and beat her lightly with their tails.

It was worth it, taking this time. If the Houses only knew how much it improved her mood, they'd be beyond grateful to these large beasts.

"Your Majesty," Sachare said meaningfully, relaying a look from a guard who had no doubt had it relayed to him across a line of people to reach her.

Time. She was out of it again.

"Yes," she sighed. "All right."

She petted Chula and Tashu one last time, leading them back to their cage. They balked, but only a little, and she laughed but insisted, so in they went. She dropped the bolt as they watched her through the bars, tails still twitching hopefully.

"I want to see the pups, Sacha."

"Yes, Your Grace," Sachare said, lips pursed in an expression of mild reprimand, which Cern ignored.

The kennels stretched the length of the long, converted stables, dogs in stalls on either side, and the new litter in the back, at the end of the walkway and around a corner. An assistant held out for her inspection her favorite of the new pups.

The runt of the litter, a tiny thing with black-tipped ears. When she'd taken the throne, she'd halted the practice of killing the smallest and weakest. Give them a chance, she'd said. Who knew what they might become?

She held him in her arms now, grabbed his snout when he tried to nibble her, let him lick her hand in apology.

After a few minutes she met Sachare's look.

"Time to go," she agreed reluctantly. She sighed, handing the pup to the kennelmaster, who returned it to a large cage beyond the stall in which they stood.

Cern stepped into the walkway, her gaze sweeping the area. Ever so slightly, three of her six guards stiffened. There was something odd about the motion. She frowned, trying to figure out what she was seeing.

Her innermost set, these six. Capable, strong. Loyal beyond question. The best of her already impressive best.

A sound from the far end of the building, out of place. A crash. A cry. A shout.

Beyond the stall, one of the pups began to growl softly.

"Sacha," Cern said.

Now distant and urgent calls. Around the corner, a shriek, cut short.

As one, her guards turned away from her toward the sounds, reaching for weapons. Half of them dropped a step back, facing the trouble, whatever it was, drawing large knives.

Tight quarters, so of course they'd draw knives. They could hardly swing swords in this narrow walkway.

But this was not quite how they were supposed to array themselves. Two lines, one close to her, one farther away—yes—but not so close to each other.

She hissed at Sachare, tugging her backwards from her guards, putting the wall at their backs. Sachare quickly drew a knife from her boot.

In a blink, two of the forward row of guards cried out,

one clutching his neck as he crumpled, bloody and dripping, another folded in half, a knife pulled out of his ribs by the guard behind him. The third forward guard turned to face the second row, a look of astonishment and shock on his face that mirrored Cern's own. In the moment in which he opened his mouth—to object, to ask, Cern never found out—the traitor guard sank his knife deep into the other's belly.

Betrayal.

Loud shouts bled in distantly from outside of the building. A deep pounding, as if someone was trying to crash through doors barricaded shut. Barking from everywhere.

"Stay back, Your—" Sachare began, then fell silent. The three traitor guards turned to face the two of them.

Cern knew them by name. Had known them for years. Trusted them. Did they really think they would survive this treason?

Only then did it occur to her to wonder if *she* would.

Where were the rest of her guards? The loyal ones?

More pounding in the distance. The guards were locked out. Some ingenious and fast treasonous work, this was.

Sachare stepped between Cern and the armed men, slashing the air in warning.

Three new guards appeared behind the three traitors, and relief flooded Cern, but no, no—she didn't recognize these at all. They weren't hers.

"Quickly," one of the newcomers hissed at the others, glancing back down the walkway. The two farthest men raised short lances, each movement fast and spare, eyes on her. Aiming for her. In quick succession the lancers snapped their weapons forward.

Sachare darted to stand in the path and howled in fury as one of the lances stuck into her chest, the other missing Cern by a hair's breadth, sinking into the wood behind, breaking Cern's momentary freeze.

Grabbing Sachare's arm, she yanked her back through the stall door out of which they had just come. She and Sachare set their backs to the door to hold it shut. It bucked against them as those outside slammed into it.

Sachare had turned white and pasty, swallowing repeatedly, hand wrapped tightly around the hilt of the lance in her chest. Cern did not think Sachare would be on her feet much longer.

Six. There were six assassins outside this stall door. She knew how many capable, armed men she could hope to break through herself, and this was too many.

As a child in the Cohort, when all the others were taken to combat practice, Cern had been taken aside to a windowless room. It had started simply enough: her father had held up an hourglass.

"You have until this empties," he said. "If you can get to the door, you can join the Cohort for the next meal. Otherwise you go hungry."

Then a large man had picked her up and began carrying her around the room. Sometimes he would set her down and let her run a few steps before catching her up again, lifting her over his shoulders or spinning her while she screamed and cried. It didn't matter how hard she ran, hit, bit, or begged, she could not get loose from him, or past him, to the door.

The men and women her father had chosen were clever and careful; they never hurt her in any way that couldn't be easily covered with clothing. Beneath her clothes were the cuts and bruises that, old and new, she was rarely without.

As the years passed, her training came to include objects of all sorts, from weapons to chairs and tables. Metal pitchers. Scarves and tapestries. Whatever was handy.

All the while her father watched.

She didn't have to defeat them, it was made clear, only to get through. To safety and help. She learned. She found ways to make it to the door.

But not always. Sometimes there were too many of them and no matter what she did, or how fast she was, she went hungry.

Too many. Like now.

One more slam and they would be inside the stall. Could she hold them off a few moments more, long enough for the rest of her guards to arrive? Surely her entire queen's guard could not have been turned.

No, it had not; distant pounding told her that outside the kennels people were trying to get in. She only had to keep these ones away a bit longer.

Some quick calculation told her that of the twenty guards who had come into the kennels with her, all were turned or slain. She put aside sorrow until later. If there was a later.

Anger could stay.

Pounding and slamming from everywhere, all around, the building shaking.

The door at their backs bucked again, hard and sudden, slamming the two of them forward into the middle of the straw-strewn stall. Sachare yanked the spear out of her chest and held it out to Cern, who took it as Sachare crumpled to the ground, blood gushing from her wound and bubbling from her mouth.

The stall door burst open, the set of assassins looming in the doorway a moment, then surging toward her.

She did not have to get through them. Just stay alive until help could arrive.

Her back against the wall, she made the first attacker gape by saying his name urgently, making him hesitate long enough for her to throw her weight into a thrust that went into his belly and through him, surprising her almost as much as him.

She tried to yank the spear back, but it was stuck somewhere inside him. She cursed as they swarmed her. She twisted with fast elbows, and someone swore in response. A quick drop to headbutt another, who backed away but not far enough. Something sharp bit into her side and she twisted again, but her ribs burned with pain.

A grab for her hair, and she shook her head. The hand slipped off her head. Suddenly she understood her own haircut.

So many things to learn. Perhaps a little late for some lessons. In moments this would be over, and not in her favor.

So fast: a hand on her arm, another on her neck, an armored body pressing in close, and she was trapped. Only a lifetime of habit kept her fighting now, as futile as it was.

That, too, had been drilled into her in that windowless room. Overcome, slammed to the ground, an adult sitting on her child's torso so heavy she could barely breathe, while another slapped her face and head until she could not think. The first time, she had wrapped her arms around her head and shouted: "You win, you win, stop, stop!"

A sharp command from her father, and all at once she was free again, adults standing back from her. She sat up from the stone floor. The expression on her father's face made her stomach feel leaden.

He stood. "You give up?"

"Yes. They are too big, ser—" she began.

"No excuses," he said forcefully. "You do not surrender, Cern. It is not permitted to you. Not now, not ever."

His disappointment was worse than the hunger.

And now, overcome by the best of her guards and three strangers, a tangled scramble to grab her tight, she still hit, kicked, squirmed, bit. Large hands struggled to gain a hold of her and finally succeeded.

She'd bought a little time. Not enough.

A knife, gripped tight, toward her. Not a threat. Held and positioned to kill.

Distant shouts. Feet pounding.

Too late.

What would her father say now? Cern, the weak two-year queen. He'd be right. No excuses.

Suddenly a streak of black and tan flashed by her legs. One of the men holding her cried out and let go. The hand with the knife opened. The blade went down with the man.

Snarling. Shouting. A scream.

The traitors turned their attention away from her to the ground.

Now she understood: Chula and Tashu had somehow gotten loose. No one would have let them out, so, impossible as it seemed, they must have smashed through the bars of their cage and crashed out of their kennels to come to her.

On the ground, one of her former guards was trying in vain to fend off Tashu while Chula grabbed him by the neck and shook powerfully. He went limp. Now two other men were down, flailing, screaming, the dogs flashing across them, leaving them unmoving and bloody.

The stall door opened.

"Your Majesty! Are you all right?"

Her guard captain stepped in, followed by another tencount of guards and Srel. The stall was suddenly very crowded.

She drew herself upright.

"See to Sachare," she said, struggling to suppress the waver in her voice. "And—no!" Cern swung her fist into the arm of a man who held a small crossbow, had raised it to aim at Tashu, mistaking the dog for her attacker.

Tashu looked up at her from the man whose neck the dog had broken. Her muzzle was covered in blood.

"Those men are traitors," Cern said, pointing to the men lying broken on the ground. "The dogs have enacted my judgment and are not to be touched."

She held out her hands to them, her rescuers, and Chula and Tashu left the bloody bodies to come to her.

They sat, one on each side, heads tilted to look up at her. Mouths bloodied, they seemed to be smiling.

A memory of her father flashed into her mind, but it must be a false memory, because she was sure she had never seen him look at her with anything like pride. Yet she could see him now in her mind's eye, also smiling.

"Your Majesty," the captain said. "You are bleeding."

Chula and Tashu refused to go back into their broken, shattered stall, growling at everyone who came close except Cern. They did not want to leave her side. She did not want them to.

"Yes," she told them, and everyone around her. "You both come with me."

"Your Majesty," someone said with concern. "You are hurt. We should carry you. You are—"

"No. I will walk."

The news would be all over the palace that there had been an attempt on her life. She must be seen. And walking. Truly, nothing could be more important.

At every step, the dogs stayed tight by her side, the warmth of their bodies reassuring against her trembling legs. Where she had been cut, she pressed her arm tightly against her side.

"Get the doctor," she said urgently to the seneschal as she walked painfully forward. "And the mage."

He left, threading through the mass of guards that now surrounded her as she slowly made her way out of the kennels, one slow step at a time, then along the walkway and up the stairs into the palace proper.

She was not only limping, she realized, she was

shaking violently. Not acceptable. She stopped a moment, took deep breaths, finding herself looking for Sachare to lean on, pushing away the dread and fear that threatened her at the thought of losing Sacha.

Drawing herself as straight as she could, head high, she refused to look anything like as shaken and beaten as she felt. Another thing her father had taught her.

The dark-skinned, black-clad mage sat unmoving next to Sachare's body, his hands on her stomach and chest. Cern sat nearby, a cloth squeezed between her arm and side, the dogs at her feet.

She had ordered everyone else out.

"Well?" she asked, when she could bear it no longer. If she lost Sachare—

"I may be able to save her," the mage said.

"You *may* be able to? What does that mean? Do we not pay you, and exorbitantly well?"

At that Keyretura took his hands off Sachare and slowly turned in his chair. He met Cern's gaze evenly. For a very long moment neither of them spoke.

"I apologize," Cern said at last. "This woman—" She exhaled. "She is my friend. That is a rare and precious thing and I cannot afford to lose it. You must save her." At his continued stare, she added: "I ask your help, High One."

For another moment he met her look. Then, wordlessly, he turned back and put his hands again on Sachare.

The assassins who had killed her loyal guards, who had cut Sachare so grievously, were all dead, every single one of them. Somehow in the violent moments following the nearly successful attempt on Cern's life, each of them had been taken into the Beyond.

This was clearly far beyond bad luck; everyone should know better than to kill those who might know about a plot against the queen. Someone had been ready for this failure and keen to be sure no one survived to reveal details.

Hardly surprising, she supposed, that whoever organized this nearly successful treason still remained at large. They would be more cautious now, at least, having failed at what must have been an impressively expensive and risky attempt on her life. They would be unlikely to try again anytime soon.

Nearly every one of her ancestors who had sat on the throne had survived such an attempt. In a way, it was a compliment: she was seen as powerful enough to be worth taking down instead of disregarding. And having survived it, she would be seen as stronger.

Could it even be one of the Houses? Would they go so far?

"The Houses love to make contracts," her father had told her. "Then twist them into strange shapes." He laughed, his voice filling the room, then went abruptly sober. "Don't confuse their obedience with loyalty."

Cern remembered thinking she would be hard pressed to confuse the two; loyalty was just a word. Looking at the unconscious Sachare, near death from having put herself between Cern and a spear, she felt an ache in her own chest.

"If you can possibly save her—" she began.

"You'll pay me exorbitantly well," he said wryly. "Yes, I heard you before."

She exhaled in a long stream and considered the influence and futility of words. Hers in particular. "More than that, High One," she said. "If you can save her, you will have the gratitude of the Arunkel crown and queen. I would like to think that is worth something beyond mere coin."

He looked at her thoughtfully a moment then nodded, his attention again on Sachare.

Chapter Thirty-five

How dare he?

Maris rode the Great Road north, stopping only for food and, occasionally, to let the horse rest. When it proved too frequent, she swapped the beast out for another, hardier animal and resumed her northward press.

It was almost refreshing, this level of fury, banishing uncertainty and extraneous thought along with the sharp concern she felt for Dirina and Pas. She rode hard, dawn to dusk and beyond when the moon or starlight allowed.

Despite the unrest, the Great Road was most direct. Those who stood in her way, thinking to thieve or threaten, she put to the ground in as expedient a manner as she could, not bothering with painless unconsciousness or even life. Some screamed as they collapsed. Others twitched and frothed at the mouth. Perhaps they lived. Perhaps not. She did not have time to care.

She came to the familiar multicolored inn where she had last left Enlon and Amarta. She stared at the building long minutes, then down at her hands, realizing they were still wrapped tightly in the horse's pale mane. The horse huffed, his breath labored. As Maris assessed the animal's body, she felt shame at the hard use to which she'd put him.

Dismounting, she banked the coals of her anger, cleared fury's residue from her body, and sought grounding in the land beneath.

Anger was power, but only when it neither blocked nor turned the channel from its destination.

She thought again of the horse. Many years of her apprenticeship had been spent studying the human body and its workings, but after she was created she spent time in hovels, treehouses, boats, grubhouses—or under sky— trying to bring out a baby, to heal a bone-break, to understand an illness—only to find that a dog or bird or a goat—in one case a stunted horse—nestled or huddled or hid nearby, more important to the person under her hands than their own suffering. Many times the fierce demand to heal a non-human companion before themselves had stalled her work. But she had learned to heal animals.

Now she dipped her focus into the horse's body, examining the heart and blood and lungs, breath and brain. She cleared out his fatigue, soothed his nerves, and touched on the places where his reserves were slim. He calmed, and so did she.

Calmed enough to think.

What in the lifeless dark was she doing? Was she really intending to ride into the palace, find Keyretura, and demand Dirina and Pas?

If she was lucky, he would laugh and mock her and tell her to go away.

If she were not, well.

For a long moment she stood, considering.

She would, she decided, leading her horse to the stables and brushing and food, sleep on her fury. In the morning she would consider again.

Dawn found her watching through the window as the town's buildings and roads went from gray to color.

What would she do if she did not go forward? Go home to an empty house?

No.

She began to dress, then instead put on the black robes she had brought with her in the half-thought that perhaps Keyretura would respect her more if she dressed the part.

Now, atop her rested horse, traveling the road north and then through the gates of Yarpin, she felt the stares. Everyone—shopkeepers, scribes, messengers, beggars—stopped where they stood, heads swiveling to watch her pass.

Let them stare. Today there were only two Iliban whose fate concerned her.

At the palace gates, those waiting in the long line for entrance flattened to the side to get out of her way. She met the wide-eyed stares of the guards who neither waved her through nor moved to stop her. At the palace's main door, she dismounted to more gaping looks. Someone, she was sure, would take excellent care of her horse and belongings.

By now he would know she was here.

As she climbed the wide stone steps, guards backed out of her way.

She could not quite remember why she had denied herself the robes for so long.

Then a particularly large guard stepped in front of her. "You can't—" he managed before she took his consciousness. He stumbled to a wall and slipped to the floor. After that no one else attempted to stop her.

She felt him then—suddenly, keenly. Ignoring the trembling in her stomach, she followed his trail, the conduit between them, the umbilical cord that she had never found a way to cut.

A flight of stairs up, a hallway east. Searching for the taste of the man who had taught her to taste.

Then his door. She hesitated, her anger tinged with uncertainty.

He had taken her people, she reminded herself, sparking to flame the embers of wrath, those that guarded her from fear, even while she knew that fury was a weak protection.

He was there on the other side of the door. She was as good as in his presence already. To stand here and consider—to waver—knowing he would know and be amused—was surely as absurd as having come here in the first place.

She depressed the latch. It clicked open. She pushed.

Keyretura sat at a low table on cushions, a writing tablet before him. So very Perripin, so unlike Arunkel, that he must have insisted on it. A cylinder of tea at his hand. Dark and bitter; she could smell it from here.

Stacks of books in the corner and too many of them.

Bought on the road, she was sure. He traveled with his books. They had that in common.

Seeing him there at the far end of the room brought the blood to pounding in her ears.

"Uslata," he said in the old language.

Summoning a certainty she did not feel, she stepped inside, shut the door behind her. "Aetur."

His gaze ran quickly up and down her, taking in the black robes. He had not, she was certain, ever seen her wear them before. She had left his side the moment she had been made a mage.

He switched to Perripin, gestured with his hand to the table. "The tea is cooling, but I can have more sent for, Marisel. Arunkin tea, but with enough honey it is almost palatable."

Of all the things he could have said, this she had expected least. What was he doing?

Trying to take her off her guard, of course.

How dare he?

"No," she said adamantly. "I—"

"A long time since we've talked."

"I—Talked? We never talked," she snapped. "You talked. I listened. I had to, because you—" Sense caught up with her tongue. She fell silent. So many years spent learning not to argue with him.

"Not long enough, perhaps, Marisel dua Mage?"

Fury restored her focus. "You know why I'm here."

"You have business with me." He put down his tablet and stood. "Your need is urgent and there is no time for useless chat. Sit with me."

"I need obey you no longer, *Aetur.*"

A snort. "Then state your business so you can leave."

"How dare you," she exhaled, at last giving her anger voice. "You broke into my home. You violated my land."

"You thought it secure? From me?" He seemed amused, but his tone was mild.

For him to suddenly rage, or become bitterly unyielding—neither would have surprised her. But this?

Uncertainty trickled through her, followed by a thin stream of cold dread.

"I thought you would respect my lands, Aetur. My doors. My wards."

"Why did you think this?"

She struggled to emulate his calm, but it would mean setting aside the anger. And then what would protect her from sense? She wiped sweat from her face. "It is . . ." She struggled for the right words. "Not done." She gritted her teeth at her own words.

"The evidence is not in your favor, Maris."

She sputtered. "Did you not teach me such trespass would be beyond unacceptable, tantamount to seeking a fight, to cross another mage's lines?"

"Ah, so you do remember that I was your teacher. You've avoided me so long, I had begun to wonder."

"Some things are best left in the past, forgotten. They are not yours."

He tilted his head. "I have them, and you do not. Whose do you say they are?"

"They belong to no one," she shouted at him, taking two steps toward him, then recoiling, stepping back again. She shook her hands open, struggling to find ground through them, down the stories and through the many basements below. Too far. Instead she groped for the corners of the room where stone might lie behind wood.

"Again, the evidence does not support your assertion, louder though it may be."

"You have no right to them. They are not some pieces to be moved about on a gameboard to serve monarchical whims."

"That is exactly what they are. You want them for similar reasons: to serve your own desires."

"No! I want them free."

"Free to scurry and hide from monarchical whims as a consequence of being the seer's blood kin? Exactly what kind of freedom do you have in mind for them?"

She felt her throat tighten. "Return them to me. I claim them as mine."

He laughed, a rasping sound. "Then it is not freedom you want for them at all, these living things you claim as yours. Are they servants? Are they your slaves?"

"You twist my words."

"Your reasoning is disordered, Marisel," he said. "I taught you better than this."

It all came flooding back: the unending failures, neverending challenges, the many and harsh consequences.

Keyretura lifted his cup to his lips and drank, his dark eyes on hers.

"I thought you might be above theft and kidnapping, Aetur."

He grimaced. "You think to shame me into remorse? You would be better off to try my pity instead. Beg me for them."

"No."

"Then what will you do to find these Iliban you are so outraged to have misplaced, daughter?"

"I am not your daughter."

His mocking amusement was entirely gone. "You most certainly are. That is what *uslata* means. I am your mother and father both; I made you as surely as your parents of blood and flesh ever did, in at least as much pain as your mother's mere days of tearing her body asunder to bestow upon you your first breath."

And that fast, Maris's balance was gone, her grounding in shreds.

"Well, Uslata? Will you fight me for them?"

She had learned much in the decades since her creation. About babies who must be coaxed to breathe air. How to repair the ill and injured. The tedious brutality of power. The foul stink of poverty. But she knew nothing about mage-fighting beyond what Keyretura had taught her.

Anger finally vanished in the full cold realization of this folly.

"No, Aetur, I will not fight you," she whispered in answer, subdued. Defeat at his hands was a familiar bitterness on her tongue. It was the taste of ash. She found herself standing at the door, hand on the wood, poised to leave.

"Shall I dispose of them as my fancy takes me, Marisel? I have a number of experiments I have been meaning to try with a woman and child of her womb. Do you leave them in my hands?"

She turned to look at him, outrage overcoming her again.

What are you missing, Marisel?

Then it was obvious what anger and fear had blinded her to: he was provoking her. Deliberately.

"What do you do here?" she asked him.

He smiled his cold smile and spread his hands wide. A clear invitation.

"Teacher," she said, voice low. "You'll kill me."

"That is certainly a possibility. But if you go, you will never see them again. Consider your actions with care."

Wordlessly she shook her head and left.

Her body trembled as she walked the hallway. Guilt ate at her, but it did Dirina and Pas no good for her to die trying to save them. Better to survive. Then, if they did as well—

Maybe he was only threatening.

Do you leave them in my hands?

They were only Iliban.

Pas held a frog with an orange stripe.

She stopped, hand against the painted walls, head down in nausea. When she looked up, green-clad servants and courtiers stared back, frozen where they stood, like terrified prey. She pushed away from the wall, took the stairs down. One flight then another and she was at the great doors leading outside.

Suddenly the line between her and her aetur came alive like a long thick rope sharply snapped at one end. As the wave found her, she felt Keyretura's grasp deep inside her.

He was not, she realized with sinking certainty, going to let her go.

Once she had stood atop a high cliff and taken a step

into empty air. He had been there, yanking her back, setting all her nerves aflame with agony. Another time he had pulled her from a lake, forcing the water from her body until she threw up, then had held her under until she drowned again, pulled her out, repeating the process again and again until she lost count.

The surround. The tighten. The pull.

The pain.

She waited for the pull, but it did not come. Was he giving her time? Time to what? To ready herself?

Too late. Any decision, too late. She walked back to the stairs and climbed, thinking of Dirina and Pas, and hoping that whatever he was going to do to them would not come close to what he had done to her.

The door was locked. He would not let her go, but he would not let her in?

So many times she had knocked on his door to be tested, to be found wanting.

That anger she put into her hands, set her fingertips on the lock and wormed her attention through the labyrinth of mechanics and magics that secured the door. First this way, then that. Back again.

It clicked open.

She stepped inside, drawing on fraying outrage. "I owe you no obedience, Aetur, yet you force me here. State your business so I can leave, damn you."

At this he smiled a little. "Show me what you've learned in the many years since you left my side."

Show me what you have learned. Words she heard so often during her apprenticeship.

The hot rush was a direct press, easily enough deflected, except that it was not only hot, but also sticky, like molten glass; she grabbed the lines from herself to the corners of the room that she had anchored earlier, bleeding into them the heat that stuck to her.

The stickiness remained. A clinging almost-wet. A heavy fog. So familiar, this.

He had not moved from his chair. "So much anger, my uslata. An impressively large reserve of it."

"You—"

Because of you, she started to say.

Something circled her, like steam trailing out the spout of a kettle. She turned the other direction. No, that felt wrong. She reversed direction, turned with it, drawing the spiral of hot steam downward.

"You should be long past blaming me for your suffering, Marisel. The study is never easy. Did I say it would be? I believe I said exactly the opposite."

He had. At great length.

"I was a child. I didn't understand."

"But you stayed. Twenty long years."

The final handful of years together had been every kind of misery; as his impossible demands intensified, so did her loathing and resistance. If there had been any way to break the contract, she felt certain he would have. By then she had given up escaping and had resolved to survive. To finish, no matter what.

Finally he had put her before the Council. She had survived, passed the test, and left the first moment she could.

"Stubborn," she said.

"Stubborn," he agreed, "and thus were you created. There is no other way."

"But you—" She wanted to say something cutting, but she was too focused on drawing down the trail of etheric steam to be able to form words. The steam kept getting stickier and thicker.

Her fingers spread, stretching lines across the room, searching everywhere for stone and metal, the children of the earth, to find and hold fast.

"I taught. You learned. The contract was satisfied. Do you have a complaint?"

She shook her head, throat tight.

The glow around him was a vast reservoir from which etheric smoke encircled her. She recognized this particular challenge: it was one they'd practiced before, in the mock battles she'd had with him so long ago, intended to prepare her for the world of mages. In the time since, she had managed to avoid mages inclined to conflict. Everything she knew about fighting with magic she had learned from Keyretura.

The surround had grown thick enough that the details of the room—table, books, teacup—were dim, as if she she were wrapped in a heavy fog. She tried to cut through it with her focus. Nothing changed.

What are you missing?

She had assumed it was an attack. A touch to the gauze. It rippled around her fingers like fog over a mountaintop. She pushed a hand through and it parted. A step through and a look back at a slowly spinning funnel.

Not an attack after all.

The floor beneath her seemed to move without moving. He was sundering her orientation to ground, she realized, to stone and dirt. She lurched abruptly.

All her lines. In a blink he had cut every one.

She groped blindly to the tile floor underfoot. Tile—just stone, writ small, baked hard. Weaker, but it remembered the ground from which it had been drawn. Small tethers, then; her toes and fingertips quested into the floor.

As he sipped at his teacup, she held tight to the tethers she'd found, and yanked on them all at once as if flying a kite, hoping to catch his attention while she cast around the room for something else to ground onto.

There was a sharp shift as every one of these new tethers was severed.

She let them go, instead latching onto the ceramic cup in his hand. It was common among mages to habitually and etherically mark and own those items they touched; the cup itself could be connected to her aetur's power lines, in which case she could perhaps find some ground through it, through him, while searching for more.

But as she reached fingers of thought for the ceramic in his hand he moved it suddenly, tossing the contents of the cup into the air. The liquid seemed to hang there a moment, then puffed suddenly out into a glistening fog, a thousand tiny mirrors all angled to catch the faint sunlight coming through the windows of the room, a hot flash of white that momentarily blinded her.

She shut her eyes, the afterimage still bright against her lids, still casting about for something in reach that remembered the earth. But he was there, everywhere, making slick each thing so that her etheric fingers could not find purchase. She grasped again and again, slipping. Slipping.

A loud knock at the door.

"Enter," said Keyretura.

As he spoke he dropped every sluice, flash, and diversion. Maris found tile beneath her; copper and silver in the lamp; rings at the posts of the bed, pewter plates and a steel knife; a pitcher of glass; ceramic pipes between the walls; iron grating in the fireplace, and the stone hearth. In a moment she had touched and secured tethers to a hundred things, trickling down her ground through the walls to the earth beneath the palace.

A sense of solidity filled her.

Srel stepped into the room, ducking his head to Keyretura and Maris in that not-quite-bow people gave mages.

"Forgive me, High Ones, I did not realize—"

"What is it?" Keyretura asked.

"The evening meal is ready for you. Shall I bring it or delay it, ser?"

"Bring. With enough for my guest."

"I am not your guest," Maris told him hotly, "and I will not eat with you."

"Then eat without me. Or go hungry."

She could feel him then, a touch within, so fast he was there and gone before she could respond or deflect, leaving a painful pressure in her stomach, making her keenly aware that she was, indeed, hungry.

Another violation. Angrily she pushed out the door past Srel, and stopped in the hallway, breathing hard, too upset to steady anything, not heartbeat, not blood, not the sweat trickling down her back.

After a moment, Srel emerged. He shut the door behind him and watched her a moment.

"Maris," he said gently. "Allow me to bring you food and wine. In the library, perhaps?"

She managed a nod.

In the library enough time passed for her to eat some of what Srel had brought her, and to find herself reading a small book in which she was quickly lost.

It was a journal from some sixty years back, by a Perripin fiddler who had decided to traverse the then-boundaries of the empire, reporting on the places he visited and the people he met. She nibbled at what Srel had brought her, drank hot wine, and read. Lost in the graceful and alluring verse she almost forgot about Keyretura.

Almost.

He touched on the cord connecting them, and Maris was yanked out of the book. She put it away, feeling him come closer to the library with each step.

"Well?" he asked, stepping inside. "What is your grievance, Maris?"

She shook her head mutely.

"You have come all this way to do what, then? Show me how well your new robes fit you? To discover that you are craven? Speak."

Even knowing he said this to provoke her did not stop it from working.

"My parents," she said bitterly.

"Ah, that. If they had survived, Marisel, you would have abandoned the study to care for them, become another Broken, making their sacrifice for your contract worthless."

"My contract was not worth their lives."

"Clearly they disagreed."

"You are responsible for their deaths."

"To refrain from healing is not the same as killing. I did not save them. Nor did you."

"I didn't have the skill to save them, and you knew that!"

"But you do now. Because of them."

She felt fury warm her from head to toe. "You are a horror," she told him. "A corruption."

"Insults," he said, with a shrug. "Not even inventive ones. You disappoint me."

"Don't I always? My grief to you, a hundred times, and a hundred times beyond that."

He made a warding gesture, an ancient Iliban sign. A superstition. An insult. The sides of his mouth curled in derision. "Is that your best?"

The door to the library opened. Srel stood there, eyes wide, expression stark.

"Forgive me, High Ones. The queen—there has been an attack."

Only now did Maris became aware of urgent shouts becoming louder. Keyretura's gaze was suddenly distant.

"So there has." He looked at Maris. "I will be busy for a time, but you will wait for me."

"I do not stay or go at your pleasure."

"Again, the evidence seems to indicate otherwise."

He followed Srel out the door and was gone.

When at last the fever pitch of agitation caused by the attempt on the queen's life eased, Maris was in the bath.

It could, she reasoned, be her last one.

And Keyretura? He would find her when he was ready. It had always been thus: asleep or awake, fed or hungry, naked or clothed, her aetur would come. Lecture. Press. Demand. Test.

Every day for twenty long years.

A bell passed. Then another. With the water cooling she was trying to decide between ending the luxurious immersion or ringing for more boiling water. The door opened and Keyretura stepped in.

"The queen?" she asked him.

"The matter is settled." He studied her a long moment. Then, his voice low, he said: "So be it, Marisel: if you prefer to depart rather than continue this engagement, I will allow it. But be gone before moonrise."

She stood from the tub, dripping.

What was this? A trick? Or was he truly dismissing her?

"Dirina and Pas," she said. "Tell me where they are."

He walked to the door, paused, his back to her.

"No."

He left.

She dressed hurriedly, eager to be gone before he changed his mind. She walked the now-darkened halls, navigating her way as much by memory as sight. At a window she paused to look at the night sky.

Be gone before moonrise.

Simple enough instructions. She would leave her belongings and the horse; it could all be replaced. She would walk. Be gone from this city and from Keyretura.

At each quick step down quiet palace stairways, she listened for him, expecting the touch that meant he had changed his mind. She paused at the palace doors, watched by wary guards who, it was clear, would do nothing to get in her way.

She took the palace grounds one quick step after another. At the gates, cloaked in shadow, she slipped by unnoticed.

Nothing stopped her feet on the well-maintained cobbles of the great square. No taste of him. The line between them was quiet.

Perhaps she was free.

At the huge center fountain, the basin of carved marble, water played out in arcs in all directions. While down-city, the poor struggled to find water they could drink, here in the realm of wealth, water flowed freely all night long. For a time she stood there, watching the streams cascade into the pool below.

She turned in place to gaze over the rooflines of the Great Houses, darkly silhouetted against the starry sky. *There*, she thought, estimating where the moon would rise.

What was she doing? What was wrong with her?

Be gone before moonrise.

She would not allow him to order her around, she decided. Never again. He could command her to go, but she did not have to—

Childish foolishness, this was. Let him command. *Go.*

Yet she stayed another moment and then another, watching the roofline where she expected the moon to rise.

Dirina. Pas. She could not simply abandon them to him.

But even that was not the real reason she stayed.

At last, a point of glowing white slid up and over the huge mansion's roofline, exactly where she had anticipated. In moments it grew into a glowing, curved white blade, the rising halfmoon coming free of its cover.

She felt him then, standing at the edge of the square, and she took a step away from the fountain, away from the palace, away from him, fear driving her fast footfalls. Nothing, etheric or otherwise, barred her way. No leash snapped tight from her gut. Maybe she could still leave.

He had not moved. He had not spoken.

But instead of leaving, she stopped at the edge of the square. She realized how weary she was of her own terror. The connection between them, the one that she had been trying to escape these many years, was not merely an etheric one.

Turning, she walked toward him, stopping a few paces away. "Aetur, let the Iliban go. They have done nothing to offend you. Please don't make them pay for my mistakes."

"They pay for the seer's mistakes, not yours, and their lives are of no consequence to me."

"Their lives matter to me. Tell what I must do to save them."

"Show me what you have learned in the years since you were created."

Pinpoints of light came from distant shadowy corners, like flashes at the edge of vision. Why he did this, she did not know, but from her earliest memories, this was one of the signs that a hard testing was to come, leaving her sobbing, bleeding. Aching in body, spirit, mind.

Pain. So much pain.

No, that was the past.

She whirled in place, trailing her outstretched fingers, pointing downward, dropping tens and then hundreds of lines of flow into the stone-covered square, down into the dirt and farther into the basalt below. He would cut these ties in moments, so she must quickly find another plan. What?

Suddenly, a hold on her right wrist. A pull, a yank, as if a mountain lion had clamped onto her forearm, locked down, crushing bones, rending and tearing her flesh. She cried out in pain, making a quick set of changes inside her body to temporarily dampen the agony, a practice she knew from her work with mothers birthing their young. She sank her grounding lines into the earth through the mangled arm as well as the good one; life would carry magic no matter how broken it was, until the very moment when it began to rot.

His next attack would come soon. What to do? What did she know that he did not?

As she finished her turn, drawing power from the earth, she sent it back down through the lines she had made, flinging the ends farther and farther from herself so that they trailed out to cross him at his feet, ankles, legs, thinking to disrupt his intention, even a little bit, to give herself time to find the next step to surviving this.

For a moment she wondered at his intention. Surely, if he had wanted her dead, she would be dead?

He might be toying with her. There was still time to die.

As the lines crossed his body, he slowed, but only a little, stepped over them, as if treading knee-high ocean swells.

A blink and then another. A line of not-quite light came from him, a strange mix of true light and the various etherics surrounding them both. It wrapped around her in dull silver, as if the moon's light had been bled to make spider-silk and she were being cocooned. In moments she felt it tighten, closing off the night's bands of grays.

Almost a pleasant sensation, like her warm bath. She was reminded of Gallelon's snug embrace. Babies were swaddled thus in soft blankets, to reassure, to comfort. Deep inside her was that memory, and some part of her was calmed.

Trickery, to take down her guard. She tried to shake away her body's sense of rightness in this cocoon, but it held tight. Then it was too tight, gone from warm embrace to suffocating wrap.

In a flash, her air was gone. She struggled to poke holes in the surrounding cocoon so that she could breathe.

But no, she realized, as a new motion began, that had not been the attack, only the base for it. Now she felt his touch on her head, neck, and shoulders, delicately worming its way inside her body as she sought her grounding tethers, but they were gone, cut away in this prison of light, no stone or tile in reach. Not so much as a speck of dirt.

It was oddly simple to still her emotions. She no longer needed to fear his coming for her, because he was here. No cause to fear death, either; if he wanted her dead, she would be dead. Her terror of him, such a constant companion these many years, was gone.

But his attack was not. A three-pronged assault came at her, all at once: the blood to her brain slowed, a rapid patter at her heart, and a near-whine inside her head that signaled a coming shock.

Killing blows, each one, any one of which she might be able to deflect or undo. But all three together? It was beyond her.

Had been beyond her, she told herself, in the days when he held her contract.

All right, then: one at a time. She drew the growing spark into the bone of her head, spreading it across the hardest part of her. It would cost her a wretched headache later, but that was far preferable. At the tattoo-touch so deep inside her chest, her heart began to tighten and clench. She held the cramp in abeyance, struggling to keep both sides of the organ quiet one moment more, to help them remember their harmony together. When she released them, they beat in rhythm.

Then the last attack, the simplest of the three. A rush of sound in her ears like a crashing waterfall. She struggled to stay conscious, head swimming as she dropped to one knee and then the other, hands flat on the ground, her vision darkening. In memory or imagination he laughed at her.

To succumb to this simplest of the three was so very disappointing.

And that was her error, she realized now, her thoughts slowing even further: she had been defending. Thinking him invulnerable, she had not attacked him, not at all.

A foolish strategy. She could see that now.

With the last of her focus she hurled at him a pinpoint of her will, like the finest of needles, piercing through the cocoon around her, sinking into his skin at the navel to find the delicate nerve that began there and wandered the body, the one that she knew so very well from her work with mothers and infants.

There it was. All it needed was a good solid push, and—

As she collapsed to the ground, she heard a sharp exhalation of surprise and pain from Keyretura. In the moment before she lost consciousness, she realized that she had never heard such a sound from him before.

Her last thought was to wonder if it had anything to do with what she had done.

Maris came awake, eagerly gulping air. Around her, the night was dark and quiet.

The cocoon of light was gone. The square was quiet. Maris leveraged herself up with her good arm, dizzy but alive, head and wrist pounding with pain. She looked around for Keyretura.

He lay some distance away, one hand on his head, the other on his chest, breathing hard. Healing himself.

Healing himself?

Had she really gotten through his defenses and stopped his assault? She sat up, for a long moment staring at him in wonder.

She had attacked her aetur. She might even have hurt him. An impossibility, she would have thought.

Minutes went by as she watched him. He moved his hands to his stomach, then back up to his chest, neck, and head. She knew what he was doing: he was repairing the damage she'd done to that critical nerve. At last he put his hands down and looked over at her. To her surprise, he smiled.

Another game?

"I abhor you," she told him.

He chuckled. "At last, the unarmored truth."

With a hand to the ground he slowly pressed himself to stand, moving like an old man, and shuffled toward the fountain. There he took a deep breath and let it out slowly, gazing at the falling water. He gestured at the streams, fingers opening and curling as his hands turned.

The sound of water ceased. A fog hung in the air around the large central marble pillar of sculpted flowers. Moonlight caught and spread among the fog, each tiny droplet of water becoming a turning, perfect prism. A mist of small diamonds, converting moonlight into millions of brilliant rainbow flashes.

Her breath caught at this display. It was nothing like what he had done with the tea mid-air earlier; this was not blinding. It was magnificent.

In Keyretura's fine mansion where she had grown up, water and glass had taken sunlight across the day to make changing and exquisite paintings of light. She had thought herself inured to such marvels now, but he had never shown her anything so splendid as this. She had not realized he was capable of it.

It put her in mind of Samnt and his hunger to see magic. She felt an unfamiliar craving to do this thing her aetur had done, to make something so beautiful.

For a long moment, the mist of moon-fed rainbows hung in the air. Then the arcs of fountain resumed their fall. Water splashed into the pool, the diamonds of light gone.

She got to her feet, bemused.

"Why do I still breathe, Aetur?"

"What do you think I wanted here, Marisel?"

"To show me how much I still lack. To end me."

"What petty motives you ascribe to me. I spent twenty years creating you. Why would I destroy you now?"

She walked to the edge of the pool and sat there on the marble, considering. "I have never understood you."

"That much is clear. Hear me, Marisel: it is no small effort to create a mage. Did you know I had two uslata before you?"

"I had heard this."

When she had asked Gallelon, he had confirmed the rumor. "Not mine to tell," was all he would say, so Maris knew little more of Keyretura's earlier uslata than that they were no longer mages. For years she suspected Keyretura of killing them.

In encounters like this one, perhaps.

She could barely make out his expression in the shadow of night, backlit as he was by moonlight, but for a moment it seemed to her that sorrow flickered across his usually stoic features. "I failed them. I created them weak and fearful." He looked back at her. "I could not bear to lose another."

His meaning sank in. "You did all this for me?"

"You are surprised?"

"But why would you trouble yourself to . . ." To what? To let her win?

"Marisel, you are my *koacha*. You are my child."

Behind her eyes was a sudden pressure. The threat of tears. No. She would not let him.

"It was feigned, then, this encounter?" She gestured to take in the night, letting herself feel the outrage of insult.

From him a guttural sound of derision. "You think I pretend to this?" He gestured to his stomach. He snorted, then held her gaze, his arms out to his sides. A clear invitation.

Never had she sent an etheric touch into her aetur's body. He would not have allowed it. But he opened the way now, taking down his protections so fast that she was dizzied.

She extended the slightest of touches into his body. There she found the nerve she had attacked, still hot and thickened, even with the healing he had done.

A killing blow, it would have been, had he not been Keyretura. It had been no pretense.

She withdrew her touch, shaken as much by his invitation as the evidence she had found.

"You must have held back," she muttered.

"How foolish that would have been, given how little you trust me already. No; I would have taken you to death's door had you not truly stopped me."

At this, she felt chilled.

"But," he added, "I would not have let you step through."

She looked at him anew, and the rest of the pieces fell into place. "Dirina. Pas. You abducted them to force me here."

A nod. "I could wait no longer for you to come to me of your own accord." Keyretura seated himself on the edge of the fountain, a pace away from her. "Maris, I am pleased with what I see in you. You have learned well."

Again his words threatened to reach through her protections. She thought of her parents, brought their faces to mind. Of Dirina and Pas kidnapped and his violation of her home. Of the decades of wrenching agony under his tutelage.

"I do not forgive you, Aetur," she said, voice rough.

"I do not ask you to. Give me your arm."

She hesitated a moment, then did as he asked. He took her wrist between his palms and the pain lessened. Next he reached up a hand to her head, and she pulled away. He waited, and after another moment, she brought her head back. He laid three fingers on her forehead, and the headache was eased.

They sat a time in silence as the moon rose. How strange, she thought, to sit by his side and not be afraid. She gave him a sidelong look.

"I would ask your advice," she said.

The flicker of surprise across his face gave her an inordinate amount of satisfaction.

"Yes?"

"I am . . ." It astonished her, that she wanted to ask him this, but she did. "I am considering taking on an apprentice. You will say I'm not ready, I suppose," she added quickly, "but—"

"You suppose wrong. Readiness comes from need, not before."

"Yes," she said, startled to find herself agreeing with him.

The need to face him. The readiness to do so. Had he said such eminently sensible things in the years before, and she not listened? He must have changed. Or she had.

Perhaps both.

"I was seven when we forged our contract. Is sixteen too old?"

"Not if he is sufficiently determined."

Samnt, stubborn? Yes. Enough? Perhaps.

"You—" She took a deep breath, looked away and then back at him. "You took everything my parents had," she said. "I will not do that. I would instead pay them for the loss of his labor on their farm."

"Then he will not survive the study, Maris. The price must be high or the student will leave to do something easier, and anything is easier. Like it or not, you know this."

"Then I will find another way to give him sufficient motivation. I will prove you wrong, Aetur."

He smiled again. "Do that, Koacha."

"Where are Dirina and Pas?"

"I will not break my contract to Innel by telling you, though I may bend it somewhat. I will say this: they are well and whole and in his hands."

"And Amarta?"

"At the Rift, where Innel has brought an army to Otevan."

"Why did you accept this contract? Did you not tell

me, again and again, to stay clear of empires and their squabbles?"

"I told you many things. Did you believe them all?"

"No."

"Good. I am here, instead of with Innel, to protect the queen, though she seems able to do that herself with some competence. Go to the Rift in my stead, Maris. Ask him about your Iliban. Help him if you care to."

"I don't."

"Then don't. Either way, I am done. I will leave after you do. I have what I took this contract to gain."

"Which was what?"

"This," he said with a gesture at her.

"This?" She exhaled. "You have an odd way of showing your care, Keyretura."

"I am sometimes fallible."

He held up a hand, fingers extended, and she felt the etheric connection between them spark and warm. For a moment she considered how she might sunder this cord, once and for all.

She could stretch it, as she had these last decades. Let it thin and fade. But no matter how quiescent, it seemed to her that it would always be there: a pressure, a touch. A connection.

It was a door between them. While she could not remove it from the world, she could, she realized, force it shut, if she wanted to.

Did she?

"Before you leave for the Rift to reclaim your people, Marisel, come and have tea with me."

The tone and words were the same, but for some

reason they now sounded like an invitation instead of a command.

She laughed at this, at herself, perhaps even at him. They sat a while in silence, watching the moon rise, as she considered how she would answer.

Chapter Thirty-six

It should not have been possible.

Innel watched the sparks and smoldering columns of smoke rise into a half-clouded, moonlit night. He strode back to the pavilion, taking Nalas aside. "How bad is it?"

"Bad," Nalas said. "Be far worse, though, if not for the—water." His eyes flickered to Amarta.

"How did they get inside our lines? Was someone bribed to look away?" He would like to think that impossible, too.

"Don't think so, ser." Nalas eyed the five Teva sitting under guard at the long table. "Their horses jumped the perimeter. Shot fire arrows. Their aim is—very good."

Better than good—nothing short of astonishing. And the horses—even Arunkel jumpers bred for the purpose wouldn't have cleared the height and width of the wagons and fencelines that were supposed to defend the camp.

Now every able soldier was on the line, cavalry on patrol, archers standing ready. A little late.

"How many days of food do we have left?"

"Four? Three? We won't know for certain until we see the damage in the light. Sunrise in a few hours."

Four days.

"How many of theirs did we injure or kill?"

A pause. "None, ser."

"*What?*"

Nalas grimaced. "The shaota move like cats. As if they can see in the dark."

Innel whirled on Amarta. "You. Why didn't you tell me this was going to happen?"

She gave him an incredulous look. "Do you think I see everything? I saw fire. That water could change the outcome. I told you this as soon as I could."

"Another few minutes warning and we could have prevented this."

"No, you couldn't," she said adamantly. "There was no future in which it didn't happen. Shall I tell you about every unavoidable thing, ser, despite that you don't listen? Very well: tonight the moon will set. Tomorrow the sun will rise. The ground will be down, the sky up. Shall I go on?"

He came close, hungering to grab her, shake her, slap her until she spoke to him properly. He pulled his hands back, remembering the last time. "Need I remind you—"

"Of our contract?" She raised her bandaged hand. "That you have my family? Which one is it this time?"

Innel wondered what Restarn would have done with her. Not have let her speak this way to him, of that he was sure. But how? "I could send a bird right now," he said, letting the bite into his voice, "directing that your sister and nephew be—"

"But you won't," she interrupted. "Don't you have

more important things to do than try to threaten me with a future I can see and you can't, Lord Commander?"

His hands were clenched into fists. "When our supplies run out, Seer, how will our troops eat?"

Her voice dropped. "They won't need to, ser."

"Damn you, give me another answer."

"Give me another question."

"How do we win against the Teva?"

"You don't."

"Unacceptable."

Lismar entered the pavilion, shot a glare at Amarta, her gaze settling on Innel. "Lord Commander, no one will sleep more tonight. The troops are angry. They know a lot of our supplies were destroyed. They don't want to be hungry. They want revenge."

Fear of hunger might be well-founded; there might not be enough to finish this campaign, even if it went well. Which it had yet to do.

The town, Hanatha, was the obvious solution. It would have supplies. Overprotected with the double walls, especially for such a remote location. Were they expecting the empire to come calling? What were they hiding?

Regardless, the town would have food aplenty and provide excellent protection for their next move, whatever it was.

He looked at Amarta.

"Attend to *me*, Lord Commander," Lismar said sharply, "not her. She knows nothing of military campaigns, whereas I know rather a lot, as you will recall, if you give it just a moment's thought." Lismar was furious, her tone far from respectful.

First among generals, he reminded himself. The king's sister. One of the oldest of the Anandynars. He needed her and her good will.

"I do indeed recall, General, and I consider myself fortunate to have you at my side. Hanatha will have food and provide a stronghold from which we can properly address the Teva. Assemble a force at first light."

"Finally," Lismar exhaled.

Amarta's expression was uneasy. What concerned her most? Her family? Her own safety? Where did her loyalties truly lie?

"We will take half the companies," he told Lismar, turning to study the map of Hanatha and the land around it. "Infantry, archers, and cavalry. The rest to defend the camp."

"That's far more than we will need to take the town, Lord Commander," Lismar said.

"That's why we brought force, General. To be certain. Ready the battalions and horses."

Tayre found it wasn't only the cook. There were also a number of axle breaks, tools gone missing, bootlaces cut. Someone was trying to make sure this campaign did not have too many advantages.

The cook had changed what she was adding to the huge stewpot. Judging from her body language this new ingredient was not as extreme as whatever was forcing soldiers to make the latrine smell so much worse than it already did. Now, instead, they were falling asleep, sprawled wherever they had been sitting, some even dozing through the Teva's night attack on the camp.

Clever. Different symptoms would confuse the mistrustful.

Tayre could think of a number of agencies that might want to undercut this campaign or sully the Lord Commander's reputation, for any number of reasons. But which was she working for?

He took her by the arm on her way back from the latrine, giving her a warm smile and whispering in her ear with intriguing gossip as if they were old friends, holding her attention long enough to draw her into a recently vacated whore's tent that he had rented for the purpose. Once inside her eyes went wide as she realized she didn't, after all, know who he was. "I saw what you put in the stew," he said. "Every drop. Now tell me who put you up to it."

"What? No, I don't—"

"Hush," he said. "You've nothing to worry about if you tell me the truth."

Her eyes went wider yet, her mouth slack. She glanced down at her left leg, then lifted her trouser to reveal a twined cord around her ankle. Grain yellow and dirt brown. House Elupene's colors.

He made a show of considering this, but the tightness in her shoulders and turn of her mouth told him she was lying. A cover story, then.

"The right answer," he said with a knowing smile, watching her already weak pretense crumble into uncertainty. "I'm only here to check on you. Make sure you have this well in hand, and it looks like you do. You didn't think we'd send you out to do something this important with no support, did you?"

The sudden relief on her face verified his guess.

"No," she said, nodding eagerly. "I understand."

"We take care of our own," he said. "We're all around you. Protection if you need it. You've done well."

At this she straightened. "It wasn't easy. I had to mix it with some of my best spices, just in case someone was watching."

"Good. Here." He handed her a small pouch. "To show our ongoing backing."

She looked inside, mouth fell open. "Falcons?"

"Not so loud. Now, we need something more from you."

"Yes, ser. Anything."

"Your loyalty."

"Ser. I'm very loyal."

"We know you are. So this, a simple thing: renew your oath to us. Now."

"I'll say whatever you want."

"No, no. Use your own words. It means more to us that way."

Her voice dropped to where he could barely hear it. She started, stammered, stopped. Started again. "I serve Helata. In this. In all things. On my life."

"On your life indeed," he answered. "Well done. I'll report to our masters you are most faithful."

He pressed her shoulder affectionately and led her out, waving her off.

So, Helata pretending to be Elupene. With all the rumors of gold, Tayre had expected Etallan to be in motion here.

Well, no reason it couldn't be both. Or more. Though

if the Houses were cooperating to undercut the monarchy's army, that would be very bad news indeed for the monarch.

Also Helata was not usually known for this sort of intrigue; to be this direct they must scent blood in the water. If the Lord Commander lost here at Otevan, with Cern's authority still so immature, Tayre could imagine a number of shifting alliances that would cost the queen dearly.

An intriguing answer, both dangerous to know and potentially worth a great deal, in whatever currency he might like.

He wondered what, if anything, he would do with it.

Amarta sat by herself in a corner of the pavilion and tried to make sense of what had happened.

She had foreseen the camp burning, quite clearly. Though when it would happen, she could not have said, until just before it did. That was how the future was sometimes: highly changeable. Built out of decisions and the people who must make them.

Before her now, one future seemed to be coming to the fore, crowding out other possibilities, becoming more vivid as the moments passed. Nearer and nearer to the same sort of inevitability as the attack in the night. Again, caused by the choices people were making. The Lord Commander in particular.

A blanket of soldiers rippled over the valley to overrun the town like ants over an injured grasshopper. A slamming, tearing sound. Piercing cries.

She could try telling him that he could not win this, but again he would not believe her.

What does he most need, to come closest to his intention?

Too big a question, the answers too convoluted. Hundreds of strands that quickly became thousands.

And now he watched her from the map table.

His face twisted in pain and fear, he gave her a pleading look.

A surprised sound escaped her.

"What?" he asked, coming close. "Tell me."

Well, she had given him her oath. "You are gravely injured, ser. You beg me for help."

His disbelief was plain, bordering on outrage. He shook his head and turned his back on her, went to his maps.

From the other side of the room, Jolon caught her attention.

If they attack Hanatha, he signed, *it is bad. The town is our children.*

What? Your children? That did not quite make sense. Maybe she misunderstood, misremembered the signs. *You care for the town?* she asked, trying to clarify.

He shook his head then nodded. *Yes, we do, but—*A gesture of frustration. *Our children defend the town. If they attack Hanatha, the children will kill them. Many will die.*

That much she already knew.

Innel did not like the look in people's eyes when Lismar was around. When he gave orders, they looked at her. He could not put from his mind her words of the previous day. *When was the last time you did, Commander?*

"I'll lead from the field," he had told her the previous

night. Was that a twitch of a smile on her face? "You disapprove?" he asked.

"No, ser. But we'll have you well-protected. I won't be the one to tell Her Majesty that something happened to her royal consort while I looked on. I'd never be invited to dinner again."

"You are welcome to lead the vanguard instead of me, General."

"No need. My list of victories is sufficiently long. Let someone else have this glory." Meaning him, of course. "You take too many troops for a town."

"A walled town."

"A double-walled town," she replied. "Even so, we send as many soldiers as the town beds. I am not overly concerned about your safety." Her tone was, he thought, condescending. "Indeed, they will trip over each other getting inside."

"I will tell them to step lightly."

She smiled at this. Tolerantly, it seemed to him.

For a moment he wondered if Lismar might prefer to see him to fail here. But that would make no sense; she must know that Innel was part of what kept Cern's rule whole, and Cern's rule kept the Anandynar line intact.

Furthermore, she had sworn her loyalty to him, in return for the safety of her descendants.

Unless that was pretense intended to make him complacent.

No—it was too easy to see treachery everywhere. He could not move forward without relying on someone. On many someones.

He missed Srel keenly. As soon as they were

established in the town he would again question Nalas on the camp's mood. Some of the troops were advocating putting the shaota carcass in the stewpot. Practical, perhaps—now especially—but not knowing how the Teva might respond to that, he had instead set a guard around the body, which no one liked. Another thing to resolve once Hanatha was in hand.

And so now he stood in the field, commanding the vanguard but surrounded by a substantial mounted guard at Lismar's insistence. He could not quite blame her; in her place, with the queen's consort putting himself at the head of an invading force, he might do likewise. Still, he could not shake the sense of being treated as a princeling at first battle.

Or would he, in her place, having been passed over for the Lord Commandership, instead look for a chance to show him wanting?

No. If he saw plots in every dark corner, he would be his own worst enemy.

Now he gave the signal to march. A horn blew. Lines of soldiers moved down into the valley.

Where were the Teva? Not around the buildings of Ote. Not on the walls of the town outer or inner, higher by some twenty feet. It made no sense. Where was the town's defense?

The infantry assembled outside the front gate of the town, lines of archers behind, all waiting for his signal.

First he wanted to give Hanatha a chance to surrender. Given his numbers, to take the town in blood would look less like a victory than a slaughter. His first real battle. What he did here would matter.

It was hard to wait here motionless, feeling the eyes of thousands on him. He wondered how long Lismar would wait, or if she even would. He could have asked her the night before but had decided not to. It seemed a small thing. Now it did not.

He wanted to move. No doubt those under his command did, too. He forced himself to count. Ten. Twenty. Thirty.

"Go," he said to Nalas, who passed on the order. Again the horns sounded.

The army surged to the wall. Ladders were set upright and men began to climb. A battering ram was pulled close to the main gate. Soldiers surrounded it and ran it forward into the large wooden doors. The deep booming echoed across the valley. And again.

It crashed through. A cheer went up. Soldiers streamed in around it.

Well, there was the first thing gone wrong: they were supposed to take the ram in with them for the inner gate, not leave it there. Enthusiasm overcoming planning. As he watched, a set of men tried to pull it back out of the way while another set tried to push it forward, while others struggled around it and through the gate. The ram stayed where it was. He growled at this, giving an aide an order to assemble a squadron to resolve the issue.

This took more time than he would have liked, but finally they were there, slowly maneuvering the heavy ram into the area between the gates, their shields overhead to protect them from the anticipated arrows of the town's defenders.

Who had yet to make an appearance.

The second wave of infantry was waiting on his signal, and he gave it. Now repeated sounds of pounding told him the inner gate was being slammed but had not yet opened.

A figure atop the inner wall. Then another, and more. Holding bows. Aiming and shooting down at his soldiers between the walls.

Well, good: something was going as expected.

"Ser," said Nalas slowly, "I think those are children."

"What? Where?"

"On the inner wall."

Innel squinted. Children? On the wall? Yes, it seemed so.

Then where were the adults? He looked around the still-empty valley. After a moment's hesitation he gave Nalas the signal to cue the line of archers. The archers drew and shot to no apparent effect. They were still just short. He signaled them to hold; no sense in dropping arrows on his own men. Best wait for the forces to breach the inner gate then bring them forward.

Then an odd sound. Metal on metal. Shouts of alarm. A handful of piercing screams. Another handful.

The ladders were yanked from the outer wall and carried long-ways through the shattered outer gate, and tilted down.

Down?

"What the—?" Innel craned his neck to see through the gates. A rider from a better vantage point turned his horse, galloped back to Innel, navigating through the opening Innel's mounted guard provided.

"A dropped floor, ser," the out-of-breath rider said. "A huge trench. Everyone inside—"

"A trench? What do you mean?"

"The ground dropped out from under, between the walls, ser. A thirty-foot drop at least."

A thirty-foot drop?

"Did we breach the inner gate?"

"No, ser. No one's made it through."

"*No one?*" he asked incredulously, distracted by fresh howls. Atop the inner wall the small figures were now tipping over large cauldrons out of which fell flaming balls. The screaming below intensified. Innel could smell the smoke from the burning tar.

A false floor over a huge trench between the two walls of Hanatha. A massive trap. How could they not have known?

Surely it did not go all the way around, like a moat. Did it?

"Take the ram to the second outer gate—" No, damn it all, the ram had fallen into the trench along with the soldiers. Hundreds of soldiers. Another ram, then. But no, that would take time. "Send the rest," he said. "All of them. Get ladders in there. Bridge the gap."

"Yes, ser," Nalas replied uncertainly.

Bridge the gap to what? The inner wall was not yet open.

"No," Innel said, waving his hand. "Wait." He had to think.

The men maneuvering the ladders downward into the trench began to fall to arrows, one by one. Shields went up and overhead, but still they dropped, some sprawling dead or injured atop the very ladders they had been trying to move. Where were the arrows coming from?

Another rider pulled alongside. "The general says retreat, Lord Commander," the rider said.

"She *what*?" he asked in disbelief.

No, he needed to see what was going on himself. He pressed his horse forward.

"Ser," Nalas shouted. "If you go any closer, you're in range of their shot."

"Advance our archers. Take them out."

"Been trying. But range and rise, ser. We didn't expect them to be able to match us for range, but it seems they can, and we can't get closer with them up there."

"How in the hells are they getting through our armor and shields?"

"Aim," Nalas said softly.

Again Innel pressed forward, Nalas trailing. If he could see what was happening, he could perhaps figure out what to do.

"Ser, this is dangerous. Any closer and—"

Ahead of him a guard clutched at his neck with one hand, gripped his horse's mane with the other, struggling to stay upright in the saddle. The horse, not sure what he wanted, backed up abruptly. Another horse snapped at its flank and the first horse whirled, the man slipping half off. There was not room for this, and the other horses, already testy, were not happy.

Innel's horse, a sensible creature, stepped backwards and out of the fray.

Now the infantry outside the wall was unmoving,

hunkering under shields to hide from the rain of arrows that shouldn't have been able to reach them, some going flat as they were hit.

It was not going well.

"Retreat!" he shouted. "Nalas, get them back. Get them all back."

How could this have happened?

How many were lost?

How were they going to eat in three days?

Innel seethed as the retreat horns sounded, riding to reach the rise where Lismar sat atop her horse watching. Her expression was as dark as he felt. He pulled his horse close by and leaned in toward her. "You set me up," he hissed at her.

"What?" she demanded.

His horse was twitchy, refusing to stand still. Agitated. Frustrated at not being able to run, to fight. He felt the same. "You knew this would happen," he accused.

Her smile turned hard and brittle. "No, Lord Commander. I told you not to take so many troops in the first place. That they would trip over each other. Do you recall?"

How many were lost?

"A drop passage between the inner and outer walls— a trap to kill hundreds—and you didn't know? You're the expert on the Teva."

"What? You think I would allow my soldiers to die just to show you wanting?" Her angry look flickered between his eyes. "I understand now. Not clever at all. Only lucky. You believed every story about your brother." She gave a derisive laugh. "And the seer, too. You don't need my help to look foolish, Lord Commander."

"Someone knew about this trap," he insisted. "If not you—"

"With how much you've spent of my family's money on spies and fortune-tellers, Consort, why didn't *you* know? You disgust me."

He did not trust himself to respond. He yanked his horse around. A tossed head, a glare—the horse was no happier than he was.

As he turned away he half expected her to say something more. Something about bloodlines. To call him the mutt. He half hoped she would say something egregious enough that he could lose the rest of his temper and release on her the coiled fury coursing through him.

But she stayed silent.

The shifting wind brought Amarta shouts and screams from Hanatha. In Jolon's face and the expressions of the other Teva she saw a mix of tension and agitation. They wanted to move, to act.

Jolon signed to her. *Again I ask your help.*

She owed him so much. Her life, quite possibly. The lives of her family, almost certainly.

To free you would break my oath, she signed, a wretched feeling in her stomach. *I'm sorry.*

Not to free us. The—A sign she didn't know. She shook her head to show she was confused. *My people.* he tried again.

The Teva. She nodded.

I hear him speak, Jolon continued, *the one who holds*

*your oath. The woman who commands beside him. My
elders think your people can be persuaded to leave, but to
sit here, to listen, is to know another thing. They will not
go away.*

"No," she whispered, agreeing.

There seemed to be so many ways for men and
women to die. But die they would; in no future she saw
did Arunkel leave Otevan with anything but straggling
survivors, heads down. Defeated.

She could not tell Jolon this, though. Not and keep her
contract whole. Not unless by the very telling him she
somehow gave Innel what he needed.

Which was what? A victory here? The empire's
borders intact? All the gold in hand?

No—none of these things walked together.

I must get to my elders, Jolon signed at her. *If your
empire has victory here, that is bad. If Teva wins here,
that is also bad. Your people will never stop coming for
us. We must find another way.*

She had yet to see another way. She looked around,
frustrated at her helplessness.

So many people in motion, creating the future, while
all she did was sit and sulk about what she could not do.

Various images vied for her attention. *A distant view
of the Rift. A sweet, quiet moment by herself.*

She stood, again sat, stood again, restlessly paced the
pavilion. A handful of guards' gazes flickered to her and
away.

*The faces of the guards, but with different expressions.
Eyes wide, mouths small. A look, at her, that she
recognized.*

Horns sounded distantly. Pounding footsteps. Angry, pained shouts. Someone, somewhere, was weeping loudly, inconsolably.

At the door, the guards' attention flickered. To the noises outside. To the Teva sitting at the table. To their own thoughts.

Dark fingers twined in her own. A trilling Teva call. A white flag snapping in the breeze.

Too much future to see it all. Even knowing a single likely outcome was not the same as understanding it.

And no one could see everything at once. Not her. Not anyone. She thought of Tayre, of how he could seem to be someone else, even when you looked right at him.

Once again she looked into the tangled future. Not distant, no, but only this moment to come. Then the next. And one more.

Now.

Amarta stood and walked out of the pavilion.

Innel raged at the guards. They cringed.

They had better.

"You let her escape?" he shouted.

"Lord Commander! I have no idea how—" one began, faltering.

"We were watching her. Truly, ser," said another.

A third tried: "One moment she sat right there, ser. The next she was gone. As if—" He fell silent.

"Find her," Innel said tightly. "Now."

The guards exchanged looks and whispers, arguing about who would leave and who must stay with the livid Lord Commander.

"You, you, and you," Nalas said sharply. "Go."

The seer. His captive. Vanished. As if by magic. In a few minutes it would be all over the camp, following hot on the heels of the disaster at Hanatha.

He glared at the Teva, the cause of all this. "Where is the gold mine?" he demanded.

"Again," said Jolon calmly, "we deny your accusations, Lord Commander, and furthermore we demand that you—"

Before Innel quite realized it, he was at the Teva closest to him, lifting him by his leather shirt out of his chair, off his feet. He hurled him across the room. A chair bucked aside, then the map table and another table on which a carafe of red wine sat, all crashing together. Wine splattered across the room, the Teva, the maps.

For a moment Innel felt a hot rush of satisfaction at this. A moment later he knew it had been a mistake.

In the quiet moment that followed, Nalas's expression was wary, as if he were wondering if Innel could be left alone for the moment it would take him to see if the Teva on the ground was badly hurt. Innel nodded his permission then motioned the guards to help. Nalas dropped down to examine the man. Breathing hard, Innel retreated behind the partition, dug into his pocket, pulled out Pohut's arrowhead.

He could not, must not, lose control like that again.

How could he have lost hundreds of men to child defenders and yet failed to take the town? It would not matter that no one could have predicted the false-floor trap, the sudden thirty-foot drop. The entire camp would be talking. The count of injured. Of dead.

Who had been in command.

He kept seeing it in his mind, over and over, despite that he had not been there: the floor opening beneath them, the crash down into the trench, the heavy ram falling atop them. Those who survived due to their comrades cushioning their fall, those who managed to keep their wits about them despite the drop, might have grabbed shields to protect themselves against the falling arrows only to find oil and fire taking them next, forcing them to choose between burning and being shot.

So many dead.

Had Lismar been right? Had he sent too many?

For the first time he understood how a commander might want the outcome of a battle kept quiet. This, his first conflict against an armed foe—a disaster. Even if no one else, even Lismar, could have led this conflict to a better outcome, he would be blamed.

The mutt who had risen above his station.

Hundreds of soldiers fallen, crushed, broken. All under his command.

All for nothing.

He tried to imagine what his brother would say now, but nothing came to him. He gripped Pohut's metal arrowhead in his fist until his palm bled.

Amarta walked slowly through the camp, slipping in and out of vision. So many were distracted now by their own injuries, by the injuries of those around them, by the loss of friends. Some saw her anyway, looking right at her and said nothing. Finally someone spoke.

"Hey," he said. "You're the captive. What are you doing out—"

A moment forward, the one in which he briefly glanced away at some shouted call. She took a quick step into the place he would not be looking.

The man looked around himself, confused to find her suddenly gone.

There were ways in and out of the camp, she discovered, that merely required patience and listening and knowing the future. Amidst the confusion of a camp invaded and grieving, it was easy to pass unseen.

Once outside the perimeter, she walked south to the rocks of the mesa, relishing the climb to the top, alone for the first time in so long. The late afternoon sun was warm and sweet, as were the lack of hard words, screams and cries. But best of all was that she was, for the moment, answerable to no one.

She looked out over the valley with bodies scattered around the walls of Hanatha, then to the rounded buildings of Ote, then the line of the far Rift. If she ignored the dead on the field and the dead to come, it was a beautiful land.

If not for her oath and her family she might have kept walking until she found a place where there was no more fighting, no more hunger, and no more Arunkel.

To rest her eyes from the close work, the elder woman in blue looked up a moment from her five-strand braid, drawing the tails from her companion in orange to her left and feeding the band into the hands of the man to her right, who coiled the result into large loops. Her attention

back to her hands and the work, she realized that
something had caught her eye. She looked up again.

He was not there, and then he was. In worn leathers,
he might have been any cattleman between here and the
distant ocean, but for the highlights of red in his hair that
marked him as something other than Arunkin or Teva.

She stopped her work and put a hand to either side to
touch her companions.

"Gallelon," she said. "Welcome to Otevan."

"Greetings, Elders," he said, seating himself nearby.
"You seem to have an Arunkel army at your door. What
did you do to inspire such grand attention?"

"We allowed ourselves to become entangled in the
empire's bridles," said the elder man as he collected his
coils and set them aside.

"Ah," nodded the mage. "Not wise to get close to that
particular snake." He looked curiously at the band the
three of them were weaving, nodding a little as the woman
in orange held it out for him to examine. "Has there yet
been a cost of life?"

"A shaota is dead," said the man flatly.

The mage waited a moment. "Any others?"

"Our emissaries, perhaps," said the woman in blue.
"Our son among them."

"Ah. And Arunkin?"

"Hours ago their army attacked Hanatha," the elder
man said. "Our children made us proud."

"I see. How many dead?" asked Gallelon.

"Hundreds," answered the woman in orange. "The
night before, we destroyed most of their food supplies.
We had thought to encourage them to leave."

Gallelon made an amused sound. "They do not have the aspect of an army preparing to depart. Indeed, they seem to be reassembling force."

"Yes. We were mistaken. Will you help us prevail?"

The mage looked around the longhouse thoughtfully. "Does this mean you are offering me a breeding pair?"

"That we cannot do. The shaota decide for themselves. They—"

"Spare me the lecture. I've heard it. Many times. From you. From your forebears."

"You are right," the woman in blue said, dropping her head. "Our apologies, High One."

"Spare me that, too. Yes or no?"

A moment's pause.

"No."

He looked at the elders, his expression one of surprise. "What? No 'shaota can only be bred by the waters of Otevan?' No, 'should circumstances permit . . .'? No explanation or negotiation? Even now?"

The elder woman in orange shook her head. "I think we have insulted you enough, mage."

He snorted. "Someone with a poorer sense of humor might say he is not your servant to come when you call, offering nothing in return."

"Again, we apologize," said the elder man. "If it were not so dire, if shaota were not at risk—"

"Yes, yes." the mage waved a hand. "And I came. All this—it's about the gold?"

"Even he knows," the elder woman in orange muttered, standing and pacing the room.

"It is the many deserters you harbor, Elders. Someone

was bound to say something. Still—" Gallelon put his hands out palms up then turned them to face the ground. "They seem to have brought rather a lot of force merely to find some gold. Is there something else?"

"Yes," the elder man said, expression pained. "A handful of years ago, one of the Arun Houses required of us an alliance."

"No choice," the woman in orange said, her pacing more agitated. "The earth had shaken herself like a wet dog and there it was. Deep and bright. To stay quiet—to keep the snake away—we had to agree."

"They were to empty the hole for us," said the woman in blue softly, "but it seems inexhaustible. Now the empire is here and the House is not."

"Give them up," Gallelon suggested.

"You think the Arunkin will believe us? After we have smuggled gold to Perripur? Forged the empire's coin?"

"Ah," Gallelon said. "The problem clarifies."

"Now we must defend our lands or the snake will take them."

"Yes, that does seem to be the way of it," said the mage.

The woman in orange spoke. "If we can find a foal to match you, mage, we will. You must spend years with us, but this we perhaps do."

"That is not what I want. What I want—"

"You cannot have," finished the elder man firmly.

Gallelon's annoyance was obvious. "Let me be sure I understand; a huge army at your door and you call me to your aid but the one thing I have ever asked of you, to that one thing you say no."

The elders seemed to consider a moment. The woman in blue responded. "Yes, you understand correctly, mage."

"Your breeding secrets are so precious to you?"

The elder man spread his hands. "Not everything is subject to negotiation."

"You assume my good will far beyond reason."

"Yes."

After a moment he spoke again. "What exactly do you think I can do for you?"

The elders exchanged looks. "You are a mage."

Gallelon laughed. "It is good to be thought so powerful, but do you really think I can stand down thousands of armed soldiers with a wave of my hand?"

The elders were silent, their looks less uncertain.

"No?" the elder man asked.

Gallelon's amused smile vanished. "No. I could tremble the ground a bit. Perhaps bring a wind. Set a handful of them to napping. But these tricks won't change the outcome. Little can divert bloodlust once set in motion. I might have talked them out of it before you took life, but now?"

"We did talk. Arunkin do not listen well."

"Even so," Gallelon said, "I am not standing in the path of thousands of armed soldiers. Not for you. Not for anyone."

"Advise us, then."

"If discussion has failed, Elders—if you have no choice but to face Arunkel in full force . . ." He shook his head. "You are the Teva. Show them what you can do."

The woman in blue shook back her sleeve to reveal the many raised inked scars encircling her forearm.

Wrapping her wrist with thumb and forefinger she drew her fingers up her arm across the many ridges of *limisatae*. "The youngers will welcome the game," she said with a small smile.

"Thank you for your counsel, High One," said the woman in orange, ceasing in her pacing.

"What will you do now?" asked the woman in blue as she stood.

"Get well out of the way. Perhaps I'll come back for the aftermath and see if I can help." He looked around the room, pursed his lips. "Then again, perhaps not."

After a time, feeling something like refreshed, Amarta reluctantly returned to the camp and the pavilion. Each step back required that she remind herself of her oath and contract.

The guards were visibly relieved to see her, stepping aside to let her in, then watching her gloweringly, as if intending to forget how they had lost track of her before. And in their eyes, that look of fear.

Innel was speaking urgently to Nalas and the general, gesturing to a set of maps. He saw her, turned a look of smoldering anger on her, held it, then went back to his discussion.

Amarta exhaled, sat down, then resolutely set about sorting through his futures. So many possibilities, all narrowing, again, to a single event, dark and bloody, a sort of funnel through which everything else seemed to pass.

Bright red on his fingers. Fear on his face.

As the light faded, lamps were lit and food was brought. Amarta ate a few bites of what was set before her but soon lost her desire for it, pushing the rest away. Tonight so many were going hungry, so many whimpering in agony, at their broken bodies and hearts, weeping for dead friends left to rot in the fields of Hanatha.

The weight of consequence settled heavily on her shoulders. If she had known more about herself and the world, would more of them be alive and whole now? There were dead and mangled people who she might have been able to save but had not.

It seemed to her that being the wolf should mean more than this.

When a servant came to take her plate away, the weight she felt warred with hunger, so she kept a bread roll, putting it in her pocket for later. The act put her in mind of Dirina and Pas. She wondered if they were well. If they were fed.

She glared back at the Lord Commander. They had better be.

As night deepened, the Teva curled up on their cots and slept. Tired herself, she found her own cot.

Some time later a commotion outside woke her.

"A messenger from the capital, Lord Commander," someone said outside.

She meant to ignore it and return to sleep, but the feeling of a storm cloud rushing toward her roused her. She stood and, ignoring the guards, walked outside the pavilion.

The night was partly overcast, a waning moon overhead giving some light to the ground. From nearby the Lord Commander's voice called out: "Cahlen. My sister. Let her pass."

At this a deep thrumming went through Amarta. She pushed herself into vision and time seemed to slow.

She began her next inhale.

The approaching mounted figure was moving, holding something, turning, a motion that Amarta recognized with a shot of dread before she understood what it was: a bow, drawn, aimed.

Her lungs still filling, she tried to think. Surely all of this, all she had been facing, would be far simpler without him. Wouldn't it?

Would it?

The queen sat on a floor, head down, shuddering with sobs. A jumble of metal rods, flats of wood, and chain fell clattering to a marble floor.

Screams echoed across the months and years. Bodies hung from scaffolding. Heads atop pikes marking the place town gates used to be.

No. He had to live. However bad it was now, it would be worse without him.

Amarta felt a thin line cross time, one of action and consequence, like an unraveling thread connecting two birds flying in opposite directions.

And still her lungs were filling. She moved, tasting vision, comparing each motion of her right hand and arm to what she had foreseen, questing forward for the one movement that could keep the thread from breaking.

Forward, then back to the present. Forward, back, shutting her mind to everything else. She twisted slightly, reaching across her body, matching how it should feel in each moment's future. Into her pocket. Taking the roll. As her lungs reached capacity and began to compress again with exhale she flung the bread at the Lord Commander.

It hit him on the neck. He began to move toward her, turning to see what had hit him. Turning just enough that he was edge-on to the horse and rider and the arrow cutting through the air toward him.

Amarta was still exhaling as she came fully back to the present, to shouts and cries and the Lord Commander stumbling, falling. Loud voices. The woman on the horse was yanked off her saddle, pulled away.

Amarta staggered back through the doorway, clumsy with the seeing haze, making room for the four men who carried the Lord Commander past her. She heard him hiss: "Nalas. Don't let them hurt Cahlen."

The doctor rushed forward, pushing past Amarta, kneeling by his cot.

"Everyone get back," she shouted. Then, more softly: "This will hurt, ser."

Innel was annoyed. By the pain, by the yelling, by having his orders disregarded. He had important plans to assemble. A battle in the morning. He turned his head to look at his shoulder, which hurt. A bolt, fletched black and red, was embedded there. But it didn't hurt that much. He was fine. Would be fine.

Cahlen, he remembered, had shot him. But why?

Oh, right: because he had killed their brother.

No, that wasn't it. That had happened years ago. In Botaros. When he'd met the seer.

The seer. Where was she now? Had she escaped again? He looked around for her.

His shoulder hurt.

His mind circled back to Cahlen. She had been trying to kill him. Why would she do that? But the seer had saved him. Why, again?

The pain in his shoulder caught his attention again. No—he could not, would not, allow himself to be distracted. He reached across his body with his left hand, gripped the hilt of the arrow, and pulled.

"Stop that, ser," said the doctor sharply, grabbing his wrist and the bolt both, separating the two. When he brought his hand back, his fingers were wet and sticky. Where had all this blood come from?

He felt odd. Numb.

In shock, he realized. He was in shock.

"Nalas," he said. His cot was surrounded by people, but somehow Nalas was not among them. "Nalas!"

"Here, ser." Nalas wormed his way between two of the doctor's assistants. He looked worried.

"Cahlen?"

"She'll be—a bit bruised, ser," Nalas said, "but she's all right."

"Why?" he managed.

"I don't know."

"You know something. What?"

"She had a message, ser. The general took it."

"What message?"

Suddenly the pain was deep and searing and Innel groaned. The doctor pushed Nalas away.

"Arrow's gone deep," she said to him. "We must—" She spoke to someone else, something he couldn't make out, and turned back. "Open your mouth, ser." Not waiting for him to comply, she leveraged his jaw open, dripping something gooey and bitter at the back of his throat. "Swallow," she said. "More. More yet. You'll need it."

"Wait," he managed, trying to get the words out around the sticky stuff. "Where's the general?"

But the doctor did not answer, calling for her tools. When she looked back at Innel, she was watching him with an odd intensity.

Why, he wondered, wanting to put voice to this question, along with the other questions he had, but somehow unable to do so. Then he lost consciousness.

When Innel woke again, he was in his bed. His head ached as if it had been in a melon press. His shoulder felt as if it had a spike through it.

Lismar sat on a chair by his side.

"I'm taking over, Innel," she said when she saw him blink awake. "You are injured beyond your ability to command."

"What? No. I can—" He tried to sit up, gave a sharp exhale as the pain wrenched through him. He lay back. "The seer," he croaked. "Where is she?"

"Your pet has escaped again, Lord Commander. Perhaps you should leash her more tightly. Try iron next time."

He wondered how well that would hold her when an entire set of guards couldn't.

"She saved my life."

"Of course she did, ser."

Lismar didn't believe him. For a moment he thought to try to explain, then he realized there was no point.

It was subtle, what Amarta had done. If he hadn't seen

the round of bread bouncing away as he turned to look at her, he might never have realized it. It was easy to miss things, even those right in front of you, if you weren't looking at them. Or looking for them.

"Cahlen," he said.

"Anyone else, I'd have her executed on the spot, Innel. Calm yourself: she's fine. Chained, guarded, but alive. I'll even allow her some food, little as there is left of it."

"What was the message she brought?"

"When you're better, Consort. Rest now."

As Lismar rose, he reached out with his good hand and gripped her wrist as tightly as he could, which didn't seem very tight. He forced the words out: "What's the damned message I was nearly killed for, General?"

He met her look. A tiny smile played around her mouth, making her resemblance to the old king quite clear. After a moment she nodded, reached inside her vest, and pulled out a scrap of bloody paper, holding it to him. He released her and took the paper, blinking through blurred vision to make sense of it.

Garaya.

Everyone dead.

"No," he breathed.

"Very much yes, it would seem. Apparently this was sent right before they were completely overcome, by some soldier at the back with the birds, setting them free. Signed by him, even. You know this Selamu?"

Selamu. Cahlen's Selamu. Now he understood.

"I need the seer."

"No, you need to rest. I'll handle this."

"Handle what?"

"Tomorrow we take Ote. Whatever cracks the Teva are hiding in, we will flush them into the open so we can bring this matter to a conclusion. We have held the empire for a thousand years, and I'm going to show the Teva how. Tomorrow night we feast on roast shaota."

"Wait, no, you can't, not without me—"

"Oh, no. I will not risk the life of the queen's consort. You will stay in bed and heal." She spoke to a guard. "See to it that he stays in his bed and heals."

"Yes, ser."

"You can't—" Innel said.

But the general was gone.

"Wait," he croaked, struggling to get up. The room swam around him and he fell heavily to the cot.

Sleep took him again.

Amarta looked at Jolon. *I might help you get free.* she signed. *I need two things.*

Yes?

Deliver something to your elders for me.

What?

Amarta struggled to remember her signs. She could not remember how to show names.

The man. Behind me. In the bed.

For a moment Jolon looked confused.

You say the Lord Commander?

Yes.

Jolon's face showed incomprehension. *I do not understand.*

The second thing, signed Amarta, *is to take me to the mine.*

✛ ✛ ✛

When Innel woke again the camp was dark, the pavilion quiet. A lamp burned low on the side table. He looked around.

Amarta sat next to him, watching him.

He was hot, soaked in sweat. For a moment he struggled to sit up, then again gave up. "Tomorrow," he said hoarsely, then swallowed. "The general is going to attack. Will it succeed?"

"No," Amarta said. "The few who survive will be ransomed back by the Teva. As you will be."

Ransomed back. To the queen. A humiliation from which his reputation would never recover.

Far better to have died.

"Why did you save me?"

"You have more work to do."

"There you are wrong," he said bitterly. "Lismar has taken my command. And Cern . . ." He trailed off.

Cern might keep him as Consort, though he could not think of why. Certainly he would not advise it. Cut away the mistaken choice as quickly as possible and find someone to replace him. A Cohort brother from one of the Houses, perhaps.

He had risen too far too fast, he realized, and it had not been an accident. The old king had maneuvered Cern into giving him the Lord Commandership not because of his ability but to see to it that when he fell it would be from such a height that he could never rise again. He had been a fool to think otherwise. "What will they say about me in the histories?"

"They will call this the Battle of Hanatha, or Innel's

Folly. They will say it was the beginning of the empire's fall."

"No." With his good hand he rubbed sweat from his face. He could easily imagine that scribed record. How the Arunkel army had failed to take a walled town defended by children. How the next day the army was bested by a smaller force with smaller soldiers and smaller horses.

Innel's Folly.

And no one would blame Lismar.

He reached across his body, groping for the arrow, thinking to drive it deeper, but of course it was gone, his shoulder and chest heavily bandaged. He looked for the bottle of tincture the doctor had given him to numb the pain of surgery, thinking that enough might kill him. But it, also, was gone.

"You should have let me die."

"No," she said with surprising ferocity. "Your empire and queen need you."

He laughed at this, struck by the absurdity not only of such patriotic words, but that they had come from her.

The motion sent lances of pain through him. When he stopped, he felt exhausted.

Cern should reconsider their Cohort brothers. Sutarnan would have been a good choice for consort, had he survived the disaster at Garaya. Mulack dele Murice, then. Despite how untrustworthy he had always been, such a union would put House Murice solidly behind the crown, and that would go a long way to strengthening Cern's rule.

Or Tok. Now that he thought of it, Tokerae dele

Etallan would make an excellent consort. With no ambition to command the army, he would also be a more manageable one. With Tok by Cern's side she would have Etallan securely in hand, the most powerful of the Houses. Her rule would be unchallenged.

But Innel remained convinced that his brother would have been the best choice of all. Prudent, sensible, and charming, Pohut would have approached the Teva with more finesse and eloquence. Not been so hasty to attack simply because Lismar wanted it. Arranged a truce that lasted more than mere hours. Charismatic as he was, he might even have persuaded the Teva to give up the gold at the very start, preventing all that had occurred.

Lismar's strange words drifted back to him, then.

Restarn thought he was playing you against each other, but you saw through it.

They had seen that, the brothers had, again and again. When he and his brother had clearly become candidates in the very long contest for the princess, there had been plenty of attempts to divide them. But the brothers were too smart for that, of course, seeing right through every scheme that—

A sickening feeling came over him.

Seeing right through every scheme that—

No, it could not be. Innel had followed the trails of his brother's betrayals back to every source. He had studied the letters closely; they had been written in Pohut's own hand, which he knew perfectly. From the brusque, insulting words to the overheard conversations, he knew beyond doubt that his brother had been plotting against him. He could not have been that wrong.

He blinked, swallowed, reconsidered.

Could Restarn truly have falsified every piece of information on which Innel had based his betrayed fury? Every single letter that had arrived?

Of course he could have.

"He deceived us," Innel muttered, fighting down nausea. "Set us against each other. Like pieces on a game board."

"Lord Commander."

Now he understood the years before Botaros all too clearly: his estranged brother, as betrayed as he was. Reading the same forged letters. Hearing the same seeded rumors.

But why? Because Restarn needed one of them to prevail. He had been tired of waiting, had taken the matter in hand. The king had told Innel that there was not room at the palace for two mutts. He had told Innel what he was doing, but Innel had been too distracted by politics and Cern to hear.

And of course, the old king had not credited the rumors about the seer, or he would have taken her for himself. She was merely a tool to force the brothers to Botaros, to have them engage in one final, engineered conflict.

He'd killed his brother for a betrayal of which he was innocent.

"I should have known," he whispered. "I should have seen."

"Lord Commander."

It took Innel a moment to realize someone was addressing him, and then another to recall who sat by his side. The seer, who, that night in Botaros, had given him the prediction that allowed him to take his brother's life and save his own.

Who he had worked for years to get in hand, yet whose advice he had ignored when it was inconvenient.

The seer, who now told him the future of his empire depended on him.

He searched her eyes. "Help me," he whispered. "Help my queen."

For a long moment she stared back. "Do you trust me, ser?"

Did he?

"No," he answered.

She nodded. "Will you do what I tell you, anyway?"

He considered these last years, this last day, and tomorrow.

"Yes."

Maris walked into the Arunkin camp in the wan light before dawn, cloaking herself in the shadowy colors of night.

"Maris."

"Amarta?" She gave the young woman a quick scan. "Someone beat you hard," she said, reaching out to take her bandaged hand.

"No," Amarta said, pulling her hand away.

"Who did this?"

"It doesn't matter."

"It does to me."

"No, I said. I don't want your retribution, Maris. I don't even want my own."

"How did you know how to find me here? Ah, of course. Amarta, I've come to get Dirina and Pas. Innel has taken them, and—"

"I know. It will wait."

"But—"

Amarta stepped close. "Maris, will you trust me?"

The question took Maris aback. Behind Amarta's usual earnestness was a sort of vibrancy and intensity that she had not seen before.

How to answer? She took a deep breath.

"You mean well, I know that, but good intention is not enough. You have so few years in you, but you think your ability somehow bestows wisdom upon you, wisdom to make decisions that—" She stopped herself mid-sentence, recognizing words that Keyretura might have used.

Or that she had expected him to use. That he had not actually used, during their recent—what? Conversation? Fight?

Reconciliation?

Go to the Rift in my stead, Maris.

Looking at Amarta again, Maris realized that this was not the same young woman she had left with Tayre to deliver to the Lord Commander. What had happened in the time since then?

"Forget all that," she said, realizing the absurdity of her own words. "In what way do you ask me to trust you now?"

Amarta reached out and took Maris's hand in her good hand, twinning her fingers through the mage's, and silently drew her through the camp.

✣ ✣ ✣

After the disaster at Hanatha, Tayre decided to stop seeming to be an Arunkel soldier. The writ of safe passage he carried would do nothing to protect him from the Teva. After changing his clothes he climbed to the top of a distant tree in the thick strands to the north, finding a good view of the field.

As the sun's first light rose above the line of the Rift, Arunkel troops marched from the camp into the valley. All but the wounded, from the looks of it, who were doubtless back at camp guarding what little they had left.

Going in full, the general was.

Teva battle histories, when scribed at all, were couched in descriptions that lacked any useful detail. Now Tayre had a chance to watch one, an opportunity he could not pass up. Indeed, this promised to be the sort of battle that many more would claim to have seen than could possibly have been here.

Depending on who took the day, that was.

Across the fields, columns of Arunkel soldiers formed into blocks, swords and spears gleaming in the dawn's light. The center vanguard was slightly forward, sleeves of archers flanking spearmen, two thick lines of cavalry on the flanks. A small company fell back from the vanguard to surround the general. She was taking no chances.

Overall, an unsurprising formation, one that had worked for Arunkel many times on many fields. Tayre found it aesthetically pleasing, almost, this geometric precision.

The Teva, on the other hand, for whom Arunkel was thus arrayed, were a bare handful, the striped shaota and riders prancing back and forth between the Arunkel army and the town of Ote, tails swishing, heads tossing. They seemed relaxed, as if out for a pleasure ride, rather than facing thousands of Arunkel soldiers intending to kill them.

If the Teva were anywhere near as formidable as rumor held, this promised to be quite a show.

He wondered what the seer was doing.

Amarta and Maris stood by the Lord Commander's bed, watching as he slept.

"Will he die?" Amarta asked.

Nalas, eyes a bloodshot red, slumped in a chair nearby, lifted his head, watching the women warily.

"Very likely," Maris said. "What pierced him was far from clean. His body is now hot with battle. His shoulder is mangled. Even if he manages to live, it will never be right again. But surely you know all this?"

"He dies, many times, in many ways, in many futures, but I cannot see everything, let alone the causes. Maris, can you heal him?"

"It would take some time."

"We don't have time. Can you do something quickly? Enough that he can move and speak?"

"I have no desire to do that. He holds Dirina and Pas as hostages, and has across the years tried to kill you. Why should I help him?"

Amarta put a hand on Innel's unbandaged shoulder. His eyes fluttered open. For a moment he gave the look of an injured animal: confused and frightened. Then he was asleep again.

"Because," said Amarta, "I ask you to."

✢ ✢ ✢

"Elders, we must leave," said Mara at the door to the longhouse, one hand on the flank of her shaota. Her horse was nosing the door open, eager to be away into the battle.

The elder man sat on the bench and motioned to the large doors that faced to the west. Two Teva children, both with fresh blood-dotted scars encircling their forearms, pulled open the doors to let in the day's light.

"Ride with the wind," the woman in orange said to them, holding her hand palm out toward them. They each ran by her on their way out the door, touching her palm with their own.

"Elders," Mara said, her voice rising. "The Arunkin are coming. We must go."

The woman in blue touched Mara's face and smiled. "Now is the time. We stay here, daughter."

"No," Mara said, putting her hand atop her mother's hand on her face. "You are not ready."

"You are not ready, perhaps," said her father. "You will be."

"I will not leave you," Mara said fiercely.

The elder woman in orange said, "You will. It is time for us to stand where we have governed, stand against the invaders. Your turn will come."

The three elders arrayed themselves on the bench that faced the open door, took each other's hands.

Mara's shaota nosed her again more urgently. Her voice broke. "I am not ready to see you die."

The Arunkin army's horns blew, again and again.

"Then mount up, Mara," her father the elder said, his voice as hard as stone. "Make us proud."

✤ ✤ ✤

Horns sounded distantly from the field as Maris reached fingers of thought into Innel. As he moved restlessly in his sleep, she sought to shift his blood to win its battle.

"Maris," Amarta whispered, "is he ready yet? Is he sensible? Can he walk?"

"Not yet," muttered Maris. "This is not fast work."

"Yes, I am," Innel answered, words slurring, blinking, breathing hard. He managed to sit up, squinting as he looked between the two of them. "What am I to do, Seer?"

"Talk to the elders, ser. Try to understand them. To listen."

"To listen," he said dully.

"Yes. Can you do this?"

He struggled to get out of bed, and suddenly Nalas was there, helping him to his feet. Maris saw Innel trembling. She put her focus back inside him.

"That is all?" he asked. "Listen?"

"Truly listen, ser."

He nodded.

"Also," Amarta said, squinting, as if peering into the distance. "I may not have another chance to tell you this: low to high and left to right."

"What?"

"I don't understand it either. If you live out the day, it will be important to you. But if you don't leave now, it won't matter at all."

"Amarta," Maris said, "I need more time. He is still very ill."

"There is no more time," Amarta said.

Innel stumbled past the two of them, Nalas half holding him up. "Bring my horse," Innel said to one of the guards. The man hesitated. Innel drew himself up and gave the man a hard look.

"Yes, ser," the guard said, dashing outside.

Innel considered the Teva sleeping on the cots. "We'll need two horses." He looked at another guard, who left as well.

"I will go with you," Nalas said.

"Not safe," Innel managed.

"Ser, when the general finds you're gone, she'll hold me responsible. I would far prefer to take my chances with you."

Innel made a thoughtful sound, then nodded, turned to stumble toward the door, Nalas holding him up.

"Ama," Maris said, still making what changes she could to Innel's body as he lurched out the pavilion door. "He is not ready."

"He has to be," Amarta said as she woke the Teva.

As Tayre watched, the sun lit up the rocks of the mesa to the south, making them glow.

The Teva had multiplied in number, streaming in from the buildings of Ote, coming out from the cover of trees, trickling in from the edge of the Rift. They now numbered in the hundreds, dashing and galloping across the area between the army and the town, darting forward and back from the Arunkel line while staying just out of bow-shot range.

It was nothing like a formation. One moment they swooped and swirled like a flock of crows, the next they seemed a chaotic mob. Yipping and shouting, singing and laughing, the sound carried like a distant mob of overenthusiastic troubadours.

Showing off, Tayre guessed.

Or warming up.

Still the Arunkel army did not move.

Tayre took a sip of wine from a skin, a chew of jerky, and shifted to get more comfortable on his branch.

Innel clung to neck of his horse, hot and exhausted. Nalas sat behind him, keeping him from falling off. The three other Teva were on the second large horse, leading them forward.

Innel made eye contact with the Teva he had hurled across the room the previous night, before his sister had tried to kill him. The man's face was covered in heavy yellow and purple bruises. One eye was swollen shut. Innel was starting to wonder if it seemed unfair to him to be hurled about like a sack of grain by someone nearly twice his size when the Teva nodded at him and grinned widely.

Innel blinked in surprise. He didn't understand the Teva, he realized. Not even a little.

He wondered what else might fall into that category.

Truly listen, ser.

As they made their way around the outskirts of the field of battle, following game trails though trees and high rocks to enter Ote unseen from the rear, war horns sounded. The signals for battalions one, two, then three, in succession. His army, even if he was not there to lead it.

Lismar would find herself in an enviable position today: she could take credit for this battle's success yet attach any failures to Innel. Through the trees he caught glimpses of the massive motion forward, the army surging to the same destination he was.

He knew what Lismar would call what he was doing now. For a moment he considered turning back, crawling into his bed and putting his faith in an accomplished general and the overwhelming force now advancing on the Teva. By everything he knew, all the years of study, the tutoring by veteran commanders like Lismar who had made the empire what it was today, Arunkel would surely win this day. Better armed, extensively trained, once again it seemed impossible his people could lose.

Whatever Lismar might think, it was only treason to be conversing with the enemy while the battle raged around them if he failed to accomplish what he had come for.

He thought of his brother. He knew what he would say now.

Don't push until you must. Then go in with all you have.

All he had.

"Hurry," he said to the Teva leading the way as he pressed his horse forward to Ote.

The sound of hoofbeats was wrong.

"Not ours," the elder man said.

The woman in blue sighed, took the hands of the other two, squeezed them briefly. She drew her knife.

She had chosen the knife because it had belonged to

her birth mother and hers before that. It was said to have touched the depths of the Rift. Maybe that was true, because all the Arunkin she had killed with it had seemed to have a moment of startlement as life left them, a deep darkness in their eyes. Or perhaps that was surprise at having been slain by a small, elderly woman. It was hard to tell.

In any case she would fight her last fight with it not because it was the most effective weapon she could take into this precious time but because it was the weapon that was closest to her spirit. A companion of many years. Almost as many as those who stood beside her.

To her right her wife in orange took a few steps back and drew her bow. To her left her husband stepped around the table and took up the curved sword of their people.

At the doorway stood three Teva, silhouetted against the morning light.

"Elders," one said.

"Nahma?" It was his voice, but he had been captive in the Arunkin's camp, so treachery was possible. She was ready.

Nahma stepped inside, followed by Makan and Rmala. "I have brought someone to you," he said. "It may be a good thing. I do not know."

A large figure followed them inside. He waved away a companion, who stepped back outside. Shuffling and swaying slightly, he took in the three armed elders.

Arunkin. Breathing heavily. Not looking at all healthy.

He nodded and spoke. "I am the Lord Commander of

the Host of Arunkel. At least for the moment. You are the governing body of the Teva?"

"We are," said her husband, his sword still out.

"What do you do here, Arunkin?" asked her wife, taking arrows in one hand and holding them ready, her bow in the other.

In the large man's eyes she saw something she recognized: a willingness to die.

It gladdened her. She smiled at him.

He said: "I have been told that I should apologize for my army's intrusion into your lands." He paused to take another deep breath, as if recovering strength to continue. "If this is so, I must first understand why. Will you tell me?"

"The fighting begins, elders," said Nahma from the door.

"All of you," said the elder in orange, "Go to your shaota. Join your kin."

Nahma paused a moment to look back.

"Make us proud," said the woman in blue softly.

"I will, Mother," Nahma said, leaving with the others. Now only the three Elders and the tall Arunkin remained.

It was clear to the woman in blue that, at least in this moment, despite that the Arunkin and their large and clumsy horses thundered closer to Ote, this man was not their enemy.

"Lord Commander of Arunkel," she said, lowering her knife. "If your army breaks through to Ote, we expect to die defending this house. If you stay, we cannot offer you safety. Not from our people, not from yours."

He nodded at this, waved it away. "Tell me about the

gold," he said, lowering himself gingerly to the bench. "Everything. As quickly as you can. Then, if we are all still alive, perhaps we can come to some accord."

Maris continued to heal Innel even as Nalas lifted him onto the horse. Then the horse left and he was beyond her reach. She drew her attention back to Amarta, who took her hand and led her and the remaining two Teva out into the camp. As they passed the guards, they looked away, as if choosing not to see Amarta and a mage and their other two captives leaving the tent.

Prudent of them, Maris thought.

The camp was nearly deserted. Amarta led them out through the fenceline and toward the high rocks. One of the Teva turned to the other and spoke. Maris's command of Tevan was minimal, but it seemed a simple order to return home. He left.

From there the three of them walked up into the rocky hills. In a small clearing surrounded by high rocks, Amarta stopped. "Here, I think," she said.

"Here, what?" Maris asked, turning in place, feeling the character and quality of the land below her.

Then she felt him.

Gallelon stepped out from behind a rock, brushing strands of ginger hair behind his ear. His expression of surprise mirrored Maris's own.

"This is unexpected," Gallelon said. "Maris, why are you here?"

His warmth drew her like a hot wind. She took his etheric touch and fed it back down and into the earth, where it found him again through his feet, the circle completing between them like a kiss and embrace in one. His easy smile turned broad.

"An explanation," she said to him in the ancient language of her kind, "would bring with it many complexities and an expense of time."

"As always," he muttered, and looked at the others. "Jolon of the Teva, I believe."

Jolon dipped his head. "High One."

"Arunkin," he said of Amarta, tone slightly puzzled. Then to Maris: "This seems a bit more than coincidence. Were you looking for me?"

Amarta spoke. "My doing, ser. I don't have time to explain, but I must convince you to come with us. Tell me what I must say, ser, to gain your help."

"You'll have to do better than that, Arunkin; my willingness to help for nothing in return has gone sour lately."

"She is the seer, Gallelon. Of rumor and truth."

"I don't care if she's the Rift worm. I'm not in a charitable mood."

Amarta took a breath. "There is a foal in your future, ser. And the way she looks at you, and you at her . . ." Amarta's eyes went bright. "I would give so much to be hers, the way you could be, if you help us."

At this Gallelon's mouth slowly fell open.

Amarta waited a moment more. Then: "Jolon, will you lead us to the mine?"

As Tayre watched, a long horn blast sounded, then another, and a third. Shields raised, the army advanced, flanks of cavalry riding forward around the sides, pulling the entire mass of thousands into a rough crescent shape.

The Teva, now perhaps four hundred strong, were still vastly outnumbered. As the advancing cavalry picked up speed, the Teva stopped their dancing, took bows in hand, and stood in their stirrups.

The forward ends of the lines of armored warhorses, the points of the stretched crescent shape, had nearly reached the town. Nimble and maneuverable as the shaota might be, Tayre was having a hard time seeing how these few defenders of Otevan were going to survive this.

Indeed, the Teva themselves looked uncertain, their horses backing toward the town into a loose line, as if they thought their single row could somehow defend their town against the rows-deep infantry and armored warhorses bearing down on them.

Then the Teva line broke apart, each side moving to meet the approaching warhorses. A bit out of range yet, Tayre would have wagered, but he would be wrong: Arunkel cavalry suddenly stumbled, soldiers clutching at sudden shafts between gaps in armor and helmets, doubling over, horses running forward without riders.

Tayre was, he knew, a fairly capable shot from horseback. The last time he had needed to call on this skill he had been riding hard along a rocky bank, aiming to miss three targets on a moving raft, and had placed the shaft right where he wanted it. But this—this was a level of capability he had never seen before. His uncle would have loved it.

Were the Teva actually laughing? He could not be quite sure from this distance, but it seemed to Tayre that they were. The riders, that was, not the so-called laughing horses. Though for all he knew, they were, too.

The Teva, it appeared, also loved this.

They were shooting without pause now, letting fly arrows in fast succession. More Arunkel cavalry soldiers were hit, folding and dangling from stirrups, slipping off their horses and being trampled underfoot.

In moments the two lines of cavalry were ragged, the riderless horses overshooting the Teva line, seeming to have other goals amidst the buildings of Ote.

Odd, that; these were trained Arunkel warhorses, here to fight, eager to engage, wanting to do damage. What could have so distracted them?

Then Tayre saw that they were following riderless shaota, out of sight, beyond the farthest buildings of Ote.

What?

Ah. The shaota must be mares. In heat.

Very clever mares in heat.

One more expensive loss for Arunkel. Warhorses were pricey investments.

The army's archers finally came in range and let fly a cloud of arrows. A few Teva doubled over on their horses, their shaota backstepping fast off the field, far better directed than their Arunkel counterparts had been.

But range went both ways. Now the Teva sent blindingly fast streams of arrows into the line of Arunkel archers, who did not get a second chance to shoot.

What cavalry remained atop horses was now closing on the Teva, swords drawn, charging the small horses and riders. The Teva waited, letting them come far closer than Tayre thought they should. When Arunkel horses started to stumble and drop, he understood why, but not how. It was such a fast move that it took some repetitions for him to work it out.

A Teva would flatten against the horse, while under them the shaota stretched its head forward, then gave a fast, round, sidekick to the nearby warhorse's legs, hitting the larger animal hard in the knee or the belly. As the Arunkel horses stumbled or fell, they took their riders down with them, mangling them underfoot.

Men howled. Horses screamed.

Those Arunkel horses that managed to get back to their feet limped away, no longer interested in fighting, let alone in giving their riders the opportunity to remount.

By the time the infantry reached the town, the cavalry lines had gaps through which the Teva might have easily ridden, leaving Ote vulnerable to the thousands of Arunkel soldiers still running toward them. The Teva had done exceptionally well thus far, but unless they had some additional play to make, Tayre's wager was on Arunkel.

Arunkel was still the larger force. Still about to overrun Ote.

He looked across the field as the time for a last-minute Teva asset ran out. Then he saw movement at the walls of Hanatha.

Streaming out of the broken gates of the town was a gathering line of hundreds, all holding pikes, billhooks, halberds, and running toward the backside of the advancing infantry. The way they held their weapons did not put Tayre in mind of determined townspeople desperate to defend their homes. No; these were soldiers who knew their trade. Who had fought before. Who were they? Where had they come from?

Arunkel army deserters, Tayre suddenly realized. Now a thousand or so strong, the mass of ex-Arunkel military were charging in credible formation toward an infantry that had just noticed this attack at their rear, some of them only now turning to meet it, while at their front the Teva were still making them into pincushions.

As the deserter army met the line of Arunkel infantry, the deserters swung billhooks and halberds, hooked aside shields, poked through defenses, tangled opponents' feet. Arunkel soldiers went down, hard, fast, and in large numbers.

Gone was the Arunkel army's careful geometries. The infantry retracted in some places, spread too wide in others, their greater numbers no longer a clear advantage. The field turned into a fog of chaos and cries and slaughter.

Tayre was no longer sure who he would bet on.

"Here it is," Jolon said, gesturing to a large circular pit in the ground, a bowl of terraced earth. At the bottom an embedded arch of tunnel led into blackness. Distantly they could hear the sounds of battle, of horns and drums and the cacophony of thousands of men shouting and howling.

Maris felt her way down through her feet into the earth, finding the trails of gold that wound through the rock below, finding also the pile of bars and coins.

"We put it all inside," Jolon said, "all that we cast and

minted. To return it to its kin. We hoped to bury it, as we had first intended, before the Arunkin came."

"Gold buried by Iliban does not typically stay buried," Gallelon said, slowly walking around the circumference of the large pit.

Jolon nodded soberly. He looked at Amarta. "What now, Seer?"

"Move back," she answered.

"What?" Gallelon asked, glancing at her as he continued his circuit.

"We stand farther back, ser." Amarta said. "There, I think." She pointed to a spot some ways behind them.

Gallelon looked a query at Maris, who gave him a look that said, yes, unlikely as it seemed, Amarta was probably right. He gave a her brief raise of his eyebrows and continued his slow walk.

She knew what Gallelon would be doing now, in addition to taking possession of the land over which he walked: he would be trying to make sense of Amarta, as Maris once had. He would delve into her with his etheric fingers, and find what Maris had: that Amarta was no mage. Barely a Sensitive.

Unique beyond reckoning.

"It will turn," Amarta said gesturing at the mine. "Like a huge pot being stirred."

"Will it, now," Gallelon muttered, the blandness of his tone a contrast to what Maris felt him doing above and below.

The distant sounds of horses, shouts of battle, all gave the impression of quieting. A weight pressed in, like the air grown thick and heavy before a thunderstorm. With each step Gallelon took, Maris felt him change the etherics of the land beneath his feet, weaving his ownership through the tendrils Maris was sending deep into the ground.

Then he began to sing, very softly, a litany of ancient words. A mage-song she remembered from her youth. Beautiful and poetic, it was the sort of thing that gave Iliban the mistaken impression that mages used spells. Rather, it was a means to focus attention, to quiet and clear one's mind, to bring one's spirit into alignment with the etherics all around. Or to bring two mages into alignment with each other.

She began to sing with him, and together they took the mine, holding the land below and the air above. The ground and air rang with their tuning, a loud sound that an Iliban might mistake for silence.

Finishing his circuit, Gallelon came to stand next to her.

"You want the mine sunk?" he asked Amarta.

"Yes, but also—" She moved her hands up and out. "Over the battlefield."

"Down," he said. "And up. Yes. Are you ready, Marisel?"

Ready to move earth and sky, to sink metal deep and raise it high? She had never done anything like this. Keyretura. That's who they needed.

With that thought she realized she had unintentionally strummed the cord that connected her to her *aetur*. She felt a distant, faint reply.

Go to the Rift in my stead, Maris.

She spread her fingers, let the gathering power she

and Gallelon were creating stream in and out of her, through her feet, palms, fingertips. Up and down her spine. She breathed in and out with the heartbeat of the land.

Perhaps even drew on Keyretura. Just a bit. Just enough.

It did not take much of a touch to bring alive the link she and Gallelon had forged years ago in each other's arms. She felt his etheric grip now: tight, secure, affectionate. An echo of their passion. She heard herself laugh a little in delight.

"Maris," Amarta whispered from nearby. "This must happen soon."

So much focus on the etherics she and Gallelon were making that Maris barely saw light and dark, sensing Amarta through the pressure of her spirit. She touched the young woman's shoulder. "Will you trust me, Amarta?"

Under the ground where she and Gallelon worked, he now took hold of her but at the same time pushed her away, creating a taut line between them, a building tension.

At the center of the pit, the ground began to pulse and tremble.

"I will," Amarta answered.

Maris went deep underground, leveraging off the building pressure between her and Gallelon to impart motion and heat. Rocks that had moved slowly for eons began to grind and push, taking dirt and roots and bits of metal with them. Under the ground everything began to shift, to turn. Like a huge stewpot being stirred.

Heat and then more heat. Motion and more motion. Together she and Gallelon built force down and up, both, drawing the many veins of gold together, creating rivulets that began to find their heavy way deeper and deeper into the earth. The pile of bars and coins, now melting, Gallelon held near the surface.

One golden mass near the surface, the other sinking below. A stewpot, yes, but also a boiling kettle.

From deep below came a rumbling, and the ground shook. Maris took the wide stance she knew from years on the ocean.

A violent sundering broke the mine's archway, and it collapsed. The ground rippled, rocked. The four of them backed away from the edge.

The earthen bowl was now churning, picking up speed, a swirling of black and brown shot through with trails of molten gold, all spinning around a central hole. The edges of the pit began to crumble, falling inward to join the fast-moving whirlpool of liquid earth and bright sparkling lines of gold.

While the swirling earth that had been the mine ate away at the land surrounding it, the whirlpool widening and deepening, the four of them backed farther and stood at the spot Amarta had indicated.

"Now," Gallelon said.

Or maybe he didn't say it, but Maris heard it clearly.

With all her focus Maris pushed down, while Gallelon pressed up. She sank the veins of gold deep into the dark earth while Gallelon took the molten mass that was once coins and bars and expelled it upward like a grain silo exploding.

With a sound like thunder, the gold of the whirlpool sank down into a small hole at the center and the swirling earth spat out a golden cloud into the blue sky overhead.

At first Tayre thought a peculiar, sudden rain shower was falling, catching sunlight. Perhaps a fast dust storm had come upon the field.

But the truth was more astounding yet: it was raining gold.

Absorbed as they were in killing each other, it took some moments for the Arunkin, the Teva, and the deserter army to take note.

As tiny flakes of what seemed sparkling sunlight floated slowly down to the field, some Arunkel soldiers stopped in open-mouthed shock. Thus distracted, many were slain by their single-mindedly focused attackers before they, too, noticed the strangeness falling around them and slowed their butchery.

Shouts took on a distinctly different tone as soldiers looked around in wonder and the dust and flakes began to cover the ground in gold.

Horses—shaota and Arunkel alike—shook their heads and snorted to clear the dust from their nostrils.

In minutes the battle had stopped. Many soldiers were now on hands and knees, sweeping up the flakes, stuffing handfuls of it into their pockets. Others simply stared at the sky in amazement or at the ground uncomprehendingly.

A warbling trill from one Teva was taken up by another and another and then all, an eerie sound that carried across the field. The hundreds of Teva pulled back and fell silent, gathering at the edge of Ote, where a figure stepped out of a long building.

Taller than the surrounding Teva, he looked very much like the Lord Commander of Arunkel. At his side stood three Teva.

He held up a long pole. At the top was a white flag.

The battle was over.

Tayre had no idea how, but he was certain the seer had brought all this about. He smiled at this thought and climbed down the tree to get on his horse and leave Otevan before the remaining Arunkel army did.

He had finally decided what to do with all he now knew about the Houses and their various treasons. While he didn't need the money or the influence, he was intrigued by the young queen and her consort's efforts here and wanted to see what they would do next. So he had decided to merely let the Houses know that their work had been seen.

Sometimes a little light on the board could make for a far more interesting game.

Chapter Thirty-seven

Innel and his company were the first to arrive at the palace. The full army, under Lismar, would follow.

Lismar was not particularly happy, but Innel was confident she would learn to be, once he made clear to the queen that her counsel had been crucial to his success at Otevan. It didn't matter if it was true or not. It was necessary.

He dismounted, one-handed, his right arm still tightly wrapped. He wondered if his shoulder would ever be right again and dimly remembered someone saying it wouldn't.

One problem at a time.

He handed the reins to the stablemaster. First, he decided, the queen. No, first the Teva.

As twenty and some Teva riders entered the courtyard behind him, the stablemaster's eyes went wide.

"Guests of the crown," Innel told the stablemaster, hoping that the collected stablehands now gaping at the small, striped horses and their dismounting riders would gather their wits and soon be useful. "The shaota are guests as well," he told them all loudly. "Don't restrain them. Keep crowds away. Let the horses do what they like, go where they will. Unlimited food and water. Do you all understand me?"

Mute, awed nods.

Jolon and Mara stood near him, looking around curiously.

"We will get you settled," he said to Jolon. "Then we will meet with the queen."

"And renew our treaty, Arunkin."

"And renew our treaty, Teva," Innel said.

He now understood the written histories of the Teva. Or rather, the *lack* of written histories of the Teva. Why the Teva treaties ended up renewed. Why the old king had warned him not to make enemies of them. The various insurrections around the empire, who was behind them, and what it would take for the Anandynars to gain Teva support again.

Yes, some things were best left out of the histories.

He left the stables, taking the walkway to the palace, trailed by Nalas and twenty Teva. Heads swiveled to follow him, mouths dropped open. Srel dashed and ducked through the tangle of people surrounding him to reach his side. The smaller man's gaze quickly ran across his visitors.

"Srel," he said, happier to see the smaller man than he would have thought possible. "I need—" Where to start? "Rooms for the Teva. Honored guests, so the best. Let me see . . . Cahlen is in chains in one of the approaching wagons and not at all happy about it. Get her to her room.

Gently, if you possibly can. You'll need a lot of men. Guards on her door until I can plead her case with the queen."

"Ser—"

"The seer . . ." Innel slowly climbed the steps to the palace's kitchen entrance, finding himself out of breath, pausing a moment. "She's not far behind, escorted by a good many guards, but not to keep her restrained. To protect her." Though he doubted she needed it. "Give her"—What? He and the seer both knew now that he could no longer hold her. He had decided to stop trying—"whatever she wants. Anything. Food, horses, carriages. The location of her family." He resumed his march forward into the palace, his entourage surging forward with him.

"Ser?" Srel sounded surprised.

From his other side, Nalas spoke up. "I'll see to Amarta's family, Lord Commander. Let me check on them and make any necessary arrangements."

Innel nodded. "Do so. Also, I want—"

"Ser," Srel interrupted. "A number of people are demanding to see you the moment you arrive. The queen is foremost among them."

There would be wild speculation at his arrival with the Teva, never mind the shaota, the striped horses straight out of children's tales. When the seer arrived—when the army and Lismar arrived, for that matter—the rumors would burn through the palace like a fast fire.

The truth, he realized, would have a hard time slipping in.

Probably for the best.

"What do they say, Srel?"

"That the Teva have joined the empire. Willingly. Unwillingly. That they won a great battle. That you did. That the fortune-teller walked through walls of stone to lead you to victory. That you found a treasure trove at the bottom of the Rift. That you made it rain gold. That you saved the queen's life all the way from Otevan when she was attacked a week ago. No, no, ser—she's fine. But you should see her first."

Innel took a deep breath. He stank of horse and days on the road. "Let me clean up."

"No, ser. You don't have time. The Houses are lining up to see her. They are most insistent. You should be there."

The Houses were wasting no time. Now that he had evidence against a number of them—and that apparently no secret—they would understandably want to see the queen before he did.

A glance behind told him that in addition to his guard he was being trailed by a crowd of aristos and clerks, all acting very important and necessary. Along the halls, people in all colors—green and cream, red and black, some from the Houses—all flattened against the walls to let them by.

One flight up. Another pause to recover his breath. Another hallway. Another set of stairs.

The queen's seneschal met them. No words from the pinched-faced gray-haired man, only a silent nod of acknowledgment to Innel as he led them to the lesser of the queen's audience chambers, the very one in which Innel had set down his brother's body, years ago.

Innel paused, saw the Teva delegates off with Srel, and went inside alone.

She sat on the raised dais in a chair of wood and bronze, one hand draped down over the side, her fingertips on the head of one of the dichu dogs. Chula. On her other side, Tashu lay on his belly, ears up, watching Innel.

"Your Majesty," he said with a quick bow. "I need to tell you . . ." Where to start? "Otevan. No, the Houses—"

The queen's seneschal stepped into the room, shutting the door behind as he spoke.

"Forgive me, Your Majesty. House Etallan's eparch has arrived. You said to send her in. What is your wish?"

"Send her in," Cern answered. Then to Innel: "Etallan waits poorly."

In came the eparch, her husband the Minister of Chimes, Tok, and another ten of them, all dressed in the charcoal and light orange of Etallan. They held before them a wide-eyed young man, hands tied, lips wide around a thick gag. He was grunting and shaking his head.

Innel drew his sword left-handed, a reverse grip.

"You don't want to do that, Lord Commander," the eparch said to him with a flat stare.

"I accuse you and your House of treason," Innel said. "You are responsible for smuggling gold from Otevan, across the empire and into Perripur. You counterfeited Arunkel coin, and brought it to the treasury as legitimate tax revenue, undermining the queen's currency."

"Innel," said Cern warningly.

"Etallan was at the helm of the infusion of forged coin

and gold into Arunkel, Your Majesty. I have proof, from marked tools to witnesses. These are traitors."

"We deny it," Tok said, hands raised in a gesture of placation. Or surrender. "A moment's consideration, Cohort brother: it was my revelations that sent you to Otevan in the first place, from where, I notice, you have returned victorious. As we knew you would."

"Innel," Cern said again, her voice a growl. "Watch yourself."

"Thank you, Your Majesty," said the eparch, dipping her head to Cern. "We are grateful for your royal wisdom. We deny any wrongdoing. However, we must confess that unbeknownst to us, one of our own, this one, named Eregin, has had dealings—indeed a sort of twisted alliance—with some persons at Otevan."

Some persons. Carefully not naming the Teva, now that it was clear Innel had reconciled with them.

The eparch pushed the man sharply and he stumbled forward. "Your Most Excellent Majesty," the eparch continued, "and Lord Commander. We present him to the crown for Your Majesty's justice."

"What?" Innel croaked.

"Alas," the Eparch said, "that he took upon himself to inveigle with those at Otevan, his actions so terribly ill-considered . . ." Her expression was a show of sorrow and distaste, copied by the rest of Etallan as if practiced. "He stole mining and minting equipment. Others helped him, of course, but they were blameless, taken in by his charm and bribery." She scowled at the gagged man, who shook his head, wide-eyed.

"Do you think us such fools as to believe—"

"Innel," Cern said sharply. "If they say this is the man, we must accept that."

"But he is a scapegoat, Your Majesty. Nothing more. A sacrifice. Let them get away with this, and what next?"

"What next?" Tok echoed. "Next we stand behind the crown, just as the crown upholds our charter. No one, least of all Etallan, wants the queen's reputation tarnished by this"—A wave at the bound man— "beast. Thus do we demonstrate our loyalty." He bowed deeply.

"We need the Houses," Cern said softly to Innel, "as they need us." She did not look pleased, but she met his look evenly. "Put away your blade, Innel."

She was right. Through the centuries the Anandynars had ruled only with the support of the Houses. If it came to open conflict, which it never would, the crown would have a hard time standing against Etallan.

But now it was also clear Etallan would not prevail, either. They had made their play and it had failed. This bound man was their gesture of conciliation, their admission they had lost.

How to make sure they would not soon forget? His mind raced with possibilities.

"Yes, Your Grace," he said, exhaling, letting himself slump as if he were complying reluctantly. His head dropped. Looking down, he gauged distance, set his expression to seem bitter and resolved, shuffling forward a little as he did. In the rounding of his shoulders, his blade tip dropped down and back.

So many hours and days and years spent in study. The Houses and their histories. Warfare and weapons.

Swinging at posts wrapped with straw, over and over, to learn to slice the straw but not the wood. Later to cut the post clean off.

It was a barely possible move at the best of times, what he was considering, even if it were his strong hand. To miss would paint him as rash and ineffectual when his reputation was already poised, ready to topple one way or the other, what with the costly win at Otevan. Even with the Teva's treaty renewed and the mine's destruction.

Flawless. It would have to be flawless, timing and motion exactly right, even though it was his weak hand. If he was not absolutely sure, it was beyond foolish to even try.

Low to high, left to right.

The seer's words suddenly came to him, making perfect sense.

He took a loose grip toward the pommel of the sword, turned his hips just so, inhaled and in one motion stepped forward, right foot compassing behind and touching down exactly as the blade in front found its target. As the metal sliced through neck and vertebrae the man's head came off his body, his knees buckled, back arched, and the bloody, open neck sprayed backward across Etallan's eparch, Minister of Chimes, and Tokerae, spattering their faces and clothes.

Innel's sword finished its arc.

There was no resistance as his blade separated head from body. It was an ideal cut.

Flawless.

A stunned silence took the room. As the blood-splashed faces of House Etallan took on expressions of complete shock, Innel drew the flat of his blade between his sleeve and side to clean it, then sheathed it.

His action was either well-done or he was in a great deal of trouble. He turned to his queen and dropped to one knee to wait and find out which it was.

The torso of the man named Eregin had fallen to its back, legs splayed. The head had rolled and came to rest at the wall, dribbling blood along the way.

In the stillness that followed, Innel could hear his own breathing and the snuffling of the dogs, who were sitting up, ears forward, noses twitching.

Cern stood from her throne of wood and metal. She looked at him a moment, then at the group from House Etallan.

"Now you have it," she said with a voice like steel. "My justice, meted out. Take the body of your kinsman and go."

The eparch urgently motioned to two of her family. When they hesitated she snapped her fingers at them, expression tight. They took the body by the arms and dragged it out the door. At her further direction, her husband, face gone white, looking profoundly ill, took the head by the hair and followed.

Innel stood as the family bowed and hurriedly left the room. Tok was last to leave. He paused and looked at Innel.

"The queen's colors suit you, Tokerae dele Etallan," Innel said.

For a moment Tok seemed confused by this, then he smiled weakly and nodded, wiping his bloody face on his sleeve.

When the door closed and they were gone, all that remained was a splattering of blood on the floor and the trail where the head had rolled.

Cern took a long, deep inhale and slowly let it out. She looked at him. "That was"—she seemed momentarily at a loss for words—"daring of you. You took quite a chance."

"Are you pleased with me, Your Grace?"

Her expression answered him, the small, growing smile on her face. Before she could speak, the door opened again.

"Forgive me, Your Majesty, but House Helata's eparch has arrived. What is your wish?"

"Send him in," Cern said, giving Innel a measuring, sidelong look. "It seems to be a good day to speak with the Houses."

Chapter Thirty-eight

"Someone's here!"

Pas jumped up from where he had been sitting and began to run the length of the long, shadowy room, from bed to door and back again. If nothing else, the room gave him a stretch in which to run, which he seemed to need rather often. Dirina wondered if she would ever become accustomed to these outbursts of motion. Amarta, she was sure, had never been this mercilessly full of energy.

He paused at the door, ear to the wood, listening. For a moment she held her breath. Then he dashed to the bed again and back.

It was a comfortable bed, she had to admit. A very comfortable captivity in which they were kept.

Still it would be awfully nice if someone would tell them something. About Amarta. About anything. The last person who had spoken with her at length had assured her that they would be taken good care of, and that he would be back soon, to say more. He had not yet returned.

A bright sun shone outside, hinted at by splashes of

light high on the other wall. For reasons that made no sense to her, their captors had made sure that they could not see out.

Did they think she would break the thick glass and drop a full story to the grounds below? Or was it to prevent them from longing more keenly for freedom than they already did?

Regardless, unlike light, sound carried perfectly well from outside. Between the estate dogs barking, and voices below in the courtyard, they knew there had been an arrival. Usually it was a delivery of supplies for the house. But it could be a visitor.

Dirina climbed up on the chair and then atop the heavy wooden table they had weeks ago moved up against the boarded-up windows, stepping between the plates on which were the remains of their most recent and, she had to admit, delicious meal. She looked through a crack between the boards and down into the courtyard.

"Mama," Pas said from below. "Is it him? Is it her?"

"I can't tell." She sighed, climbing back down.

Her. Amarta, he meant. The reason they had been yanked out of their beautiful, warm Perripin home, abducted by a mage who didn't seem to care about Dirina's warning that Maris would come after him, who had forced them to a hard ride through what must have been the entire length of the empire. He would answer no questions, the annoying Perripin mage, regardless of how she asked or addressed him. But it took no special insight to know her sister was the cause.

Amarta, who must surely be alive if they were still being held here.

Pas had made the ride with the silent mage bearable. From all appearances it had not even occurred to the boy to be afraid. Rather, he seemed to delight in the horse, the lands they passed, and even had some fascination with their taciturn captor.

The next time Pas ran by, she grabbed him and lifted him into her arms, propped him on her hip, and kissed his forehead. He wrapped his arms around her neck.

"I think it's him," Pas said in her ear.

Him.

"You're heavier every day," she muttered at the wriggling child, letting him slip to the ground. He took her hand, pulling her this way and that with surprising force.

A knock, and the door opened. In the doorway stood a tall uniformed man, hands on the doorframe. He looked at her a moment, then stepped inside. He was breathing hard. He had the look of someone who had rushed to get somewhere, but having arrived wasn't quite sure what to do next.

Pas pulled out of her grip and ran to him, taking his hand.

"Nalas! You came back!" He pulled the man into the room.

"Are you well?" Nalas asked her, resisting the pull but letting Pas draw him one step closer.

"You said you were coming back soon," Dirina said accusingly. "Sorry," she added quickly. "But no one talks to us."

"I wanted to. I meant to. There was a—" He waved his free hand, let Pas draw him another step closer. "It's a long story. But you're no longer captive here. You are free to go."

"Amarta?" Dirina breathed.

"She's fine. On her way here. Not far behind."

Relief flooded Dirina. "Oh!"

"She's"—he allowed himself to be taken another step forward by Pas's relentless pull—"free of her contract. She means to take you home to Perripur."

"Will you come with us?" Pas asked him.

"Ah. No," Nalas said, grinning down at him, the smile vanishing as he looked at Dirina. "I am sworn to the Lord Commander. I can't."

As if he needed to explain anything to her. "We understand."

Still Pas was tugging at him. Nalas stepped again in her direction and stopped, ignoring the boy's repeated snapping of his arm.

"Why did you come ahead of her?" Dirina asked. "Are you not her escort?"

"She'll be fine. She has a substantial guard." He scrunched up his face in that way he had, as if trying to sort something out. "I wanted to ask you something first."

Outside dogs began to bark again. Horses' hooves sounded on the stone road.

"That's her," he said with a tilt of his head. "I should go." He began to turn away, but Pas held him tight.

"Ask, ask, ask," Pas said, bouncing.

At this Nalas turned a sober look on Dirina. "I have no right to ask you anything, let alone this."

If this kept up, he'd never get to it. "Ask, ask, ask," Dirina repeated softly.

"Would you stay? Not here. The palace, if you want. Just for a time. Free to come and go, of course. Go back to Perripur whenever you wish. I only thought—I just wanted—" Again he fell silent, his mouth opening and closing silently.

"What? What did you want?"

"Time. To know you better. Both of you," he said to Pas, who was still inexhaustibly tugging on his hand.

"Yes, yes, yes," Pas said, now jumping up and down, still trying to move him closer to his mother. "I want to see the palace!"

"So," he said to Dirina, "do you think you might—"

The door opened again. At first Dirina didn't recognize the figure there, dressed in riding leathers, oversized red and black vest, hair cut short. "Amarta?"

Her sister ran to her, wrapped her in an embrace. "If they hurt you—" Amarta began.

"We're fine, Ama," Dirina muttered through her sister's hair into her ear, emotion overcoming her from the familiar, warm scent of her sister. She swallowed hard, held her tight. Below, Pas was hugging them both.

"I was so worried," Amarta said.

"What?" Dirina took her sister's shoulders and held her at arm's length. "Worried? You?"

Amarta laughed, eyes bright with tears. "There is a distance between vision and what will happen. Sometimes"—the smile left—"the gap is filled with blood." She took Pas's hand. Then she noticed the man watching.

"Nalas? You came ahead of me?"

"I did, Seer," he said.

She frowned at him as she picked up Pas and held him in her arms. "Why?" She looked at Dirina, then back at Nalas, letting Pas down to the ground. "No," she breathed, her expression falling. "Diri, he's—no. Do you know who he is?"

"Ama—"

"We have a home in Perripur with Maris. I came to fetch you. To rescue you."

"Ama. Yes, but. He—" How to explain what she herself didn't understand?

"I want to see the palace," Pas said earnestly to Amarta.

"You can't stay in Yarpin."

"Why not?" asked Pas.

"Yes, why not?" Dirina asked. "It's all right for you to wander off anywhere you like, on dangerous adventures, but we must stay safely tucked away until you return for us?"

"That's not what I meant. But I worked so hard to keep you safe."

Dirina took her sister and her son back into an embrace. She whispered into Amarta's ear. "Ama. I like him. Pas likes him. Is he not a good man? Tell me truly, will he treat us well?"

A returned whisper. "But we've always stayed together."

Dirina stepped back and gave her sister a reproachful look. "No, we haven't. And he will treat us well or you would have said otherwise."

Amarta gave Nalas a glare. "You had better, ser, or I will come for you."

Nalas held his hands up, a gesture of surrender. "Seer, I know."

"Ama, you could stay with us."

"No, I don't think I can."

"Then, but—what will you do?"

Amarta looked around the room, took a deep breath. "I don't know yet."

"How can you not know?" Nalas asked. "Can you not"—he waved a hand—"simply look to the future and see?"

Amarta laughed a little, shook her head. "First I must choose. Like everyone else."

Chapter Thirty-nine

Maris stood at the edge of the small farm, inhaling the scents of mountain lily, spiceflower, and pine. The sun had just risen over the high mountains to the east, bringing the fields of amaranth to brilliant shades of pink and gold and green.

Under a thickly canopied alder, Maris borrowed the tree's shadow and a dusting of magic to stay hidden as Samnt walked the rows of tall plants nearly as tall as he was, inspecting them, every now and then toeing one aside to look at the earth below.

Sending her focus through his body, she dipped into his blood, tissue, bone. Except for a tooth that needed attention, he was sound and strong.

Had Keyretura done this, she wondered, for the first time, watching her before he sat with her parents to create the contract that had changed her life? Had he asked himself if Maris were worth the devotion of so many years of his life and such consuming labor?

Was she herself really ready to make such a sacrifice?

Readiness comes from need. Not before.

She stepped forward and dropped her stealth. "Warmth of the season to you, Samnt."

He whirled and stumbled backwards into the high stalks of flowers and green, brushing grain off his shirt as he stepped forward again, out of the high stalks and onto open grass. His mouth went slack with astonishment. "Maris," he said at last.

"Good looking crop you have here," she said when it was clear he wasn't going to say anything else anytime soon.

He nodded, expression uncertain. Wary.

Afraid.

For a moment she remembered the deep chill of winter as the door stood open after he had fled.

Magic. Now you've seen it.

"I went by my old cabin," she said. "I see it's been rented out again."

"We still have your things," he said quickly. "Someone suggested we sell them, but no, of course we wouldn't do that."

The familiar, deferring tone. He had not forgotten how she had treated him. Did she expect him to?

"You should have sold them," she said. "Not the books. Those you should have kept."

He shrugged a little, looked away. "I went back to your place after you left. The door was open. I thought it might be you. It wasn't."

"Who was it?"

"I don't know. A mage, I guess. Dressed in black. Dark, like you. Asked me where you were."

Keyretura had been looking for her. Not long ago this would have filled her with a craving to run, deep into the forests, in case he was still nearby. But now?

Now she might willingly have tea with him again.

"What did you tell him?" she asked.

Samnt sucked his top lip uneasily. "I should have held my tongue."

"No doubt. What did you say?"

"I told him I didn't know what shithole you were using these days and I didn't care. Told him it wasn't his business anyway." He looked at Maris. "I was angry. Not thinking clearly."

She shook her head slowly, found herself smiling. The courage of ignorance.

"What did he say?"

"Nothing. I ran as soon as the words came from my mouth, realizing I'd made a mistake. Half expected him to set me on fire or melt me into wax or something."

Had Keyretura sensed her touch on Samnt and let him go without consequence because of that? She could not imagine he would simply forgive such an insult.

Then again, she was no longer quite certain she knew him as well as she'd thought.

"Really," he said, "I should have known better, after—" He faltered. "After—"

"After our last exchange."

"Yes. That." He crossed his arms, looked at his feet. "You tried so hard to teach me. I wasn't a very good student."

"I could have been a better teacher."

"No," he said. "It was me. I was young."

Maris laughed. He rolled his eyes, grinning.

"Younger," he corrected.

"Younger," she agreed, smiling back.

"I practiced letters, as you taught me," he said. "In the dirt. Not much. Some."

"Good. You should do more."

"Maybe," he said with a shrug and made a show of inspecting a nearby plant. "Maris, do you remember how I kept at you to teach me magic?"

"Keenly."

He toed the dirt, kicked out a divot with his toe. "There's a rich merchant in town. So rich, he can do anything he wants. Not a big man, but he seemed big to me, with all his money and his painted carriage. I used to watch him at market and think: if I could be like him, have that carriage, that would be enough."

She nodded, waiting for him to continue.

"Last month I saw him watch a carriage go by. So magnificent I could barely think. From Yarpin, I suppose. Shiny and black with silver designs and sparkling red bits on top. Made his carriage seem ragged by comparison. I realized he was looking at the owner of that carriage the way I was looking at him. That's when I knew there was always going to be someone who—how do I explain—"

"Someone with a bigger carriage."

"Yes. That's why I pestered you about magic, Maris. I thought it would be like that. Like having a bigger carriage. But it won't, will it."

"No," she said.

Instead it would break him, rip his world to shreds. Change everything he thought he knew.

Teach him to build roads.

"If I had it to do over again—" he said.

"You don't," she said. "Bury your remorse." She considered him a moment. "I have something for you." She knelt by her pack, pulled out a book, held it out for him to take.

He dropped down beside her in the grass. "Oh, Maris." He opened it, looked at the first page, his expression falling. "I can't read any of this."

"You merely need practice."

"Sure," he said insincerely. "But no. It would be wasted on me." He held the book out to her. For a moment they stayed like that, him offering, her refusing to take.

His stubbornness seemed intact, in any case.

At last she took the book back. Together they stood.

"Who was he?" he asked, "The man at your cabin? Tell me I didn't insult a powerful mage."

She laughed. "But yes, that's precisely what you did."

"Good thing I'm just a farmer's brat, then. He'll forget me. Won't he? Mages don't carry grudges, do they?"

The warm sun reminded her of Perripur, of the years with Keyretura. Days of hard words, nights of harder silences.

How easy it was to be sure of what you thought you knew.

"Some do," she admitted. "But I don't think you need to be worried about that."

"Look—the sun's already moved, and I haven't offered you anything. You hungry? Thirsty? Come to the house and we'll find you something." In his eyes was the hope that she would say yes, the fear she would refuse.

She went to pick up her pack, but he was there first, hefting it easily, grinning, turning to walk with her on the path to the house.

"I'm glad you're here," he said, voice low. "I thought I'd never see you again."

Well, if she were going to prove Keyretura wrong, she had better get started.

"Samnt, do you want to study with me again?"

He shook his head. "I don't want to disappoint you. I'd waste your time."

"Then answer my question."

"Yes!"

Maris smiled. From the farmhouse came a call. Samnt's mother. She waved.

"Then we will talk. All of us."

"About what?"

"Feed me first."

He darted in front of her, animatedly stepping backwards to keep her in sight, her bag swinging from his shoulder. "Maris, talk about what? Tell me."

"Be patient," she said. "If this leads to something, you're going to need a whole lot of that."

And stubbornness. And many other things.

"What something more do you mean?" She could see his clever mind casting about for answers.

But she would not answer, not yet. First she would tell him what it had cost her.

Chapter Forty

Amarta dismounted, aware that the many uniformed riders dismounting around her were attracting a good deal of attention in this seaside town. Some townspeople stood and stared. Most backed away.

She inhaled the scents of the town in summer: hot stone roads, rotting garbage, sluggish sewers. Then the winds changed: sea breezes, woodsmoke, baking breads. A strange world, where things could change so quickly and thoroughly.

She thought of the Lord Commander and their last conversation. He had held the reins of the horse on which she sat. A gift, he told her.

"Stay," he had urged. "Your queen and empire still need you."

"I can't, Lord Commander. And I will not."

"Seer, things are very different now. Your family—free to come and go. You, likewise, at full liberty. Stay with us, Amarta al Arunkel, as our guest. I can offer you—"

"I want none of it."

He nodded, seeming unsurprised. For a moment he studied her closely, and she had the odd feeling he was seeing her now. For the first time. "What, then?" he asked, voice low. "Some apology or reparation? Would that change your mind?"

She thought of the years behind her. Of being hunted. Of being afraid. Of the lives she had cost.

"Or perhaps this?" He held something up to her, and she took it. For a moment she didn't recognize it. Then she did.

A blue and white seashell. Her mother's seashell. She found herself smiling. "No, ser. You can't give me what I want."

"Name it."

She looked at the squadron of guards he had put at her disposal and thought of all the things she could ask for, and how each one would bind her more closely to him and his queen.

"I want to be free of all this, ser."

"Ah." He took a deep breath. "So be it. One last question, then: what do I most need to know about my future?"

Amarta had come to very much doubt that answering this question did anyone any good at all. Even when she saw the future clearly, even when it changed little between prediction and outcome—even in those rare cases where people did as she directed—what did they gain?

Were they not then her tools, as she had been his?

In any case, people usually did what they wanted to, regardless of what she said.

And there was wisdom in that, perhaps.

As she considered how to answer him, she looked into the future and what was to come for Innel sev Cern esse Arunkel. Images of him with his queen. Of Arunkel soldiers alongside Teva on striped shaota. Of Houses of metal and stone and ocean, of people and colors moving across the land. Children to be born, deaths to come. A rich tapestry.

But she was done being one of its threads.

As he waited for her answer, she realized that no matter what she said now, whether based in vision or fully invented, whether smoothly spoken or absurdly clumsy, her words would carry influence far beyond anything she might expect or intend, and once said, they were out of her hands entirely. What could she possibly say to him now that would do more good than ill?

She laughed a little. "Listen, ser. Try to understand."

He was silent a time. Considering, she hoped.

"The crown offers you hospitality, Amarta al Arunkel," he said, handing her the reins. "We welcome your return."

Her return. She did not want to think about that, but as long as Dirina and Pas were here with Nalas, she would feel the pull. But for now—

She had left the palace, then, and the city, with a guard of red and black trailing her along the Great Road, past houses and hovels, shipyards and markets. The ocean was to one side, sometimes close enough to be booming with surf, other times only sending a distant salt breeze her way.

But always the gulls overhead. She remembered once envying them their freedom.

And now Amarta stood on a cobblestone street, one

hand on the warm neck of her mare, the summer sun in her eyes, the distant roar of the ocean in her ears.

The captain of her guard dismounted, strode to her.

"Go back to the palace, ser," she told him. "You and all your men."

"Are you sure, Seer? We can wait on you, as long as you like. The Lord Commander instructed us to—"

"Give him my thanks, but no; I no longer need your escort." She could not imagine the world was more dangerous to her than an army camp, or a battlefield. But if it were, so be it.

"Seer, we were told to make sure you—"

"And you have. Now you are done. Go home."

"If you're sure, ser . . . ?"

"I am."

With reluctance he mounted and led his squadron away, looking back repeatedly at her until they were out of sight. Amarta led her horse to the inn's stable, leaving it with the hands there, and walked inside the many-colored inn and upstairs to the rooms where she knew Maris would be.

She knocked, and the door opened. A young man she had never seen before stood there.

"Yes?" he asked, seeming as startled by Amarta as she was by him.

Are you ever surprised?

All the time.

Maris appeared at his shoulder. "Amarta, come in. This is Samnt, my"—she laughed a little—"apprentice. Samnt, go downstairs to the kitchens and arrange dinners for the four of us."

"Arrange? What? But I don't know how to—"

"What a good time to learn," Maris said, putting coins in his hand, closing his fingers around them, and pressing him outside while bringing Amarta in. Maris closed the door on the bemused young man.

"You probably already know this," Maris said to Amarta, "but he's here."

At the far end of the room by a draped window Tayre stood.

Maris was right, she had known. But she had stopped looking at the future, the moment she saw that much. Some things, she had come to realize, were too important to foresee.

Even knowing he'd be here, she felt a shock go through her at the sight of him. Knowing the future, it seemed, was nothing like living it.

Her left hand still ached where he had broken her fingers. Her bruises were almost entirely healed. She worked her fingers, remembering the things that had been said in that room.

"Hello, Seer," Tayre said. "I have come to speak with you, if I may."

Maris looked at Amarta, a deepening frown on her face, and made a displeased, thoughtful sound. "If you want privacy, Ama, I can stand outside yet still protect you."

From her tone, Amarta realized that somehow Maris understood the connection between Tayre and her various bruises and breaks.

"I think you should stay, Maris," Tayre said.

"Yes, I think I should, too." Maris said, pulling a chair around to sit.

"You came with a royal guard," Tayre said to Amarta. "Is your contract with the Lord Commander intact?"

"It is finished. He released me," Amarta said. "But now, of all things, Dirina and Pas want to stay at the palace, while I am free to go."

At this he gave a small laugh. "Are you? Have you done what you came here to do?"

Had she? She had changed the Lord Commander's path, for a time, anyway. If stability and peace across the empire were truly her goal, possibilities existed for both where they had not before.

And Dirina and Pas, well. They were as secure as they could be, if they were going to stay in the queen's palace. After all Amarta's efforts to keep them safe, leaving them in Yarpin seemed the strangest of outcomes, but she could not argue with her sister's determination to find her own way. Amarta would not tell Dirina where she should go, or what she should do. Or whom she should do it with.

She exhaled. "I think so."

He pulled the drapes back and glanced outside. Through the window, the ocean bay glittered. "There are curious tales being told on the streets. Large sums of coin being offered for news of the true fortune-teller. Rumors of a young woman with the queen's ear who has fortified the treasury and secured the borders."

"That's absurd," Amarta said. "That's not at all how it happened."

"It rarely is." He looked back at her. "So, Amarta, what will you do now?"

She wanted to go away, far beyond the red and black. "I don't know," she said. "What will you do?"

"That's why I'm here, Seer. To find out what I do next." He took a step toward her and paused. "Do you," he said, advancing another slow step, "still want my help, to learn to live in the world?" Another step. "To help you understand what you are?" One more step, and he stopped. "And, should you decide, help you to die? Do you still want all that from me?"

Flashes of metal points in candlelight. The smell of hot iron. The sound of a knife being sharpened.

A palm-sized, glinting coin on a table top.

His finger on her lips.

"If you have a contract to offer me," he said. "Now is the time. If not, I will leave you in peace, and never trouble you again. On my word and oath before a mage who I am certain will hold me to it."

The room was very quiet. She could hear her own breathing.

"How much?" she asked, her stomach trembling.

"What do you offer?"

Her heart sank. In all the time she had been at the palace and at Otevan, she had taken nothing of value. She had refused the Lord Commander's offers of payment, had stood watching the mine swirling with vast quantities of gold, had walked across flakes of gold fallen on the battlefield like bright snow.

She had taken nothing, had asked for nothing. It had not even occurred to her to do so.

In desperation she reached into her pocket, felt something hard, and pulled out a single copper nals, the very one the Lord Commander had given her to seal their contract. The Grandmother Queen sat dour, a dog at her feet. On the other side, the great Sennant River, the very river down which she and Dirina and Pas had fled years ago.

Fled this very man.

She held it up for him to see. "I can get more." How, she wasn't quite sure, but there must be ways to get the sort of coin someone like this would require. "Just give me some time." She looked at Maris. Perhaps the mage would help her.

Then she looked back at him. His hand was out, palm up. Her breath caught.

He could not possibly mean that he would accept a single nals for this contract. That would be absurd. Unthinkable.

Was that what he meant?

"For how long?" she asked.

"As long as you need me. Until you release me."

"No. You can't possibly accept this for that."

"Yes, I can."

She rubbed the coin nervously, feeling the imprint there. What to do? Put the coin in his hand or tell him to go away? What might happen?

No, she thought firmly, pushing vision away as it tried to answer. She would not look to see what she would do or what might happen. She would decide for herself.

He had given her a promise to leave her in peace. She could be free of the Lord Commander's hunting dog. Truly and finally. Did she want that? To never see him again?

Still he waited, unmoving, hand outstretched. How long would he stand there?

He would not move, she realized. Not until she answered.

She stepped close, close enough to see the scar on his face, the gold flecks in his light brown eyes, the stubble on his cheeks. To taste his breath on the air between them. "As long as I need you?" she asked. "That could be years."

"Then it will be years."

Fear is a shadow.

So be it.

Holding his gaze with her own, she put the coin onto his open palm. He curled his fingers around the coin and her smaller hand. With his other hand he covered them both. "Maris," he said. "Will you witness?"

"I will," Maris said, surprise in her voice.

"Are you ready, Seer?" he asked her.

Again she held herself back from foreseeing. To glimpse what might come was nothing like being prepared for it. To be sure you could face the future was—what?

An impossibility, is what it was.

"There are things I can't be ready for," she said.

He had a hint of a smile on his face. "Many of them."

"Then . . ." She glanced at Maris and back at him and took a deep breath. "Then our contract is made, Tayre. Enlon. In all your names and appearances."

"Our contract is made, Amarta al Arunkel. Seer."

And what now? There were places she wanted to visit, things she wanted to understand, far away from this land of red and black. This man, this hunting dog, this shadow made real, would help her find them.

Despite how Amarta's heart was speeding, despite

how tight his hands were clasped around hers and the coin, a smile spread over her face.

"I am," she said. "ready."

IF YOU LIKE...
YOU SHOULD TRY...

DAVID DRAKE
David Weber
Tony Daniel
John Lambshead

DAVID WEBER
John Ringo
Timothy Zahn
Linda Evans
Jane Lindskold
Sarah A. Hoyt

JOHN RINGO
Michael Z. Williamson
Tom Kratman
Larry Correia
Mike Kupari

ANNE MCCAFFREY
Mercedes Lackey
Lois McMaster Bujold
Liaden Universe® by Sharon Lee & Steve Miller
Sarah A. Hoyt
Mike Kupari

MERCEDES LACKEY
Wen Spencer
Andre Norton
James H. Schmitz

LARRY NIVEN
Tony Daniel
James P. Hogan
Travis S. Taylor
Brad Torgersen

ROBERT A. HEINLEIN
Jerry Pournelle
Lois McMaster Bujold
Michael Z. Williamson

HEINLEIN'S "JUVENILES"
Rats, Bats & Vats series by Eric Flint & Dave Freer
Brendan DuBois' *Dark Victory*
David Weber & Jane Lindskold's Star Kingdom
Series
Dean Ing's *It's Up to Charlie Hardin*
David Drake & Jim Kjelgaard's *The Hunter Returns*

HORATIO HORNBLOWER OR PATRICK O'BRIAN
David Weber's Honor Harrington series
David Drake's RCN series
Alex Stewart's *Shooting the Rift*

HARRY POTTER
Mercedes Lackey's Urban Fantasy series

JIM BUTCHER
Larry Correia's The Grimnoir Chronicles
John Lambshead's *Wolf in Shadow*

TECHNOTHRILLERS

Larry Correia & Mike Kupari's Dead Six Series
Robert Conroy's *Stormfront*
Eric Stone's *Unforgettable*
Tom Kratman's Countdown Series

THE LORD OF THE RINGS

Elizabeth Moon's *The Deed of Paksenarrion*
Shattered Shields ed. by Schmidt and Brozek
P.C. Hodgell
Ryk E. Spoor's Phoenix Rising series

A GAME OF THRONES

Larry Correia's *Son of the Black Sword*
David Weber's fantasy novels
Sonia Orin Lyris' *The Seer*

H.P. LOVECRAFT

Larry Correia's Monster Hunter series
P.C. Hodgell's Kencyrath series
John Ringo's Special Circumstances Series

ZOMBIES

John Ringo's Black Tide Rising Series
Wm. Mark Simmons

GEORGETTE HEYER

Lois McMaster Bujold
Catherine Asaro
Liaden Universe® by Sharon Lee & Steve Miller
Dave Freer

DOCTOR WHO
Steve White's TRA Series
Michael Z. Williamson's *A Long Time Until Now*

HARD SCIENCE FICTION
Ben Bova
Les Johnson
Charles E. Gannon
Eric Flint & Ryk E. Spoor's Boundary Series
Mission: Tomorrow ed. by Bryan Thomas Schmidt

GREEK MYTHOLOGY
Pyramid Scheme by Eric Flint & Dave Freer
Forge of the Titans by Steve White
Blood of the Heroes by Steve White

NORSE MYTHOLOGY
Northworld Trilogy by David Drake
Pyramid Power by Eric Flint & Dave Freer

URBAN FANTASY
Mercedes Lackey's SERRAted Edge Series
Larry Correia's Monster Hunter International
Series
Sarah A. Hoyt's Shifter Series
Sharon Lee's Carousel Series
David B. Coe's Case Files of Justis Fearsson
The Wild Side ed. by Mark L. Van Name

DINOSAURS
David Drake's *Dinosaurs & a Dirigible*
David Drake & Tony Daniel's *The Heretic* and *The
Savior*

HISTORY AND ALTERNATE HISTORY
Eric Flint's Ring of Fire Series
David Drake & Eric Flint's Belisarius Series
Robert Conroy
Harry Turtledove

HUMOR
Esther Friesner's *Chicks 'n Chainmail*
Rick Cook
Spider Robinson
Wm. Mark Simmons
Jody Lynn Nye

VAMPIRES & WEREWOLVES
Larry Correia
Wm. Mark Simmons
Ryk E. Spoor's *Paradigm's Lost*

WEBCOMICS
Sluggy Freelance… John Ringo's Posleen War Series
Schlock Mercenary…John Ringo's Troy Rising Series

NONFICTION
Hank Reinhardt
The Science Behind The Secret by Travis Taylor
Alien Invasion by Travis Taylor & Bob Boan
Going Interstellar ed. By Les Johnson